RANDOM HOUSE
LARGE PRINT

MOON
WITCH
SPIDER
KING

MARLON JAMES

MOON
WITCH
SPIDER
KING

RANDOM HOUSE
LARGE PRINT

Copyright © 2022 by Marlon James

All rights reserved. Published in the United States of America by Random House Large Print in association with Riverhead Books, an imprint of Penguin Random House LLC.

Maps by Marlon James

Cover design: Helen Yentus
Cover illustration: Pablo Gerardo Camacho

The Library of Congress has established a Cataloging-in-Publication record for this title.

ISBN: 978-0-593-55644-3

www.penguinrandomhouse.com/large-print-format-books

FIRST LARGE PRINT EDITION

Printed in the United States of America

1st Printing

This Large Print edition published in accord with the standards of the N.A.V.H.

Shirley

TABLE OF CONTENTS

THOSE WHO APPEAR IN THIS ACCOUNT   XXIII

1. NO NAME WOMAN   1

2. A GIRL IS A HUNTED ANIMAL   391

3. MOON WITCH   551

4. THE WOLF AND THE LIGHTNING BIRD   755

5. NO ORIKI   925

ACKNOWLEDGMENTS   971

THE SOUTH LANDS

HIGOGO FLOW

NJUBWA RIVER

GULU MOUNTAINS

CHEETAH BAY

YELLOW LAKE

BUNDIBAYO RIVER

WHITE DUST MOUNTAINS

WEME WITU BAY

GREEN LAKE

N'KOOKO RIVER

KILUMI PASS

BLACK LAKE

LWAMPA KEYS

N

KEY

1. WAKADISHU
2. GO
3. NIGIKI
4. LISH
5. SUNK CITY
6. MASI
7. WEME WITU
8. OMORORO
9. MARABANGA

KONGOR

KEY

1. MISTRESS WADADA'S HOUSE OF PLEASURABLE GOODS AND SERVICES
2. BASU FUMANGURU'S HOUSE
3. ALLEY OF THE PERFUME MERCHANTS
4. TOWER OF THE BLACK SPARROWHAWK
5. THE OLD LORD'S HOUSE
6. KONGORI CHIEFTAIN ARMY FORT
7. GREAT HALL OF RECORDS
8. SINKING OLD HOUSE
9. NIMBE CANAL

NYEMBE

TAROBE

BORDER ROAD

BORDER ROAD

BORDER ROAD

BORDER ROAD

NIMBE

IMPERIAL DOCKS

OLD TAROBE (FLOODED)

GALLUNKOBE/
MATYUBE

N

FASISI

BAGANDA

MIJAGHAM
(The Floating City)

TAHA

IBIKU

UGLIKO

TO MANTHA

TO REALMS SOUTH

TO THE RIVER TRIBES

KEY

1. THE WORLD BAZAAR
2. BIMBOLA'S TAVERN
3. THE FLOATING DONGA
4. ARMY BARRACKS
5. KEME'S HOUSE
6. HOUSE OF NOTICE
7. THE ROYAL ENLCOSURE

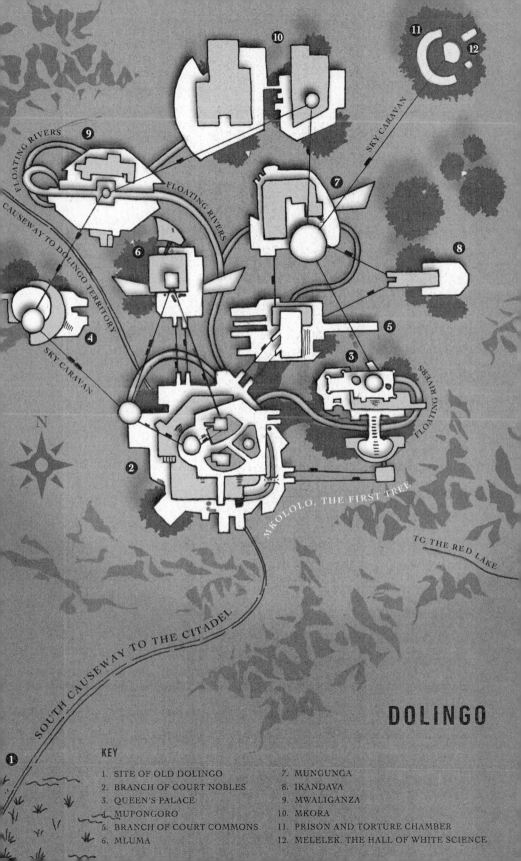

DOLINGO

KEY

1. SITE OF OLD DOLINGO
2. BRANCH OF COURT NOBLES
3. QUEEN'S PALACE
4. MUPONGORO
5. BRANCH OF COURT COMMONS
6. MLUMA
7. MUNGUNGA
8. IKANDAVA
9. MWALIGANZA
10. MKORA
11. PRISON AND TORTURE CHAMBER
12. MELELEK, THE HALL OF WHITE SCIENCE

MALAKAL

TO THE HILLS OF ENCHANTMENT

GREAT NORTH GATE

CLIFFS

SLAVE ROUTES

FOURTH WALL

SENTRY PORT NORTH

THIRD WALL

LOOKOUT

SECOND WALL

FIRST WALL

SALT ROUTES

LOOKOUT

SENTRY PORT SOUTH

LOOKOUT

SOUTH GATE

LOOKOUT

OLD MALAKAL RUINS

N

TO THE UWOMOWOMOWO VALLEY

KEY

1. NORTH FORT
2. THE HOUSE WITH NO DOORS
3. HOME OF BELEKUN THE BIG
4. EAST BARRACKS
5. WEST FORT
6. TRACKER'S INN
7. THE COLLAPSED TOWER
8. VICEROY CHAPEL
9. SOUTH FORT

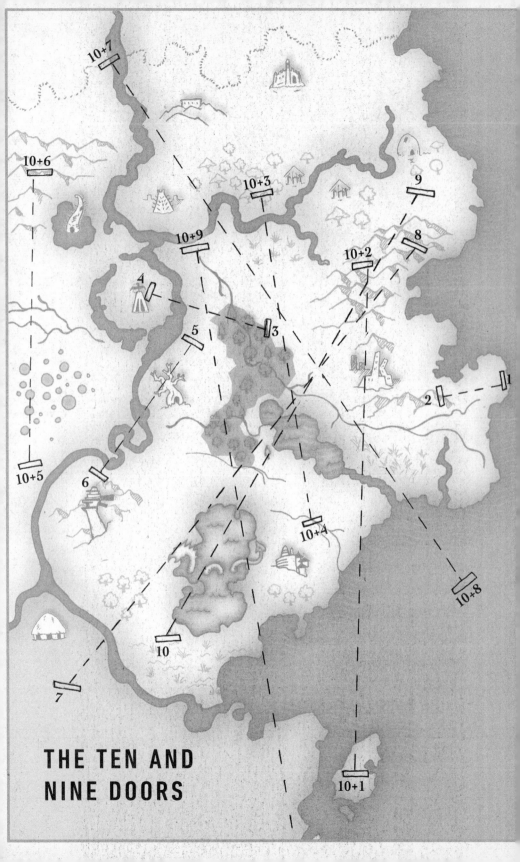

THE TEN AND
NINE DOORS

THOSE WHO APPEAR
IN THIS ACCOUNT

IN MITU AND KONGOR

SOGOLON, also called Forbidden Lily and Moon Witch
    HER FATHER
    OLDEST BROTHER
    MIDDLE BROTHER
    YOUNGEST BROTHER
    PYTHON WOMAN
MISS AZORA, owner of a house of pleasurable goods
    and services
    YANYA, one of her whores
    DINTI, another one
MISTRESS KOMWONO, an imperious woman
    MASTER KOMWONO, her husband
    LADY MISTRESS MORONGO, her sister
UKUNDUNKA, a monster tied to a talisman
THE COOK, known as Cook
NANIL, a slave
KEME, royal scout, marshal of the Fasisi Red Army

WANGECHI, Basu Fumanguru's wife
  MILITU, also his wife
OMOLUZU, roof-walking shadow demons
MOSSI OF AZAR, third prefect of the Kongori
  chieftain army
THE MAWANA WITCHES, dirt mermaids, a.k.a. mud
  jengu

IN FASISI

YÉTÚNDE, Keme's wife
  KEME, son
  SERWA, daughter
  ABA, daughter
  LURUM, son
  EHEDE, son
  MATISHA, daughter
  NDAMBI, daughter
BEREMU, a lion
MAKAYA, another lion
LADY MISTRESS DOUNGOUROU, courtier of the Fasisi
  royal house
LADY KAABU, courtier
  LORD KAABU, her husband, also a courtier
THE SANGOMIN, apprentices of the Sangoma, a sect
  of necromancers and witchfinders
KWASH KAGAR, King of all the North and father of
  Prince Likud, of house Akum

QUEEN WUTU, his second wife

JELEZA, his sister

LOKJI, his sister

KWASH MOKI, son of Kwash Kagar, formerly Prince Likud

ADUKE, his twin son, later Kwash Liongo

ABEKE, his twin son

EMINI, princess, his sister

MAJOZI, prince, her husband

KWASH ADUWARE, Liongo's son

KWASH NETU, Aduware's son

KWASH DARA, Netu's son

THE OKYEAME, the King's messengers

THE AESI, chancellor to the King

ALAYA, a southern griot

DJABE, mercenary, the Seven Wings

OUMOU, Keme's friend

BIMBOLA, bar owner in Go

OLU, war hero, commander of Kagar's army

VUNAKWE, attendant to the princess

ITULU, attendant to the princess

THE HEADWOMAN, chief servant to the princess

ASAFA, a general in Kagar's army

DIAMANTE, another general

SCALA, a dead elder

KANTU, a berserker

THE DIVINE SISTERHOOD, nuns of the fortress of Mantha

IN THE SOUTH

BUNSHI/POPELE, a water deity
NSAKA NE VAMPI, a bounty hunter
   OSEYE, her sister
NYKA, a mercenary
BISIMBI, murderous water nymphs
BOLOM, a southern griot
   IKEDE, his great grandson, also a southern griot
YUMBOES, grass fairies
CHIPFALAMBULA, a great fish

IN MANTHA

LETHABO, a nun
LISSISOLO, Kwash Dara's sister
NINKI NANKA, river dragon
PRINCE OF MITU, as it says
BASU FUMANGURU, elder of the North Kingdom
SISTER REGENT, head nun of the divine sisterhood

IN DOLINGO

JAKWU, tactician for the Southern King (deceased)
NNIMNIM WOMAN, master of healing and restorative
   magic
THE QUEEN OF DOLINGO, as it says
   HER CHANCELLOR

THE WHITE SCIENTISTS, darkest of the
  necromancers and alchemists
IPUNDULU, vampire lightning bird
ISHOLOGU, a masterless Ipundulu
SASABONSAM, bat-winged ogre
ADZE, vampire and bug swarm
ELOKO, grass troll and cannibal
THE BOY, Lissisolo's son, unnamed

IN MALAKAL, LATER KONGOR

THE SEVEN WINGS, mercenaries
SADOGO, a very tall man who is not a giant
AMADU, a slaver
  BIBI, his manservant
THE TRACKER, hunter known by no other name
THE LEOPARD, shapeshifting hunter known by a few
  other names
FUMELI, the Leopard's archer
ZOGBANU, trolls originally from the Blood Swamp
VENIN, a girl raised to be food for the Zogbanu

1

NO NAME WOMAN

K'hwi mahwin

One night I was in the dream jungle. It was not a dream, but a memory that jump up in my sleep to usurp it. And in the dream memory is a girl. See the girl. The girl who live in the old termite hill. Her brothers three, who live in a big hut, say that the hill look like the rotting heart of a giant turn upside down, but she don't know what any of that mean. The girl, she is pressing her lips tight in the hill's hollow belly, the walls a red mud and rough to the touch. No window unless you call a hole a window and, if so, then many windows, popping all over and making light cut across her body up, down, and crossway, making heat sneak in and stay, and making wind snake around the hollow. Termites long ago leave it, this hill. A place nobody would keep a dog, but look how this is where they keep her.

Two legs getting longer but still two sticks, head getting bigger but chest still as flat as earth, she may be right at the age before her body set loose, but nobody bother to count her years. Yet they mark it every summer, mark it with rage and grief. They, her brothers. That is how they mark her birth, oh. At that time of year they feel malice come as a cloud upon them, for which she is to blame. So, she is pressing her lips together because that is a firm thing, her lips as tight as the knuckles she squeezing. Resolve set in her face to match her mind. There. Decided. She is going to flee, crawl out of this hole and run and never stop running. And if toe fall off, she will run on heel, and if heel fall off, she will run on knee, and if knee fall off, she will crawl. Like a baby going back to her mother, maybe. Her dead mother who didn't live long enough to name her.

With the small light coming and going through the entry holes, she can count days. With the smell of cow shit, she can tell that one brother is tilling the ground to plant new crops, which can only mean that it is either Arb or Gidada, the ninth or tenth day of the Camsa moon. With one more look around, she see the large leaf on which they dump a slop of porridge last evening, one of only two times every quartermoon that they feed her. When they remember. Most of the time they just let her starve, and if they finally remember, late in the night, they say it's too late anyway, let some spirit feed her in dreams.

See the girl. Watch the girl as she hear. It is through her brothers yelling about when to plant millet, and when to rest the ground, that she learn season from season. Days of rain and days of dry tell her the rest. Otherwise, they just drag her out of the termite hill by rope bound to the shackle they keep around her neck, tie her to a branch and drag her through the field, yelling at her to plow the cow shit, goat shit, pig shit, and deer shit with her hands. Dig into the dirt with your hands and mix the shit deep so that your own food, which you don't deserve, can grow. The girl is born with penance on her back. And to her three brothers she will never pay it in full.

Watch the boys. Her brothers, the older two laughing at the youngest one screaming. Boys like they were born, wearing nothing but yellow, red, and blue straw pads on their elbows and shins, and tiny straw shields over their knuckles. The older two both wear helmets that look like straw cages over their heads. Helmets in yellow and green. The girl crawl out of her oven to watch them. Her oldest brother spin a stick as tall as a house. He swirl and twirl and jump like he is dancing. But then he roll, jump up, and swing the stick straight for middle brother's neck. Middle brother scream.

"Whorechild!"

"We from the same mother," oldest brother say, and laugh. He turn away for a blink but still he is too slow. A stick strike fire on his left shoulder. He swing around, laughing even though the hit draw blood. Now he going to do it. He grab his stick with two hands like an ax and run after his brother, raining down chop after chop. Middle brother strike two blows but oldest is too fast. Swing and swing and swing and chop and chop and chop. Slash to the chest, slash to the left arm, slash to the bottom lip, bursting it.

"Is only play, brother," middle brother say, and spit blood.

Youngest brother try to tighten the big helmet to his little head, but fail. "I can beat the two of you," he say.

"Look at this little shit. You know why we go to donga, boy?" ask oldest brother.

"I not a fool. You go to win the stick fight. To kill the fool who challenge you."

Both brother look at the youngest like a stranger just appear in their midst.

"You too young, brother."

"I want to play!"

Oldest brother turn to face him.

"You don't know anything about the donga. You know what this stick is for?"

"You deaf? I say to fight, and to kill!"

"No, little shit. This is first stick. When you win, you get to use your second stick. Ask any pretty girl who come to stick fight."

He grin at middle brother, who grin back. Youngest brother confused.

"But you only use one stick to stick-fight, not two."

"As I say. Too young."

Middle brother point at youngest brother's cock.

"Ha, littlest brother's stick is but a twig."

The two brothers laugh long enough for rage to come over youngest brother face, not because he still don't understand, but because he do. The little girl watch. How he grab the stick, how far he pull back the swing, how hard he strike, right in the middle of middle brother's back. He yell, older brother spin around, and his stick quick smack youngest brother on the forehead, swing again and clap him behind the knees. Youngest brother fall, and oldest brother rain down strike all over his body. Youngest screaming, and middle grab oldest by the arm. They walk off, leaving youngest bawling in the dirt. But as soon as he see that nobody is watching him, he stop crying and run after them. The little girl creep farther from the hut and take up a stick they leave behind. Stronger and harder than she did expect, and longer also. Longer than her height three times over. She swing it back, whip the ground, and wake up dust.

We wait for mother to scream four times, that is what we do, say the oldest to her. Day gone but night not yet come, and he yank her chain twice to allow her to come out, though most times he just pull her out without warning, and by the time he reel her in, the girl is choking. Palm wine is spinning his head, which mean he is going to talk things that nobody is around to listen to. He yank the chain like he is pulling a stubborn donkey, yet it is the only time he allow her near the house. And when she do, the girl meet up on a loose memory, that of her father picking her up and smiling but the smile go sour in the quick and his arms go weak and there's one little blink where she float in the air before she fall in the dirt. We wait for mother to scream four times, he says, for four times mean it's a boy, and three mean it's a girl. But mother didn't scream.

Oldest brother is telling the story, but palm wine make him tell it with no form. You see my father? You see his pride when mother's belly start to push forward like it is leading her? Three sons soon to be four, and if it is a daughter then he can marry her off if he get rich, or sell her off if he get poor. Your brothers watching your father count till the baby is born, for she gone to bear child at her mother's house. All of us waiting to hear news of a boy, but your youngest brother the most, for finally he can be older brother and do the things older brothers do. Your father wait for news but he also resting, for he did finally listen when his wife say, Husband this small house will not do. And make it bigger he do, knocking out the wall to the grain keep and making it a bigger room for the two oldest boys, then building another room for the younger boy and the boy coming, and another room for mother's seamstressing for she is the most glorious of women. And one for the grandmother who he hate but cannot allow to live alone. We wait for the mother to scream four times. But four screams don't come, and three screams don't come either. When we get to Grandmother's hut she say, The baby, she come out foot first with the birth cord around her neck. My daughter bleed and bleed and bleed until she all bleed out, then her eye go white and she gone. Ko oroji adekwu ebila afingwi, Grandmother say, but it was not yet her time to rest. Little devil, motherslayer, you are like the one speck that drive the whole eye blind.

Look how you bring down curses on this house! My father take to weeping one morning, dancing the next, then screaming to the ancestors at night for their wicked sport. We speak to the priest, he say. We wear the amulet, we invoke the gods of thunder and safe journey, we don't eat fat, or bean, or meat killed by the arrow, so why the gods bring tribulation on us? She rejoice in her belly, she rejoice in her husband, and we don't lie with each other for six moons, so why the gods bring tribulation on us? Why, when we pour libations and give praise to the goddess of rivers who control the water in the womb? Nobody call him mad until one day we see him curling upside down, knee past chest and pissing into his own mouth. After that, mad is what we call him. The third day after birth is the naming ceremony, but nobody come and nobody go. Nobody dare name you, for you are a curse and the only thing worse than birthing a curse is to name it, for every time you call the name, you invoke woe. So no name for you. Also this, little one, nobody spit crocodile pepper in your mouth to prevent you becoming a shameful woman, and nobody make you a necklace of iron to cut you off from the world of spirits.

A new night. The little girl feel the tug of the chain on her neck, which turn into a pull, then a yank right out of the termite hill, a yank so fierce that she burst through the small entrance, leaving a bigger hole. So the yanking go, through the mud and the dirt, and the chicken shit, almost breaking her neck until she grab on to the chain, until the girl see that she is moving closer and closer to the house. She flip around to see nobody pulling her, but hear a slither on the ground. A giant white and yellow python hitch her tail to the chain as she moving to the house, not knowing that she dragging the girl. The girl, she fear what the python will do when it get to the house of her sleeping brothers. But no scream come to her mouth, no yell, no cry.

But then the python tail slip from the chain. Not slip, for she seeing it in the dark. The tail getting smaller and smaller as if the snake is sucking in herself. The tail getting smaller as the snake get wider, bigger, like a cocoon, for much movement is rumbling under her skin. The white and yellow lumps twist and stretch and turn and roll, until two hands burst through the skin and tear the whole body open. The skin slip away and a naked woman rise up. This woman don't look back once, just head to the house and around the side. The little girl follow her from several paces behind, to the back of the house as the python woman climb through the middle brother's window. She sit in the dust and the dark listening to silence, until a man's cry come from her brother's room. Louder and louder, this cry, loud enough to make her leap to her feet and run to the window, which is too high for her, so she scout in the darkness for something to stand on and find only a stool with one broken leg. An oil lamp light the room dim. On the floor is her brother and riding her brother is the python woman. She jumping up and down like she trying to catch something, the brother jerking and writhing like somebody is beating him rough. Then he yell that she finish him, he dead, and his whole body collapse on the floor. Then he start to cry, while through all of this, the python woman say nothing. Nobody come here but this whore witch, he say. I not no whore nor witch, you just cursed, she say. You and your brothers and your mad father and dead mother. So cursed that only whores come near you.

"You should kill the girl," the python woman say.

"Try to kill her already, but she come back," the brother say. The little girl nearly fall off the stool.

"Four days after she drive my father to madness, and drive my mother to the otherworld, we, my brothers and me, take her out to leave her in the deep bush. But do you believe that the cursed girl find her way back? She not even crawling yet. People in the village say that Yumboes, grass fairies, feed her nectar and crushed nuts. Little sorceress, they call her. Sake of her, the village shun us. Blame us when rain don't fall, or the crops yield small. Listen, I say to the people, come take her if you want her. I don't care what you do, but nobody come. We three raise weselves with people leaving us food until we can grow our own. She is the reason why they shun us. She is the reason why I not going have any wife but you."

"I not your wife," the python woman say.

Many moons come and go and take with them years too. She is bigger now, with hair in dirty clumps that hang until she tear them off and a voice that sometimes trick her brothers into thinking they hear their mother. She learn the ways of big people for not a loose word slip past her. More than twice the youngest go to slap her but she catch his hand and slap him back. Nobody teach her songs, so she make her own, and start to see a sky beyond the end of her rope. Yet still she is living in the termite hill, still she is plowing dirt and goat shit, still she is getting the whip for sport, and still she is having the youngest kick her to the ground and stomp on her back and push her deep in the mud. For if you are going to kill our mother, at least you should have come out a boy, he say. She feel herself moving through many moons and summers, but the brothers still at the day she was born, the day her mother die.

Whenever the two older brothers would travel east,

for they say no woman would have them in their own village, the youngest would come for her. His face would tell her that he's been thinking evil the whole day. My older brothers are lucky they have the ceremony before we mother die, he say. They lucky that they both turn man. But you take my luck. No elder will circumcise me and make me a man, for all of we cursed. After stomping her in the ground every day for eight days, on the ninth, he stomp her down in thornbush.

She know why they hate her for they tell her every night. Little demon, motherslayer, when will Mama stop bawling, they ask. When will she stop bawling in the otherworld about the little devil who slash and burn through her koo and kill her. The girl listen for her mother's cry from the land of the dead but hear nothing. Silence, then. She is silent as they beat her for asking for more food with less rot. She is silent when they say, Don't make us go to the otherworld and beg its lord to take you and give us back our mother. She is silent, for she already know that they try. So say the middle brother to the python woman on another night.

Three brothers, all wicked. The oldest whip her, leaving two marks on her face. The middle one starve her, saying she think she is woman, so let she cook her own food. And the youngest, he is the worst, because nobody will give him the ceremonial circumcision to make him a man, and is all because of her. I will kill you before you become a woman, he tell her. He say this also. I will take a knife and cut out your koo head myself for no woman will dare touch you. With it still in your slit, you neither boy nor girl. You is a monster.

The girl take it to mean a different thing each time. When they first call her a monster she scratch her skin until it bleed, angry she could find no scales to scratch off. She bite her nails to stop them growing into claws. When an itch come between her eyes, she think a third one is growing. Or that hair is going to sprout all over her like the tokoloshe, the black, bushy hair demon that oldest brother say will attack her while she sleep. One day she poke her head out of the termite hill to see a woman passing by the hut and laughing at her brothers for they in such a bad way that somebody must did put a curse on their curse. Maybe she is a monster. Little demon. Motherslayer. Girl who the python lady say grow up without knowing breast milk. No wonder her little titties don't grow. Her brother say plants grow the yield of their namesake, so surely if they say she is a monster, then a monster she will be. And when years fall away and she see how loose people use that word, the girl come to think that if she is not a monster, then she is a curse that her mother give birth to. Not even pretty, the middle brother say. The little girl run her hands over skin, feeling every harsh bone poking up, the hip bones being the biggest and the worst, and ugliness move from what she fear to what she know.

But her brothers lie too. Watch the boys, how middle brother steal a necklace that oldest brother win at the donga, then whisper that it is the youngest who steal it. Then two nights hence a giant python will slither away with a brass necklace around her neck. And oldest brother beat youngest brother, and the youngest beat the little girl in turn, but he not done. Youngest brother set poison in the creek where the python woman always drink and she get overcome with so much sickness that under the wind's breath come the messenger of death. The middle brother shout, Who is this poor, sick stranger, for he cannot tell anybody, not even his brothers, that every night he do a forbidden thing, and that he smash the eggs that the woman sometimes give birth to in the tallgrass down by the riverbed. And the oldest, always when he is under palm wine, talk of the man he murder and the woman he rape, and the man he rape and the woman he murder. Moons pass and years pass before this little girl see that nothing that come out of the mouth of these brothers could ever pass as true, not even if they say the water is wet and the fire is hot.

So there. Decided. She decide ten and two moons ago. Around her neck is a shackle and tied to that shackle is a rope. That rope is long enough for her to leave the hut, walk the yard, edge to the fence, slip past grass, hogs, chicken, mouse, and whatever other animal live in the pen. So from ten and two moons ago and at every dawn she chew at the rope near her neck, the end they never see for nobody want to see her up close. Only a little at a time, sometimes only a bite, and between chew and spit she gnaw through the rope. Then she put up pretense to be still bound, tying a weak knot and wincing as if they pulling her too hard. But planting season is nigh, and the brothers would soon be coming, shouting, Little one, dirty one, time to plow. No. This is time to run.

The day she pick get dark, and the sun turn black overhead. Dark like night. The shackle is still around her neck. But she crawl out of the hill and wrap the long rope around her waist until it look like a squeezing snake is killing her. The little light trick her into thinking the sun done gone, but it is still high in the sky, still not far past noon, a ring burning around a black center. She look at it for too long, and when she try to run, her eyes blind with light. There is glow in the air, a glow on the dirt. Everything bright and burning into white. The chickens squawk, stunned as she kick them out of the way, and as she run for the gate, the girl run right into his chest.

"But this not looking right, little dung."

Youngest brother.

"Where you think you going?" he ask.

First he think that she just running out to romp with the hogs, the only beast dirtier than she, but then he see the rope wrapped around her. Little piece of shit, he say and grab her by the hair. The pain make her scream but she don't want to cry. She yelling and kicking and he shout back, Yes, yell and buck like an animal, as he look for the end of the rope to spin her like a gig. But then she kick him in the shin, a good kick, and he drop her. A fierce look he give her, without saying anything. Youngest brother drop his cutlass and pull the leather strap from his sarong to beat her. Smile so wide his face look slit in half. She grab one of the little things she is carrying and as he pounce on her like a cheetah, she squash it in his face, a little goat bladder filled with her piss from too many moons ago, mixed with the dust from ground stones that scratch when he try to wipe his eyes. He scream-ing, his eyes swelling shut. You blind me, he bawl, and he coughing from some of the fire piss in his mouth. She try to run again, but in the scrambling he grab the rope and pull. And pull and pull and she can feel herself rolling out yet getting dragged to him, and nothing is stopping it, digging her heels in the dirt, mud, chicken shit, and pig shit. Little dung, he screaming, I going take what I always take and then I kill you, he say. Don't look for my brothers, none of them here to stop me. There. The fear stop. Brothers wouldn't be coming to save her but to stop him. Like somebody seeing you about to step on a thorn and warn the thorn. He still blind and pulling the rope one arm length then another. She let him pull, and then she grab the cutlass. Not far now, I can feel it, he shout, and she really is not far. The rope pulling at her waist, dragging her, squeezing her, but she let both happen and now he is smelling hog shit on her. She take all her might to swing and chop.

"You cut me hand off! Little bitch! Little bitch!"

Youngest brother braying and wailing and cursing and looking for his hand. This little girl finally run.

The rope dancing behind her, the hand of her brother still grabbing it.

And then there is more sun baking the skin and blinding the eye, and a trail wide for two chariots, and the numbness of feet walking too long. Running from shed to shed, path to path, bush to bush, and tree to tree until finally a forest to hide from her brothers, who would surely be looking, and asking others to look. Four days since shelter, more since food, and one more moon before she fall. The girl can feel sleep though she is not dreaming, and when awake she is moving, though her legs are still. The rope was so tight it was killing you like a snake, say a husky voice belonging to a woman bending over her. Where your mother be? she ask, and the girl shake over and over as if air slapped her out of a daze. One day more and the bounce of the cart cut her sleep. The woman ask, Where were you going, little girl, but the girl has no answer. No matter, the woman say. They are going to Kongor.

See the girl. The woman in the cart live in a house on a street where everything is blue. A house with two floors and two ladders, and with ten women also. Women with the bewitching koo, the men call them. The woman from the cart, who call herself Miss Azora, dub them her whores, for she was never one to hide behind pretty word. Why you bring another girl here, ask one of the women who in the seven days since the girl come never once put on clothes. Business steady but business slow, say Miss Azora, who look at her like she is herself wondering why she pick up extra cargo.

"A spot round here soon need filling."

"I can't work clay," the girl say. The other girls laugh, but Miss Azora mouth something silent, like she is counting.

Year jump over year when she count the days with Miss Azora, but sometimes she wish they would jump back. Year jump over year and throw a curve into her sides and flesh on her bottom. Years crack her voice then smooth it new and sometimes she don't know herself. Years make the same eye see the same thing but read it new. Read men new. Read Miss Azora new. No, read her for what she always was, and what she see a girl's for. We is women together, but don't call us sisters, one of them say. That first year two women leave, the year after, one come back. Three men die at the house, one while inside Dinti. Two of the men, other men come for, but the third man was a traveler they had to pay a merchant to burn. The young girl Miss Azora bring home have no name, but since she is the only girl among women they just call her Girl. Girl is who they send to the butcher for guts and trotters because he take pity and give her more. Girl depend on the kindness of some women, and stay away from the wickedness of others. Girl hide when a woman say hide and don't come out, for certain man come with certain wish, and while

Miss Azora love her children, she like money more. Girl play in the dirt, in the back room with a stick she call her sister until the day she wake and leave stick sister on the floor. Girl watching the whores be everything but a whore until night. Meanwhile Miss Azora watching her. Say she about Girl, You been growing through the years, but your face is too hard, like all you can see are people who wronged you, and your chin too sharp, your eyes too deep, nose too big, titty too small, legs too long, hands too crafty, and tongue too quick. Then she grab Girl and pull her shift over her head. She shudder, for in the years covering up in a house where women cover nothing, she learn shame. Let go of that shit, Miss Azora say while she inspect the girl. Shame is something you can neither buy nor sell. Your koo change also, she say, and tell Dinti to bring some rags.

"The moon soon come to you for what she want," she say.

"And the men coming after that," Dinti say and cackle.

Miss Azora's words come to pass soon after, and the first time make Girl's nipples sore, swell her belly, pain her head, and leave traces of blood everywhere she sit for three nights. Her lower belly punching her from the inside when it feel to, and the pain echo across the pit of her back and down her thighs. Girl don't stop crying. Me never see anybody have it so heavy, Miss Azora say, before they lower her in a tub and pour warm water over her shoulders. Miss Azora smooth the back of her head with her hands and sing the girl to sleep. Don't despair, Girl, you are woman now, she say.

A half moon later Miss Azora move her to the smallest room in house, the one they call the Cupboard. Is her first bed, a thick sheet stuff with feathers, and in the corner a basin and a jug of water, not for drinking. The same night one of the ten women climb into her bed from the window right above it. Is me, Yanya, she say. The woman look at her, sigh loud and long, then say, Don't mistake what Azora doing for charity. She only grooming you to be the next forbidden lily. Forbidden lily is for the man with peculiar needs, but nothing peculiar about these men, other than a huge purse. The kind of man who see the friends his young daughter playing with and can barely control the lust to grab one and drag her to the back bush. But first she going wait, watch you grow a little, fatten you up little more. Then what she going do is this. One night she will send a man in on you with no warning. She prefer it that way, to set them loose on you, then explain afterward that if you don't take to it, you can always leave. That is what she going do, for she do it to all of we. But this is what you can do, Yanya say, even as she say nothing about what happen to the last forbidden lily. Instead she slip Girl a pouch and say, Mix only as much as your fingertip in that bowl, and make sure they take a drink.

The first four men all leave a fat pouch and a big smile with Miss Azora, saying that lying between that one is like lying on a cloud. That cloud is not between her legs, but the pillow on which all sort of man fall asleep. But the fifth man rape her for as long as two songs humming in the back of her head before he take a drink. The men always wake up spent and proud, thinking surely they leaving bastard twins inside her. But after the fifth man, she start robbing them.

Her sack is getting full. Gold, silver, iron, cowries, and ingots. And earrings, nose rings, finger rings, necklaces, kola nuts, miracle berries, talismans, charms, a dried heart, animal bones, Bawo pieces, jade gemstones, wood fetishes, kaolin, and a small figure cut from onyx. The man tell his wife it must have fallen out on the road, in the river, lost to sea, or got picked from their robes. Far easier to let them go, even if they knew who took them, for the only thing worse than saying something precious is gone is to explain how it come back. They still come calling and ask for the girl with the cloud between her legs. Azora thinking something strange is afoot, for this girl don't have anything about her to entrance a man, but can't hiss at the coin she bring in.

Certain things come to pass. Maganatti Jarra, the twentieth night of the Cikawa moon. Man is doing what they feel they must do, and woman is making do. And at the house of Miss Azora, the mistress is cursing about the slow night. Most of them in the hall where Miss Azora greet the men and settle accounts. Yanya and another woman seated facing each other, two other women standing together by the right window, Girl sitting on the floor at the far end of the room and out of Miss Azora's slapping hand. As for her, she can't stop walking up and down the hall while cursing. Superstition about the night sky, one of the women say, but this don't please Miss Azora. She began to wonder if there is a new rumor about the women, one stronger than all the ones before that never stop any man, but make their wives feel better. They saying we have nasty woman disease again? She ask, but nobody there can answer, for none of these women keep the company of women other than themselves. If man not coming to the koo, then the koo must go to the man, Miss Azora say and ordered Yanya to go out on the street and pull down her gown so that any man passing can see her breasts.

"Why me, Miss Azora?"

"Why you think, girl? Because Dinti's titty lanky like goat, and because I not saying it twice that's why. Now go—"

Slow yet quick it happen. One long black finger wrap around Miss Azora's neck, then two, then three, then four. Before any of the women scream, it grab Miss Azora, yank her off the floor, and fling her into the wall across the room. She on the floor and still. Now the women scream and run. Nobody hear it coming, nor see nor smell it either. Two steps in, one can see it is a male one, one that shriek so loud that some women's ears bleed. He look like something that would move slow, but in a blink he grab another woman trying to run and fling her away too.

He shriek and mash a chair. He, the thing. So high his head scrape the ceiling, one hand thin and weak looking, the other thick as his body and touching the floor. Two legs tall as trees but one shorter than the other. He shift and scramble like a spider, slamming down his big hand and smashing tables and urns and vases, and throwing whatever he wrap his long fingers around. Then he see the girl and shriek again. He go straight for her. She climb the ladder fast—she never climb anything so fast—and run to her room. The smashing, the shrieking, the screaming moving closer until the little door get rip off. The beast, still screeching. The girl is shaking so hard that each blink scatter tears.

"Better thank the gods you're not a boy thief. Or I would be calling ten men to pull the Ukundunka out of your little shithole," this woman say.

She, a lady looking like somebody of great nobility and importance. Her dark lips and wide nose in a frown, her annoyed eyebrows sitting below a pattern of white dots that run down her left cheek. An ighiya on her head like a large black flower, and a long white Basotho blanket around her shoulders with the black pattern of a warrior with spear and shield. A tall woman, and wide, though she is not fat. She look like she can hold all her children at once. Cheeks of a woman who laugh without warning, without joke. The little girl is still trembling. The Ukundunka pawing at her sleeping sheets, as if trying to pull her in.

"Where is it, little girl?"

The little girl can't get the words out. "Where . . . where . . . where . . ." she say.

"The talisman, little fool. My little figure in onyx. Don't make me ask for it again, or I will let him search you."

The Ukundunka lower his head right in front of her. A head long like a horse, eyes like a wolf, teeth like a crocodile. Breath like she don't know.

"They are one, you understand me? The Ukundunka and the talisman, they are one. Let me tell you a story. Once after we long married, I say to my husband, Dearest husband, everybody know that you are an important man. Everybody know that is important business that keep you out late at night. The gods know how I worry. I worry so much that I ask a conjurer close in spirit to the gods to make me something to keep my husband safe. Yes husband, I say. You carry this talisman always and Ukundunka will protect you. An important man like you, with enemies everywhere, why, you could be in a ditch! So every night, if I flip the hourglass more than five times and there's no sign of my husband, I send the Ukundunka searching for the talisman. To keep him safe, you understand me? Lo, one night he not only come home late, but he come home without it. Lost it, he say. He say don't bother find it for I don't know where it gone. I say don't worry husband, I soon find it and deal with who take it. Now look at it resting in the bosom of a whore."

"I not a whore."

"You're in a whorehouse. Odds not good that you're a nun."

"I not a whore."

"You're not a cook."

"I not no whore, oh."

"Then why this room smell of men?"

The little girl have no answer. She could have said that yes, the room stunk of men, but none of that stink is on her. But a talk of sleeping poisons would lead to Miss Azora finding out. The noblewoman eye her deep, inspecting her.

"Maybe you can give him a child. I'm certainly not about to suffer one, certainly not with him. Ha, the shock on your face. You really are a child."

"I never whore. I never whore with none of them."

"Never, eh?"

"I rob them."

The little girl is getting more disturbed by the woman's stare than by the Ukundunka hiss. But then her frown break into a smile.

"Gold? Cowrie? Money notes? Talk to me, girl."

The little girl can do nothing but stare at her again. She wonders if this is what grown women do, unveil and unveil, surprise and surprise, until the only thing one can expect from her is wonder.

"I take whatever they have that shouldn't be hanging loose. And I keep it, for Miss Azora give us nothing."

"Nothing at all? Your clothes?"

"We buy. I say she don't give us nothing. Except for one thing. She give all of us a rape the first time she sell us, and charge the man triple money. So I mix them a potion, then I rob them."

"Eh. So they take nothing from you, but you take plenty from them? See here, girl, you in the wrong house."

"I not leaving one user for another."

"Who say you even have use?"

The little girl leave with the noblewoman that night. Miss Azora say nothing. Miss Azora don't move from the spot where the Ukundunka throw her, so who knows what is the fate of her. The noblewoman ask the girl her name.

"I don't have none."

"What? What do people call you?"

"Little one, little dung, little girl, little whore, girl, forbidden lily."

"Enough. You choose a name and that is what we will call you."

"I call my mother Sogolon."

See the girl take her dead mother's name, one hundred seventy and seven years ago. One hundred seventy and seven times that the great gourd of the world spin around the sun.

Sogolon.

TWO

"Sogolon, stop walking into walls. You not a little girl anymore."

See the girl. She want to tell Mistress Komwono that she not running into walls by habit, nor is she seeking self-harm. But it is curious, the feel of smashing yourself against something so stiff, that don't take in the hit like cotton, or silence the hit like dirt, or allow you to sink in it, like mud, or scoop some away, like clay. It is new to feel what will stop you no matter how hard you run. For the way forward cannot be through if the barrier is stone. No bounce, no echo, no sound, final. Yet it is not stone, even if stone help to make it. Rough and grainy, but not like dirt, more like sand, as if somebody find a way to put sand together so that it is stronger than wood. And cold, the wall is always cold, like an axhead in the early morning that the cook would drop in the jug of wine to cool it. Two mornings, maybe three, maybe ten, she go to a wall, perhaps the dark end of the cookroom, the back wall facing the garden, the inside of the grain keep, anyplace nobody can see her, and lick it.

Walls like these, taste is not the only difference. From the first day Sogolon come through the back door, and nearly every day after that, the mistress boast that this is no ordinary house. And certainly not some vulgar Kongori house, but a dwelling fit for any great lord above the sand sea. No expense we spare to make our house look like something out of an eastern dream, say the mistress. Sogolon don't yet visit no Kongori house, so she have none to compare it to. First, the ceiling, which is higher than a man standing on another man's shoulder. Walls rough like stone but still shaped by hand, like a mud house from Mitu. Bigger windows than in any Kongori house, where they look like a hatch. Sharp wood support beams, high and out of reach, like whiskers on the wall and on which belts, swords, masks, fetishes, and shields hang. Lower, but still hanging high, textiles from all over the North and South Kingdoms and beyond. Right by the left window, the master's stool, which he don't allow nobody to sit in. A slave sit there once, the cook say. The master have a magistrate flog the boy until the little fool can't tell water from piss. All over the house, rugs and cushions on the floor for whoever wish to sit. Everything in red and yellow and green and blue pattern.

But many a day Sogolon wander and find herself in a new room. Or rooms that look big a moon ago but small now. Rooms once hot, but now feeling cold. Rooms once right beside the cookroom, now far down the hall in the part of the house not even the master go. The room didn't move, that she know, but it feel that way because there be too many to remember which is which. Perhaps that is why she couldn't count how many people live there. The mistress and master. The fat cook, whose name she don't know, and who never see the need to share it. The thin slave girl, who introduce herself as a slave before she reveal her name, Nanil. A boy who take care of the master horses, this she learn from the cook. Then one day she see this boy leading out a horse and sweeping the roof at the same time. Twins, but nobody tell her. Unless they have to, nobody talk to her.

But you not a little girl anymore, Mistress Komwono say, and on a different day that mean a different thing. For the girl find herself wondering not when she stop being a little girl, but when she start. The chicken never once say she was a little chicken, nor the goat say look how I was a feeble goat. Who was there to tell her but her brothers and Miss Azora? And to Miss Azora, girlhood was a waste of time, a clumsy state that a smart female should shed quick. But be joyful she would say, for some of them prefer you look like little girl.

Mistress Komwono tell her several times that her ultimate use is beyond this house, but she like this house. And her words leave her wondering if the mistress training her to be a gift to a nun house, or a camp of elders in exchange for a life with more gold coin, which the mistress love to count. Hear Mistress Komwono. Imagine it, eh? she say, grabbing some coins. Imagine a house where all the master bring to it is his name. Not coin, not note, nor cowrie. His name is his only use. Griots, who record family history in verse and song, can trace his line right to the forming of Fasisi itself. Komwono, the cheetahs of the old savannah. If only they was real cheetah. If only they was a real anything that one can buy or sell or give. But still many doors open, and few shut when you have the name Komwono.

And this master. They did all become one man, the men who come to her room, so she couldn't tell him from another. They fall asleep on her cloud before they even bother to talk, and those who try to talk didn't think she was worth talking to. After all, that hole is not the one they pay for, unless the woman is Dinti. And the one who didn't talk and didn't drink the wine rape her. She leave a mark in her mind, a memory of their smell if not their faces, and a vow to visit them one night with a knife. But when she see this master, she couldn't determine if he is the first man, or the last, or any of them. See him, that is, not meet him. She never meet him, even the first time she see him. The slave say to her, Girl, don't even look his way for he is man who used to get summoned to the royal court. And when Sogolon ask why he don't get summon anymore, the slave just say who are you to expect a lord of the middle lands to lower himself by explaining anything to you? A girl like you must be like the air to a man like that. Which mean I must never be in his way, Sogolon think, for though she saying them, none of those words come from Nanil.

But while she can't remember this master, she mark how he remember her. See it all over his face, especially his eyes that pop open when he shocked, shift when he crafty, squeeze tight when he angry, go blank when he pretending, and close when he deny. At least it never wink with desire, which she still fear will come. All of this the mistress see as well, and take so much pleasure in it that Sogolon start to wonder if this is a game. Hear them, in the bedchamber where the master is setting to go to his second rest, and the mistress is dressing and doing her own umchokozo, dotting a line of white ochre from her left brow down her nose, her lips, to a final point on her chin. Someone of prominence she is about to meet, or something of prominence she is about to do.

"Wife, you just find this common girl and bring her back like she is some pet a family dash away?"

"Husband, you are the one who lose the talisman. I merely go to find it."

"And end up with this girl?"

"So it look. Maybe the gods have decided to bless us with some fruit. Good too because I found her—"

"Maybe the gods find you a thief."

"Then she is most crafty, dear husband. How did she pick it from around your neck?"

The master quiet for a while. Then he ask, "W-w-where you find her?"

"Just some ditch, husband. There she is right beside the talisman like she keeping watch over it. Looked like a sign. Trust the gods."

"Some ditch? Which ditch?"

"A ditch is a ditch, dear husband."

"She can't stay in this house."

"And where shall she go? She is just a girl not being put to use. The house is getting bigger, the need for servants greater. What is she to you?"

"Me? I don't even know the girl."

"Well, you always say you want a child."

"I never say that, oh."

"True. The word from you was, Barren bitch, where are my children? You going to kill my family line. Well it is a new day for you and for this house. Children may come yet. Or one is already here."

"That is no child."

"She's somebody's child."

"I don't like her."

"You don't know her."

"Fuck the gods, woman. You setting to spite me?"

"Spite? How so, husband? She said she found the talisman in the same ditch we found her. Surely this is the gods' work. I say to myself, Wife, why would your husband be walking near some ditch? In the Gallunkobe quarter? How the necklace fall off his neck when the string is not broken? Why would he be walking at all? But the gods always say trust the husband to lead in truth, so trust is what I choose to do. But given how this girl protected what is safe to me, to us, surely a man known for his good works as you are, would see good done to her."

"Then throw her three gold coins and send her off."

"Like some whore?"

Master Komwono cough. He say he don't know nothing about bartering with whores. Sogolon listening from the entry hall, out of sight. Nobody hear her giggle. This is a cunning woman, even if all she ever say to Sogolon's face is what she doing wrong. Girl, you eating wrong. Don't chew your cud like a cow. This is how you eat. Consider the piece of bread before you tear it, and don't tear any piece wider than the palm of your hand. Scoop a piece of goat stew no bigger than a fingertip. Chew slow and don't make nobody hear or see what you chewing, for that is how you disgust whoever looking. Girl, you clean yourself wrong. Which is to say that you don't clean yourself at all, except for when I threaten to kick you and your stink out of me house. This is how you clean. Go in the water stall by the grain keep and scrub your skin with sand. Scrub between your breast, scrub under your foot, scrub your elbow so it don't look like chicken heel, but dab your koo gentle, with just little water or you going ruin it. Girl, your head wrong. Don't even try the ighiya—you not from no dignified family. Take this cloth and make the cleaning woman teach you how to wrap a gele. You don't have plenty hair and that little hair not pretty. Girl, you walking wrong. This is how you walk. Watch the ingxangxosi, how he carry himself, wings fold away like a man clasping his hands behind his back, chin cock out, head high like he balancing a bottle of oil. For each step regard the knee first, which rise, but not too high for a woman, and the feet when it touch the ground, do so without disturbance, like a tiptoe. You want me to be like the devil bird? Sogolon say when she see the same fowl stomp a snake to death and eat it. Mistress Komwono reward her with a slap. That is shit-hut woman talk, she say. You leaving you girl years soon enough and you need to be ready.

Ready for what, Sogolon don't ask. As far as Miss Azora did say, she already pass her girl years. She don't want to upset Mistress Komwono and end her kindness. But she know the mistress is grooming her, even if she don't know what for, and that don't sound much different from Miss Azora. Sogolon take to watching every man or woman who visit, and that is plenty. She wait in the darker hallways to hear about who lose a cleaning woman, who need a daughter, which boy just complete the manhood ceremony, or which chief disappointed in his latest wife. Or, because Mistress love to count coins, who just come into good money. Years with Miss Azora don't make her into a fool. She know that without a dowry she is useless to a man. Unless the man want son and more son, and don't care what hole they pop out of.

See the girl as she see the world from out her

window, still rubbing her hands all around this thing called window. A wide roof, maybe a place where men meet and discuss wise things, or drink. A roof with steps to another roof, perhaps a family already big and getting bigger. Roofs sometimes no different than the wall leading up to them, with traces still of the hands that smoothed the mud out. Farther off, a tall thin tower, a prison, or maybe where the city stores sorghum in case of famine. Or perhaps the home of the thinnest, tallest people in the nine worlds. She count the floors by the windows. Three houses three floors tall with windows above windows, then a fourth house only one floor high, with no window at all. Three families rich and one poor, she guess. She wonder what kind of woman live in them. A city of roofs that she can't judge by the height, for most of them the same. Which is why the few six floors high, and even eight, poke the sky. Same color though, all these walls. Brown, ochre, sand or hard dirt. Windows not following any master craft but seeming to pop open like a bee house.

And the city change at night. Now it look like the back of an animal, black with shadow and spikes, but in the shadows windows where orange light flicker. Several lamps in several windows all looking lonely. More with dim light because the fire is farther away, in an oven cooking meat, or a floor pot brewing coffee. Farther off, deep into the city, the lights don't even flicker. And far north, in the center of Kongor, on top of that tallest tower, a statue of the bird perching on

the pinnacle as if about to fly. The Tower of the Black
Sparrowhawk, the cook call it when she take her out
into the streets. All she remember is the road curling
and twisting and spreading so wide that three carts
on one side can pass three on the other, then squeezing so narrow that only one woman can fit through
at a time. To leave Tarobe quarter, which the cook tell
Sogolon with pride is the richest in the city, means to
either go south to the drying riverbed, where slaves
go to coax water from the mud, drenching cloths and
then wringing them over buckets to separate the dirt,
or it means to go north to everywhere else. We take
the border road along the imperial docks until we
come to another road, wide and busy, that take us
deep into Nimbe quarter, where man keep records of
everything that walk, breed, and shit, the cook say.
Sogolon already tired, but the cook never seem to get
weary. Sogolon have to shout that she not walking no
more, for her to whistle down a cart, which take them
across, past the Tower of the Black Sparrowhawk, into
Nimbe quarter, which is where the cook plan to shop
all along. We need a new oil lamp, two if we saving
money, she say. And here in Nimbe was the finest
lamp maker, the finest maker of everything if you
must ask, she say, though Sogolon never ask. Sogolon
marveling over how these walls so high that the sun
can't see the street. An argument pull her back to
the cook, screaming at a merchant on the price of
a lamp. They curse and threaten until the cook finally say that if she wanted to deal with thieves she

would have taken her backside north. North. That is where they go next. Gallunkobe quarter, where most of the houses look fat, squat, and same. And all the people with the same frown. Don't tell the mistress where we go, the cook say. And don't ever come back here. The cook take her hand through the streets and frown when Sogolon say that long time pass since she is a little girl. I let go your hand in Gallunkobe quarter, you never see the mistress house again, she say, leaving Sogolon to marry the sight of selling, shopping, drinking, laughter, cloth rolling out, meat chopping up, noblewomen with guards walking behind as tall as trees, haggling over prices, with the warning that she could leave herself to danger.

Danger is back on a farm in a place she never learn the name of, with three brothers waiting to kill her. Danger is man who visit Miss Azora to bed the Forbidden Lily, man she couldn't get to drink the potion before he push her down on the bed. Danger is somewhere in the otherworld where according to her brothers, her mother is screaming for them to take revenge on the little dog who claw out of her koo and kill her because she selfish. Kongor? This land is a wonder. And it sadden Sogolon because she don't want to leave. Even if the master still walk right past her like she is an old ghost in the house. Mistress do more than enough looking at her. And fussing. Sogolon is somebody for the mistress to fuss over, and worry about. Somebody to dress in good clothes so that people think of her as coming from a good house.

She is somebody to instruct, correct, rap on the forehead, slap across the buttocks, scold when she speak
like some Mitu river rat, which is what the mistress
call her when she work out where exactly Sogolon
come from. But she know. The mistress is preparing her for somewhere else. Somebody else. So she
learn days and start to count them. Twenty and nine
and you have a new moon. Then she learn moons
and how to count them, glad when she count one
off, scared that it will be the last moon she count in
this house. Stand tall like a woman and not some
lazy fool, Mistress Komwono say when she catch her
slumping, but her slump don't come from laziness.
Meanwhile the master still don't look at her.

Then one night the master come down into the
quarters near the cookroom where she and the slave
girl sleep. She not asleep, though it look that way, and
so be the slave girl. He trying to be quiet. Tiptoeing in
slippers that slap the floor with each step. He nudge
the slave girl with his foot. She don't move and he
rouse her hard. She groan and roll away from him
but he follow, then nudge her with his foot again.
She groan again, a groan that turn into a mumble.
Enough for the master, who lift up his nightshirt to
show nothing underneath, but that nothing black in
the dark, making him look like a ghost under a dress.
The nightshirt keep falling down and he keep pulling it back up. The master kneel and pull the slave
girl to him. She groaning like she want to go back
to sleep, and roll onto her belly as he pull her across

the floor. The master push her robe past her buttocks up her back, and lift up his again. He slap it on her skin until he think he ready. Sogolon turn to watch them, interested in seeing what she think he think he did do to her at Miss Azora. He thrust and push and stop to brush off something pricking his knee, maybe a pebble, but she don't move. She grunt none, but he grunt plenty.

The city is the city. Where she come from, sometimes the sway of grass in the breeze can feel like the land is opening itself up to her. Especially with nothing but a hole in the side of the termite hill to look out of. But Kongor don't offer nothing. And when sleep don't find her, she get up and look out the window. A street near asleep, but boys always on the road, looking like they going somewhere. Some in wraps, some naked, all wearing or carrying straw helmet, or elbow brace, shin brace, in bright color that defy the dark. Trappings that she know, but can't place why. But something hit her deeper than knowing. And something about the boys, strutting in the city like they own the street, make her feel freedom, which just wash up to her feet, is now running away. She out the door before a devil could blink. A door with no lock or guard, for the master's name is his protection. Too much time pass before she realize that she don't know where to go. Or how to get back.

But she in Tarobe quarter, and that the way south is to the riverbed, so if she moving the other way, to the Tower of the Black Sparrowhawk, then she must be moving north, or north and east. The night streets in Tarobe quarter all lined with torches for light. But soon Sogolon on a street she don't know, where the only light carrying her is the moon. Sound is carrying her more than sight, for she catch up with the boys. The Tower of the Black Sparrowhawk is getting closer and closer but still far away. She approach a clearing where a large market bustle by day, but is now filled with voices and torchlight. She come around the corner and see the bonfire blazing as high as a house. And the boys, but is not the boys that strike lightning in her chest. Is the trappings on their head and their elbows and knees and fingers. The straw armor of the stick fighter. She is in a lane that open out into the bonfire square, as the roofs cut the moonlight and cast her in shadow. She step back from the flicking bonfire light and watch from the dark.

Boys jumping, yelling, laughing, and braying. Not like her brothers, where every move is marked with wickedness. Men here too, some dressed like Seven Wings with black garments on the outer, white on the inner, some in illustrious agbada, some looking like lords, others looking like beggars. But more than them, boys, most of them naked or taking off clothes. Many in stick-fighting armor. Some wearing nothing but white clay and a belly chain. See the boys. One on the ground blocking another who hammering down his stick on another boy. The hammering boy shiny and quick. The boy on the ground have no finger shield, and a strike to his knuckles make the stick slip his grip. One whip of the face and another to the cheek and a man run in to stop it. Some boys cheer. They run in and lift the winner on their shoulders. The loser, nobody come for.

The second fight longer but still too quick. She want to watch the boys, but that is not all she want. Watching them leap, yes, but Sogolon imagine her feet off the ground. Thrilling her it is, to watch them swing, sweep, dodge, and parry and strike and strike again until blood spray, but she swing in the dark, and sweep and dodge and parry and strike also. This is what dancing can do, for even when they strike blood, there is bounce and lift and grace. Sogolon want a stick, more than anything. One thin as her thumb, tall as a tree, and tougher than stone. Sogolon want to go down empty street with evil waiting to pounce. Another fight. When she leap in the air, just as a boy also leap in the air, it is like she stay there.

Sogolon thinking the way back home is south, but Kongor streets don't play by those rules. She don't find the house until noon, and everybody doing what they doing, moving with the course of the day. Misery chase away her relief when it come clear to her that nobody miss her. What a place, where everything go on without her as if nobody counting on her for nothing, as if she of no significance to nobody. Truly it make her want to scream.

One day Sogolon is walking down the entry hall
and happen upon people in the welcome room deep
in talking. Here is truth, Sogolon didn't happen to
walk there. She know that the secrets of the house all
come out in the welcome room, for everything find
a home there, confidences most surely. Not that the
mistress and master didn't keep things private. It is
that nobody walking down the entry hall ever stop to
listen to people's business, for surely she must be busy
with business of her own. And if the cook did ever
see Sogolon there, she would give her cheek a hard
slap and report her to the mistress. Sogolon mark the
ways of nobility. Not for the noble to be secretive, but
for the lower born to not walk in on the secret. That
don't stop her from sneaking toward the entry hall
to listen.

"How I must go to him? How that supposed to
look?" the master ask. More agitated than Sogolon
have ever hear him.

"Look to who, husband?" the mistress ask. "Nobody on the street at noon."

"You mocking daft, or you daft for sure? Nobody
on the street at noon. You think I don't want go because I afraid of people?"

"No, husband."

"And then telling we to walk, when he know I have
cart, chariot, and the finest horse in Kongor."

"He is not far, husband."

"Is not about distance, you fool. He want me to

come to him on foot to show me that his house is in favor and our house is not. Otherwise this bastard, who is not even from a real jesere family though his house full of instruments, wouldn't dare summon me to his house. And as if injury not enough, the swamp cow choose to add insult. Not only must we go to him, but we must walk, like we are his servants. You know he have the entire household waiting to see it, you know that don't you? He might even call friend and neighbor, saying, Come watch! Come watch the Komwono family crawl to my door with dust on their feet. How you don't see any of that?"

"Because I already looking beyond that. One season soon pass into another, but you are there bawling about how the season hot."

"That don't make no sense, woman."

"The way forward is sometimes through, husband."

"What?"

The mistress let out a loud sigh. Sogolon watching the burden of woman. Having to act stupid to make a stupid man think he smart.

"Is like you say, husband. The destination is all you need to see. Don't even look at who on the journey because we walk past all of them. So let us walk, husband. Let us walk right past them."

"You always have too much word."

"What he say to you exactly?"

"He don't say nothing to me. You didn't hear? Me not worthy of his voice no more. He send his messenger. 'I have word from the palace. Favor might yet grace the Komwono family.' Might yet grace the Komwono family? My grandfather liberate Wakadishu all by himself in—"

"In the first war. Yes, husband. Maybe that is the problem."

"Look at this woman, she turn diviner now."

"Husband, neither you nor he is young, so surely he would remember how our King take Kongor by force."

"And?"

"Fasisi born nobility, living among the Kongori. Some widows live on this street."

"Don't be daft, woman. Joining the empire was the best thing to happen to Kongor."

"But they didn't joi—"

"I say don't be daft. Kongor is not Bornu. That realm's impertinence got it scratched out of memory. This place never raised a single voice against the King. Meanwhile this piece of jackal shit didn't even have the respect to simply send word that he have an urgent matter. He share the matter with his servant. A messenger, wife! A messenger!"

"We waiting for this news for three years, husband. Who care how we get it?"

"Must you always betray your lower birth?"

Sogolon wait on the mistress for a quick word, something short and sharp to shut down the next words out his mouth. Nothing come. The space go so quiet that she wonder if one of them did leave. She shudder, thinking suddensome that somebody is creeping up behind her.

"Well, husband, next time flog the messenger if you wish."

"Won't be the last one I flog today, you can be sure of that. Like some banished dog, they treat me. Like some banished dog."

"Husband, you are wise in all matters. But if they want us to be dogs, let us be dogs. They won't know when we bite."

Another pause. Sogolon know that the master is finally hearing something he can use. She know little about men, but little is enough to know what come next.

"They treating us like curs? Is that what they will do? Then let us be curs. Let them know that this cur has bite, and will draw blood!"

"Such a wise man, my husband," the mistress say. "We wear white. Take your dagger."

The mistress and the master don't tell nobody where they go. If the people they are going to is low then we are even lower, and do not deserve any report, the cook say. Sogolon wait until dark to go looking for stick-fighting boys. She hide and watch until a man shout that is time they end this donga, and they all go. This time somebody leave a stick in the dirt. Like a thief who can't believe her luck, that is how she snatch it. She should run home now, she know it. Run before whoever forget his stick come back. But she can't leave. She crouch down low, a cheetah in the bush, leap up in the air and fight the dark.

Because she learn to name days and count moons, Sogolon know that four moons come and gone since she living in the house. The day before, she count the end of one moon and now she sit in the welcome room wondering what this moon, Gurrandala, the last of the year will bring with her. Only six days before, the sun bring heaviness on her with swelling and blood, which give her nothing but worry, because even in this house moonblood is to mark that your use is to breed. Though the master never look at her, she never forget when the mistress say that with her coming to the house, perhaps one day will come children. The cook see Sogolon acting uncanny, and instead of asking what her problem be, just give her some leaves and quiet is how they keep. Sogolon hoping. Many ways to describe a woman, but as soon as blood show, she get leave with only one.

No time, she say. No time indeed to take you to a fatting house, indeed from the looks of it you too old and it is too late. So Mistress Komwono forbid her from cooking, saying that her hand should be put to gentler ways. That mean combing the mistress hair. The mistress hair is coarse where she think it fine, and every time the comb snag a knot, she slap Sogolon's hands. But this is also where the mistress give over her time to train the girl with more than just telling her what she doing wrong. Stand tall girl, curve your hip up like you want it to fold on your chest.

Now walk. How many fingers to pick up the bread? Two, fool, not three. Next thing I know you going to scoop up the meat. I sure I show you how to eat raw goat from cooked, and when to choose which. Stoop to the floor girl, your knees together. Don't kneel, don't bend, and certainly don't squat, nobody want to see you like you about to cut a shit. Listen to you, with your stooping is hard. It not supposed to be easy. You don't yet know how much your legs going have to bear, yet you whining for bearing air. Now comb out my hair.

"Yes, Mistress."

Sogolon combing the mistress hair when she grab her hand. "The master, he look at you?"

"No, Mistress."

"He don't come to you? In the night, girl, he don't come to you?"

"No, Mistress."

"Strange. Then where he going, I wonder. You might be right. I fear he may be too embarrassed to ever come to you."

"You want me to do something about that, Mistress?"

"Oh by the gods no. His shame and guilt is what keeping him under manners," she say and laugh. Then she say, "But if he come to you, don't refuse him."

"Mistress?"

"You hear me. The man is your master, girl. Don't go forget that."

———

The first night of the Gurrandala moon she wash, thinking she would go to the street donga. A day full of sun leave the water warm even in deep night. Neither cook nor slave wash, so the stall is empty, three walls on three sides that open into the backyard. They build it between the grain keep and the cookroom, which can mean many a thing, but mostly that no man will see a woman when she being private. Since no man, surely none with standing like the master, would ever go near the cookroom or the grain keep. Mistress Komwono say that out loud one day, and from then the master don't bring himself to the room. Is Nanil who take herself elsewhere when morning come near. The mistress make sure the stall is a place with beauty and purpose, with a pattern of gold coins in a row, then shells, then back to gold and so on. The floor, cut from stone, is smooth, and at the top of the middle wall, rising just above Sogolon head, is a thin, hollow bamboo that water run through. So she wash. Longer because it is late night with nobody awake. And when she done washing, a sight she see in the stall. Herself.

The cook say the mistress buy the large silver food plate over seven moons ago, but not to present her bountiful food. She hang it in the bath stall so a woman can see herself. Sogolon can't guess why any woman would want to watch herself when she wash, yet watch herself is what she do. Long after stepping out of the way of the water, she still in the stall, regarding. Miss Azora make sure none of her

rooms have nothing that would cast an image lest a
man see himself and lose his nature over either the
sight of his flabby body, or the weight of his guilt.
But this is not a place for any kind of man gaze. So
she gaze. She lower her head to see the hair, almost
to her shoulder until she roll them into bumps. The
face that make her guess her age, except that is not
her guess, but the mistress. The cook say to Mistress
Komwono, Surely Mistress she can't be more than
ten and one. To which the mistress say, No, her mind
too crafty for somebody that young, but too raw, too
much heart and too little mind to be older than ten
and five. Ten and three then, Sogolon whisper to the
dim mirror of herself. In the dim torchlight she can't
make out much. Her shape, still strange to her, with
shoulders that remind her of a young stick fighter.
Narrow waist and narrow hips, not the hips to promise a man eight children. Legs looking ready to run
with little heed. The torchlight throw itself on her
breasts, which she never see reason to look at, but she
catch the mistress looking, plenty a time, and suspect
she thinking of the master. She really wish she could
remember him, and what kind of talk he bring to the
room before she quiet him. Something scatter across
the yard, and her heart jump. A cat.

See the girl regarding herself. Sogolon touch her
neck, her breasts, touch her koo and think about the
mistress words coming at her again. She feel to touch
each place of her body and ask it, what is your employ? Nanil the slave say her body is for plenty babies.

The cook say, This little slave whore is already beginning to show, but Mistress won't banish her from the house, even when the master demand it. How it be that this woman don't do as her man will it, she ask the cook. Because he have no will, and in Fasisi, where the master and mistress marry, a bride keep her fortune if she wish, so the master have no wealth either.

Three women. The mistress, the cook, and the slave. Sogolon regard all three and think perhaps this not about who she is, but what she want. The mistress want a good word to one day come so that she can return to Fasisi with no loss of face. She wait for that good word every day, listening for the faint beat of drums, watching for boy heralds passing her house, or pigeons flying overhead, but never pitching on her roof. The cook want nothing more than to cook and laugh at people. What the slave want, she don't know. What Sogolon want, Sogolon don't know. Perhaps she want to talk, to flee, to walk up the side of that Tower of the Sparrowhawk, all the way to the top, and see as far as the end of the world. She tell the cook for she need to tell somebody, only to hear her say, Listen to this, girl. Is because you have no grooming. No mother to raise you. Sogolon listen but hear **No mother raising you to never ask what you raising me for.** She look at herself and shudder at the thought that these women make her glad she don't have no mother.

She think of the cat that just ran across the yard who only live to eat, piss, shit, just like the master.

But her koo is a hole and he have something to put inside it. The mistress don't want children, it seem, but fine with how to make them. She and the master go at it like war every quartermoon or so. Otherwise he fuck Nanil until it start to look like he bothering her. Then he go harder. Sogolon standing in this water stall for too long, and the night is going deeper, darker. Trying to think about what she want only to have thoughts of the master overthrowing it. She want to move. She don't know what that mean, but she want to move. She want people to know her only by her trace.

Who tell you that you get to want? a voice from inside her ask. No woman in Kongor get to want. One time she hear the master in the welcome room tell other man that there are people who ride the edge of the sand sea on horse and strange beasts, and they cover their faces with a veil, and their hands with witch marks, and sometimes men will love men, or the beast that they ride, or sometimes their sisters. But they call no land home. They plant no grain, and build no keep, and even when they stand still, they moving slow. Sogolon like that. Moving slow while standing still. She see it and know it. She was already moving, running, leaving, coming, vanishing, dashing, walking, slipping, all of it is moving.

Sogolon is not a whore, that she say to any who will hear. But the girl is a thief, that she don't say at all. When she leave Miss Azora, Sogolon bring all that she take from the men, and every other night since then, when Nanil get up to go find the master, she pull out the sack from where it hide, a loose tile in the floor, in the corner of the room where she sleep. Beneath the tile is a few of her clothes, and on top of that few is a rag stiff with old blood. Moonblood, she whisper once to the slave girl so that she, or whoever she tell would have too much disgust to ever trouble it. Kongori women take some strange things for truth, such as if you touch another woman moonblood you going to be barren for all your living days. And living days is all Sogolon think about. Ever since she start to count days, then quartermoons, then moons, then whatever is beyond moons, she already putting herself ahead of it, already thinking nobody going to do anything for her but her, despite being under the mistress kindness. **Kindness** is a word the mistress use, not her. She under the mistress pleasure, is what it is. Pleasure.

Hot night at the donga. Heat demons that chase away rain and crack the riverbed land on the city from before dawn break and by noon even the roads sweat. The kind of day where beasts either fall down or run to foul water, where people have nothing else to do but sit in shade and curse that shade don't block this kind of unseeing fire, and where old people's eye roll in the back of their heads as they die. Night bring nothing but discontent because when the light leave it don't take the heat. The mistress gone to her sister, and Master go to sleep only after the cook rub him down in a leaf water that she let sit for weeks until it taste like wine. The rest of the house make do. Nobody really sleeping, but everybody fussing about they own and nobody else. She wrap herself in a blanket and leave through the front door, into the night, fighting the thick soup of turbid air until she get there.

Sogolon take her place, sweat running down her face and her tunic, between her buttocks and down her legs, leaving her fearing that she leaking on the ground. People wiping away sweat before it blind them, and the whole place working up a wicked man funk. Three fights pass, two in the style they call Kongori and one in the western style. Western style she like the least. Two men jump into the circle and attack, with whipping and thrashing and slashing and cutting, with nothing but force until the weaker one grab his bleeding forehead and switch from giving to blocking blow. The thicker one keep thrashing until the other stop blocking. Stop moving. The donga quiet as they pull the boy away, then a corner burst out cheering. The thick one win every night. But only that corner like him. They run to grab him, to put him on their shoulders when somebody shout. A man Sogolon never see before step out from the crowd and walk to the center of the ring. Sogolon ignore her own mind and move closer.

The man wear a blue skirt tied high up his waist and flowing lower than his knee. His headdress, a lion mane. He standing proud and speaking a tongue Sogolon don't know. Closer now, among some men in the darker part of the square, but clutching the blanket tight over her head. The thick man jump back in the ring, waving to the crowd to cheer, but the whooping and hollering only come from his corner. The new man shake his head and laugh. Also this, he wielding two sticks. A long one that he grab in the middle, the other shorter. The thick man shout that he could have ninety and nine sticks it still going be only one defeat. The referee dart in the middle but the thick one push him out of the way. He start to wail and hammer the new man. Thrash, thrash, thrash, up then down on the man, who blocking them with one hand. If you only blocking then you losing but this man laughing like he winning. Then he spin the stick until it blur and every strike from thick man bounce off and slap him in the face, sometimes in the mouth. Thick man cuss. He swing and he slice and the man block and hop and block and dance. Thick man pull back then charge, but new man block the charge and whip him in the face, right then with the small stick. Right beside the mouth. Thick man spit blood. He jump down into the fight, smashing the stick quick, striking the dirt more than the man. New man hopping, he spinning, he dancing around him like a mosquito. Thick man trying to spin as fast, but drop twice. New man turn his back and raise his hands to the crowd like he win. The crowd roar like he win. Sogolon look left and see a man looking at her. The new man soaking up the cheering like they soaking up the heat.

"You bring a blanket to summer? Heat not hot enough for you?" he ask but she don't answer.

"You the prize?" he continue. Sogolon move away.

The new man still rousing the crowd and the crowd still loving a man that they can like. Thick man get up. Even Sogolon thinking, Be like the lion in the bush, fool. But thick man thick in all his ways. He roar and charge but the new man don't move. Thick man charging with the stick straight out like a spear. Sogolon gasp. The new man don't even turn around, but stand there until just a blink when he drop to the ground and shove his small stick between the thick man feet. Thick man fall hard on his chin and don't move. Long cheering and the man still don't move until his corner pull him away. Nobody but Sogolon hear him screaming that he can't move anything below his neck. She walk away but see the man who question her now following her. She dash down a lane, turn right down another and left down another.

When she get back, the house quiet. Mistress not yet returned from her sister, so she must be staying the night. Master, being the master, must did thank the gods for sleep in his own bed. But Sogolon unsettle her head too much to sleep. Master and Mistress keep only four doors in this house, the grand entry, the bedchamber, the back door, and the master library. She already gone through the bedchamber more than once, more than five times, and never find anything interesting in it. The master library she stay away from. But it is night and everybody sleeping. Most of the room is like any other in the house, empty mostly, but with fabric, and textile and pouf and stool. Near the one window is something all covered up with white cloth. She know what it is, for the cook talk about it whenever she wishing for a turn in her luck.

Sogolon run her hand on the canvas covering. She feel it pull against the thing underneath and worry for a second that it is a beast keeping still. Sogolon grab the canvas with both hands and pull it off. He keeping a boli in the house, the cook did say. She jump back at the sight of it, for it look like an animal. Four little legs holding up a round and fat base like a young hippopotamus. When she come in close the legs look more like that of a stool. But the shape still taking the body of an animal. The boli carry a hump on the back, and a bump to the front of the body working as the head. But the head is round like the hump, with no feature of any animal face. The boli is thick, with rough skin, like mud cracked under sun, or old leather. This is not like the sculptures she see all over the house, or a fetish, or the body of a god in the shape of beast. The boli look like a god was in the middle of creation and didn't finish. But the way the cook and the slave whisper about it, she expecting it to be magnificent and terrible. So she touch it.

"Power might come through and blind you."

Sogolon flinch. She jump back quick, but there is nowhere to flee to. The master is in the doorway. She bow her head and nod to him. The master walk in, not looking at her.

"Or turn you into fool for thinking you can handle it."

He walk right up to the boli and touch the hump.

"When the boli first come here, it is nothing but a piece of wood wrapped in cloth. And look at it now, eh? Ten and nine years of offering to the gods. Clay, sand, dirt, shit, and some things no decent tongue should talk about," he say and laugh.

This is the first time he say anything to her, and Sogolon know it is best to say nothing. Not even Yes, Master.

"I . . . I . . ."

"You are nothing but a thief?"

"No, Master."

"Then you looking to sap the boli for yourself?"

"No, Master."

"You don't even know what it is, and why would you? What is a power object to one with no power?"

The master start to stroke it. "Try you head to understand," he say. "The nyama of the world, that run in and out of your nose when you breathe, that bring rainfall and drought, that bring life and take it, all of it come together in the boli. The gods take a look of everything and squeeze it down to this like a potter squeeze down clay. It keep safe the spirit, you understand? It hold the nyama for the community."

"This not the community. This your house," Sogolon say. The moonlight land on his frown.

"Not everything deserve to be had by everybody," he say. "Come over here."

Sogolon is shifting a little to the door, but now she stop.

"I don't repeat commands in my own house, you understand?"

Sogolon walk toward him but stop when her foot touch a rug. Halfway from his finger beckoning her to come closer.

"How come I supposed to have had you, if I can't remember you?"

Sogolon don't answer.

"You passing so many days as my wife's little pet that you forget that whoring is what you do. How lucky you must be, to leave Miss Azora right before somebody break into her house and kill her. Break her neck like a twig."

Sogolon gasp. She didn't know what did become of Miss Azora that night, and didn't have nobody to ask. The mistress clearly don't care what her monster do.

"You the one who want to come into the presence of the boli. Then come into the presence."

Sogolon is back where she is before he come in. The moon shift since and now it cover the figure in silver. The master tell her to touch the back. Her fingers come back from it wet.

"Goat blood, all along the back. Some chicken blood too. You understand? You can't add nothing to it that is not a sacrifice. For it to give to you, you have to give to it, and for you to give to it, you have to take from yourself. What you going add to it?" he ask.

Sogolon stare at him.

"You think your stare is an answer?" he say.

She turn back to the boli. She say to him that she could go to the cookroom and come back with some kola nuts to chew and spit on it, since she hear that some gods take that as offering.

"My money buy that kola nut. How is that your sacrifice?" he say. Sogolon step back from the boli, but he step back with her.

"All your mistress care about is getting summoned back to court, you understand? All she living for is that one day the royal house of Akum show her favor. Never mind that is her poison mouth why we are banished."

Sogolon grab the canvas to cover the boli.

"Never mind that. Get out."

Sogolon turn to leave as quick as she can walk.

"One more thing," he say. "Washing water right outside by the grain keep. Don't come in here smelling like the donga again."

Don't act like you shook. You shook, but don't act like it, she tell herself over again.

"Look at me and my mood that I should say this with some goodness. From the first time you go out I follow you. Or was that the second time, or third, or even tenth? First thing my mind whisper to me is look at this whore going out with her unsatisfied self. But lo, look at where I find you. Now I don't even have to follow, when you come in here smelling of men."

Sogolon just standing there. She don't turn around.

"You like see man set 'pon each other like wild

dogs? Is that what excite you, girl? How you take to a man wearing nothing but himself?"

Sogolon don't turn around.

"I tell you to get out."

She don't get five step when a blow to the back of her head knock her down. The master drop the carving, then drop on her before her head stop spinning. He grab her by the shoulder and roll her over on her back. Sogolon head still spinning and won't come to a stop. The master saying something but it come out a snarl. Her head come back just as he grab her top to rip it off. But the top won't tear, he yank it again and again, and yank her again and again. She try to push him off, but he slap her. She gasp, she about to scream, but he say, Scream and you out on the street before the sun even rise, you understand? She squeezing her legs together and he, with one hand grabbing her neck, try with the other hand and his legs to spread her. She whimpering and struggling and free her hand to scratch him on the neck. He snarl again and punch her in the face. Stunned too long, she is stunned too long. She try to push him off, try to roll over, but he already pull up his nightshirt, ready to slap himself on her skin. Stop with your fight, you not bred to win, he say and sink his finger. She close her eyes and think of the loudest, wildest, noisiest thing. A storm, with clouds gray and churning like cow milk in coffee. Rain breaking loose and flooding the pasture. And wind, whistling, then howling, then screaming, then blowing away the trees, the house, the land, the blue sky, the dirt, and the Tower of the Black Sparrowhawk, breaking the statue from the foundation and making the stone bird fly. A cough then another coax her eyes open. Wind, a whispering demon, whip up papers on a stool, float the canvas like a sail before it fall gentle, and slip past the boli as it escape through the window.

Right across from her is the master, head near the ceiling, his back pressing against the wall, his legs loose as if floating in water, his arms shaking, his hands trying to hold air. And bursting through his chest, a wall beam, sharp like an arrowhead.

THREE

Bezila nathi. They mourn with us. By the evening of the next day, Mistress Komwono's eldest sister put down the multitude of tasks the gods are expecting her to finish in order to offer her open bosom to her grieving sister. This sister short where the mistress tall, and fat in the front where the mistress just wide at the side, and anybody looking at her would say, Praise the gods for they bless you with another child. The mistress have no children so the sister bring nine of her own, all boys, the oldest scraping the doorway with his head, the youngest leaving the smell of baby shit in every room he enter. Three to six cry, two to three shout, eight or nine yell, four or five laugh, and at least ten times somebody bawl out, Stop it at once! None of this from grief.

But the sister make it known to everybody in the house that she come to shoulder the burden of her sister's sorrow. And what a burden it is, praise the gods, for they know of the multitude of things she have to do. Which is why she demand fufu every day, both from yam and plantain, three kinds of soup, two chickens every morning, a fresh new goat, and millet porridge because all but one of her boys hate the taste of sorghum. And no meal too hot or you will get a slap, or too cold or you will get a pinch. The cook say to make everything the warmth of baby piss, and all ten will be happy, which prove true. The mistress eat nothing.

And Mistress Komwono. She was the second to find the body after the slave girl get up from the kitchen floor at dawn and sneak to the library expecting to do what the master always summon her to do. Instead scream and wake up the house. The mistress, coming home from her sister's, where it had been cooler but far too noisy to sleep with all nine of her sister children waking in turn and disrupting the night, go quick to the room where the screams come from, hoping to catch her husband in the act of something awful, something he only bold enough to do when she gone, that she can hold against him. She reach before the cook and the twin boys, who arrive right in time to grab her arms before the mistress faint and hit the floor. Mistress Komwono bawl and keen and weep and scream and holler and spit, and laugh over her husband all in a manner unbecoming of a noble lady. This come from the cook, who say that only a moon ago this same mistress would have said the same thing about somebody else. Since the discovery of the master's body at dawn, she, the cook, take it on herself to run the household, with no direction from the mistress that she is now to run the house. That running come to an end at noon when the mistress's sister arrive yelling, What happen to my brother-in-law? Though nobody at the house remember sending word for her. The first thing this sister, who call herself Lady Mistress Morongo, do is demand they move the body from the welcome room to one of the end rooms that Sogolon can't remember stepping foot in, after all they can't have his body in these chambers. It have a hole in it.

Mistress Komwono take to her bed through most of the day and don't have the will to tell her sister and her nine nephews to keep quiet, you disrupting my grief. The cook, she begin to worry about her eating less and less until two days later when the mistress eat nothing at all. Her sister say, Yes, what a shame but give the bowl to my middle child for between those above him and those below always forget him, and no food should go to waste. That night, the cook go to the mistress to check if sorrow is making her ill and find her fast asleep, not on the marriage bed, but the floor. The cook, thinking she fall off, rush to wake her and steer her back to the bed. But the mistress box away her hands and say it cooler on the floor. But the room already cold, Mistress, why you looking for colder? the cook ask. She look on the floor and see a headrest and all sort of linen, spread out like a bed.

"A spirit in the bed," Mistress Komwono say. "He didn't die good and now he on my bed. Last night he reach under my nightdress."

The cook overstep her station and say perhaps it should bring her some happiness to know that even in the next world the master still have a raging desire for her in this one, to which the mistress say, "I never say it was him."

The next day the sister waddle into the cookroom, fanning herself and asking what is to be done now, for the poor woman talking to herself. One of the twins say, "Maybe she talking to the ancestors, Mistress. Maybe she seeing about her husband's safe passage. I mean to the otherworld."

"Who in the name of gods wise and stupid permit this boy to talk to me?" the sister ask.

This is witchcraft and evil, the slave girl say and the thought take life in the house. The cook declare that she will never leave the mistress at her weakest, for that kind of disloyalty would get out and poison her search for new work. The slave can't leave for she bound to the Komwono name. The boy twins refuse to leave but they never sleep in the house, but with the horses, and Sogolon don't have nowhere to go. They close the library after the twins pull the master to the welcome room. Everybody wait in their own fashion for evil signs and malevolent wonders, but none come.

Though nobody call them, the magistrate come,

along with two deputies who look like their balls still waiting on hair long past due. The mistress was in no mood for talking, except to say that the Komwono name surely buy her privacy to grieve her husband. And the cook was in no mood to watch strangers turn upside everything in the house, especially when the first thing he do, he knock over the boli, then marvel at how it didn't break. Crime not some boat in the night. It can't just pass by like that, he say. Good, then find the devils who hoist him up right up to the ceiling and drive them out, since you clearly of the badder sort, she say. Everybody in this quarter know the magistrate is as cowardly as his deputies are stupid. Me not done with this house, he say, but done he surely was, for he never come back.

In two more days the families of both wife and husband arrive. The number so large that the house swell and burst, and some have to find lodging nearby, while others curse and say they going back home. Lady Mistress Morongo whine and curse because all she's thinking about is the well-being of her sister and these people come to take everything, eat everything, and sleep everywhere. But her voice now lost in the house, this she say to the cook. Mistress Komwono have three sisters in total and they all come with their large families. But the master have three brothers and three sisters, who come with their children and their grandchildren all in dozens upon dozens. This overwhelm the cook, who have to call in two women to help, two who never see inside Mistress Komwono's house before.

The master's family different from the mistress's in ways plain to see. Here is where it come clear that they are an old family, for they carry themselves that way. Head high like they don't look down to count money. They squat despite stools everywhere and none of them is fat. But shifty, like the master, as if they all keeping secret, even from each other. The oldest brother, he who bring five children, already take it on himself to make arrangement for the rites. The youngest brother, without counsel from anyone, decide that it is witchcraft that kill the master and as soon as he find her, drag the slave girl right into the middle of the yard to flog her until she confess. He get one of the twins to tie her up with grass rope, ignoring her bawling, begging, and screaming. Talk 'bout your necromancy! Talk 'bout your malcontent! he shout. He lash her twice before his sister yell at him to stop. The brother shout that this is man business and to keep out, to which the sister say, This is business of man with sense and in all these years you never show any. The man grab the stick and march to his sister as if about to beat her too. My husband can break your back with one hand, you little piece of dog shit, she say, loud enough that the whole house hear, for now most of the house up and bored. Who else have reason to go against her master but a slave? he say and scowl. He is still thinking at the end of this argument is his victory. This little stick of a girl look like she know witchcraft? She look like she know any craft? The little thing can't even read, his sister say.

"You all think your brother impale himself?" he ask. He let it come out, how he seem to be the only one concerned that his brother didn't die right. "Maybe all of you been wishing for him to be dead," he say.

"Maybe we waiting on the investigation from the magistrate, brother."

"He already come and gone. They speak of it at the markets."

"Maybe he solve it, then."

"The question still unanswered, sister," he say.

"If you still don't know what she doing in your brother's library before even chicken wake up, then no wonder you have only one child."

"Must be some reckless fucking you putting on, sister, if you thinking is that cause his death. What he was fucking, a bat?"

The brother let go of the slave, but not the matter. It don't take long for the word to leak out in the street that devilry set upon the Komwono house. Especially when the leaking is the youngest brother's doing. One of those bitches in the house studying evil, he say to a pillar that in his drunkenness he mistake for an agreeable man. Get your stinking paw off me, he say to one of the twins, who go to fetch him.

This brother summon fetish priests and Ifa diviners to the house at his dead brother's expense. They sweep the library with their eyes, then sweep it with a

broom, collecting dust, and paper, and whatever piece
of a thing they can't identify, coin that nobody can
spend, and whatever is now dry from whatever spill
from when man and woman fuck. And all the dry
blood on the floor. They also cut some of Nanil the
slave girl's hair, and ask for articles of her clothing,
but she only have the one cloth she have on. And they
take some of the master's precious books, though they
don't say what they need those for. The library is the
only room empty of people. When the brothers decide it is time for umkapho, the youngest curse and
say, What is the use of sending word to the ancestors
if nobody can tell them where his soul be or where it
going to go? Then give no speech at the rites, the oldest brother say and the men of the house leave him.

Meanwhile Sogolon stay in the grain keep, out of
the eye of everyone. Because nobody call on her, nobody see the dark swelling right below her eye. She
set her mat in a corner so small that the girl have
to curl in like a baby just to fit. Then she pull her
dress over her head up to her waist, leaving the rest
of her body to the flies and itchy grain. Nobody have
need for her, most of all the mistress, who stay in her
room and sleep on the floor, except for once when
her sisters break into the chamber with two urns full
of water, saying if you won't do nothing at all that is
your choice, but first you going to wash. Her sisters
and sisters-in-law all grab her like they capture wild
game, and strip her while she struggle and scream,
and all Sogolon, the slave, and the cook can do is

watch. Until they close the door so that no man or lower woman see how uncleanness and grief bring a woman down low.

The eighth night Sogolon jump up like something wake her. She roll on her back and look out the window. The house full, yet everybody is asleep. Everybody is able to, even the mistress, whose grief is driving her mad. But not Sogolon. See the girl. She take herself out of the grain keep and go into the courtyard to see even the chickens asleep. If you go past the corridor on the other side, stooping below the cookroom window and staying low, you will get to the same gate the back door lead out to, and from there you can run away. **But run away to what?** another voice inside her head ask. **Not run to, run from,** say another voice. **Run before they find out. Run because soon they know.** Wind outside slip in, like a whisper she overhear from another room in a tongue she do not know. A whisper that sound like a giggle, then a cackle, then a growl, and all around she feel the dirt start to shift and the grain shake. A rumble, a crack that open a sinkhole and swallow her full.

Sogolon wake up choking hard. She hack a cough in the dark. She is on the mat in the grain keep and can hear flames waking up the cookroom. Dawn. She remember just then that is not that she cannot sleep. Is that she don't dare.

Right after noon the men come back with some elders and a cow. They slaughter it right there in the courtyard, letting the blood run where it choose to run, this perhaps a message from the god of judgment and revenge. The youngest brother point to a stream of blood heading to the cookroom and say, I too tired to tell you that witchery coming from over there, but by now people stop listen. This is what the men do. After they kill the cow, they cut up the flesh, chop the bones, and cook the whole thing in three pots with neither flavor nor spice. Then every person related by blood or by law eats. They sit on the floor in the house, in the walkway, in the dirt of the courtyard, and out in the street. They hiss and frown at the awful taste, but say nothing for fear of angering the ancestors, who are watching and making judgment of both the living and the dead. Cook, slave, servants, and Sogolon just watch.

The same afternoon the women curse each other out. Send the children away, say the mistress's sisters, for they have fewer children, even when you add Lady Mistress Morongo with her nine. And yours are the loudest, the most vulgar, the most spoiled, and the most getting into fights, the Komwono women, the master's sisters and wives say. Lady Mistress Morongo say the dead not yet gone and when he carrying messages to the ancestors, his behavior attracting spirits. Besides, everybody know that bad spirits love funerals. But the master's sisters reply that all of you daft, just like your husbands. Light a lamp in every window and no bad spirits will come in, that is all. Lady Mistress

Morongo heave herself in front of the Komwono sisters and wives like she is about to brush back dirt with a hoof, and snort. Who you all calling daft? None of you bush pussy used to cover up your titty before your brother marry my sister's money and property, she say. Komwono the legendary warrior clan. War done fight, oh. This appall the Komwonos, for their grand name is all they have. You all just afraid that your children still have eyes to see what they shouldn't see, they say. A sister, seeing her across the courtyard, shout to Sogolon, the first time any of the relatives on either side so much as say a word to her.

"How old you be? Yes, you, the one covered in the grain that bitch cook make me eat. How old you be?"

Sogolon is standing by the grain keep, but now with all eyes on her, she don't know how to be.

"Me, Mistress?"

"Then who else, girl? How old you be?"

"Ten and three, Mistress?"

"Hmph. You . . ." She let that point die before going to another. "You still a child then. Tell me, young girl, tell all these precious, intelligent ladies. You see any spirits round here these nights? Anybody bother you?"

Sogolon take a good look at the sisters and the sisters-in-law, the master's kin and the mistress's, and forget which is which. Four on one side, three on the other, and they all look like each other more than the master or mistress.

"No, Mistress. I don't see nobody," she say.

For all Sogolon do is watch. Then she watch herself watching, watching to the point of knowing deep
what is not her business. So in two days she know
which brother and which sister-in-law, and which sister and which brother-in-law is closer than the married couple was in this life. She spend all the time she
can looking out, and with the crowd ever growing
there is always somebody new to watch, to study, and
to follow. But she know that is not why. After two
days nothing more is curious about the people or the
world. And yet still she up all night through dawn
and sluggish in the day.

Sogolon watching herself for the change, for she
know it coming. She know it might already be here.
A change in her voice, a change in her walk, a change
in how her face look when people ask her a question. She don't know how she know, that being in
the same room to see death come and leave, taking
a life not yours must stain you. She feeling different.
Sometimes is a heaviness like what will happen to her
body in two quartermoon. Moonblood. But this is
not like that, this come on like a quick sickness, linger for longer than anybody would want, then leave
when it choose. She can't describe it even to herself.
Not a heat, but it feel like heat burning her head slow.
Not an ache, though it feel like a hurt. More like a
disquiet. A vile disquiet. A most uncomfortable thing
that won't decide if it is a thought or a feeling. Like
something at the back of her head, not unlike the
first time somebody give her coffee. She wish it is

coffee. She feel bad at comparing it to something so light, but what there is for her to compare it to? At night it feel worse, a thing that take over a side of her head, quiver down her shoulders, and tremble on her fingertips, a thing that make her want to cut her skin open and climb out of it. She want to get out of it so bad she would peel herself to do it. That is the only way she can think of it, this creeping heat that is not heat, pain that is not pain, madness that is not mad. Just this . . . she don't know. And thinking over and over don't make her know any more than before. Sogolon see the flame in the cookroom and wonder if she stick her hand in it, not enough to burn her bad, but enough to hurt her so, then this night creeper, for that is what she start to call it, would creep away. Chase away pain with pain. When her brothers forget to feed her, sometimes her head would fly up in an agony as if furious with her, and all she could do is beat her head on the dirt over and over until one pain defeat the other, and sometimes both vanish. The creeper in her head make her want to beat it out. No. She know it will never go out. It come upon her every evening and steal away her sleep. Sometimes it come in the morning when she gathering grain, or when she see one of the master's brothers, or at a thing connected to nothing, like finding a hole in her dress, or seeing a sunset deep not with orange, but purple.

See the girl. Count the days. Her own mind yanking her back in the library touching the boli and coming away with goat blood. Chicken too. Blood is streaming down the wall. Follow where it come, go the other way, up where it going down and you see his toes, then legs, then nightshirt. The beam sticking out of his chest, the arms open wide, and the eyes still looking but not seeing. She too frightened to call his name, or to call for help. She turn to the entrance and he is walking in with a frown, eager to get to work and hoping she will get out without him having to tell her. He is walking in, noticing her, and he scream, **You are nothing but a thief.** This is not happening, look at him on the wall. Seeing his empty eyes up there make Sogolon wonder what plot he did have for the day. What he mean to do as the sun rise, like it rising now, where would he be around noon. When a person dead, you kill the future too. Not her, she thinking, she didn't kill nobody. She need to walk backways out the room, yes back out, erase every step she make into the room, undo herself. But as she reach the doorway Sogolon still. The master, still and stiff. Sogolon already wondering what lie at the end of this day when his left foot twitch. Then his right. Then he lift his head and try to scream, but out of his mouth come blood thick like honey. His head jerk, his hands jerk, Sogolon run.

Outside in the courtyard she make it just beyond the entry when her whole body lurch forward and she vomit. She retch and retch, even when no vomit coming. The day is approaching and nothing is stopping it, and Sogolon, once her belly stop trying to empty her, remember that people soon be up, who never wake before her, but always get up first to sneak off and do business with the master if he didn't come to her in the night. Sogolon jump up, kick dirt over the vomit, and run back inside. She sneak over to her bed cloth and cover her dusty feet. Sogolon turn her body away from the slave girl, and stare at where the floor meet the wall until slave girl shuffle. The fuss of her brushing dust off her nightclothes, trying to walk silent to the bowl of water in the cookroom, dipping her hand in the water because she don't want to make splash, and sniffing herself, then sniffing again, under her armpit perhaps and wiping them, then her chest and her legs and her koo, grabbing her bed cloth, rolling it up and walking over to the cupboard, opening it up to a creak, closing it, tiptoeing, pit-patting out of the room, her feet getting quieter as she walk farther until there is no sound, just Sogolon counting footsteps she don't hear, and wondering how many steps take the girl to the east side of the house, if she moving constant or stopping, because Nanil is always careful not to rouse nobody, then counting how many steps from the outdoor passageway to the indoor passageway, past the welcome room, past another corridor leading to the marriage bedroom, past some cracked tiles that the mistress keep nagging the master to replace, until she finally in front of the library. Nanil will knock their secret knock on the door. She will wait two breaths, maybe three. She not looking at anything but the ground, and step into a spot, pull up her dress, kneel, go on all fours, waiting for three blinks, maybe four. Sogolon still lying on her side, on the floor watching where the floor meet the ceiling, and waiting for it. She wondering why it don't come. Maybe in the room is possibility and something else happen in there, or nothing at all. But then Nanil scream. And scream, and scream again, and Sogolon stay still as the tears run out of her eyes. Nanil still screaming. Then nothing. Then a quick creak from a door swinging open, follow by it slamming into the wall. What kind of devilry going on in my house? the mistress say. I going to discipline that damn girl and that damn . . . The mistress trail off. Sogolon waiting for it to come and it do. Now the mistress bawl, and bawl and bawl again, and now footsteps thunder through the corridors. The twins running into the street to find help. The feeling seize Sogolon again, and she jump up and run outside just in time to vomit in the archway.

So the mistress cry the whole day. She summon Sogolon little after noon, and say, Amuse me with something you learn in the bush. Sogolon confused. She say she don't come from no bush but the mistress say, Then why you always smell like tallgrass? and laugh out loud and hearty though Sogolon didn't find it funny. She used to smell like dirt, and now she smell like whatever flower she can find, but she never smell like no grass.

"Amuse me," the mistress bawl, and fall off her own chair and stay there until the cook and a twin run in and pick her up.

"Why you didn't help her up? Is any fool anywhere so worthless?" the cook say.

Within three days the smell coming from the mistress room is beyond stink.

She never supposed to be in the library. She have no business in that room. The master have every right to be in his own chambers, she do not. She come through the door of her own will, which make her the subject of his. Those sound like words that would come from the master, not her. But if the master didn't touch her, he would be here right now, ignoring her. A voice that sound like her remind her that the mistress tell her not to refuse him. If she didn't go in the room without permission like some common thief, nobody would be there to tempt the master but Nanil. You bring evil on yourself, and you bring evil on him. Shut your mouth while he show you what your holes is for and just say to yourself that these are the things that must happen to you. No. I didn't do anything, the wind do it. The wind do it.

The weight of thinking turn Sogolon into a stick. She don't know she in the cookroom until the cook shout more than once, Get out the way, you stupid little girl, don't you see everybody busy with their sorrow? Just then the mistress stagger into the cookroom, with her sister shouting behind her. She can barely

walk, and her eyes look lost, like she looking at yesterday. She almost fall on Sogolon, grabbing the girl's
tunic and almost bringing them both to the floor. "Is
you kill me husband, talk truth! I say to talk truth.
Is you? You done kill my master, you done kill him."

The mistress breath is foul. Sogolon, still holding
her, blink once and tears run down her face. The mistress pull herself away and grab the cook. Is you kill
me husband, talk truth! I say to talk truth, is you?
You done kill my master, you done kill him, she say.
She grab the cook and try to shake her, but the cook's
figure is mighty and she only shake her dress. Sogolon
watch her staring at the cook and realizing she not demanding, but begging. The mistress let her go and set
off outside when she see one of the twins. Two sisters
cut her off. They don't have to drag her this time. The
mistress hands fall to her side, and she walk back to
her room.

Two things happen in the quick. The burial of
the master and the summons to the royal court. The
night of the funeral Sogolon wake up to see that the
lamp in her window blow out. On the morning of
the rites, the sisters dress the mistress in black. She
is to stay in black for nine moons. Near evening the
men come back with another cow. They slaughter it
right there in the courtyard, letting the blood run
where it choose to run. This is what the women do.
After they kill the cow, they cut up the flesh, chop the
bones, and cook the whole thing in three pots with
guinea pepper, garlic, soumbala, peanut butter, and

salt. Then every person related by blood or by law eat.
They sit on the floor in the house, in the walkway, in
the dirt of the courtyard, and out in the street. They
swoon and marvel at the wonderful taste, and speak
words of praise for the master, who now become one
of the ancestors, watching and making judgment of
both the living and the dead.

The priest sprinkle all the relations with blessed
water, and rub them with herbs to banish the shadows following them that their body didn't cast. But
not Sogolon, or the cook, or anybody working in the
house, for they are not blood. Just as well, the cook
say. Their devils is their own business.

The house of Komwono is finally restored in favor,
the bearer of this good news say, a boy with a smile
too wide. He carry the words in his mouth like he
don't know what he is saying or who to, which is true.
He don't know he is coming to a house in the middle
of mourning, or that he would be telling this news to
Sogolon. May the gods bring you consolation, he also
say, before leaving quick, all the while looking up at
the ceiling as if he catch a bad spirit watching him.
Tell me everything he say, Mistress Komwono say,
and they watch in shock as her bad mood burn off
her skin quick, fire set to wild bush.

First thing she do is drive everybody but her staff
out of the house. What about those of who come
from far, sister? say Lady Mistress Morongo. That

don't include you, sister, you live up the street, say the mistress. But all of you need to go by noon, for I will have back my house. Sisters and sisters-in-law deem the whole thing appalling. Brothers and brothers-in-law all sigh, nod in relief, for spirits is visiting between their legs at night, and none can swear that they are female. The mistress sisters one by one refuse to go, saying, Dear sister you will be in ukuzila for nine moons, maybe even a year if the ancestors don't welcome your husband in time. A woman in ukuzila can't do what is expected of a woman wearing red or yellow. The gods demand that you not be bold in action or thought. You need your sisters, say her sisters. The Komwonos say the same thing, but they add, And we need to see about what our dearest brother has left for us.

"Ukuzila doesn't bind the feet, nor the hand, not even the mouth," she say to her sisters. "And you chigger foot bitches forget that the one with the wealth is not the one dead," she say to the Komwonos, though the look on her face say that all sisters are scavengers. They leave that afternoon. Sogolon still don't believe that the mistress could be back to her old wits in just a few turns of the time glass, not when she couldn't even take herself out of the room to piss only a day before. But she know that wits return to her mistress by the evening hour, when blood and law relation set to leave on their feet, horses, chariots, carts, and caravan only to see seven warriors of the Seven Wings, mercenaries in the service of the Black Sparrowhawk, standing at the gate to check one and all for pilfering. The rest of the evening Sogolon hear the cling and clang of gold, silver, iron, and ivory thrown out of thieving carriages, with the mistress laughing and saying, See that? See that? As if somebody is watching with her by the window.

Mistress Komwono now consumed with preparations and readiness. The herald leave nothing but the trail of his own voice, with the message that the master (and Mistress Komwono) is invited by the grace of the Most Excellent Kwash Kagar, King of Fasisi, Emperor of the Northern Lands, Regent of the Valley Territory, and Imperial Cleric of the Divine Regions of Earth and Sky, to an audience, of course at his regal pleasure.

Mistress Komwono is no fool. She knows that "at his regal pleasure" is both promise and trap. That his pleasure might change at a whim and the trip from the royal enclosure to the royal dungeon can be within the wave of a finger. Or that his pleasure might just be to taunt them further by declaring himself too busy to see anyone. Them, for she not sending news that the master is dead. For a King whose blood is in the divine line of gods has very little time for silly mortal business. And who is she to think she had right to be in quarrel with the King or anyone in the house of Akum? This she say to the room as Sogolon enter it. Sogolon taken aback. The mistress, in a tone almost like a girl, like somebody wanting somebody to like her, but not sure what to do. The mistress yet to say what get her banish from court.

"The master, he is the one she like, you understand. She loved how he would call her pretty. Not beautiful like a woman, or handsome like a horse, which indeed she was, but pretty like a little girl. That must be why she giggle. What she say to me was harsh. What she do to me was harsher."

"Who, mistress?"

"The goddess of love and poetry—who else I talking about but the King Sister, you walking imbecile? When I was one of her ladies-in-waiting, she was always cursing me, calling me slow, saying that I even wiped her ass slow."

Sogolon is a girl. Grief look like carrying a house on your back, so she is nothing but perplex that the mistress not buckling under the weight. Maybe she hide it, or maybe a big woman can carry grief as big as a house on her back and it look like she carrying everything else too. Sogolon wonder how she do it, because her mind buckling nearly every night. She think she is in the dream jungle, but night jump to morning and leave her with the feeling that either she never wake or didn't sleep. Grief and guilt mixing, brewing into something like a lump under the skin. Something monstrous.

The night before they set out for Fasisi, Nanil approach her outside the grain keep but don't turn to show her face. Bold for a slave to talk just so to anybody free, even if it is a foundling girl of no use. I know is you, she say. I know is you surely. The master go down to the library waiting for me, and nobody else would have any use, not the wife, not the cook, and not either boy surely. Sogolon think to say something. **Girl, shut your mouth until the mistress permit you to talk.** She open her mouth, the words right behind her teeth. Then she look over again and see nothing but the lonesome yard. It must be her head running from her. It must be.

Two more day come, then they up and leave in a caravan, on the way to Fasisi. Right at the edge of town they pass the magistrate, who shout that he don't forget and one day he heading back to the house.

"Head there right now," say the mistress. "But if you don't find out who kill . . . no, how they kill my husband, I will get a decree from the King himself to have you flogged."

And so they go. The royal escort tell the mistress every morning how many more days leave before they reach Fasisi. Quartermoon done, a whole moon to come, if it is the will of the gods. This is what the mistress take with her. Silk cloth she is saving in a chest with four locks, and from a land where people keep worms in their hair that spin the thread. Sogolon see it once when the mistress open the chest and white and purple flutter out like it was going to fly away. Sogolon know from that one day, the greatest pleasure in the whole world will be to touch silk. And these things also, ukuru and aso oke cloth, indigo, a bottle of myrrh she oftentimes use on herself, leopard skins, a cow for beef, a lamb for mutton, gold nuggets that she take out on occasion and slip between her breasts, sighing because she still thinking again about not parting with them, and a monkey that used to amuse the master. This is who come with her. One of the twins, three from the Seven Wings that she pay for in silver, the royal escort leading the way, and Sogolon.

The mistress at the back of the caravan on cushions and rugs and skins and fur that even a woman like her could get lost in. Like a Bintuin tent. Fabric of every make running up the walls in patterns that say Gangatom, Luala Luala, the river people of Wakadishu, and more from above the sand sea. The perfume in the room so thick that it turn into a feeling. Two windows on both sides stay shut most of the day, but open for sunrise, sunset, or whenever the mistress feel there is no dust. The mistress don't eat much, certainly not much of what the twin cook at night by the fire they make. She nibble the dry meats and fruits that the cook give Sogolon to serve her, but many a time she just drink wine. Sometimes she talk to the master in her sleep, and ask why his cock is sticking out farther than the beam bursting out of his chest. The only other thing she do is look at Sogolon. Every single time she turn to look at the mistress, by the time she see her apart from all the fabrics and furs, the mistress is long looking at her. Sogolon don't know what to take her face to mean. Looking like she

know this girl is the cause of her sorrow, even if she
don't know how. Because of that, Sogolon don't fall
asleep since they set out. She lie on her side, at the far
end of the caravan, behind curtains that the mistress
told her not to draw. At her back, a stone with many
edges jagged, and meant to prick her if she fall over
asleep, which she do sometimes in the day. The mistress look at her like she notice. What you afraid will
happen if you fall asleep, that the sleep will set your
tongue loose? That wicked tongue, living inside you
but never truly obedient. What is it waiting to tell
me, deceitful girl? Sogolon turn away from answering, until she realize that all this talking is passing in
her head.

Third night of the third quartermoon. By light of
lamp she see the mistress staring at her again. The
mistress not in any mood to talk to this foundling,
but still want her wishes known. Sogolon open a cupboard just as the caravan fall into a rut, which throw
her and the contents to the side. She hear the twin
curse and the escort laugh. She put the food back in
the cupboard and take a wineskin over to the mistress,
who all this time never stop looking at her. Annoyed
now, most surely, but still not thinking she worth the
labor of a good scold. Sogolon walk over to the mistress, bracing herself against the bumpy ride until she
get to her. She about to present the wineskin, when
she see that though the mistress eyes wide open she

deep in sleep. Miss Azora had a word for this kind of thing. A god watching what you do at night will take over somebody's sleep, and use their eye as a window. The next day the mistress say, "Is a trick. Must be."

"Mistress?"

"All of this, sending for the banished one. Is a trick to embarrass me. You don't know her ways. The King Sister, fool. Or Princess Jeleza, I don't even know what she call herself. Royal born mean royal in their pettiness. And the gods know that it not beyond her to have me travel for so many days just to make me the joke of court."

"Then why you want to go so bad, Mistress?"

"What? How dare this little girl think she can ask me such questions? Intolerable. That is the word, intolerable. I should have you flogged."

"Beg pardon, Mistress."

"Yes, you should beg. Not that begging ever got me a damn thing."

She look at Sogolon plain, like she just noticing her in the space. "I really should have sent you to a fatting house, so you could become an accomplished woman. Some dancing, some embroidery, even a little bit about child-rearing, instead of all this rawness."

"Mistress?"

"Girl, you tire me, go ride outside."

Sogolon can't even pretend she sad about it. The escort take off half the burden on his second horse and let Sogolon climb up. This horse tie to the escort so there is nothing for Sogolon to do, but this is still the first time she on this beast. She adding up all the things that she feel once and want to again. Sinking into silk, riding a horse, thinking she is free.

They stop in open space, almost like sand, with no trees, and in the night the cold turn bitter. Still Sogolon now sleep under two blankets in the open with the other men. Each day nearer to Fasisi, the mistress get more and more excited. Fasisi not like most places in the North, with every custom tie up in the nobility of the man. Women keep their wealth when they marry in Fasisi, and the power that come with it. Even the King, when he chooses to become a god and join the royal ancestors, pass the crown to the firstborn male from his oldest sister's house. Maybe this why the mistress seem to miss Fasisi even more than the master did, why she had been hungrier to return. But she still wonder out loud why they was summoned back at all. The mistress say more than once that surely the King and Queen didn't invite them only to hear the master's dull mouth. Sogolon don't know how much burden any of this carry. Or which is worse, a secret or a lie, and if a secret is hiding enough of the truth that we see a different story, is that not lying too? The mistress banish her to sleep with men and insects, but she still feel sorry for the mistress, and rebuke herself for thinking she can pity anybody.

But now that she is out under sky from daybreak to nightfall, the way to Fasisi showing her things she never see before. The road come and go. Sometimes for a half day the road is stones cut perfect, but right after that is nothing but dirt and sand, and thorn-bush. The second time they come up on a stretch of old road, the escort say that this is all part of the old kingdom, long before Fasisi, long before any man yet living. They pass villages perch on hillside with small houses people build from mud and stone, with thatch roofs and no door. They pass villages that look like the people all run away or die off. At a turn with two trailways ahead, the escort shout that they will stay along the rivers, since that is the wisest way to avoid bandits. A Seven Wing say he ready for any fight, to which the escort say, So go off and fight, then. My King give me orders to bring back cargo alive and unspoiled. The mistress, listening at the window, hiss at the word, **cargo,** and make sure he hear. Guests, he say. They ride along the river and pass the walls of Juba, where every few lengths stand a horse with a man on it, man who dress soldierly, like the escort.

And this escort. The wingsmen cover themselves in black tunic and blue sash even on the hottest day, also hiding most of the face. This man look every-thing the opposite of Seven Wings. Firstly he almost all in green. A bronze and black shield that he wear on his back. Sogolon notice the blade next, a scimitar she will soon learn to use. Green chain mail, green tunic, leather sword belt, and a long flowing green cape that he wrap around himself like the mistress and her blankets. Fire-golden hair and beard, almost wild, and a thin face with thick lips looking like he grin ten times more than he scowl. And the voice, like river flow. This is not the sort of man to visit Miss Azora. Sogolon looking at his face, sharp, perhaps a little mischief hiding in that beard. Mischief? This is not the sort of man that come to whorehouse, because he would never need to. Handsome? She barely know the word or when to use it. Sometimes she blink and all she see is hair, cheekbones, and lips. And skin like coffee making peace with milk. Is the eyes that keep grinning when the rest of his face don't, and is the grin that stay on her even when he turn back around to lead the way. They stop along the river route twice. The first to rest the horses, the second because the mistress halt the procession for they would get to Fasisi too early, which would be an irredeemable loss of face, her words. Both times he wash, when nobody else do.

"The water is best here," he say to Sogolon as he walk to the bank. Sogolon grow up all these years taking stock of what man say and weighing it for danger.

"I not bathing," she say.

He look at her once, with nothing in his face, not disappointment but not indifference either and say, Suit yourself. He don't think once or twice about it and take off his clothes. Sogolon would swear to whoever ask that it look like the opposite, like the clothes take themselves off him. The men who come to Miss Azora look like men who need to come to

Miss Azora, and not like the boys who win the donga. But the boys of the donga look like dark, shiny sticks with long and thin arms and legs. This escort look like his clothes commit wickedness by hiding him. Shoulders broad and chest heavy with muscle. The thin waist of a stilt walker, the thick legs of a young horse. Sogolon know she is going to think it, and want to meet the thought before it reach her head and stop it, but she fail. The cock one hope to see at the center of a body like his. Hanging over balls, thick, loose, proving nothing. He raise from the river and stretch himself at the edge, then walk a little, not to show Sogolon nothing, for he already forget that she close. But she watching a man walk as water drip away from him, and after so many years in a whorehouse she didn't know that when a man move one way, his cock move another. Up and down, jiggle like it dancing to quicker music. In the whorehouse there is only two kind of cock, violent and limp, and neither a girl prefer to see. But the escort either don't see her, forget she is there, or walking like this is no different from waking up, or paying for beer. Paying for beer. She wonder if this is always with her, body shame. Can't be, for that is not the people she come from. Curse this whorehouse that give her something she would never expect from such a place. Modesty. Sogolon stringing together thoughts in her head that don't make no sense. He stand and stretch his arms out like he saluting the leaving sun.

"So Sogolon," he say and the girl jump out of herself. "Not so, your name?"

"So indeed my name be," she say. Turning her whole head away from him, and wondering where this turning coming from. He don't turn around to see her. But his buttocks, big and darker, look like they are all that is holding wayward arms and feet and back together.

"You plan to ride this horse, or you fine with this horse riding you?"

"What?"

The escort turn around, his back to the sun. The water can't even bear to leave his skin. Look at it trying to stay on him a little longer. Sogolon don't know who doing this kind of thinking but say out loud, Hark, you need to stop it. He is coming to her, what is that he say? Coming to her, and she can't look up to his face, but looking down not better for now she gone past between two nipples and roll up and down the washboard that midway, erupt with hair that roll down and down and down.

"You want to ride?" he say.

Sogolon is a stick now. She is a stick.

"We carry another saddle in the back. Strap it onto the horse, then strap you in it. The saddle, not the horse. A girl should know how to ride a horse, do you not think so?"

"I don't know."

"Never know when you might need to get away.

Horse feet faster than your own." He smile again. She think he is going to get the saddle right now. Teach her right now. Grip her in his mighty hands and place her on the horse, as if she weigh as much as a reed.

"Tomorrow," he say and walk to his clothes.

And so, Fasisi.

FOUR

So this great god of sky, who cry with the rain, ride on lightning, and shout with thunder, had two sons. One son he have with the sun, and when she lay with him, orange light burst from their fuck and make what is gray sky purple, then blue. The second he have with the moon, for night come after day, and the god in his naked darkness fuck the white moon and turn the sky silver. The god of sky lay with one without telling the other, for their hatred is long and deep, and if you see the sun, all alone by day, and the moon with her hundreds of twinkling children by night, you soon know why. Sun and moon bear their swelling bellies for four years, and both almost fall out of the sky, for the weight of carrying a godchild is too much. But since they don't visit this god the same time, neither did know the other is with child. The world is so new that plenty things don't yet have name, and because they don't have none, nobody can claim them. Things like fire, nakedness, emeralds, and beasts of the sea. The gods, still making the beautiful and terrible world, did not have time, which they also didn't name.

The sun and the moon give birth on the same day. Both hand their sons to the god, for neither mother would make space for mothering, not when the sun constantly standing watch over the earth, and moon have more than enough. A baby demands from you the world, they both say to the god, though at different times, in different rooms. Neither wants to feed the child and starve the universe, for a universe and a baby want the same thing. The god of sky name his sons Dumata, meaning he of the orange and purple light, and Durara, meaning skin of he who comes with night rain. But even a god is still like the man he did not yet create, meaning he raising his sons wild and careless, meaning he not raising them at all. Soon it come to pass that these boys run rough through the kingdom, thundering with so much weight that clouds split open, and sparking so much lightning that it kill anything that would have been lying under a tree, if trees and such things existed. They make mischief with the sun, who set the sky on fire, and then torment the moon, who hide behind darkness more and more, so that by the twenty and eighth day, she gone completely for four nights. These boys are a problem, oh.

So the great god of sky, who shout with thunder, ride on lightning, and cry with the rain, send his two sons down to the world. Call it not banishment, he say. But no, you can never come back up to sky, he also say and throw heavy weight in their feet to make sure. He send them with three things, but since none of those things have names, none belong in this story. Dumata of the sun land in the north, while Durara of the moon land in the south. Nowhere is there to stand, for such a place no god create yet, so both boys pull something from their bag and sprinkle it before they land. Where Dumata land is yellow, and hard, and glitters in the daylight. Dumata is an impatient one, he has no time to wait on the pleasure of the gods, so he name it gold. Durara land on a hard land of white that he mistake for hardened clouds. The land is pale and empty and have no glitter. But when Durara lie down on his belly, he stick out his tongue to lick it, and the taste is pleasing. Durara, of the other mother, is still too much like his brother, and he also name the land himself, calling it salt.

And so it go that the two boys become men, then kings. King of Gold, and King of Salt. Both grow fat and greedy, keeping near everything for themselves, and leaving none for the people, who by now are all over the earth. But gold and salt is more than gold and salt. For gold is all that is beautiful, and salt is all that is useful. And though the north is beautiful lands, with beautiful wealth, and a beautiful king, more pretty than his Queen, not much is there that serve use. Not even food, for whatever there was always looked magnificent, but everything taste the same. But nothing is great in the south either, for they never have a single thing that is not put to good use. Nothing in the kingdom that they would look upon and admire, or even love, not even the king. Not that the king is ugly, but nobody in the lands see anything beyond the use of his eyes to see, ears to hear, nose to smell, and mouth to speak. Even intimate congress is always for breeding and never for pleasure, which is why they call it intimate congress. As for the food, it satisfy the taste and make boys strong, but people shut their eye before they put food in the mouth.

Reason tell us this. The north could use much from the south and the south have much to gain from the north. Trade is what many think would happen, but the kings fulfill the destiny of their mothers and declare war on each other. The north invade some of the south and that is why they have salt and spice. The south plunder the north, and that is why they have castles rising from the ground, and necklaces in shiny gold. And so go the times of war, until the old names for the north and south kingdoms, the names of the two boys get lost to all but the southern griots and the forgotten gods. Everything woman and man learn they learn from the gods, including this. That whether spirit or flesh, people is the only creature who, even if they know better, never do better. And for what they do, they outrage every other beast but the horse, camel, donkey, pig, pigeon, goat, and dog, and from that day all other beasts is enemy to most man. Meanwhile the sun and the moon shine down on both kingdoms with equal light, lamenting that people of the earth too stubborn and stupid to get along, how they must have learn all this warring from each other.

"Reason tell you that too, pretty man?" say this mercenary from the Seven Wings, as they all sit by the fire. They, the escort, the twin, the wingsmen, and Sogolon. The mistress rest in her caravan and soon fall in sleep so deep that her snoring scare every little creature sleeping under it.

"I just repeating what the gods tell me," the escort, whose name is Keme, say.

"War don't need no reason, war is just war," say the wingsman.

"War is just war? Or war is just money, mercenary?"

"Listen to this, soldier. King after king declare war and never lead their own man in battle. Why, when he have fools like you think he be the strong arm of the King? Then you fight and get kill, and your wives all get one coin. Money at least is something, guard. What you fighting for?"

"I fighting for what worth fighting for. For her," he say and nod to Sogolon.

"She don't name mistress. Who be this one to fight for? What you fight for is like air. You can't grab it, or hold it, or even smell it."

"And yet if you don't breathe it, you die."

"All this talking about air. That where your head live?"

Him from Seven Wings laugh. Not long gone are the days when she didn't think they talk at all, much less laugh. Sogolon want to say that she like them better when they still cover their face and say nothing, but that is a lie. Even before that, she never like them at all. Keme should be annoyed, that is what she is thinking. Be so annoyed that he punch one of them, knock out his filesharp teeth, for nobody would blame him if he do. But Keme sit with them by the fire, laughing and smiling as if he enjoying their company, as they mock the man cooking their food. For a while she more interested in watching him be a man among other man. Everything is new. Like how man sit with man in the grass and dirt. All finding their spot around the fire, waiting on the meat, whatever it is, and laying down sword, and spear, and helmet, which they take off like they are laying down babies to rest. Then lying back on their elbows, or sitting up and resting hands on knees, and head on hands, and spreading their legs wide, as if telling the fire to come in between and warm it. Sogolon is thinking things about men, and is not sure if she would be thinking of them either way, or if the escort is setting her thoughts afire. For neither her brothers, nor the master, nor the twins ever stir anything like him. Sogolon can't remember when they stop calling him escort and start calling him Keme. She don't know how she feel about the name. No, not the name, but calling it. She sitting away from the caravan, but not in the circle by the fire and wondering about men. That if they spend any time together, say on the same pursuit or just going in the same direction, do they always become brothers?

"But look at Keme in the firelight. So pretty you could be a girl."

Everybody laugh. Including the escort.

"Careful, mercenary, Fasisi don't give pass to man lovers the way Kongor do," he say and everybody laugh but the Seven Wing who call him pretty. Sogolon mark him. She look up and see the escort marking him too, even as he laugh. In the quick his eyes land upon her and she look away not as quick.

"What do you think, Sogolon?" he ask. Sogolon spirit nearly jump out of her mouth.

"You asking the girl if she think you pretty?"

Sogolon quiet and looking away in the dark. The truth between her and sky is that she ask herself that question many a time in her mind. And answer it.

"You were smarter last quartermoon," Keme say.

"I didn't talk last week," the Seven Wing say.

"That is what I say. Now, Sogolon, do you fight for a cause or for coin?"

"Woman don't fight," the Seven Wing say.

"You trying to become one, that's why you answer? I talking to Sogolon."

She don't know if he defending her or mocking her a little. Maybe both. A man can be two different things at the same time, just like a woman. She come out of her head to see all the men watching her.

"What is the cause?" she ask.

"Go again?" he say, curious.

"You say fight for a cause. But what is the cause? Fighting for it don't make it good."

"She talking sense, escort," say the other Seven Wing. "You didn't say if the cause good."

"Pick one," he say. "Pick a cause that you think is good."

Sogolon don't want to look at him, but she don't want to turn away. He looking at her, not angry, or sad, or mocking, but not like he waiting on her either. Soon the talk will change, and he will change with it, laughing and joking as he is before. But will he think of me less? she ask herself, but not with those words. When the escort look at her she don't have no words.

"Stupid escort, stop trying to get a girl to think," the first wingsman say, and everybody laugh. The escort laugh and the sound of it cut her. But he don't stop looking at her and that make her feel like her clothes is burning off.

Sleep will not come this night. No, it will come, but trouble her anyway. All the way till morning her eyes wide open, watching the fire die, and him lying there with a gentle snore, making her think that all she is good for is to watch him sleep.

"Don't let those men trouble you. All they do is tell stories," the escort say to her in the morning. "So much shit about gods and monsters."

You was the one telling them, she don't say.

"It don't trouble me."

"Men in a ring all trying to be the loudest. None of us louder than the gods."

"I not troubled."

"I'm troubled a little," he say, and pick up her saddle. She follow him to the horse. Morning come out full, and everybody is waking up. Keme throw the saddle on the horse and is about to strap it on when she say, "I can do that."

Keme back away, hands up like he is a capture, and smiling. "Sogolon. Do you know why you going to Fasisi?"

"Of course. I go to keep the mistress company."

"If company is what you're supposed to be keeping, how come you're not in the caravan?"

Like river flow. The girl open her mouth but say nothing. He reply with a nod and hid it in his cape.

"Last night I didn't pick a cause because I don't want war," she say.

"Girl, war is always upon us. And if not war, then the rumor of war. Your King likes peace but your prince?"

"I don't know anything about the King or prince. Fasisi always so far away from us."

"Now it getting closer by the day."

He teach her how to ride so that the horse don't throw her off, or bruise inside her legs. The mistress don't know what she doing outside, but glad to not wake up seeing Sogolon watching her. As for her, Sogolon and her horse at the front of the trail one evening, when she find herself wondering where Keme be. But as she turn around Keme ride up close and spike her horse. The horse bray, take up on two feet, then tear off.

"She will not scream, she will not scream."

To not scream she has to say it out loud. But the horse is bounding and bouncing, she is slipping and they are moving so fast. So fast. Faster. He will throw her off, this horse. She will break her neck. She squeeze the reins and pull, but still the horse gallop. He jump over a rock and Sogolon feel her entire body leave the horse until she land in the saddle again. She pull the reins tighter and tighter until she realize that make it worse. Each pull make the horse shudder. Make her more afraid. And still it won't stop. Sogolon try something else, pulling the left rein, firm yet gentle, pulling until the horse turn his neck. The turning slow them down. Calm the horse. Soon they in a trot, and Sogolon, for the first time, breathe. In her mind she flip the time glass three times before the caravan catch up to her, standing by the horse. When he see her, Keme make a quick gallop, stop when he right before her, and dismount.

"Sogolon! I was starting to fear bad things happen to you," he say, the smile on his face never wider. Sogolon open her mouth to say something but all that come out is a snarl. She charge him and swing her arms. He duck. Just as she want. He don't see the knee coming up until it hit him straight in the face. He fall flat on his back and don't move.

"Keme?"

Sogolon fury turn to mist. She drop to the ground.

"Keme!"

Keme open his eyes, he turn and spit blood, and when he smile his teeth still red.

"Fuck the gods, you're a horse lord now, aren't you?" he say.

And so, Fasisi.
     Fasisi, like Malakal, is a city where you know you are close when you start to climb. The air turn thin, then cold. The Wings mask their faces again, and the twin try to wrap himself in a caravan curtain. Keme still in green, but he switch his cape for a blanket like what Mistress Komwono sometimes wear. White and green of course, Sogolon say to herself when he wrap it over his shoulders. White like the cold dirt of the mountains, but the green pattern, corn popping out of the husk. He throw another blanket to her.

"Fasisi coming in closer," he say.

"We should wake the mistress?"

"No."

The sudden steepness jolt the twin. Something roll and drop inside the caravan, but he don't stop to check.

"He taking after you," Keme say.

"What? How you—"

"Don't reply to everything with **what.**"

"I say how you mean?"

"At the start of this trip, if he hear something in the caravan, he would stop everybody to check. To make sure all is the best for his mistress. Now she could be breaking her neck, and the boy just carry through."

"Is a long trip."

"No lie you tell there. I already feel older just for making it."

"You going be glad when we done reach, and you done gone."

He turn to look at her.

"Not totally glad."

The road winding as soon as they set on it. Soon they riding through mist, but only when they get far enough past it that Sogolon see that they riding through clouds. The road is twice as wide as the caravan, and at the horse's feet is cut brick that go as far as she can see. Almost red, and clean as if rain just fall. The road is a snake, with turns leading up to turns, and little of it straight. Sometimes the road hug the mountain, for this is a mountain, and sometimes it lay out along the very top, with a steep drop into mist on both sides. Sometimes the roadside is bare with nothing to stop a wayward carriage, or a frightened horse. But right around another turn the road narrow down even more and on both sides a stone wall rise high. Sogolon never gone this far, never climb this high, never see mountains in the company of so many mountains, so green that they blue. Maybe this really was the work of the son of the god of sky, pushing aside dirt and making hills and valleys as he turn and toss in sleep. This is the back way, he say. Less use, but leading direct to the royal enclosure and cutting a day off entering through the city gates. They come to a turn that go almost full around before it straighten again. Every two hundred paces or so they pass through a brick archway.

"You a child of your mother or father?"

"Wh—"

"No more with your **what.**"

"That is one of those questions that people of learning ask each other."

"You asking or telling?"

"Yes."

"Well I was asking. What would people say? You, your mother's daughter or your father's?"

"I don't know."

"How? Mark it, next time me and my father meet, he will also meet this dagger. But even I have to admit I have his stubbornness, his mirth, and gods forgive me, his sins. We even like the same kind of woman. I know this because he almost stole mine." Keme laughed. "That is too coarse."

"I prefer it."

"I know."

They let the horses trot on their own pace.

"My mother, she midwifed the crown prince, and

then his sister. They call her special among women, for she delivered he who will one day become a god."

"Blessed hands, the mistress would say."

"Not so blessed when she whip us like she driving out devils. Ay the gods. They must know how you can have a great love and steeping dislike for the same woman. They consume you, both of them, love and dislike."

"So who you both hate and like, then?"

"What, there's no such thing. I—"

"No more your **what.**"

He laughs. "Clever, clever girl," he says.

She says, "Father or mother it don't matter. I don't have knowledge of either."

"None? None at all? But you're not an orphan?"

"Three men out there looking for me will say I am their sister. One is the worst man I ever know, and the other two worse. But I never know my mother or father. People say devils infect my father's head."

"Maybe he was just sick. How do they know?"

"He put his cock to his mouth and drink his piss like wine."

"Fuck the gods. Vile yet impressive. And your mother?"

"I take her name. I leave my brothers with nothing but that."

"She let you leave?"

"She dead. Die giving birth to me. Also what drive my father mad."

"Ah."

"I don't want to hear it, that I am cursed."

"What sniveling son of a hyena bitch tell you such a thing?"

"My brothers. And everybody in the village. Their words jump over the fence and come to me."

"Oh Sogolon."

"What is that? What you doing?"

"Taking pity on you."

"I don't want it. Who would want that?"

"I wonder if these will always be your ways. You see it and you call it. A vulture is never a hawk with you."

"Is that good?"

"Most of the time."

"When they call me cursed they bring pity with the scorn. The village burn the last woman somebody call a witch."

"Fuck the gods, and the witches, and the belief in witches. A motherless child and a brotherless sister. Instead of one life, you already live three. Do you think on these things?"

"Why? Living is living, and that alone take so much to do. Who have time to do anything else?"

He stop the horse to look at her.

"I will not soon forget you, Sogolon the motherless."

The mistress wake up with a wild beast appetite. She mouth, "One whole day?" to herself over and over,

for she cannot fathom how she sleep away two sunrise and one sunset. Or why this stupid girl didn't
wake her. Sogolon leave the mistress to her lonesome
as soon as she start checking to see if she piss herself
while asleep. The rest of the afternoon, she catch the
mistress looking outside the window, like she trying
to find the day that slip away. Sogolon thinking of
the many teas in the caravan, and how she brew too
much of the wrong one. By accident, she tell the escort, then herself. Sogolon feeling monstrous for what
she do, but every time her eye catch the escort he either giggle or laugh loud.

"Shut up," she say.

"Nothing come out of my mouth."

"Trouble is what you setting for me, I know it."

"Not going be around long for that," he say and
take both their smiles with him.

The caravan is just ahead of evening when they
reach the great wall. Sogolon was expecting cut stone,
perhaps even brick, but the wall smooth as clay. This
also, a pale pink where the sun still hit it, and almost
purple where the light throw shadow. Big turrets and
little windows, and from one window, brown water
flowing down. Sogolon guessing that the wall ten
and two times as high as the guard standing next to
it, and at the top and every few paces apart stand a
guard wearing an iron helmet and holding a spear.
They come upon another gate that open as soon as
they see the escort approach, looking like he about
important business. Sogolon try to hold her head high

as well, but too much is there to see that she never see before.

They enter Fasisi. Before she even think about what she see, Keme say to her that this is the nobles' enclosure and not the city proper. To get to the other edge of Fasisi would take half a day. Sogolon thinking that she is seeing more than enough on this street. She can't help but compare it to Kongor. And Kongor walls are so much like dirt that the whole city can seem as if it rise from dust. Perhaps it is because her head is darting left to right so fast and so often that at first all she see is color. The blur of white, red, purple, green, and blue settle into white robes on the men and women; red dirt, bricks, and walls; purple fabrics flowing from the bazaar as they pass; green grass and trees crowning courtyards hidden behind walls. And blue walls down the road Keme take them. **Settle, girl, settle,** a voice sounding like Sogolon say, but she imagine Keme saying it. He already gone ahead, not too far, but far enough that the city know that a soldier returns.

She look up to the sky first and below it, the city draping around this grand mountain like a mighty dress. Farther up, at top, she guess is the palace but it is so high that all she see is shapes and lights. The street ahead of her is wide enough for three caravans to meet and pass. Brick again, all the world's brick just for one road. Groups of boys in white skirts and breeches and wraps, groups of men with gold shields, spears and sword, and wispy headdresses from feathers.

Every man wearing a beard and some have mustaches that drop even lower. She pass a little girl staring at her, wearing brown goatskin and a tower of beads around her neck. And three more women, all in white, all with hair large like cushions on their shoulders. Two carry shiny gourds with leather straps as bags, and one carry a large orange sash holding a baby. So this is Fasisi women. She know nothing of them. The women whisper to each other and laugh above the noise of the city that she don't notice till then. Shouting, laughing, haggling, swearing, invoking, praying, demanding back my money you cheat, settling that dowry now that you have included a goat, leaving now to a scolding wife so best I not leave and drink some more beer, and is that who I think it is, with his mess of a wife, oh yes I hear she has been called back to court. And other loose words, and annoyed calls and drunken verses that almost pulled her away from seeing so much that is new. She swing around, almost prompting the horse to look also at the women, who did not see her.

Fasisi is not about to sleep, and neither is Sogolon. Houses in Fasisi stand taller than most in Kongor though they have fewer floors, because on a mountain no matter how high you climb, there is a part rising higher. The nobles' district, Keme say. And very different from the rest of Fasisi, he don't say but she guess. And if this is the nobles' quarter, then it was clear who would be living higher. From where they are, all she see is walls like the one they passed through. **Palace, court, king,** all words she know of but can't keep steady in her head. Master and Mistress are the only nobles she know. But here they be, moving in closer.

The mistress finally stick her head through the window. Sogolon slow down her horse. She is waiting for it to come from her, a command or a curse, but the mistress say nothing. Her lips part open and stay open and her eyes barely blink. The street too noisy to hear it, the mistress's sigh. Ahead a wall stand higher. Not the palace, for the wall hide all but three towers, all with a nipple for a roof. They make her chuckle. Keme look at her, as if about to ask a question, but he say nothing. The palace walls not far ahead now. But then Keme rein his horse right and all follow. Another blue street, on the walls, the door, the windows that some are now closing. They pass buildings as grand as palaces, with stone arches, stone steps, dome roofs, and in some of them, men in blue robes moving up the steps slow with heads down. Monks, she remember their ways at the whorehouse. This is a house for the worship of magnificent gods. The escort lead them down another street more narrow than any before. The Wings, who was riding alongside the caravan, pull back. Two women with baskets on their heads squeeze by and one man dodge through a door. Sogolon is riding beside Keme but her eyes are on these houses on both sides, all with balconies and hanging gardens, two things she don't have words for. And from the balconies men and women and children shouting at the horses.

Some kind of fuss stop them at a crossroad. A rumble. Two lazy men jump out of the way. Two chariots race by, each carrying two men. In both chariots, one standing and cracking a whip over the horses and the other sitting and examining something in his hands. Both men in white robes draped over one shoulder. All this commotion draw the mistress to the window.

"Stop. Stop at once," she say. She shout twice more before the twin hear.

"Sogolon. Sogolon!"

Sogolon dismount and go to her mistress.

"Stupid girl, you didn't hear me call you?"

"I had to dismount to get to you, Mistress."

"Of course you had to dismount. This street is so narrow that only a woman with no damn breasts can pass through. And this street, what is the meaning of this? Talk quick, girl."

"I don't know what you asking me, Mistress."

"If I am stupid, then I am stupid. But I sure even my stupid eyes can see this is not the royal enclosure. We reach Fasisi?"

"Yes, Mistress."

"Then what is this place?"

"Fasisi, Mistress—"

"Girl, don't make me drop like thunder on you. You know how long they been waiting for me at court? I swear I will whip the skin off the backs of all of you if you make me late. And what with night coming."

"I will ask Keme, Mistress."

"Keme? Well suck the teat of a barren cow, who is Keme?"

"The escort."

"The escort. Listen, girl, you not to have any other name for this escort, but escort."

"Oh."

"Oh is right. Your days with Miss Azora long gone, girl."

"I not—"

"I didn't ask you no question, so why you replying to me? That escort's head as soft as yours?"

"I don't know, Mistress."

"I will speak to him. Now, girl."

Before Keme even get to the caravan, Mistress Komwono lighting fire on him, wanting to know if his eye is in his pants and two shitholes are flanking his nose. And if they not near the crown of Fasisi then they in the wrong place.

"And what place is this?" she ask.

"Ugliko."

"This is not Ugliko. All I see is trade."

"The merchant side of Ugliko, ma'am."

"Merchant side? Is that what money does now, buy nobility?"

"It is with the grace of the King, ma'am."

"They going to buy princedoms next? How much

to be a priest? God alive, somebody will even pay to be a griot. Anyway, please to take me to somewhere else."

"Here is where you stay until the crown call you to court."

"What you just say to me? Stay? To put my feet down here? Stay?"

And on she go, about if she is to really believe that a woman of noble birth, a woman married to a lord chief even nobler, a man whose blood one can trace to the great warrior kings of the North lands, must take up residence within Ugliko prefecture, among men of trade. Trade, she yell again and again, saying it the way another would say shit. And as if to let him know she mean shit, the mistress go on about how the trade prefecture smell, how merchants always smell, how the smell going to infect her if she stay here even one night and what in a million curses is to be done with this ghastly blue. All Sogolon can remember is the mistress loving to count money. The escort listen to it all with patience and calm.

"Lady Komwono. All who see the King, all who will enter court, whether noble, peasant, family, or pet, must go through the house of notice, where they will be vetted before given permission to be in the royal enclosure."

"But I am—"

"Not deaf, I know. That's why I don't need to repeat myself. I'm sure you view the safety of our King, Queen, and princes as paramount, or perhaps you do not?"

"What?"

Sogolon almost say, No more **what.**

"Of course I do. May the gods always protect our King and princes."

"And the Queen?"

"Gods alive, of course protect her too. This must be new."

"Not so, ma'am. They started it the month you were—you leave court. The wisdom of His Excellency the chancellor. Mistress, we must go. The Ugliko is a different place after dark."

"What kind of place? I would never know."

The escort nod and go back to his place at the front. Sogolon turn to follow.

"Not you," the mistress say.

Two days pass on the merchant street. They stay at a compound as large as a palace, but the mistress use every chance to curse about how vulgar the place be. Everything has the shine of the new, she say. The glare of the coarse and the bought, instead of the elegant coat of generations of nobility plus the original blessing of the gods. Sogolon thinking the place more grand than any room in the mistress house. Each room have a fire, each room telling a story with paintings on the ceilings of devout men doing what look like devout things. A room with a bath for the mistress and three more for whoever have use. And servants that come from the crown's service, but none working in the palace. This they know because the mistress ask. Keme is with them as well, for his duty is not complete until he has done what the court send him to do. To deliver those of the house of Komwono. Sogolon attend to this mistress until she grow tired of praising the King Sister for her bottomless forgiveness, then cursing her for her petty vindictiveness, then falling asleep. But Sogolon never sleep.

The second night she go out in the courtyard and see the escort with a lion. She sure she never see one before. A male lion looking almost white in the dark. Big as table, big enough to crush Keme just by lying on him. The lion grunt and growl, and Sogolon jump even though she out of sight. What kind of place is this where beasts run loose? Mistress Komwono never say anything about this kind of danger. Sogolon don't know what to do, confusion seizing her, terror also, but then she notice that no such thing seizing Keme. **This?** Keme seem to say. Then he dash across the courtyard and the lion growl and chase after him. Keme don't get far. The lion pounce just as he turn around and both fall to the ground. Sogolon about to scream when Keme laugh even louder, and shout, Watch where you lick, man lover, to which the lion growl again. Keme scratch the lion's jaw and he purr like a cat, rubbing his face against the escort and almost knocking him away. All this make Keme laugh even more. They roll and tumble in the dirt.

"A mosquito getting into that body before you," Keme say and the lion purr before trotting off.

"Good thing you hang back while you were watching," he say as he turn to her. "Because Makaya looking for a new mate."

"How me to marry a lion?"

"No ceremony. He will just bite onto your neck and take you away."

"Woman like that?"

"Noblest of creatures? You could do worse."

"I wasn't watching."

He brush the dirt off his clothes.

"You looking at nothing at all, and the lion and I just walked in your way?"

"I going to bed."

"But you not going to sleep. Or you wouldn't be out here talking to me."

"I don't—"

"Stop disagreeing with me for disagreeing's sake. Not every man want to fight you."

"True. The dead ones give me peace."

Keme burst out laughing so much he had to shush himself.

"You going wake up the mistress," Sogolon say.

"Fuck the gods, let us not have that. Tell you something. We should go around the back. I can show you something you will like," he say.

Sogolon stop and look at him long and deep. The frown that come over her face even he can see in the dark. Her frown hold him there, in the space and in the night.

"I not going around any back with you."

"Suit yourself," he say and walk away. Sogolon will spend more time than she will admit wondering whether she should follow. But she go back to her room and enter that land of neither asleep nor awake. Things moving as if she under water, but everything she see and know. This house with the beds raised off the floor, and with blue and green parrots flying in the ceiling and drawings of holy men in the ceiling that sometimes, in the corner of her eye, move. It's a trick, she thinks. At this time of night, at this point of tiredness, the mind too weak to keep anything still, including what one see.

Oh no, that woman losing her head. A decree is a decree," she say. She, the lady who this morning pay a visit to Mistress Komwono. The mistress keep calling her "dear sister" when they speak, but did call her a foul mouth, lanky breast bitch before she come. She been calling her all sorts of curse as soon as the herald leave, he who wake up the whole household that morning to give message with shouting and drums to expect her visit after noon.

"After noon, meaning prepare a lunch," the mistress say.

Mistress Komwono set the cookwoman working,

and before her guest arrive, mpotopoto with mackerel, herring packed in salt—for sea fish is a rare thing in the mountains—sweet yam eto, fresh figs, and rings of fried klouikloui are all ready. From when she sit down on the cushions, Lady Mistress Doungourou complain about how everything is so sweet, too sweet, even the herring, and how the cook must not be the sophisticated sort from court. For at court, savory is the old thing that new now, which would have sent up the price of salt, but since we no longer at war with the South, the price stay firm, and even though a woman like her, with a noble name like hers, would never associate with any form of tradesman or merchant, they did dabble a little for their own amusement in the markets, so what a sad thing for many, but not for them really, that peacetime make salt prices drop so low. And then she complain about the food again, but don't leave a drop for the mistress.

Sogolon watch them and observe a new thing. The friend enemy. She don't understand it, so she watch more. Lady Mistress Doungourou, the dearest sister, the lanky breast bitch, for she did wear her dress the old way, with her breasts uncovered. This lady remind her of the mistress sister, who also cling close, but who the mistress also say she can't stand. Seem to her that this kind of friend and family is all Mistress Komwono have. But Sogolon can't find anywhere in her head to place it. What hold them close if not love? Not that she know that love be any sort of thing, much less a thing to hold people close. Her brothers hold close because they don't know how to live any other way, and as soon as they learn one, she sure they gone. This is some other big word that the dead master would use. Sogolon let the thought of the master leave as quick as it come. What pull them women close? Maybe this is how it is, where people of all sort surround you but you have nobody. Keme have a lion that he play with in the dirt. She let the thought of Keme leave as quick as it come. Maybe it is a show, a dance, a ceremony between the two of them.

"Oh yes, ever since the Sangomin taking seat at the foot of the crown prince. Now every other woman beyond blessed if she don't get call witch," say Lady Mistress Doungourou.

"They calling Lady Kaabu a witch? Then what they calling her mother?"

"A word a proper woman don't use."

"Then don't trouble your head, dearest sister."

They both sprawl out on cushions like women who don't have to worry about male company. Lady Mistress Doungourou wearing a dark green gown and a heap of bead necklaces that come all the way down to her dark nipples. On every finger, a gold ring. On some fingers, two. The lady mistress talk as much with her hands as she do with her mouth, and both make her look like she raising alarm.

"They summon the Ifa priest after a week of divination, and all then nobody could say for sure."

"But why they think she is a witch?"

"God's words, Njaaye, you don't get news out in that lower province? Two of the lord's concubines have baby that come out foot first. One strangle on the mother cord, and the other one kill the mother. All the servants say Kaabu filled with wickedness and bad spirit ever since all she birth is one slow girl."

"And Lord Kaabu just let them take his wife?"

"He the one who accuse her. The priests couldn't find nothing to say she is a witch, so the lord call a Sangoma."

"And now this nasty river shaman come reach all the way to the throne? Things really different."

"You no want to hear the story?"

"Of course."

"Oh. Well the lord ask for redress from the King and that, good sister, is when the chancellor get involved. God's words, that man make me shudder. He's the one why all this happen, if you going fire an arrow. I don't believe no rumor, but I hear is sake of him, the chancellor why the court now showing the Sangomin favor, and why now there is to be judgment to all things witch. This is how the things happen, sister. The white clay man, this witchfinder who never ever bring comb to his hair show up unannounced at their house. Man look like skin and bones I hear, and hear this, he also come with seven others. Listen sister, all seven of them be children and lo, the strangest children you ever going see. One of them skin red, one crawl sideways on the wall, and another have two head! They just drop in the house like thunder and seize Lady Kaabu saying she is a witch. Two guards I hear, two guards go to defend her, for they thinking this must be some attack, and the children set upon them like somebody throw raw meat to a pack of hyena. My lady, I hear when they pull away, one guard is bones and the other have all him parts scatter all over the courtyard. Demon children, but they in service of good now, so they good? Two other concubines they find to be witches too."

"How?"

"The white clay witchfinder divine that they sharing lusts for each other."

"So? Ignored concubine make do. That not new."

"It new now. The witchfinder himself have the children hold down and spread the two woman while he correct them himself."

"I don't know what you meaning, my sister."

"Yes, you know. That nasty hair man and his demon children set upon the house like it is war they come to fight. They even grab the master and beat him little bit until somebody realize who he be."

"But you not leaving out something, sister? When it come to pass that witches now evil?"

"How long since you . . . since you gone, sister?"

"Long enough."

"Of course. And poor Master Komwono. I didn't even know until last quartermoon, sister."

"Witches, sister. When since that any woman can get called witch?"

"But they are witches, sister."

"You don't hear what I asking, sister."

"You will have to ask my husband. He is the smart one, even the crown prince is impressed."

"That is the second time you mention the crown prince. What about the King?"

"The King? You didn't hear. Dearest sister, I thought that is why you come. For your husband was always in the King's heart. Even after you . . ."

"You make it sound like—"

"He leaving, sister."

"Leaving to go where?"

"He leaving, sister. Leaving."

"And I say where . . . he . . . oh. The King near done dead."

"Sister! You gone too long. That kind of talk is treason. The King is about his business with the ancestors, you hear me? Good for you to never talk that way again. Is treason now. To say what you didn't say, for I didn't hear it, is to wish to kill the country. The lord chancellor say it, and the crown prince approve it. And the scribes put it down in parchment which mean is law now. The King is about his business."

"Nobody going dead, so nobody need no last respects."

"Now you sound like you learning."

"I learning many things, Njaaye, and this only my third day. Is it new tradition also to not speak of her? Or am I not worthy until she receive me?"

"Who, sister?"

"That certainly answer the question."

When the lady is setting to leave, she say to Mistress Komwono, Make sure you ready for when the chancellor come. This just cut loose one more question from the mistress.

"I still don't understand this chancellor business. The King don't have his own mind?"

"It puzzle me that it puzzling you, sister," the lady say, and frown to make her eyebrows say what her lips won't, that she done get too many questions now.

"Kwash Kagar never used to have a chancellor. He used to lean on the fetish priests and the King Sister."

"Your meaning in the dark, my sister. Surely the chancellor was always here? Is always here."

"No, not five years ago. His Majesty's sister is his great counsel. Who is the chancellor?"

The lady laugh. "Sister, you in the provinces too long? Or night devil take your memory? Oh . . . wait . . . is the grief. That must be what taking your recall. The Aesi is with the King from there is a King. And the King don't have no sister."

"I think I would remember the one who had me banished."

"No need for us to go back to that, sister."

"The Princess."

"Princess Emini? Surely she would be too young. You perplexing me, sister."

"Not any more than you're doing me. King Sister, Jeleza. The note of banishment came from her own messenger."

"Not a name I ever hear anyone speak."

"What? This is the most stupid . . . Oh. Of course. I'm not yet worthy to speak the name."

"You done leave your mind back in exile. Didn't you get banished by mark?"

"Yes, on papyrus, but what that matter?"

"So the mark come from the royal house. Who cares who, especially now that you shall be restored."

"Certainly, sister."

"But take heed. Now His Majesty take counsel from his daughter, but everybody at court already complaining that she acting like she is the crown prince. Even after Kwash Kagar marry her off."

"Forgive me, dear sister. Clearly the Kongor air has given me memory sickness."

"Is the grief playing tricks, sister. It taking the wrong things from memory and leaving the wrong things behind."

"That must be it. Be blessed with bounty, dearest."

"The same for you, sister."

As soon as Lady Mistress gone through the gate, and Mistress sure that her palanquin take her far beyond earshot, she turn to the courtyard and say, "Oh Jeleza. We were women together. We were women together, oh. Sogolon, come out from behind that damn door."

Okyeame in the streets. The regal polyglots, what the heralds hoping to become when one of them die. All of them wearing the sacred kente fabric that they wrap around the body twice then over the left shoulder, for the right shoulder is for the King. They walk in the streets carrying staffs. Keme point one out to Sogolon as they leave a market with the cook. The Okyeame speak Kwash Kagar's tongue today, he say to her. Judge them for their verse, for the beauty is what come out of their mouth even if they describing a puddle of mud. Sogolon see one join another, but nothing there is of interest to her, not even the gold staff they both be carrying. Keme drag her with him to get a closer look, to see what the staff saying, he say, but she don't know what he mean. They cut through the crowd until right behind them. A senior Okyeame and an apprentice. At the top of the staff is a carving of three men, one covering eyes, the other, ears, and the last, mouth. Keme about to say something else when the Okyeame say, "Most magnificent Kwash Kagar is about his business! The King is being about the ancestors' business! Most magnificent Kwash Kagar is about his business."

Sogolon see it and still don't believe it. The whole market, every single woman and man, every single mouth go quiet. Most excellent Kwash Kagar is about his business, he say again. The market stay still. Even a seller woman handing a woman a fruit and the woman taking it. Then just so everybody moving again, buying, selling, haggling, quarreling, cheating, catching while the Okyeame move on.

The second cook run out to meet them, out of breath.

"They at the house! They didn't send no word, and this mistress already frighten," she say.

"Fool girl, who? Tell me before you swallow your tongue."

"The Aesi."

They all rush back to the compound, but when they get to the gate a different kind of wind blow past Sogolon, harsh and cold and smelling like a dead fire. Two strong gusts, then what sound like the flap of huge wings. The sound startle her, but only she notice. The cooks run back to the cookroom, and Keme run to take his place with the palace guards standing at attention. Sogolon run past them, and across the courtyard to the hallway leading to the welcome room. Two guards stand by the entryway, with large bead necklaces around their necks, bare chests, and white robes that start at the waist. Inside, two more stand by the window. And on a stool but facing the mistress sit a man with red hair rolled into bumps all over his head, and wearing a black robe with no sleeves. Sitting, yet taller than most people standing, his neck and arms black like the dark of green moss. The mistress about to say something. Sogolon can't read her face. The Aesi turn around and smile.

"Wait outside, please," he say.

The time glass in Sogolon head flip three times before a guard come for her. He point to the stool for her to sit, then leave the room. The two guards are still standing by the window. The Aesi enter the room and his cape flap up even though Sogolon don't feel no wind. She wonder if the bright red hair making his skin darker, or his charcoal skin making his hair brighter.

He clear his throat. "You. The girl with no name."

"I—"

"Don't speak unless I ask you a question. And don't make me repeat a question once I ask it. Do you understand?"

"Yes. Yes, Master."

"Only Kwash Kagar is Master. We all serve him. Do you understand?"

"Yes, Mas— Yes."

"Call me chancellor, or call me Aesi, or call me nothing at all. Titles are for all the vultures around us. I don't care."

Something catch the Aesi's eye and he look out the window. He look out the window long. Sogolon fidget.

"Do you know why your mistress is banished?"

"No, Aesi."

"But you were there when Master Komwono died?"

"What?"

"In the house, little girl. You were in the house the morning Master Komwono die?"

"Yes, Aesi."

"Do you know how he died?"

"The slave find him on the wall, Master."

"No master here."

"Oh."

"And now you are . . . not slave, not child. . . . What are you, a ward?"

"Yes'm."

"Do you know what it is, a ward?"

"No."

The Aesi laughs. It sounds like a sneeze. "Your mistress desires entry into court. Reentry for her. And I am inclined to give it, for the crown prince will be known as ruler with mercy. Who knows, maybe she is now a better ruler of her tongue. Is any witch her friend, girl?"

"No. No, Master, she hate witches. No witches come to us in Kongor."

The Aesi nod and laugh again. Quick as a blink he turn and stare at her. Sogolon try to hold the stare. She not trying to be defiant or strong, but she tired of men working their strength over her, even if is just a stare. She stare back and blink once. The Aesi hold the look and don't seem to blink at all. It is there so quick she know that most wouldn't see it, but she do and she don't know why. Right before he smile again, he frown. It take over all of his face, then vanish.

"I would tell you to remind your mistress to control her tongue this time, but you don't have the liberty to say such things to her," he say. "Who name you Sogolon?"

"Me name myself, sir."

"That is a lie. The mistress call you by that name."

Just then one of the guards grab his belly and vomit. It distract Sogolon, but when she turn back to the Aesi, he is staring at her.

"Take him out," he say, then get up to leave. "What happen when the master finds you?" he ask.

Sogolon's jaw drop. The Aesi smile.

"Wrong question. Wrong person," he say.

The mistress take to her bed the rest of the day and keep to it until morning. Sometime before dawn she shout, **Your words are the same for any woman whose dress you don't lift up,** then wake up. Sogolon is in the sleeping chair by her bed.

"What you watching over me for, girl? I not sick."

"Sleep just catch me here, Mistress."

"Don't make it catch you here again. I will not be watched over. Anyway, what a glorious day. Why ruin it with malcontent and bad temper? Nobody has time for such. Sogolon, go to the cookwoman right away. I will have eggs and not some muck she surely cooking. Glorious day."

Sogolon walk off when the mistress call her back.

"And when you come back we'll pick which of these fabrics suitable for a gown and gele."

"Yes, Mistress."

"Sogolon do you . . . No, go on girl. No, wait. . . . Why am I asking you, you are nothing but a bush girl."

That didn't even bother her. She turn to go.

"I just don't know what to say to her, not as a subject, but as a friend. As a woman."

"I don't know what word you last say to the King Sister, ma'am, but—"

"King Sister. Silly girl, I am talking of the king's daughter. Kwash Kagar don't have no sister."

Sogolon blink away the shock.

"Kwash Kagar don't have no sister, girl."

FIVE

Reading? You must think you're in Juba. No reading happen in Fasisi. And what do you need to read for?" Keme ask.

See the girl. See how her face drop when this man among men in her mind tell her not to bother with reading for he see no use for it in himself, and no good that can come out of it for her. She don't know why she ask him. He making her sour lately, and it is everything and nothing, like laughing at her wanting to understand what it means when a man make a mark on parchment. And wanting somebody to teach her for she can't teach herself. He make her lose memory over why she want to read in the first place. In Kongor, there is a great hall of records, a great egg built from thatch and plaster that stand ten and three men high and that contain the records of every Northern king and kingdom. People from Juba talk about the Palace of Wisdom, where people from far and wide, some as distant as lands across the wild sea, come and read their way on to knowledge of natural science, mapping of stars, healing arts, surgery, and mathematics. The Palace of Wisdom only care about the mind, and don't bother with the body carrying it. But neither place is Fasisi, the seat of the empire. Here knowledge is for those who wish to prosper and if you already of noble birth then what in the nine worlds is there to prosper to?

Somebody tell her that man have might because only man have burden, somebody with a voice that sound just like Keme, which further sour her. All she see is man going through life so easy that he can even scratch his crotch when it itch no matter where he be. Or walk into a place smelling ranker than a dead corpse and expect that a woman will not deny him her koo. Even her brothers used to look at her as nothing but a burden, though she is the one carrying everything from a bag of grain to a big leaf scooping up all the cow, pig, and dog shit. If man want to think he have the burden, let him think it. She see scrolls and loose parchment, and engravings, and leather-bound books in a dusty room of this house, and want to know what lay in them. To know because she is beginning to despise the feeling of a book opening up only to lock her out. A scroll unrolling but keeping itself shut, an open parchment showing everything but revealing nothing. But she cut the wish loose. A burden is upon her that have nothing to do with what make her knees buckle.

Now every invitation from Keme sound like

something else. **We should go around the back. I can show you something you will like.** Sogolon young enough to know she not yet come into her full growth, but old enough to know not to trust any man to lead her anywhere in the dark. Lessons she done learn from living with Miss Azora. When she ask him why he is still here, he ask her if she wish him gone. Before she decide if she is to answer or not, he laugh and say that his instruction is to deliver the house of Komwono to the royal court and from where he and the crown see it, she not delivered yet. Come learn archery is the last thing Sogolon look at him and say no to.

Sogolon is in the room they place her, feeling like iron as she sink into the sheets. The Aesi leave him smell behind in the welcome room and hallway, but she can't tell if it really is a smell or just a memory. She wondering about memory too. Two days ago, the mistress worried about the King Sister. One day ago and the mistress say no such soul live. No, not that, for to say no such soul live is to consider that she did once. Bad enough for the mistress to think she lie. Worse for her to think Sogolon invent, which would beg the reason why. Sogolon know she didn't make this princess up, or have any reason to, especially when the rest of day the mistress have a sharp memory, scolding her for eavesdropping yesterday. But the way the mistress first reply to her make her think that dream and memory is blurring, and now she wonder where else

she confusing the two. The thought weigh her down
in the bed, but then she doze into light sleep, which
bring on a light dream, where she see a flash of that
hair, red like the head of a weaver bird. In the dream
memory he turn around to face her and is about to
speak when she wake up.

Three days after the Aesi visit, the court send message that they will receive the house of Komwono the
next day. As soon as the herald leave, the mistress
fly up into a wild cursing, complaining and yelling
at Sogolon, for she now see that all her fabrics are
from the last time she was at court and it would be
an appalling loss of face—Appalling, you hear me,
girl, that I set into court in such out-of-fashion rags.
Better I come back dressed like a slave, she say to
Sogolon, even though the girl have nothing to do
with her dress. To a real bazaar with you, she say,
and throw coin at the girl. Sogolon in fear, for she
don't know what the mistress like, don't know what
would please the court, and don't know if that is one
and the same thing. She send Sogolon with Keme,
who hiss when he hear that this is an errand for
woman dress.

The fabric and gifts bazaar is in the Baganda district, at the end of a long causeway that connect the
four other sections of the city. And downhill. They
leave by the west gate before noon, both on horseback though Sogolon still nervous about riding. At
the great road, they set off. For most of the causeway

run along the peak of the mountain with nothing
but a steep drop on either side, and nothing to see
but blue mountains on top of mountains. One crossroad lead to another, and with that a turn that dip
down along the side of the mountain, which then lead
to a steaming lake that they ride around. One long
turn and soon they hit a straight road to the district,
home to blacksmiths and claymakers, merchants and
tradesmen, markets and bazaars, buyers and beggars.
People buy and sell in the Ugliko too, but they all
have to close up and empty the street by sundown, or
they spend the night in dungeons that plunge so deep
that some never come back out. In the Baganda section, nearly every shop and smithery have the owner
and family keeping house above or behind it. But she
never see a place like Baganda. This must be where
the mistress's silks come from, for here she see fabrics
in colors that have no name that she know. And patterns that come alive—fishes swimming, lions prancing, patterns that dance to a drum she don't hear.
Foods sizzling and foods raw. At one stall a man is
selling live yellow cats from across the sand sea, **Pet
them, cook them, pick your choice, both will be
nice.** More than one seller woman shout that her
wares just come off the ship from a land where men
spin in one spot for ten moons. From a land where
the fish walk and the horses swim. She almost walk
into a stall selling live snakes and scream. Keme laugh
and pull her away. Sogolon and Keme at a trot, and
she seeing people who are not merchants. Women

buying for families, traders on their way to markets of gold, emerald, pelts, musk, and salt. Boys carrying scrolls for old men hobbling far behind. Craftsmen carting tools, carts pulled by donkeys, carts pulled by mules, carts pulled by oxen. Oxen snorting at boys with switches. Heralds spreading news that the King is about his business.

"I soon join the buffalo legion," Keme say, nervous when he say it.

"I don't know that legion."

"You know any legion?"

"I know I can ride off in peace."

"Your problem is that nobody ever bother to tell you a joke."

"I see jokes all the time," she say.

"Everything is a fight with you all of a sudden."

"You going to tell me what is this legion."

"Fuck the gods." He frown, then smile. Sogolon still just looking at him blank.

"They march to the battlefield and lead the way with war. Skilled in all manner of combat and report to no one but the King."

"You already have skill. Buffalo legion, eh? Maybe you turning into a buffalo already."

"That would sound like praise from everybody but you."

"What it sound like from me?"

"I don't know, Miss Sogolon."

"It look like there be at least one thing redeemable about you," the mistress say. She inspect each fabric

Sogolon bring back, frowning on all, but caressing them nonetheless.

"These three will suit," she say, pointing to the pile on the left. "These we will just have to make do," she say, pointing to the pile on the right. "I mean for you, girl. Surely you don't expect to go in the presence of the King looking like a swamp rat. Tell the house-keeper to get me a seamstress. Tonight, girl."

Inside, the whole house cringing from the mistress yell at the seamstress. So Sogolon go outside. She lose count of which night it was, but it is either the second or third with no moon. Sogolon bored. This must be the time of night where men read, she think. Well, she can't read and nobody is here to teach her. The mistress more interested in teaching her how to sit, and eat and stand and be, that it is a wonder that she don't try to teach her how to shit. Her mind is being cruel. The thought don't even come that much, that tomorrow she will be in the royal court in the presence of a royal somebody, and this is an honor not many, certainly nobody like her, will ever see. A thought come to her to look over her life up to this moment, to go as far back as she can remember, then travel to this point, just to marvel at the whole thing. But she not interested in going back that far. Or going back at all. Not even to this afternoon, much less.

What interesting her is Keme, leading a horse, slip-ping through the gate, gone into the dark. Not think-ing about it much either, she do the same and follow.

They on the same causeway to Baganda. The night scare her until she grasp that darkness not dark. That the road is right there, bright from dust, as are the trees, like shadows against a sky that is not black but the richest blue. And her ears do the seeing when her eyes cannot, following Keme at a good pace behind, but never losing his trail. At least in the dark she can't see the steep drop on either side of the road. She turn left at the first crossroad, which take her around a bend that go down the mountain. In the middle of the bend, a path on the right, where dust is still floating after Keme's horse wake it up. She coming near the end of the road, where she see his horse tie up to a tree, but no Keme. Now at the road edge she step off into the trees and bush. No answer from Keme, though she call his name twice. The cliff drop off steep and she stumble. A stump break her roll, a good thing, for beyond the stump is air. At least she feeling air around her legs. She seeing something else. Blinking five times, then seven don't change what she see, so she watch Keme, though that don't make her disbelieve it less.

Keme is walking on air, over clouds. No, he is walking on tiles, some taking just a tiptoeing foot, some as big as a door, none tethered to anything but open sky. Tiles, bricks, rock, chunks of floor all making a trail leading out into open air. Sogolon is on the first floating block before she considers what she is doing. It sink a little and she slap her mouth to stop the scream. The second block sink a little too. She can't go. Below her she see mountains and valleys and the air not promising her nothing. Is Keme, walking as if this is just another path, who is making her do it? But she stumble on the next tile and almost fall. A yelp come, but not loud enough to catch Keme's ear. The tiles, planks, bricks now feel as solid as ground. Clouds float below her and the dark underneath send terror into her chest. Keme is walking like man who trod this so often that he don't bother look. But she do look, for the first time, beyond the trail and beyond the wind that take on the color of a ghost in the night sky.

The trail longer than it look. Longer than two time a glass flips. She would wonder which God with such scattered thinking make this trail, as if cobbling together anything he can find, as if she can wonder about anything other than how she walking on sky. The end of the trail more mystifying than the beginning. Her head is brimming with things she is seeing but not believing, even if there is something insistent about Keme's steady walk. Clouds come together and pull apart as they go, and something is on the air, a whisper maybe. Keme is gone. She rub her chest and stop a panic. Clouds pull apart and she see smoke first, seven trails going up into the air and below that roofs, some pointing, some flat. Seeing and believing won't come together and it shake her balance. Houses, shacks, taverns, bridges, shelters, all huddled close like any section of Fasisi, and all floating in air. Doors connect to paths, which connect to doors, which connect to paths, and all along them, movement.

A quick step cost her. Only sky beneath her now. She is falling. She stop falling. A hand catch her wrist and pull her up. Keme.

"I not going around any back with you. Not that you say? And loud too. So why you following me?"

"Is this you was going show me?"

"You continue to make no sense, girl."

"This place, what is it?"

"You frown like you smell something stink on my tongue. I here thinking, This girl thinking I trying to rape her or what? Is that what you did think?"

"No."

"You lie better in daylight."

"Children of gods live here?"

"No." Keme continue walking. "But children of Go do."

She don't ask him to explain, figuring him too annoyed with her to do so. He never did give reason to believe he mean to do her wrong that night. Like man need reason. But he wasn't like any other man. But he is a man.

"I don't understand."

"No, you don't. Try don't slip again."

She follow him, striding where he stride, shuffling where he shuffle, hopping where he hop. They soon in the middle of the town, for what else it could be but a town? Nothing in Fasisi look like these roofs or walls, and nothing in Mitu or Kongor either. Clay walls, white, but dark in the night, and covered in patterns, and scratches, and drawings of war, hunting, swimming, fucking, dancing, all of which glow red and yellow in the night like a blacksmith's iron. Marks reaching past the first window and the second up into the sky. Flat roofs and walls from the same clay. Houses taking any shape they please, some with wide more than high, some a tall needle in the sky, some with a curve like an egg or a bosom.

"What you mean?"

Keme stop by an entrance with much shouting and laughter going on inside. A tavern.

"Go. The Children of Go. You hear of Go?"

"Nowhere name Go."

"So you never hear of it."

"Yes I hear of it. I say nowhere name so, other than in story woman tell her child."

"You never know any such woman."

"You going tell me the story?"

Keme laugh and shake his head. "The people here, they descended from the people of Go. Come here ten generations ago. When they left Go, they took everything with them, even the clay, even the wood and stone to build their houses. But everything from Go, whether wood, or stone, or metal, or dirt, behave as Go do. The legend is true, girl. It's not even a legend. Everything of Go and from Go float as soon as the sun set, and sink as soon as sun rise."

"You saying the entire city rise in the air as soon as sun set."

"That is exactly what I just say."

"I don't believe it."

"And here is a town floating on air whether you believe it or not."

He turn and go inside the tavern. People shouting, Keme! She about to follow him, but can't pull herself from all that is in front of her. Everything look like one suppose it to, unless you look down. At the edge of a wood or stone path is a gap separating one part from another. What happen when somebody fall off or through? Maybe people from Go fly too? People pass by, going about their business, but they look no different from anybody else in Fasisi. And this is a tavern. What befall the drunk who walk? Three man pass her, too much into arguing about what a look from rich maiden might mean, to notice her. Her eyes follow them until they turn left and vanish behind a wall, with glowing red patterns all over it. She is tempted to touch the glow to see if it burn. This is a big district she is seeing, looking like houses on top of houses, many boasting the glow of firelight. People in their homes about their business. She go inside.

At every corner hang torchlight. Under every torch-light, people gathering, laughing, shouting, cussing, yelling for another draw of wine or another mug of beer and bring your naked self with it. What you going do with my naked self, yeye man? the server girl ask. Come back naked, the man say. Come back and I drink you like how I drink the beer. You mean only glug half because you can't handle the rest, the girl say and everybody laugh. Through the laughs Sogolon find Keme, for his is the loudest, a shout that end with what sound like a sigh. The room puzzling her. Music, from kora and oud, but no players of instrument. A dim light, enough to see all for who they be, but the light is a blue blanket, landing on every face gentle. Everybody on carpets, carpets on the floor. Everybody leaning against pillow and cushion, or sitting up straight. Like Keme. He burst out laughing and slap the lion lying right beside him, who growl and raise a paw like he about to knock Keme over. Keme laugh louder, and the others join in. An old man with a staff he still holding and whose back is to her. A bare back, and scrawny with his ribs poking through the skin. Also laughing, one of the wingsmen with his head wrap off and his bald head shiny, another man dressed in the armor that Keme usually wear, a woman in a long gown with gold stripes, but the gown so thin that what not gold show right through to her skin. A woman brush past Sogolon on her way to them, a beautiful woman that she thought is a serving girl until the woman sit beside the old man.

"Sogolon, meet my friends," he say.

The old man turn around to look. Keme start with him.

"That is Alaya. Don't be perplexed when you go

to Malakal or Mitu or where else and you see a man looking just like him. Some say is his twin."

"More than eight mean more than twin," the old man say.

"More than eight mean an inbreeding daddy," say the woman beside him and they all break out into laughing again.

"The wicked woman beside him, Bimbola."

"Every woman get call wicked when she realize man stupid," Bimbola say and point to a spot for Sogolon to sit. Keme continue.

"You know the Seven Wing, but this must be the first time you seeing Djabe's face. To my left, Beremu, the foulest-smelling lion in Fasisi."

The lion growl again.

"And to my right somebody nobody need to know."

Out of the dark, something hit the side of Keme's head.

"Woman what in two fucks you hit me with?"

"Something Beremu can eat," the woman say as she come into view.

"Oumou them call me. What they call you?" she ask.

"Sogolon."

Keme look at the old man and say, "But Alaya, how fare the King?"

"You the one who serve the palace. I just a griot."

"Who have news of the realm even the realm don't know."

Alaya pound the carpet two times. "The King is

about his business," he say and the lion roar. "Yes, Beremu tell him again not to peddle that shit."

"You must think we in your bedchamber."

"Shut up, Oumou," Keme say.

"I not saying nothing."

"But you thinking it. Beremu, what you know?"

The lion growl, then he purr, then he make a sound that Sogolon don't know.

"People up in the sky don't care about the King, whoever that is," Alaya say.

"What that mean?"

"It mean your prince already acting like the crown sitting on his head. And the King, he getting more busy and more busy. Two nights ago he almost finish he work. First time in three moon, the prince come to the palace and nobody summon him. But then Kwash Kagar decide there was more work to do. He even get up and walk a few paces before we put him back to bed. You should see that prince face when his chariot take him away. Man have a look that can melt silver."

"Chariot don't take him far enough," Bimbola say. "They have to pull him off a girl in the Taha section when she stop moving. Right there in the street and he don't care who see. Then the Sangomin find her house, and burn it down. Only this week them children—"

"Bimbola," Keme say.

"I talking the things. Ever since that witchfinder get the ear of the Aesi, ever since the Aesi bring him and his whole brood of demon kin, all of Fasisi on the edge of a knife. Running loose, disturbing everything, taking what they want. You see them in the market, grabbing any food they desire. Last week a woman make protest and one of them burn her tongue out. Another one just slap a man face, only for people to see that he slice off his head. And gods help you if you just in their way, for who don't stomp on you will walk right through your body and make your heart explode. A lucky day is when they only take a finger. Call a magistrate, they just walk away. They running loose in the kingdom."

"They not running loose. Somebody set them loose," Alaya say.

"What a land this going to be when this King—"

"Shut up, Oumou," Keme say.

Beremu roar.

"Beremu, you watch your mouth too," Keme say. Beremu rise, growl, and leave for another room.

Alaya turn to Sogolon. "That is the lion saying stop being such a coward."

"And he lucky it's him or I would drag my knife right across his face. How the fuck he going to call me a coward?" Keme say.

"Tu loju," Bimbola say.

"My face not hot," Keme say.

Keme take a drink of his beer. Oumou look at Sogolon and say, "So Sogolon, girl, you plan to be Keme second wife?"

Keme shout something but Sogolon don't hear.

Second wife. It go through her head, leave her head, come back to her head, and leave again. Her mind don't know what to say to it. But it keep bouncing in and out of her.

"The poor man can barely take care of the first one," Oumou say.

"Come out of the girl face, Oumou."

"I not in her face. If I was planning disrespect, I would have asked you."

Sogolon look away to the group on the right, the two old men smiling but saying nothing for nearby ears to hear. To Bimbola, who go over to the counter to pour a man more beer. Of course he have a wife, look at him. He perhaps have even two. What is it to you? Between him and you is nothing but breeze. Sogolon want to be a big woman, who already understand big woman things. But this make her feel like she just a girl. No, not a girl, a fool. Not just for feeling a way, but for feeling at all.

"Which of the nine worlds you just gone to?" Oumou whisper to her.

Sogolon don't answer. The air thin here and she want to leave, she think.

A crash, a roar, a scream, a snarl, more crashing, a scuffle, and something running. Then something chasing it, then a slam into a door or onto the floor. Nobody know which until the lion come back with a little white girl in his mouth. People in the bar jump and scream and run, but nobody by Keme move.

Beremu's jaws around the girl's neck, the girl skin white like kaolin.

"Beremu, drop the girl!" Keme shout.

Beremu still shaking the girl. The girl not moving.

"Beremu!" Keme shout again and grab his spear. Beremu drop the girl and roar louder than she ever hear him roar. Everybody rush out, leaving just those with Keme.

"You kill her?" Oumou ask. Beremu growl again. "But she look dead."

Beremu look at Keme and roar. Keme still clutching his spear. Bimbola go over to the girl, head to toe in white, even hair. She stoop down and look at the girl, just a child with her eyes open but seeing nothing, mouth open but silent. She touch her forehead and all of the girl crumble into powder.

"The gods!" she say.

Keme lower his spear. To Beremu he say, "Sangomin?"

The lion growl and mumble and hiss, and growl again. Keme stare at Sogolon. She don't like the look on his face.

"Powder. Nothing but powder dust," Oumou say.

"He or she already change into someone else. They gone," say Alaya.

Sogolon afraid to go look, but everybody do except Alaya. "If Sangomin come up here before, I never see them," he say.

"Alaya, who you anger now?" Keme say. "Soon somebody will follow him."

Powder is slipping out of Oumou's hands. Now they all looking at Alaya.

"Beremu is the one that kill him," he say.

Beremu start to growl, but then Oumou say, "Whatever that was is nothing more than a husk."

"And you, Mr. Castle Guard. You can't stay here," Bimbola say.

"But I didn't do a thing."

"This need to cool off. Leave."

"Alaya is the one that need to leave."

"I look like I was asking?"

Keme don't look back when he say, "We gone." At the doorway he pause. "Sogolon," he say, and leave. She run after him.

Outside, Keme walking real fast the entire way and it is a while before Sogolon catch up with him.

"All I want was one peaceful night."

"I not the one who take it from you."

"Even when nobody bringing fight to you, you fight anyway."

"You the one in there fighting with your friend then."

"Oh I forgot. You don't have friends. You going to the palace tomorrow. From then on you're another guard's problem."

"Oh is problem I was. You teach all your problems how to ride horse and shoot arrow?"

"Go home, Sogolon."

"I don't have no home."

"Then go to wherever will have you. And don't follow me."

"Look here, I—"

"Don't follow me again."

SIX

Understand that the King don't live in the royal enclosure. The walls of this place hold those noble, and those close by blood, those rich and those powerful, those of old coin and new, those in the King's favor and in his service. But in the enclosure is another enclosure, with high curtain walls and sitting on the peak of the mountain. Is there that sit Kwash Kagar's castle, and the grounds where seven other castles stand. Seven of them leaving behind stories of the seven kings of the Akum dynasty, for it is forbidden that any heir live in the house of a dead king. A prince can live in any castle he want, and a princess too, or Queen Mother, or those with blood but not title. But a crown prince must build his own when he is to become king. And in the erecting there must be wisdom and care, for if he build too late, the old king will die leaving the new king with no house. If he build too soon, then the living king will see the insult of the son already trying to take his place, and banish him to a mountain fortress farther away than even Mantha.

Kwash Kagar build the biggest castle any eye did see, big to match his ambition, and to house his many legitimate and bastard children, as certain mischievous griots sing. Curtain walls of brick, four floors high with battlement as high as a man. On every floor, windows set in an arch, and as tall five men. Four tower corners to the wall with sentries standing guard, and within that the castle, and on the top floor of the castle stand two more floors half as wide where the King and Queen live. You look at Kwash Kagar's castle and see that this King did come with one ambition, which was to be greater than any other king, and if not, then to look so. Each brown brick marked with the day he was born. Each brick wall four footsteps thick. People say the castle is so wide that when night come to the east wing, it is still evening in the west. And as his kingdom and family grow, he add room onto room, hall onto hall, and what not part of the castle spread out to the enclosure, including the servant quarters for those who feed him, clothe him, wash him, cut his claw-looking fingernails, clean his crusty eyes, and wipe away loose piss before the royal bed goes rank. Also close by, the ballroom, theater, and bathhouse. Then the barracks for the ten and two imperial lions, a library as big as the first palace, and an archive hall. A guard with spear stand at every battlement, and sometimes there be two. Guards also stand, four at the gatehouse, and one on every step of the staircase leading to the entrance.

In the keep, and sometimes out in the enclosure if they annoy the King, stay those who are at court. Some stay only a quartermoon, some stay half a year, some never leave. The mistress won't say which was she. But she gain intelligence from dearest Lady Mistress Doungourou, who is at court now. The King, Kwash Kagar, old and feeble in his ways, is keeping himself to bed. His wife, the first Queen, dead years before him, with her spirit haunting the same tree of the ancestors, even though she is not blood. Kwash Kagar's second wife, Queen Wutu, who he marry two year ago, but who when he could still walk would stumble upon her like one do a stranger in one's own house and ask which concubine she be. So beautiful that people think she foolish, but all the while she plotting, so say the cook. So say the cook also: Last year she is claiming baby-bearing sickness, but stop when the Aesi count back to when she claim to conceive and discover that the King was already too weak to do anything in bed save sleep. Also present is her sister, who have four children all claimed by her husband, but all looking like the King; her pompous father and lecherous brother, who think himself a favorite of the crown prince, even though the prince keep mistaking him for one of the King's men, asking him at every chance if it is not his duty to wipe the King's

ass before all of the court can tell that he shit himself.
As for the crown prince, Likud used to share a castle
with his sister, Princess Emini, but both grow tired of
each other's ways. At the prince's dwelling and living
with him are four men and three women, who might
or might not be betrothed to each other, since the
servant always see a different mix in a different bed,
or floor, or railing, or roof, or that one time, cage.
At the princess's quarters, five women who know her
since birth, since they all used to attend to the dead
Queen. Both princess and prince complain to who
will hear of how this still new Queen infest the house
with family the way lice infest hair, for also at court
is her uncle, aunt, and two cousins.

At court also, several of the King's bastards that he
have great affection for, and Commander Olu, the
King's greatest warrior, who now live at the palace as
reward. He survived a spear going right through his
head, but it take nearly all of his mind with it, and the
new Queen ask often if there are two fools at court,
not one. Commander Olu keep to his own company,
but wear a marriage necklace, and nobody can tell
why, not even he. At court also, four other men in
close service to the King; seven more noble ladies still
in service to the dead Queen; players of drums, and
harp, and kora; one fool; one Ifa diviner; and many
Sangomin, all of them young, some even younger.
And the Aesi, but what is there to say about him?
Everybody know who he be, and know it always,

though nobody remember when they first see him, or how he come to be chancellor. They just know it always as so.

The two wingsmen ride at an easy trot until they get to the castle gate. They out in front, the twin handling the caravan, Keme at the side, about to talk to Mistress Komwono, but peering through the window.

"Why this escort looking like he lost something in here?"

"What, no—no ma'am."

Sogolon wish she could see his face crumble on itself from the embarrassment. But it won't, for is not embarrassment he feel. He looking like he lose something in here and trying to find it. Sogolon at the back sorting out the mistress's gifts for the King, which include the myrrh she never stop using, though she say it is rarer than a baby jengu in a jar. Keme looking through the window and Sogolon having no interest to look back. Mistress Komwono looking at them both and satisfied, for that at least take care of the worry that this girl is going to come to court already ruined. Sogolon look down on the dress she wearing, the first time she wearing one. And the gele, she still not accustomed to something on her head more than hair. The dress blue like morning sky with a pattern like chicken feet scatter all over it. The gele, the same. Sogolon feel like a doll or like a frame storing the dress, not somebody wearing it. Is hard walking in a dress, is not easy, she say to herself over and over as she gaze at the narrowness at her knee that sprout out below, and making it impossible to walk without looking like a clumsy fish.

"We coming to the first of the grand castles, ma'am," Keme say. "On the right, past the trees the castle of Kwash Jafari, the second of the Akum kings. Kwash Kalifa, his father conquered these lands, but died before he could build on it. People call it the Red Castle, because, well you can see why."

Sogolon want to look outside. She want to see castles, and road, and guards, and things that would make her swoon. But she don't want her eyes to meet his. The caravan swing right.

"Now we coming up to Kwash Jafari's castle, a palace to tell true. And where the Princess Emini live. One of the two castles built from stone where everything else is brick. And—"

"Why this escort think I need learning about a place I already know? He think this is my first time at court?" the mistress say to the air, for she would never lower herself to address him directly. Or complain to Sogolon. She leave the window, sit back in her chair, and close her eyes to ready herself. The caravan stop. The mistress wipe her eyes and grumble for some water, which is when Sogolon see she is crying.

From the gatehouse all must travel by foot. Or palanquin, which the mistress curse under breath for coming without. Keme escort them through the archway to the great welcome hall, with guards in red armor standing at the door. Keme not stopping for nothing, and neither is the mistress, so Sogolon can't see anything long enough to marvel at it. She can only look ahead, at two purple doors in an arch that open as they approach, into a room with tall curtains touching high ceilings gone wild with painting of men at worship, at battle, and on the hunt. Two more doors open into another room with full urns by the windows, vases in the window sills, small trees inside vases, and chairs waiting for people to sit. At the head of the room, a platform in gold, and three chairs, with the one in the middle being the biggest. A purple chair with words in gold that Sogolon can't read. They come to another door, but at this one two lions stand guard. Even with seeing Beremu twice Sogolon frighten that they get so big, both of them reaching the mistress's shoulder when they step in first. They don't seem to bother her, even as they make Sogolon uneasy. As Keme pass the one on his right he scratch his head. Beremu? He say something as she pass, not a growl but not a purr either. Halfway through the room she realize the two lions following them. In the next room, there are less chairs than the one before, and tapestries of kings and queens. Kwash Kalifa, the first King, on a white horse. The same King on the throne, beside his Queen. Kwash Kalifa again, in front of his multitude of children and subjects standing on the first mountain. Kwash Kalifa again with sword and spear, leading a great red army in a clash against the green enemy, with dead men and horses at their feet. And there again, the last two, on both sides of the hallway leading to another set of doors. On the left, the one of Kalifa slaying the fire-breathing ninki nanka, whose long scaly body and tail wrapping around the whole frame. On the right, the King, Queen, and baby prince surrounded by lions.

Two more lions join and lead them in the next room.

"But this don't be the King's palace?" Mistress ask. Keme turn around, but he don't reply.

"Kwash Kagar won't take residence in a dead king's palace even if he—"

Two lions roar. The mistress shut up quick.

The two doors open to a burst of sound. People. The court. Chatter, laughter, gossip in a hush, rumor in a whisper. Air flowing in and out and around, and sending to Sogolon's ear loose talk she didn't ask for. **Which forgetful god suddenly remember she . . . mark it, when he go the peace go with him . . . conducting herself quite like a man these days, look how she soon take wife . . . war? No no no no war.** But she look around too late and can't tell who say what. All she can do is see women and men dress up with so much finery that the whole room glow. Some even wearing gold. Women in patterns of every color and shape, and in competition for the tallest and widest ighiya. Men and women in every color and pattern of Basotho blanket, so much that Sogolon catch the mistress looking at her own outfit, different because she choose so, and frown. Sogolon know. The mistress want more than anything else to stand out, but now she is ruing because stand out is exactly what she do. Sogolon as well, for she is wearing the same style. Whispers come to her, too quiet to hear, but she know that none of them mean well. For now everybody looking at Mistress Komwono, who nod slightly at a few of the people she know. Two men darker than blue smile. A few people nod, a few women frown, and many do nothing at all. Farther back in this gathering than the airs she put on would suggest is Lady Mistress Doungourou.

This is the procession now. Two lions in front, two wingsmen, Keme in full armor, the mistress, Sogolon, and two lions in the back. As they come up to the throne, this happen, the lions crouch down. First the hair go wild like wind rippling it, then their back skin grow darker, and darker as the back widen, and muscle build on muscle, and limbs stretch into legs and hands, and four naked men, dark in skin and light in hair, rise and stand. The mistress quick hobble to the high steps leading up to the throne and throw herself down on the floor. The room quiet, save for whisperers who think they quiet.

"The house of Akum, descended from the divine blacksmith who spoke to Bakali, the god of lightning and fire, who killed his own family in error and from that night shares his fire and his melancholy with the world, but his triumph also," a deep male voice say.

"As it was and is and shall be," the gathering join together to say. The voice continue.

"Bakali put his eye on Kalifa the blacksmith, and

found him most pleasing of all men so he elevate him to the corner of kings, who one day join the ancestors, who one day join the gods. In his name, Kwash Kalifa."

"As it was and is and shall be," the gathering join together to say.

"Blessing to those of you who seek divine counsel," he say as he come in from the west door. He, the Aesi. He step into the room wearing a flowing red cassock. Long sleeves, and a white tunic peeking out from the chest. Seven or eight bead necklaces, orange and yellow, and all of them around his neck like rings circling. A straw-weave cap with two bead tails going past his ear all the way to his waist.

"Blessings," the people say.

Sogolon watching the mistress. First she is all flat on the floor, her forehead and nose pressing into the tile. But now she raise her head, as if music nobody else hearing catch her ear. The Aesi turn to her without moving closer and say, "The King is about his business today."

The mistress either don't hear or don't know what he mean, for she stay on the ground.

"Get up," he say much louder. The mistress struggle. Sogolon rush to help her up. The mistress grab her hand, and soon as she find balance slap it away. The lion men hear something, and they all drop to the floor, rising as cats, standing by the four corners of the throne platform. Another commotion come from the west. The room all bend the knee until the princess sit on the throne. Princess Emini, in no regalia at all, and dressed more humble than anyone in the room, in a tunic and cloak as if pulled away from some sport that men play. Regal she leave for her head, a gold headband around the forehead, with a fringe hanging over her brow, gold and cowrie beads dividing her long, full, and curly hair in two, four or five necklaces in four or five patterns, and hoop earrings twice as big as her ears. Following her, a pale wet rat of a man, shuffling to catch up with her.

"Your Highnesses, Princess Emini and Prince Majozi."

The prince set himself to the right of the throne. The princess throw herself in it.

"Your Highness, the King's throne is—"

"Cold. But it will do. What kingly responsibilities did the crown prince leave with me today?" she ask.

"Duties of the throne, Highness," the Aesi say. Sogolon watching his broad back.

"So much for my brother's sense of duty to his people," she say.

"The crown prince is busy—"

"And I am bored. But you don't see me hoarding killers and killing whores. Or perhaps I should, eh, Aesi? You don't seem bothered by boy transgression half as much as a girl's."

"But you're a woman, Princess."

"Save that flattery for a wife. Or a slave. One can never tell with the women around you."

Some people, the one who look like they don't

know better, laugh. People like the prince. The Aesi
make a motion to turn around and everybody stop
quick, but the prince. He giggle for so long that the
princess have to glare at him to stop.

"And of course, my father is busy. If only the crown
prince would be so busy. Aesi, is that treason?"

"Not yet, Your Highness."

Sogolon watch his back as he nod. But as he
straighten himself he look off to the side, almost turning around. Like music just catch his ear. Sogolon
clear her throat and he turn again.

"The King is about his business every day, not so?"
say the princess. "What I would give for people of
Fasisi to speak freely. Or maybe just this room."

"They speak as you demand it, Princess," the prince
say with a laugh.

"Are you deaf today, dear Prince?"

"I hear everything, dear Princess," he say, but the
princess already looking at the crowd. "Who brings
tribute from our friends?" she ask. Keme and the
wingsmen step out of the way, and prod the mistress
to do the same. Sogolon shift to the side, between two
women with gold-striped clothes and noble noses.
From there and for much of the day people come
bringing trunks, bags, sacks, palanquins, barrels, and
cages. Carrying birds and beasts, and horses small as
cats, and two boys who shift into an animal never
seen in North or South. A prince from Kalindar who
can't prove what he is prince of come with an offer of
marriage, which make the princess laugh and ask if

he knows that she is married. The whole court gasp, and Prince Majozi hiss when the man say that he know. Prince Majozi glare at the princess to do something but she laugh and say, Besides, my real husband is my father's responsibility, but you never know, my prince, are we not people, and people's lives change in the quick. Then she wave away the prince with a wink and a smile. And still more come from lands across the wild sea, and the sand sea, the last one smelling of the myrrh that he bring. Sogolon wince for the mistress, who bring the same gift.

"I think I am near the end for today. My room is overflowing with all your tributes. And complaints," the princess say.

"A few more, Your Highness."

"One more."

"As you wish," the Aesi say, and spread both arms as he bow. It look like too much to Sogolon, but too much of what, she don't know.

"Returning to us, the lady mistress from the house of Komwono," he say and the mistress shuffle forward before anybody prompt her. She bow.

"Returning from where?"

"Kongor."

"From so far? That's a month and a quartermoon. Why were you gone?"

"I . . . if, if it please Your Highness," Mistress Komwono say, now nervous as she look around at the people of the court. She turn and look at the Aesi as if asking for help.

"Lady Mistress is pleased to be with us," the Aesi say.

"But why was she gone? Were you not at court once? Here, then gone, and now you've returned. This is not a hard question."

"This is before you grew in your royal responsibilities, my princess," the Aesi say.

"Taking a very long time to answer my question, both of you."

"Lady Mistress Komwono—"

"Komwono. Komwono. Oh . . . oh yes, I see it now. I see it." The princess stop and think for a long time, glancing at the mistress, then glancing into space. "You're the one who was banished. By my mother if I remember."

Mistress Komwono bow her head again.

"The lady mistress—"

"Can speak for herself, Aesi, unless you enjoy me constantly interrupting you. Lady Mistress, the crown and the court welcome you."

"Thank you, Most High."

"Most High would be my father. I'm a considerably lesser light."

"With permission, Your Highness, sad and sick was my years away from court. I sit many days in fear and trembling, missing the light of his presence. Oh the misery, oh the regret. My late husband—"

"I was about to ask his whereabouts. Especially since the invitation would have gone to the husband, for him to bring his wife. Or whoever. Up to now nobody seemed to know you are a widow. Did you think we would have retracted the invitation?"

"No, ma'am."

"Then you would have been wrong. The gods set the rules, we simply follow them as best as we can, don't we? Sometimes we have to do without them. Take your case, Lady Mistress. The invitation was for your husband and his guest, not you, but here you are without him. Since you sent no word of his death, what can we conclude here but that you have committed a lie of omission? And since this invitation is through the grace of the King, indeed you lied to the King. And lying to the King, Lady Mistress, as you well know, is punishable by death. But as I said, rules, sometimes one must do without them, not so?"

"Yes, yes, yes, Your Highness."

Sogolon wonder if the mistress nearly piss herself. She know she come close to it.

"My mother is dead and my father is . . . busy. I am afraid there's no royal to reminisce with you, Lady Mistress."

Sogolon feel a knot at the back of her head so tight that she look down just to let her neck stretch. When she look up, the Aesi looking at her. She look away, at the gold trim running up the canopy shading the princess and at the chair arms, both carved into lions. And the four lions who did just stand as men from before the sun turn color. She turn back to the Aesi still looking at her.

"Is an honor to return to court, Your Highness."

"We will see what you think after a day of court with these beautiful ladies and learned gentlemen. In the meantime, gifts? I shall see the gifts you have brought your King."

At this the wingsmen come forward with two chests and place them on the floor. One open a chest, and the silk cloth wake up, and start to free itself before he lock the chest back shut.

"You present these chests to the King?"

"A chest filled with silk from across the wild sea, my princess. Silk as worn by nobody in this court, for none go on no ship to bring it back."

"That might be true."

"And a nkisi nkondi made from gold with gold nails."

"For when my father wishes to make a golden curse," the princess say. She is looking bored, not for herself but for her father.

"And this girl, Most High. I bring the King this girl."

At that a wingsman grab Sogolon by the arm and drag her to the front, right between the chests. Sogolon leave shock and dismay back in the spot where she was. She can't take either of them with her now that she is standing before the princess. Except she don't know where to stand, where to look, where to be. The wingsman kick the back of her knee and she fall on one leg. She want to look at the mistress to ask, Why? How can you? Or, Fucking bitch, is slave you just turn me into? The other thoughts pile on top of each other. Maybe if she run. She wouldn't get far, but at least she did try. Kwash Kagar's face fly up into her head, or maybe it is just some other face, for she never lay eyes on the King. She don't dare look at the princess, for the voice in her head tell her not to. Tears well up in both eyes but run down one, and she refuse to wipe it. Sogolon is shaking, she know it. At the back, a laugh. She think it's a laugh. Something like Middle Brother's laugh. She tried so hard to escape people working their will over her. She try so hard. She leave a man on a wall and another without a hand. She not only trembling, but pulling away from herself to see herself standing there crying with nobody caring, and seeing her skin flush in a rash and her hands shaking. Slave. The mistress trick her into slavery. She want to look at her and say, I trick you into widowhood. She can't stop the shaking, or the tears, and now a shadow is upon her.

The Aesi. He's right before her face, looking at her blue fish dress. She remember how men at Miss Azora look at a woman. Slow, from foot, to waist, to belly, stopping at the breasts to linger, then maybe at last, the face. Many she remember don't look that far. This Aesi look straight up to her face and she try to see nothing in him doing it. Not frowning, but his eyebrow raised, and his lips part, like he looking for something hard, but still not finding it. **Maybe he looking for your beauty and not finding it,** say the

voice that sound like her. He grab her neck, just so.
Not squeezing, but firm. She clutch his hand and try
not to cry. She slapping his hand, trying to grab on
to something, to pull it away, but his eyes not showing no might, no force, no nothing. Sogolon listening for some word from the mistress behind her but
hear nothing. She listen for footsteps to approach and
do . . . she don't know what, maybe Keme's footsteps but hear nothing. Is not like he's strangling her,
but he is making her know his power. His fingers are
warm and getting warmer. It feels like he is lifting her
up and her legs are flailing, but she is still standing
on the floor.

"Oh put the damn girl down, Chancellor. Every
face you see, you go looking for a witch."

"Witches are not the only threat to the kingdom,
Highness."

"Of course not. There are also rainbows, baby
chicks, and the color yellow. Or whatever it is that
you divine this week. But a little girl?"

"A little girl can be—"

"Hark how this man is about to tell me what it is
that a little girl can be. Maybe you know a little too
much of little girls."

Some in the court laugh. The laughter catch on
and the room roar. The Aesi smile. He let go of
Sogolon's neck.

"Lady Mistress, step forward," the princess say.
Mistress Komwono walk around them to stand in
front. She bow again.

"So what is it you bring as gifts to the King? A gold fetish, coins, women's cloth, and a slave?"

Sogolon eyes widen.

"She . . . she not a slave, Your Highness, only a gift."

"A gift to do what? Have you not heard, Lady? My father is not for much doing these days. What is he supposed to do with her?"

"Whatever he wish, Highness."

"Whatever he wish, you say. The King's harem has over four hundred women. You think he would notice one more? Ha, look at her face, joining the harem sound like news to her."

"Harem if His Majesty wishes, Highness, unless you find for her other use," Mistress Komwono say.

"Other use? You're supposed to be telling us what that is. Looks like you doing nothing more than dropping off a burden, Lady Mistress. And look. Again, this is news to her. Maybe you will have some use for her, Prince."

"She don't look very useful, Princess," the prince say.

"Maybe the kitchen, Highness," the Aesi say.

"You expect me to send this girl to the cook? You forget who really rules this palace. Can you cook?"

"No she don't, Highness," Mistress Komwono say, just as Sogolon open her mouth.

"Also since when is this court in the business of placing concubines or cooks?"

"Forgive me, Highness."

"Forgive what exactly, Lady? You dropping off this gift hoping that it would have been a man you're giving her to. A gift to the King will soon mean a gift to the prince and . . . well, well, well, well."

The princess stands up. She is done for the day.

"Look at this girl. Nothing of the slave, nothing of the servant, nothing of the cook, no art, no craft, not pretty, perhaps not strong, no gift other than staying alive." The princess shake her head. "Keep her away from my brother," she say and leave.

The people raise all sort of fuss, with petition after petition, and what can't wait, and what she must hear today, but the Aesi say, with barely a whisper, that when a royal leaves the room, the room leaves with her. They know what he mean. Right after the princess take leave, but before the court, the Aesi give tidings that Mistress Komwono's gift will be accepted, and to consider her good standing with the King restored. Now the crown wishes her the blessings of the gods on her journey back to Kongor. Tonight. The mistress shook. She start crying, but shut her tears down when she see all the people of the court bearing witness. Mistress Komwono hold her head high, and walk out without escort, not looking once at Sogolon. Sogolon want her to look. She want the mistress to read her face. Quiet take over the room and the people retire. All but Sogolon, who don't know where to go. She wrap her arms around herself, though she not cold. The room is different with everybody gone. Gray seeping into it like the room hosting night. Quiet, but silence like a hum, like being under a tree swarming with bees.

"You are the no name girl."

"I have a name."

The Aesi laughs. "But no sense of who you can speak to and when." He steps up to the throne, then turn around to face her. His robe turn slower, following him like a wave.

"You ever see it, such magnificence?"

"I—"

"First thing to learn, girl. When somebody of high birth pose you a question, they not looking for an answer. But look around you, look at columns of gold, tapestries of velvet, and ceilings, and walls telling the story of kings. How unlikely that a girl such as you would find herself now in such halls. I know what you would say if you had the words to say it, that none of this is your doing. But the gods must have taken a special interest in you, child. Very special interest. What do you know of your King?"

Sogolon stand there, her mouth shut.

"Out there in conquered lands, a no name girl like you, why would you know about kings, any more than the conquered lion or buffalo?"

Sogolon stand there, unclear.

"Now you are among peacocks. And peacock shit."

There is a shame in Sogolon that last the whole quartermoon. She stare out at sky from her window, stare out from morning till midnight, for there is nothing more to do but jump out and let her body land where the gods wish it to land. She wish to scream at the lady mistress for her wickedness and deceit. She was never her slave, she can say that to her face. She want to shout that this is why her husband is where he is, but at least he touch her when he try to violate her. This mistress abuse her with no touch at all.

See the girl, in a room at the third tower of the princess's palace. Not doing anything but waiting. On the sun each morning, on food three times a day, on the change of guard though the housemaid say she is not a prisoner. But everywhere Sogolon wish to walk is forbidden, so confined to room is what she be.

From her window she see dwellings she is waiting to learn the names of. All of them wonders compared to a termite hill, whorehouse cupboard, or the cookroom floor of a lord. Mistress Komwono not gone so long that she should start to forget her face, but forgetting it she do. From her window she see steps leading out of her own tower. This she also see: part of the battlements and tower of the busy King's castle, guarded by sentries. The rest is out of her window's view. Direct ahead a paved path to library, a castle to itself, but with four walls like a box, two floors, and no door that she can see. To the right of that, the banquet hall as big as a field, where at night she hear music, dancing, shouting, and screaming. If she look hard enough past the trees, the grand archives, twice as wide as the library. Right in line with the library, the unfinished castle of Kwash Abili, who die one moon after he become

King, and beside that, the finished castle of Kwash Kojo, his brother, and this King's great-granduncle. The line of kings confuse her, but the castles do not. She just wish she could look inside them. But even this place they lock off from her. Farther off, left of the living King's castle, is that of Kwash Kong. Not the oldest, though it is the only one falling into ruin. No house is as narrow, yet no house climb as high. She can count four rows of windows above the trees, leaving her to wonder how many are below. From her window she see halls and the roofs of halls, covered hallways and the ruins of hallways, people and beasts dressed for court, guards and soldiers, orchards and pastures, peacocks, and lions.

By dusk light, five women all wearing white come for her. They come by morning light as well, to take her to the dining hall, where they stand while she eat breakfast or dinner, and say nothing to her.

"Your tongue cut out?" she ask them but they don't answer. Sitting in this dining hall that can hold a hundred, but now holding only one, make her feel like a queen of nothing. She can feel it hounding her thoughts, jealousy, loneliness, the knowing that this is food and drink for many, as is this room. At least she never see the Aesi. That man unnerve her with just his robe alone. Nor do she see Keme, except once when the princess decide to mount a horse and ride, and the palace guards, none of them horsemen, shout for him and two more, and two lions to follow her. Maybe what she is seeing from her little window is how the palace work? Seeing is all she is left to do. Sogolon is losing count of days, but the last day of the third quartermoon since she get leave in this room, the princess demand to see her, the girl somebody thought to present as a gift.

"Her head have a nice shape," a woman say.

Sogolon assume she is of noble blood, by the way her chin is jutting out so far from her neck. She is in a room and can't remember how she get there. Through a doorway she see a bed, which make her think this is a bedchamber, but the princess is sitting in the windowsill, while the other women relax on stools on the floor. This room could be where any of these women stay, all of them in fabrics of big fashion, their foreheads and cheeks in white umchokozo dots because they visiting something or someone important.

"A nice shape for what, Vunakwe? From what kind of mouth come such shit?" the princess say.

This Vunakwe looking like she want to say something but think better of it.

"Stop thinking better of saying something, and say it," the princess say.

"I just saying the girl head look good, Princess. When you have nothing, even a little something is a big thing."

"Hmmm. And what do you have, Vunakwe, but my indulgence?"

Vunakwe eyes say it all. Better for her that she don't speak.

"And listen to me, being so cruel to my mother's

favorite," the princess say. "Lady Vunakwe, you must forgive me."

"Of course, Princess."

"Say it."

"I forgive you, Princess."

The princess laughs. "The thought, that I would need forgiveness," she say. "Fuck the gods, if I can't joke with my dearest friends. Must I have no mirth in this place?"

The four women laugh. The princess cross her legs at the knee and Sogolon just now realize that she dress herself like a man.

"Nice shape head? I find her head odd," the princess say. "Come forward, girl."

Sogolon hesitate, but step forward before the women mark her insolence. She standing nearer to them, all reposing on rugs and pillows on the floor, than the princess. Sogolon standing there, feeling women eyes on her and how it different from men's eyes. Neither nice, but this is not nice in a different way.

"Itulu, what can we do with her?"

Itulu lips are shiny from chicken grease. She tries to talk as she chew, not seeing that this make the princess frown.

"You asking me, Princess?"

"I called your name and asked a question. What do you think? The gods are trying me today, with my mother's women."

"Perhaps offer her up as sacrifice to Baraka, Highness."

The princess stand up and laugh. She walk all the way around Sogolon before she say, "Itulu, that is for people who still cut out their women's koo. Don't be a savage. I know your mother was from Bornu."

Itulu laugh with her lips, but her eyes not doing it. The other women try to look busy by eating chicken, drinking nectar water and wine, fondling fabric dolls, tickling a baby lion, fanning themselves, but what they really doing is watching the princess, trying to get where she going before she get there, so they can be ready for whatever she going to say.

"She is studying us," the princess say, amusement on her face. Sogolon's eyes dart away, but the princess is laughing now.

"Precious girl, look around if you wish. Nobody here is worth your study."

But study she do. Reading how much these women hide feeling from their faces, whenever the princess say something that, judging from her face, she like to say to women such as these. It make her wonder if anywhere in the lands are two women like Keme and the lion. Maybe they too spend the afternoon eating chicken and being cruel to each other. No, just she, the princess, being cruel. But Sogolon is reading faces. A small smile, meaning hiding hurt, which turn into a big smile when the hiding work, and a droop when it don't. Two eyebrow raised mean what thrilling news, but one eyebrow mean there go this bitch. If the eye under the raised brow roll, then it's the same road we going again. And no matter how quick it shut, a gaping mouth mean I didn't see that lash coming. A quick look away, a turn for tears. A quick turn away while still looking, to see if anybody going to witness it.

"What she learning from us, Princess?"

"I don't know. What are you learning from these esteemed women? I speaking to you, girl."

"Such insolence. Answer your princess," Itulu say.

"Girl, you want us call for the whip? Answer Her Highness."

"I . . . they tell me never to speak to the princess directly, noble lady," Sogolon say.

"Who tell you that?" the princess say.

"Noble lady Mistress Komwono."

"That banished woman? She might as well lift you up, tear your legs apart, and plop you down on my father's cock. I wouldn't heed anything she say."

"Indeed, Princess," say one of the women. "I still remember when she tell Queen Moth—"

"If I need to remember it, I will ask you."

"Yes, Princess."

The princess walk around Sogolon again.

"But you are a puzzle, girl."

"Maybe she should be your new attendant, Princess."

"Attendant? But then you women would be useless to me. Look at them, girl. I keep mistaking them for my friends."

All of this is too much for Sogolon, who don't know what to think, what to feel, or even where to look. She try to look out the window at a guard she hope is Keme but is just some other sentry.

"I know, Princess," say a woman who might be Itulu. "Marry her off to Commander Olu."

To this all the women laugh, a loud laugh that get louder and louder until they realize the princess not laughing.

"Can you imagine? The way he keep twirling that wedding necklace, as if he ever married nobody. Poor old madman," say another.

"Mad, mad, mad."

"Leave him alone, he never trouble anybody."

"Viper don't trouble nobody until you step on him."

"Then leave a man's snake for once."

More laughter.

"Indeed, he already married to the air, or ghost, or demon maybe. I hear he moan for her at night, even though he can't name her in the morning," say another.

"Put them together and then you have two people who won't know what to do. All he can do with it is piss in the bush, and she look like she come from bush," say one more.

"That man is the reason you can all sit here eating chickens and being as stupid as one," the princess say, which shut up the whole room. Indeed, so quiet it is that Sogolon can hear the guard outside telling somebody to use the third gate.

"Commander is that way because spear gone right

through his head, leaving a hole to be taken up with devils. Why are you that way, Itulu? My stomach goes sick from the sight of all of you. Get out. Get out!"

Sogolon watch all the women leave, then turn to go.

"Watch them, watch the hawks and vultures. Every single one from conquered territory. The horse-looking one who served my mother lost her husband when we restored Wakadishu. I didn't dismiss you. Where are you from, girl?"

"Mitu, Your Highness."

"Tell me something of that place."

"It . . . ah . . . I . . ."

"I'm already bored. Sit down. Eat chicken."

In the middle of the next quartermoon, right after the sun slip away, Sogolon leave her room. The guard warn her many a time not to leave her chamber, but he can't stop her if she go. She run down the stairs, around and around until she is at an archway, which lead to an archway, which lead to an archway, which lead to huge and heavy double door that she push open with all her strength. Outside she find herself on a path that branch out toward the King's palace, the library, the amphitheater, and to steps going down to Kwash Abili's ruins. A crowd of court-iers in fine dress and loud tongues are walking toward the castle where Crown Prince Likud stay. A voice she don't hear that sound like her say, **A gift for the King is a gift for the crown prince.** She head opposite

way to the library. But the voices seem to follow her.
She never seen the prince and already know that she
never want to. But she already know this is impossible talk. She will most certainly see him soon. He
is the crown prince. All paths in the palace must lead
to the crown. The voices are getting louder, laughter, like everybody laughing at her. She wondering
how in this place with the least threat, she is the most
scared. She turn around to see them still walking to
the prince's castle, farther away now. She turn back
and walk right into his chest.

And books. She knock the books out of his hands.
That is what he say, not mad or sad, but like someone noticing sun leaving sky. "You will be the one,"
he say. "You will be the one to knock the books out
of my hand, and try me." They are at the door to
the library. They, Sogolon and Commander Olu. The
King's greatest warrior, who now live at one of the
palaces as reward. The women talk, even after that
day in the room with the princess, about how there
still be a hole in the commander head that go right
through, that if he stand sideways you can see clouds
in the sky. These women's tongues no more refined
than any whore at Miss Azora, but it tempt her, she
know it, to pull down his hood and see for herself.
Instead, she stoop down and pick up the books.

"Sorry," she say.

"Books won't care that you're sorry," he say. He serious for a blink, then he mumble something.

"What?"

"You can pick one to read if you like. I read all of them already."

"So why you have them?"

"I will forget them all. Burden I bear, not true? I will read them all, and I can't go to sleep because I close the book and one hundred men and beasts won't leave my room. I will wake up the next day, and guess what. They gone. All gone. So I will read the book again."

"If you forget all of them, how you know you reading the same books?"

"Pick a book."

"I never learn book reading."

He look at her like she say she never cure her leprosy. Old, thin, he already stooping in the back, and his eyes look almost like they are river blind, but in his way, Commander Olu more handsome than Keme.

"Then what taking you to the library? Nothing in there of use to you, not true?"

"I go the archive then. That a library too?"

"No. Common mistake of the fool, to think a library and archive is the same place, but they not. A library is a place to read a text. An archive is a place to hide it."

"I don't know what you mean."

"Of course you don't. Walk with me. I will go to my room at the back of third palace, but I shall forget my room, which palace, and maybe even you by the time I get there. We must hurry."

They set off walking.

"What would your name be?"

"Sogolon."

"Sogolon. Who call you that?"

"Nobody."

"You look like you don't even know your own blood yet."

"You look like that is not your business."

He laugh. Louder than she expect. The grin wake up his face and make him look younger. She want the hood to fall off.

"Soon, when I ask you again what your name be, take no offense."

This is the longest she walk so far. He forgetting? She wonder. They take a brick path, which lay out in swirls that take them through a confusing garden, for the path split into paths, which split into more paths, like branches, though it look like a dry up river and streams. Plants and flowers, some she never see before. He look like he still remembering, for she wouldn't want to get lost here. The garden path lead to a bridge over a river that look too neat for the gods to make. The bridge lead to three flight of steps that he bounce up quick, but it make her heart threaten to burst out of her chest. They get to a landing, which lead to three more flights, and another path, and the thin castle. Now that it is near, it is even taller, the top floors lost in clouds.

"You, why you following me?" he say, not mad or wary, just curious.

"You tell me to follow you. That you might forget."

"Ah yes. I don't remember, but your face look like one to believe. Follow me."

Inside his room, which is one whole floor. As wide as that room with the princess's friends, with large windows, and tile floors, and great chairs and stools and benches, and rugs. Also this. Everything covered in black writing, red in some parts. Every wall marked in coal and ash, and ink, all the floor tiles mark in dye, all the cushions marked as well. She don't know how writing read, but starting to see what it might mean. Some of the writing is smooth and full, and so fat with ink that it drip, while other writing like scratching, like he trying to write as quick as he think. She don't know, but those scratches so mad they blur out. Word, glyphs, marks, drawings of horses and spears and chariots and war.

"Sometimes when I start a line, I forget what it's about before I finish," he say. "Then I wait a day, I think a day, then just finish it with something else."

"You rush because your head fleeing from you. What it say on the jug?"

"Ask for milk if it's the end of the quartermoon. Is it the end?"

"No. On the table? You carve it with a knife."

"We? We . . . treaty with Wakadishu. Never sign."

Sogolon is liking this. A whole house telling her things as it is telling him things. Sometimes she can see a mark and guess the word or part of it. "This is grand what?" she ask.

"Grand hall. I don't like banquets. People make a game out of what I remember."

"You remember that?"

"The fetish priest tell me that my curse is that I still remember that I forget. Peace won't come until I forget that I forget. Or die."

"This is great what?"

"Great backside. The lady Itulu has a great backside."

"But a small mind," Sogolon say, and he laugh.

"What your name?"

"Sogolon."

"Sogolon. Somebody name you that?"

"Leave my name be, old man. You write all this?"

"I write all what? Wait. Hark. Look in the window."

On the window is the gentlest looking writing. It make him smile.

"Yes, according to the window I write it all. Funny things. Soon as I read it I remember some of what I write. Especially all the things in red."

"Blood?"

"No."

He pick up a cushion, read it, then go to his bedroom. Sogolon follow, though her first thought was not to. He lift up a rug of zebra skin and on the underside is small red writing.

"What it say?" Sogolon ask.

"It say not to share it."

"What is it that you not to share?"

"You think you clever?"

"I just a girl."

"You don't look like you just anything. You could be their friend."

"Whose?"

"I don't . . . I don't know."

"I not nobody friend," she say and turn to leave. "I gone," she say also.

"Wait! I mean no. When evening come, being alone is a sickness. I don't know why. That memory never comes back. It says don't trust them. That is what it say. Don't trust them, especially the Aesi."

Sogolon don't know what to make of that. All she know is that the Aesi watch her too long. Not like the other men who want to mess with her koo, but he want to get inside her too.

"She say I can never go," he say.

"Who?"

"I don't know, but she say it to me every night when I dream. Sometimes when I wake up. I can't go because nobody here will know her."

"What she look like?"

"A dream. Don't sit there."

She jump quick from the stool, then turn to look at it. Like any other stool.

"For sure a sadness wash over me when I sit there. But I know it. It feel like it is for me alone, like some part of me is over there. Some part of me that gone now. You want to know why I telling you deep things. Soon I won't remember that I tell you. I might even forget your face," Olu say.

Still looking at the stool, Sogolon say, "So tell me, then. Why that thing around your neck?"

"What?"

"The necklace. Around your neck. Why?"

He touch it light and look come over his face that she can't figure. He press into it deeper, tap it, then press again, all the time looking like is his heartbeat he pressing for.

"A necklace. Around my neck."

"Who put it there?"

"Must be me. Who else? I don't know. I don't know what it's for. Why does it need a for?"

"Then take it off."

"No."

"Women who attend the princess say is a wedding necklace."

Olu laugh. "The only thing I married to is war. Woman don't know nothing, she is woman. I am tired."

He lower himself to a cluster of cushions and fall asleep quicker than a blink. Sogolon know she should leave, but want to stay. She should leave things alone, but want to look. Again, at the walls and curtains and floor all covered in his writing. She look at the zebra skin and wonder why he have to tell himself not to trust the Aesi; perhaps a warning from the Commander Olu of an older day. She look at him again and make quiet steps to the bedchamber. Inside is a bed, a large one, too large for even a man of mighty size like the commander. But clean, where everything that make to shine, shine. But the floor cover with writing, and smudge from where he rub out with his foot. Right above the bed another of them is hanging, and she almost miss it, for the silver is now pale. A wedding necklace exactly like the one around the commander's neck. He mumble from outside and startle her. Back in the welcome room, the cushions and rugs make a pool and he floating in it. Over by his side Sogolon feel to sit by him, to watch over him, to take care of him, even. This here lover of war.

"War too important to leave to soldier," he say on a breath, startling Sogolon again. But his eyes still closed, and he still above and below the cushion pool, one leg under a rug, the other kicking out.

"War too important to leave to soldier. . . . You think you can . . . no, no, no, I leave purple for your sort . . . no, no, no, woman, no. Ha ha ha . . . feather make you look like the peacock. . . . How can I mock the likes of you? A nose like yours?"

He turn on his side and what come next, come out as a sigh.

"Oh Jeleza. Jeleza, Jeleza, Jeleza," he say.

SEVEN

Troubling sleep. Sogolon wake with nothing to do. She don't want to get out of bed and get a drink of water. She don't want to go to her window and look out at the moon. She don't want to rouse up the guard by her door, and for what? She don't know where the cookroom be or worse, the well if she have to fetch water herself. Nothing for her to do but lie right there above and below sheets, and look at the ceiling.

But then the ceiling look at her.

Everything jump but her body. Even the scream die in her mouth before it reach past her teeth. Something like this happen before, the not being able to move, and she don't know if she have time to think of it when the ceiling have eyes and eyes are upon her. Waking up but unable to get up. Willing everything to push away the sheet and stand, but cannot. So she trying crawling but that don't work, and rolling, but that don't work either. And when she finally pull herself up on her elbows, the tears rolling down her face feel as if they pop out from will, not just distress. The ceiling looking at her, with yellow eyes that glow. Wide like it curious, not even wicked. The eyes pull out from the dark, eyes set in a face still black. The face lower itself from the ceiling, pulling two arms, then a chest, then a belly, lowering out of the dark as one would lower from a pole. Face round like a plum. Like a child. One leg flat on the ceiling and sticky to it, but long, too long. Then his dark, skinny arm reach out to touch her face. Scream, is what she do.

Sogolon roll and fall out of the bed hard, on her chest and chin. The hit shock her all the way to her toes. Movement in the ceiling sound like a scrambling animal. Sogolon jump up and run for the door, but something catch her shirt. This darkchild, the color of tar, his long finger grabbing the neck of her dress, not with force, but just curious. Sogolon scream again. She try to run, but that gentle grip is firm, she running nowhere. The dress tear, she is pulling away hard and screaming for the guard, but he pull her back so easy she might as well be a feather. He let go. She think it is a he, but won't turn around to see. She is trying to run out of her dress, but he yank her again, pulling her to the ground. Sogolon's head start to spin. Her head is thumping, and the room is turning and tossing her around. The floor shift underneath her, and won't stop. She roll again and fall when the floor turn all the way on its side, becoming the wall and the wall becoming the floor. She roll near the window and stretch out her hands to brace against it before she fall through. And still the room shift, but only she is falling. Everything, the bed, the stool, the lamp, the rug, the jug all still. So it must be that her head alone is spinning. But then the room spin again, and she tumble again, and roof become floor and floor become roof. And there he is, standing instead of hanging. She grab a column, unsure of herself.

And the boy, looking like a boy now. A boy blacker than shadow, and skinny. His arms and legs long like a giraffe, his chest and middle small, and his head big. The only light in the room, the dim lamp on the side table, a teapot with a single flame. And his eyes, his yellow eyes. Glowing like incense burning. Down on the floor he bend at the knee and the elbow, a spider now in his movement. Sogolon eye the door now on the other side, which mean getting past him. The boy stomp one foot and hiss. He crawl up the wall, scamper to the ceiling, and just so, he gone. She in a tower and the ceiling is high. But the ceiling is the floor, and floor, ceiling. Or everything right-side up and she is upside down. She stumble to the door and grab the lamp just in time to see him crouching on the floor. Ceiling. He jump at her so quick that she don't think, she throw the lamp at him, which hit him in the chest. On his chest a flame flicker then burst out all over his front, back, and neck. The boy is shrieking and the noise is a knife, cutting through her ears. Like a spider, he scramble to a window and climb out. Sogolon run down the peak of the ceiling and back up to the door. Only when she is outside that she hear her own yelling. Beyond the door, floor is floor and roof is roof, and the guard is sleeping or dead. Sogolon run down the stairs and through a hallway. Down more stairs and through one door, which lead to another door, which lead to another door, and finally into the first throne room. Not the one where she meet the princess, she can tell, even though nothing much is there to see in the dark. But she see them, three lions asleep in the middle of the room. Keme already warn her. Not every lion is a shapeshifter, some is just a lion. Sleepy, tired, fearful, or just done, Sogolon creep in between them, sink to the floor and sleep.

She wake up the next morning in bed, the sun warming her face, the lamp beside her with the flame out. Sogolon can't help herself. She dash out of the room and slam the door behind her, waking up the guard standing at the head of the stairs.

"Young mistress, everything good?"

"I not a mistress," Sogolon say.

"Of course."

"Where he is? The guard from last night."

"Last night? Change of shift, young mistress."

"I not a . . . never mind."

"Young mistress, you not supposed to—"

Leave. But she do it anyway. Down the stairs, past the rooms that she walk by at night, wondering how this palace sometimes feel more empty than Mistress Komwono's house. The King is about his business, and so are all the servants, somebody will tell her if she ask. But she won't ask. Each day waiting on whatever the princess decide to do with her is enough for her to wish the boy on the ceiling did take her away. Two of the lions are still sleeping but the one awake follow her. They walking side by side, and when she ask, "Beremu?" no answer, not even shaking of head come from him. Truth, it might as well have been fart as much as a call. Sogolon shudder. This is not a shapeshifter, but a lion. She is out of words, to name what it is when thrill and terror happen at once. He accompany her half the way to Commander Olu's quarters, when something catch his eye and he run off.

Leaving Commander's house as she get there is a woman she never see before. Dark skin, bare breasts, and a wrap around her waist. Both hands full with gold plates, jugs, goblets, and an arrow that Sogolon remember him saying is a present from the King, or Queen, or somebody who love wearing a crown.

"None of that is yours," Sogolon say.

"And no part of you is me mother," say the woman.

"He already pay you."

"He don't even remember where he keep his money. I take my own payment."

"I don't believe you."

"Little girl, me look like me give two shit, or even one? Don't make me drop all of this and cut you."

A roar, so quick and so loud that even Sogolon jump. The woman drop everything and run away.

The lion trot after her a few paces and she run even faster. He follow Sogolon inside and she see no reason to stop him. Commander Olu sprawl himself out on the floor. In the quick she think him dead until he roll over. Keme is enough, she don't want to see another man naked.

"Commander Olu. Commander Olu, wake up. Commander Olu."

He shift a little and mumble something but don't wake up. The lion roar and he fling himself out of bed. Sogolon surprised to see a spear so near where he sleep. He grab it like about to throw when he see Sogolon. The lion roar again. The commander drop the spear and rub his eyes.

"What you two doing in my house? A man can't sleep."

"Your whore was robbing you," Sogolon say.

"Who?"

"Your whore."

"The court lion and the court jester in my house this early. Must be a joke."

Sogolon not trying to look at another naked man, but there he be right in front of her. This old man thin and muscular, like he from a roaming tribe, but on every limb be scars. And not a pattern or craft, but the rough scars of war. Hair on his chest and above his cock like the hair on his chin, black with some white sprouting all over. When their eyes meet, he is frowning, knowing she is inspecting him.

"I know you, but I don't know your name," he say.

"Sogolon."

"Sogolon? You from the bush tribes?"

"Leave my name, old man."

"Who your friend?"

"A lion."

"Clever. You going to look in the air and tell me that it's air next, or scoop out some water and tell me look at water?"

"Why everybody so rude in Fasisi?"

He laughs. "Because it is Fasisi. Everybody breed for war, even the wet nurse. No delicacy among us."

"Maybe if you don't lie with whore, you won't wake up rude."

"Look at this little girl, thinking she can try me in my own house. Now who rude?"

"I didn't—"

"Don't dare step in my house again thinking you can judge what I do in here."

Sogolon pause. She hope her face say sorry without her having to say it.

"Lion, I feel like I fought by your side in war. Or maybe it was your father," Olu say as he walk over to the lion and scratch behind his ear. "I am going to make coffee."

"You don't have woman to make it for you?"

"Little girl, why you in me house?"

"I mean, I see how the cook do it. I can make it for you."

The commander go find his robe, while Sogolon go to the hearth, wake up the flame, and brew coffee.

They go outside on a landing, where the lion roll over and sun himself.

"Sogolon," Olu say.

"You remember."

"Sometimes."

"Somebody come to my room last night. If I go to anybody they will say my head take up with devils," she say.

"Who come to your room?"

"He look like a boy. But only in his face. Legs long like a spider and his arms too. And he was crawling along the ceiling when he come for me. Black boy, black, black, black. He run along the ceiling like it is the floor. Then, then he come for me, but I throw the lamp on him and he catch fire."

"And?"

"And he escape through the window. That's when I leave the room and go sleep with the lions. With him. When I wake up this morning somebody put me back in bed and fix my room. The room, is like nothing happen there last night but sleep, Commander."

"Olu. I not commanding nothing."

That is when she see his head. The head is always in front of her but this is the first time she look at it. Not a hole going right through, but a scar with points like a star where no hair grow.

"Strange shit afoot since . . . I don't know how long now."

"Since when?" she ask.

"I say I don't know, child."

"Who are the Sangomin?"

"When you say that name, all I see is his face. Him, the Aesi."

"A lady tell my mistress that he bring them here, when nobody could cure what ailing the Kwash Kagar."

"I remember something like that. They didn't cure him. No, they didn't cure him, they only say witchcraft is upon the King. I don't remember anything after that."

"Maybe you write it down."

"Maybe."

They search the walls and the floor for words. Look for red letters or the dog with the tail of the snake, he say. Sogolon find one to the side of the privy, another under the rug hiding the warning about the Aesi, and one more in the middle of a garment that she drop when he say, Leave my underwear. He grab it from her, and she smile as modesty come over him.

"I hope I didn't just take it off."

"If you do, then you cleaner than most man," she say and he nod. "What it say?"

"It not in order. Something come before it."

The king is under a different kind of enemy, lord redhead say. Throne calls for a different kind of warrior, he say. Maybe he is correct.

He just do it, this Aesi. He sack all the throne guards, even the lions. A public outcry it take, to bring them back.

Only the Aesi and the Sangomin allowed near the King.

Nasty children, let slip dogs.

"You find another with the dogsnake?"

He lift up the rug higher than before.

And then the princess send for the herbswomen, the nuns of deep bush. We wait. Some of us wait. The prince is constant in cursing, and complaining and whining, truly this is a man who will never know war. The king is not worse today, but by the gods not better.

Six herbswomen come but four disappear. We couldn't find them anywhere. I would find them, if anybody ask me. I am a commander, I have use.

"I must have . . . when I wrote this . . . I . . . the next one, where is the next one?"

The king is worse. The Aesi demand the execution of the herbswomen, and the prince agree. Witchcraft is the problem, he say.

Blood, so much blood. By the gods, that herbswoman bled. The Aesi.

I will never forget how to wield a sword, by the gods. Maybe I use it on him. Why do I forget everything, but him?

"Him who?" Sogolon ask.

"Who you think?"

What a boy to have hair that look like a dead snake. The hair is white clay. The face, the neck, the legs, everywhere like moonlight. The Aesi bring him and he come along with the strangest children in nine worlds but though he is bigger, he is child too. Many would swear it. I count nine, but later I count thirteen, and one day later, eight.

"Is there more?" she ask.

"I have to look. Maybe they tell the same thing. Maybe," Olu say.

They look some more. Sogolon starting to see marks and words and know what they might mean if she can't name them. "That mark, I see it ten and one times already. What it say?"

"Jeleza," he say.

"Oh. And who she to you?" she ask.

"Is a she? I don't know who that is."

A voice that sound like her say, **Those words pooling your mouth should not leave it. Never.**

"That thing around your neck. I know what it is," she say.

Three days later Sogolon still wake up shocked and mad. She think back to the fear as well, that moment, short as a blink when it look like he would do something to her. Sogolon didn't know what to expect from him, but Olu flying into such a rage that the lion had to come between them and roar him off is not it. All she do is tell him that Jeleza is the sister of the King, and his wife, and she don't know where she is, and how she can be gone, but everybody seem to think this woman never lived, everybody but me. And you, Olu. She thought he would show relief, that at least he know why this strange name haunt his dreams. At least he would know that he have good reason to distrust the Aesi, and she do too, for all that stand between her mistress remembering the King Sister one day, then the next acting like the woman was never born, is the Aesi. Except for Olu. He don't fully forget. She linger on in him perhaps because love is a thing that linger, and maybe it is something no force from the Aesi or whoever can smite out. As for that force, she don't know. She don't know anything about the Aesi. She barely know anything about this court, or this King. But maybe Olu do. Maybe it is written in red or in black somewhere in the house.

She wasn't expecting a smile, for this is not cheerful news. But she did expect some satisfaction from knowing both the truth and that Olu is being deceived. Instead he start screaming. How nasty and wicked one girl need to be to make up some whole lie about a fucking King Sister when she know everybody at court think he is a madman who make up things every day? Is this mockery? Is this from the prince? From the cruel bitches at court who make up stories about a hole in his head?

"Is my head, not so? Is because you hear that I will forget most of what you will say, that you come in here to say any vile thing you can. How many days you doing this now? How could you put so much wickedness on a man when all he ever know is loss, you little—"

He come at her and the lion come between them. Then he scream for her to leave.

On the sixth day of the third quartermoon, Princess Emini hold court to hear all entreaties and petitions to the King. Sogolon don't know if she is to go until a hard knock on her door tell her all she need to hear. Now she is in the throne room hearing the same people, looking at the same people asking for the same things. The princess look as bored as she always look, and the Aesi almost turn around when Sogolon enter. She stare at his back even as she lose herself in the crowd. Turn around, she think, but then shudder, wondering how in all this forgetting, his is the name that one hear over and over. He half turn again and Sogolon shut up her mind. She look around and the feeling come on like a flood, that she the only one in the kind of clearness that only come at night, when skin and sky, person and spirit is all the same color. While everybody still in the blindness of high noon, daylight burning everything into nothing but white. This time he do turn around to look straight at her, but she shift behind a woman with a large ighiya.

"He bringing them?" somebody whisper. Two women gather by a window and whisper. Sogolon want to see what they looking at, but then a door swing open and outside light rush in. Also with it, three of them. The black one from that night, or perhaps another, crawling on the ceiling, stopping to poke his head down and scare the women of court. Another one, red as sunset from head and neck, blue as sea from chest to feet, and a yellow fork tongue slithering from her mouth. Somebody whisper that here also is he, the oldest of them, but entering the room is just a boy, older than the others. Tall and lanky, with hair on his face, but a boy nonetheless. A boy who make some people tremble. He sit at the foot of the throne steps and the princess glare at the Aesi.

"Move," the Aesi say to the boy.

"Everybody giving orders, and yet I am the crown prince," he say. Prince Likud, entering the room. The first time Sogolon seeing him. The court drop down on one knee so fast that only Sogolon standing. She stoop too quick and nearly fall back. Prince Likud skip up the steps to the throne and stand right beside it, looking down on the princess until she move herself. He smile at the crowd, and Sogolon take him in, his thick eyebrows above small eyes, his beard and whiskers below thin lips, but no mustache. Strong head, the shoulders of a man who do labor, and not a prince. A skull cap in black and gold and a cape draped on his right shoulder, the other shoulder bare. She's not been in the knowledge of royal customs long enough, yet even she know that only kings go shirtless, with a robe drape over the right shoulder. The princess frown and shake her head. She know it too. Meanwhile Sogolon watch the children, and how they circle, hop around, and enjoy how people pull back. A girl from a farm know what this is. Herding. She not sure if they are Sangomin, but she sure they are one thing.

Pets.

Even the older one, the white clay one look on like he's waiting for the prince to throw him scraps. The red and blue lizard girl clear a whole path to the throne just by walking through the people. The ceiling walker is still scrambling across the roof, as if looking for her. Sogolon bow her head. The prince fling himself onto the throne in the same way as the princess.

"So, sister, give me news," he say.

The ceiling walker eye the chandelier, then crouch to jump on it. But then he see the Aesi looking at him and pull back. He crawl down to a window and sit on the sill.

"And good news," he add.

"Give you news?" she say.

"Not like that, Emini. Not like you're about to spit out something sour."

"How about I—"

"Nicer. Like a poet."

"You cannot be se— Verse?" She is standing now. Both of them looking like they talking not to each other but to the court. "How about a riddle? Guess who just left your royal court."

"Never liked riddles. Why choose to make your brain hurt?"

"Chiki of Gonyo."

"Did I have her in the front or the back?"

"The back is my guess, brother, since Ambassador Chiki is a man."

Sogolon look up, expecting a scowl on his face, and that is just what she see. But she also see the ceiling walker eyeing her. He change from a sit to a stoop and touch the wall, ready to climb it. To crawl back to the ceiling and right over to her, she think.

"Ambassador Chiki. Of course."

"He gave you the red horse for your birthday."

"Yes, of course."

"The ambassador from Wakadishu."

"Good, good."

"No, not good. Wakadishu expecting us to sign a treaty that we will not invade. That we make no move counter. Otherwise they will get help from the South."

"Father always said that Wakadishu is North. The gods did tell him so."

"Father also said that any land south of the Kegere River is South."

"Father must have meant southern in their ways, sister. Backward people, backward. Their women put their men's things in the mouth."

Sogolon look up, expecting murmurs and chuckles from the crowd, and that is just what she hear.

"They want to know why we're assembling armies

near the Blood Swamp. I told him nobody is assembling anything. That the drill is custom. If anything, we're protecting the east coast from pirates."

"Is that what we doing?"

"No. We assembling armies."

"Devious, sister. Look at my sister the warmonger."

"Everybody leave."

"What? But I have not seen such old friends since . . . yesterday," he say. Then sigh and say, "Yes, you all bore me, leave."

Everybody leave but the Aesi. Sogolon step out but stay by the door. The courtesans and their chatter fade down the hallways and then in the quiet, the voices from back within the chamber come to her. This is the first time she do it. Usually when the wind wish, it blow all talk to her ears. This time, Sogolon close her eyes and think about the wind carrying voices to her. Soon, a cool breeze blow past her ear.

"Brother, stop performing. The audience is gone."

"When there's a crown princess and I'm the one fucking a title-less prince you can give me orders. Though there have been rumors, sister. Rumors of unsatisfaction. Frustra—"

"Our spies say the southern King looking to invade Kalindar by sea. Wakadishu either giving them help, or their armies safe passage," Emini say.

This seem to stagger him. He take so long to reply that Sogolon crack the door and peek inside to see why.

"You have proof?" Likud ask.

"I just said we have spies. Drums in the North and especially in the South telling everyone the King is about his business," she say.

"So, the King is about his business."

"The King has been confined to bed for ten and two moons. Everybody knows what busy means, brother."

"Then we fortify Kalindar and crush Wakadishu for betraying us. Send a sign to the whole empire."

"Nobody betray us yet," the Aesi say.

"We need to send a message, not so? A message needs to be sent. Crush Wakadishu."

"No reason to crush—"

"And set an example, sister. I hear the South King is going mad. Kind of thing happens when your mother is your sister."

"Diplomacy is clearly your gift, brother."

"But sarcasm is not yours. Every time we say the King is about his business they hear the King is weak. Then the ambassador comes to court and find he has to deal with a woman, so of course he take step with you."

"I only filling a seat you supposed to take, but watch it now, brother. You are on the throne, so rule. Rule, brother."

"No, sister. This still looking like your time. Running out, but still yours."

"The King is still busy. Also before we send out swords and spears, you should know that war don't pay for itself," Emini say.

"Condescension also not one of your gifts. Tax the people. Ha, tax Kalindar. They should pay for their protection."

"We should consult the elders and the—"

"Only thing those elders have is age. And . . ."

Sogolon lose what the prince say next. She lean in closer, right to the edge of the door, when a black hand grab the back of her neck and yank her all the way up to the ceiling. She scream. The ceiling walker. The darkchild. He giggle and shriek at the same time, while Sogolon keep screaming. He swinging her like a doll and they scramble from vault to vault to the throne, and Sogolon can feel herself slipping out of her own dress. The darkchild scrambling now, and in Sogolon's eyes the whole room blur.

"Stop," the Aesi say.

"Chancellor. Did I ever tell you how much I appreciate these gifts you gave me?"

"Gifts to your father, Highness."

"And I am the crown prince. My point, dear Aesi, is that once you have given a gift, it is no longer yours. I tell him when to stop, not you. Right now it seems he found a new toy."

"Tell him to stop," the princess say. The prince laugh as the darkchild let Sogolon drop a little, then catch her. The floor rushing toward her and then jerking back away as she scream and scream.

"Likud!" she say.

The prince nod, and the darkchild lower her a

little, then let go. She fall on the ground when he say, "Who is this? A southern spy? Kill her."

"She's a gift."

"Stand, girl. A gift? Looks more like scraps. Kill her still."

"I said she is a gift, brother."

"To who? To me?"

"To the kitchen. She brings uncommon skills from the Malakal cookhouses."

"Then how is she not in my palace? I see, you wanted to try her out first. My sister, up to her crafts again. Aesi, is my sister not crafty?"

"If you say so, Lord."

"Fuck the gods, for making the two of you so tiresome."

Wind, rising outside and starting to blow wild inside.

"From where comes this gale?" Prince Likud say. The Aesi looking like he wondering too. Two servants rush in to close the windows and get a fight from the force of wind. The prince almost look at Sogolon when he say, "Aesi, am I to inspect the guards today?"

"It is your duty, Prince."

"My sister loves duty. Let her do it."

He goes to leave but stops by Sogolon, who bow her head.

"And such a stick. How do I trust a cook who doesn't eat?" Likud say.

The redhead girl leave last, tasting the air with her fork tongue. Sogolon still on the floor, not sure if she should stand, sit, or kneel, desperate to make herself smaller.

"I never seen a man so want to be King, but so don't want to rule," Princess Emini say.

"Sangomin are turning into a distraction, Highness," say the Aesi.

"You're the one who brought them here, and can't even control them. Talking about saving the King," the princess say.

"Protecting the King, Highness. Save, I never said."

"So you think he is beyond saving."

"That is not my answer."

"I didn't ask a question. What is your purpose here, Aesi, other than to tell me things I already know? Advise on things that need only good sense? Give wisdom that we already have elders for? Between you and my father, all the elders have been sent away, but your counsel is no wiser. All the healers have been sent away, but my father is no better."

"You father is safe from—"

"Witches, yes safe. And every day brings a new kind of witch. Yet my father is dying and my brother has nine new pets. You can't control them and he won't."

"My lady, Wakadishu."

"You're dismissed, Aesi."

He stand there for a while before he go. The wind die down as soon as he start walking, and the whistling through the windows stop. Sogolon notice that he notice. The princess is back to the throne.

"Stand up, girl," she say. "Come here."

Sogolon stand right before the throne steps, not looking up at her. The princess step down and slap her hard across her face. Sogolon stagger but don't shout. She feel the tear coming and bite down on her lips to stop it, but that fail.

"Spy on me again and I will have you burnt. Why are you crying? You should be glad the crown prince finds you ugly. You want to see where we put the ones he found pretty?"

Sogolon wait another quartermoon before she go back to Olu's house. Early morning, and the lion go with her for protection. Olu don't remember her name, but remember that he supposed to remember her. She remember him saying that one day he going to forget that he forget. Something heavy pass between them, he say when he see her, something that leave him sour but it's lost, whatever it was. Sogolon look at him and say, I chase away your whores, that is why. He nod and agree. She ask him to teach her words. He don't know why he feel to trust her, since he don't trust anyone at court. He point to markings on the wall, chair, bed, and floor, and she say nothing when he skip those in red.

Sogolon's head is getting heavy. Too many things for just a girl. Learning words from Commander Olu, but also learning about Commander Olu. The darkchild, who don't visit her room since, but haunt her mind making her afraid to look up. Then there is the Aesi of the palace court, and the Aesi of Commander Olu's wall, both of them frightening her. The King

Sister who used to be, but never was, though her name leave a mark on Olu's wall. Maybe all of these things is what she get from learning, that he is not only leaving words in her mind, but a weight attached to every one. Yet she don't stop going, not even when wind blow a rumor her way that the commander putting his big commander into action again, with some scrawny girl who don't look like she can take a flea's cock, much less the Berserker of Bornu. And still more things. The princess, who have her around because she is intrigued by a girl who don't come with a use. Maybe your use is to eat all my things, she say. But she watch the princess in her mirth and her melancholy, and find they both come from the same place. Too often she joke that Sogolon don't have use as a slave, but she have plenty use as a Queen, yet watch us both, in the wrong palace. She reaching out to Sogolon, at least that is what it look like, until her words make Sogolon gather that she is a pet too. The princess saying deep things because she think they will fly past her ears as they would a dog.

Too many things swirl in Sogolon's mind. Too many things. So she shed the sister of the King, the wife of Olu. Nobody remember her but two, which is really one, for Olu don't know that what he is saying is her name, and Sogolon never even see her, don't know what she look like and never hear her voice. And she shed Keme. Days now come to pass where she don't see him much. And when last she see him, his words were full about how he get his desire to be an elite palace guard, and not a ceremonial one, like the lion shapeshifters. It is all he talk about and don't stop until he go far past annoying her. And still he go on about throne room that, castle keep this, and securing that and protecting this, that after a while all she see is a suit of armor talking to her.

"Maybe she can fan you, Highness," say the head-woman, the chief lady waiting on the princess.

"If she was a slave. I am not going to make her a slave," say the princess.

"Well, Highness, she is a gift to the King. Long time now she should have gone to the Kwash Kagar's palace."

"Didn't you hear? Any gift to the King is being claimed by the crown prince. The arrogance. The King is still al—"

"Busy?"

"Yes, busy."

"You not in any debt to this girl, Highness. You are royal blood of the throne of Fasisi. She is no one."

"Not even a no one deserve this prince."

A hot night with wet air. Sogolon get send to the castle where Prince Likud stay until his own is complete. Two male servants escort her to the rear welcome room, carrying next to nothing, for the girl have next to nothing, other than what the mistress leave behind. No light but two torches. All Sogolon can see of the room is that the walls and columns are high and they arch into darkness. The male servants are tiptoeing their way in, and jumping at the slightest sound. Sogolon can't tell if they are fussy, flighty, or afraid. A shout come from another room and they both cry out, drop the small sack with her things, and run. Sogolon look around but there is nothing to look at. Then, off in a distance she can't tell in the dark, flickering lights swirling around and around like slapped bees. As they move closer, Sogolon see flapping wings and wonder if they really are bees or some great fireflies. Soon they are flying above her, a kind she has heard of but never seen. Yumboes, as big as her head perhaps, ten and two of them, maybe more, maybe twenty, maybe more than that. Fairies with blue and green wings like dragonflies, and beating so quick that in the dark is a low hum. A few slow and hover above and around, as curious of her as she is of them, male, female, and some she cannot tell. And the lights, jars containing multitudes of fireflies. **They will all die by morning,** she hears on a tiny whisper. They fly up into the ceiling, lighting the walls, and for a blink there are people, a crowd of people on the ceiling, until she recognize the frescoes of kings, and knights, and beasts, charging, drinking, feasting, and battling in the vaults.

More noise approach, this time the shouts, cheers, and laughter of young people. Another light, this time a naked boy made out of nothing but it. He is walking ahead of the others, but a chain around his neck is slowing him down. Holding the chain, the white clay Sangomin who don't seem to have any gift other than being the oldest, or the biggest. Let me hold the pet, a boy say and grab the leash. In the quick he pulls the chain so hard that the light boy fall back. Careful, Prince Abeke, all suns carry heat as well as light, the Sangomin say to the boy ignoring him. Behind those three many more, including the red and blue girl, boys older, boys younger, two girls, maybe three, and the watcher women who lost control over them. Running, skipping, drinking, taunting the women, creating games, looking for trouble.

One of the girls notice Sogolon first. "My prince," she say, and two boys say yes. Twins.

Prince Abeke, the one with the light boy, approach her. The light make the boy appear harder, all chin, cheekbones, and brow. Sogolon glance above, hoping a hand don't come for her from the ceiling. The other twin catch up and they both look over her, the new and strange animal.

"Where you come from?" say the other one.

"A witch conjure her, Aduke," a girl say. "Or maybe a devil."

"Devil don't come in the night, only in day, fucking fool," say Aduke. The girl jaw drop when he say **fucking.**

"Who agree for you to come with us?" say his brother. "And who tell you that you can call my brother

by his name? I am prince and so is he. Who are you?"
The girl drop her head like a sheep and shuffle to the
back of the group.

"Maybe she is a devil," say Abeke as he look over
Sogolon and toy with the leash. "Who are you? I am
a prince."

"Your father is the prince," say Aduke.

"The son of a prince is a prince also, fucking fool."

"You is the fucking fool, fucking fool."

One twin jump the other and they tumble to the
floor. One roll on top and try to punch. The other
grab the hand and try to kick him off. Another girl
scream for them to stop and they do. When I become King, I going end you first, one of them say,
Sogolon don't know who. We born the same time,
the other say.

"But I come out right before you."

"She still won't say who she is," say white clay, the
first she hearing his voice, which sounds like a whisper and a groan.

"I come from the princess house," she say.

"But you not the princess."

"I name Sogolon."

"She name Sogolon," a girl say with a giggle.

"Sogolon," say Abeke with the leash, as if he is pondering on it. "Sogolon, shall you come with us?"

"Where you going?"

Nearly everybody laugh.

"Stupid girl, the question is for us, not you. You
do whatever we say," say the other twin. "We are

ibeji, divine twins who come one every ten and two generations—not so my father say, nurse?"

A meek woman hiding at the back say, Yes, Highnesses.

"Give me truth," he say, turning around. "My father just love to hear himself running his own mouth."

Sogolon around enough mistresses and nobles and people of the court to know that whatever next come out of that woman mouth could be what send her neck to the chopping stool.

"His Highness says exactly what he needs to say, Prince, not a word less and not a word more," she say.

"Boring. She bores us. Somebody remind me to have her flogged in the morning."

Some of the children—they are all children—start to chant **flog** in a whisper. The princes look back at them. Not much taller than Sogolon, and perhaps ten and five years in age. Tomorrow they might be men, but every time they open their mouths and that whine comes out, they look younger than an infant.

"Boring. Are you boring, Sogola?"

"Sogolon she name."

"Nobody asked you. So, Sogoli? You boring?"

"No, Highness."

"How do you know? You come from nowhere and have nothing. It's boring just to talk to you."

"She own these," say white clay, who point to her sack.

"Look like some river girl things," say Abeke. The other prince grab it and laugh.

"She really is from just bush," white clay say.

"You know how to fight?" ask Abeke.

"I know how to win," and know she say a wrong thing.

"Sogolon, eh? Maybe you not so boring after all," he say and release the leash. "Let us have fun with this one, brother. Clubs!"

Those two girls hand Prince Abeke two clubs, one almost as long as half of him. Aduke steaming but stay quiet. Sogolon don't understand what is going on, not even when everybody start to surround them.

"A fight? This is boring," say Aduke.

"Not so, brother. Not when I kill her," Abeke shout with a laugh.

Sogolon jump.

"As a joke, girl. I only going to break you little and hurt you more. Brother, watch how I go as easy with her as I do with you. This fight might even last more than a blink."

"You not giving her a weapon?" somebody ask, but nobody reply. The girl try to eat her fear, but it is too big.

The white clay man is beside her ear just like that, and he whisper, Remember he is a royal, only to be touched by the gods. Sogolon still don't know what is happening until all of them start to chant and cheer, and Abeke rush after her.

Three days later, Princess Emini still laugh when she look at her, saying, Alas, the little girl find her use. Two days before, the princess herself come to rescue her from what the Aesi call a detention cell, saying to the crown prince that she is gift to the kitchen, not to him, and that he knows full well that this is his boys' fault, so build either better fighters or better sons. As for touching the prince, surely, my brother, even you saw that it is the staff that touched him. She did not lay a finger on His Most Excellent, one day to be divine head. None of that make Sogolon feel happier or safer. Two nights in a cell where she still hear a woman moaning, laughing, and screaming. Two nights after the Aesi said she will be flogged, not killed and consider that a great mercy, girl.

But she would not say much on what come to pass, not even after an order, so one of the princess's guards catch one of the Yumboes in a net and bring him to court. He is no taller than her arm, and the hum of his wings drown out the chirpy voice, but she understand:

He coming like a bull, my Prince Abeke, running and coming, coming, and coming and no god or demon ever see a girl move so fast, she dodging him and he ram like a rhinoceros right into the wall. He raging now, yes he raging, this little brown bull, he raging, he come at her and

swing one club here another club there, ay he
swing swing swing and she dodge dodge dodge.
He swing so hard he almost strike himself. But the
girl, she only dodge blows, she not landing none. It
make the prince more mad, you see, like a woman
in the night trying to kill a mosquito. She duck and
weave, and dodge, and jump like wind is lifting
her up. Lo, Prince Likud enter. Prince Likud and
plenty from court, including some who wicked to
the Yumboe. Yes. They all come in and the crown
prince tell them not to stop for no prince, no heir
to the throne run away from a fight. He even say
this, that the whole court shall place bets, he on
his son, of course. This is what he say, this for true.
He even say this too for I hear it—we hear it, that
if he placing bets, they should fight to the death.
Hear him, he say, Son you must kill her, but she
can also kill you. Father? the son say but nobody
hear. And a woman say, Most Excellent, that's not a
fight, that's an execution, for no soul may touch he
of royal blood, and the Most Excellent says, Am I
not crown prince? I waive it, and Abeke look at his
father a way, for he is counting on her not touching
him but him touching her. Father? he say. What is
this? But she has no weapon, the crown prince say,
and as there be gods, he throw her his staff! All
of we see it, he throw her the royal totem of his
own power. The whole place gasp when she pick it
up. Fight, Prince Likud shout, and he watch it keen.

How his boy have no skill, just rage and might, and he swing and flap like a headless chicken. And this girl, by the gods this girl, she float like a bird and like a wasp she sting, dodge there and strike, leap there and slap, jump there and whip, roll on the floor out of the club striking bam bam bam bam bam bam bam and twisting the staff between his legs and lo he fall on his back. She walk away from him but he get up and rush, he is a rhino again. But this girl drop and let him run right into her staff and knock a tooth loose. She swing so hard she nearly drop herself, hear what me telling you. Prince Likud laugh at his son, laugh I tell you, then he wonder how this girl learn to stick fight, and which man would dare teach a girl, yes that is what he say. Then he say off to the dungeon with her for touching the young prince. So it happen, as I say.

"Truth is I cry when the guards grab me, and I bawl when they take me to some place with iron doors. But it was no dungeon, just a cell. I could even see the stars from the window. He come to see me, the Aesi," Sogolon say, then hang her head low, for she speak out of turn.

"Oh so he do?" the princess say, as one of the women try to hold on to Mistress Komwono's silk that is still trying to escape. "If I make a dress out of that, it will fly right off me, no?"

The princess turn back to Sogolon, who stand beside her now. My new bodyguard, the princess call her when she free her from the cell. Sogolon know that it is mockery, and yet she still grin wide when she hear it.

"When the Aesi come to see you, what he do?"

"Look," she say and get a pinch from the head-woman beside her. "He look, Your Highness."

"That is it? That all he do? He say nothing to you?"

"No, Highness, he just look at me."

The princess eye her up and down. "You don't look like his kind, so . . ."

"Dear Highness, what his kind be?" ask the headwoman.

"Nobody ever seen the kind," she say.

Sogolon only now coming in audience with the princess, for before that her head was exploding. An ache like a torment at the front of her head, that happen as soon as she get left alone in the cell. The pain so mighty that she is bashing her head against the wall in the dark. But then the princess free her and order her to bed.

"Expect him to come soon," she say.

"Who, my princess?"

"Likud. Watch it come to pass. Those twins soon remind him that he promise to kill you. And he will have it, girl, your head or your heart to throw to his dogs—I mean boys. Those two boys. Word is that their mother didn't give birth, she just shit twice."

"Is that word coming from somewhere near you, Highness?" ask the headwoman.

"Must be wind. I hear the wind also promising to execute all who take what I say out of this room."

"Death to all spillers of secrets, Princess," this lady say. Sogolon don't know her name.

"Leave the killing to Likud," the princess say.

Behind Princess Emini's back, Prince Likud speak to several elders about crushing Wakadishu. All is talk, and talk is wind, but the crown prince is playing king for size, for fucks, for laughs, or for the pleasure of wrapping himself in the royal cape. All tiresome to the princess, for she is spending too many days telling elders that the crown has not lost its head.

See the girl, finding herself back in Commander Olu's quarters, for she find herself with questions that he can't answer, but maybe his wall will, or his bedsheet, or his curtain. He not there when she let herself in, but it don't startle him when he come back to see her.

"I can't remember your name, but you seem to know my house," he say.

"You teaching me to read."

"And can you?"

"More than a moon ago."

"So I'm a teacher?"

"No."

"Priest?"

"You are a commander."

"So people tell me."

"I looking words for something."

For he have words on everything, if one know where to look, she continue in her mind. Every time she step into his house she stepping into what his mind used to be. He is a man who see and note everything. He know that he is the one doing all the writing down, but some days he forget why. When she say that to him, he smile, which surprise her. "You starting to forget that you forget," she say, frightened that it is coming so soon.

"Why the princess and the prince at each other so?" she ask.

"They do as brother and sister do. You don't have a brother?"

"No."

"Your mother must curse her luck."

"A boy is no luck," she say.

He go on about how the princess have to do the work of the King, but the brother will see the glory, and that must be why she have hatred for him. Why all this on the princess? she ask but he don't answer. Commander Olu's house is become a better version of Olu. In the written word he don't hide under diplomacy, a word she just learn, or memory, and he don't have any code for prince or princess. Then she remember what lie under the rug, the note on what happen to the herbswomen. Sogolon search. She compare a word on the wall to a word on the floor, to a word on the windowsill, until thoughts start to come. Some so clear they come with the sound of Olu's voice.

Some already throw ten and six sacred palm nuts into the Ifa bowl to divine the gods' will for the future. The time to come, taking too long yet too soon. The princess when she become the King Sister will restore.

"Restore what?" she ask.

"Eh?"

"The princess when she become the King Sister will restore what?"

"What you asking, girl?"

"You the one who write it down. Come look at your mark and see if it strike a memory."

"I too old for anything to strike me."

"Commander."

Something change in him when she say that. He stand taller for certain, but something else.

"Oh, that. You don't need memory for that. That is just the way of kings. Any griot would recite that." He pause as if waiting for a question, but she just stare at him.

"Prince Likud is not supposed to be King," he say.

"What?"

"He is the son of the King."

"Yes, he is the son of the King. So?"

"You under whose rule? Don't you know anything about your King and ruler? Kwash Kagar grow with no sister."

It come to her there. That the King of Fasisi is not like the Chief of Kongor. When the Chief of Kongor die, his oldest son become chief, no matter where he

fall in the line of children as long as the chief ac-
knowledge the mother. The King of Fasisi is never
the son of the King, but the firstborn of the King
Sister. That is the way it always was, and always is.
Except for when no sister is born in the King's family.
Then his oldest son become King. The elders and the
priests pray that he is a wise and just King, he who is
not meant to be, but even if he is not, restoration will
come as soon as the King Sister produce a male heir.

"No sister?" she say almost as a whisper, but let
it trail off. Wedding necklace on Olu's wall match-
ing the pattern around his neck. **Jeleza, Jeleza** in his
sleep. Maybe everybody in the world is right and she
is wrong. She try to shake out the thought but it won't
go. It can't go with him standing there, with his eyes
looking baffled like the river blind, feeling he lost
something that he don't know is gone. In her head,
that word **gone** is starting to fade. **Taken** slip itself
into that spot and rising higher and higher in her
mind, insisting that it won't go. She look for Jeleza
on his wall. Her name is all over the house but she is
not, making Sogolon wonder if Olu forget her before
he lose her.

Meanwhile, the King is yet busy. Another woman
long in charge of his care but dismissed by the Aesi
four moons ago get sent to the dungeon, for one of the
Sangomin visit her house and nearly choke to death
on the fumes of witchcraft, his words. As the gods see
and hear all things, in there smell like when witches
cook my brother, he say. And while the sister is ruling

in all the ways that the realm demand her to, it is the prince who take it on himself to render judgment. So he ask the Aesi, who say that if indeed the smell of burning flesh is coming from a woman's yard, then yes it must be that she is roasting a dismembered baby for witchcraft. But how do this Sangomin, and a boy with a hump in his back at that, know that she is cooking necromancy? The Aesi ignore the prince. When people cook a living thing they season and prepare, the Aesi say. When they just burning flesh for a sacrifice they don't care that they burning nails, or shit in the bowels, or hair, and nothing smell more foul than baby's burning hair. The woman scream that she is cooking goat and at the beginning, goat flesh always smell foul. The Aesi declare that this is another of those women who put a curse on the King. The prince condemn her to die in the way she kill babies, but slower, longer, and for three nights all of Fasisi come under the smell of burning, screaming woman. The smell reach every woman who nurse the King and even some who bathe him or wash his bedding, and they flee, knowing they not safe. Most don't get very far. Sogolon walk into the cookroom one noon to see the headwoman crying. She don't say why, for why would she lower herself to Sogolon's level, even in distress, but a cook tell her that nearly all her friends either lock up or executed for putting a curse on the King, and it is only because she never serve in the King's house why no accuser ever come for her.

"And not because she not a witch?" say a woman peeling yam.

"The only difference between who is a witch and who is not is one man's mouth," say the cook.

Now the princess starting to take Sogolon wherever she go, making her think that they looking at her as a bodyguard for true. And she start to ask where Sogolon go when she missing in the mornings and sometimes evenings, and the girl say she go to the library. But when the princess ask why, for she cannot read, Sogolon say she go to smell the paper, for it smell like intelligence. It smell like old age, the princess say. Sogolon know the princess not watching her, so is either the guards or somebody else in the castle giving her news. The winds are changing, don't you feel it? she say once at court to nobody. Sogolon, who feel all kind of wind, don't know what she mean.

So, this. The headwoman come to her room without knocking first. Darkness cool the air, and the night is already old. She throw a dagger on the bed and say, Follow me. How you know I wasn't sleeping? Sogolon say, but she don't answer. So she follow the woman out the castle, down a long outside path, far past the lights still flickering in Prince Likud's castle, down to the ruins of Kwash Abili. In the dark it look like a row of cracked giant teeth, but at the base is a door, which the headwoman go through, expecting her to follow. They go down a corridor, long and cold and so

dark that Sogolon can't see her hands in front of her.
They stop at a cross path, where two torches blaze.

"Take one and continue. When you get to the door,
wait for four knocks, then let him in. Bring him back
to the cross path," she say. Sogolon leaving questions
for later, for her heart beating from just being in the
now. Four knocks come far apart. She open the door.

A guard in armor is standing there, looking around,
not sure if he in the right place. The torchlight turn
his face into just cheekbone and brow, but the armor
look green, not the red of royal guard. She don't dare
speak to him. Sogolon head back to where she come
from, and listen for his footsteps crunching behind
her. She want to turn back and look at him again, but
don't. At the cross path, the headwoman is waiting.
She take Sogolon's torch and hand her one with two
flames. "Leave it behind the green door and enter,
don't wait," she say. "Bring her back to the cross path
and go where you see me going." The headwoman
and the guard turn right and go off.

At the green door she pause when she hear sounds
that men make when they dream. Or the other thing,
which is what she see when she enter. The bed wide
as a room and full of so many pillows and cushions
that the two of them almost lost in them. The prince
consort standing by the edge of the bed, between the
two legs of the princess. He is the one making the
sound, the grunt, the mumble. The princess left leg
as still as her right, and both of them bare like a slave
girl's. This prince thrust and thrusting, his buttocks

sweaty in torch and lamplight. She mumble too, like she keeping her voice out of the reach of somebody else. At Miss Azora, the woman shriek and bawl that **the man is tearing her in two, two I say, don't destroy my little koo now, big master.** A grunt take her back into the room. She move over to the side, kicking a silver basin, which make her jump. Neither turn around. The prince consort continue with his grunting and thrusting, and in the dim light Sogolon see the princess tapping her fingers on the bed. The prince grunt into a yell and try to pull back, but the princess wrap her legs around him tight and he almost pull her off the bed. The princess burst into a laugh and the prince let his nightgown drop and he climb into the bed. He throw himself down on the pillows and there they stay. The prince, his head on a pillow at the head of the bed, and the princess, lower down than him, her legs still hanging off. And so they stay for what would be many a flip of the time glass. The princess remain nothing more than two legs still wide apart. The prince consort lie still for a while, then sit up, take off his nightshirt, look at Sogolon, then lower back down on the bed.

As soon as he start snoring, the princess raise up and gather herself in the robe she still wearing and leave through the green door. She stride so fast that Sogolon have to trot to keep up, but at the cross path she stop and wait for Sogolon to take over the lead. She still thinking about the rat she sure she step on when they come to another green door. The princess don't wait. Inside the guard is just taking off his breastplate. He see the princess and start to take off his armor quicker.

"Even the night is taking her time, officer," she say.

Standing in a dark corner is the headwoman, who shake her head at Sogolon when she try to move from the door. The guard remove his armor and under-garment. The princess already ready when he climb on the bed. He is unsure for sure. A princess is not a woman, he must be thinking. The princess pull him to the bed, his back down, then straddle him as if on top of a mule and ride. Sogolon watch the princess controlling how fast he stroke, what he can touch and what he cannot, how far up in her she allow, and who get to cry out. Olu's words return to her right there, that restoration will come soon.

s a long time since it happen, but Sogolon catch herself looking at herself. It happen when over by the princess's bedroom window she learn of glass. Truth, she never even know of such a thing before she try to push her hand through the window to feel rain and nearly break a finger. Glass, like amber that trap the fly, but the same color as air. She tap it, rub along the iron frame holding it, and at one time, lick it. By day she watch outside as the ladies of the bedchamber ready the princess. By night, when lamps bring more light inside than out, she look at the glass and see

herself. Sogolon pull back, for what she see is a boy.
The tunic with a strap around the waist, the little
knife, the hair that grow up and out, but never down.
She think to ask if the princess is bringing her up as a
boy, but know she will say she is not bringing her up.
Right now the ladies of the bedchamber are washing
the princess in another room. **What are you, her pet?**
say a voice she don't recognize. The voice ask again,
and again, and again until she realize it is Middle
Brother. The thought make her jump. She dart left
and right, looking up and down for him. But there
is no way a man like him would ever find himself in
any royal bedchamber. That fact make her look at her
life in the quick, at how none of it make any sense.
But maybe her path to here leave a trail for her brothers, maybe dead Miss Azora, maybe spirits of the un-
peaceful dead. Boys who can slice a skin open with
fingers, boys with two arms for legs, and girls who
turn to dust. A boy black like a night spider, with
the legs as well. But she is just a girl, just a girl who
neither ask for nor want notice. Now she at court and
feel safe in the eyes of the princess, but unsafe everywhere else. The prince will demand that they send
her to his court again. She is sure of it. And the twins
will again ask for her head, or with the help of the
Sangomin just snatch it.

"Now we wait for the day of no moonblood,"
the headwoman say when Sogolon ask what they
are doing.

"You know what I mean," Sogolon say.

"But you don't hear what I mean. Her reasons be her own, but she let you into her inner room and I don't mean a place. It mean now you see more and talk less."

"Why me?"

"You asking royal blood to explain their ways? If it was up to me I wouldn't pick you."

"I not a problem to you."

"You not a thing to anyone. I hear say you are a foundling. Everybody here have something to lose, but what you have?"

"I wouldn't pick me, either."

"Her Highness possess wisdom from the gods. God wisdom sound like folly to many. But make me repeat it, lest you let your head take you somewhere foolish. You are a woman of the bedchamber now. It mean we be the ones who see more and talk less. If the seed don't take, we do this again. What any of this mean is not for you to think, much less say."

But talk is all the princess want her to do. Princess Emini ask Sogolon her opinion of other ladies of the court, whether Mitu is a land of river people or lake people, and what certain guards look like with all their clothes off. She laugh at the shock coming over Sogolon face when she ask how she figure general this or commander that fuck. Other times, the princess ask a question that need a long answer, such as why you think you are born as woman in this age and not another, not to hear the answer, for Sogolon take too long and make her yawn twice, but to hear her Mitu bush girl voice and giggle. "You are a puzzle, Sogolon. In your face there is nothing you have not seen, and nothing that you have. Teach me, girl. Teach me how to be one year old, and one hundred at the same time," Emini say. Another time, in the middle of an audience with the people, she grab Sogolon by the arm and whisper, "Nobody raised you. That means nobody can fool you."

A quartermoon later and in the quick, the King die. Pass on to the ancestors silent, like an afterthought.

EIGHT

Sogolon do the work of forgetting Keme so well that she don't recognize him passing right by her in the funeral procession until near one hundred soldiers also pass. By then he is gone too far, and she is nodding at man who don't nod back. Kwash Kagar when he die become an ancestor, for there is no such person as a dead king. Nor do he return to his name before kingship, for that is lost to all but the griots, and most griots now in hiding, for it is said that they are in league with witches. Only Alaya, from the floating district, dare to show his face in the streets, singing truth until somebody send a stone straight to the side of his head to shut him up, and others come after him with sticks to drive him from the street. Nobody like the songs he is singing, about age, and disease, and weakness, and death. But nobody want to say what everybody thinking nonetheless. That whatever lead to the King's death, even if it is disease, or the call of the ancestors, evil is going on. So they call him Ancestor Kagar and hope that when he reach the final house, those long gone recognize his name.

Mourning rites for Ancestor Kagar should take seven quartermoons, but Prince Likud chop that down to three. That displease many who say that Kwash Kagar, the uniter of the ten and one kingdoms, the great and terrible lion, the master of war and peace, and the dominator of the South deserve seven years of weeping and wailing, but here the court won't even give him seven quartermoons. But people speak their displeasure in the bedchamber, whisper it under tavern light, or share with their reflection in water and shiny silver, for word travel on wind much these days, and a secret is not a secret even if the only person you tell is yourself. That she learn from the princess, the night before her father's funeral. When she ask her brother by whose authority does he cut short the time of mourning for the King, Prince Likud laugh and say that there is no King, only a spirit, waiting to be called an ancestor, and until then Kagar is neither man nor spirit. He is nothing. Princess Emini leave him, for that outright blasphemy make her choke. She leave Likud, already sitting on his father's throne shouting that funerals, like wars, also cost plenty coin. Grief must be driving him mad, she say to Sogolon and the women.

The princess, when she is not crying, is wailing, and when she not wailing, is cursing anybody who cross her path, and when she tire of all these things

she is at the window staring into sky until it start
to shimmer with stars. One of the chamberwomen
whisper to Sogolon that she crying because her time
pretending she King is over. Sogolon mark her, remembering her face and name. The King is always
the King Sister's firstborn son for a reason, for all that
is truly kingly, not the seat of power, but the strength
and wisdom to bear the burden of responsibility, come
from the sister. But Kwash Kagar lose his only sister,
Lokji, to malaria when she was just nine in years, and
no more sister come. That is the common knowledge
to everybody but one. Sogolon.

Sogolon try to let go of this Jeleza, who is nothing but a name that Olu whisper in his sleep. But
two nights before the funeral, Sogolon find herself
in the dream jungle, and that bush lead her to castle
grounds of the house of Akum. Or what look like it.
She assume before she can know for sure, for she has
seen no other castle. She follow a white vapor that
vanish into a trail of just sound, a mumble that fade
into a whisper, that fade into something that not until
she walk past palace, library, archive, banquet hall,
one more palace, and the ruins of another to reach
the lion cages do she realize is the silent sniffling of
sorrow. A lioness alone. No, not alone, beside a lying
lion, stretched too loose and sprawled too wide open
to be alive. Louder than her weeping, the buzz of
flies. But the lioness don't even see the lying lion, for
she looking down at her own belly, where womb must
be, and instead of belly is nothing, no skin, no flesh,

not guts, not even air. A nothing like a hole but hole is
not what Sogolon would call it. She search her mind
but can't find no words. The lioness with a hole in her
belly, she know something is there, but don't know
what that is. A flutter of huge wings and a blinding
splash of red wake her up. Sogolon pull the sheet over
her face before looking, then pull it down slow and
quiet, while she look at the ceiling for moving eyes.

This is woman's work. Queen, princess, freeborn,
or slave, it don't matter. That is the answer she get the
three times she ask the question. The question still on
her tongue though she run out of people willing to
answer, and she certainly not going to ask the princess. The question consume her all the way down the
corridors and walkways, past the ruins of Kwash Abili
and the towering castle of Kwash Kong. The question
fill her mind and avert her eyes from seeing all that
is different in Kwash Kagar's palace, the guardhouse
as wide as a throne room, the grand entrance, the pillars of gold rising in the halls, and the lions standing
guard, shapeshifter and beast-born, outside his chamber, where all the murals, frescoes, and tapestries are
covered in purple cloth and no light is allowed in.
And when the headwoman stride in first, in a slow
mourning march, followed by two death midwives,
then the princess, then six more chamberwomen, and
Sogolon, the question is right there in the bed. So
she ask herself, knowing no answer is going to come.
Why must they be the ones to wash his body? Sogolon
won't cut the question loose, and now, when she in

this great lion's bedchamber, which call for silence, she whisper it again to a chamberwoman who look younger than her. The woman whisper it to another woman, who whisper it to another, and another until it reach the princess.

"Sogolon, come here," she say without looking or turning behind her. Sogolon barely in front of her before the princess swing her hand with force and slap the girl in her face so hard that she stagger backways. She can't stop it, the tears that run down her cheek.

"Is so it go, that you are too good to wash your King? What it be? A King's blood not as noble as yours? Or maybe you turn King last night, and is the King who turn into a no name girl fucking a mad commander by lamplight? Hmmm? Girl, tell me, since it is I who need to hear from you, and not the other way, so tell me. Tell me!"

Sogolon hang her head low.

"You get called to clean the King's shit, you fall on your knees and ask the gods why you so blessed. Every woman in this room born, raised, and trained for this day, including your princess. You the only one here because I was in a good mood the day I first see you. Now all you do is prove that my kindness is a gift to a fool. Go stand over there. I don't want you touching my father."

She stand in the darkest corner of the bedchamber and watch the women. Sogolon want to cry whenever she think about herself and what a loose tongue get her, so she look outside herself at these women working. Two women at the head of the bed start to sing a praise song barely above a whisper. **We thank the Gods for the ntoro, for through this the King is of his people and the people of his King.** Two women on left and right of the bed roll away one bedsheet, as the princess and the rest of the women stand at the foot. All the women humming if they not singing. **We thank the god for the mogya, the blood of kings that come only from woman, for it is through the sister that come the King.** The two women roll away the second sheet. **We thank the gods for the sunsum, which is all that our King is and will be when he is called to the ancestors' tree.** The two women roll away the third sheet. **We salute the okra, the soul given by the gods, which returns to the gods for it cannot die, but will rise to the ancestors' tree and decide our destiny.** At that the princess wail and two women catch her as she stumble. **If there is wickedness, if there is evilness, if this is not his time, guide him to the tree of ancestors, so that his spirit not roam the world in fury and disturb the living.**

Then a woman step forward, one Sogolon never see before this day. This woman, a cousin of the King on his father's side. A woman from an old and noble family that help found the empire but run afoul of the King. She stand by the left side of the King's body, the side of the father's kinfolk. On the right should be the relatives from the mother's kin, but Kwash Kagar's cousins are too old and he have no sisters, so the duty fall on his daughter. Sogolon try to picture it, even though she is about to see it, the princess washing her father's body. The women all gather and lift him up with their strength. They take his body to the center of the room to a sheet on the floor. The women remove his death mask, his tunic, and his undergarment and slippers. The flurry of women's robes block her view but then they pull away like a flower spreading open. The King, pale and death thin, with bones poking under his skin. His head drooping more like a drunk man than a dead one. The princess wail again and the headwoman touch her shoulder, the only woman allowed to do so. Women on the left and right dip washcloths in a bowl and hand them to the cousin on the left and the princess on the right. The cousin wipe the left side of Kwash Kagar's face, while Princess Emini wipe the right. They move down as the women sing, **We are your kin washing away your death, banish all illness and ill will, bring us health and send us children.** The princess wash the right nipple while the cousin wash the left. The women keep singing for his okra to bring them health and send them children and the two women scrub down. Princess Emini reach his penis first and drop the cloth. As you would a child, Highness, headwoman say, but the princess refuse to pick back up the cloth. Is the cousin who dip her hands into his cock and sack and between him like she cleaning a baby. They put a fur to hide his maleness and the princess continue. When she get to his feet, as much tears as water wash him. They finish by washing their hands with rum and pouring the rest of the bottle down the King's mouth. That will keep you happy, Kagar, she say, before crying again that now that he is dead he is not Kagar anymore.

"He lost his name," she say.

The other woman dress him in black and white robes streaked with gold, and a crown of gold crocodiles and turtles. They place the funeral shroud on the bed, then they place him on the left side, like a lover turning to talk to you in bed. A pillow prop up his neck, and his left hand is open to receive whatever he will need for his journey to the ancestors. Then they leave him, all of them, none saying anything to Sogolon, who stand so still in the corner that nobody see that they leave her alone in the room with the dead King. Why she didn't speak, whisper, or cry out will bother her all night. Something in the princess's voice make her think that her mouth is the last thing that any woman want to hear. The day moving on without her, but Sogolon don't know what to do. She could just leave, but she in the corner under order of the princess. If she leave now, somebody might see her and accuse her of theft, or something else that people who get caught with a dead king do. And the princess will be back in her castle, no longer caring about the affairs of this house. Or worse. They could accuse her of worse, acts treacherous or indecent, for she is a no name girl, and the only people outside of the court of the princess who know her are the twins, who want her dead, and the prince, who might give them their wish. Or Commander Olu. Or Keme. None of this mean a thing for girl in the bedroom of a dead king who is washed, dressed, and ready for all who will pay tribute.

So she stay all night. It strike her first with confusion then with bitterness that she not even trying to hide in the corner, and yet nobody see her. She just standing there. By late afternoon, two men wearing purple enter with plates of food, which they place right by the reach of his left hand. They leave, walking backways. Sogolon settle on being in the corner, for how long she don't know. The sun dip lower and lower until rays coming through the window hit the King's face. His eyes are shut but he is frowning at having her in the room, she can feel it. Lying there on his side with the trays of food by him, he is a man disturbed from his feast. Outside drums boom like thunder and startle her so much that she slip out of the corner, tripping in a spot of water the cleaning women leave behind. Hit the floor hard she do, her shoulders and the back of her head the most. Sogolon barely up on her elbows when loud footsteps come straight for the door. She scramble to the bed but there is no hollow to slip under, so she try to cover up with the leopard-skin rug on the floor.

She feeling breeze on her feet when the door open.

A commotion of footsteps march in, but only one go all the way up to the bed.

"You all plan to hold my cock so I can piss as well?" Prince Likud ask. The motion to the bed stop.

"Get out. All of you."

"Your Highness, it is tradition that no one who sees the King wi—"

"There is no King."

"Of course. But with respect—"

"Respect? You have as much respect for me as I have affection for you. Or as any of you have for the crown."

She hear him before she see him, the darkchild with yellow eyes glowing even in the daylight, scuttling on the ceiling, the shadow spider. As she pull the leopard skin over her face, she can feel more air on her bare feet.

"You lords know the way out, or shall I have him show you?"

More scuttling. This time on the floor as the men all back out of the room. Everything is quiet. The darkchild scuttle across the ceiling twice, then settle somewhere beyond her feet. The room is again quiet, until she realize that the prince is sitting on the bed, and only after he spit a seed on the floor that he is eating the food.

"Come," he say. Scuttling she soon hear, from the ceiling to the wall to the floor. Then a laugh like a shriek, and scramble back up to the ceiling. She lift the leopard skin off one eye just to see him, feet on the ceiling, hands free as he devour a full roasted fowl in four bites.

"What unfortunate vagina spit you out," the prince say and laugh, but it wither into a sigh. She feel him adjust his weight on the bed.

"Kagar of Akum. Look at you now," he say. "Look at you now. Look at you."

Another sigh. Another silence.

"Try the goat. Raw, as you like it." He laughs. "I know, you don't like no goat. You don't like a single thing on this plate. What shall we serve your father, they ask me, as if I know what my father likes. Then I remember the first time you spit this out. Who be here mistaking me for some mountain man, you say. You, a civilized King. So civilized that you don't know what thought calls for 'be' and what calls for 'is.' So here it **be,** Father, I serving you raw goat.

"Nobody believe that I want none of this, except you. I run all the way to Omororo to not be you. My memory comes back like a dream, Father. That is the one time you ever looked for me. Whatever you try-ing to drive out, my general will beat back into you. Beat back into you. Beat back . . ."

He laughs again, so long and loud that he start to cough.

"You lying in rest in the same bed I took your last nine concubines. The last two didn't take me, if we speaking true. Truth, Father? This bed is as wet from me as you. Ponder the horror, old man. Tell me what upsets you more, that I disrespect you or your bed? Spill away the line of the house of Akum on bed linen washed by slaves. I will bet you've never seen your own sperm, have you, Father? Not a drop of seed wasted with our Kwash Kagar. I woke up this morning thinking, Has ever a man had so many bastard brothers as I?"

He throw a chunk of meat at the darkchild, who catch it with his teeth. The child sniff, picking up the scent of something. Sogolon shudder under the fur.

"The elders say it is a curse to speak directly to the dead. It confuses them. They think they're still alive and then they start to meddle in the living's affairs. Meddle? That would be a start, not so, Father? Meddling would speak of fathers speaking to sons, the one having care in the affairs of the other. But when did such thing exist between us?

"Meanwhile everyone speaks of the line of King. It comes from the sister, did you know, Father? Your brilliant daughter. The woman who will spit forth the next King from between her legs. You should hear talk in the street, Likud the incorrect. Likud the proxy King. Oh King Sister, bring forth a boy, and restore the line. They calling her King Sister even before they crown me King. Oh King Sister, bring forth a boy, and restore the line, even the children sing it as verse. If she ever has a firstborn. If your father had more care about who he fucked, I wouldn't be burdened with your damn throne. You think I want it? I hear what you tell the elders. You still think you know what I want. I want many things, Father. I wanted to be the one who when you see him, you say you see the sun, but no more. That Likud, that fool, if only he loved duty as much as he love power. That's what you tell the elders just three days before you die. You tell people a lot of things you think I won't hear. But I have something to tell you, Father.

"Do you know that I'm not raising my sons to be King? My twin sons, my ibeji. Make them meet you once and even that is too much. My sons look at the lions and look at you and cannot tell the difference. No, that is not praise.

"Father. That is not what I have to tell you. What I will tell you is this. Your daughter. Noble Emini, dearest sister. Plotting against me, she is. You didn't know, and as much as you wish she could rule, not even you want to break tradition. Listen, old man, and don't tell anyone. I said she is plotting. Even now she speaks to some of the elders, promising them a boy child before the rain season. And when that child is born, we crown him King and her as regent until he reach ten and five in years. Oh yes. But know this, Father, that does not offend me. I will destroy her plan and wreck her ambition, but I admire it. But Father, that is not what I come to tell you.

"I come to tell you about the prince. Your son-in-law from Kalindar, you know, that prince with nowhere to rule. Emini is his third wife, and as for concubines, he has more than you. But hear this, Father. After all this time, all these seasons, all these years, not a single child. Not even a girl. Not one. But your daughter is crafty, Father, after all, she takes from you. Yet not even you would think to have your husband fuck you odd nights, then go to some secret place and have some soldier lay his seed in you again. Your daughter is crafty, Father. She will have a child, a son, and nobody would even know that a bastard would soon sit on the throne of Akum. She do it with every new moon. She is doing it tonight. Send your spirit, I know it still walks. Go see for yourself, how this whore will end the house of Akum, end it with no one even knowing that she killed it, just to get the throne that I don't even want. Because I don't want it, Father, but unlike her, unlike you, I can think beyond myself. So, you might never have liked me, Father, and this is fair, for I abhor you. But I'd see you rot on this bed, and rats feed on your lips, before I make a bastard the next King. I take your silence as gratitude. Who knew the day would come when your unworthy son saves your fucking throne? The knight she will have tonight? I send him myself. Tested him on one of your concubines, who found him most satisfactory. Eh, Father? Even the King Sister deserves some sort of pleasure at least once."

Sogolon feel the bed rebound from losing his weight. Likud is at the door when he say, "Oh, and the generals you had beat me? They shall all be beheaded tomorrow. I will arrange to have their heads buried with you. You really should try the goat."

He leave. She almost get up when she hear scuttling

across the ceiling. Under the leopard skin she stay until night fall. In the room she stay until dawn break.

As much as she fear the darkchild, it is only by thinking herself as him that she escape the King's palace. Sliding from wall to wall with her back scraping against the stone, crawling along shadows, slipping into dark corners, behind loose tapestry, waiting for people to leave a room, taking on the shape of statues and craftwork, and standing in places where no person highborn would look. She almost make it out until she come to first set of guards stationed by a doorway. Nothing to do now but walk. She grab the smallest urn by the tapestry and take it with her as if she and it have purpose. The third guard stop her.

"No servant supposed to be in the palace," he say. Sogolon have nothing to say, so she say nothing. She lift the urn to him, hoping it would mean something.

"That urn have no use," another guard say. Sogolon almost drop it before she hear a roar. The guards stiffen up. Her lion. He trot right up beside her and they leave together.

At the princess palace she tiptoe through the cookroom. When to speak to the princess? Should she tell the headwoman? The first question both will ask, How you know? How you hear these things? Maybe she will tell them that fall asleep is what she do. She wonder why nobody is in the cookroom until a foot slip right into her way and trip her.

"Where you going, little bitch?" the headwoman ask as she come from around a corner. "Grab her."

Sogolon turn to yell, but a guard slap it out of her mouth. They don't wait for her to stand but grab her hands and drag her along the floor and up each stone step. She struggle for five steps, then quit, her head hanging low and saying nothing. The headwoman saying something about all of last night, but Sogolon not sure what she mean. In her room, in her bed, is the princess, looking sour.

"I told them to wake me as soon as you slither through whatever hole wretches like you slither through," she say, as she sit up on the bed. "From where you come, girl?"

"Your Highness, I—"

"What did you take?"

"Highness, I—"

"I say, what did you take?"

Sogolon lower her head. The guards pull her up to stand, but still grabbing arms.

"A part of me always suspect this about you. Watch that girl, I say. She plotting something."

"Your Highness, I never do nothing."

"Imagine. Every woman entered that room in reverence. To do the gods' work."

"I—"

"Shut up! How dare you speak when I am speaking. Every woman in the room is there to dress him for the ancestors, but you? What are you even doing there, you have no woman skill."

"Highness, it is you—"

"You in the room to steal. From a King. From

a dead man's room? What kind of bitch give birth
to you?"

The princess nod at the guard, and the one on the
right quick as light punch her in the belly. Sogolon
bowl over. Her legs buckle and her knees hit the floor.
She cough and cough as the men pull her back up.

"Thief, what you steal? You spend all night in my
father's room, or you break into some other room? The
thieving, girl, what is it? Don't make me beat every
spot on you until it fall out. What an embarrassment."

"I didn't take nothing, Highness!"

"Steal from the dead. Are you a witch? Only a witch
steal from the dead."

"I didn't take nothing."

The princess nod again and in three pulls, the
guards rip off her clothes. They shake out her clothes
but nothing fall out. They nod to the princess.

"What you take, girl, a trinket? An amulet? One
of his rings? What kind of devilry going on in your
mind that you slip away from me to search my father's
bedroom? What gall. Honestly, what gall. All that I
give you and all you think to do is take take take."

"I didn't take nothing."

"You didn't take nothing, what?" say the headwoman.

"I didn't take nothing from him," she say, quiet and
cold. The princess look at her, appalled.

"You not done with your search," she say to the
guards. "The little witch have three holes, fools. Take
her from my sight."

Sogolon have no strength when they take her, so

they drag her along the floor. When the guards report that they find nothing in her, the princess declare that either she is lazy, is defiant, or is doing something with her father's corpse, all of which fill her with anger again. She order the guards to whip her, then leave her in the stables, for that is where she will live until all of this is over and the princess heart grow warmer. Sogolon say nothing when they take her away. The guard about to swing the whip when the headwoman shout from the stable door that the princess change her mind. The girl is not to be whipped, but to be left in the stable to sleep on hay. The guards are about to leave when the headwoman say, I said not to whip her. I didn't say not to touch her. Before Sogolon can scream, one guard knock her down and the other guard kick while the headwoman watch. Her lips crack open. She almost smile.

Sogolon in the stables wondering why the wind never come. It come as it wish, but even when it do, it seem to rise from some part of her desire. None of that mean anything now. Wind if it working is fickle and testy, and about as trustworthy as lightning. Or maybe she is like those stupid old diviners always looking for signs and wonders and the only wonder here is some lazy young god having fun with her twice. Or three times, now she don't want to remember. Nor do she want to think of it, for how foolish it sound now that wind is her guardian, her protector, how different is that from men who say they hear god's rebuke in thunder? No sense believing in that, no sense believing in nothing. The world is what it is. Soon as one see that, then one can live in a world with pain, lonesomeness, and betrayal. The two things always coming from people that you never see coming are surprise and disappointment. Sogolon look at the horses and ponder this all night. Surprise and disappointment come from the same place where also come a sudden bump on the cheek, or a lightning strike. While her belly ache and her shoulders burn from bruise, Sogolon thinking she looking at this all wrong. It's surprise she can expect, and disappointment she can depend on. The other things, goodness, kindness, fairness, loyalty, decency, those are the things that come out of nowhere.

She feel like something new enter her head, or that she find some place in there she didn't notice before. A place that make her consider her years, which she never knew for sure, but it don't matter, for now she is the one age that will always count and never change: old enough. Only yesterday she thought she have news for the princess. But there is nothing that a girl from the Mitu bush could have that a woman of royal blood could want. The princess would say so herself. The world is what it is. And this stable is what it is. Sogolon consider the night, and how only one night ago she is already crafting what to do to get back in the presence of the princess that she get cruelly cut from. One night later she remember who is behind the cruelty. Besides, the stables feel warm, don't smell much of shit, and horse don't do much other than stand and look magnificent.

One night turn to two, two turn to three, and three turn to a number that she stop count. The stables are as long as any palace and the horses count to over one hundred. It is the night she gone walking and counting that at the last horse's stall she discover steps that lead up into the roof. And up in the roof a floor, a pile of rugs and pillows, a jug and a bowl for water, and in a dark corner under hay, some small fetishes. Other than the groomsmen, no other person come to the stables and those who come don't speak to her even when they see her. Since she sleeping up in the roof no man come to rest here and nobody put it to use. So she do. Twice a day somebody decide to show her kindness, and send her scraps from one of the royal tables, and twice a day it shame her how she devour them. She don't want to need anything from the princess ever again. Never ever. There. Decided. She will never need again. Season of plenty, season of famine, same face. People kind, people cruel, same face. So when Keme march past her during the funeral procession she don't see him, for it is with the same face that she is looking at every soldier. At everybody.

The morning of the funeral, masters of stable come for the brown horses to drape them in red and black. Nobody tell her to come to the funeral, so she don't go, which might make her the only person not ill, or old, or dead to not go out in the street to mourn and celebrate the passing of Kwash Kagar to the ancestors. Sogolon think of the dead King and what come to her is goat flesh. Now she is on her bed of carpets and hay, thinking about this day and about Keme passing by the stable. Morning it was, with sun already high but not yet hot. Drums beating from dawn send tidings of great mourning from one mountain to the other. The drums draw her to the wide stable entrance, where the procession beginning at the King's palace would pass the stables, all the palaces, and through the grand guardhouse and gate, then down the main street of Fasisi, looping around the capital three times through all the districts and sections until finally it descend the hill and march to another hill, that of Sigray, the mountain of the tree of the ancestors, where the body and the body alone is tied to rope and pulled up by divine-chosen bearers, who live in the mountains all their life. Up the steep slope they pull, so high that they pass clouds. The bearers will pull the body up to the hole in the mountain, one that the gods already dig out, right below the ancestors' tree, which is old beyond a dozen ages and more. The bearers will speak in a tongue that only they and the gods know, entreating those divine to welcome Kwash Kagar to the land of the ancestors. **I will arrange to have their heads buried with you.** The words come quick and at first she start to shake them out, but then stop. Let words land where they want to land, she say to herself. None of this burial she see. All of it she remember from a conversation between an old cook and young milkmaid about how they bury a king.

The rites begin at dawn, the birth of the day, and end with the King's burial at dusk, the death. Neither princess nor prince pass the stables, though she see many from court walking in procession. From the stables she hear the drums getting louder and louder, and another sound, louder than that, the earth rumbling from the drumming of feet. She know it's the death masquerade, though she don't see them, one hundred masked dancers, maybe more. For an instant that feel as long as a season she take her mind there, to the ground, where the feet riling up dust. Bells on their ankles, their chants rising with the wind. First the band of the biriki bearers with masks as tall as a giraffe to bridge earth and sky, the original house of the gods. Then pass the wanaga bearers with masks not as tall, leading the soul into the afterlife while the body go elsewhere. Two bars on top of the mask, one for land, the other for the underworld. Groups of six dancers or ten, they hop, stomp, twirl, bend until their masks touch the ground, then sweep and spin so that the wanaga touch the four points of the universe. Seven hops and they do it again. And on and on. All the same to Sogolon, for morning is morning and night is night, and nothing any person can do to challenge their march.

Then come night and rain.

Sogolon lying right under the ceiling, right under

the patter of rainfall on the roof. The sound soothe her, even when it grow louder, into a pounding on the thatch. The hum sweep over in a wave, she is sinking deeper into the rugs and hay, even as she feel lighter and lighter, as if someone slip her wine. But a screech down below rip her from all that. She jump up to see the stable door sliding away and the full spray of rain coming in. A man as well.

"Sogolon. Girl."

Keme. She roll to the edge of the bunk and jump down, too quick to think that she moving too swift for a man's sake. He notice her landing quiet on her feet. "Like a cat," he say.

"Don't call me that."

"But is it not uncanny?"

"What?"

"You jump from all the way up there. Ten and one, ten and six . . . seven . . . ten and eight rungs on that ladder. Then look at you landing like a feather."

"Everything to you is uncanny."

"Not everything, just you."

"I know you think I like hearing all the time how strange you find me. But I don't."

"By the gods, girl." Keme raise his hands as if expecting a blow. He turn around before she can study his face. "I know I once called you a horse lord, but Sogolon."

"Yes, I choose to live in horseshit. Just like how everybody here get to choose what they want."

"I've heard of your fortunes, lately. How sorry I am, Sogolon."

"Fortunes? Like I lose a game? Yeah, the kick to my forehead did feel like three moves on a board."

"I'm so—"

"I don't need your sorry."

"Of course. Sogolon never need anything."

"I need one thing. For you to take your wit and fuck off with it."

"Fuck the gods for this vile temper!"

"Gods can go fuck themselves too!"

"Sogolon!"

"What you want?"

"I . . . I . . . now you've flustered me. I forget why I come."

"Then leave."

"What kind of strangeness get inside you?"

"I don't know. Is it different from the last strangeness you find? All you seem to look for in me is strangeness. In what way is Sogolon the freak this week? What new curse you find that you can tell your friends in the floating bar?"

"By the gods, how you misjudge me."

"I think I judge everybody just right. For the first time."

"In the court of Sogolon, where all are judged guilty. How will you punish us?" he say with a smile.

"Fuck off."

"Do not speak to me that way."

"Or else? Which side of my face you want to punch? Maybe a kick. How my belly look? How about a bruise over the left eye to match the one over my right one?"

"By the gods, no. Sogolon."

"What you want, guard?" she shout.

"Alaya is vanished."

"What?"

"Two days ago some people in the tavern called him a manwitch for writing words. We tell him it is safer if he leave, and he look at us like we are the ones calling him a witch. Nobody answer his door two days now."

"Look like he run."

"Not like him."

"Nothing is like it is."

"Nobody is behaving true."

"That is not what I say. Maybe everybody behaving true for once."

"Who did this to you? The princess? Why?"

"It don't matter."

He stare at her for a long time until she look away.

"Now Beremu tell me they are dismissing the lions. The new King want his own imperial guard."

"Sangomin?"

"No. Me. And a few others chosen by the Aesi."

"At least you getting what you always want. Praise the gods."

"Fuck the gods, Sogolon. I don't know what times

are these," he say and sit down in a pile of hay as if the strength just get knocked out of him.

"You still think you fighting for what worth fighting for?"

"You think you've cut me enough for one night?"

She bow her head, but no words come. She feel the rain drawing her, so she go to the stable door. The air is crisp, cold, and thick with spray. She close her eyes and let it wash her face. Keme take a deep breath.

"The gods are wise, and the gods are stupid," she say.

"That sound like old woman wisdom."

"I know the things that old woman know."

"It brings you no happiness?"

She laugh.

"What?"

"I never have a happy day ever."

"That is the most piteous thing I ever did hear."

"I not sad about it."

"So you say."

"Look like we all here at the grace of the prince. The princess too."

"Careful. The prince is to be the King and the princess, the King Sister. Word is the King already take a new name."

I have a few names for them, she think but don't say.

"Maybe the same people making you rise, making Alaya fall."

"Speak of what you know, woman."

Something come to the tip of her tongue and she swallow it back down. She don't want to ask him again what he want. Though his voice is still like river flow. The rain spray is making her clothes wet but she is still standing there, feeling that one spot of peace.

"You getting wet."

"That is what rain do. Get people wet."

"Sogolon."

She jump. He is right beside her. She didn't hear him get up. His helmet is in his hands and his hair is wild. The armor make him taller.

"They've been rounding up witches, so many women plotting that the King die early. Word was—"

"Word from who? If there is a word, then somebody saying it."

"Word from the people. The people think that the King's days were cut short because witchcraft let loose in the kingdom. They round up twenty yesterday."

"If a man look at anybody and call her witch then she is a witch. Go look at that stone and call it a witch so you can throw it in a dungeon."

"I think—"

"Don't worry your head, thinking is not for you. You a guard now. Doing is all you do."

"Fuck yourself, girl."

"Practicing what you going say to Alaya when they catch him? 'My friend, how I love you, but I love my ambition more.'"

"I really could strike you."

"For the last time, guard, why you come?" Sogolon ask.

"Because nobody is around to make me feel like a flea."

"Not that what wives do?"

"You do better to ask my father about my wife. He the one who pick her."

"You just fat her up with children."

"Don't speak of things you know nothing about, girl. You don't like when I do it to you."

She can't bring herself to say anything like sorry. So she hang in silence instead.

"Nobody care about my ambition here. I am just a peasant that slip through some crack they forgot to seal. You hate it. At least that is something."

She grins.

"At least I get a laugh out of those lips," Keme say.

"That is no laugh."

"That is something. You will be restored to the princess palace soon. And then she will be the King Sister screaming at you. You say nothing."

"Nothing to say. It is all their will, truth?"

He touch her shoulder. She jump and he move his hand away just as quick.

"There is a power in you, Sogolon."

"Spite the gods if this man call me strange again."

"I didn't say strange. I say power. One day you will see it."

"You turn prophet now?"

"Maybe. Look, call me a fool. But I see people pretending power all the time. I know what it look like when somebody don't have it."

"The world is what it is," she say. He nod and they both stare at lightning far off.

Maybe nobody is looking, in all the fuss over the King's death and burial, and the hunting down of witches. Or maybe nobody is looking at the point where night is an old woman and day just a baby, the point where gods of sky and gods from underground show divine favor and lay stone upon stone, stones too heavy for a hundred slaves to lift. That is what the headwoman say about Prince Likud's palace when she bring scraps to Sogolon to see how she fare. That gods and divine craftsmen finish the prince's castle overnight, for that is the way for every house of the King and no living men could ever place stones so huge in walls so high. Maybe the gods showing this new King much favor, she also say, but Sogolon wonder who in the living shit she speaking to. I don't know who in the living shit you speaking to, she say to the headwoman, who raise her hand to strike her.

"Lay that hand on me and I promise you, you won't get it back," she say. The headwoman taken aback.

"Wh-what you say?"

"Your ears deaf or your mind slow?"

"The impertinence! You think I would lower myself to come give you food the dogs don't want? You lucky this headwoman come to bring you glad tidings."

"Of what?"

"Of Her Highness, soon to be Her Excellency, deciding to forgive you and indeed show you favor. I was to tell you that you returning to the royal household, but maybe I should tell them that no part of you change."

"Suit yourself, headwoman."

"You don't care?"

"I don't care if you walk back, trip, burst your head on stone, and bleed to death."

The headwoman's jaw drop so low that she cover her mouth. Then she giggle, though her eyes fill with so much distress that tears well up. She bite herself but the giggle force itself out. She jerk and cover her mouth, but can't stop it. The headwoman cough and choke but still can't stop giggling. She run out.

The morning of the coronation, masters of the stable come for the white horses to drape them in white and gold fabric. The stable busier for the crowning than the burial. Best for Sogolon to stay out of the way, so she keep to her perch. For in they come, slow graceful horses with two humps, of the like she never see before, with riders like nomads. Horses taller than trees, with manes that reach the floor, and hair bushing up their hooves. Chariots with two, three, and four horses, including one made of gold and two made of ivory. A cart carrying players and another carrying horns longer than the cart and also made of ivory, that take two men each to lift. Five elephants, a prophet who travel by ox, and warriors from Juba on rhinoceros, and from Dolingo in a massive wagon scraping the ceiling of the stable, pulled by men.

Escorts, guards, horsemen, knights, and servants all leave their beasts by the guardhouse, for this is not a place for people of the court. But several times some disembark in the stable and not the guardhouse. Men and women who didn't earn the grace to be in the radiance of the soon-to-be King. Sogolon watch in hiding on high, and hear their grumbling, their disagreement, and their blasphemy. Two cousins dressed like monks who not happy one bit about this horrible banishment, but already see some new virgin at court to sink their cock into. A brother of a cousin of an uncle who nine generations before try to seize the throne from the house of Akum and now live in inglorious banishment in the Purple City. A prince on a chariot who is magnificent because he say that he is magnificent and will see title now that a new King with sense will sit on the throne. Another cousin who is thinking that this invitation means a restoration of favor until he hear that his horses are to take him to the stable and not the throne room. Four men and three women who grumble and cuss that the family of the Kwash Kagar's wife should be at the side of the throne, not here with the field mice. A blacksmith who joke with the stable hands that he don't know why he is here, but hear that the first ruler from the house of the Akum is called the Blacksmith King.

Around noon Sogolon hear wings flap and a wind, cold and quick. She is rubbing the neck of a black

horse when he step in alone. The Aesi. The urges to
slip away and to stand firm both come over her. He
halt when he see her, surprised she is in the stables.
This is what you come to? he seem to ask but don't.

"That one will do," he say. She step out of his way.

"The gods don't look down on honest work, young
Sogolon," he say.

This is not my work. It coming to her mouth, she
can feel it in her mouth, ready to leave, but it don't.

"A saddle, girl."

That is not her work. The saddle in her hands before she think better of it and he watch her saddle
the horse. Before he mount, the Aesi stop and grab
Sogolon by the cheek, not hard, but firm. She grab
his hands and struggle, but he is a rock. He stare at
her and she stare back, even with her mind wanting
to do something else. The Aesi is on his horse and out
the gate before she realize he let go. And still a while
after before she stop feeling his grip on her face. Little
after that a headache hit her so hard that she collapse
in a pile of hay. She press her temples but the pain is
throbbing from her forehead as if some demon is forcing his way out. She crawl over to the nearest wood
post and bang her forehead against it until her mind
go dark.

Sogolon tell herself that nobody would permit her to
the ceremony, so she should be neither angry nor
sad. And when it do come to pass that nobody take

notice of her, Sogolon tell herself over and over to be neither. And over and over she repeat it until the thought become words, and the words become fierce, so fierce that when she grab a bowl full of water and fling it against the wall and it shatter with a crash that rile up the horses, two stable boys rush back in shouting where is the fire. Instead they scowl at the girl, for they know she is there by royal order, but also that she have no business in this place.

At least she can ride a horse, is what she want to say. Indeed, she should just grab any horse and put distance between herself and Fasisi, for it was never her choice to come, nor is it her wish to stay. And the princess say to more people than her that she is not a slave. But if she can't move of her own free will and she is not a slave, then she must be a prisoner. But girl, all your life you been bound to something or by someone. Chains been on you so long that you believe the shackle is part of your neck. **Maybe Keme did come around to free you,** say a voice that sound like her. She would rather just see him naked, to speak truth. To look at him rather than to want from him. Him walking to her naked with a slow stride. His broad smile, and sweaty shoulders, and head with a helmet on. Off. Blocking cock with his shield then not blocking it, his chest catching sun, his bare legs about to leap off the banks into the river. Sogolon thinking to stop herself, but **stop** is just a word from her mouth, or a mark on Olu's floor, not something to do. He marching across her mind.

No, he is on horse and marching past her door. The horse and him almost one, for they wearing the same robes. The horse draped in that white and gold. A strip running from mouth to ear and a gold headpiece above that, and the rest of the fabric wrapping his neck, covering all the way to his tail, and as long as his ankles. At the ankle, stripes of gold and white with shiny diamonds. Keme, the same in white and gold stripes under a full suit of chain mail, his helmet in white silver and so broad and high that it rest on his shoulders and reach down to his chest. She watch as the procession swallow him up.

Sogolon run. Out into the courtyard, down the trail still dusty from marching soldiers. She hear the far-off rumble outside of the procession long gone and as she come to the grand gate and guardhouse, notice that nobody is there but sentries stationed at the gate and the battlements. She at the slot to let herself out when guards begin to open the gate. Four men approach carrying a covered palanquin and as they pass Sogolon, stop. She pull the curtains apart and stick her head out. She, Queen Wutu, last wife of Kwash Kagar. Sogolon mark how she don't look much older than her, just a girl under the burden of so much gold jewelry. Her face still round, her cheeks still full, but her eyes tired.

"I don't know you," she say.

"Your Excellency," Sogolon say and kneel quick.

"No. Not anymore. Not by the time the day go out. Then I just a woman."

Queen Wutu tap the handrail and the men lower the palanquin to the ground. The Queen point to the wide seat.

"Let us be women together, then," she say and she bid Sogolon to climb in.

"I smell like a horse, Excellency," she say.

"The only beast in this compound that I can stand," she say.

The men take lesser-known roads and reach the city center before the procession. Sogolon expect the Queen to leave the palanquin, but she stay within, pulling back a curtain to see outside, while unseen in the shade. From there they see the platform, covered in red velvet, leopard skin, and zebra skin, while seven elders stand on the platform chanting and singing and burning sacred herbs. One elder brush his large feather broom over the stool in the center of the platform, and another drape it in leather skin.

"Ceremony of the leopard skin is here," the Queen say. "Then one ceremony of the bark cloth, down in the Baganda district, one for the calfskin in the blacksmith's row, and the crowning on his father's throne before they burn it."

Drums and horns move in close, while kora and lute follow. Then dancers, not in masks but wearing talismans on arms, elbows, neck, and waist, and spinning in mushrooming pantaloons that fill up with air and lift them off the ground to land slow. The dancers leap higher and spin faster, clearing the way of dust and spirits. Following them, soldiers in ceremonial armor, red chain mail for the troop on the left, green for the troop on the right. They split and march around both sides of the platform. Taking their place at the side of the platform too, the princess and consort, and Prince Likud's twin boys. And others close in blood to the house of Akum. The drums stop thundering, but the horns continue to blow.

Two fetish priests, both painted blue, lead the way, chanting and throwing smoke, and then it is him, Prince Likud, in a silent march wearing nothing but palm oil. He stand at the foot of the steps, straight and looking ahead, his skin dark like burnt wood and shiny. The prince is a tall and strong-looking man, but he is thin and women of the court seeking to be concubines make promises aloud to nobody that they will fatten him up soon. Beside the twins is a woman Sogolon never see before, but who she is guessing is his wife, soon to be Queen. Two of the elders, both in headdresses of feathers and gold, take the prince by both hands and shout that he is no prince, no father, no son, no one. No prince, no father, no son, no one, until he is right before the stool draped in leopard skin. Then they speak for long in a tongue Sogolon don't know.

"The tongue of priests, kings, and gods," Queen Wutu whisper. "Only they know how to speak it. None of them ever teach it to me."

Sogolon don't think to say nothing to her, for until this prince is crowned she is sitting beside a Queen. Sitting so close that their arms touch, and this Queen

don't seem to notice. Let us be women together, she
did say, but Sogolon can't take those words to mean
anything.

"Sword-bearers, soldiers, guards, soul washers,
drummers, horn blowers, umbrella men, priests,
chiefs, kings of the lower lands, none of them come
to see me marry the King," the Queen say.

The two elders, still holding Prince Likud's arms,
turn him around to sit on the stool. The drummers,
hundreds of them, beat harder and faster, making the
ground shake and waking up the gods of the underworld and the spirits of the land, while the horn blowers blow loud enough to reach gods of sky.

"He is incomplete until he sit on the stool, they
saying," Queen Wutu say, even though she say before
that she don't understand their tongue.

The dancers in mushroom pantaloons spin and
spin until they lift off the ground again. Prince Likud
close his eyes and the elders guide him to the stool.
Another elder standing behind the stool, remove the
leopard skin and hold it up. The elders release the
prince, for he must by himself sit, with the mystic
coolness that every wise and strong king must have.
He must not hesitate or falter, and he must resist the
urge to wave his hand behind him to make sure it is
there. Prince Likud sit in one movement. The drums
and horns stop. The people cheer, chant, and sing,
and the drums and horns return. The elder holding
the leopard skin drape it over the prince's shoulders.
Mystic coolness. The prince's face show nothing.

"Not a king, not yet," Queen Wutu say.

"Yes, Your Excellency."

"If you want to follow to the Baganda district, don't let me stop you. But I go back to the palace until I am no longer Queen. You wish to go?"

"No, Your Excellency."

"Like me, you done see enough."

They wait for the prince, now wearing leopard skin, to leave the platform with the elders. As soon as the family leave, Queen Wutu tap the handrail.

The prince return to the royal enclosure as King, under the new name Kwash Moki, meaning **he who will still the winds.** Princess Emini return as the King Sister, but for that there is no crown. Sogolon return to her bed of rugs and hay. In half sleep her mind run on the twins, on how they are crown princes now, and all she can hope for is that they long forget her, or they gone past bored with seeking revenge on a bush girl. Celebrations for the new King go on for three quartermoons, with the stable overflowing, emptying, then overflowing again with people and beasts. Sometimes the feasting get so large that it spill into the stalls, with drunk men and loud women eating and drinking on the grounds, and tossing meat, bread, and wine. More often than not Sogolon wake up to the sound coming from a dim corner of fucking; men, women fucking whoever in the dark. Royal inside commoner. Priest atop sorcerer.

Friend astride foe. Chief and girl who don't want his cock. And then there would be feasting again, or the departure of somebody whom this new King and kingdom has left most bitter. The stable keepers, when they get used to her, start to supply Sogolon with food. Before the celebrations end, Sogolon start grooming the horses to earn her stay.

Nobody from the King Sister's palace ever come for her again.

NINE

Bobo, the white one. He is the one she talk to when the hands take leave and the stable is empty, except that the stable is never empty. More nights than not it fill with the most agreeable beasts in the whole kingdom, more pleasant than any man she ever meet. **Will ever meet,** say a voice that sound like her. She lose count of how many quartermoons back she realize that this is the most agreeable place she ever stay. And horses the most agreeable company. If horse could shapeshift like lions, then maybe that person would be the perfect friend, or maybe all that is man would ruin all that is horse. She talk to all the horses as she feed and clean them. But Bobo, the white horse with the black patch on his left eye, is the one who listen. Sometimes he reply. Talk of people he don't find to his liking rile him up, especially Keme, maybe because Bobo is male too, and he don't want to hear of anybody else when she brushing his hair. But she would ask him a question like, Should I present myself to the King Sister even though she don't ask for me, and he will shake his head fierce. A strong no.

"Because she don't want me to come, or you don't want me to go?"

He whinny and swish his tail as an answer. She feed him hay and, when the stable hands leave, sugar. It is enough to make Sidiki, the horse in the next stall, jealous. He kick the back wall, threatening to bust through the stable itself unless she give him some sugar too. Demanding, these horses. But their demands feel simple, and simple is perfect for a girl reducing herself. The girl was once in the termite house, but that girl is looking for a way out. A way higher than the dirt her brothers stomp her down into. Now see the girl who wake up for the horses, who mark a day's passing through which horses leave and which horses come back, who eat two times a day, who wash once a quartermoon if she feel to, who take notice of no one, and even when she do, don't listen, and even when she hear, don't care, who then go to sleep in fresh hay to wake up and do it again. And if she do visit the dream jungle, she forget as soon as the sun come up. Dreams that she remember, she tell to Bobo, who whistle, neigh, whinny, or just nod and rub his head against her when he sensing sadness.

"No, the lioness with no belly don't come back. Different dream this time," she say. "Near all of it gone, Bobo. My mind don't want to remember it. Maybe I dream I dead. Or maybe I dream blasphemy."

The horse swish his tail.

Time is the cobra, coiling and coiling. She feeling it in the stable, even as the stable give her peace. It is a moon and a half since Kwash Moki made King. Night it is now, and the first time she leaving the stable in a while, so she take a small oil lamp and go. Sogolon know where she is going but don't know why. **Yes, you know,** say the voice that sound like her. Outside, the night is shadow-blue and gray, but white stones in the paths glow. The tall, thin castle is a stick in the dark. She walk past the back door to a window.

"Commander? Commander? Olu?"

His door usually open, but she climb through the window. She almost fight with the curtains the last time, which is why she notice quick that they are all gone. All the walls and doors look strange. Sogolon hold the lamp right to the surface and see why. The writings and markings done gone. All the tapestries gone and all the rugs too. She kneel to check the floor but everywhere is clean, even under the chairs and stools, and the one rug still in the room. Olu's bed-chamber is the same, no bed, no rugs, some sheets, and the one bowl that he don't cover in writing. No Olu. She think to search one more room, but he is gone. Or taken. Or vanish into the air. Or something else. It make her . . . angry is not the word, for she also sad and afraid. And lonely, something that stay behind her in the stable but lap around her now. Leave is what she must do, leave now. Leave the way she come. She try to push herself up to the window but the planks right by the wall wobble. She feel along the edge of the wood until it pull free. Words frantic but clear on the underside of the wood. Sogolon set herself to climb through the window when faint voices come upon her. Guards. She blow out the lamp and wait until they pass.

Back in the stable, and under more light, the writing on the plank tell her too much and not enough.

This King is coming ... own alone ...
and the Aesi ... Gods know why
Jeleza, Jeleza, Jeleza

She read it five times before she notice that he write the words in blood.

Everything she would want to know about the happenings of court Sogolon learn from the movement of horses. A white horse for Queen Mother Wutu, dressed in blue and gold finery for a quick wedding ceremony, and given that is only one horse, a quiet one. Three horses from Wakadishu that leave the same night with riders hissing and cursing. One moon later, two horses from Wakadishu and two riders who didn't come back. A horse late at night for a knight who the headwoman see off with harsh whispers. Two young horses dead from slashes and stabs up down and crossway, horses stolen out in the morning by three who walk with the twin princes. A horse long gone to Kalindar many moons ago just coming back. And a black horse that she rest

and prepare for two nights' ride, for the Aesi, alone.
A horse for climbing mountains, is the only request
he send, and the only mountain two nights away
have Mantha sitting on top. Many horses leaving
that don't come back. One gone in finery, only for
somebody to bring back the horse the next afternoon
and tell her to take off everything of gold before the
horse leave again. A mule leaving buckling under salt,
another arriving buckling under gold. Chariots for
the princes.

The problem with a simple life is that the repeti-
tion is endless. The same every day is making Sogolon
bored. Not every boredom is the same, but what kind
of living is this where she can tell the many boredoms
apart? She remember that time before, when she meet
Olu on the way to the library even though there is no
tongue she could read. But now she read a little. The
library is a farther walk from the stable. Olu would
read a book in a day and forget it by the following
dusk. She don't know enough words to read a book
in a day, but love the idea of forgetting. And beginning again. Maybe she will walk in with a stern face,
and the book master will leave her alone as she grab
a scroll, or something bound in leather.

Sogolon walk along a covered pathway when a
scrambling along the ceiling start to follow her. A
gasp leave her mouth, and she try to walk faster. Not
run, for running would mean that whatever is behind her is real. But the scrambling on the ceiling getting closer and chilling her so hard that she shudder.

Running ahead of the scuttle is the shriek. Sogolon run to the library doors, looking up once to see the darkchild catching up to her, then hopping ahead. If only she could get to the doors. Nothing about the library ever say it was safe, but if she could only get to the door. The boy with red ochre skin hop onto the path and spread his fingers, each popping a claw as long as the whole hand.

Then they stop. They don't just halt moving, they halt everything. The red ochre boy, who raise his right foot to run, still have the right foot off the ground, the left foot on his toes and ready to pounce, both arms open and his smile wicked, wide and stiff. The darkchild in a crouch, but he don't move either. Now footsteps is coming behind her.

"If you're not frightened yet, make no sense to be frightened now," he say. The Aesi. "Where you head?"

"The library."

"Why?"

"A book."

"You can read?"

"No."

He walk a few paces ahead of her before he stop.

"Hope you are a better reader than liar. Come then, come get your book."

As she pass the red ochre boy she shudder again. He don't move, not at all.

"What you do to them?" Sogolon ask.

"Why you think it's me?" the Aesi ask.

"I don't think it."

The Aesi laugh as he stop at the doorway.

"The blue scrolls will bore you. All this stuff about politics and money."

"And the red scrolls are about what? Squatting to drop a baby?"

He laugh again. They go inside. She turn back once to see two of them still there, not moving. She look twice before she see that the book master not moving either.

"Do you know where Kwash comes from? The title, not the—"

"I know you mean the title," Sogolon say.

"Of course. Well?"

"No."

"It comes from the founder of the line of kings. Not a man, a woman. Back when the world was young it was custom for a man to put the name of his mother before his own. Kwash was the mother of the blood of all kings, so we put the mother's name before all other names. Of course that knowledge only live in parchment and paper, not even on the lips of griots. All great kingdoms come from the great mother."

"She a Queen?"

"Nobody know."

"Fitting."

"Listen to you, you already sound like life leave you fed up."

"People talk a lot in Fasisi."

"And saying nothing?"

"You the one saying that."

"You are a peculiar one, surely you know."

"I know man keep calling me strange. I not strange. Strange is . . . strange is . . . the princess. The next king not supposed to be her son?"

"Of course. That is tradition."

"Then how come she not regent until she give birth to a king? When she give birth to a son this King going leave?"

"So you have been reading the blue scrolls," he say, laughing. "What you know about the regent?"

"I listen."

"To who?"

"And why you call her the King Sister when she is Queen Mother? Sound like what she is instead of what she do. And man always get call by what they do even if all they do is be first. But the King didn't come first, not even in birth."

He approach her, close enough to see eyes she never see on either woman or man. Almost green, they look. He stare at her long but look away first.

"Her mind won't move," he say, but low, talking to himself. He mutter it again twice before he see that she hear.

"It not supposed to go anywhere," she say.

"Indeed. Indeed."

"The freak children keep following me."

"The Sangomin? Do they have reason?"

"Ask them. But tell them to stop following me."

He turn to leave, but stop and say, "Look for something bound in leather."

"Who is Jeleza?"

Quick, quicker than a blink, but she see it. That he pause before the steps right as she say Jeleza. But he keep walking as he answer her.

"Jeleza? A whore's name. So common in the Ibiku section that you might as well say girl."

"Oh."

"One of Commander Olu's sluts, so you—"

"Where Commander Olu gone?"

"What is his whereabouts to you?"

Sogolon say nothing.

"Time is a cobra. Coiling and coiling," he say.

As soon as he pass them, the red ochre boy run to a stop, all confused, then run again. What become of the darkchild, she don't see. Sogolon lose her appetite for books and is about to leave when her head light afire again, painful, but not as heavy as before. She grab a pillar to steady herself, but the agony vanish in just a few blinks. The Aesi. Him it must be. He is working craft on her, but her mind won't move.

When they come for night horses she is watching stars on the roof. First the commotion sound like a fire, but as Sogolon go to the latch door, it sound like thieves. But who would dare steal from the King and how would they pass the guards of the royal enclosure double in number since the coronation?

"You have to take the reins, Excellency!" the head-woman say.

"Ride the damn horse myself? Where is the caravan? Where is my chariot? No," say Emini.

"This faster than a chariot, King Sister."

"This King will have me like a dog? Is that what I am lowering myself to?"

"You have friends, King Sister. Some still know the King Sister rule—"

"Watch your mouth. That is blasphemy."

"Excellency, we must go."

The King Sister Emini standing in a long black cape while the women-in-waiting fuss around her.

"No dress, no slippers, no food, no nothing?"

"All is prepared, Excellency, we have—"

"No. This bastard will know there is one in Fasisi who is not a coward."

"You need to get out!" the headwoman shout.

Even Sogolon jump. The waiting women silent.

"Please, Your Excellency. Please."

A shout and a commotion, the scrape of swords drawn and the thump thump thump of arrows hitting bodies and bodies hitting the ground. Her two guard don't draw their swords before so many arrows hit their face that there is no more face. Her women scream, then her women all fall to the floor. The King Sister is stiff. She try to stand tall but her knees buckle a little and she grab the horse to steady herself.

"You killed them!"

"Every woman will be seen to her bed and will rise tomorrow," say the Aesi.

"Everybody scared of witchcraft when they should be scared of you."

"They return you to your own chambers, Excellency. Escort her back," he say.

Sogolon hear the King Sister breathe out heavy and see her shoulders slump. The soldiers clear a way and not a single one move until she leave. The Aesi's red cape is as wide and flowing as the King Sister's. Why do nobody burn in this heat? she think, but then he look up. She dodge out of his view quick.

In two dawns, it is all that people at court whisper when they fear being overheard, and joke when they don't. The stable hands recount what they hear in the streets. One of them start to sing a song about how many men get trapped in her royal koo, but stop when they see Sogolon brushing a white horse, all silent. The prince consort, he don't show his face, one of them say.

"Then you would show yours?"

"How you mean?"

"How you mean how I mean, the meaning clear, yeye boy."

"Clear it for him, brother."

"Maybe King Sister born slut, maybe she turn whore. Or this here prince not no prince in the royal bed."

"The royal spear not even a dagger. Not even a toothpick."

"Not so I hear. Dagger plenty fine, but he can't stab nothing."

"Nothing go so. Man can do the stabbing, but sperm might as well be piss."

Laughter.

"Perhaps the King Sister barren?"

"Then he would be fucking the barracks full, not she, fool. Plus this here prince have plenty concubine, yet not one son. Not one. Not even a daughter."

"They arrest General Asafa yesterday."

"Why? He station in the Blood Swamp. Near two moons' ride."

"'Cause he be General Third Leg is why."

"And what, it stretch all the way up north to slap her poomsy?"

"So the word go in Baganda. They arrest him in the Blood Swamp."

"What a world. Man going burn because he cock too long. What a world."

Three mornings later they come for her. Nobody grab her or even call her name. They march right up to the foot of the ladder and wait. That frighten her more. She can't dress so she wrap herself in the blanket. Coming down, she almost slip off the ladder. Guards in red armor. A cold morning and her teeth chatter. She think of women who have different clothes to wear for the different things they get called for, and try not to look down at the blanket. Uneasiness make her tongue slip, and the chattering teeth getting louder, because the morning cold, she think. Because the morning cold. There is no fault with me, she promise herself. "Where are the lions?" she ask, but no guard answer her. For the better, she think, for with the times being the times, she might not like the answer. Four guards, two in front and two behind. She try to keep up with the march but have to trot several times. Most of the time she watch only the backs of the guards in front, but at times she look away and see people of court watching her. Men and women, some she see before. Some stare, some glare, some look away. Eyes on her making her feel guilty of something everybody is hiding from her. Some of the women she remember from the princess throne room. King Sister. Whatever it is that they now call her.

Rumor spread by voice, pigeon, and crow. Not by drum, for drums would make such tidings official. And word is that they calling it an inquest, not a trial. They, the counsel. Commander Olu is the first name they call alongside the King Sister, but victim is what they call him, not perpetrator, for she take advantage of his disappearing memory. And his love of whores, say a female voice. Rumor is news and news is rumor. How we going to fight any war if the King execute every cock that fuck her? That mean all the mightiest warriors in the kingdom. A general of the Green Army. Three warriors from the Red. Two berserkers, who never wear clothes, so the whole of Fasisi know why she choose them. Some even see wisdom in breeding with a warrior instead of a prince. But none

in a chief in the West from the Purple City, or two
men of the King's chamber, including one who know
him from childhood. Or that apprentice to a fetish
priest, or that apprentice to a griot. Maybe that one
fuck her with verse, say another voice that wind keeps
blowing to her ears. Even Olu is the Butcher of Bornu.
But nobody know what they accuse her of, since this
is an inquest and not a trial. The bewitching koo.
Many a woman and a few men already see the executioner's blade for witchcraft against Ancestor Kagar
and other people. Many a husband have been getting
rid of wife, wife getting rid of mistress, mother of
daughter, and Sangomin against anybody they divine
to be witch-born or witch-bound. The fear infect the
people. The fear infect the court. And still nobody
can find Commander Olu.

The guards take her past the arch standing in front
of Kwash Moki's castle. Taller than any castle, higher
than she can guess, maybe more than ten and five
men standing on shoulders. A road leading straight
through it to his castle. Red Guards flanking it
all the way up to the steps. They lead her to the archives, the first time she seeing it. Musty dust floating
on the sun rays. A wide space full of books, scrolls,
and papers stacked from the ground to ceiling, like
a library nobody use. Not just books, but also birth,
death, and masquerade masks, gold bracelets, spears,
and arrowpoints. Glass jars on high shelves with
red, green, and blue fluids, maps on a faraway wall,
and in a corner, robes, capes, tunics, and chain mail

of old kings. They pass a shelf full of stones, busts, and bowls, all floating above the board. They walk between pillars covered in patterns, glyphs, and words, some she recognize. The crunch of the soldiers' metal and leather on the mortar floor. By the stairs, a sleeping lion. An archway and a door already open. Diviners, priests, noblemen, chiefs, and elders waiting for her.

Ten and two men in all. Some sitting on stools, some sitting on cushions, none telling her to sit. Most of them old, two as young as the King, but none younger. One on a stool, with mighty white hair and a beard just as long, another bald and hunchback with smoke coming out of his mouth, another tall and skinny, his arms like branches.

"You the one they call Sogolon? What is your name?" say a noble.

"You just call it," Sogolon say.

One of the men, a diviner, walk up to her holding an iron plate with ashes and twigs and an eggshell burning. He walk around her twice, then blow the foul smoke in her face. She try to fight the cough but fail.

"This room have the power to challenge a king, little girl, so treat yourself to a favor and fear us," say the one.

"Fear provide as good a testimony as torture, man from Malakal," the white hair one say, though nobody show any sign that they agree. "How long you stay with the King Sister, Sogolon?"

These men making her afraid. Then angry that she is afraid. Then afraid of what she might say because she is too angry. She don't want to tremble or for her voice to quiver, for they will know they are the cause of it.

"Six moons."

"How it is that you stay with her?"

"Mistress Komwono gift me to her."

"Mistress Komwono?"

The men turn to each other and talk in a mumble.

The man from Malakal look straight at her. "Talk true, girl. You are no gift to the King Sister. This mistress present you to the throne, but the King Sister take you for her own use."

"Well, she look more like a milkmaid than a throne room guard, brother," say the white hair one.

"I not your brother. As for you, girl, why you? You play any instrument? Sing any song? You know any verse, girl? You have skills in midwifery or even know how to clean silver? You have any skill with a weapon to protect her?"

"N—"

"No. The answer to all these is no. So what we have here is a nothing girl. A girl that if the princess make her into something, she would be grateful indeed."

"You yap so much, maybe you are the witness and she is the inquisitor. Brother."

"All the years this elder been eldering and you don't pick up much wisdom, friend. I taking us somewhere."

"Wherever you flying, perch soon, brother."

He approach her.

"Did you not injure Prince Abeke?"

"Prince who?"

"Only the second in line to the throne, girl. You injured him with a stick and would meet justice had the King Sister not taken you in. Do you deny any of this?"

"I didn't injure nobody. His father—"

"Don't even dare!" he shout.

Sogolon jump.

"Don't dare think you can call His Excellency anything other than King."

The white hair man sigh, wondering how much more of this he have to take.

"I say to perch, brother," he say.

"You are in the King Sister's debt. Perfect girl to keep her secrets."

"She don't tell me nothing."

"Wait until I ask a question to talk."

The bald hunchback one rise, his cane wobbling. He walk not to her, but to the window. Only when he get there do Sogolon notice that she can see right through him.

"A woman don't have to speak to you to tell you something, little Sogolon. You was a woman of the bedchamber. How come we fetch you from the stables?" he ask.

"I . . . I . . . the . . . the princess, the King Sister grow tired of me."

"So it go?"

"Yes."

"Not so other women say, but everybody know how woman lie, not so?"

Sogolon don't have no answer.

"She banish you for theft, girl. Don't waste our time. We are talking before that."

"I don't know nothing."

"You don't—"

"Scala. Everybody appreciate that you so dedicated to the elders that not even death will keep you from duty. But living affairs don't concern you. Now, girl, we asking what you see, not what you know," the man from Malakal say.

"I don't see—"

"You not blind. A fool, maybe, but your eyes have use."

"Or perhaps afraid," say the white hair one. "You have nothing to fear. Lady Emini will be stripped of King-Sisterhood. It is no treason or blasphemy to speak out against her."

So say the hunchback ghost, "Kantu the berserker? General Diamante? Commander Olu? So many virgins that one devirgin. In my day there was competition between—"

"Scala! Shut up!"

"I don't know them men," Sogolon say.

"But you see others. Listen, girl, again, it's no treason to speak against the King Sister, but to be false is to be treacherous to all that is good, and all that is good is of the King. You understand? Nobody here care about the adultery, let aggriever and aggrieved sort out their own mess. But we cannot have a bastard on the throne just to keep the house of Akum in power."

"If is the end of the line is the end of the line," say the man from Malakal with a wicked smile.

"That is not what is happening, friend. We already have Kwash Moki as King and he is no son of a sister. The law is the law. If there is no sister, and Ancestor Kagar have none, the next in line is the son of the King. If his sister produce a son, then he is the next King. If she having a bastard, then she violating the rule of gods to keep the throne not in the house of Akum, but her very own roof. You can cuckold a man but you cannot cuckold the kingdom. A plot to seize the crown is treason against the crown. If you lie or we find you in league, then you commit treason too. Besides, the only kind of woman who trade in secret is witch. So again, little girl, what did you see?"

In her mind is a name for these shrivel-cock buckets of shit that keep calling her girl.

"I don't see nothing. Sirs."

"Send her to the Aesi. Let him get what he want out of her," the man from Malakal say. The hunchback nod, agreeing.

They leave her in a room in a temple off the royal enclosure. The room is misty and white, but green also, a forest with plants reaching, spreading, snaking, coiling, popping yellow flowers, and standing still. No windows but inside is bright as day. Glass ceilings resting on a wood frame, Sogolon never see the like, not like the beads in all colors that people wear, but like the windows she kept tapping, thinking nothing is there. She hear a flutter and there he is in the room, though she don't see him come in. She don't see a door either, but know she come through one. He point to two stools in the clearing and tell her to sit.

"You think it will rain tonight?" he ask.

"I . . ."

"Speak up, child."

"I . . . I don't know."

"No? Even the market woman reads the clouds before she sets out."

"Never have a reason to look up in the sky," she say.

"Little girl, we both know that is not true. Are you not a farm girl? How else does one tell the beginning or end of days?"

She don't answer.

"Such a refreshing rudeness in you," he say. "Ignorant, but refreshing."

Sogolon enter the room expecting anything. Questions that cut into her flesh. Or a knife. She don't know what this is, but it feel like circling. **Turn him into something in your head, reduce him, ask yourself why he only wear red and black and if he look like a fool in pink,** say the voice that sound like her. I didn't see nothing, she say to herself. That is what she going to say. Not that she loyal to this King

Sister, surely he must know of how she mistreat her.
Then she think of what she do know, which is not
much really, nothing that the lowborn is required to
make any sense of, and what she really want is peace.
No, that is not what she want.

"Be here now, child," he say, and raise an eyebrow
because he know a response was coming to her lips.

He grab her hands with one hand, and she jump.
The other hand at her jaw, forcing her to face him as
he stare deep. She can't look away because his hand is
still on her face. She try not to blink, but then her eyes
start to burn. Sogolon don't know what he is doing,
but know he is doing it. Your mind won't move. She
remember him saying such. Sogolon try to stare right
back at him but the brown in his eyes gone leaving
white. Answer me, girl, you think it will rain tonight?
he ask. She hear him ask it—she know he ask it, but
his lips didn't move. He staring deeper, moving in
closer and she try to stare back, but the plants start
changing, yellow flowers turning purple then gray,
snaking plants twisting and coiling and reaching for
her, but he have her hand and her neck. He is squeezing her hand now, hurting her. She try to pull away
but his grip too firm. She won't complain, she won't
cry, she won't scream. She can feel a heat at the back
of her head moving to the side and making her left
ear burn. The plants turn green again, but he is slapping her forehead, one two three four times. No, one
hand is still grabbing hers and the other is still at her
neck. And then it come, a sharp agony in her forehead

that jump to the back of her skull. The tears coming
for real now, but he not saying anything. Inside her
the voice is screaming. **Fascinating, just fascinating,**
the Aesi say, but soon he quivering too. There he is,
squeezing his brows, squinting his eyes, and gnashing
his teeth with spit clumping the corners of his mouth.
Locking me out only going make it worse for you,
he shout though his mouth don't move. He look like
the one things getting worse for, but then he push her
off the stool and she fall to the floor.

"Get up! Get up now!" he shout. Sogolon pull
herself up on a plant, away from him, but he grab
her neck and push her into the wall. But he is the
one shaking and it start to shake. The stools tremble and tremble until they both lift off the floor. His
frown tightening his face so hard, a tear pop out of
his right eye. Both her ears are on fire but her forehead is cold and numb. Then they rise and she feel
as if they are spinning. He is yelling now, or screaming, or braying like a beast. Sogolon think to pull
his hand from her neck, to fight him off, but instead
she release her face. She don't know why she do it,
why the best fight feel like no fight, but she release
her jaw, her brows, her eyes, and her chin. His eyes
roll into the back of his head and he scream so loud
that they fall to the floor knocking over some of
the plants.

Sogolon pick herself off the floor, out of breath.
The Aesi pull himself to a stoop, but do not stand.

"Get out," he say.

"There is no door."

"Get out!" he say. Behind her is a door, standing open.

The King Sister don't confess to nothing. Kwash Moki say his own sister has blanched out the name of Akum to nothing but white. She wash away all honor, all dignity, all that is next to divine just so she can take her hands and strangle the crown. Oh I am not meant to be your King, he say. I am not who the gods wish, but I will be your best King until the same gods have blessed a generation with a virtuous sister, pure in heart and mind to produce a vital heir, and not some bastard that she can control. Oh how she violated the sacred space of the King Sister, the highest of all titles, for from her loins come the King. Maybe I shall produce a first daughter and from the first daughter comes a true son. I was not raised for this, nor are my sons, but the times have called me to serve and serve is what I will do. For Fasisi and for the North. None of this he say officially, for the King Sister has been accused of nothing. So it go out on the lips of the messengers as a rumor of what he might have said, to what might have been the court, at what might have been an official address. But when the King is ready to give an official word, by the gods, he will give it.

———

Two doors open to the burst of quiet. No people, no servants, no lions, no magnificent birds, no monkeys, no court. At first Sogolon hearing chatter, laughter, gossip in a hush, rumor in a whisper, only to realize that she is walking through the memory of all of it. Air flowing in, sending to Sogolon's ear nothing but breeze. The stone walls look cold and naked, for the tapestries of Kwash Kalifa are gone. Sogolon expecting at least one lion to come up behind her, but none come. She get to the final doors to find them gone, the hinges too, and remember that the doors are purple. The thought spin her around and now she see it, the purple chairs, also gone. Gone too, all the drapes that have even a hint of violet, every needlework with a purple flower, all fabric with a purple pattern no matter how small. And all the rugs, all the garlands, every drape of silk around every gold pillar to mark royalty. Stripped. Gone.

Nobody in the throne room, and from the gatehouse to here, no guards. Nobody to escort her or point where she is to go. But this is where they send her to await the King's pleasure. They, the council. To await further direction from the King or from his right hand, the Aesi. Sogolon pick a room beside the kitchen that used to be the grain keep and throw down the only other dress she own. No servants, which mean they send her here to serve, for she see servants. Perhaps also to spite the King Sister who punish her. With nobody to tell her where to go, she d upstairs.

"You still studying us?" the King Sister ask when Sogolon step in. She is sitting in the windowsill, looking at the doorway to the next room, where Sogolon remember a bed used to be. Disturbed sheets on the floor make her guess that this is now where the King Sister live, not where she visit.

"This is where one of my father's whores insulted your head. Or my mother's wet nurse. Sometimes the same women," she say and laugh to herself.

Sogolon barely in the room before Emini hop off the sill and walk over like a drunk. Sogolon about to ask if she need help when in the quick the King Sister grab her throat.

"Who send you? Who plotting against me, bitch? Who send you? Nobody would choose to come here."

Sogolon frightened, but the King Sister's grip is weak. Her eyes look heavy, with crust at the corners, and her breath is foul.

"The council, Highness. The council send me."

"To do what? You all come to some agreement to damn me, is that it? They send you to spy?"

"I don't know, Highness."

"You don't know. I ask if you are a spy and you say you don't know? Who has ever said such things to a princess?"

"They just send me here, High—"

"Of course. How fitting. I send you to the stables, they send you to court. You must be happy."

"I rather be with the horses than any of you!"

Sogolon gasp at herself.

"Well look at you. It all comes out of little Sogolon. Even the stable girl think she can take liberty with a princess."

"My apologies, Highness."

"Don't apologize. That is the first honest word I hear in more than a quartermoon. Besides, I am not a princess, I am not a King Sister, I am not even Emini. Not even nothing."

"Highness."

"You know what you are when you are nothing? You are bare but you not clean. A sheet, a parchment with nothing but intention. A whiteness."

The blanket around her shoulders is but a rug, which she let drop to reveal her flimsy white gown, as misty as breath on glass. Sogolon could see her skin and a flat belly.

"My headwoman. I don't even know her name. From when they send her to me she is always Headwoman. Not even Lady Headwoman, just Headwoman. Maybe that is why."

"Why what, Highness?"

"Why she send word to the King. About the tunnel. After she help me do the very thing she send word about."

She didn't help you. You command and she obey, Sogolon think but don't say. She shocked but only for a blink before the thought rush in that whatever come by surprise is, when you look hard enough, a long time coming. Besides, this King Sister acting like she is kind when she is simply not wicked. Still the betrayal shock Sogolon. Some who serve take the role like it is a blessing from the gods, and believe in the throne more than the one sitting on it. The head-woman seem to be that person, even as she used to sneak food into the stable. This make her feel sorry for the King Sister all of a sudden and the pity leave her mouth sour.

"Me, I don't know if I'm sick of the gods or if I have dawn sickness," she say as she rub her belly and laugh again, a long loud choking laugh, then when it turn into a cry Sogolon barely notice. Emini wobble as if about to stumble and Sogolon run over to grab her shoulder.

"Don't touch me! I am royal blood. I am still . . . still . . ."

The King Sister legs give out but the stool by the window is right behind her.

"A piece of purple silk is stuck in the floor in the throne room. They chop into the floor, just to get that one little speck out. You understand? One little speck. First they say I was trying to poison the crown. Me. I am the only one trying to save it. What choice did they leave me, eh? I asking you, what choice did they leave me?"

"Highness, you should rest."

"Show me the princess who choose her own hus-band. Show me the woman. This prince with no damn princedom, this prince with no damn seed. Kagar choose him, not me. The man have three times ten the number of concubines and not one ever drop child, yet it is the Princess Emini who must be barren. As for plotting, the only one plotting is Likud. He trying so hard to get his headslow twins the throne, that the only joy I have left will be seeing them kill each other over it."

You both plotting, Sogolon think. **You both scheming to get the throne, thinking yours is the way the gods smile upon.**

"Look at you, eh? Like you I am a no name woman now," the King Sister say.

"I have a name," say Sogolon. The princess smile and grin bitter.

"They tell you I am nothing now. That's why you can be rude to me with no fear. I not excusing my trespass. But my son would have been a warrior raised by a Queen. Instead we going to have rule by snake. Never seen battle, never fight in any war, never even seen blood, but want to start a war with Wakadishu because my brother loves to win and he must win something. Anything."

"Commander Olu."

"Man don't know his right hand from his left leg, and they think I lay with him too."

"He missing."

"You won't find him here."

One day later they execute General Asafa and Kantu the berserker. For me to commit such a sin in Fasisi, would I not have to be in Fasisi? the general plead right up to his death. The guards strip both him and the berserker to nothing, and Sogolon watch from her window as the court women examine why they call him General Third Leg. And this execution, right by the King Sister's window they do it. Slaves erect two poles made from tree trunks in the yard and guards bind the general and the berserker to it. The general submit, for he had dignity and honor, but the berserker slouch and stagger. Farther off Sogolon see Kwash Moki and his men, all on horses and riding to the gate. Watching the execution is the Aesi, who say something about it being a new way to justice no one has ever seen before. The people of court, at least two hundred, she guess, start to look around, at each other, at the sky and the ground for the new way, until a boy break from them and walk to the two men. General Asafa close his eyes in prayer, but the berserker's eyes wide open. Too wide, and the boy too close. Kantu pull a hand free and grab the boy's neck. The men shout and the women scream. Even the Aesi jump. Kantu bellow a laugh and squeeze, forcing the boy to clutch on to his hand. But the boy calm, he let Kantu lift him up into the air, and as the crowd panic nobody but Sogolon notice that the boy don't resist. Instead he change, slow at first, so slow that it look like he is sweating and shiny, until it come clear that he is not reflecting light, but burning it. The same light-filled boy from that night, the one on the twin princes' leash. The brown skin burn away to orange, then yellow, then almost white, and the berserker's hand start to smoke. He scream and try to flick the boy off, but he won't flick. He swing and swing but the boy grip him hard until the berserker's hand burst into flame, then his chest, belly, head, and legs. The berserker bellow until fire consume him whole, and burn him to a black husk, which break away as flakes of ash. The Aesi look up to another window, in which Sogolon guess is the King Sister watching. Then he nod to the boy, bright as the sun, who then go over to General Asafa. The Green Guard, who keep scream- ing that he was following the command of the King to go to the princess's room, is executed for treason and slander.

Days pass hot and long, and night flee as soon as it come. And a womanservant bound to the castle but not happy about it say all of Fasisi stinking of dead flesh. Traitors to the crown, traitors to the King, lech- erous lords who share their cock with the royal whore. A new witch or a man, woman, child in league with witches. Sogolon ask her when did Kwash Moki issue the edict to rid the lands of witches and witchmen and the woman look at her like she speaking a river tongue. Everybody know that Kwash Kagar's mysteri- ous illness—he was a mighty man at the front of each charging army before—was the result of witches. And as for the other maladies and misfortunes that afflict Fasisi, from the house of Akum to the house at the end of the poorest street? Sorcery. Babies leaving wombs foot first and already dead. Sorghum crop falling to blight. Wives talking back to husbands. The truth is, they didn't see the work of witchcraft until the Aesi reveal it and punish the first people responsible. After proclaiming it in the markets, and the fields, and the chambers of nobles, no man had to light any flame against witch or she who rumored to be witch. The people's hate now too ready, too coiled and waiting to strike, be it moons, years, even generations. So when the Aesi first bring the Sangomin to Fasisi, he say here they come, the gifted children from above the river, the apprentices of the great Sangomas, and the sworn enemies of all witches. And now, slashing bodies and starting fires are the Sangomin, who set themselves against all that is witch.

But children is what Sogolon see. And nobody seem to be in charge of them. Not the King or the Aesi, who either let them run wild, or can't stop them, even as they point to any woman and call her witch. Aesi give them power to judge, which they take as the power to persecute and execute. Sogolon don't hate witches, but then she never meet one.

"They smell like burning hair," the womanservant say as she gut a fish for the King Sister's dinner, answering a question Sogolon didn't ask.

"Then if woman burn at the stake her hair will burn too."

"Not when they burning. More time than not is so they smell."

Sogolon stop talking, hoping the womanservant would stop too, but she keep on. She stop listening but hear the tone and know it, a tongue set loose now that what she saying is neither treason nor blasphemy. But it make Sogolon think on the King Sister and how it been days since she see her. She have no reason to go to her, and the King Sister have no reason to call, so that mean two women in a house that don't set eye on each other for days. Concern rise up in her, care even, and by the gods she hate it. Regarding who would never ever regard you is a fool's exercise. As for regard, Sogolon looking at her reflection in silver as the thought take over that nobody regarding her, mean nobody seeing her, and if she is out of sight then she can leave. If I am a no name woman, then let me be a no name woman. If nobody care that I am here, then by the gods nobody should care that I leave. Back in Kwash Kagar's room she don't even try to hide until the darkchild show himself. She is the girl who stand anywhere and nobody see her because the sight of her is neither pleasure nor benefit. Far from making her sad, the thought tickle her, almost make her giggle. That she can flee and all she have to do to is walk out the gate.

There. Decided. The next moon. Sogolon find a sack in the kitchen mudroom and every morning before sunrise she look around for a new thing to steal. Nuts. A wineskin. Goat bones. A drape ripped from the wall and left on the ground. Gold rings. The girl let loose in a palace with no guards but those stationed outside with crossbows ready to fire. But the tunnels never leave her mind, and if some of the men who fuck the princess come from far, then the passage must go farther than the royal enclosure, farther than even Fasisi. None of this she know. But she know it is there, and there is not here, and that is enough.

"She want to see you," the womanservant call out, and Sogolon jump. She shove the sack behind her, but the servant is not looking into her room. Sogolon wait until she leave, then hide it. As soon as she enter the King Sister's room, she slap her. Sogolon stagger backways, not because she lose her balance but because she had to push her own self out of slapping King Sister back.

"You want to, don't you? You think you can. No, that you will."

"You summon me, Mistress?"

"You can if you want to. Anybody can do what anybody want to in this new world."

"If you ready for lunch I will go fetch it."

"You can be cruel too. Tell me to get my food myself."

"I can close the window if the draft getting cold. Is that time of year."

"You can say to me, You have no purple. No proof you are royal."

"How can I help the mistress?"

"Mistress? Mistress? I should be King Sister. Let me tell you something. These past days is the first time I see my own shit. Can you imagine? What a sentence to tell another woman. Eh? Of all the things that say to me, royal blood, of all the things that tell me what royal is, it's not the curtains or the crown or the fucking purple. It's that with nobody to take away my own shit before I even rise, I now see it. That's what royal mean, I understand it now. She who never sees her own shit."

"I don't know what you want, Highness."

The King Sister walk right over to Sogolon and slap her again.

"I want you to fight me. I want defiance. I want somebody to tell me that I am nothing now so that I can wake up just once and believe it."

"No, Highness."

"Don't tell me what I want. I want you to fight me."

"No."

She slap Sogolon again.

"Fight me!"

"No."

"Fight me, you road smelling, dirty fingernail, cut koo bitch!"

"No."

"Why no?"

"Because if I fight you I will kill you. I will grab that scepter you hiding under your bed and bash your head in until everything leak out. And even when you dead I wouldn't stop. Then I would break every bone in your body, and shove this scepter up your shithole. And even then I wouldn't stop. I would stomp you until your bones crack quicker than eggshells, and

I would take that precious oil from the kitchen and pour it all over you and set you aflame and the stink of you burning would be the sweetest thing."

"Sogolon, stop."

"But I wouldn't stop. I don't stop until I burn down this house and—"

"Sogolon!"

"What!"

"You gone past me, girl. Anything else you say is treason. Stop."

Sogolon out of breath, surprised it take so much out of her.

"What is slapping somebody? That must be some treason too."

The King Sister about to say something, but stop and grin instead. "Mind, you start to sound like me. Like these are not the times you born for. And—"

"Where is she? Where is the grand whore of the North?"

He enter the room still shouting where is she, even though she is right there. The prince who is her husband, Majozi. The King Sister look him over and sigh, a loose toenail she forget about.

"Grand whore of the North? You can do better than that," she say.

"Vile Fasisi trash."

"I stand corrected. What do you want?"

"Only to give you news. I understand you have no one to give you anything. Except her."

"Sogolon? Trust me, husband, whatever she is giving, it's not to me."

"I am not your husband. Listen, I am not your husband. The marriage is annulled. Like I said, I thought I would give you the news since you have no one to tell you."

"No, you thought you'd give me the news because it would please you. Revenge agrees with you. Makes you look less fat."

"You would have me raise a bastard?"

"Raising? You? Oh no, husband."

"I not your husband."

"No, you're not. What you are is an idiot and a cuckold."

"What you are is a whore."

"I wish I was a whore. For then I would know that there is more to it than you being a slug on top of me until it is over. If I was a whore then I would know that my hole is just one more place that you don't get for free. I wish I was a whore. Instead I was a fool trying to save this realm."

"And how is the realm? Is it saved?"

The King Sister don't answer. Sogolon reading the prince's face. Too much rage and contempt there. It is too much, making dark circles around his eyes, and drooping his face, and eating him alive. He want to hit her. She can see it in his clenched fists.

"Is it saved, wife?"

A breeze outside rattle the window. He turn to leave.

"Annulment on what grounds?" the King Sister

ask, but he keep walking. "Is the annulment your idea or the King's?"

For that he stop and turn around.

"Fuck the gods if that matter. We not married, that is enough."

"I hope it's enough for you. Because you should have divorced me. For a divorce, my prince, gets you any province west of Luala Luala and your entire family's weight in gold. To annul the marriage is to say it never happened. You get nothing, you fool. Really, Prince, you're a fool's idea of a fool. An idiot's idea of an idiot. An imbecile's idea of a—"

The prince curse and charge her. The King Sister steady herself, for these are the things that must happen to her. A mighty wind, a near storm, blow past her on the right, knock him over, fling him up in the air, and slam him so hard against the window that he burst right through. Sogolon scream. The room is on the ground floor, so he don't fall far. But for a long time, both women watch him lying there still. Soon he twitch and shake and bolt up and start to cry. Blood running from his arms. He stagger to his feet, and try to run, but fall twice.

"Now is not the season for witches," the King Sister say.

"I not a witch," Sogolon say.

"You are something, for certain. Maybe you should join the Sangomin."

"I would rather go back to Mitu."

"What is in Mitu?"

"Death."

Prince Majozi out of sight now. The window will not be replaced. Neither say it, but they both know.

"Commander Olu still missing," Sogolon say.

"Who?"

"Commander Olu."

"Who?"

"Never mind."

TEN

See the girl as certain things come to pass. Nobody is watching her and she is watching nobody. Sogolon here thinking that it feel like freedom until she remember that every freeborn person is here at the King's fancy. Nobody watching her, but they all watching this house of the King Sister, where nobody bother to visit no more. Whatever disgrace visit Emini visit her too, for Sogolon pass by the gatherings of court with no greeting and talk switch to whisper as soon as they see her. The womanservant stop coming and a new one replace her. Her smile is too wide, Sogolon think, for there is nothing in this place for anyone to grin about. She thinking it mockery that this woman keep calling her Highness, but it is that the woman don't see too good, certainly nothing farther than three arm length ahead of her, and at night she totally blind. But she cook, and clean, and serve with such pleasantness that Sogolon start to wonder if she is sometimes deaf as well. How could she not hear about this house of a fallen woman? Who is this woman with nothing but kindness in the heart? Sogolon is about to believe that there can be still goodness because of this one woman until she remember the Aesi. The work of the Aesi—she smell it all over her.

Sogolon would tell the King Sister, but Emini no longer remember Commander Olu. Forgetfulness spread through this enclosure like a sickness and she know who is the cause. And he know that she know. And she know that he know that she know. Any more knowledge would be a kind of madness, so Sogolon quiet her head. Besides, it is not forgetfulness, for forgetfulness means feeling there is something to remember. Is like Commander Olu gone to the place that Jeleza gone to, the place of they who never born. Like never knowing sight, instead of going blind.

Meanwhile Sogolon watching and plotting. Emini keep to her room, coming out every odd day to go to the battlements and watch hawks. All of the court awaiting the judgment of Kwash Moki but that is so long coming now that the anticipation pass. Maybe that is the punishment, that her bedroom is a prison. But Sogolon hiding, saving dry food, a dull knife that she sharpen, a cowskin that she cut out holes with the knife to wear over her head and see without being seen, and a small wood fetish shaped like a man that she find in the old cook's room. In it she drive two nail to make her own nkisi nkondi. And other things, like a potion in a green bottle she find under the cook's bed that she said would heal a cut in one night, a lodestone shaped like an egg, and sandals too big for her feet but with straps as long as a child's height. She wonder what the guards tell the cook that she had to leave the palace in the quick, without her stashed things.

Should she tell Keme? Better not since he is the King's soldier who forget his griot friend as soon as he go missing. No, better to leave like a secret. Nobody will care that she gone, but they will punish her for trying to leave. The King, that is. But she already seeing where she going and it is not a place, not a city, not any lands or sea, just a place that is not here. Or Mitu. Or a house of whores, or a mistress married to a master who go hunting for whores. A night with no moon, that is when she should go. That way a white blanket won't glow in silver light. A day before, she follow the wastewater to see it pouring down the back side of the castle and into an aqueduct that cut through wild field and lead all the way over a gate. This is what she will do. Tie together her sheets and whatever rope she can find. Climb down the back wall of the castle and follow the wastewater.

She move back to her old room knowing nobody would notice. All that is left is to pick the night. She have no other way of picking it other than when she feel ready. That leave it open to be tomorrow, but also two days, two moons, two years from now. Not years, not even a year. No. She need a better plan than that. There is no such thing as the right night, no such thing as ready, and more and more guards are setting up station around the enclosure walls each day.

This day wake her with a monstrous stink. It rush to her nose and pull her eyes open. Yank up her sheets she do, then rush over to every jar in the room to smell it, then unroll a linen that is holding all her dried food to see if any is rotting. But rot of just handful of food could never whip up such a stench. Outside her room it is worse, a torment of smell with something almost sweet underneath it. Flesh, maybe. The smell lure her down the steps, through the great hall and one more after it, and then a third, which frighten her when she remember that the lions used to sleep here. The stink come over her in gusts, but it is sound that lure her farther. Flies buzzing. Ripe. That's what the smell is, ripe. And the flies making a dinlike swarm. Across the room, the curtains are flapping, hiding the open window. Sogolon stop breathing, but taste the stink on her tongue. She pull back the curtains.

Somebody plant the stake outside the open window and leave the rest to wind. The face with eyes open look at Sogolon, the hair clumpy and wild, the cheeks thin with the skin cracked, and the lips pulled back like a grin but the teeth red from dried blood. The hands loose and the legs free. The stake invading through a hole, Sogolon can't bear to see which, dislodging her spine and bursting through the side of her neck. Blood like ink cover her chest, breasts, and belly. They impale her like they been doing witches. Her, the headwoman.

Sogolon vomit. Each time she try to cough, she hurl instead. She run to an urn and vomit again, then look up to see the King Sister in a chair, staring out the window.

"Sometimes when sorrow and anger war for space in your head, neither win," she say. "I tell myself, Emini, you should feel sorrow, but I only come up with pity. I say, Emini, isn't rage rising up in you? What say you to fury? But what coming out of my mouth is disgust. So much disgust I want to vomit. At least that is something. Most times I just come up with nothing. Silly, stupid cow, how did she think this would end? She do the King great service by betraying me, but doing that only get her marked as a woman who betrays. And if the princess is wrong to trust her, why would a king? Learn that lesson, girl, especially if you thinking only for yourself."

"She have something in her hand," Sogolon say.

"Must be her bracelet."

"Not on her wrist. In her fingers like she holding it. It look red."

"Must be blood."

"Blood would look black by now."

"Sogolon, who cares what the dead bitch have in her hand?"

But something make Sogolon care. A voice that

sound like her ask, **What you think you doing?**
when she approach the window. Then the King Sister
say the same thing. Sogolon pretend she don't hear.
The curtains blow out of the way, and there is the
woman, looking like she is crouching and about to
rise. They leaned the stake so that she almost come
through the window, and the woman look as if she is
about to climb in. Sogolon tell herself she don't want
to know, but as she reach the window, she see which
hole take the stake. Sogolon still herself, stop her belly
from expelling through her mouth. The red thing not
shining, nor glimmering, just red, like a bold fabric,
like living silk, unlike everything else on her.

"Fetch it," Emini say. Sogolon turn around and
the King Sister look down on her feet. Things done
change in this house and they both know.

"Do fetch it," Emini say in the closest she is going
to come to begging.

It move Sogolon, not out of pity but amazement.
The King Sister use as much will to say those three
words as others would to row a ship. Sogolon almost
pitch herself out the window trying to lean out to
grab the red thing. The stink rise up anew and make
her eyes burn. The headwoman is smiling at her with
her damn red teeth. Sogolon lean out the window
again to see that she is not smiling, her lips are eaten
off. She won't get the red thing unless she lean far out
and pry it from the headwoman's hand. Sogolon sigh.

"Is a key. A red ribbon tie to a key," she say.

Emini whimper a **what?** and jump from her seat. She rush over just as Sogolon climb back in. She stare at the key and her mouth quiver. Fear rush over her face and she start to back away slow, as if a beast about to corner her. She almost stumble, the way she trembling. Is just a key, Sogolon thinking. Maybe she don't see that it is a key and red ribbon. Nothing else. Sogolon make one step to the King Sister, who cry out and run.

Only a certain kind of woman get a key with a red ribbon. It open a door that few come to by choice, and that choice no woman ever make. Sogolon still remember the King Sister crying, and how in her running she have to stop herself from falling. It perplex her, for every abuse this woman suffer so far she take it by laughing at her abuser. Her mighty mouth and savage tongue, which can wither elders, sages, priests, even her own brother, fail in the presence of just a key. Brass and not even shiny, is all she think when she look at it. And heavy. Sogolon never see one before and don't know what it mean until the womanservant, the one who always smiling, come to the kitchen to cook. The grinning annoy Sogolon so much that she want to slap it off the woman's face.

"You don't see what outside?" she almost shouting.

"What outside?" the womanservant ask.

Scream at her, maybe. Or drag her to the window.

Or just ask the dim-light bitch if she can't fucking smell. Sogolon thinking all three, and they run back and forth in her head until she remember that this woman would never have a reason to see the back or even the far side of this palace. As for the stink, she can't tell if it gone or if she get used to it. Or if the smiling woman just ignoring it. Truth, sometimes the womanservant look like she smiling by force, mouth wide in a grin though her eyes not grinning, and showing her teeth for too long. She rolling dough to bake bread on stone when Sogolon place the key on a table. The womanservant turn around with a smile that drop from her face as soon as she see it.

"W-where that come from?" she ask. Sogolon mark the stutter, and the way she shifting slowly away from the table. "How you come by it?"

"It come to the palace," Sogolon say.

"The gods," she whisper. "It come for you?"

"No."

"Trust the gods. Trust the gods. You have to trust the gods."

"I say it don't come for me, oh."

"Then who it come for?"

"She run when she see it."

"You should run from it too!"

"What the key mean?"

"You really is a swamp girl."

"Now look like a time to be rude? I ask a question."

"Girl, if somebody get a key, you know somebody get a death."

The woman walk over to the window, still talking but not to Sogolon.

"So it go. She is the sister to the King and the King is a death away from being a god. Who going kill the sister of a god, eh? Who?"

"Woman, make sense."

"When a woman condemned to death but no hand can kill her. When a man tired of the old wife but she won't make space for the new, or when a rich man hiding a bastard girl-child, or one who born slow, or deformed, or born looking like the moon. They send them there, girl. The key with the red ribbon open the door. I hear that the key can let you in, but no key can let you back out."

"You one of them woman who when she explain something leave everybody more perplex?"

"Guards soon come to take you away. By the gods I hope they don't take me too."

"But I don't do nothing."

"But you with her."

"So are you."

"Trust the gods. Trust the gods."

"Take her to where?"

"Mantha," say the woman, looking at Sogolon with monstrous pity.

Is still night. The great crocodile done eat half the moon. Sogolon jump out of the bed, for the voice that sound like hers say tonight is the night. Yes now, when the night getting old and it still deep dark. She shove the dry food into her sack, strap on the knife, and grab the cowskin to slip over her head, when they kick the door in. She can't tell who they be, men or women, just wearing white everywhere but a slit for the eyes. Sogolon back up to the window and they fan out around her. She wave her knife, but a staff swing at her in the dark and strike her hand, making her yell and drop it. She back up more to the window, right until her bottom hit the sill. They coming in closer and saying nothing. They prefer it when you fight, the womanservant had said. Two move in and Sogolon slap one in the face and kick another before two more join in, grabbing her two hands while the third punch her two times in the belly. They let her go and she drop to the ground. Hands grab the cowskin and yank it over her head, grab at her tunic until it rip off, tie her hands with rope and drag her down the stone hall. The way she is screaming and the way they paying her no mind make Sogolon think they are deaf until one reach over and slap her mouth. A mighty one in white grab her by the waist and fling her over the right shoulder, and so it go.

The white robes take her and Emini from the palace, while a few stay back. Both she and the King Sister struggling against the ropes, thumping against the carrier's back and trying to kick in the front, but neither act slow them down. Emini curse and grumble until a robe walk up behind her and shove a wad of cloth in her mouth. One approach Sogolon with a wad, but fall back when she quiet herself.

They take them to a moon-shaped pool waiting on rain to fill, tie their hands to longer rope, and throw them in the water. Sogolon can hear Emini screaming into the gag. Is the only thing stopping her from screaming as well. Two robes walk into the water, seize them by the head, and shove them under, making Sogolon choke. A big hand span her whole head and grip it so tight that it is no use to struggle. But struggle she do anyway. The hand hold firm and shove her deeper under water until right before she release herself to drowning when the hand pull her out. At the bank of the pool, two robes present themselves holding something Sogolon don't know. They shove them down on the bank, one holding down their arms and two a leg each. Then the white robes scrub them so hard, Sogolon believe she bleed in the dark. Like a block of sand it was, the thing they scrub her skin with. They scrub her until her skin burn, her neck, her back, pulling her buttocks apart to scrub deep, then her breasts, her elbows, and her knees. One take two fingers to pull her koo wide, splashing it with water but staring at it, looking for it, feeling for it, and pulling out only when it get found. Sogolon know why. Most woman from the mud tribes and the hut tribes get it cut out before she reach her ten and third summer. Remove the man born within the woman, they say. But nobody from where she come from care about what Sogolon grow into. And not every mud and hut tribe cut girl, she want to scream at the robes. After the scrubbing, they rub them with oils and herbs then scrub them again. Satisfied, they drag them back into the pool and nearly drown them again.

They take them back to the palace dripping wet and naked. Sogolon count it as rare kindness that Kwash Moki don't have the court lined up to see this sort dragging them back. The King Sister quiet, but Sogolon want to rage, at her, at them, at whoever decide to punish her because she nearby, and Mistress Komwono for bringing her here as gift. She want to rage at the wind, who only help when it see a way to make things worse. Fuck the gods. In the great hall of Emini's palace they dress the two in white robes and for the first time one of them speak. Like a woman the voice sound, but it could also be a eunuch. Or a young man. The voice say that now that they have been washed of everything they are nothing and should wear nothing. But nakedness is not nothing, for it is how we born, and how we are when we make life, and no two nakedness is the same. But all nothingness is the same, and since you are both nothing, you should wear the color of nothing. White.

They take everything, even the beds, even the bottle of wine that Emini hide. That do it. For the first time she scream that she is a princess and King Sister and they will all be beheaded for what they do to her tonight. Her and Sogolon. The robe who sound like a eunuch walk right up to Emini and slap her twice.

"Submission!" she say.

"Who fool you that you get to command me? You think because I going to your stupid nunnery I am a nun? They send me there to get out of the King's face, not to become one of you."

"We won't tell you again."

"Or else what, you going to kill me? Hark this fool who think that because she wash my skin, she wash out my blood. I am house of Akum. My ancestors rule your ancestors."

The robe nod at two others and they grab Emini. She laugh at them, still shouting that the gods will drop like an ocean on them for defiling royal blood.

"Submission. If you can't see submission, we will take out your eyes. If you can't show submission, we will cut off your hands. If you can't hear submission, we will cut off your ears."

One robe pull Emini's hand behind her back while the other shove his fingers in her mouth and pull her jaws apart. Another approach her with a clamp. Emini try to scream. Sogolon jump and they grab her too. They clamp her tongue and pull.

"If you can't speak submission . . ."

A robe approach her with a dagger. Emini struggle. Even in the dark, Sogolon can see her eyes and she cry too. The robe push the dagger across Emini's lip, ready to slice the tongue off, when she stop and sheathe the dagger. They let her go and she collapse on the floor. Emini can't help herself, she cry and wail. Sogolon can't help herself, she run over and hold her.

"Make your peace with your dead life," the robe say. "We leave tomorrow."

Kwash Moki, King of great might and even greater love, retire to his chambers rather than watch his sister go. For though she goes to serve the gods, it is with no shame that he confess that to lose her to the nunnery feels like losing her to death. And how fortunate are we that he who will one day become a god shares feelings akin to the woman and man of this world. This the Okyeame tell the people in the square, from the roofs, and in the streets. Here is truth. Kwash Moki would not visit his sister, so he send the twins.

"Now that you are nun, Aunt, are you poor?" a twin say.

"We are all poor in the sight of the gods, even your father."

"My father has lions and a chariot of gold."

"Look like so."

"So he is rich."

"He is something."

They look like princes now. Before, they would wear what they wish, which would mean nothing but a haircut, or whatever somebody else is wearing that they command he take off. But now they wear the loose, flowing black robes that their father used to wear before he become King. As is tradition, now they grow their hair long.

"Will you be chaste now that you are a nun?" say the other one.

"What? Who feeding you words, boy?"

"Women talk at court. Then they laugh. They don't care who hear. They say you not here to hold their tongue any longer."

"So the pit of vipers get back to hissing. Will you miss me?"

"No."

Sogolon enter the room, but they call at her before she can turn back. She still can't tell them apart.

"Will a nun have a slave, Aunt?" says one. Emini pause before she answer.

"She is not a slave," she say.

They look the same, but Sogolon feel older. In this white blouse with long sleeves and this long skirt that blow up like a fish in any wind. And the white wrap around her head, so much white that her skin feel white even though she can see what it is. But maybe it also hide her from these boys who would see her get a whipping or a killing.

"You look like a girl it don't take long to forget," the other twin say.

Sogolon bow twice, too long and too quick, then turn to leave.

"Nobody here dismiss you," he say and approach her. Sogolon try not to tremble as she stare at the ground. She is not sure which of the twins this is. They both taller than her, and thin but not showing bones, and handsome with eyebrows always arching and wicked smiles always grinning. You the one who still have a whipping coming, he whisper to her. Sogolon try to walk away but her legs won't move. The twin look her over, then walk back to his brother. Sogolon start to walk right back where she come from.

"You still not dismissed," he say.

"Go about your business, Sogolon," Emini say.

"My father say you are no longer royal. You cannot give commands anymore."

The King Sister bow her head. "Of course," she say.

Sogolon standing there wishing for her sack, wishing for her nkisi nkondi, and a nail to drive in. A nail for every single woman in white, with a curse that they wither from within right down to a husk. Or that they die by lightning, or thunder, or their own foolishness. Sogolon have to stand there until they leave. She stand there until Emini come up behind her and put a hand on her shoulder. Those two going to destroy this kingdom even before they destroy each other, she say.

A woman who is but air to everybody can do what air do, slip into anything, enter any room, and be anywhere, with nobody giving a care. But a woman in white can't hide from nobody. Men think that there go a woman who just asking to be spoiled, which must mean that she is spoiled already. Women think that she lose all use as woman and banish herself to the land of women who work their koo with their own hands and produce demon child. Children think she is a ghost, and the King's sons think she is a target for the arrow. Two arrows zip past her as she get to the library door. She run as two more hit the door and boys who usually follow the twin princes laugh and chase her. One of them shout that is a pity His Excellencies choose to be boring today because the hunting was meager until now. Sogolon running back under the aqueduct and them chasing. Another arrow, and a spear with feather fly past her and land in the grass. She turn back to see them chasing, turn around to see Keme dash past her. They coming in closer, but Keme stand firm, draw his bow, and release. The arrow land right at the foot of the tallest, who look down and cackle. Then a fire burst out, catching his clothes and blazing a circle right around the group. Some of them yell and scream. Two who try to run burst into flames. Keme grab Sogolon's hand and they make tracks.

In the garden leading to the steps up to Olu's house, they stop.

"You should leave them to kill me."

"You don't want to die."

"You don't know what I want."

"I know people who want that, and they don't look like you."

The last person she want to see is this man. Sogolon start to walk away.

"People like that look like Alaya. The magistrates impale him."

"He is a griot, not a witch."

"A witch is whoever a Sangoma or any of the Sangomin say is a witch." Keme walk past her as he talk, expecting her to follow.

"I don't need an escort," she say but he ignore her.

"It take a certain care, if you do it, knowledge of some sort of sick white science, to know how to impale a man so that he don't die for days. By the second night everybody can hear how he moan and cry. I beg the guard to look the other way the third night and stab him in the heart. He smile at me. That damn, damn man, he smile at me."

"Alaya is not a witch."

"He blaspheme the King."

"You used to say he speak the truth."

"I never say that."

"So now you saying he speak lie, or me?"

"I never say that either."

"Make one wonder what use your mouth serve."

"Why must your fucking tongue always snake around me? Either way, it don't matter what I believe."

"First thing which we agree."

"I save him from suffering."

"Why you didn't just save him?"

He look at her like she say the most wild and stupid thing anybody ever done say. And still he look away.

"This King Sister say I should always have faith in my enemies. They the only ones who will never disappoint you," Sogolon say.

"I can—"

"I know where I going."

When she take the front, he halt for a blink, then follow.

"They will tell the princes about this. They will come for me and you," Sogolon say.

"So that the prince tell their father, who will have them all whipped for hunting? Nobody telling nobody. How fare you, Sogolon?"

"You serious? This sound like the question to ask a woman? I fare well, guard. I never fare better. I faring so well that I going to be banished to some hill nobody can find over something I didn't do. How you faring? Good as me?"

"Please believe I have so much sorrow."

"I look like I need your sorrow? Nothing anybody can do with that."

"Sogolon."

"Help me flee."

"What?"

"You hear me. Help me flee. I can't go to that convent, Keme. No blame on me so why I have to go?"

"I . . . I . . . that is our lot, those who are not kings."

"You mean cowards?"

"I not no coward!"

"Everybody in this empire is a coward, including your King."

"You don't even know what that mean."

"I know people who not coward and they don't look like you. They look like Alaya."

It stagger him, even if he don't move. It stagger him.

"If you flee, all you do is set men on the hunt. The King won't care if all they bring back is your eye, he might even join the hunt himself. Don't turn yourself into their favorite sport. Sogolon, don't."

She regard his eyes, pleading.

"You can help me flee."

"You listening to what I telling you? This is not Kwash Kagar's men. Slaves trying to escape is all they are looking for."

"I not a slave, oh!"

He jump. Then he glance left and right, looking to see who hear. The afternoon quiet for everybody in the court of the King.

"But you bound. Just like me."

"Boy, you have anything to show me but surrender? No." A bitter laugh is what she give him.

"You a divine sister now. No man can touch you again," he say.

"You have any purpose for seeing me other than to make every bad feeling worse?"

"Girl, I not trying to make you suffer."

He pull something wrapped in linen from inside his tunic, look over his shoulder, then hand it to her.

"Take it."

"What you giving me?"

"Don't open it. Not here."

"I not taking anything from you."

"Is a dagger."

"What? What you know?"

"I don't know anything. Roads are treacherous, Sogolon. People too."

"They searching we every morning. Where you think I going hide it?"

"You don't want to go to Mantha without protection, Sogolon. Find a way."

"You deaf? They search we every day, I say."

"Then hide it where they won't check."

"They check there too."

"I say hide it where they won't check, Sogolon."

"I don't have no use for damn knife. If you want to help me, tell them you want me to be your second wife."

"What? No, it's too late."

"Too late for who?"

"Sogolon, what you mean?"

"I say take me for your second wife, or third, or whoever."

"I can't—"

She step toward him, he step back.

"Everything about you is what you can't. A whole day waiting for when you can."

"Sogolon."

"I can be good with the wife things. I not no little girl."

"What is this? Who is this?"

"You think I don't see how you look at me? Every time me turn to look at you, you looking at me first. Tell them that you find me agreeable and want to have me for wife. Tell them."

"It not going to make any—"

She step closer. He don't step back.

"Tell them, oh. You think me can't do the wife things? You already have bitch to cook and clean, me can give you other things. Stop looking for a little girl, she gone. The woman you waiting on right in front of you."

She move up to him, almost pressing into his chest.

"People teach me woman things. Thing you don't need no big breast for."

She do it. She reach out, push through the front of his armor, and grab his crotch, too hard, then squeeze too hard, then caress, too slow.

"I can't go with them, Keme. I won't go. I won't go. Don't make me go."

"Is not by my hand—"

"I won't go, you hear me? Take me, move me, hide me, I don't care what you do, you want to sell me too? Sell me to a good man, give me to your father, or your brother, or somebody, anybody. I can't go to this place I can't go I can't go I can't go."

Keme pull her hand out of his crotch.

"You mistress did say you are late of a whorehouse."

Sogolon stop with everything, her thinking also.

"Told me that one morning when she thought I

was taking a liking to you. So collect yourself and find the girl who just vanish. She must be around here some—"

Screaming wind storm from behind her, knocking down a young tree, breaking off new flowers and ripping their petals apart, and punching Keme into the air and spinning him head over heels and flinging him right off the landing.

"Sogolon!" he yell.

But he don't fall. He still in the air, spinning in the sky, shouting at her to help him. She doing it, she don't know how and yet she know is she. For more than a blink she just watch him, feeling her mind race and him spin, her mind calm and him slow. He still yelling, and if he make any more noise somebody will come running. Sogolon think about a gentle wind coaxing him back to the ground, and that is what bring him back. When he land, he stagger, almost fall, coughing twice. Sogolon reach for his shoulder.

"Don't touch me, witch," he growl as she pull back from him. "Make distance between you and me."

Sogolon run off.

Later, in the night, she discover his gift on her windowsill, still wrapped in linen. The knife is no knife, just a piece of wood like a stick. She go to curse Keme and grab the thing to throw it when a sharp and shiny blade shoot through from the tip. Sogolon drop the blade and wince at the noise. She pick it up and see a blade so shiny that she is looking at herself. The handle firm, like ivory, but the side sink when she grab it, like she is clasping a wrist. She examine the handle, rolling it around in her hand, and touch the pommel. The blade vanish back inside so quick that she drop the dagger again. She put the pommel to her hair, her elbow, and neck. Nothing. She touch it with her finger, and the thing, shiny like a mirror, stab through the dark.

Both women wake up surprised that the night didn't pass in troubled sleep. Emini say she take it as sign that over her has come everlasting peace. Sogolon take it as warning, about what, she don't know. Sogolon tear away a strip of the bedding and wrap the dagger around her arm. The caravans leave at dawn. Emini scoff when she see what the caravans be, two carts with a wooden box built on top of each, with a door with a cut out window and a cloth roof. Everybody else is on donkey, mule, and horse. She shout her demand for two horses, one for herself and one for Sogolon. You ever been on a horse? she ask, but before Sogolon answer, the woman who yell submission into them before—she recognize the voice—shout at them to get in the first wagon. Sogolon go to climb but Emini go to defy, shouting that she is not going to lie in someplace that men sleep with their lice and fleas and ticks. This woman, who is about to ride a horse, approach the two of them. She swing hard but Sogolon jump in the way and take the slap meant for the King Sister. She don't know why she do

it. The woman look at her perplex before she shout
that they both get in the wagon.

"Why you take my slap?" Emini ask.

"I don't know."

Inside the wagon everything is white, even the
runes marked all over the covering. Too low to stand
without bending over, even for a woman. Furs, two
cushions, and a jug that smell foul, that is all what
inside the wagon. All for a trip that she hear would
take a quartermoon traveling at this pace. Sogolon
pull back a drape at the front to see seven riders ahead
of them, all horsewomen. They are the first divine
sisters she see with weapons, brandishing sword, dagger, and spear. The cart hit a bump that pitch both
of them forward and knock them down, where they
stay. Downhill they go. Sogolon only need to look at
Emini to know they gone past the final gate.

But then all around her again, a monstrous stink.
And not no flash of rankness that mean they pass-
ing it by but one that go on and on, so endless that
Sogolon turn to lift up the covering.

"Sogolon, no!"

The wagon swerve so close that she could touch
one. She yank the covering down, shaking, but then
scramble to the other side, where she pull up the cover
again. Emini shake her head slow and look down at
the wood floor. On this side also, nothing but dead
women and men, as far back as she can look, as far
forward as she can see. Naked women dressed in
their own blood, women losing flesh to maggots and

flies and crows, women and men melting in the sun, and whispering rot on the breeze. Alaya? For some the impaling stake burst through their chest, some it burst through the side of the neck, one or two the stake burst right through the top of the head, but for most it burst through the mouth, and they look as if vomiting out something big and vile. Stakes rampaging through koo, and buttock hole, and place where there is no hole but the stake make one. Several bodies and she is sure it is him, Alaya. And all of them swinging like they are flying, or crouched as if somebody catch them sitting down, and some swaying in the wind. Some with eyes closed, some with eyes frighten, and some with eyes that just stare and stare.

"Witches," Emini let slip with a whisper.

"People they accuse as witches," say Sogolon.

"Who is 'they'?" say Emini.

"All of you. All of you is they. Anything you can't fathom you call witchcraft and anybody you can't fathom you call witch. You will see a fish swimming against stream and say a witch do it."

"Look at you, thinking you better than us now."

"You the only one in this whole damn caravan who still think that."

"So two men take away my birthright and I must just wave it gone. Never, you hear me? Never."

"Look at you, thinking you rebellious now."

Emini laugh.

"What give you joke?"

"You. I just jump in your skin to hear how you sound, taking all kinds of liberties with me. How it must thrill you, talking to a royal this way."

"I don't see no royal."

"Then you're just like them."

"No, you just like them. Only people like you do things like this to people like you."

"After all this, you still don't see no difference between me and my brother."

Sogolon turn away, watching the window but not looking through it. Not seeing where this trail is taking them.

So to Mantha, seven days west of Fasisi. To everybody not from the kingdom, or those who never hear of it, Mantha is just a mountain. It rise high like a mountain, have rocks like a mountain, and sprout loose bush like a mountain. You have to get close enough to see the steps, and the windows, and the battlements, and the arrow slits, and if you get that close it already too late. Halls and chambers, and rooms and baths all carved out of the mountain rock. But cut with the mountain to look like it is the work of the gods. The highest tower, the great lookout at the peak of the mountain, you cannot get to by path, steps, or ladder. Word is that long before the house of Akum, Mantha was a fortress from where the army could see the enemy coming close without them knowing they are being watched. But that is over seven hundred years ago and nobody know where rumor end and record begin. So say the King Sister, who also say that every king from the house of Nehu, the royal family before her own, would send his old wife to the fortress as soon as he marry a new one.

"But now it seem that the hill get overtaken by this sisterhood."

"Sisterhood? All of them is woman?" Sogolon ask.

"All save the scout and this wagon driver."

"You not the first woman from house of Akum who get send there."

"I don't know," she say, but Sogolon wasn't asking. No way a house with such deceit and wickedness only send one woman to her fate all these years. She rub her left hand all the way up to her elbow and down, then all the way to her upper arm, and the strap hiding Keme's dagger.

Each day right before dusk, one of the white women come to a chute near the front and push in a gourd of hot jollof. The warmth always surprise Sogolon, for not once did these people stop, but the blandness of the food—what a sin salt must be—don't.

"Put a pinch of spice in these women food, and one by one their koos will explode on their donkeys' backs," Emini say. Sogolon laugh, though the look on Emini's face say she wasn't joking. She keep on laughing until the King Sister laugh, late to hearing how funny her own words. Rice in the morning, rice in the night, a gourd the next morning so they can shit out all that rice. Neither woman feel to eat, so neither woman ever feel to squat. So little shitting going on that they finally stop the caravan one evening to see what is taking place between those two women. Has any woman ever heard such words? Emini say to Sogolon when the white woman ask how come neither woman leaving no stinking snake in the pot. They take them to a bush with reeds as tall as a man, and have them squat until they feel enough time pass, then shove them back to the wagon.

"They say Commander Olu was one of your lovers," Sogolon say when they return.

"They say I spread my koo open to swallow fifteen in the Red Army all at once, so what's another lie?"

"Except he did live for true."

"No matter what the court want to think, I know the name of every man who would father my son, and none of them named Commander Olu."

"I know."

"You know what?"

"I know you didn't take him. I also know why you forget him."

"Forget is what I do with my mother's father's name. Nobody knows any Commander Olu."

"He cut him out of your memory."

"He?"

"The Aesi."

"Ah. So the Aesi cut into my head and slice away the memory? Where is the scar? Where is the blood? Why that memory and no other?"

"He take other ones."

"That is not his ways."

"But you agree he has ways."

"I agree that I never liked him, and I know he is behind all of this. But the only craft he working is politics."

"Basa Ballo, the ten and fourth day, eight moons ago. He come to my mistress, asking her questions. That is the last time she remember Jeleza, the one who banish her in the first place."

"Who?"

"Your aunt."

"I . . . the way you look, I'd almost believe it true."

"I don't care what you believe."

"Then why you keep talking?"

"That day is first time I ever meet this Aesi. Tell me when first you meet him."

"What? From I was a child there is the Aesi."

"But when?"

"From I was young."

"You remember when you young? First gift your father give you? When your grandmother die? How you get that cut scar under you chin? Yes? Then tell me when you first remember the Aesi."

She look at Sogolon, eager to be gone from something so tiresome. She look in the sky, rub her lip, scratch her head, and furrow her brow.

"He is always with the court."

"But the first time. How about the second time? How about five years ago? Any memory no matter how small. You don't remember a thing, for he take it from you. He take it away from everybody."

"This sound like madness."

"Madness only because I just a girl, and he know math and science and sit on the right hand of the King. You still trying to find memory. Nothing going come to you."

"I don't understand."

"Everybody have beginning and end. Except him. Now everybody forget you father's sister, and the man who marry her."

"What happen to them?"

"He take them."

"How?"

"I don't know."

"And how it is that you're the only one who know?"

"I sure I not the only one."

"Disappearing aunts, and their—"

"Who win the battle of Bornu?"

"We win, girl. Every child sing that song from they can sing."

"But who is the commander? Who win the King's favor for that victory?"

"The King win that victory for Fasisi. You forget, I was there. I saw the roads line in silver and gold. I see every man get a cape and every woman get gold and salt."

"And you still can't tell me which commander—"

"I said my father win the damn war!"

"I not talking about war, I talking about a battle."

"Stupid little girl, how in the name of the gods would you know?"

"From you. You talk about your father all the time,

so that everybody would know that Kwash Moki is nothing like him. Your father win war because he can be wherever and trust his commanders all over the realm. A good army of men and a better army of pigeons is all you need to win a war, that he say according to you. That's why he can be fighting in Mitu and win a war in Omororo. So you say to those women you used to think is your friend, back when I was just a fly on outside shit to you. But I remember."

"I don't remember no damn Olu."

"Is not that you don't remember any commander. You don't care also."

Emini laugh. "And the Aesi is to be blamed for that too? Maybe I should put blame on him that I don't care for jollof. I tire of this talk," she say.

"I tired long before you," Sogolon say.

They travel over a small hill, cutting through thick bush that don't see much people, before going down into a valley that nobody tell them the name of. Rain come down gentle and soothe her, even as water drip through the linen. Outside and not far off, apes are keeping their distance, but frowning as if expecting deceit. Sogolon pull away from the window. This part of the forest is so thick with dark leaves and gray mist that it throw upon her the mood of evening, even though it is noon.

The wagon stop. They look at each other for an answer that won't come from either face. A crack at the back of the wagon and they both jump. A door neither notice before open, and the curtains hiding it blow out of the way. A divine sister step in, her head wrapped so tight that Sogolon can't make out her face, even though she hide neither nose nor mouth.

"On this day you wash," she say.

Sogolon not washing again. They better kill her first. **When they find that dagger on your arm, they will kill you for sure,** say the voice that sound like her. She don't move. Emini don't move either.

"On this day you wash," she say again, louder, and strike the floor with her staff. Neither woman move. The sister start to wave her staff, as if she expect to use it. These women love violence. They want it, Sogolon know. So she start to rub against the strap around her arm to loosen the dagger hiding in the robe.

"Don't make me say it three times," the sister say. Sogolon rub and push against the strap. Emini stand and sigh.

"I thought the sisters were pure," Emini say.

"Nobody is pure, but yes, we work toward divine purity, like the goddess who has never been touched. Clean on the out as we aspire to clean on the in."

"Ah. So woman blood clean now?"

The woman face drop, like she just taste something rotten.

"I on my moonblood, which make me impure. And if you touch me, you impure too. Maybe you sully yourself just by coming into this wagon. How long it take to purify yourself after being sullied? Three moons? Five?"

The sister say nothing. She look as if she is about

to hit her own face with the staff. She turn and leave without saying a thing, her slam of the door being the final word.

"On my way to becoming a nun and yet I still lie. What kind of sister am I going to be?" Emini ask. Sogolon still standing there, holding the dagger in her fingers.

The route through the valley forest stretch from dawn to dusk. Emini never look out the window, not even once. Sogolon working out that bafflement in her head. How it is to head to a destination, not wanting to know anything of the journey. The King Sister don't want to see all that she will have to forsake. But seeing what she will forsake is all Sogolon want to do, for she didn't choose to forsake nothing. She look at the forest outside, knowing these people will ask her to abandon bitterness as well. She won't do it, even if she have to pretend to. The bitterness burn at the base of her throat and sometimes leap into her head like wildfire. The bitterness make her know that she is where she is, and someone is responsible. Her mother, her brothers, Miss Azora, the man she couldn't drug who then rape her, Mistress Komwono, Master Komwono, Master Komwono's cock, which lead to the princess, this royal whore, these women in white and their nasty, cleansing hands, spirits of ground, spirits of river, gods of land, gods of sea, even gods of sky and the otherworld. All of them. Bring down lightning and thunder, because she blaspheming and she don't care. The bitterness is new blood, green maybe that rush through her legs and straighten her back. The bitterness make her hold on to herself, even as the white women try to take that away. Let them take it away from the King Sister. The closer they get to Mantha, the more she seem to want it all gone.

"Who you murder in your dreams?" Emini say. It rouse her up, though she would swear sleep never reach her.

"W-what?"

"The look on your face, like you want to lock somebody in a hut and burn it."

"I wasn't sleeping."

"Who say you was?"

The wagon start moving. Sogolon don't remember when they stop, so now she wonder if indeed she is in some kind of sleep, and if her face is showing so much what her mouth is telling. The King Sister scratch right under her rib again, something that Sogolon remember only when she do it. At first she think that it must be because she never wash, for there is nobody to wash her, and what a thing it must be to never have to wash yourself. The thought wither when she remember that she don't wash in a while either and the white women who washed her put rancor between her and water. Emini scratch the second time.

"This don't feel like mountains. We not any cooler," she say.

"We still in this bush," Sogolon say and pull the curtain. "They not going to stop until we reach Mantha."

"Good. Lend your eyes to this," Emini say, look left and right, though nobody can see her, and pull off her whole gown. Then her undergown, then a long, wild cotton fabric wrapped around her chest and belly, going down on her hips, roll after roll, scrolling around her body. Sogolon not ready for whatever it is this woman is about to show her. The King Sister stand tall, her shoulders and breasts free, but what wrapped around her look like papyrus. Emini pull at her back and the scroll unwrap itself, falling to the floor in a pile that now look like linen. Sogolon had handled many papers and scrolls studying with Commander Olu, but had never seen a paper like this. It must have been made especially for the royal family of Akum. Emini check the windows again. Come look, she say, as she spread the scroll on the floor.

Math and science is all Sogolon can think, though neither she know. At the beginning of the scroll, numbers and marks, and glyphs and words, some in black and some in red, some not more than a quick scratch. Emini guide her finger along the length of scroll.

"What all this be?" Sogolon ask.

"The future. A future. A dream. I don't know," say Emini.

"The future of where?"

"Wherever want it."

But Fasisi done forfeit it, is what she don't say. What use to Fasisi, the ideas of a banished woman? Or any woman? Emini don't say that either, but Sogolon know. And this city she is keeping around her waist. In one drawing, trees tall enough to touch the moon, tall as the world itself, a city or citadel reaching even higher. In another drawing, the houses, halls, and palaces all shaped in the same smooth curves, like the hips of women lying side by side. In another, roads that look a day long, but go up toward sky. A city in the tree, and another farther off, and ropes connecting the two, ropes carrying cargo, carts, and beasts in cages. Another drawing of just rope in knots, rope tied to wood, rope wrapped around big wheels connecting to small wheels and big wheels again. And still more. With each roll, out come something new. House on top of house on top of house again all the way past clouds into sky.

"So high they would frighten the gods," Sogolon say.

"Now you know why they gift such wisdom to a woman. So nobody will ever look at them, and even if they look, they will never see. I showed them to my father and they give him nothing but sorrow."

"Why?"

"Such bold vision will never come from Likud," my father say. "Likud sleep every night, but never dream once."

"Me sure he—"

"You know what I mean."

Sogolon pick up the scroll.

"The rope and the wheel. They work together but that wisdom still dodge me," Emini say.

"Talk plain and true."

"Who else going to show me these dreams but the gods? Who else would show me a new land rising from dirt, then give me the hands to draw it? Then they whisper a secret about rope, how rope will move mighty things, build towers to touch the gods, and summon a river greater than the Utumbi falls. You will never open a door again, for the rope pulls the door open. And a wagon, even one full of ten oxen, rope will pull from floor to floor. Even pull water to the city. Who else but the gods would give me so many answers, only to curse me with one question? If rope pulling everything, what pulls the rope?"

"If the gods show you that, you will no longer need gods."

"True. True. Hark at Sogolon, the blasphemer," Emini say and laugh. "Maybe they will send me divine oxen. This is too much work for a hundred slaves, even a multitude upon a multitude of slaves. Maybe we catch fire, maybe water, maybe whatever pull the sea away from the shore at night only to release it by day. You ever think of such power? It would be like getting a whole storm down into a bowl."

"That sound like mad talk."

"Some people think the world flat like bread, not round like a womb. That is mad talk. This is just the sight of what to come."

"So you are soothsayer now."

"Third-eye magic? Only man need a third eye.

Woman fine with two, sometimes one. Look at this. We feed the tree until it spread wider than a lake and rise past the castle of the god of sky, or we give it magic."

"This is Fasisi?"

"No. Not after all that come to pass. I see that now. They decide not to take, so I decide not to give."

"That is all you affair. Meanwhile sun burn and rain fall. Make no difference," Sogolon say.

"I am the one who lose her throne and yet you are the one bitter. Difference to who?"

"To me. Difference to me. Make no difference to a woman from a termite hut. Of course you building city up in the trees. Of course you want to live higher so that the rest of we can live even lower."

"Woman, if that is how I did think, I wouldn't have been banished."

"You banished because you share your husband's koo and conspire to put a bastard on the throne."

"You really don't understand the Aesi. You still think this is about some memory-stealing witchcraft? The chancellor have a vision for the empire, for the world, and that vision don't have nothing to do with what the gods tell me or you. Put a half man, half donkey on the throne and they wouldn't care. As if this would be the throne's first bastard. As for you, Sogolon, late of a termite hut who reach the very foot of the throne of the North empire. What place is there that you cannot go?" Emini smile for she know

Sogolon don't have no answer. "My book is written and closed, but yours? Yours is not even a book," she say.

The road to Mantha is hills and valleys and this new valley is damp and cool, bearing the weight of rain. Sogolon can tell without looking out the window, for the last valley smelled of a salt mine all mined out with nothing but holes for the wagons to dodge. This one smell of rain, which mean water, which mean the caravan stop. Yours is not even a book, the King Sister say to her, but now she wondering if she say that only because she think Sogolon cannot read. Better keep it secret. Better keep it safe. Better to take it and run.

And that thought never leave her for long. Running, that is. There are things the King Sister will say, and sometimes just how she say it, that make her think there is a place near her side. Or close. That they are women together. And yet there are other times when Emini will drop something, a spoon, undergarment, hairpin, and expect Sogolon to pick it up. Women might be equal here, but she is not the one this princess equal to.

And so the caravan come to a stop in this wet valley. She wait for Emini's little snore, and the big nose cackle from the sleeping wagon driver. The door hiding behind drapery at the back is locked from the outside, but some fool put a small window right on level with her eye, wide enough to shove her hand through. Now she is down the little ladder to the ground lost in ferns that swallow her up to the knee. All around her the darkness is blue and misty. Tall tree trunks rising up into the dark and necklaces of vines hanging down. Two fires, weak in all this wetness but still going, horses and mules tied off to trees and the women sleeping under furs while two stand watch holding one torch. Farther off. Her wagon is so far back that they wouldn't see her even if they turn around, and those behind her, all over the bush like white spots, all asleep. **Now is the night, girl,** say a voice that sound like her. Now is the night to make distance between you and every white woman. Now is the night to run.

But where she running to? say another voice that sound like her. Sogolon hear this voice before, one that sound closer to her, a voice that slow down her step and calm her heart. No. Calm is not what it do to her heart. The voice don't slow it down with peace, but with confusion and fear. Right here is the bad she know, out there is the good she don't, which could be worse than bad. Worse than worse. So the voice telling her. But Sogolon getting tired of that voice, tired of its mosquito buzzing in and out of her ear. No bad that she know sound better than the bad she don't, when that bad is her brothers chaining her around the neck and putting her to live in a termite hill. The bad that she know is Miss Azora training her to be a whore, then auctioning off her koo to the first rapist. The bad she know is the mistress giving her away like a trinket, and the master and his wicked cock, the sharp point of his rage. The bad that she know can go lie down and spread its legs and get ripped open by a buffalo's cock. She would rather run off a cliff, wade into the deep part of the river, run down a road with no marker, or where there is no road. Is not where you running to, she tell that feeble voice, getting feebler. Is the running itself. Not knowing where to go is what stop too many from going, keep too many staying, and leave too many not knowing that it don't matter where you running to as long as you run. Not seeing what lay before them never stop anyone from running in the dark. Girl, nobody here give a care for where you go, not even you, so make distance between you and them. You cannot stay here.

See the girl run, but the running is hard. Everything turn into nothing in the dark, and no fire burning to light up these trees. And the ground is tricky, soft and muddy, sucking in her foot with one step, then rocky and sharp, scraping her ankles with the next. Sogolon don't know where to go other than away, but there is no sun to tell her east from west and she never learned to read the stars that she cannot see. And this is a new moon, so no grand light is in the sky. She try to run but the mud hold to her feet too long, not letting go unless she pull. The ferns wet her calves, and the rough leaves begin to scratch her. Then her toe buck something and she trip. The scream burst through her throat before she even think it and she break through some branches as she fall. Sogolon squeeze

her eyes tight, hoping in the quick for mud, but she
don't hit the ground. She wasn't falling slow—nobody
falls that slow when the ground hungry to take you.
Maybe she already fall and it is so hard that she lose
feeling. Or maybe the fall knock her out and she is
lying flat in the dream jungle. Sogolon realizing that
her face is still in a wince and her eyes still closed.

Her eyes open to the same darkness, with wet ferns
brushing against her face. Sogolon can see leaves at
least, and hear night insects. She can even smell the
damp dirt. But she can't understand how she is not
feeling the dirt, nor any hurt from the fall, nor mud
on her face or in her mouth, or the firmness of the
ground. She squeeze her eyes shut, then open them
again, but there she is, lying almost flat, a breath away
from the ground, but not touching it. She gasp, not
in fear but in wonder as her clothes hang loose, away
from her. Sogolon wiggle her toes only to realize that
she is wiggling in air. She stretch her hands out and
the tips of the ferns tickle them until they no longer
brush her skin. She is rising, higher than the shrubs,
higher than the ferns, higher than the plants, rising
into cooler breeze, now higher than Emini is tall. But
what if she rise all the way up to the gods of sky? The
wind could be playing with her, or toying with her.
She hit the ground. Mud in her mouth now. Mud and
fern, bulky and bitter, she think to swallow it just to
remind her where she is. Is not where you run to as
long as you run, but what if there is nowhere to run?
It come over her, a sadness that feel like tiredness that

sink her. All she seeing around her is nightfall, and all she hearing is insect. She not hearing the others who move at night, snakes, and hyena, and beasts that would dig their teeth right in her neck until the skin burst and her bones break. Nothing big moving through the bush, but if something shift or shuffle Sogolon know she will scream. **Just because you're too fearful don't mean something not coming for you,** say a voice that sound like her. Maybe those who can see in the night already see her, already size her up, already thinking this one will do, now that she is no longer in the safety of numbers, weapons, and fire. A voice that sound just like her say, **Girl, you have no memory of this bush.** She turn to go back to the caravan only to realize that she can't see the way back. Sogolon wrap herself in her arms, and tell herself that all that shaking is the ground, not her bones. Nothing to do now but wait until first light and hope nothing out here is waiting for her.

Emini convince her to wear the scroll of cities. They will visit things on me that they won't on you, she say. Sogolon think it is a big thing carrying something for the princess, bigger than the small bother of living with the itch. The itch come through in the dream jungle. And with it heat, first faint, then like ten summers all at once, and the sound, crackling, rumbling, then roaring. And smell, a sharp, stinking, burning odor that make her frown, and smoke that make her choke. Sogolon cough herself out of sleep to see that she wasn't sleeping.

Not sleeping or dreaming, but burning. Fire racing up the side of the wagon, gnashing teeth and eating away the roof leaving a rib cage, gobbling the floor leaving bones, sweeping up and around, and under, and above her. Sogolon jump up, right as part of the roof tear away and fall right on top of her sleeping pile. Smoke blinding her as she try to run to the front of the wagon, burning her eyes, grating her throat, and masking fire that rush at her and pull back like wild dogs. She dash but trip on something, falling hard onto burning wood, but feeling the wood, not the burn. This fire is going to get to her hair, get to the oils in it, get to the perfume she steal from Emini to rub under her nose. The flames crackle and Sogolon scream but it fall into a cough. Then she see what trip her.

A leg right beside another, a burning leg attached to burning hips, to a belly black as coal, bursting woman juice and popping off skin and fat. Like a fallen torch. Emini. The fire burst her open and there it is, the little one that is already growing in Emini's belly, a ball of flame and a black husk. Sogolon yell her name, and the yell attract a laugh from the front of the wagon. She look up to see the boy at the reins, an unmoving clump of ash. Bright hands yellow like the sun let him go, hands belonging to the young shoulders of that boy from the palace who is all light, the one the twin prince used to pull on a leash. Now not light but fire rolling inside his body like storm clouds. Bald yellow head, yellow eyes, yellow teeth that switch from smile to a sneer when he see her. Run, girl, run now. Jump out and land on ground, or sand, or stone, or a nest of ants, anything is better than fire. Fireboy let go of the wagon driver and he crumble. Fireboy hop back into the wagon just as the axles break and the whole thing crash to the ground. Sogolon fall, and the wagon fall upon her, but nothing touching her skin, not even her hair, and this boy is a breath from her face. He reach for her neck and Sogolon feel the heat wrapping around her neck, but he try to grab her throat and his hand slip off. The more he grab, the more it slip, but slip off air, for he not touching her. Air slip between her and him, but it don't feel like wind. The boy hiss and crackle. Sogolon work her fury into one wicked look, not even thinking, when the wind (not wind) kick him in the chest and hurl him up in the sky, tumbling him head over feet until the wind (not wind) let him go and he slam into the wreck. The King Sister burn to nothing and Sogolon mind go red. The fireboy come at her with a leopard leap, but ram into a shield of nothing and they both hear a crack. The wind (not wind) seize him again, fling him up in the air, then slam him down again, and again, again, beating breath out of him like washerwomen beating out clothes. It slam the fire out of him, the light out of him, the breath out of him, the blood out of him, and the flesh, leaving nothing. It, meaning her. She do it. She who is beyond words. She, Sogolon.

Two voices scream for the fireboy. A brown blur like a hand flashing across her face zip over the burning wagon, then stop for blink, then blur again. Sogolon could swear she see eyes, mouth, and hands. The blur dash to the fireboy's body and snarl until it form two heads on one body. They shout at the fireboy, then turn and growl at Sogolon. She scramble, try to run, but this two-headed boy blur into nothing. Then the blur rush straight at her, knocking her down. This boy with two heads is upon her, oxenstrong, one breath fouler than the other, speaking a tongue she don't know, but as one head talk, the other head nod. Then they both glare at her. Sogolon summoning wind in her mind, saying, Wind I summon you, then saying, Wind I demand you, then Wind I beg you, but it don't come. She would curse it and its fickle ways, but their hands are on her throat, two hands feeling like four and she can't breathe. She can't cough. Sogolon fumble for the dagger in her arm, but she already going dark. Her arm flailing as they shove her in the wreckage. The dagger finally slip into her palm and she press it against his neck. "A stick, she come at us with a stick," they say. They still laughing when she touch the pommel and the knifepoint burst through to the other side of the left one's neck. The right one look and scream and his body die on him.

Words flee from her. She look around and see only

fire and destruction. Nobody watching the no name woman, easy picking for the fireboy. The wagon in front burning too, the horses, mules, and donkeys fallen, some on fire. Most of the white women dead and the few left trying swordplay against the Sangomin, but they count themselves as nun, not warrior. She is just a girl. She should run. Terror beat into her heart, pound against her temples, and make her hands and legs tremble. **Run, girl,** Sogolon tell herself. **This is not your fight, these women are not your friend, and whoever fighting them doing you kindness.** But the King Sister is burning. They kill Emini and the baby inside her.

In the ribs of the other burning wagon, two white women swing swords at one of the Sangomin, one for the neck, the other for the leg, and both miss as he leap up in the air, level himself with the ground, then swing two swords that slice the white women down. The red ochre boy with razors for fingers slice and cut and chop and carve his way through four women, who explode blood and drop their swords before they realize they dead. He making his bloody way to Sogolon but taking his time, enjoying each kill. A fat boy with no legs but tree trunk hands that he use to run all over, knocking away some and smashing others into the ground like insects. And still the women in white fight. A mighty one run with a spear in hand, and hurl it right into the back of the tall man, white as stone. He stagger, choke, stiffen, and then crumble. Fire jumping to nearby trees and green grass turning red and redder. Three white women retreat to a tree, fighting back with dagger and sword the red ochre boy, who grow back a blade finger as soon as they chop one off. But from the top of the tree come scuttling down the spiderlike darkchild, who grab two by the neck and scoop them up. The third look up to see parts of one rain down on her. Then one red blade finger burst right through her throat.

See the girl run. See the girl look through tearblind eyes. Hide behind trees too thin and under ferns too low. Where to hide in open land? This is not the rain forest, but the rock hillside leading out of the valley. Nowhere to run but down, and skipping through rock that jut out to knock you down, and pop through the ground to cut up your feet and trip you. She try to skip down the side of the hill that fall away from the narrow trail, trying not to break her toe, break her legs, tumble all the way down. But she coming down too fast and can't stop, her toe hit a rock that send her up in the air and she stay there for a blink before she fall and tumble, bump, and clack into a rock, and roll again, until she lie out in a field of tall grass. She lose the dagger. Blood run from a cut in her head into her eyes. Through them she see a black figure hopping through the leaves, the darkchild getting closer and closer. Sogolon first try to crawl but then try to rise on her feet, but her left foot won't let her. She try to lie low and hobble away but on the third step a black hand grab her ankle and leap into the air with her. He let her hit the ground twice, to knock the dagger out of her hand and the wind out of her.

They all bend over looking at her, as she feel her back on the ground. Her head woozy and her right eye only seeing red, for when the darkchild is dragging her back up the hill, he don't care what her back tear against or her head bang into. One saying to cut her up, while another saying that to burn her while she alive will send a sweet aroma of fear to the gods. Another say, Fuck your gods, we are the gods of this hill and valley now. Through one eye she see the fat ball of a boy yell and stomp toward the skinny one, the first she seeing him, and as the fat one swing his arm to knock him down the skinny one turn to mist, then switch back to flesh and knock the boy down so hard that he can't stop rolling away. They all laugh, the Sangomin. Laugh so hard with each other that Sogolon limp to her feet and stagger away. One scream to catch her, but another say no, delight in his voice.

See the Sangomin hunt. See how they chase her. Up this narrow trail falling off on both sides there is nowhere to go but through the fire and wreckage and dead bodies and body parts scattered all over. She dodge out the way of a rolling wagon wheel, but don't see the girl behind it, the girl whose skin won't settle. The white rolling over her chest and breasts and legs and breaking up in spots all over the brown. The girl have a dagger in each hand as she step to

Sogolon, who move back, step for step. As the girl step, the white in her pool into one whole half and start to push against the skin until another girl, white as an albino, pull herself from the brown girl, who now stalk Sogolon with four knives. The white one jump her and slam into this nothing between them that crunch her bones. The nothing, the wind (not wind), hit her in the face and twist hard and quick until her neck break. The white one fall to the ground as the brown one gasp. Before she even bawl, the wind (not wind) seize her up and slam her against the rocks until there is nothing to slam. Five hands of white stone grab her by the neck and throw her down. The tall man who just crumble. A white stone girl in the floating city flash through her head. Somebody with no form, taking form out of stone, in the shape of a long man. Sogolon roll and roll and roll until something stop her fall. The foot of the red boy with the razor fingers. You supposed to be seven, she mumble. A wicked smile rip across his face as his finger grow long and longer. Coming behind him, the fat boy stomping his hands, the skinny one made of air, and the darkchild hopping from rock to rock. Farther off the red and blue girl with the lizard tongue throw a dead woman onto a pile of white. The fat boy giggle, asking if they see what this one can do. This one special. This one almost like we.

"Nobody is like we," say skinny one.

"Enough of this," say razor finger and he move in to slash and cut.

It all happen too quick, her anger kicking away fear as she look at them all through her red eye. Wind ripple through her skin—she feeling it now—then her two eyes go red.

"What she doing? What sh—"

ELEVEN

See the dark pack in tight and crush her face. The dark squeeze her legs, squat in the cradle of her belly, and shove against her two arms that she cross against her chest in a burial pose. Like she is dead. Nobody tell her that death is just darkness, pressure, and waiting, but all three pushing against her head and pulling her right leg in a wrong way. She can't remember what is the then before darkness, only now, and now is dark, dark, dark. The dark have a smell, like fire and bush and worms and mud and shit. And taste, spilling into her mouth, rock, worm, mud, shit. Her eyes can't open. Won't open. Her mouth can't close. Won't close. Her arms can't swing, won't swing. Her legs, where her left leg be? The right one hurting because it is bending the wrong way. **Get out, girl, get out, whatever you name be, go go go go.**

She twist her hands around and claw away clumps of dirt, claw and claw until the arms stretch and the

dirt fall in the space it leave. She claw and kick and
spit out dirt, and claw and kick and spit until her
body is moving up, climbing up, sometimes rolling
up, sometimes slipping sideways. Mud smear against
her chest and rock scrape and cut her hip. And still
she claw and claw and claw, up and up, dirt slipping
all around her until her right hand grab a clump of
wind. Then the left, then both pull her out of the
ground and her head burst into the air, which rush
into her so hard it nearly knock her back into the hole
that she dig her way out of. Dirt stuck in the back of
her throat make her cough, and terror make her shudder. Sogolon is crying when she pull herself out of the
dirt, but the weak sun open her hazy eyes, and what
she see stop it.

Is the dirt on the edge that she see first, all around
and uneven like somebody just dig a grave. The light
shift, or her eyes shift, and they look like a range of
mountains far off. It take her a few blinks to see that
she is spinning slow, turning around and around to
see piles of dirt on the edge of a pristine circle. The
edge far above her, a height she cannot measure, so
she follow the dirt down until her eyes reach her feet.
Gods must have done this, she think. Gods must have
heard her screaming and send the moon to smite the
fight and crush the ground, then with divine fingers
pull her back out of the earth and fix her back in the
sky. For there be no other way to explain what she see.
What she is in the middle of, this crater wider than

a lake, this smooth bowl that she will have to climb out of.

Slippery, the dirt and rock keep rolling down and taking her back down with it. Sogolon grab clumps of rock but they come loose and roll down with her. The second time she hit a rock with her knee and draw blood. This hole so wide that the sun is leaving it behind even though the sky is still clear blue. Sogolon finally make it to the rim of the crater and almost slip back down when see them floating, first the top half of the razor finger boy, his entrails dangling, his eyes gazing into nothing, and his legs nowhere to be seen. Slabs of loose white rock and cut white stone—the big man shattered in a multitude of pieces. She climb out and walk past the red and blue girl with the lizard tongue, her hands and legs swaying as if underwater, her face sleepy, the back of her head exploded with all of her shooting out. Perplexing it be, all three floating in air like they underwater, but everything stuck as if whatever happen don't finish. All of the lizard girl bursting through the back of her head, but it stay there, not going farther, not falling to the ground. Just there. As be the pieces of the boy that had two heads. And rocks, and trees, and two wagon wheels but no wagon, and bodies in white robes, and food, and dead horses, dead donkeys, dead mules, even dead birds. And the legs of the razor boy sticking out of a tree trunk as if it is how trees grow. Nothing rising higher, nothing falling, and Sogolon running to what is the front of the caravan, then all the way to the back, and seeing that everything that prove who they were and what happened is broken to pieces and floating in sky. Even flame. Even some of the rock leading up to the mountain look gone. She can't tell for sure, can't tell anything other than that her head hurt and her legs going to buckle. They buckle.

Cawing set off and wake her up. She doesn't know how long she was asleep, but she wake and all that float in the air fall to the ground. The caws rise to a din. Crows. They swarm like bees, crows all over the trail, picking on the remains of the caravans, on dead bodies, and also this—pecking corpse and carcass to make sure dead is dead. More land, and her legs are sticking out. Sogolon panic, then catch herself. Near her is the body of a sister with her legs missing. **No use in crying, girl,** say the voice that sound like her. Crying will only draw them. See them close. Hopping at their pace, the crows. They shuffle past her head and the corpse at her feet. Her eyes open a crack just as a crow peck the sister's chest. Another hop onto Sogolon's head. Sogolon shut her eyes tight and hold her breath. A jab first, the point of a nail on her forehead. Sogolon dig her fingernails into her skin but don't move. Another jab. Another. Another. One more and tears will break her. Then just so, the crows fly away in one monstrous flutter. All of them, in the quick, gone. She don't dare open her eyes until she can hear wind rustle weed.

Sogolon wake again. She find the dagger lodged between rocks. Evening come around soft and cool and she wake under two wagon wheels leaning against each other. Mantha must be only a day away, she hope. A day by horse, something else by foot. But if it was only a day, for sure somebody from Mantha would have come looking for their lost sisters. Somebody must be expected. Somebody must be missed. Somebody must need them found. This from the girl who is going to run, the girl who say to herself that where you run to don't matter as long as you run. Now here it is that you have nothing to run from, and must.

Cold air drop down on the trail and she start to tremble. The later it get the colder it become, and then a wind rise and cause a shudder so hard that she can hear her teeth. Air so bitter that it feel like her skin is burning. She dash from wheel to wheel, wreck to wreck, until she come across the white-wearing bodies of two divine sisters. Their cloaks as ripped as their bodies, but still white fur. Sogolon try to pull one off half a body, but the corpse appear to hold on, refusing to let go. She scream as she yank the half cloak away, now white and brown and splotchy from dry blood. Don't think, just wrap it around you, wrap yourself into a ball, she is thinking. She is a cocoon until morning. Stars and moon spin away into the dawn but Sogolon don't sleep none, only walk, past shapes and forms and pieces that might be person, beast, or something she can't imagine. The trail look like what she think after a war would look like, a place with no peace even in quiet. The only quiet she find is at the bottom of the crater, and is at the bottom of the crater that wisdom come to her that all of this she did do. Or maybe the gods, or the moon, or that wind, which refuse to be her servant or master. Her mind run over those thoughts, but only one feel like when a key unlock a door—that it is done by her. But when it is coming up from her hands, the last thing she remember, it don't feel like wind leaving her skin, but like something on the boil and bubbling up. A mighty thing that knock everything out of its way, not a wind that blow everything down. Like two attracting pieces of iron, when you turn them around, push them together and they scatter. Her mind wrapping itself around this, not the metals, but the scatter.

This thing, this it, that push everything away with the might of a hundred battering rams, this thing that punch out a hole in the ground as wide as a field, and blast a man head north and his heart south, and some of him it just blast away into air. This great might that she been feeling all along, and mistaking for breeze or gale, this thing that prevent her from hitting the ground when she fall, and prevent everything from hitting her. Witchcraft? Devilry? She don't practice one and she not in service of the other. Her mind working deceit is what this is. Her mind working deceit. How many a woman or a man for how many an age think everything strange be the work of magic or the gods, when it is just the sky, or the sea, or the air, or the water, working in their ways, and we be the one to think it must be us, or gods or devils because we have misfortune and stumble upon it? Or wishing for good tidings so hard that when it happen we think it is through our will, and not that we just lucky? Heavy thoughts pushing her back down into the ground this evening. The sky telling her nothing.

The days are not warm, and the nights cold as spite. She scamper around the trail trying to find anything of use or anything to eat. In a patch of shrubs she find a wineskin filled with water and the faint taste of wine that made her want to drink all of it in one gulp. In the same patch, pieces of dry bread and piles of crumbs, a few dates, dry bones, and a hand with three fingers. Only two nights before the sight would have made her vomit. Now she pass by with neither heave nor sigh. Before sunset, she find one of the two headed boy's heads among rocks, and the splatter of dried up yellow in the spot where she killed him. The splatter start to glow in the dimming light. At one of the fallen trees she tear off a thin, straight branch, as tall as she, and shed the leaves and bark. Two times she wake up to beasts scurrying, rummaging, and feasting through the night. She clutch her new staff, but none come close. In the morning she gather all she can find, scrape some of the yellow into cloth and set out.

But where to go? A voice that sound like her say, **Trust the gods.** But from what she been seeing since the termite hill, trust is one thing you should never put in the gods. Better yet to come to them in fear and trembling. Better even yet to not come to them at all. As for hope, that sound like it can be a good thing for those who need it, but for she, the only hope she need from the gods is that they never find her to make sport. Sogolon look back at what she is walking away from and wonder if that hope went lost many moons ago.

Here is truth. Sogolon can't tell west from east or north from south, despite the sun. Above she can tell from below, and only because her thighs hurt from the climbing. One morning bring her mountain sides so steep that she climb with hands more than feet, and hang on by just a finger as rock and boulders tumble over her head. Feeling the side settle, she look up and dodge quick a rock coming straight for her face. How is a wagon to climb this? She take too long to tell herself that she gone off track and need to get back to the trail. The same day she slip through a passage so narrow that it rip the back of her fur. Worse, the narrow passage only lead to one narrower. Sogolon curse when she get stuck. Curse so loud that a rumble drown it out, the sound of the passage-way shifting, opening wider as if both sides of the rock grow afraid to touch her. The push loosen rocks above that bounce and shatter right above her head. By the gods, this thing inside and outside her that she don't understand and can't control. That come one day when she need it, only to abandon her the next. It feel like temper, but sometimes all she have is empty rage, and her scream is just a scream. Maybe it is not a gift from the gods but a god for true, doing what they do mostly, which is to fuck with people.

Sogolon let the thought steer course to its destination for once. She is in a wild expanse of mountain and clouds, all the way to the end of her vision. That the gods, as is their nature, fuck with we of a mortal life because they envy us. Yes, those same gods, perfect in their ways, but they not perfect. They petty. And irritable. And flighty. Foolish. Childish. Vengeful for no real grievance other than being annoyed. But envy is the thing, she know it now. Envy is what they have for us because we have one power no god can ever have, and that is the power to surprise oneself. The wisdom shake her. She wonder where it come from. It sound like somebody whisper it from the mountain-top. Or maybe this is the day she is born, but don't know. She can no longer picture it being a god's work bubbling under her skin. **It is you,** say a voice in her head that sound like her.

She want to get off this mountain, which turn into mountains. Or reach Mantha, though she have no purpose there, which is why she don't think often of reaching it. She is lost and alone and hungry, and all three will soon work to kill her. The divine sisters made it seem like this is just one narrow road always winding up, but she already walk through two small valleys, the second showing her some mercy with a stream to fill her wineskin. And what look like the peak of the mountain become one of many peaks, with nothing to tell her which is Mantha. Trees start to get scarce and rocks loose and firm stand in her way more and more. It only take her a day for fear to lose itself to wonder. Uncanny, even her own mind think so, that she start to lose interest in finding or being found. And this thing inside her coming to an understanding of her. Or maybe she is coming to an understanding of it. That don't mean it not still too wild. She will think of walking on air and curse herself because she still feeling pressure underfoot. But then she will look down and see herself a horse's height above the ground. Not a wind blowing but something pushing—perhaps she should call it the push. She will stare at the ground and not think, something beyond think, and the push will hit her in the chest and fling her up in sky. She will shout as she fall, but not hit the ground, just float right above it. She will touch rock and wonder if the push can come from inside a thing and the rock will explode. She will come to a trail blocked by fallen rock and see a new one where travelers had to make do, and without thinking, the rocks will scatter from themselves.

Climbing at night. A voice in her head that sound like her say, **Now you do it, now you cut all wisdom loose.** All sort of beasts roam the land at night looking for flesh and blood, even on the mountains. Sogolon cut loose something else—fear or care, she not sure. That is how she come to the place unaware. Dirt is dirt, stone is stone, rock is rock, all the same under night, so where she make bed don't make no difference. Sogolon wake up before the sun to her fur, her face, and the ground covered in white dust, cold to the touch. She pinch a little and put in her mouth. White water dust. She scoop up handful after handful and devour it. It is only when the sun start to peek out that she see rocks all around her, standing up and fallen down with too much craft to them to be just rocks. In the night a younger girl inside her thought they look like a fallen giant's hand. But masonry they be, all in ruins, all over the ground. Not like castle ruins, for those she know, but pillars, some four or five times as high as she, some shorter, most leaning as if either sinking in or rising from the dirt. All ravaged by weather, some covered in moss. Three stand tallest, as if whoever build this place knew that those three would withstand as testimony to whoever lived here. Columns, three huddled together. The shortest is the widest, but it lean to the right, the top ravaged away to just a mound. The middle one, the tallest, higher than a house with four floors, with a worn-down swirl going around it, once a staircase, she reckon. The third the thinnest, but with a wide head that narrow at the top. Not till noonlike do she see the big round eye and long jaw of a snake. But they all carved up with drawings, lines that look like runes or science, words and glyphs whose meaning hover around her head but don't become clear. She almost come to read them, only for the meaning to open up, then close back down. On the first she find House of Lords, on the second, House of Kings, and on the third, just House. She run her fingers over the shapes, feeling them for meaning, wondering if this is a temple, palace, fort, or something else of glorious use. Also on this mound, four trees, dotting the hill careless-like, with bitter fruits that she still eat, and leaves that taste better. This is where she put down the little she have and rest.

What to do with a blessing and curse? Run wild and laugh like a mad old woman and send her cackle on wind only for wind or not wind to send it back to her? To run up to a cliff and leap and fall as wind or not wind rush so hard that she feel it through every strand of hair, only to land a finger's length from the ground and stir up a cloud of dust. To hop off one rock and land flat on another, and screaming from the pain of her busted ass, and cursing the push for saving her from death, but little else. No matter. Sogolon is running on sky, and sleeping in the cool under earth, and wondering as she sit at the bottom of a stream, dry, the push forming a cocoon around her, if this is from her mother. The only gift her father ever show is to contort himself to piss in his own mouth. Madness, which her brothers blame her for. No matter, she would forget their names. But here she is, on a new night, trying to remember just one

brother's name, only to grasp that she never knew it.
The fire crackle and it sound like laughter. Then another sound, like the crack of a branch or tree bark.
Sogolon look around her at the three giant fingers,
then quiet her mind to listen. The fire crack and
crackle. Nothing.

Sogolon wake up deep in the night to the fire
still crackling. She think to kick dust on it so that the
crackling won't wake her up, but don't want to move.
Sleep claim her quick, but a crackle wake her up
again. She throw off the fur and kick dust on the fire
until it is only smolder. The yawn come big and loud,
but as she stoop, a crack cut through the silence. Not
the fire behind her. She turn around to look between
the two skinny trees, and between the two trees look
right back at her. Piss-yellow eyes blink to black. She
jump up to run but the big black thing knock her
down hard in the dirt, paw pinning her right hand,
other paw squashing her throat, belly crushing hers.
The thing roar and shake its head, its long tusk teeth
scraping Sogolon's chest. He roar again. Sogolon
scream. He open his mouth wide and spit hit her face
and chest, and breath burn her nose. The dark hiding
too much. Sogolon see ears pointed up like a bat, skin,
fur. She smell sweat, river funk, mud, rotting flesh
every time he roar. Shuffling in the dark. More. Eyes
so yellow they glow, wicked. Sogolon shudder. Eyes so
yellow, and nose huffing vapor, and a mouth big as
the moon. Another roar to the left and coming in
closer. The one pinning her roar back. She can't feel

her right hand, which is slapping the beast with no notice. The other ones closing in, he need to claim his kill. He throw his mouth wide open, his eyes on her neck. Sogolon press against his belly.

The other beasts gone, taking their shrieking all the way where they come from. There is no sleeping now, not with all of this side of the mountain covered in exploded beast. On her chest, warming her legs, slicking her face, leaving the taste of iron in her mouth. Sogolon lie there looking at the sky as night flee. The next morning she cook the biggest strips of beast she can find.

Two dawns later, with her ear to the ground, another rumble wake her up. Riders. She grab all that is hers, but the land is too open. They are almost upon her when she hide between three pillars, throwing herself in shadow.

Sogolon watch them through an opening in the stone. Ten riders she count, but more coming up behind, three, five, two, and two more. Before several dismount, their armor make plain who they be. Red Army, from Fasisi. Archers, spearmen, sword wielders in full chain mail and gold helmets, smooth and close to the head, flares at the ears like wings. Three chariots pull up, then two more. From one of the last, a dog as tall as half of a warrior jump out, sniff the ground, and race off, away from her. A sigh, too loud, escape her lips. The warriors are among the ruins now, and there is nothing she can do but calm herself, be like the earth, and hope that her brown leather and dirty skin they mistake for dirt itself. Sogolon wonder what they looking for, since nobody have any reason to seek her. But they are from Fasisi, in service to the King, and the word to kill all the divine sisters could only have come from the throne. No, that is not it. The word was to kill the King Sister and make sure there are no witness to give report. Even if scouting for witnesses would take days. Survivors, if there are some, to make sure they are none. But there are enough soldiers here for a small siege, much too many just for picking through dead bones. A soldier crouch and sift through the dirt with his dagger. Some of the men spread out, but most stand still, looking around at the sky and the mountains, as if they never seen this view.

And the dog, the dog is behind her. In front of her when she turn back around. Gray, with a white chest and nose, and shaggy, like rug wrapped around a dog. Truth, the dog look as big as the lions of court. He stand there, looking at her, tilt his head like he hear her remark, and so quiet that Sogolon thinking that maybe he is friendly. But then he growl, low and wicked, then louder, baring his teeth like he already decide what to bite into first. Sogolon stiff as wood, frighten that any move would make him pounce. He growl again, then bark and won't stop barking, and moving in closer and would be upon her if a soldier didn't pull him back.

"You don't look like a cat," he say and grab Sogolon's arm just as she set to scamper. The soldier pull her to him and she swing around to slap his cheek but hit the side of his helmet. She yell at the pain and the soldier shake his head, telling her that inside these new helmets sound like a bell, and you, young girl, look like you sprain a finger. He drag her along, and Sogolon still yelling and cursing and trying to kick his legs.

"I can either cut your throat, break your arm, or leave you untouched. Which it going be, girl? Choose fast."

Sogolon calm down and relax the arm still in his grip. They walk past the soldiers spread out, past four setting up camp, and down to the last of them, where three men on horseback is looking at the sunrise. Larger gold helmets, meaning marshals or somebody with authority over other men. Two of them turn around, one she seeing for the first time in red armor.

"Ke—"

It leave her mouth, but her throat snatch the rest of the name back. Sogolon don't know why. Maybe because even in all this some of the court stain her ways, and she think better than to address a soldier like she familiar. But that wasn't why. Keme clear his throat.

"Soldier, this is neither lion nor cobra. Who is this you bring?" he ask.

"Find her hiding behind the obelisk, Lord."

"Everything here is an obelisk."

"Behind them three over there, Lord."

"Alone?"

"So far, Lord."

"Marshal," Keme say to the one beside him. "None of the river tribes live near Mantha?"

"You would need a river for that."

"So from where come this girl?"

"She could have been—"

"Everyone there is dead, and everyone is wearing white. This girl, she's wearing whatever she can find, it seems."

Sogolon would say something, but even now he don't say one word to her. Or look at her longer than one would look at a fly. Things didn't end good between them, but he leave her with a gift. Why pretend not to know her? Some game this is that is afoot.

"Marshal, she looks like she don't know where her next meal is coming from," say one next to Keme.

"Marshal, we are brothers in rank and thought. And we have too little food as it is. Soldier! Kill her," Keme say.

"What? No! Keme!"

The soldier grab her arm again, but Sogolon struggle. Keme is about to turn away but stop.

"What did you say? Girl."

"I don't say nothing."

"You did not just say Keme?"

"No, I—"

"Is my ear a fool or your mouth?" He dismount,

march right up to her, and grab her chin. "How do you know my name?" he ask.

"I—I—I don't know it."

"You just called it."

"I did—"

"Gods of chance just whispered it in your ear?"

"I don't know—"

"You'll know this blade soon enough."

"One of your men, he just say it."

"I have no man that would address me such a way, not even this man," he say, pointing to the other marshal.

"Marshal, every whoreson from here to Kalindar have the name Keme. Stop acting like you special," the other marshal say and laugh. He is one of three men naked except for the marshal's helmet, and he is the only one on a horse. The other two spread out farther than the other men, going down the rocky slope.

"Besides, when Kwash Moki shows a man favor, all of the Kingdom knows. Your name precedes you, and that is no bad thing," he say.

Keme release her chin, but the frown don't leave his brow. "Bread for this one. From the looks of that poor tree over there, she's been eating famine food," he say as some of the men laugh.

The name come out like a curse, so she thankful that it leave her tongue as a whisper: the Aesi. But the name still have weight, and even to whisper it make her buckle. She stumble to the ground and two soldiers rush to pick her up. She don't fight them. One tear off a piece of flatbread, scoop some lentils, and hand it to her. She don't want to need to eat. She don't want anything from these men. But she swallow it in three gulps, leading one soldier to shout that a crocodile eating its own young take at least four bites. The camp laughter shame her, but she sit in the dirt wishing for another bite. The crackling fire take her back to all the kitchens she know. It lull her to sleep, for how long she don't know, but Sogolon jump when she wake up to Keme watching her.

"Is this what you seek?" he ask and wave her dagger. His dagger, looking like just a piece of stick. "Ingenious thing. What would happen if I put it at your throat?"

Sogolon say nothing. Keme throw the dagger to her and mark how she catch it.

"You didn't even look," he say. "Perhaps the trick of dim light? I would swear the knife found your hand and not your hand the knife."

"Night have plenty tricks," Sogolon say.

"Is that a wise saying where you come from?"

"No."

"Where do you come from? Why walk you on this way?"

"You asking me where I going?"

"I asked you quite a few things."

"We live on the Ubangta River."

"No tribe lives on the Ubangta River."

"Never say we are no tribe. Just a family."

"Ubangta is east of this trail, yet you walk from the west?"

"Never say I was coming from there."

"You never said anything."

Sogolon is hoping, she admit to herself on the quiet, that this hashing and sparring would wake up his memory.

"Talk, girl."

"I . . . I was hoping they would take me in. The nuns of Mantha."

"The divine sisterhood? You?"

"No damn thing wrong with me," she say louder than she intend, and the frown return to his brow.

"Who was that for, mother or father?"

"Yes."

He laugh.

"One does not just go to Mantha, girl. One is never even invited."

"Then how you go?"

"Don't ask me, I'm not a nun."

There, decided. She hate this Keme too. The same smile, though. The same damn smile shining out of that same damn beard, hugging the same firm chin of that same damn face.

"Did your father beat you hard? Perhaps your mother?"

One thing Sogolon learn from the people at court. Give them just enough about you and they will build their own story. So to his words she just nod.

"Perhaps you are the kind of riotous girl who needs such firm instruction."

She feel it bubbling under her skin and quiet herself with a long breath.

"And now you're running away to a place where the women are even more fond of whips than your father. Or mother. So you run to be rid of him?"

"I run to be rid of the man he want me to marry."

"You're even wilder than I thought. Why would a maid run from marriage? The pain you must be causing your parents. Does a girl wearing skins and furs not know what she is for? Dowry, is it? Did they struggle to meet it?"

"You ask plenty question."

"Better I know. Because who I don't, I kill."

"Even a girl running away?" she ask but all he do is smile. "You already tell them to kill me," Sogolon say.

"I did. I did. A scout saw smoke in the direction of Mantha, so we rode for four days. A day past, we saw what might be the source of the smoke. Do you know what I speak of?"

"No."

"What is your name?"

"Chibundu."

"Chibundu, next time think more careful about what you say as truth, and what you say as lie. For your neck's sake. There is nothing left of this caravan, nothing that the hyenas left behind, anyway. And here comes you, first soul we find in many a day, and you're walking away from it."

"I don't see nothing."

"Only one road, girl, no matter where you veered off, judging by those bruises. And every trail lead back to the road. That was to make sure that women fleeing to be nuns didn't lose their way and die."

"I don't see nothing."

"We can see the blood on your little half cloak."

"I don't cause nothing."

"Didn't say you caused. I said I saw. I didn't even have to ask. Tell me news that is truly news. Like why were you there, and what befall you?"

"Traders. That is what they do."

"Did. Not you?"

"I is a trader's slave, not a trader."

"Why you didn't say that before?"

"I not being a slave again."

"I see it now. Whatever bad tidings hit them was good tidings for you. And what tidings, eh? We found wagon wheels but no wagon, horse reins but no horse, women's fingers but no woman. My scout says he takes this road two times a year, sometimes three. And he remembers no lake bed without a lake. Such a perfect bed, like a god sat down on one perfect ass cheek. On this you have no news?"

"I . . . I . . . It knock me out. Whatever it was. I don't remember nothing but people screaming and then waking up."

"And you, the only survivor. What blessed sleep. I know what this is."

"You know?"

"A merciful god has taken your memory. How else can you not remember? And who would want to remember this? All you recall is being someone's slave. Rest safe, girl. Under Fasisi law no person can be enslaved twice."

"Sangomin."

"What?"

"I remember my master shout Sangomin."

"Why would the Sangomin attack some traders?"

"Because they wicked and murder for sport."

Keme burst out laughing, enraging Sogolon, who shut her eyes tight to hide it.

"Sangomas give us the muti, girl. Of the field to bind us to spirits, of the beast to give us all the courage of lions. The Sangomin is why none of us have defect or illness, why none of us have lost our minds. Every warrior among us wear the muti on their face, or chest, or arm. Here is a secret, some even rub it on their cock. What you say is almost blasphemy—or somebody bewitched you."

"None of this was witch."

"You accounting for all kind of witch? What about the ones half woman, half viper? The ones washing in the blood of the dead? The ones living under the ground? There are as many witches as there are stones in a pond, girl."

"I didn't see no witch."

"They also didn't see you, or you'd be a rattling corpse. Where is your master heading?"

"You say this road go only one place."

"Mantha? Nuns make trade now?"

"Ask the trader. Slave don't know master's business."

"When they sound as smart as you? One thing you certainly don't sound like is a slave. We leave tomorrow. Some of these men have unease lying with dead kings for too long."

"Dead kings?"

"How long you sleep here?"

"Some days."

"Days alone? And you are untouched? Unspoiled?"

What a question to ask a woman, she think but don't say. "Yes," she reply. She don't mention the night beast.

"Uncanny for such a place. This is the necropolis of kings, girl. Dead kings and princes from long before the Akum dynasty are buried here. The Giant Kings going back a thousand summers, back when leopards had the tusks, and elephants the spots. When man was taller than that tree. Look behind you," he say, pointing at the same three she hid between. "The middle one is Kamak the Wicked, the right is Barka the Good."

"The third?"

"Not even old men know."

"Marshal, stop looking for a second wife," he say as he approach. He, the naked marshal. He probably thinking he shut up Keme, but who he really quiet is Sogolon, who ready to ask him what a slave sound like, not because she care about his answer because

fuck the gods and fuck him too, but to curse him
for thinking a slave is a slave because they are stupid
or ignorant, and not because they ill-starred, or conquered, or under wicked bondage of people like his
King. Or maybe even him as soon as he can buy one.

"Even you can do better than someone smelling of
beast skin," he say. Sogolon look around for who he
must be speaking of and come right back to herself.
She know this one too, but no name coming to her.

"Marshal, every man wearing a piece of beast skin
somewhere. The strap around your helmet, for one."

"Not like her," he say, walking away.

"A care for the marshal," Keme say to her. "How
would you feel if he is wearing your mother's skin?"

Sogolon miss the meaning until the marshal appear again in her view, as he stand by the fire, fall
to his knees, then to the ground to rise as a lion.
Jump is what her heart do, for it could be Beremu or
the other lion who become her friend, but she don't
recognize the man, and the other lion she is sure is
no shapeshifter. Both spark the same sight in her
memory. Lions in the Red Army, which mean that
Kwash Moki find a use for them after all. But that
is court business, and now she is annoyed at herself
for thinking of royal things, as if she belong there. A
change in policy, how strange a turn of words, the
kind of words she can't imagine ever saying again.
And for why, there is nobody to say them to. **Wake
up early, girl, will yourself,** say a voice in her head

that sound like her. **Wake up and leave this place before them. Nobody here will miss you if you go. Wake up early.**

A cold splash of water to her face and Sogolon wake up. Shocked and blurry, she didn't see who throw the water. But then men are tossing water on fire and men gathering up to head out. At the front Keme and the marshals already on horses, ready to go.

"You're on the horse tied to the marshal's horse," Keme say.

"I going to Mantha."

"No, you going to Fasisi."

"No, I not going b—"

"Not going where? They sent us on a fact finding mission, and you are the fact that we found. They will want a deposition, our commander. And you as a witness will be the one to give it," he say.

"I not a witness."

"Put that in the deposition if you wish, but we go."

"What if I don't want to go?"

"I don't really care what you want, you're coming with us. Free or in chains is your choice. So choose."

2

A GIRL IS A HUNTED ANIMAL

Bingoyi yi
kase nan

TWELVE

Let us make this quick. Kwash Moki, eager to prove that he too is the Lion of the North and not the Cobra, invade the independent country of Wakadishu. They been conspiring again with the South, planning iniquity and destruction, say the Okyeame. Forces from Omororo and Weme Witu conspiring with Wakadishu to cross the Kegere River and invade North. Kalindar. The southern King don't declare war, nor do he come to the aid of Wakadishu. The southern King didn't bother himself with matters of war, for lilies was growing from his toes, his own shit was demanding not to be tossed, and his grandmother needed to be burned alive, for she was no grandparent but a tokoloshe gremlin. "You have to ask if nobody in the South ever think to crown a new dynasty, since this one been going mad for hundreds of years," people in Fasisi say and laugh. Wakadishu now occupied territory. But the flames of Bornu, the country Kwash Kagar wipe away from memory, start to flicker again, with random attacks from no attacker, burnings with no flame, knockings down with no battering ram, and assassinations with no arrow or poison. Rumor flicker too, that it was witches.

Keme and the Red Army ride back to Fasisi, which was the last place I would ever want to go, but there I go. And I make no protest, telling myself to make distance between me and this man as soon as my feet touch Fasisi soil, and to never see his face again. Instead, I end up living with that man gone five years. See me now, shaking dust from my sandals every time I am about to enter his house, a house I return to every time I leave. Watch my hands, though hungry for bow, club, dagger, or sword, instead grabbing a broom to sweep away dust shed by the running, screaming, and laughing children who come out of my womb. From his seed. My hands, hungry to grab a dagger and plunge into some man's eye just so I can see he spurt blood in my face, instead is smoothing clay onto the outside walls after rain season, shelling peas, grinding grain, and smashing to juice a spider that sneak into the house and frighten the children who come out of my womb. From his seed. Hands so hungry to grab a knife and slit a throat, or to touch a head and make it explode, instead is rubbing the sick bellies and wiping the runny noses of children who come out of my womb. Every night when the great crocodile almost finish eating the moon, I look at myself in the water and wonder how my life twist and turn into this.

Like I say. The Red Army ride faster than a caravan of slow women, so it reach Fasisi in just two days. When we get to the grand gate, night reach before us, but I still didn't feel safe. A voice that sound like me say, **Look at you, a girl with no name and yet all you know of Fasisi is the royal court. As if you was higher than a servant, as if you was higher than slave, or anybody.** I shake out that thought and fill it with this: how to get away from this army and this man who done forget me. By the time they get all the way up to the royal enclosure I slip off my horse, which was trailing theirs, and try to vanish into the crowd, when all I walk into is a growling lion. Don't make us take you back in chains after all, Keme say as he grab me. And here is how things go. Keme and the marshals take me to a guard house and leave me there, for the commanders who send them to investigate the smoke on the mountain will certainly want testimony from whoever they find up there, especially this girl who clearly have more to tell, say Keme. And then he leave me with three bored constables who point to the cell I supposed to stay in. You can't put me in a room with man, I say and they laugh. The two men in the cell, they laugh too. The next morning, the guards shocked because one man is dead with a broken neck and the other near dead with two broken arms. All night they fighting over who would take me first, is all I say.

Two nights pass before the constables tell me there is nobody to carry out the inquiry. All who is of top rank either in Wakadishu or on a dhow sailing there. The King, gone to the south border to celebrate his victory, which mean his chancellor, commanders, counselors, winemakers, White Guards, and a few concubines are gone too. Nobody here to interrogate and no charges against me, so they let me go. One of the constables ask, What about the marshals? To which the one opening the cells say, If they want answers so bad, they should have questioned her themselves. And just so, I am back in Fasisi. But this place is different when you not walking the streets as one of the royal house. Take away the protection of your station, as well as that of the guards, and before you is a city that won't hide that it is out to get you. A city that flash and wave a fabric in your face to hide the dagger coming to stab you underneath. People outside of Fasisi think this King have such an iron grip on the land that no crime happen unless he order it. People outside never know anything.

Evening. Mothers, wives, and young girls of good name all running home. Green Army patrolling the streets, which make me look for the first alley to hide. So I turn down one with a chariot blocking the way, one with a tired horse and no rider. Day not yet done, but night reach this alley early, with candle and lamplight sneaking out of the back side of taverns, inns, and as the door swing out, a whorehouse. Two stagger out, tight like they are born as joined twins, for joined is what they was before they even stagger out the door, the man with his robe up to his chest, and the woman he was fucking from behind. I press my back to the wall on the other side of the alley and pass them quiet, but the woman see me. I recognize the face. Not the face, the look, one that I used to see in myself years ago. Inside Miss Azora house, hearing women moaning and bawling to remind the man that she is here with him, even though her mind long gone to another place. The look on her face saying either join me or tell me how to get where you are going. But I keep walking.

Three nights later it stop astonishing me that I was about to find a safe spot in some alley, or street, or tree to sleep. I try not to think of beds, cots, or even cold, clean floors. The second night I try to sleep in a big tree and wake long before dawn to a monkey pissing on me. It screech and run, but my wind surround him, then tighten like a snake and I watch him stunned silent as he float in air. Then my wind slam him against the tree. The fourth night, I walk until I reach the western edge of the city, or so it look, for it was a low wall, and beyond it, mountains. Others already on the ground curling under whatever they could curl under, while others just wrap up into themselves. I wrap myself in fur and go off to sleep clutching my stick and my dagger.

The rough touch on my shoulder come first, and I dismiss it as dream. Then the breath unsettle my neck hair and I remember that it is rare that I dream.

Somebody was trying to curl up with me, somebody big, and foul, and wet. When a hand touch my thigh I will it in myself to work force to knock him away, but nothing come. I think harder, squeezing my face and gritting my teeth, but the hand start to rub my buttocks. No force, no wind, no nothing. I curse loud, spin around, and point my dagger at the man's neck. He jump back and stray light mark two breasts. A woman. I yell at her to move but she stay still, even stoop down again like I was going to allow her. I press the two side of the handle and the blade shoot out. She jump at first, then laugh, showing black stumps where teeth used to be. She grab for my fur and I stab right through her hand. The woman jump back, shriek, then cry, then laugh. She charge again and I swing my stick straight for her forehead. She fall back, then run off.

White mean nothing, but it mean something when a man wear it. An afternoon of a day I forget to count. I am running down another alley because street boys take to chasing me even though after just one night sleeping on dirt I no longer look like a girl. Kill the beggar, cut the thief, they shout as they chase me. And I run, which make them think I am fleeing out of fear, when the truth is I just don't want to have to kill a stupid boy today. They chasing me around the Ibiku district, which I get to the night before, not knowing that this was where I would throw myself down to sleep. At least the ground was cooler and for the whole night no dog, beggar, or rapist bother me. Somebody once say, not to me, that Ibiku was a district swarmed with whores, but walking and running down these street I don't see none. No anybody else either, no cart to scramble up, no goats to jump over, no horse to run under, and no people but these boys. I squeeze my dagger and think to stop, for if they looking for a fight maybe I will give them one. But then two doors swing open and white rush out like a flood. A temple. Pilgrims and worshippers. Whichever god or goddess demand white robes and quiet I don't know, but I start walking with these men and women, though my white is now dirty as rust. I trail behind three women with long curly hair looking like honeycombs, and as they break from the procession for a house, I skip ahead of more people, still so quiet, and stop behind four men. They are whispering, but the wind blow their secret words to my ear. Floating district. Place bets before flip of the time glass. Bet on the reds. Donga.

The first three nights come at the end of market days, so food is not hard to come by once you forget shame and fight off beggars, madmen, and dogs. By the fourth night I chasing away rats only to see that they were eating another rat. Food start eating food, and my belly is stabbing me and knocking me down. The cloth I turn into a sack keep showing me how empty it is, even though I keep looking. The bitter bunch of leaves I eat force itself back out my mouth, which only make me more hungry. Too hungry to walk all the way to the floating district to feed myself on the fighting. Besides, to get in I would need more than this fighting stick. The fifth morning I pass by an apple seller and try to beg with my eyes, for my mouth wouldn't move. He threaten to beat me and call the magistrate, then have his shop boy chase me down the street to the yam seller, who yell and have his two pet apes chase me several streets across town, until I come upon the mango and guava seller, who scream that he don't run no almshouse and fling throwing daggers at me until I run and run, right inside the floor of the bazaar of a spice seller, who don't notice me until my belly growl fierce, and who then set a white dog on me, who chase me down the merchant road, over carts and under horses, and don't stop until he tear away my fur coat, mistaking it for a beast, and ripping it to nothing. I run until I come upon the roast goat seller, not far from the gate leading to the royal enclosure. He don't see me. A voice in my head who sound like me ask, **Why be a nasty beggar when you can be a filthy thief?**

A big man, he throw three cuts of meat on a sheet of iron that look like a breastplate. I wonder how it don't yet come to my head to steal. Fasisi is bursting at the seams with gold and salt and if you was to take three dates, nobody would know. I try to stop the thought from running away with my head, how in the place that take everything from me, I didn't yet think to take something from it. He sprinkle it with salt and pepper and irú, then turn his back to slice off more. I watch him take his time, not turning around but listening to the meat. Ten people pass by before he turn around and flip the pieces of goat. The raw side wake up the fat, which raise a noise like clapping, and lift up flavor into the sky. At the sound of the sizzle, my belly stab me, and a groan leave my mouth before I could stop it. His back is to me, the goat seller. If I grab it now, the meat would be half raw, maybe, and the oil would burn my fingers off. But if I wait, he will scoop up everything and put in that basket by his right, and my belly will kill me. No time to think about how bad the idea be, I say, and run to the stall, grab one chunk of meat with two fingers, drop it because it was so hot, pick it up again though it burn my fingers, drop it again, and scoop it up again, just as the goat seller turn around to see me trying to hold on to a piece of goat covered in dirt.

"Thieving little bitch!"

I drop the meat and run. This big goat seller chase after me and all I could think as I jump on cart, and tumble, and fall to the ground, and run, is Who minding the fire with him running me down? I skid under horse, run around donkey, kick away pigeons, and dash down one narrow alley that lead to one more narrow, and one more narrow than that. Still the goat seller after me. He get so close that I can hear him screaming that I will be the last one. He strike a wall with his cleaver, which make me turn around while running and stumble. The goat seller knock down an old man and push two women out of the way. I take off, turning down the first alley I see, and now I am knocking down old men and pushing women out of the way. Stalls of fruit and vegetables and meat, I pass them in a blur when they all flip over one by one and flood the street with red, green, and yellow. My wind finally, I think. People pounce, beggars grab, two sellers pull knives and one a whip. And still I run, and still the goat seller, jumping over fruit and kicking away vegetables, follow me. I turn around once to see two boys join him in the chase. I hear them screaming for a magistrate. As I run right into a line of sheet and tear the whole thing down, and scramble to get up while the fabric seller take a switch and start to whip me. All I do is look at her and my wind knock her off her feet, and I curse it for how random its ways. The three men right behind me, I can hear them. But a horse galloping above me, this I can hear too. I don't dare look, for no horse can ride on sky. Then the back of my head explode in pain and I fall. The ground feel hard, but it moving like waves. The three upon me, but their faces stretch and shrink and swirl, and I can't hear what they say. Then just so, each back away and scatter, quicker than roaches in the light. The ground still feel like it is spinning, and tilting so low that I spread my arms to not roll off. Under my neck is warm and wet and I know what will be on my fingertips if I touch it. I lie there thinking there is nothing to do but gaze at the sky and wait for the warm wetness to run out of me, or I run out of sky to see. They dismount, which I can tell because hitting the ground rattle their armor. I stay on the ground, feeling my shoulders getting warm, and watching sky, when the riders three all bend down and block my view. I can't make out any faces, but I know they are Red Army.

thought you hail from Fasisi," he say.

"I never say where I hail."

He and his men giggle at me like little boys. Here is truth, I've never seen no lion or hyena or giant lay waste to a whole loaf of bread and a quarter of fowl like this one, a soldier say, but not to me. The whole room giggle again and annoy me so much that I almost shout that they should at least laugh like men, and not like some damn hyena. But then it run across my mind that one or two of them might actually be hyena, so I stuff my mouth with more fowl. The back of my head pound when I think about it, but one of the men say it was just a bump. We at a giant table in a room of a fort made of stone. No doors, just archways. Cut stone, each one bigger than a wagon wheel, and mortar that still smell wet. I want to say how surprising it is that it's not cold, but not a single face look like one you say loose words to.

"Then why stay in a place you don't know? Have you no people here?"

"No."

"Nobody?"

"Why would a slave have somebody?"

Two of the officers mark my tone.

"Of course. What is your name again?" Keme ask.

"Sogolon."

"Well, Sogolon, as warm as these walls be, you cannot stay here either. Our . . . accommodations can't hold the likes of you."

"Man don't frighten me."

"Men down there don't care that you have no fear."

That is when I gulp. He notice. What to do with her? he ask the others, but the lion ignore him, one man say he don't run no almshouse, another say that the wife wouldn't believe him even if he say she was a new slave, while the others just nod and leave. He about to leave when a soldier from Green Army enter and stand still. I recognize the black fur trim on his cape. Royal guardhouse.

"Yes, soldier," Keme say, which surprise the guard, who don't look like many people call him soldier.

"From the palace, Marshal. Orders to escort the Queen Mother—"

"The Queen."

"Uh . . . yes, the Queen. A personal escort to the lake temples so she can pay tribute to her gods. You go by boat."

"Escorting is for the Green Army, I should know. Why bring it here?"

"The Queen is leaving the enclosure, Marshal. This come direct from the Aesi, sir."

"The Aesi requesting marshals as bodyguards now?"

"Is not a request, Marshal," the guard say. He say other things too, and I see his mouth move, then Keme's, then the guard again, but I not hearing anything they say. The Aesi. The first I am hearing his name from somebody else's mouth since before we head to Mantha. I am watching these two men, hoping they don't turn and look at me trying to gather my head before it fall apart. I am watching them but I'm seeing Emini's face smiling, sweating, screaming, bursting into flames.

Later that night, on the way back to his house, with him on a horse and me riding behind him, he say to me, "Sogolon, eh? You called yourself Chibundu only four days ago."

"I . . ."

"Best you settle on a name before you meet my wife."

They live in the Ibiku district, above Ugliko and east of Taha. They don't keep a lock on the door. Keme dismount and walk in, leaving it to me to tie the horses, which make me cuss silent.

Voices inside, voices I don't know. A woman's. I turn around and see only an open door, and inside a shelf full of lamps, fabrics on the walls, and a nkisi nkondi bigger than a small child. "Welcome."

She is shorter than her voice would make one believe, with a blue-pattern headdress almost as big as the nkisi nkondi, and the same fabric wrapped around her body and tied at her breast. Arms strong and bare.

"You look underfed," she say.

I could say that a man like Keme leave you with a picture of what his wife might be, a picture that take up space in your head as soon as he talk, as soon as he walk, as soon as he emerge from the river naked, even as soon as he eat. This is not the woman I did see in my head, but now I can't remember who I did see. Deep in the house children are squealing. Delight. The wife sigh, not from contempt, for no such look come over her face. Tired, I was guessing, until she say that she too tired for the excitement tonight with him and them, and they going want to play with you too. I still trying to steal look at her. Among the river people some women have plates in their bottom lips bigger than a dish. She have two big as the palm of my hand in her ears, her lobe stretched right around them. Skin darker than coffee ground of the deepest roast with a line of beauty scars running along her brow, which is all I see in the lamplight. She turn and walk into the house, expecting me to follow. I pass a room where Keme was on all fours growling like a big cat and mauling his children while they squeal, jump all over him, and growl too. The wife hiss. I want to say that a grown man playing is something I don't like either, but I quiet myself, for this woman looking like she just can't wait to tell me that I and she are not and will never be friends.

"I don't have nowhere to go," I say. "Is the only reason I come with him. Give me some food and I will leave."

"Nonsense. You just say you have nowhere to go," she say and walk to the kitchen, still expecting me to follow her.

How you reach this far in years but don't have no use?" she say, Keme's wife, who answer to the name Yétúnde. A woman he steal from Wakadishu is what she call herself, and right now in the kitchen, crouching around a steaming pot of ewa aganyin, she is telling me how every woman from Wakadishu can cook before they reach nine, otherwise how they going to find husband at ten? She see my face.

"That was a joke, girl," she say. "No father send off his daughter to get crush by some big, smelly man until she is at least ten and two in years."

Her laugh shake the room, and a slap on her own thigh finish it off. Right before, we both was coughing, for she tell me to watch the yam and I look away only once, to turn back to it burning and smoke filling half the room. But the question linger with her for too long.

"Woman in Mitu don't cook?"

"Never live long enough in Mitu to become a woman," I say.

By then I was staying under this roof for two moons. Six moons later I stop saying staying and start saying living, when I hear the wife say to Keme, You set that ship asail long time gone, she living here now. She was answering a question I didn't hear. I am not much use around the kitchen, can't clean the floor without leaving half the dirt behind, and don't know what I supposed to do with dirty clothes and water to get them clean, but I can pound grain and if I stay still the children, all three of them, roll, crawl, jump, and walk all over me. Wherever I go they all scream and beg to follow even though all I do is walk, and all they do is follow behind me in a single line like little ducks. Look how they take to you, Yétúnde say whenever we come back. She tell me all the time, Look how you made for raising children. But whenever I ask what kind of raising she see me do, for I not seeing it, she just laugh. Whenever the children ask me where I come from, I tell them I sprout from the middle of a yellow bush lily.

Sometime four nights would go before I see Keme, then he appear in the room I stay at sunset. Or in the room I play with the children, or in the small field behind the house, the reason why he live in Ibiku district, though most of the Red Army live in Ugliko to be nearer to the King.

"Chibundu," he say.

"Is not my name."

"You the one who choose it."

"For two moons your name was the Marshal, and I didn't give you no fuss."

"Mouth full of mirth even when you not trying to be funny," he say to perplex me. I can't think of no other reason. He shed his red armor somewhere, leaving his red tunic underneath, and I almost tell him to keep on the helmet for I like the wings. He sit in the grass while I pound corn to powder. I don't have to look up to know that he is watching me.

"Chi . . . Sogolon. This new fetish priest send us all home with totems. Says we're to pray to them and ask for abundance from the gods. I say to my general, What does he care about the food we eat, or the number of children we have? Beremu says to me that the general wants me to pray for abundance of soldiers, so we can go to war. Now, I would be the first to agree that peace is an ill fit for North and South. But war? Again?"

"Show of armies don't have to mean readying for war."

"So it go? Then what else it mean?"

"Men like showing off their weapon just for the sake of showing," I say.

"Ha, I would take those words a certain way, if the look on your face didn't say different."

"What you mean?" I ask, but I know what he mean. Keme don't answer.

"So, you want a fetish?" he ask.

"No."

"Why not?"

"I have no view on the gods."

"You don't trust the gods?"

"The gods don't trust the gods."

"Is so it go? Which one whisper that in your ear?"

"If I was a god knowing how other gods behave, why would I trust them?"

"Girl, you sound like you've been thinking about this long."

"What is any sort of god that you should spend any time thinking about him?"

He look up into the sky.

"Sango, when you send lightning please spare my house and strike only her," he say and laugh. "What you have against the gods?" he ask.

"What you have for them?" I reply.

"Don't answer a question with a question, girl."

Keme sprawl himself wider on the grass, clear to me that he is enjoying himself. He beckon me to sit, but he look different in his own yard, like a master, and I not sure what I am yet.

"I don't have no reason to pray to the gods," I say.

"No reason? Listen to this girl. Food? Shelter? Good robes? Success in war? Rain? And that's just for what you want. And then what about thanking the gods for all the good, and for being good."

"No god good."

He frown, then he smile, then he say, "Put down the mortar and speak, little miss sage," and I try to not let it annoy me.

"I used to hear Mistress Komwono—"

"Who?"

"Nobody. I used to hear her say, Trust the gods, for in the end the gods are good. And yet she still get banished. Seem to me that the gods say they are good only because they are gods and nobody can challenge them, even if they really wicked. Or good is good and evil is evil whether there is a god or not, and if is so that go, then calling a god good is worthless too."

Keme look at me like I say something fearful, and I look away like I say too much.

"Sorry," I say.

"Don't be sorry because your mouth run. Be sorry only if it stop."

I take the new grain into the kitchen while he follow.

"You remind me of someone or something. Something I don't know . . ."

I used to think that certain things have a way how they supposed to be done, or a way you supposed to do them. Even when I don't know what way the custom, there should be a custom and somebody, an older woman perhaps, who should know. But what to say about a woman who born in a hut with boys, and only know of woman who try to use her? And what to say when the only older woman she can think to ask about what come to pass is the wife of the same man she is about to fuck? We wordless because I don't have any and he choose none. I thought I would think these are the things that must happen but I not thinking at all. He move over to me like he is about to leave the room, but he brush close, even though great space there be between me and the doorway. I smell iron on him, chain mail marking the red tunic, and he sniff me like he hungry. My nose follow a trail around his neck, my hands bolder than his, under his tunic and pulling down more cloth and grabbing his cock and feeling all the way to the loose skin and squeezing and moving down until my fingers discover balls that I grab too hard and he moan and shiver. I push him to one side of the doorway and he push me to the other side and I listen for squealing children but only for a blink, for his hands circling between my legs, then gone inside me, then circling me again, and then my gown is off so quick I don't remember when it was on. And then he sucking my right nipple so hard he pull out a cry and I yanking the red tunic off his body but it stuck at his neck, and through the cloth he hunt for my nipple again and I watch a gluttonous red shroud suck me. I want to discover him, since I yet to discover a man, I want to run my hand over the washing board between his chest and his cock but can't leave his cock for it is growing in my hand. And growing. Bigger and bigger and bigger still, and if I was a thinking woman I would remark on how big it getting, and not quitting getting bigger. Big not in way of thinking what it going do to me if I let him, but big in a way that you want to whisper to another woman so both of you can squeal in the marketplace, and she can tell you nasty things like when he burst he going to knock out your womb, fly up your neck, and launch through your nose. A noise bring me back, something like a growl, like an animal but it gone, and I say get out of your head, no name woman, and he lift me up and I wrap my legs around him, and I smell dinner on his breath, dinner that for once I help cook, and this make me feel that I make him ready for this night, and he hold me with one hand and take the other to guide his arrow straight into me.

This is not a big house, but in it we always find space unbothered by anybody. Times come when I feel we in another house, or a room set off from the rest, for I shout when he fuck me now, and nothing go tumbling and nobody come running. He take it for sport, I start thinking, for he don't work my body until I done work his mind first, so much that certain afternoon before it even go dark, my mind worried about what small thing I can make deep, what stupid thing I can make smart. It is enough for me to wonder in the days what he truly come to me for. All of this I forget when I squat down onto him or he swim into me. Two moons later when I tell him to squeeze me harder and fuck me stronger he don't take it as invite to war, or to best me, just something for a gentler hand, and for drawing runes on me with his tongue, and hammering me with his hips. I hold his buttocks and play in between them and make him moan to me the way I moan. The moan make me look up, to a brass shield in the corner, so shiny that I often catch myself. But this time I am not the woman that I catch in it.

"Gods!"

I jump off him to grab the nearest thing that look like cloth, a zebra skin that stick to the floor. I try to hide behind it, supposing that in a blink I going to get a slap, or a scream, or a knife through the neck. Or see a dagger cut through to his neck, but he just lie back and put hands behind his neck, not looking at anything while cock still stand tall in the dark. His look say to me that he would like me to climb back on top of him, but if I didn't that would be fine too. When I look again at the shield, the sight gone. Is another four moons of the two of we stealing fucks that she come up to me in the grain keep. We doing the things for so long now that I forget to think about her, so I am thinking she going to cuss about how much sorghum go to waste when I trick the children into thinking pounding grain is the greatest game.

"Soon and very soon you going to feel sick. Whatever enter your mouth going leave through your mouth more than your back hole, you understand?"

"No, I don't understand."

"A little sicky-sicky is usual business. But if your sickness get worse then we have to see the potion master, you understand?"

"I don't know what y—"

"If you more sick than usual, he going be happy. That mean is a girl, girl."

Yétúnde gone back in the house before I catch what she mean.

You would think that with all of this, you would cut such thoughts loose, say a voice in my head that sound like me. **Look at how your hands get full with three children who are not yours but are now**

yours, and with duties around a house that always end right as another one start, and with something like a purpose, and with a man who send you past the brink four or five times a night before he leave your room, or his room, or the kitchen, or behind the big tree, and with a first wife who don't raise fuss when you start to act like second wife or first concubine. Look at how your hands are full, but you empty out your mind every morning to make space for him. Him who you don't want to meet in a dream for he will rule you there, but who take over your mind many times when awake, so that when you're still burning the food, or wasting the water, it is because you make him take up space in your head. And you don't let him leave until you think of another way to kill him.

The Aesi.

I say his name under my breath like I am trying to catch it. I look at Yétúnde and think surely I not the first woman who have to learn to let a thing go, but I cannot let it go. Some sores heal and some sores fester. More than one night I see him trapping himself in my wind as I slam him into tree after tree until he is as flat as a leaf. Or I kidnap the goddess of rivers and springs and tie her to the grand gate of the royal enclosure and whip her until she release a flood that drown everybody within those gates, especially the children, so that evil don't reproduce. I sit in the little room I sleep in and wonder what to do with burning rage before it start to eat away at my heart, my humors, my gut. Some nights I climb on top Keme and I become hammer and he the one who beg me to stop for he going to slip out right as I hammer down and break it. One moon later, one of the boys turn over a jug full of milk that I fetch myself since no space there is to keep a cow. He turn it over because I say I don't have time to play, and he say you will make time because I want to play and I don't care what you want, and then he turn over the jug and as I turn to strike him, he jump back, and fall, and scramble away and scream. And Yétúnde run in shouting what you do to my child, and I scream at her that I didn't do a fucking thing, check the little shit for yourself. Check she do, despite what I say, and no mark she find, but that boy stay with her from then on, and don't come to my room.

Meanwhile rage turning into a friend that come at night and sit with me. It come on like a fever, while other time it come out of nowhere, like something that I hope would pass. Other times it come like a reminder, like some herald that I didn't pay for to hark back to me why the gods return me to Fasisi, and it wasn't to be no second wife raising children that was not mine. **Girl, you slipping,** the voice say. **You think you can forget what your life is for.**

Any bird looking down at Ibiku would think that the district is sliding down the mountain. Which is to say that I didn't have to go far to reach mountainside and woods, and forest dense with tall trees, but still cold and dry. Wind sending tidings from tree to tree perhaps, or maybe breeze is just breeze. I approach a thin tree with next to no leaves left on it and break off a long, thin branch. I peel, and strip, and rub, and shave the branch until it is nothing more than a long, thin staff. A fighting staff. I rob the tree a branch, then I fight the tree. In the dark, through trick of moonlight I conjure a tree fighting me back with her hundred branches and stinging leaves and blinding thorns, which make me jump, slide, skip, duck, roll, and strike. And do all of that again and again, until I gasp all the strength out. The next night I come to the tree not with rage but with craft. Like somebody who wield the staff instead of grapple it. Like the boys in the donga who leap in the air without secret wind and strike like a scorpion.

So of course that night come to pass when I wait until everybody asleep. Keme don't come to my room that night and neither do the children. I creep past their room to see that even in the marriage bed, he roll off onto the floor, not once waking up. I get to the edge by riding across town and cutting through Taha district and a long, dark causeway until I reach the cliff. No cloud hiding the floating district this time, every window is orange from lamplight, and every wall glowing patterns. Nigh on a league the distance to the first landing, but it feel shorter. On the landing, I steady myself as if coming from sea, and look to a view that still mystify me, houses, shacks, taverns, bridges, shelters, all huddled close like any district of Fasisi, and all floating in air. Doors connect to paths, which connect to doors, which connect to paths, and all along them, movement. This time I know where I was going.

Two silver coins get me confirmation that somewhere in the floating district some night entertainment is coming to pass. Two silver coins more get me knowledge that it is a late-night donga after one silver coin get me someone to stop denying it. Three silver coins get me to a gate, and five silver coins get me a voice at the slot growling at me to go fuck a tokoloshe. Three more silver coins and one gold get the gate open, and a knife to the guard's throat get directions and a laugh. Here is why he laugh. I didn't see that past the gate was no ground, only floating tiles and planks, until I slip between two and fall right to my waist. Nobody in the dark to see mean nobody around to hear or help me, so I curse. I watch the tiles while my ears guide me to the shouting, cursing, and cheering.

Two platforms facing each other, like the stands at the King's amphitheater, with the shouting, cheering, and cursing men, both sides packed so tight that the barriers look to burst in a blink. In the center a wood platform as long as is wide, and tiles, rocks, and doors lying flat and river stones all floating. It don't take me long to hear that all the shouting was people cheering a fighter's name on one side and insulting it on the other. Many men sitting on rocks and planks, so I creep behind a rock holding six men. The two men causing all the cheering and cursing finally appear.

Torchlights light up the platform but I can't make out either man in the dark, only the red, yellow, and blue helmets, elbow, knee, and shin guards. It is so dark I don't even see the ringmaster start the fight.

The next night that is me at the gate, with my stick, my breasts bound tight and flat, and my loincloth I swoop up between my legs and tie at the hips. I think to stuff a fruit in there lest anyone doubt I was a boy, but put more linen instead. White linen wrapped around my arms, wrists, thighs, and ankles and a scarf around my head like a hood, covering everything but eyes. Another late night where I leave the house fast asleep, with Keme and Yétúnde naked on the floor.

The crowd jump up again, roaring. The man at the gate say that every fight booked. I think back to early in the day when that little boy piss in my water jug, even after telling Yétúnde that he don't want to play with me, and I fly up in a rage so wild that I did know right there that I could kill a child. My wind, she don't have head nor mind, so a little storm rise up, blow him out of my room, and slam the door shut. In the evening I go into the woods to fight the tree but they all start to cower, or so it look. Rage was coming out of me whether I like it or not, and even though I know who I mean it for, it was starting not to care. I tell the man that I will challenge who win, and I come with gold if I have to pay.

"You paying me to fight? You mad?" he say and laugh. But he open the door. "Pay me now," he say and I realize he was trying to steal more coin, but I pay him anyway. The donga already shouting and raging from a fight. I reach just as one fall down on the platform and the crowd start to chant. The chant get louder and louder, in a tongue I don't know. I touch a man beside me.

"What they singing?" I ask.

"You new?"

"I come from the east."

"Ikipizu. It don't belong to no tongue. It mean kill him."

So there be the crowd. Looking down on one man standing, one man on his back, and shouting Ikipizu! Ikipizu! Ikipizu! The fighter raise his fist to the crowd. Then he turn around and push the man off with his foot. I run back home.

A whole moon pass before I leave the house again. In the noon of that day, the house is most lazy, and those who not sleep, lie down heatdrunk and fan themselves cool. I going through a bundle, for I have enough clothes for a bundle now, and come across what I done forget. The linen paper that Emini used to keep secret by wrapping around her waist, the cloth that she wrap around me because none of the nuns did see the need to inspect a no name girl's body. Her dreams, her plans. Trees tall enough to touch the moon, a city or citadel reaching even higher. Houses, halls, and palaces curved, like lying women, roads a day long, going up toward sky. A city in the trees, and bridges of ropes. Home on top of home all the way

past clouds. Drawing of dreams I still don't understand, but I do understand that somebody out there
so wicked that he murders dreams, even the dream of
a womb-dwelling baby.

I go back to the donga that same night.

Third match is where they put me. They ask for
a name and I say call me No Name Boy. "This one,
he call himself No Name Boy," the announcer shout
to the crowd and rub the fat belly under his white
agbada. The crowd start to chant No Name Boy! No
Name Boy! Until my challenger leap from out of the
darkness and land on the platform so hard that my
side of the platform whip up and almost throw me
off. Love him, this crowd do, for they are roaring
so loud that I don't hear Pig Destroyer until the announcer say it. Then Pig Destroyer is all that I hear.
His skin red like ochre, which could have been from
the torchlight, but it look like he want people to think
it was blood. A whiff come on the wind and I smell
that blood is exactly what it is. Pig Destroyer! Pig
Destroyer! is what the people shout, and when he
stand tall he is taller than me by at least four heads.
Before I even wonder where his stick be, this man
hold out his hand and something from the dark give
him a hammer.

"Hark, this is no stick fight," I shout but in this
crowd it is a whisper. The crowd roar again and
he is a buffalo, charging after me. I slip to the side
quick, but he quick too and I roll out of the way before his hammer smash the platform. He hammering

and hammering and I rolling and rolling so fast that everything blur and I roll myself off the platform. I scream. I grab a floating boulder and for the first time look down into the darkness that clouds pass through. I try to pull myself up, but there is nowhere on the rock to climb up. So I swing my legs, trying to catch a small platform, really a door, and push myself from the rock. Pig Destroyer's back is to me as he whipping up cheers from the crowd. I leap from the door back to a bigger rock, controlling myself this time, letting it sink, and waiting for it to rise when I use the push to leap off and land back on the center platform. Pig Destroyer still bathing in shouting and whistling and singing, so he don't see me swinging my stick with great force and striking his back thigh. He shout, turn around, and run after me in a rage, hammering and hammering his club. That when I realize that despite a club instead of a stick, he is still fighting northern-style, where warriors just wail on each other until one get whipped up so bad that all he can do is block blows. I jump out of the way of a blow, for there will be no blocking that club. And then it happen. I leap out of the way, but I don't land. I leap high above his head and the crowd all go **wooooo.** His head, my stick, I whip-whip-whip his left cheek, then right, then left, then right, then his neck and slice his lip, and spin-spin-spin like a gig and rip up his chest. The wind, my wind, decide to help me, I know it. **Your dagger for the streets, not this donga,** a voice sounding like me say, but I shut it down. He block his

belly, but that is not what I was going for. Yet instead
of drawing blood, my stab at his crotch draw a spark.
Iron armor. The crowd laugh at him and boo me for
hitting where man not supposed to hit. The thought
take me out and he come at me again, northern-style
like everything was an ant, and every hit a hammer.
He throw his weight down, trying to knock me out
of sky, but wind shift me sideways and I slice across
forehead and down nose. Pig Destroyer scream like,
well, a pig, and clutch his face, falling to one knee.
He roar something but I all hear is something about
women liking his face. He come for me and I dodge,
but he ready for me and I dodge right into the swing
of the club, which clobber me in the belly.

   I fall and roll, on the brink of vomit. He come for
me and I have to move. I have to think. Too late, he
grab my ankle and it slip out of his hand. He grab
me again, hook his finger in my belt, and fling me
off the platform. I land on floating rocks, and roll,
spitting blood. That is when I realize that if I come
back with any mark Keme or Yétúnde will ask how. A
voice in my head that sound like me say, **Stupid girl,
you lucky if you make it back to the house alive,
much less with flesh wound.** People shouting Pig
Destroyer, No Name Boy, Pig destroy the No Name
Boy. Pig Destroyer crouch low and leap in the dark
and I see nothing and hear nothing until in the quick
two giant feet come straight for my head, and I roll
out of the way and off the rock.

   The crowd go quiet. I hear the crowd go quiet

before I even see that I am falling. I miss one rock, then two, then three and start to scream. A branch block my fall and I grab on, and it sink with me fast, too fast, then stop and bounce back up. Stop thinking of sky, stop thinking of falling, stop thinking of below, all is just floor. The darkness, the thick black make me forget the sky and I hop from one rock to another, run up ten stacked like steps, and jump back on the platform. Pig Destroyer see that he didn't kill me and curse. He try to hop from rock to rock but slip and fall, and the crowd wash in a wave of **ooooh** as he clutch one and pull himself up and jump to the wood plank and leap again, but this time I ready. He jump for the platform hoping to capsize me, but I leap right before he land, with wind (not wind) pushing me higher, and he smash the platform, tilt it hard, and capsize himself. I am a cat, landing on a tile. There be the big man, hanging on to the platform by one hand, but the platform still tilting and his hand slipping. If this platform right itself all he have to do is climb back on. I hop to the tilted edge of the platform, skid down, kick his fingers off, then stab into the wood to stop my fall. Pig Destroyer screaming until the wind suck away the sound. The crowd so quiet that for the first time I hear a flag flapping on a nearby roof.

No Name Boy! they burst into. No Name Boy! No Name Boy!

The fight master come over to me and say he thought for sure he was sending me to the ancestors because I choose reds. You mean the donga, I wheeze out, but he say, No, reds is the name of the match. Red band and white band fight, with white band being combat until one fall down or yield. Red band fight was to the death, well till one fall off, but on the way down is no cushion. I limp home.

Later in the quartermoon, Keme come knocking, cock in hand and smile on face but I close the door on him. Moonblood, I say. Look how my wicked belly keep cutting me. Moonblood disgust many a man and this one no different. Every body part with a bruise, hint of a bruise, or the fear of a bruise, I cover up in muslin. Nobody see me in half a moon, which was the same time I return to the donga to the crowd shouting No Name Boy! I lose two fight, one white and one red, but skip death because the other fighter too weak to strike the final blow. I draw two, one because we grapple long but neither winning, and another because the crowd was jumping and shouting so raucous that a part of the stand break away, a part not made from Go wood. The fighting continue. I win all the others, nine in number, five of them red fights. Keme start to remark how frequent this moonblood was coming, sometimes not yet gone a moon.

"A woman body do what it want to do," I say.

"But I forgetting what your body look like," he say.

"Nothing on it memorable," I say.

Blood. More time than less I leave the donga covered in it. Six moons pass and the wondering come to me that I should let slip that I am woman, not boy,

until I look into the crowd see all the women and
know that not a single one there by their own choice.
No Name Boy is a champion, but not the only champion, and I stay away from any man twice my size.
The fight master promise me more money, but stop
when it start to seem that I care little about it, for I
forget to collect three times. A voice in my head that
sound like me say, **Look at you and how you like the
taste of blood.** The last one was like Pig Destroyer,
hanging on a little rock by just two fingers, which I
cut off. **I don't kill nobody, they kill themselves,** I
say. **One kind of killing can't fill the spot that the
other kind is to fill,** say the voice, to which I say,
You don't know what you talking about.

"But I didn't say anything," say Keme's little boy.

I cover my mouth. Two children are right here
playing in the room.

The same night Keme come to my chamber, saying to me, "Look, woman, not another complaint
about moonblood. Is only half moon since, I count
the nights," he say also, but I don't close the door.
Quiet is how we keeping it, as I go down on the floor
and pull the muslin up my waist. Keme mock a laugh
and tell me to turn over, and though I don't want to, I
don't want him to ask me why. The muslin not coming off, I thinking. Keme say, Be a nun, if that is your
wish, and push himself in me so quick that I jump.
Nothing to stop, he is on top. No time leave for thinking, only to grab his backside, hand to cheek, hoping
to guide him slowly in and out of me, but he fuck

me hard and hungry. My wince, my groan, my little cry out, my rush of breathing, my everything he is mistaking for pleasure, but every single one is a pain, sprain, and bruise waking up. How much more of this I can stand, I don't know, but stand I going have to do. **Fuck anywhere else, even the mouth,** a voice in my head tell me to say, but he would ask why, and what is going on with me, and perhaps even ask that I take the muslin off. **Push up on him then,** the voice say, **press in to his press, wrap your legs around his hips and take control. Man like surrender when nobody watching him bow.** I fuck myself upon him, and he moan and say, Take what you want from me. Squeezing the sheets, squeezing my shoulder, Keme is going wild, but I just trying to stop my mouth from screaming the way my chest, hips, arms, and belly been long doing. Nothing to do but bear it, to hold on to the actual sweetness of us fucking each other good. He sleep in my bed that night, but I take to the floor, then climb in the bed in the early dawn, right before he wake up.

Moons coming, time passing, soon one year gone and the Aesi is still alive. And this King, and his boys, and the good people of the court. Certain streets start to smell better now that the bodies of impaled witches all rot off. The North make peace with Wakadishu without a long war, even though the territory say they is neither North nor South. One day I pass by fabric seller's stall in Baganda district, a day hot though it is not the season and the sun gone past noon.

"Purple? Is only for royalty," I say and pick up a shawl.

"Only the womenfolk, and the Queen Mother say she hate purple. I mean the Queen. Stepmother one day, wife the next, who knows what she will be to-morrow? Why this King need two wife is what people should ask," she say.

"The King Sister used to love purple."

"Sister to which King?" she ask, and I didn't know what to say, so I say nothing, hoping the talk would just die. "Girl, which King Sister, me say. Girl? Girl?"

I don't stop walking until I am back in Ibiku.

Here is truth. I try to forget, and living in Keme house make it easy as long as nobody ask any question for which nobody have any answer. Yétúnde's children still ask who I be in this house since I don't stand for discipline like a mother, nor share in their mischief like a sister, but they don't ask me. One time, past a year now, I am in the granary pounding grain as I do, and two of them run to their mother in the kitchen. The two of them have a bet about who Sogolon is. So who she be? they ask. She say, Ask your father. Certain things about the father I asking too, not to him but myself. A voice in my head that sound like me say, **Look at you, your questions used to come with an answer clear as night or day, but now you can't tell if is dusk or dawn.** I curse myself because I don't know what that mean even though I am the one saying it. I curse until I understand myself. That is, not long ago all questions in my head was simple, with yes or no, come or go, hot or cold, good or evil. Now come questions that don't have one-word answer, when they have an answer at all. What is the yes or no to the question of the linen paper that I sometimes wear around my waist to remind myself of Emini? What it mean that I have to remind myself now? That my memory fade faster than the ink on this royal parchment? My first thought was to stop going to the donga because I working off too much of my rage in a place that it not meant for. My second thought is that rage is not what bothering me, but other things that I can't name. Won't name. Keme. Me and Keme. There is no me and Keme. There is Keme and his wife, Yétúnde, that is her name, which I say over and over. I live with a man and his wife, and yet I know exactly which mushroom remind me of the tip of his cock when I pull the skin back. **Nasty girl,** that voice say to me, but the quiet voice say, **As long as he is cock, then he is not man, and as long as he is not man, he is not . . . what?** He don't bring marriage promise and I don't bring dowry. I don't look like a concubine, and me and the wife is not sister. We not even friend. We not enemy either, but yet one more thing in this house that is just too gray. And Keme still hungry for my mind, though I don't see what he find in it. It make him feel like a brother, but I don't fuck my brother. As for fucking, is this fucking when it move so slow, slow meaning he mean it, slow meaning he care, slow meaning that this must be how people who lucky to meet in a love match fuck? One time he make me holler with just his finger, and afterward all I could think was that the least of him touch me, yet that was the most of him I ever did get. This man is making my thinking messy. That is what he is doing and I going to need him to stop it. Except I don't.

Night come and I wonder who put it in my head that I supposed to be the instrument of anything named vengeance. If the divine sisters' spirits crying out for justice, that is a cry for the ear of devils. I never sorry to see a single one go. And Emini never look at me as no sister, but how could she, being the princess? Maybe she did try as within her strength, even if that was never good enough. I wrap her linen paper around me without thinking, until I think about it. Sometimes I wear it before a fight, but I don't want to think about that either. Sometimes I have even been hit, slashed, right where the papers are wrapped around my body, but never once do they tear or smudge. What am I supposed to think of that? Thinking come anyway. Of that time riding in the wagon on the way to Mantha, me waking up from every bump, Emini not sleeping. Me seeing her looking at me every time I open my eye. Before she even talk, I get this feeling that she was trying to know me and that was new to her and for me too. For the only way I could know this was because I knew the opposite, her not showing no interest in me at all. Her and everybody.

"What is it like to be alone?"

I don't answer. Being alone still perplex her. For her it mean just her and the servants, or the lions, or whoever been there so long that they are one with the drapes. I see it, that from she was born, Emini have people watching her, following her, caring for her under threat of their own life. The same women who follow her to chambers, undress her, and try to amuse her also hold the bowl under her when she cut shit loose, also wipe her, and also make the whole concern go away. They hide her stink from her, but they always in her company. Even after they take everything from her, I was with her alone. The thought, her on her own in a room of her own, perplex her spirit until she have to say out loud, Good riddance to all that. She will die alone. By the moment I witness it, she was already dead. Some dawn she will come back to tell me she is roaming the lands between death and life because nobody come to sail her to the otherworld. She cannot book passage because her spirit won't settle and neither will her baby.

Fuck the gods and drown her in a well of piss, for I don't owe her a thing. Nothing about my life from the day Miss Azora find me was my choice, and if I did have the choice it would never lead to no royal house, and no royal house would even know of me. This is how it really go: The princess, the divine sisters have one thing in common, that they both take me against my own will, and all of them dying and leaving me alive mean the gods love to make joke. Then why on certain nights and certain mornings a whisper come to me saying, **Woman, you delay. And undying quiet will never come to your head until you make haste. You think what you have now, when Keme come to your bed and you listen him sleep, is peace, but that is not peace, that is comfort. Comfort is a lie that shame the gods. Comfort is how you fool yourself. Comfort, like happiness, can't last.**

I lose the fight that night, but it was a white band fight. I lose because I hear news among the crowd that steal my mind from everything else.

Ugliko district. Call it dusk. Two men back in the donga crowd said a word and a third agree, saying, They making a mockery of justice, a mockery of decency, hark they soon make a mockery of mockery if nobody do anything. You see those two, last quartermoon? No, but we hear that they killed a woman because the two take it for a joke to throw her up into the sky, higher than birds fly, but not catch her. Flap, flap your wings, they say. Laugh at it they do when she land and burst open in the street. Next time be like the cat, the green one say, we hear it. Her husband and three children take it to a magistrate but he say, Where are the witnesses? Hear me now, they take what they want to take, eat what they want to eat, last moon they rape a boy with a knife so no need to tell you how fare he. You would think things would be better after the witch purge, but they worse. And this King, this better we not say, for I know one of their kind can hear from over a thousand paces away.

They, the Sangomin.

So, Ugliko. A district that is no district, according to the people who live in this district. Prefecture, they call it, to make you know that it is more than just some other place in Fasisi. But it is nothing more than the place to smell the fart of the King. No house more magnificent than anywhere in Baganda, no garden as beautiful as the hill gardens in Ibiku, but it is the backside of the royal enclosure, and the home of all in service to and in the favor of the King. But it is evening, and I am here in a street I don't know, three streets over from where I tie the horse. My feet take me to the center, and a garden that make me feel too unmasked to stay. Nobody here would know me any more than they would know Emini, but the fear still creep up and push me back into an alley. Is not like the men at the donga promise me anything, since none even talk to me, but I take their word as promise anyway. The drum in my chest pound until there is nothing left, then start pounding again. The Ugliko is a different place after dark, Keme say to Mistress Komwono once. Right now I counting on it. The alley too quiet for me to just stand, so I start walking up another, down the next, cutting across three, to trail up two, to go back up to the first, then do the whole thing again. I wait for the wind to send me some distress, anyone, probably a woman suffering at the hands of one of them. Or two, I add, and the thought make me almost grin.

Quick as you think it a cry come on wind, down a street, not even an alley. They do their deeds in the dark with no reason to hide, these children. In the time since going to the donga I stop counting off the nights, then quartermoons, then moons since they murder the caravan to Mantha. Soon I will start counting summers, **and Emini's cry going turn into a whimper, then a whisper, then nothing,** say the voice in my head. But it don't know that this is not even about Emini. She never was my friend, and even her trying to know me was only because she see the fruit of things coming to pass that she didn't know.

In the time since I stop counting night, I go back to the Ibiku woods and chop down the straightest branch a tree would give me. Then I strip it, paint it with stolen ochre, sharpen one edge to an arrowpoint, and whisper to the gods that it is a spear now, a spear that I plan to throw only once. The cry come again, three streets over, maybe four, as do a big laugh and a small one. I run. A long, dark street with carts but no horse, stalls but no sellers, doors but all shut, and no light but the green smoke coming from one of them. They stand over two people, one a crying boy and the other someone bigger on the ground and not moving.

First all I could think was Watch this come to pass, for this is not what you want. What you want is for them to lead you to the royal enclosure. To him. But then the boy scream.

Any man would call this spear a good weight, even if it bend and twist a little. Between the two of them come a green smoke that light up the alley. I move back five step, then run as fast as I ever run, then sixty paces or so, dig my heels, and my whole body, not just my arm, throw the spear, which burst right through the taller one's neck and kill his laugh. I don't see his face. I want to see his face right then more than I want to live, and to have the darkness take the sight from me make me so mad that I don't even see the other one until he upon me. Little, but he running along the wall as if it is the road. I turn to run just as he knock me down harder than a battering ram. A mask covering his nose and mouth. I try to get up, feeling wet on my chest but not knowing what it be, but it not warm so is not blood. Then he pull the mask and green vapor blow from what is neither mouth nor nose, from what is nothing. Green vapor bright like lightning. He blow and blow and the wild bush all round me shrivel to nothing, and an owl flying low drop from the sky. But his eyes going wild. This not supposed to happen. More weeds die and more bird and bugs drop, and the skin on my arms start to dry out, but around my face the wind (not wind) blocking the smoke. I reach up and grab him, since he still but a child, poke the dagger right to his chest and press the sides. He jerk and fall, smoke still coming from the lower half of his face, but now he coughing up blood. He say something, that he could never get the smoke to stop, but stop it do, only one little wisp coming through a hole that was no mouth and two holes that were no nostrils. Then he die. Just like that, and it come over me like a massive weight that this don't feel like nothing. I don't know what it is, the something I was looking for, but this is not it. This is worse than the donga, for at least there I earn the victory. I did want a fight. I did want a punch, a scrape, a stab, or a stomp, something that make me fight for my life and come within a blink of losing it. But Sangomin when you take away their gifts and their wickedness is just children. Nothing about killing them feed the hunger. Hunger for what, I don't know, but is that thing that feel fed when I kill in the donga. But the feeling never last, and the hunger won't go. It come when the children say something stupid or wicked, and I yell at them so loud that they run squealing like pigs, which make me feel like I am a mean woman who deserve no kindness. Sometimes the hunger last for many moons, and I lapse into forgetting, but it always come back, as if such a thing would ever quit a woman. Which lead me to Ugliko, because a Sangomin, no matter who, is a Sangomin responsible, but the hunger is saying to me that if you think an arm is the same as a finger or a head the same as a nose, then you are a fool. Dogs run loose

because somebody let slip the leash. Now you acting like rage causing your hunger when you did have
anger from long before. This hunger only come after
you pick up the taste for blood.

I didn't even look back at the boy or his mother.

THIRTEEN

Three years it take me, and the first thing I wonder is why it take me three years to find out that Keme fucking other woman. I almost scold myself for calling it a shock, when I don't feel anything like surprise. Of course he entering the house of other woman—I was three years ago that other woman. I not even trying to follow him when I see him, but think that he was following me. After all, why take the border road of Ibiku to come all the way around to Taha when many a road simply cut across? I was ready for whores or other man's concubines, but not for a house owned by a widow with children and donkeys and one of the few camels in Fasisi. It make me wonder if in a man's mind different kind of woman lay in different kind of way, and to get what he need he go out. That evening I follow only because my curiosity get hungry. He leave with a smile on his face and the thought that it was from a pleasing fuck didn't bother me, but that it could come from a pleasing talk bother me to a fever. Wind was running ahead of me to trip him up and knock him down before I whisper through my gnashed teeth to stop it. Maybe Yétúndé know. He not under any duty to tell me nothing. Besides, she not the only one.

I not making note. But the second one is younger than me, and sell roots in Baganda district. I follow him that time, as he go from high Baganda, which sell all that is beautiful, to low Baganda, which sell all that is useful. That is why she selling yams there, for nobody in high Baganda want to see anything that remind them of dirt, especially food. She look like a woman who don't wash. I wonder what Keme see in her, and what is it he getting that he not getting at his house. Maybe not getting it at a house was enough, for he never fuck her in one. After she close up her stall, I don't even count to ten before the whole shack start to shift and shake and she start yelping like a small dog.

And he not the only one I follow. A voice that sound like me say, **You looking for story, that is what you doing, and is because you don't like your own.** What story? I say back to the voice, to which she only say, **Yes.** But the children I follow too. In the day, of course, I see them playing in the dirt, with the youngest shouting, I am ninki nanka! Look at my tail! Look at me breathing smoke, and then he hold ash powder to his mouth and blow it. One child squeal, the other laugh, and the other curse out words he not supposed to know, but in the quick they all go quiet, turn and leave the house through the back. Is not the leaving that make me follow, for children will be children, but the quiet, for that is not like them at all. They weave through the Ibiku backwoods, past trees a hundred times taller than them, from a clear trail onto one that still hide in the bush. Not total silence, for the smallest one is singing something. But they keep walking like something unseen luring them until they come across five mounds, in what was a clearing before grass run it over. On these mounds they sit quiet and play quiet games, barely talking to each other. It look like a thing to let pass until a half moon later when they do it again. The third time I follow them halfway and grab the youngest.

"Your mother know you go in the woods?"

I expecting her to be in some sort of bewitchment, but she answer me clear.

"But we always go to the woods. Or they get lonely," she say.

"They who?"

But she smile and push my hand off, gentle. I quit thinking bewitchment fall on them, and that it was all play.

Maybe I was looking for malcontent, or at least something more sinister, but that they was just children being children leave me feeling a way. The voice in my head would be disappointed if I did allow it. Or unsatisfied. Or whatever it is that lead me back to the donga, and that night I didn't even fight. A man who take to wearing blood, like Pig Destroyer, defeat

another man who go by the name Shit. Two fight to
a draw and one get disqualify when in the quick he
shift into a leopard and snap the other man's neck
with his jaw. No shapeshifting in the donga, the master shout, only fair fights in this arena, which make
me laugh. I sit in the crowd as they shout and sing
and curse and shake the floors, and there I recognize
the smell of people hungry for blood. I stay for three
more fights—quicker when you watching them instead of fighting them—until a man with foul breath
say to me, Is you name No Name Boy? Every time
you win, I lose.

I get home hoping he don't come to my room tonight. Morning is still a good while away, I am thinking, when my back get such a clobbering that I barrel
into an urn that crack. I roll over, frightened that it
was a thief or murderer or demon, but is Keme, his
lips wet with rage and his eyes red and furious.

"This is what you do at night, eh? This is how
you betray my house? Is my money you betting on
death match?"

Before I say anything he reach for my own stick
and stomp toward me with it. I can't ask myself how
he find it, or how he know what it be for. I try to roll
out of it but the stick still reach my thigh, my buttocks, and my back. I scream, and scream again, but
he pull back only to beat me again.

"Stop!" I cry. And I shout it again, but he growling
like some sick dog and turn to beat me again, like
me was the most wicked child he ever did see. He

still shouting and I wondering how he not waking up the house when he swing the stick again, not looking where he going to hit. I crawl away and he strike my back and I cry out. He say something about me loving to watch stick fight, then I going get one, and he swing the stick again. But this time I catch it.

"Stop," I say.

He is the soldier, but I am the one who been killing people. He don't know this, but I going to learn him. Still holding his end of the stick, he try to slap me but I raise the stick in his way and he hit it. He drop the stick and curse something that I don't hear.

"I going show you who is master in this house," he shout.

"You is not my master," I say, which enrage him more. He stomp to me again, but the wind (not wind) push him back. It drive him to shock, as the hunger come over me and I swing with the stick and strike him on the chest and the neck, top his head, and face, and he fall and I start to wail on him and didn't even notice that the one screaming was me. He try to fight but I too fast, I whipping him until the stick come back red. He grab my foot to pull me down, and I kick him but he catch that foot too and he pull and I fall on my back so hard that I cough out the breath. He growl something about fighting him in his own house, defying him in his own house, and slap my face left, then right, then left again. He on me, pressing me down and as he rise to his knee I see an opening and kick him straight in the balls. He bawl out, drop beside, and curl like a baby still in the cowl. I jump and scream at him that no man get to call me property, no man, but then it come, another blow to my head that shatter clay. Yétúnde is yelling at me. I don't say anything. All I do is turn to face her and she go flying into the wall and stay there. But that is not enough. My wind (not wind) pull her from the wall, then slam her back into it, pull slam, pull slam, until she stop moving. Keme get up but I scream at him and in the quick the wind grab his head, about to twist it until the neck break. Both of them rising before me as my breath race. I raise them higher, twisting her neck and wrenching his hand behind his back and bending every finger, waiting for ten snaps, then his wrist, then his elbow, which was going to bend in different way until it break, then break off, and as for she, her head drop but it wake up my anger and I slam her into the wall again and there is the ceiling so fling them up until they burst through their own roof straight toward the sun and—

"Sogolon, please!" he shout, then whimper. "Sogolon, please."

They both off the ground and I not hearing them. But then I turn around and there be two of the children, the youngest girl perplex, the older girl just looking. The wind (not wind) drop the both of them. I out of breath. The children still stare at me, following me with their eyes.

The morning birds have not yet woken outdoors and I gathering my things. By now I did save enough coin to afford a room somewhere in Baganda district, or one of those lonesome streets heading north, or anywhere that I would never see Keme again.

"No inn will have you," Keme say. I don't know how long he at the door, or how long he watching me.

"Who will have me is my business, not yours," I say.

"I mean none will be open." His right cheek have a long gash and his right eye won't open right. It look like he is limping. Or that standing up is paining him.

"Then any street can have me until then."

"Nobody saying you should leave, not even Yétúnde say so. You knock the memory out of her. She wondering which cow knock her down last evening. I think she think it was a dream." Keme laugh, but it come out like a wheeze. Great pity come over me when I look at him, so I look away.

"If I was you, I would tell me to go," I say.

"Good thing that nobody in this house is you."

"I don't bet on the fight. I am the fight," I say.

"I don't understand."

"At the donga. I am the one fighting. The people call me No Name Boy."

"But you are—"

"Too young. They don't care. Since my first fight any man who lay him hand on me, I kill. Not just in the donga but out of it as well."

"I see."

"No, you don't see. If Yétúnde at peace with a man who beat her, that is her mind. But I will surely kill you. Either right there or in your sleep, and I don't care if your child sleeping with you."

"You seem sure."

"I don't seem."

He grin again, as if I was some woman saying something that was all heart, that he had to laugh off with his manly patience. It annoy me.

"You learn to fight in the donga or before?"

"What you really want to know?"

"How a woman beat me up, to be honest," he say with a painful smile.

"Because you fight with the pride that you will win."

"You don't?"

"I tell myself either I leave alive or we both leave dead. Either outcome fine by me."

"You also have spirits fighting for you. God or demon? Or do I live with a witch?"

"Witch work spells, and gods don't care about no girl."

"So you're like the Sangomin."

"I nothing like them!" I say and he jump. Then he hold his hand up as if blocking a blow. Also annoying.

"But it's true. If a Sangoma found you as a baby, you would be Sangomin now. Very few like you ever pass their notice."

"Nobody looking for gifts in a termite hill. They looking for somewhere to shit."

I forgot how bothersome it be when he is correct.

Then he ask, "You don't fight to the death, do you?"

"Yes."

"Sogolon, no. You can't. . . . You can't. . . . I . . . What will I tell the children the morning you don't come home?"

"I not going lose."

"Because you fight with the pride that you will win? Maybe one day somebody will come with more reason to be angry than you. Maybe even a woman."

Here is truth. I never even think about that until he say it.

"Who you really trying to kill?" he say.

"One thing don't always mean something else."

"One thing always mean something else in this world. You not that different, no matter how special you think you are."

"I never say I was special."

"I never say you say anything."

"Something about you like having a woman around who can beat you."

"Perhaps," he say and smile, and I start to lose grip on what all these smiles mean. Some man seem to like it when the woman put up a fight, even when she get in some blows, but only if he hold down, overpower, and charge himself inside her koo. Keme is not this kind of man, not even in this fight.

"But don't leave because some stupid soldier try to be overlord with you. He will never do it again," he say.

"I won't stop going to the donga."

"I know. Who in this house can stop you? There

is a power in you, Sogolon," he say and for the first time this night he hit me. I wish it was a punch but it was with those words, words he say before but will never remember. Words I can't forget. What he see in me now is what he see in me then, and he was always looking deeper, and even when he looking twice he find the same thing. I will not soon forget you, he also say to me once, before he forget it.

"What is the matter? What did I do?" he ask.

"Is nothing. Is nothing. I just tired."

"Beating up one of the King's warriors will take the breath out of a girl."

This time I smile.

"If I was you I would turn me out," I say.

"But I am not you, so that settle that."

"I going back to the donga."

"I know."

"Perhaps tonight."

"What if I want to come to you?"

"Not the first time I do two in one night."

There he go, laughing again, though I didn't try to be funny. He turn to leave when I say, "Hit me, or Yétúnde, or any of the children and I will kill you."

"Look at you, the champion," he say and close the door behind him. He did limp for sure.

So this also happen in the third year, the year where I stop counting years, for a year of moving forward also mean a year of leaving things behind, and the leaving behind feel like accepting fate, the times, cowardice, or just the slow move of days from dawn to dusk to dawn again. So I tell myself as year jump on top of year. But come to pass this do, near the end of Gurrandala, the tenth and second moon, and the first thing I remember was some years back when Yétúnde say to me, A little sicky-sicky is usual business. Morning malady that send me outside to vomit out breakfast, and evening malady that force back out dinner, and strange leaves which only old woman can name that Yétúnde have me eat. She look at me and say, I was starting to think you was one of them ill-equipped women. But see it there, look at what finally come over you.

"You with children," she say.

"Children?"

"That is what I telling you. This man seed never breed just one."

The news fill me with dismay, for how I was going to fight man with a bother in me belly. How was I going to fool anybody now that I really am No Name Boy? But it fill me with wonder too. After all, how could something growing in you, with little care for how you feel about it, not make you feel something? I start to sound like Yétúnde, wondering how it take this long to occur. Even Keme take the news with a face that said both **Oh?** and **At last** at the same time, which make me wonder if this is how he plan to imprison me. See him here in the welcome room, stretching on cushions and looking at me and my belly, and seeing himself. Seeing this man's work.

"By the gods, you must be the first woman to see motherhood as a prison."

"You lock me away inside for the whole spell, so what else I supposed to call it?"

"You could at least pretend this bring you some joy."

It did bring not joy, but delight. Sometimes. Like those times when I catch myself rubbing my belly and grinning to myself. But it bring fear too, fear of almost everything. Fear of what this birth going to mean for me, and for this child, or children, as Yétúnde keep claiming. It leave me with waking dreams of running and dodging in the donga while two thin babies dangle from my two breasts, holding on with their sucking lips. The children take my swelling belly as some great illness or some massive, nasty bump about to burst, for they avoid me as soon as they wake and head to the mounds, where they play all day.

I know the way of mothers was nine moon, so it frighten me when on the third day of the seventh moon, wetness run out of me down my legs. Outside I stand, watching evening come, shelling peas and wondering if any man at the donga was asking what become of No Name Boy, when a shift happen in me. Shift is all I can call it, for everything that happen to me up till now I know of, or feel before. Every single thing that come next is a new thing and I hate it. I run to Yétúnde, for she is the only person I can tell.

"Go outside and walk around. The real business don't even start yet," she say.

She don't tell me when to stop so I keep walking, and the children, liking any activity, start to walk with me. Later that same morning a horse kick me in my belly, a scorpion sting numb my legs, and a demon hand shove itself into my back, grab ahold of my backhole, and pull. So it feel when this child coming out of me. Children, this wife say to me again, and I scream at her, then say is the pain that make me do it. One everlasting pain that lead me to throw myself off the hill would be better. Better still to cut me open, take it out, and leave me to die. But this pain coming down like assault, then to retreat, only to come back again, make me want to search for Keme and kill him slow. This is when Yétúnde send for a midwife.

"She can't speak," is all she say.

Is not true when they say that all that come before the baby you forget after. I still remember the horse-kick pain, and my body screaming to push, and the midwife waving her hands to say not yet, not yet, not yet, and me howling at her, Then when, you shriveled, silent bitch! And I still remember each time Yétúnde and the midwife look at the time glass, then each other, then at the time glass again. And I still remember one of them saying that is not for the man to be here when me scream out for Keme to come so I can kick him in the face and knock out at least two teeth. That make the midwife laugh, but no sound come out of her mouth. Is total dark when Yétúnde shout that I must push for real now, and I scream, What in the fuck you think I was doing before, but my body start push without me. And the top of my belly want to rip open too, and I want to shit out the world, and my knees gone numb in this squat and everything is wet wet wet and red red red. None of this this bitch tell me, not even that moment when you head bout to tell the body to surrender only to see that it surrender long time, and all I can do is huff and puff while a voice that sound like me say, **These are the things that must happen to you.** I still remember how much I cry in front of this wife, and how she look at me blank like I was giving her a gift that she have no use for. And then one slip out and the mute midwife come at it with a knife and I slump over, but then Yétúnde say, Another one, and I think, Fine, if there is another one, so be it, and then though she don't say anything more she reach under me to catch two times more.

And one have strong cry that would wake people asleep a day away, the other cry too, not as strong, but nothing coming from the other two and I shout, Is what? Is what? Tell me if they dead, tell me, you silent bitches. And there they go again looking at each other, then at the swaddling cloths.

"Is what?" I shout again.

"Trust the gods," she say to me.

"I want my children. Give them to me."

"Rest now, girl. You—"

"Give me my fucking children!"

Yétúnde give the midwife a look and she nod. I am on the floor, trying to sit up. They bring over first two babies all wrap up, one with eyes closed, and the other open but looking all over, for everything is new. Then the midwife bring over the other bundle, but walk so slow that it look like she about to faint. I yell at her again to bring me my children, and she hand the bundle to me. I had to pull it open and even then I nearly drop them.

Inside, one is sleeping, the other is awake, both of them lion cubs.

Outside I can hear them pacing and twitching, wondering what they going to tell Keme, when they should be wondering what Keme is going to tell me. My head won't settle, it get wicked and full of ill will, but then it get fearful, then it get mournful, and then all of that vanish in wonder. Everything run through this unsettling head. That Yétúnde is about to walk right back in and say, Is a little joke I did play on you, one of them jokes only she find funny. That this is witchcraft, meaning I fall under the curse of witches. That this is witchcraft, meaning I am a witch. That some enemy put a curse on this house or on Keme and nobody see any need to tell me. That a shapeshifter is nothing strange in Fasisi, especially lions, and anyway my middle brother used to fuck a snake. I think to grab both of them and smash their heads against the wall, but they also fumbling their way to my nipples, hungry, and I can't do nothing but let them feed. The other two, a girl and a boy, both have skin dark as me, but the boy already have hair on his arms and legs, he open his eyes and look at me, waiting for whatever it is that I don't know. I don't know what to say or do, and Yétúnde not inside to teach me of mothering, so I push him to my left breast and he suck too. There I be on the floor, but I can see myself looking at me on the floor, the afterbirth in the corner luring flies, while a cub and a boy feed to their full off me.

N one ever come out of Yétúnde," this man say to me. He step into my room like he come home from war, or from conquest of something that I don't want to know about. His helmet off, but still in chain mail and irons, his way of saying to me that wherever he coming from, he soon gone back to, so don't even come with any fuss.

"You come into my room and that is the first thing you say?"

"Is you they come out of."

"Is you who put them in there."

I still on the floor, getting furious that this is what the man say to me after him make me squat for four.

"How—"

"Don't even dare say it."

"I was going to say, how it come to pass that me own wife never . . . but you . . ."

"What you saying? You think me out there cuck-olding you with some cat?"

"No. What? Of course not. I thought it skipped," he say but it don't sound like he saying it to me.

Which is when I say, "That sound like you telling it to yourself."

"I was."

He pick up one of the cubs, fur clay white with dark spots almost like a leopard, and purring at the touch of his daddy. At who must be his daddy. The cub, from nose to tail, reach from Keme's elbow to thumb.

"You must have some enemy who bewitch me," I say.

"Hardly," he say as he help the cub climb his shoulder, then cradle him before he fall off. Then he hold the cub right up to his mouth and lick his head and little feet. I wait for him to speak because suddenly I can't find words.

"You not a . . . You couldn't . . . How . . . What?"

"I said I thought it skipped. Meaning skipped a generation since none of Yétúnde's ever born this way. My father never show anything, but grandfather could change, and my granduncle was a full-on lion."

"What you saying? That they might turn into boy and girl?"

"They already boy and girl," he say to me, harsh and sharp. "Don't call us beasts."

"Us?"

"Yes," he say. He place the cub on his head and grin as he seek out his hair. He, not it. He.

"I never see you shift to nothing. Never hear you roar, even when you play with Beremu. You don't even take to meat much." He laugh, hoping the laughter will warm me. I can see it in his eyes.

"No lion at court ever become a general. All of them are playthings of the King, even Beremu. They say they have no ill will for us. They say we are not lower, yet I don't see any shapeshifter leading an army, or giving counsel to the King, or deciding the tactics of war."

"We not fighting any war."

"You know what I mean. Ever since a hyena troop turn on their own men near a hundred years ago. Well I not about to become either palace toy or army berserker."

"That man who ride with you all them years was a marshal."

"He was a scout. And there at my pleasure, not the army's. Plus he don't ride with us anymore. Don't you hear what I am saying to you? Where I want to go, being me can't get there."

"Then go somewhere else."

"You and your simple head and your simple answers." He give me a bashful smile, but he is insulting me, and he know that I know. He annoy me so much that for the first time that day I try to stand up, but my knees buckle. He rush over to grab me, forgetting the cub on his head, who jump from him to me as he grab my waist.

"Where you think you going? You still too weak," he say. I really want to make distance between me and him, but my knees don't agree. He help me back down on the rugs, all tender, which surprise me still. Outside, Yétúnde is still talking to the midwife, who still don't make a sound. I know they talking about me, talking about how I try and fail to become number one woman, even though that is something I never want to be. I know that before these children come, she was worrying about losing favor with her husband, but now that two of these children born beasts, she is still the reigning woman of the house. It don't matter how many times I tell her that I don't want to be in charge of this house, she could never hold the thought in her head for long, the thought that a woman could want or would want anything else. I try to be a motherly woman and not think of the donga.

"And you think nobody know?"

"The lions know. Maybe. Perhaps. Didn't ask."

"They know. How you can think they don't now? I would know a woman even in the dark."

"Fine. As you say, they know."

"Is not about what I say. Is—"

"Quit this talk, Sogolon."

"Or what you going do, roar?"

He furious for one blink, but then burst out laughing. Funny it is for real. He stoop down to me.

"This was long time past. Kwash Kagar send troops to smash a rebellion in the Purple City. Every general say take Lake Abbar by night, by boat, sail east and storm the city. From behind, they say. Beremu was the only one who say that Lake Abbar's current always push boats west, and people would see us from a day away. And what is the Purple City but one big lighthouse. He even told the general about the caves running under the lake. You know what that general say? **The only sound I need from a berserker is a roar.** Five hundred soldiers slaughtered before they even reach land, because nobody want to take the counsel of a fucking cat. They even lock him up for unruliness because he wouldn't stop growling about it. You know what it is like to never be listened to?"

A hundred and one things I could say right now. A hundred and one things.

"Well, that fate is not for me, you hear? I refuse it. I have standing in this form."

I laugh.

"What? What now?"

"You call it a form. A shape like any other. Who is me to tell you who is you?"

"You know the work, being me? You know how you never have to think about breathing, but you have to think about how you dress, or what you say? That is me wearing the skin of a man. I have to will my own skin to settle."

"Is it so as a lion?"

"No."

"Shame can never settle."

"Is not shame, woman. I know . . ."

"You know what?"

"Quit this talk, I say."

"You have three others," I say, and he hop over

to the other bundles, while this cub find my breast again. Keme grin so wide as he look inside each bundle, his brand-new children. Is the first I seeing it, but the feeling come to me that many women see it before me, the look in his eyes and his grin that say, These come from me.

"Look at the hair on this one, and he not even the lion!"

"Not yet," I say to myself. He is cradling all three now, shushing the first girl as she start to cry—I know her cry already—and there it is on his face, a new look I never see before, that I can't find words for. Like surrender, but not, or like sweet bliss that come after he cum, though it is not that, or like relief, or satisfaction maybe, though I don't know what that look like. Or maybe it is a look that only fathers get when they see their pride—the word just come out of me, as if I was already accepting all this. He is grinning and grinning, and cooing and making a sound that take me too many blinks to see is purring. **Who is this man before you, the new man who come to the house for the first time in three years?** say a voice that sound like me. Here is truth. With his other children he really is the lion, now that I think about it. He play with them as be his pleasure, he tell them which street not to walk on, and which men not to trust, and jump in front of them when a snake slither into the yard, but most day he don't even see them.

"Show him to me," I say.

"Which one?"

"Not the baby, you. Show me he that you hiding."

It take him a while before he see what I mean.

"Here?"

"Listen to you, you sound like a virgin around a boy."

"You don't know a thing about that."

"Stop delaying it and let your children see you as you."

"This is me."

"That is how you want people to see you. Them two things not the same."

"Girl, I tell you I don't change for—"

"This not the army, and I not your commander. Children should see their father, even if is just once."

He look at me with a battle-loss face and place the children down. I sit up, not expecting anything, but expecting everything. He clutch his stomach and start retching so quick that I jump, thinking he is going to fall or vomit. He cough and choke and cough, then jerk, and jerk, and jerk again, then do a drunk sway, about to topple, then fall hard on one knee, his back to me. He heave again, and moan something low and death-slow. I try to get up, but he wave his hand behind at me fierce, telling me to stay. This thing come over him like waves, reminding me of me only this morning. He start to huff and huff, blowing out whatever punching him down inside. I regret that I ask him. In all these three years I never see so much of a whisker, which mean if he ever did change, it was from a time even further from that. Not true, my voice say. He been changing every day since before I know him. The Keme that I see every day, that is the change, that is the form that never can settle. He throw off his chain mail and pull off his tunic so hard that it tear. His buttocks I see first, spread wider and long, as if water is rushing under his skin, filling out his thighs and his legs and packing muscle upon muscle and sinew upon sinew. Then hair rush down his lower back and race down him past his cheeks into a tail while he growl and howl. Hair burst from his head, lighter and straighter than his usual hair, a grain field growing wider and wilder. Not hair, mane is what to call it, and it ripple across his back and meet his hip, while his skin burn off the brown for gold and his back widen like the head of cobra. Keme turn to me as his neck turn into a tree trunk and his ear pop open big, and round, and furry. The black in his eyes vanish and his forehead rush over his face, shoving his nose down as it widen and he snort out of it. Whiskers sprout above his mouth and gold hair sprout below. His little belly, which come after three years of two women taking care of him, vanish in a washboard. He try to stand and stagger at first, for he was still changing, but stand he do as a fire of gold hair break out on his chest, spread to his belly, and gush above his cock. Twice the man he was before and the most beautiful of anything I ever did see, woman, man, or beast, considering that Keme's looks give me fire from before he first forget me.

"Bigger," I say and look right between his legs. For a blink I think he is Beremu and without voice.

"Trick of the hair," he say.

"Such things never trick a woman," I say.

He stand up before me, fearless looking, but fearful too. He look around twice, though this room have no window. He scratch his chest but the hand stay there and I know he is unsure what to do with it, what to do with himself.

"You don't change into a full lion."

"I am a full lion."

"You know what I mean."

"Some people neither night nor day, Sogolon. Some people not—"

"Set-out point or destination, some people is journey."

"You know words like that would never come to me. What you looking at is the only way I don't feel like being me is labor, like I holding myself together all the time."

His words making sense to me. I want to say I understand, though some people can't abide by or afford staying in the middle, for that too costly, but I push that away. Besides beast or man, perhaps the problem really is **or.** The hair, the tail turn his buttocks into a tease. I wish right there that I was friends with Yétúnde so I could ask her woman things, like how it is that I lying here torn open from what this man do to me, and all I want is for him to come over to me right now and do that whole thing again.

I want him to rush me and smell like me like prey, and lick all the way around me neck. I come this close to whispering that there is more than one hole to a woman, and more than one use for such a kingly cock. The thought make me laugh out loud and then wince in pain for letting my head run wild when I know not a thing going happen to this body for at least six moons if not longer. Nothing other than sleeping, crying, avoiding death, and surrendering milk to four who know nothing but hunger. That first moon, the suckling also bring on a pain that make me almost scream for goat milk. Here is truth, one night of birthing leaving me so spent that I thank gods that these babies too young to know that sometimes I so tired that I think twice about feeding them. And the pains from my body trying to decide what shape it will be in from now on, is enough to make me feel that thinking about fucking is foolish. The lion standing in my doorway all but make me forget that this was a mighty day and nobody more surprised that I survive it than me.

"You making me forget that this night is about you," he say.

"I going own many more nights. This one can share."

"No clothes fit when I look so."

"Cowskin will stretch. Besides, you see no lion in clothes? Call your children."

"For what, for them to see me like this?"

"They little, not slow. The way they crawl, scratch, and romp, you likely wasn't fooling them neither."

He turn to the doorway, still unsure. He still buckling a little. He still the young boy who decide one day that only way he could show himself was to hide himself.

"Keme."

"By the gods, woman, wait," he say. Even his snap has the mark of a lion. "Children," he shout.

"No, not like that. Call them, I say."

He turn to me again, and I smile, hoping that it will wash the doubt off his face. Then he lift his head, and roar.

FOURTEEN

I see the Aesi. Two times now it come to pass.

The first was the day of the Nanosi, the eldest of the elders, the oldest people of the North, who still live in the dry plains between Fasisi and Luala Luala. Kwash Kagar decreed it so, that those who first broke stone to build the North should have one day where they take to the street and conquer the city once more. In dance and drum of course. And even if they did sharpen the dull spear, switch the ceremonial sword for a real one, and take the string from the kora and return it to the archer's bow, they would have no use for this kingdom anyway. At some time in the age, three or four dynasties before Akum, the Nanosi abandoned the city they build, and returned to the dry plains to hunt, gather, and run with the oryx.

"To this day, nobody knows why," Keme say, except I can hear the wonder in his voice and the envy in his sigh. He looking like himself as we wait with the crowd for the Nanosi, but still take to soldier form when he head to the royal enclosure, or when his men come for him. I forbid him from wearing anything but himself around me or his children since that first day, and the last time he approach them as a man, they all scream. Even his older children grab and tug any hair they can grab, and squeal when he growl and pretend to gnaw them. Sometimes he greet them as lions do, rubbing neck to neck. My shaggy son, who we name Lurum, now have hair the color of wheat. One of the cubs, who we name Ehede, sometimes speak one word, sometimes two, but two years later neither cub change in any way other than growing bigger, and a two-year-old lion no woman would call small. Lurum's eye grow from brown and white to white and brown, and he stop hiding that instead of fingernails, he have claws. The children have that sweet blindness to each other where they don't care how each one look, even if playing rough with a lion soon lead to scratches upon scratches, bawling because a tail get yank too hard, and crying because one child's pet turn in to another child's meal. I start to wonder if there be any chance of schooling for any of them, for who will take to teaching a child that could kill her with one bite? The house continue as the house do, for all but one.

"You take him looking like that?" Yétúnde ask me one time, almost a year after my children born. Surprise me she do, for other than to ask about grain or if I going to kill a fowl for dinner, she stop talking to me. I don't know how to answer her.

"Well you know what them say. Silence mean consent," she say.

I want to say to her that only man who force woman say words like that, but she is the first wife and I not even a wife. She snap at Lurum once, and when I say to her, Don't snap at my boy, she go and tell Keme that I call her sour. Twice she scream at the cubs to take their nasty stinking self out of her kitchen for they bound to piss and shit on her floor, and she wonder which of their parents they get that from. Ever since that night, Keme take to walking like the man he is, even reporting to the barracks, where he say some don't speak to him anymore, some speak to him for the first time, and some asking if he can still drink masuku beer. No complaint come to him in word or rumor. If anything my eyes, ears, and nose even more keen, he say. But walking out in the city like a true lion was another hump to climb over. I say to him that leopards walking tall in Taha district, and everybody know how loose and without morals they be.

"I can't stop thinking I am naked," he say.

"Be like the lion," I say.

"Stop thinking I naked?"

"Stop thinking."

He look at me with the face that say, Only you like to think so crazy. But I watch him stand up straight and catch himself in the underside of his shield. You not taking off clothes, for nothing should be on you, I whisper to him, which somehow make him listen better. So many questions come to my head that I stay myself from asking, including one about his balls that make me laugh. Furrier than before, the voice in my head say, and he look puzzled when I giggle.

"Whose permission you waiting on?" I ask him.

"Permission? I don't need permission. I am the lion."

"Then go be the lion."

When he finally go outside as himself, Beremu jump him in surprise. Half lion and full lion they lunge at each other in love, rubbing head and neck and side together before they both frighten the whole street by running off. And the house continue as the house do, for all but one.

T hen go find woman who love fuck beast," I overhear one night, not loud, but clear enough that it reach the person she intend it for. He don't seek my bed that night, but he come after, and I say that it is indeed true, that this is the only way I will take him. Poor Yétúnde thinking that as a lion he would maul her, when he is even more gentle. And he lick every single thing. Indeed one night he didn't even see that his tongue was fucking me to the point where tears set loose. True it is indeed that I never could get my fill of him that way, the crown of hair glowing in lamplight, the whiskers against my neck, the breath waking up my skin in the cold night, the field on his chest, the twin mountains of his bottom, and the tuft of tail between them that I grab as I look down in the shadows to see his cock going in and out, up and down inside of me. Perhaps he is too gentle, for I want him to roar when he cum but he never do. And Yétúnde find reason to burst into flame over anything. If you want raw meat, go eat from your mother, she shout at the cubs when they spit out the cooked lamb, but to tell true none of the children, not even hers, like cooked flesh much, and is not because she couldn't cook. Yétúnde is the kind of woman who would never say anything to a grown woman's face, so she say to the children instead and hope the message get back to me. One time Lurum, for he speaking now, ask me what his name be. I say silly boy it is Lurum. Lurum from who? he ask and I ask why.

"Miss Yétúnde say we can't take our father's name. Take it where, Mama?"

"I don't know where she want it to go," I say to him and smile. "Anybody ask you, you is Lurum of Adu, just like your daddy. And listen to me. Anything you want to know about yourself, you ask your mama."

He nod and run off, the matter rolling off his back like water. My fury take me all the way to outside her chamber when I remember that she is the first wife and I am no wife. I leave her to her ways but shout so much louder when Keme and me fuck that night that Matisha, my young girl, start shouting that a bad dog is in Mama's room.

Which is to say that a day would surely come when this woman turn so stink with malice that the whole house decide it have to get away from her, her own children included. First I am thinking, What luck of the gods is this that today of all days there is ceremony in the streets? But right before we leave I realize that is not luck at all, but Yétúnde sensing laughter and light, and pleasantness in the sky, and deciding to be all things opposite, for that is how she is now, hunting down smiles like prey and mauling everyone. "Come, children, who want to see the great hornbill?" Keme ask and they all jump and hop and tumble and shout.

So, the Nanosi. This, the day where they reconquer Fasisi, is also the day of the Doro, the initiation rites that happen once every seven years for their boys and men. Hearing this wipe the smile from my face, for I long gone tired of ceremonies for only boys, but when I say that to Keme, the words vanish in the crowd. That look rush over him again, and I can see it even in his lion face, his open mouth and wide-open yellow eyes. Something about the Nanosi make him hunger for their ways, perhaps, or their thinking. Meanwhile this crowd reach hundreds upon hundreds and more after that of man, woman, beast, shapeshifter, ancestor in the form of smoke, ghost in the form of dust, and some another people would call monster. They line both sides of this Ugliko street, and who is not in the street is in a tree, or terrace, or rooftop, most of them with children and old people trying to get a look, but there is one littered with rugs, grand umbrellas in red, white, and gold, and a big chair waiting for the King. But you never know with this King, Keme say. The street, bouncing up and down with chatter, just then drop to quiet all around me.

"This is no longer a street. This is the sacred wood, one time the holiest place in the kingdom before it was a kingdom," Keme whisper.

Lurum is on his shoulders and the two cubs are standing between him and me. Matisha already asleep on my shoulder, and Yétúnde's children plant themselves in front of us after I warn them of a beating if they wander off. Only one line of people stand before us and the street, the sacred wood. This is Keme whispering to me.

"And coming down the sacred wood you soon see the children who will become boys, boys who will become young men, and young men who will become men. By those means they rebirth the way of the universe. First you will see the Nyara, boys who start at seven going on to twelve. After them watch for the Nigogo, who begin at ten and two, and end at ten and eight, but you will know them when you see them. After them come the Comoro, the final class, the ones finally ready to reach Iologo."

"Iologo?"

"Manhood. Every boy go through three ceremonies, Iologo being the final one."

I wish it was for me what it is for him, but I done tired of every kingdom making ceremony for boys. None of them coming from any kill or any war, so this ceremony look like nothing more than a salute for just swinging a cock. But Keme is looking at the whole thing the way Commander Olu would marvel at a falling star. The rumbling music drown him out, so he stop whispering, and along come players beating little drums for the bap, and big drums for the boom. Right behind them come boys, some younger than Yétúnde's youngest, most older and taller but still far from man. All walking naked except for some white and red spots on the chest and rattling anklets on the right foot. Each boy passing have six more behind him and is not until they all pass that I notice that they moved as batches, all marching the same, and looking in the same direction, even in the quick. It come to me right there how many they be, and that right outside Fasisi live a people who all but forsake Fasisi, and not just the place, but the way they live. You watching? Keme ask me, and I want to slap him.

More drummers fill the gap between this procession and the next, until there they come, bigger boys, boys at the age when my brothers thought they were men, which quickly make me feel sour, then sorry that I taking my feelings out on boys I never see before. Keme tap me three times, so excited. These boys are flowing in yellow tunics with black stripes running up and down, but at the top each head sit magnificent bird. Three times as big as the hornbill, this bird they make out of cowries, beads, wood, and gold, though at the front is a real bird beak. The headdress sport a tail that reach down behind the knee. Keme is whispering something to me about the great bird being the helpmate of the original man, but something catch my eye, a glimmer, or a shine, something that vanish before I can look good.

The boys about to become men pass next, but by now it is a movement in the crowd, not the street, that catch me, for other than the cheering everybody is standing in place. And crowd is who I am thinking they are, on the other side of the street, but they keep moving while the cheering people stay. My eyes follow and before I realize it, my legs follow too. We all marching to the same drum, these boys with a hornbill on their heads, me weaving through the crowd and on the other side, the royal delegation, which I know from the colors. Men of the court wearing their flowing white, and soldiers from the Green Army flanking them ready to draw the sword. All of them in court colors save one in black and red. With them, in the middle, falling behind to talk to one, and still talking until the others slow their gait and he is back in the lead. The sudden cheering mean the King is waving from the roof, so this is not the King.

The Aesi.

This is the first time I seeing him, I am sure of it, but the voice that sound like me is remembering Taha district at night three years ago or maybe two, Baganda district three quartermoons ago, or maybe two, robe fluttering like wings from a time I cannot place. And it keep happening, him almost coming into my sight, my heart about to jump, then the cheering crowd block him from me. I trip over somebody's

foot and nearly stumble, but don't turn back when
the man curse after me. We gone far past the King's
roof. Where he going? come out of my mouth as a
whisper and the Aesi stop right there, as if he hear
me. I stop, hold down my head, and shuffle behind a
man wrapping his huge arm around a woman's shoulder. The Aesi not making it plain why he stop, and
he is not looking over at me. But I wonder about it,
him stopping. For that in turn stop me from thinking too hard about why I am following him. I mean,
I know. But then I don't. I searching for fury in my
heart and find only the memory of it. Same too for
revenge, or just blood. I can't find the will for blood,
only the memory that I used to have it. It is gone,
but not like when the Aesi take away some people's
recall. I working to find the fury but instead of fury
all I discover is work. He start walking and they start
walking, so I start walking and I hear **shame,** though
nobody speaking it. If I don't have no more fury, then
shame over not having it, which lead to fury for having shame, will do. He is looking at me.

Through the crowd, looking straight at me. No,
in my direction, but fear jump up and stop me cold.
My head stay down but I glance across to him still
looking. The people in front of me squeeze together
tight, cheering as the King do or say something that
I neither see nor hear. But the Aesi is looking over,
looking hard, knowing he is supposed to see something but not seeing it. And I know what it is that
is making him look. For I know that he can read

people, see what they don't show, and is something that he take for granted, but on a street where every window is open you will notice the one shut. The voice in me whisper, **What you think you doing, girl, you don't have a knife, and even if you did have one, children weighing you down for years now and all your moves are slow.** I stoop and watch him through the spaces between the crowd. The men with him holding their tongues until he finds what he is looking for. A whisper roll through the crowd that I catch the end of: elephant bull, elephant bull, elephant bull.

Elephant bull. I don't know what is coming and there is no Keme to tell me. I done gone too far off. The drummers slow the rhythm, but the beat boom bigger. Between that and the foot stomp, the road quake. Whisper turn into chant, **elephant bull, elephant bull,** until the women and children scream while the men laugh. Two of them, charging up the road looking as wild as the buffalo, they keep calling elephant bull. Two servants running with them, guiding them, telling them where to go, sometimes lying down in the road and daring them to trample. Both bull costumes sporting a mask of buffalo horn, crocodile snout, and warthog tusk that they fix in front of a cloth body as long and wide as two elephants. The first bull, with beads and cowries on a thick brown covering, with red and white circles like dots, the second in a black and yellow square pattern, and both of them with a long bush skirt to hide the legs of the men running underneath. A different kind of drumming is coming from under the skirt, a thunder. The children thunder back and I am losing sight of the Aesi. All I am seeing is the flurry of white robes and red until they stop again. The Aesi turn around, but not to find me.

Elephant bull! everybody roar. A bull servant now in the middle of the road and daring the buffalo to come. Come he do, running and stomping, and the servant try to jump out in time but the buffalo knock him down, trample over him, and charge into the crowd. People thinking this is part of the ceremony until the buffalo pull back and charge straight at the crowd again, knocking down woman, child, and man. Children scream. People still thinking this is the ceremony. The servant lying still in the middle of the road until two drummers pick him up and drag him away. The second buffalo that everybody forget, he charge into the crowd with the other servant shouting No! The second buffalo pull back and ram straight into a woman who fall back on a man who fall back on an old man who crack his head. The first buffalo break from the parade and start rampage through the drummers, swinging like he drunk into the crowd, then out in the road again. Coming toward me. Now people run. The second buffalo ram into the district of the crowd that I just leave. I know what he is doing, the Aesi. What he can see is not what trouble him, so he trying to attack the blind spot. The there that is not there. I gone.

The second was before the first time, but I remember it after. The donga, when I was fighting as No Name Boy. Right before my fight there was a commotion in the dark at the end of the stands. Not a noise, indeed it was the quiet that strike people. Men rising up to leave, most in white, but one lost in the dark, until the red cape flutter into the torchlight. Running through my head at the time was how I was going to kill this man who been threatening to kill me for three quartermoons, fighting his way up to my class. Something about his threats, how he was going to pierce me, come inside, split me open, punch up to my brain, made me wonder if he knew something. Keme was in my bed most nights around that time, so there was no way I was going into any death match, not with him seeing my naked body the next night. But I get so taken with how I was going to humiliate this man, which would be worse than killing him, that all I notice was the sound of the big black wings. And even then it would be near six years before I realize that it was him. Word about this donga was bound to spread, despite it being a secret, and he certainly wouldn't be the first man there hiding in the dark. I wonder what make him leave early. I wonder if he would recognize me under the bandanna and all this binding. Or if he would just be disturbed that he read nothing at all.

But because I didn't spot him the first time, it make me wonder how many times agone that I didn't see him, mark him, hear him, smell him. Two ways it make me mad. One, that I allow all these things to take me away from what I come back to Fasisi to do, and two, that I now so far away from the royal enclosure that I am not even who he need to bother about. Some people eyes never even see downhill, some people say, meaning anybody who live higher than Taha. As for the things that take me away, I stay away from what that might mean, before the voice come after me with, Things? You mean you children? Your love? Your blood? Your duties as a wife?

I not his wife, my own voice say, loud enough to fill the room.

And there was another time, not even six moons ago, when Kwash Moki decree a start to his birthday celebrations even though that day was six moons away. Him being Kwash Moki the magnificent, but also the generous, did mean that he was opening the doors to the royal enclosure so that the people could enter and celebrate with him, in ceremony and dancing and delicious spreads of food. Them being all men of military stripe, and nobody below the north of Taha. I tell Keme to take Yétúnde, though I was the more presentable wife. She been feeling undesired for a long time now, and is the good thing for a husband show some love to his wife, I say to him. Take her alone, for a woman get tired of having to share all her love with all her children all the time. Make she feel special just for herself, even if for once. Yétúnde look older than him, and she grow fatter still, but this make her straighten her back, smile three times in one day for no reason, and even throw sides of raw lamb to Ehede and Ndambi, my daughter, who roar in thanks, something she never allow in the house. She even say her thanks to me in her way, which was to say nothing at all, not even after I lend her the fabric that she wrap herself into and wrap the ighiya around her head the way I see Mistress Komwono do. Doing something nice for her did feel good even if no thanks was coming, but I do it for me, not her. Here is truth, I didn't want to see the Aesi. He have a way to make people forget things so complete that not even the memory of forgetting remain, but I didn't know if that mean that he forget also. I was the one with grievance, yet I was also the one who didn't want to face him, and it was not because of what he could do, for the man didn't scare me. Yes there would be danger if he remember, but that still felt like a better fate than if he didn't remember me at all. Something about that did feel all the worse. I swallow them thoughts as I watch them leave. Keme, more bolder about looking like himself, usually walk around with no clothes—for which lion need clothes?—but for the first time he keep himself true while wearing a uniform to fit the real him. The voice whisper to me, **If you say that this is not the most desirable you ever see him, then woman, you lie.**

See this now, how motherhood change a body. I losing hunger, I can feel it, but I still want to fight in the donga, and not any fight, but a red fight. The thought come to me that I have children now so I can't do none of that kind of fighting, but the thought not as strong as I would expect and that worry me. So I fight one night and win. A white fight, but a win is still a win, especially when I wrap so much cloth around my waist to even it with my hips that I couldn't even bend for the whole fight or on the way back to the house. Binding my breasts was harder, because now I did have breasts, but they didn't make me feel no way. Too many years thinking that all of me must be of use, I think. And even now when I start to see the harm in seeing any soul that way, I still think about it. My use. Who have time for use anyway, when I seeing my children growing older, the lions big and full already? Nobody tell me yet if these lions will live as long as lions do, which is not as long as shapeshifters do, which is long indeed. But nobody is around to tell me, not even Keme, who know nothing about his kind and refuse to learn. Keme call Beremu old friend, which must have been more than ten years perhaps, maybe even more than twenty, which I hold on to, because as soon as the thought run and hit me that I might outlive my children, I gnash my teeth and shake it loose. I picture them getting the wind (not wind) from me and the thought of flying lions make me laugh.

There is this about the children, the lions for sure but all of them too. No tomorrow. They pay no mind to it, have no stock in it at all. When I used to live in that termite hill, tomorrow was all I could think about. Something about a next day just being next make me believe that whatever come will be better than this, even if I didn't know what better mean. But these children, all they think about is where can I play today, what I going learn today, what will I eat today, who make me cry today, what will Father bring today, Mother bring the switch so I hate her today, Mummy give me a stick with a wad of honey so I love her today. Yesterday they have no reason to remember, and tomorrow they cannot grab or squeeze or lick. First I think that this is just the province of children, but I was a child in the termite hill. Maybe they have no reason to lose faith in the day. Maybe that is it. I do know that living only for the day lead them to ask the same questions over and over, try to escape work over and over, play the same games over and over, bruise the same knees over and over, and tell the same lies again and again, no matter that it didn't save them from the switch the last time.

Over and over they go through the Ibiku backwoods, more than I remember them going before. Ehede and Ndambi stay away at first, and both of them shudder the first time I ask them where the other children be. I don't know what come to pass, but it soon happen when they all go to the backwoods. Truth is I did only want to see how these little children play with these already big lions, and if they heed me telling them that they have to be gentle with their brothers and sisters.

From behind a low tree with huge leaves I watch them on the five mounds playing games, rolling in the sun, and keeping peace with each other, all of which perplex me. I am here thinking that little people get away from big people so they can be more little, but there they was, acting like Yétúnde's idea of perfect children. Matisha is the one singing something that I don't know in a tongue foreign to me. Nothing about this feel like mirth, certainly not like childhood mirth, and the sight of them start to disturb me. And then Matisha say, "I don't know that game." I am thinking it was to one of the others but then she say, "Lurum, you know this game?"

Lurum shake his head, and Matisha, now sad, pat the mound she is sitting on.

"Nobody know it," she say, and even the lions' face downcast. But then she jump up. "But you can teach us! You too."

Ehede shout Yes, one of the few words I ever hear him say, and Ndambi do something between a purr and a growl. Then they all play louder and harder than I ever see them play before. And also this, one or two of them would share a giggle with nobody, or whisper a secret to the space between two trees, or shout No I am the tree! to what must be the wind. Children will be children, but Yétúnde's children not babies anymore. Then Matisha burst out crying and shout, I not playing with you anymore, which make me jump out of the bush and demand to know who trouble her. None of them take the blame, and Matisha making it look like none of them guilty. The worst part is that I did already know, for I was watching the whole time. It never trouble me that spirits could be in the bush, even spirits that want to play, but this is the first time I thinking they might be wicked. And even that thought don't last, for if they planning wickedness, they certainly taking their time, and Matisha look like she was bawling from the stupid things that children do. Nevertheless I tell them to stop playing around and get back to the house. Whoever out here messing with them was going to have to mess with me. I sit on one of the mounds expecting to . . . I don't know. Feel something maybe, but all I feel was tough dirt under my bottom. Smell something maybe, or wait for the wind (not wind) to send me words from a tongue near or far. Nothing.

Something wake me up in the deep night. That time for the ancestors that I have no use for. My legs now compelling me and my hands too, and I know I am doing it but I also feel myself looking at myself doing it and not wondering why. The voice that sound like me is silent, when I want her to ask me what I think I doing and to stop it. But what telling me to go outside is not a voice, is not words, is not even a message, but the demand is clear. A feeling then, or an urge, like how we know without either of us saying it that Keme is going to be inside me certain night. So I get up, wrap a blanket, go out in the welcome room, and grab a torch. I am down in the backwoods before good sense catch up with me.

The air feel wet and the ground soft, and the branches slap me gentle. The darkness start out black, but as I walk, it smooth into different kinds of gray and blue, and I can tell grass from ground, and branch from leaf. Ancestors I don't want to see, I say this under my breath, but who among them would trudge all the way from Mitu? Rid your mind of questions, rid your mind of thinking, and walk. You know where you going. I know. But Yétúnde never once plant a living thing, so I have no tool other than my hands. It wash over me again, me coming back to myself and wondering what I doing out here in the dark, in the bush, still wild no matter how close to Ibiku it be. But the space between the trees that Matisha and Lurum speak to, the nothing that the children hold like hands, the joke they share with open space, the patting and stroking the mound as if the mound can stroke back, all leave in me a disquiet that get fierce. Disquiet is what it is, the thing that troubling my head and disturbing my sleep and even now won't leave my mind alone, even as between my toe sticky with mud and my nightdress smelling of bush. It leading me over to what might be a mound, or a little hill, or a trick darkness playing with me.

Disquiet telling me to take my two hands and dig. The soft dirt take me by surprise. I scoop away a handful, then another, then I link my fingers together and dig. I dig until I couldn't see my hands anymore, until I have a hole that I almost tip over into. I dig until the dirt coarsen up, and smooth out again, and stone scratch the skin off my knuckle. I dig until my hand grab a tough piece of cloth, which turn out to be swaddling cloths coming loose but still holding something.

I take the bundle back up to the garden, and under the torch unwrap it slow. The bones at the front lie so loose that is only when I put them together that I see they were legs. Which mean the other two were legs as well. The long, thin cage of ribs, and the longer jagged bone snaking from top to bottom, the back and the tail. The skull jut to a point and poking from it is two teeth. I don't know what it is, and curse myself that I was digging up some pet, or some nuisance that neither Keme nor Yétúnde wanted to burn. No man's dog ever wander into this yard, nor stray cat either, even with this being a house full of cats, and maybe this was why. But the disquiet wouldn't leave me alone, and I curse it. Again, before my wiser self could stop me, I go back to the woods and before sunrise I dig up three more mounds. Graves. Dusk shoo away night so quiet that I didn't notice until I finally stand up. With all of them, the swaddling cloths come loose with barely a touch.

Trust the gods. I don't know why that stupid uttering float through my head, bothering me even though it come as a whisper. I know I am doing what I don't want to do and where my legs taking me I don't want to go. I could be wrong, I think. **You could be wrong,** say the voice that sound like me. **You should go to her and let her put your mind at rest.** Except the only person whose rest Yétúnde ever care for is hers. Right there the thought fly up in my head that this is because of me, that she welcome me in her house and didn't even curse when I welcome Keme in my bed, and when his children come out of me. She is the one who stop him from being a lion, and she was the one who complain that he roam and wander, and won't stay long enough to father his children. And yet is when he did become the lion that he turn into the father she want to him to be. But instead of being grateful, she look at me with sourness since then and take out her malcontent on the children.

But none of these bones have anything to do with me, for all of this happen before I come to this place. Somebody looking from some window bound to know. Five graves, surely a neighbor did see. Now my fear is waking up the lion, for the last time he scratch my thigh. It is the one thing I warn all the children to never do. Yet see me here, going back in the house to do it, whispering to myself, Trust the gods.

Everybody still asleep. The gods are merciful, for this morning he not with Yétúnde, but Ehede and Ndambi, on the welcome room floor. I stand a good distance from him and poke his neck with a staff. First he just roll over. I poke him harder, behind the ear, and he wake up swiping the staff so hard he nearly bring me down with it. I rush over and cover his mouth before he wake up the children.

"Come," I say.

Outside he look at all five of them.

"I don't know if there is more."

Keme circle them again, stooping down to poke his finger at one. The strap give way and his finger touch bone. He pull back quick.

"By the gods, when she set her mind to it, she can be a vile woman."

He say it like this is something he long know, but look at me like it was news.

"We must be lucky," he say.

"Lucky?"

"Of course. That no man on this street come here looking for their dog, or pig, or whatever beast unlucky to cross her path."

I try not to look at him when he say that, but I still catch his eye.

"Keme."

"What?"

"You look at the last one? The dirt was kinder to that one."

"What you mean, woman? Why you pull me out of what was a sweet sleep?"

"Look."

"Sogolon."

"Look."

He walk over the last bundle and stoop down. The earth pound it flat but the white, spotty fur was still there. And some of the tail.

"Is a—"

"I know what I see," he say. He turn to look at me again, his lips sinking and his eyes wet. He touch the bundle again, this time gentle, like something living in it.

"First I thought it just skip a generation. But this, this. Not every woman is suited, you understand? Not every woman, not every person . . . to tell the truth I surprised we have any children at all. And then you come along."

"I didn't come along."

"I know. You are here, and you give birth to them, and poor Yétúnde, poor Yétúnde and her four miscarried lions—five. You have to be kinder to her, Sogolon. You and the children, especially Ndambi. Make a bond with me on this."

"Keme. Oh, Keme."

He stand up, still holding the bundle. "What else?"

"You didn't see it? You're holding him and you didn't see it? The neck."

"I don't know how much desecration you think a man can stand, Sogolon. You're starting to make me angry, digging up her shame, her guilt. You plan to gloat this over her now, is that it? We need to bury them back."

"Stop being a fool and look."

Instead he look at me like I am mad. Then he open the straps again, looking with an probing eye until he find it. Keme gasp. He drop the bundle, and stiffen worse than a rock. I watch his whole body tremble with terror. He try to say no, but it vanish in his mouth. He knees go weak but the wet ground cushion the fall.

"No. No. No."

He keep saying it over and over, each one more like crying until crying is all he do. I pick up the bundle and move it away from him. I have to look again, the cub's body demand it. For Keme's sake I want to be wrong, even though I am sure beyond sure. I look again, willing to have him curse me as a cruel, wicked woman, for even that would be better. But the skeleton don't deceive. In the middle of the neck, cracked bones, with a head hanging too loose even when lying flat. Anybody who ever been in a cook room, a farm, or anywhere that people keep beasts know what we looking at. Yétúnde wring the necks of her children, killing them all.

"That mute midwife know," I say. I don't know why that is the first thing to come from my lips, but so it go. Keme scoop up the bundles in his arms and cry over all of them. The cry turn into the loudest wail I ever did hear. Then he drop the babies. From a kneel he crouch into a squat and dig his fingers into the dirt. He snarl and growl, and snarl again.

I call his name but he past hearing. This I never see him do. Fingers and toes swell into paw and pop claw, legs shorten as they grow thick and twice as much gold and brown hair burst from head, chest, and belly. Hair rush down behind him and a tail sprout until full. Nothing of the man left in him anymore. I try to say his name, but the words don't come, and I don't think he would know it. A total lion this is before me, as tall as me standing, and full of fury.

"Keme, don't—"

He roar at me and storm into the house.

Yétúnde's doorway don't have a door no more. He break it down when he rush into the room, and now the room full with roar and scream. I run to them thinking he full gone now, he full turn, and no kind of word can reach him. He roar again and shake the floor. In the room rugs and cushions scatter. Yétúnde in the right corner, her left arm bloody and just hanging, while her right hand swinging a torch. She screaming and screaming for Keme until she see my face, then look back at him with nothing but horror. She swing the torch at him again, but the lion don't retreat. He leap up on two feet and try to swat away the torch. I shout his name and he turn in the quick and rush me. I stand still though every voice in my head say run, and he run right up to a hair from my face, snarl, then pull back. Yétúnde swinging the torch like she blind in the dark and attacking sound. He going to do it, I know. He going to lunge for her, knock her down, and bite into her neck until dead. I squeeze my eye and my knuckles hoping for wind (not wind), but it don't come. Won't come. I curse it, for several moons now it seem to be following my will. Yétúnde waving the torch too fierce and the fire is going out. Keme lunge again straight into the way of Ehede and Ndambi, who I didn't see run into the room. They push him back with their paws and he almost swipe Ndambi. Keme try to rush Yétúnde again, but them two stand between him and her and they not moving. Keme growl, they growl, Keme roar, they roar, then Keme hiss. He turn and trot out, almost knocking me out of the way. I watch Yétúnde peel herself from the wall when Keme burst in again, running straight to her. Ndambi jump in his way and they slash at each other and tumble on the floor. Keme pull back, quiet in the quick, then leave, blood on his jaw.

Yétúnde leave at dusk, before he come back. "He know your smell, he will still come after you if you don't make distance between you and this place," I say to her, as I watch her bandage the arm in the kitchen, the cloth already red, even though she not done. She struggle to tie it off but I don't help her. I say nothing, hoping she don't say anything to me, but talk she do. She couldn't stop herself, yelling at me that I got no cause to judge she, for a woman low like me have no fear of falling lower. But what was she supposed to call herself if she turn out to be the mother of beasts? Who she was going share those tidings with? Everybody around her saying that shapeshifters deserve better life and shouldn't be living low like beast or witch, but nobody ever see no lion king. Or leopard knight. Or cheetah chancellor. Which suitor going come knocking for a four-legged daughter's paw in marriage? And how must she, a woman, put a cat to her breast to watch it feed? How was she to pretend that this was not shame, especially when this same lion never bother to tell her who he be before they wed? Who going give me justice for his crime? She give him three children, three beautiful children. The rest was a curse. The rest make her stomach sick, for she would rather succor shit. "Look at them," she say, "look at the two you drop. They don't even look like real lions but some kind of joke to the gods." And he wouldn't stop giving them to her. Breeding her like some bush beast who was only here to drop his children and bring his food. Well no. That is not what was going happen to her, and even now if one of them was to come out of her, she will kill it in the quick.

"And look at you," she say to me. "Look at you taking his word, and calling it murder. Is slaughter. No different than when I kill the goat all of you eat."

"He didn't say no words to you," I say.

"None of you have no cause to drive me out of my home. I make it somewhere people would live. If it was up to him you would be crawling over shit and if it was up to you . . ."

"What?"

"Don't have nothing to say to you."

"So stop talking, then."

"They have laws in Fasisi. Laws against people behaving like wild beast. And wild beast who think they is people."

"I sure one of those laws forbid murder, but you would know more than me."

"You think I won't tell people that is he kill them? Me is but a poor, weak mother. Look how that beast murder my babies."

"You gone full mad."

"You see it yourself how he ashamed that he is lion. He is the one who kill them, that is what I going say."

"Why would a father kill his children?"

"Because he is a beast. That is all people need to know"

"Beast only kill for survival and food."

"Look at this, eh, gods? We agree that he is not people."

"Think what you want."

"I coming back with a mob, you hear me? I coming back with a mob."

I walk right up to her face. All the windows and doors swing open, then slam shut. I keep walking, she keep stepping back.

"A mob? You sending a mob for Keme? You shitting yourself because you afraid of the lion. Listen, you dry up, swamp-smelling bitch. The one you should be afraid of is me. Anybody come for my man or my children, I come for you."

She swallow whatever she set herself to say.

I watch her look around her room, considering how to pack a life. My thoughts leave me, even though I not no stranger to making haste or to seeing my life change in a blink. But I can't remember when I was ever the cause. The thought take hold of me and run. My thoughts shoot to moons ahead of me, wondering what would I grab if the day stop on itself and everything that I was doing have to halt, every plan I have for the moment, the day, the week get chopped, and the ground that I take for granted as mine tell me to run. Now. The new thought push away the old one, that she is a baby murderess.

"No word for you children? The ones living."

"They your children. They your children from you step in this house and take them away from me. See it there now. All of this is yours. You come in and take it. Is yours."

"I didn't even want to stay."

"Show me the chain we put around your neck to stop you from leave."

I don't say nothing.

"Coming in here with your eyes and your silence, thinking you can judge me. Any woman around here with a baby hyena is a woman with a dead hyena. Any woman round here with a baby leopard is a woman with a dead leopard. What you think the gods see when they look at the backwoods of Ibiku? Behind shapeshifter wife's house is a buried carcass. I can tell you what they don't call it. None of them call it a graveyard. At least I give each one their own grave."

"First you say people will scream for justice. Now you say every woman around here doing the same thing."

"Don't talk me like that."

"Bid your children goodbye, Yétúnde."

"You better find a cook with no hips or no teeth. Or he going leave her with nasty cats too," she say.

"None of them ever take to cooked flesh, not even your boy," I say.

She nod, but I can't say if is in agreement. "Is you

going have to raise them," she say, as she pick up her sack, balance it on her head, and leave. I not walking in her steps or seeing with her eyes, but even so, even with knowing that Keme would certainly kill her if he see her, her leaving still seem too quick. Like that bag was half-full from before, and her sandals clean and ready. None of we would ever see her again. Keme scrub her memory from his house so clean that sometimes I wonder if he did think his older children sprout from him. Nobody speak of her since then, not even the children. Here I did think forgetfulness was a spell somebody wreak on Fasisi only to see that it is also a gift, that nearly every soul here seem to have.

Either way, the woman gone. He never find her and I know many a night he go searching. Hunting. We bury the five cubs in one grave, a hole I dig. The children all but carry their father, who stagger three times, weak from grief. None of the children play in that part of the woods no more.

FIFTEEN

I am a woman with children. Hear me call their names. Ehede, Ndambi, Matisha, and Lurum children of my womb, and Keme, Serwa, and Aba children of the woman whose name we no longer call in this house. Keme wanted to name the dead children in the backwoods, but lose his voice to grief when none of us could tell who was girl from boy. Truly, the man mourn them like he watch them die one by one, and my own fear arrest me, fear that I will never show for anyone such woe. The King Sister was the only one dead that I could imagine showing sadness for, and even with her no sadness come. Anger yes, and the feeling that the gods deal with her in wicked fashion never leave me, not even now. But grief? Not once.

See me call my children's names out in the dark when the whole house gone to sleep. In my bed lie Keme and Aba, that woman's youngest, who take to sleeping between us and refuse to lay her head elsewhere. I say to him one morning that I done forget what it look like when it big and stiff, and he say, Woman, you can't be saying those things around your children, which shake me, for he was the one who used to like what he call my coarse mouth. That is a lie, or it is not the whole truth. He never like my coarse mouth, he just accept it as the price for having me, but not making me the number one woman. Now that I am this woman, he want me to be more like a mother and not like one who drop out his children. I don't bother to tell him that I was always the only mother in this house. So see me waking up when it is still dark and walking around the house calling my children's names as if keeping a record that they still here.

Aba, the youngest of hers but still the third oldest of all, start acting like a baby ever since that woman leave. Nothing like a lion but with black hair long and wild as one, skin the closest to coffee, like her mother but not her father, and with two spaces in the front of her mouth waiting for second teeth. She soon take to screaming in the night when sleeping alone, and sucking her left thumb when sleeping between us. Two strong apes couldn't pull that thumb from her mouth, and I know because every other night I try.

Serwa, the oldest from that woman, look like her mother too, but her wily ways are indeed of her father, though I never once see any of the cat in her. She is a big help to her kin and even to her half kin, and she be the only one that can convince them to wash themselves, but like her mother she don't like me. A dislike that grow bigger as she get older, which make me shrug and say this must be the way. Maybe I would have been a sour little shit to my mother too. Defiance would never come from her lips, nor disrespect either, so she pound the grain when I say pound it, and set aside raw goat for those who want it raw, never wash reds with whites or blues, but I know, and she know that I know, that if I should fall into sinking sand, she would never offer a hand, or even a stick.

I walk through the house because ever since that woman flee, sleep leave me sometimes as soon as it come, never taking me safe into the morning. Is a mercy that I never wake anybody, but a curse that I can't go back to sleep until I can see light peeking up from the ground. Sometimes that make me slug through the day, but even when I force myself to stay awake, to get as tired as I can get, not long after I fall asleep, I fall awake. So I get up and walk through the house. And when I tire of house I walk outside, and if there is a moon I lie down in the grass and watch it dodge behind clouds. My children's names slip past my mouth as if sharing a secret.

Keme, namesake of Keme, who was a namesake of Keme who was a namesake of Keme. In these years, six now, he grow almost as tall as me, as tall and skinny as a boy can be before the changes visit him. Which mean that he is the rare seed of Keme who won't see body hair before he reach a certain age. In this house most of them born with hair already, even the girls. He do as he is told, follow me everywhere, and carry whatever load I buy. Calm and cool, he is the walking Itutu, but a flash of the father's temper come out whenever I say that is long time now he should be in some school. Even the lions of court can read, I say, but when he ask how I know, no answer come from me.

One day in Gardaduma month, when the sun start baking the room way too early, I rush out of door to cool my face only to see a naked boy squatting in the dirt with a dead beast, a monkey perhaps, hanging from his mouth. The scream come out of me before two things appear to me at once, that I never see this boy before but I know him all his life. I scream, he jump, and as the monkey fall out of his mouth, he catch it and clutch it close, as if I was coming to snatch it. Right before the yellow eyes flash back at me, right before he growl, right before he even bite off the monkey's head I know is Ehede. But the way he crawl, and growl, and roll in the dirt tell me that he didn't know he change into a boy. A beautiful boy with gold hair like his father. I shout for Keme to come look, but by the time he rouse himself, Ehede change back, his gold hair running just along the top of his head.

Ndambi, my little lion girl, who reach near my waist before reach three. She was the one who make me worry, for lion years is not people years and one year for me might be ten for a cat. Maybe even more.

I say to Keme, Since you are as much the man as the lion, is year but a year for you or it is more? But he couldn't answer for anybody but himself. I have to take comfort in that he age as a man do and hope that in another ten and three years I will not be burying my children. Unlike Ehede, she never say anything with a human tongue.

Matisha, my loud little woman, miss the spirits of her brothers and sisters the most. She sometimes run out into the backwoods even though they never come to greet her. I tell her that they gone to the otherworld for good now, but perhaps one night she will see them up in the tree. She say to me, "Then I will never see them, for I sleep at night." Unlike her brother walking on two legs, Matisha feel the most distress when any of the lion show up in her. She fear that as part cat she will have to marry a lion, and she already had enough of lions among the ones she grow up with. She hide it from me but I already know that instead of fingernails she have claws and sometimes she cannot control when they stick out.

Lurum can only claim to be the first out of my womb, but that boy act like he the first one born in the whole house. Hair short, unlike every other child, and tight to the skull, and a grin so wide it take up all of his face. If that boy just cry out it is because the back of his head just receive from me a slap. Sly, too sly. Wise, too wise. He is the one who I soon see build a new room on top of this house, or pull one little thing to bring whole house down. Wise, too wise, so wise that I ask him questions that I would the old, and with him there is nothing happening out in the street that I have to go out in the street to know. But he is not the oldest boy, and too often now fight break out in the house because little Keme try to remind him that he is the oldest. **Oldest boy,** Lurum always spit back at him, which just make them fight more.

I am a woman with children. Which mean that now I get as much joy running away from them, even if is for two or three flips of the time glass. And yet Keme is why I leave them for Taha district, on horse-back because nobody look down on a woman when she is up this high. The boy did need learning, more than what his father could teach him, and even to that he would grumble how the boy didn't need it. He was starting to sound like little Keme.

"All a warrior need is a sword and spear to con-quer," he would say.

"How you know what to conquer when you can't read a map?" I reply.

Now I am in Taha district. The district in Fasisi with the most people but the least difference between them. Different in what they do, for the number of those trades higher than the sun. But not different in how they be, for they are not the nobles of Ugliko, or the sellers in Baganda, or the soldiers in Ibiku, or whatever one call the people of the floating district. Taha might have the most people living there who work somewhere else. For this is the district of ser-vice, of craftsman, builder, guard, teacher, midwife, apprentice, and poet. And they all have the same class, which is just one way of saying they all making the same coin, Keme say.

Taha district is where I go looking for a teacher for my boy. A master, like the ones I used to see at court running down the princes, trying to teach them things that they never need to learn. Somebody must be out there teaching the sons of warriors, and I was going to find him. Seven streets I cross before the thinking come to me that this is folly. Nobody who live here work here, remember? I stop at a post and tie up the horse, for road was as narrow as lane in this part of Taha. Halfway down a medicine men's alley words come to me that the only people right now in Taha are new mothers and wet nurses, beggars with no one to beg, old people, and witches. That last one not a thought, but the mumble of a small crowd in the middle of the street that I walk into. Here be a witch, there go a witch, catch the witch. Is been so long since the great purge that I done forget that purging is still going on.

Somebody called a witchfinder. The same white clay man from the Sangomin. I look at him now, lower now than when Kwash Moki sons used to call for playmates. Maybe at some moment in the years the Aesi get tired of this not-boy not-man easing himself into the King's favor, trying to stand on the left side of his right, when all he could call gift is the ability to smell out witches. The spider already have eight limbs, he don't need four more, I picture him say as

he banish him to low work, and it make me laugh out
loud, so loud that people glare at me, for they gathered here for a serious matter. There he be near the
archway at the mouth of this alley. At least the Aesi
allow him to wear the white of his men-in-waiting.
A thin tunic like that of a woman indoors, thin enough
that you can see his scrawny backside and his elbows
through the sleeves. The kind of man who don't get
much favor with other men in Fasisi. Except at night,
and only in the floating district. I silence myself.

A crash, a scream, and then out the door, two
Green Guards with swords out, then two more grabbing the arms of a struggling woman. She naked.
Why they always naked, I wonder as first she kick
and kick, then do the opposite, make her legs go life-
less as they drag her from the house. No woman in
Fasisi go about their daily business with no clothes on,
not even the whores. But every time soldiers come, or
Sangomin, or guards, or men looking to rein in a
wayward daughter or wife, they always rip her clothes
off before dragging her in public. Is not like people in
Fasisi have any feeling about nakedness, but the sight
of it irritate me like nothing ever before. So much
that I don't realize that the wind that whip up into
a twister with enough dust to hide them is coming
from me. Some of the crowd scatter, the rest root their
heels in the dirt to throw stones, hurl spit, and scream
at the witch who take away too many men, cook stew
with that missing girl's heart, and hoist her ass up in
the air on night with no moon so that street dogs can

fuck her from behind. Plus who know what craft she was doing this very morning with her moonblood? A woman throw a stone that hit a guard, who strike her straight in the face with the blunt edge of his sword. That push the crowd back and hush them to a grumble. Another day they would leave their outrage for this witchfinder, who don't care that people can see through his thin cotton and know which body parts wearing jewelry that nobody ever see wear jewelry before. And the woman, older like they almost always be, and judging from the whispers and grumbles, alone. A punch or a kick to the chest of all four Green Guards and they all stumble, bringing the woman down with them, but she get up first. Some people watching say, You see the witchcraft? Is like she just bounce back up and run. Which she do, and a Green Guard jump up and hurl his spear, but trip before he let it go, sending it upward. The crowd scream and scatter when they see it coming down toward them, bursting through a Green Guard's calf. The others try to chase her, but the little dirt and mud burst from the ground and blind them. I walk away before anybody see me sweating from all this doing, when ahead of me I see him.

Now I thinking of necromancy, or what people in Kongor call white science. For all I seeing is the back of him, and yet that back is sending me so far gone in memory that even his smell come back to me. Seeing the past blinding me, and I almost run into a cart as it barrel away with the driver cussing. He still ahead, down this lane, but then he quicken. I quicken as he walk to a trot to a slow run, though he not once look back. I don't know if he's running from me, but now I running, and carts, mules, donkeys, old men keep barging into my way. If I stay in this lane I going to lose him. He break for a left and I cuss, knowing I going to lose him until I get to that side lane and see a dim dead end.

Nothing but garbage, rats, broken wood stalls, and the back side of shops, storerooms, and taverns. No sign of him. I am almost at the wall when a twig snap behind me. He holding a thick piece of wood with nails sticking out of it.

"Who you? Turn around—slow! A woman? Why you following me?"

"I didn't want to think it was you, but look at you now. Where you been keeping, Olu?" I ask.

He glare at me, and even when he ease his face, a slight frown remain.

"Olu sound like a man you know," he say.

"You don't remember me?"

"Yours don't look like a forgetful face."

"What you saying?"

"I saying that I know that everybody taking to rob the old these days, even woman. And I only look weak. Only thing you going get from me is this plank in your face."

"Soon, when I ask you again what your name be, take no offense. You say that to me once. Say not to take offense when you forget me," I say.

"I don't know you. Or this Olu."

"So what you name?"

"How this your business? I making tracks between me and you. Don't follow."

"Wait? It really all gone? I here thinking you dead, that they finally wash you from this city, and you been here all this time. The gods take away your memory finally, eh? You finally reach it where you forget that you forget."

"Forget. I know what today is, and yesterday, and the day before that. I know the King birthday gone and the Queen's coming. And I know my address just as much as I know not to tell it to you, thief. I warn you, send me to the gods and you coming right with me."

"Fuck the gods. He get to you. He couldn't smudge you out the first time, but nobody did believe a word you say anyway, not even you. Call yourself mad when he was the one that take away everything that make sense."

"You sound a whole heap of mad right now."

He turn to leave and I dash after him.

"You really don't remember nothing? Nothing at all?" I say.

I grab his elbow. Maybe he see that I grab him as if I know him, but he didn't turn to strike me.

"Woman, I really want to wish you well."

"How the Butcher of Bornu get brought this low?"

He pull away from me. Desperate to grab anything, I take his hand.

"You still have charcoal under your fingernails."

"Lady, let me go."

"You have three scars on your back, same length, and slant."

"W-what? How you know that?"

He grab his back, feeling for a hole in his shirt. I feel both at once, that he is slipping away and that he already gone.

"You tell me that it was a warrior with a three-blade dagger. You kill him with the point edge of your shield."

"Now I know you mad. Kill? Dagger? I faint just from the sight of chicken blood. Make tracks between us, woman, or I going shout that you attacking a fee-ble old man."

"You not feeble! You is Olu."

"And you is mistaken. Or mad. Either way that is your business."

"Jeleza."

"That your demon? Praise the gods, why you send this woman to torment me?"

"You don't have no yesterday? You don't ask how you come to a warrior's scars and a fighter's body?"

He laugh so loud it bounce off the walls.

"This body? Whoever fought me did clearly win. Be off with you, woman. Better yet I will be the one who leave."

He back away from me as he leave, eyes making four with mine. Back in the lane he turn and dash off. I don't follow.

Two moon pass since I see Olu, yet my mind won't leave him alone. He take up so much space that I forget what I was doing in Taha district. Olu perplex me when he not troubling me, and it take two moons to see why. At first I was thinking that it was because he still handsome, because whatever burden he was carrying vanish from his back. Before, at the royal enclosure, Olu was a sign for me to remember; uncanny since he forget his own wife. And yet his wife didn't forget him. Couldn't leave him. His wife make me think that memory was sometimes a ghost offering a gift you don't always want, instead of a possession you already have. I didn't know why such a sad situation give me mirth until I realize that it was not mirth, but relief. That somehow the ghost of not forgetting triumph even if nobody see or understand the victory. The ghost win in dreams, which is why he used to chant **Jeleza, Jeleza** in his sleep and not know what that mean when he wake. Somebody might call this hope. Just a speck when despair is an ocean, but maybe that speck is all one need. That speck but a pebble in a shoe, but it prick at you with every step. Somebody drive that speck out of the commander and take not just his wife and his name, but even the memory that he forget. The Aesi.

Sogolon, the last thing you have time for is fresh hate. I think this until thinking fail, then I chant it until chanting fail, then I sing it until my children think I mad, then I hum it. There must be a space in me that this hate is filling, so I take it up with

housework. The clay floor never have no shine before, but it shine now. The iron shields don't mirror anybody in years, but they look shiny and new
now. The children ask for goat so I kill and butcher
it myself, right down to each child-size piece. The old
beds need new linen, so I saddle the horse and ride
out to Baganda district before the shops even open.
A band of starving Yumboes scurry among the flowers in the backyard for some nectar, so I open the
cookroom window and lay out bowl of honey mixed
with water and magic berry. I watch them drink until
drunk, too drunk to fly straight, and when they dip
and tumble and bump into the windowsill, the laugh
that come out of me feel so strange that I didn't even
recognize it.

Which is to say that I was looking for anything to
squeeze into the space that hate was carving out for
itself. I wonder if this is how I would feel if my brothers find me. Or some disease that you think is gone,
only to see that it just in the dark, waiting. Is not like
the Aesi was ever gone, but my years was full—is full
and with so much time passing new loves and hates
take over from old ones, and all one can do with a bad
memory is forget it. Like the name of the wife who
used to live here. Like Olu. Whether you choose forgetting or forgetting choose you, both take you to the
same place, this place of peace. A voice that sound like
me say, **You betray your purpose. You come back to
Fasisi for only one thing, but you take everything**

and leave that one untaken. I hear a laugh come in from the street and can't tell if it was loose talk from people passing or the ancestors or devils.

I search for other things to make me mad. Matisha whisper one evening, not even on purpose, that she forgetting if her father hair gold or brown, for the little time he spend here, he spend with the lions. Two things make me mad, that Keme have no eyes for his daughter and that she calling her kin the lions, like they live across town. He change full with them, and they run off in the night to hunt whichever careless antelope or wild goat stray too close to the mountainside. Then they feed on the whole thing right there in the bush, not even caring that the other children love raw meat too. Except Matisha.

Salban Dura, the twenty and fourth night of the Bakklacha moon. This is what I say to him when I go searching for them in the dark: Look here, you have five other children or perhaps you forget? I say it to him as a shout too. He can't talk to me as full lion or won't, so I have to wait until he remember that he can change, and watch the children watch him change halfway, before he say, I know the names of all my children.

"I didn't ask for a roll call, I ask that you show your face. Matisha starting to wonder if she even have a father," I say.

"Fine, woman, I hear you. No need to start snarling."

"I look like I snarling to you?"

"Sogolon."

"What me sound like to you? Like some beast?"

His face change in the quick, and not a shapeshift.

"And what is wrong with sounding like a beast?" he say.

"Nothing. Nothing at all."

"Good, for you sound like my first—"

"I not your second."

"Fuck the gods, woman, you really itching to have it out tonight."

Ndambi long run back to the house.

"Where is Ehede?" I say. Neither of us see him leave.

"He gone down in the bush," Keme say. "No lion foe down there."

"He is your son. He don't need a foe to start a fight."

"Some bee gone up your backside, woman?"

He approach and rub his fuzzy hand on my face. I want to brush him off, but I also thinking that maybe if Ehede already in the house we can take our time before we head back.

"Ehede! Boy!" Keme shout and ruin that thought. I tell him I going back up to the house to check.

"Right now, he is stealing meat from Ndambi's plate if I know him," he say.

"I didn't see him."

"I saw him run right past you."

"When?"

"Right now he's making a nuisance in the house like he always do. I am sure of it."

"I don't know. I—"

"Woman, how many times must I tell you what I telling you?" he say with a grin, and the grin open my eyes wider. Half lion, half man, no clothes, full cock.

"It even bidding me good evening," I say.

"It not bidding you anything so chaste."

I meet him, and he meet me and we touch halfway. The time lost to me, when last I grab this part of him and delight in it growing bigger and bigger in my hand. No, here is truth: I didn't lose no time—motherhood snatch it from me. Half the man and half lion, he do something between a moan and a purr. That woman who we don't call by name used to cry disgust when he come to her like this, saying he even smell like a beast. But the smell is a road to map him, and I follow it to his lips, behind his ears, right under the arm, and the gold forest right above his cock. My nose, my forehead, even my ear I let press against this bush so it can hear the rustle.

"Women from Omororo, they take it between the lips and fuck the man," he say.

"That must be why we call them southern women," I say. We sneaking around the back like young boy and girl too full of sex to wait on wedding rites, and I can feel his desire grow in my hand. My dress rise above my hips, my breast, my neck, and before the next breath rush out of me, he gone inside me. Motherhood give me more breasts to grab, he say. I reach behind him and grab his buttocks, pulling into his pushing into me. Trying to stay quiet is its own kind of noise and we fucking so feverish that this quiet is all I hear.

"Keme. Keme."

He grunt.

"Keme."

"Busy right now . . . fucking you. . . ."

"You don't hear?"

"I don't hear nothing but you. Woman, the children going rush out the door soon, then only the gods know when next—"

"Is that me talking about. We not hearing nothing, Keme. It too quiet."

He stop. We pull from each other. I turn to see him look in the direction of the house and frown. I forget how quick he be. He at the door before I even reach up the hill. But the house is still, which begin to frighten Keme.

"Matisha!" he shout, only to see her peek from under the wedding stool.

"Shhhh, we hiding," she say.

"Hiding from who?" I ask.

"Shhhh, they coming," she say again.

"Matisha, come from under there right now. And where is—"

I don't know what come first, Keme leaping faster than a flash, him knocking me and himself to the ground, or the three arrows that zip through the window **zupzupzup** and pierce his arm, shoulder, and the thick skin at the back of his neck. Matisha scream so loud that I don't hear my own. From the other room the children start bawling, but I don't have time to think how young they are. Matisha, she is the one who tell them to hide before the killers even come. My mind want to think on this, but my mouth still screaming. Still on the floor, Keme pull the arrows out of his flesh and crawl to the doorway. A shadow come in, which Keme bite in the leg, bringing him down, then bite in the neck to rip his throat out. I scoop up Matisha and throw her in the room with the other children just as an arrow zip right past my nose to stick in the wall. Keme take on two, and the second roll with him outside. At the side window near the kitchen two shadows climb through. Not shadows. Red Army. Once Keme's own men. They move quick and quiet, drawing swords. The wind (not wind) is neither master nor servant, but I yell for it. They both come at me, and nothing for me to do but dodge when they swing, dip under the table when they strike it until it crack, and throw vase, urn, and bowl at them because they still approach. I run to my children's room, trip, and land on my chin, which send a shock through my whole body. Moving not happening. One of them grab my ankle and I see nothing in his face. Everything is there, but nothing at all. I kick him one, two, three times and he spit out a tooth with the same blank look. One more kick make his hand slip and I scramble away. Nowhere leave to go but in the room with the children. So I yell and the yell grab the soldier and throw him up into the ceiling so quick I barely hear his neck snap. The wind (not wind), finally. By the door of the room stand a staff that Keme was making to pass an idle afternoon, and as I grab it the donga come back to me. Then it leave, the memory laughing at me trying to be the long gone No Name Boy. But when the second one swing the knife at me I didn't even have to look to block it. He is a soldier, and he is lightning quick. Keme roar from outside and the dagger slice across my chest before I even realize. I yell again and the yell knock him in the chest and send him flying out the door until I hear him smash into a tree. I look at the two doors, the children behind me, and Keme outside and run to the front door. The darkness hiding nearly everything but sound, so I run back into the room to see my children huddling in the center and trembling together. Then two battering rams burst through the wood shutter and four men jump in the windows. This is it, my heart say. Nothing to do but cover them and hope no sword or spear kill them by going right through me. I close my eyes and hear an explosion and walls crumbling. One window where there was two, and pieces of the soldiers floating around before they fall on us.

"Run!"

They run out the door but stop, and I almost knock Lurum over by running into him.

"You," he say. "Of all the people that mad commander would lead me to, I never thought it would be you."

The Aesi.

His black robes spread like wings to reveal the red underside. I glance at the table, and the glance do what my yell do before, lift it up and hurl it at the Aesi, who swat it away, breaking it into pieces. My wind (not wind) throw stools, jugs, ceremony daggers at him, and he swat away them all, sometimes without his hands.

"You are one of them with her mind locked to me," he say. The words come tumbling to my tongue, words screaming to get out, but nothing leave my mouth. I grab who I can grab, but Ehede and Ndambi howling too loud.

"Mother of shapeshifters? For such an unremarkable girl, remarkable things seem to happen to you," he say.

"What you want?"

"You the one taunting me. What do you want?"

"Nobody here trouble you."

"Yet your troubling reach me. You know who I am."

"Everybody know."

"You know more. It's like a disease, what I do with people. Infect them with forgetfulness. I can even send it on night air. And it pass to everyone, even the King. But not you. Never you."

"I not any threat to you."

"If everybody forget for the better good, the one who remember is always a threat. You were in the caravan with the King Sister."

"The King don't have no sister."

"So everybody in Fasisi would believe, but you."

"I don't believe."

"You don't need to. You know."

"Don't kill my children."

"If they forget this night, I won't have to. Olu, though. Pity you followed him."

"All that man ever do was serve his King."

"And he will still. He was like you with the remembering, you understand? She must have been a magnificent wife. I never took a wife."

"You never take a grown woman either, from what I hear."

"Do I also cut out people's hearts and drink their blood?"

He smile and I am thinking that this man really expect me to laugh with him.

"I came to him in dream, you understand? I can't see your mind, so I will guess that I can't visit your dreams. But Olu? Dream is keeping what little memory he have. Hear me now, a little trick that I didn't even teach the Sangomin. If you enter a man's head while he sleeps, you see with his eyes when he wakes. And who I should see, but you running him down, proving that you're not dead. You frighten me, can you imagine? You frightened me. If she of such low stock is still alive, could the princess be living and hiding as well? But it was only you. You and whatever spirit help you to lay waste to that mountainside. Who you?"

"A no name woman from Mitu. Just leave us be. I never once come near you."

"You and I know that is not true."

Keme come running back to the house. I can see him out the doorway, see him shift to full lion, but then the ground start to shake under him, rocking this house. The shaking trip his balance and he stumble, but just as he rolling over to get back up, the dirt break apart, suck him in and swallow him whole. Keme force one paw out of the dirt but the earth claim him, pull him under, then close up.

"Keme!"

"No use screaming, there will be much still to scream about. Besides, he might even claw his way out."

I want to run to my man and dig him up with anything I can find, bare hands if I have to, but I cannot leave the children. Ehede and Ndambi growling and won't stop, but the other children quiet. The ground outside so flat, as if it have no memory of what just come to pass.

"I wish I could study you," he say.

White science. Outside, two from the Green Army gather. Or more, I can't tell in the dark. Then the Aesi do something. I can't tell what he doing, dancing, prancing, working up some heat between his hands and trying to throw it at me, whatever it is he do it frustrate him so much that he yell at the men to attack me. That do it, that make both lions leap at them. Ndambi swipe her paws left and right and slash the soldier's head clean off. But Ehede, my lion, my boy, leap right into the spear that the other soldier raise in the quick. The point burst through his chest, then his back. My son slump and I scream again. Everything I then see, I see in red. The Aesi talking about how regret is flooding him, how he is so sorry it have to end this way, but the world is moving forward and one who can pull us back to the past is a danger of the worst kind. But everything I seeing, I see in red. My daughter ripping and ripping at the soldier until I see his ribs poke out, the Aesi somehow deeper inside my house and still waving, dancing, conjuring something, and something coming to my house. Flutter of wings booming like thunder.

But my boy.

My lion won't move.

Something in me, it don't have a name but I feel it popping under my skin. I wail for him and the wail lift me up and hurl me against the Aesi. The soldier's dagger is in my hand and I going for his throat, but the floor break off into rocks that fly into my face and chest, knocking me down. My head swirl and sounds rush in and out, and before I can make out his face, he grab my neck and squeeze. Lurum skip over with a stick but he swat him away. Serwa rush him but Aesi swat her away too, his hand still squeezing my neck. The wind (not wind) not coming, and I can't even curse it. Instead I think of my son breathing, of him pulling air in and blowing it out, of him blowing a goat stomach out by blowing in, and I look at the Aesi's face, which have determination on it, but no malice, and I know.

He squeeze tighter and I grab him. The Aesi smile with his eyes, enjoying my weakness, already bored. But I not trying to pull his hand from my neck. I want him to touch me. My skin on his skin even if he is colder than a Waxabajjii morning. Strangling somebody won't happen in the quick, so he try to release me, but I don't release him. My hands grip his wrist and all his pulling won't set him free. The ground start to rumble, and right then black birds fly into the room, pecking at my children. But I don't let go. The Aesi don't feel anything at first. But then he gulp, and belch, and belch again. He look down on himself, then gasp at me. He can't believe his state as it begin, his belly swelling and pushing and rolling and churning, like a fat fish swimming right under the skin. The Aesi gurgle. His eyes widen. I release him and he try to get up but fall to his knees. A loud rattle come out of his mouth and he clutch his buttocks in a fright for the sound coming out of there too. Then he look at me and know that this is my doing. He try to reach for me again, but the wind (not wind) is with me, doing my will when I want it for once. The Aesi grab his belly but can't stop it from blowing up bigger and bigger and bigger, his neck too, and his buttocks and his balls. Because I grasp that while my boy was blowing that skin that if wind (not wind) can birth itself from without, then it can from within too.

Aesi losing grip on himself and he start to float. All over him his skin start to tear and bones crack. The birds, no longer under his control, fly into the walls and each other. Then a small, gentle hand touch my shoulder. Matisha. She say no words but her eyes tell me plenty. Whatever I am thinking, she is thinking too. Together we turn to the Aesi and his eyes and nose pop blood as his tongue flop loose. Then he swell, and swell, and swell, and then he explode. A loud big blast that shake the house, a loud big burst so mighty that all that leave of him is red spray.

New breeze blow in and take the spray away. Young Keme, who was hiding all this time, come out from under the bed to see me and Matisha standing in the air—both of us still in the air but slowly moving to the ground. Matisha run to the doorway. Only the gods know why as her crying get louder and louder, I turn my back to all of them and try to cover my ears. Yelling don't matter. Screaming don't matter. All of the bawling for their mother don't matter. As long as I don't turn around, my lion not dead. There. Decided. I was going to face this way for the rest of the night and the morning too. And the morning after that, and the one after that too. Mama, Matisha shout. Mama, look. But I not looking. I won't look. I can face the wall, or look out the window into a night where Ehede and his father are out hunting prey. Hunting prey, that is it. They will be hunting all night, all quartermoon if they have to.

I hear a rumble and a kick and a big man coughing. Keme dig his way out of the ground. I can feel him take up space in the doorway.

"Sogolon," he say. "My love."

Don't call me that. Don't call me anything right now that you didn't call me at noon, or in the morning, or a moon ago.

"Sogolon."

I stare at the wall and remember a woman who used to claim that I lick them. A hand touch my shoulder, a bigger one this time.

"Sogolon," he say

"Don't touch me! Don't touch me!"

"He's—"

"Shut up shut up shut up shut up. Leave me be."

"Woman, no."

"I don't have no use for your words. You hear me? I don't have none."

He grab my shoulder this time and all I can think is to get his furry paws off me. But when I spin around to slap, there at the door be my boy in his sister's arms and a long spear sticking out of his chest. My lion changed back into a boy. A boy so little that I allow my mind to ponder how such a big lion was also such a small child. Like all of my small, beautiful children. I want to yell at him to get up and stop making his sister cry. Get up, boy, enough of this foolishness, enough of it, you hear me?

"Sogolon."

And I still don't know that I shouting all of this, not thinking it.

"Ehede, game time long done. Get up and stop scaring your sister."

Matisha look at me, the most confused eyes I ever see, a confusion that interrupt her tears for a jolt, which make her cry harder. The children gather around Ehede and all I can say is, "Give the poor boy some air. You going to crush him. Move, I say!"

Now I furious. These children not listening to me, not giving my boy a chance to cough or to stand. I push Keme aside and march over there, knowing which child is going to get which kind of punishment. The children sense my anger and pull away, leaving Ehede to fall back on the ground.

My boy with the spear that nobody will take out of his chest.

My lion.

He is lying on the floor and he won't get up.

Get up, I say five times in my head before I decide to let it slip from my lips. But instead of words, what come from me is a scream.

SIXTEEN

Bezila nathi. They mourn with us. But there is no they, only us. This is what come first, a voice that say, At least you have nobody to answer to. Nobody to wish you well or ill. Nobody to split apart the wealth, and no wealth to split. No woman to remark what a curse it is, what a knee-weakening, heart-shaking curse to bury your own who come after you, so unnatural, even though what mother in these lands don't know the death of a child. Nobody to speak what they think is a balm but is really a razor. For the lion's family is scattered, and the mother's family is no family. And yet, I say to myself at night, even that I would choose over nothing. Words no woman think they would say, until the time come to say it. For when the people flock to your house in mourning, people joined by blood or by law, it don't matter what feeling you carry for them, if you carry any at all. For grief is a burden that don't care about anything other than we bear it. You don't need love to withstand it, you need shoulders. I didn't discover this until now, that mourning is the work of many, and we have only us.

Meanwhile every dead moment, no matter time of day, Keme come at me, pointing his hard thing straight in front. Everybody have their own way to bear what they need to bear, that is what I tell myself, because it feel like wisdom. First I believe it because he seem to believe it. That wherever you find relief, then take relief. So we fuck. We shoo spirits of sadness, who see scandal in people fucking who should be crying. We lock away the children, or send them out into the bush, or just draw a curtain, or close a door, or leave it up to them to flee, so we can fuck. There be no thinking about it, or thinking ahead of it, or even thinking after. I would be walking outside to throw away wastewater and he come up behind me and lift up my dress. He would be set to leave and I push him down right by the entryway and don't care who pass by in the morning. One time I was cooking for the children because I forget that they all prefer meat raw and he come in with his fingers and start to rub the little me inside of me and I wrap my fingers around his stick, and we stagger like we drunk as our fingers fuck us and the food burn until smoke choke the room. Too often the children have to make their own food because I can't leave the bed and he can't neither. All the time we fuck silent, but quietness come between us even when we not fucking. Quiet lurk around us like a whispering enemy, so we start to fuck loud, so loud that two times the girls think some wicked spirit sneak in the room to murder me. They never yet have reason to wonder why they father naked, for all lions naked, but is more than four times, more than five that they see him with it big and stiff and I start to wonder if they start to wonder what is the purpose of that. These children starting to see us like no child should see us, and the little relief from a whole day of whatever this is feel worth whatever we losing with them. **Shame, woman. Shame is what you losing,** say the voice that sound like me. Shame.

The shame swoop over me like a fever. It infect me so hard that I believe for sure it will infect Keme too. But shame don't stop the fucking, and I find myself wanting it until I don't. His want is my want, I tell myself, and he want anything else, even if it is down an alley or behind the stalls of Baganda district or in the bath chamber of a general from the Red Army who wouldn't raise fuss because we still mourn. I tell myself that he would stop if I tell him to stop, but I don't tell him to stop. Then one night he yank me from near sleep with his penis rubbing against my back, insisting. I turn over my body but leave my face where it was in the sheets, looking away from him. Keme grunting and snorting but is his whimpering that disturb until I look past him to see Aba crying in the door.

"Keme, Aba," I say. "Keme, it is daughter. Your girl. Your girl."

He keep fucking. I finally kick him off.

"I say your daughter right there."

"So?"

"What you mean so?"

"This bush girl all about modesty now?"

"This bush girl seeing to what your daughter need, since you—"

"I giving her what she need. She need to know how I going to make more brothers. Might as well learn now. Girl, you see how this still hard. This is what man going put—"

"Aba, go to your bed. I soon come."

"No. Stay."

"Aba, go to your room."

Aba turn from looking at me then him then me, and her face wrinkle into bawling.

"Daughter—"

"Don't call her that. You never call her that before," he say.

"Aba, go to your room."

"My fucking girl going stay and watch if I say to stay and watch."

The wind (not wind) slam the door.

"Watch what? You think I doing this with you? Your head take with devils?"

"We didn't finish," he say and rush at me like me is prey.

"Don't come near me."

"We didn't finish."

"And I say don't come near."

He grab me by the shoulders and push me down

on the sheets. I feel him reaching to grab himself and slapping it, waking it back up to hard. I can make it happen. I can blow him straight through the roof. I don't say nothing but he hear something because he look at me, frightened. He roll over beside me. We don't talk for a long while.

"If . . . if we just have another one we will—"

"You can't replace your son."

"He was a lion."

"Keme."

"I am a lion."

He don't say nothing for a while, but I can hear him weeping as faint as Aba. I want to tell him that this is no pride, this is a family. I want to tell him what I don't have words for, something about trying to fill an empty jug with the wrong spirits because we so sad to see something empty that we will fill it with anything, but those words feel foolish and wrong.

I am the woman who scream for three days into sheets and furs for I couldn't have any neighbor direct a magistrate to my house. My mouth stop screaming after three days, but my head scream for two more moons. I am the woman who exchange one heaviness for another every day. The voice in my head say, **What kind of a wicked bitch you must be, where you don't grieve because you have no time.** I am the mother with hands too full to shed tears. I am the woman who make her man bury her son's killer with him.

And I want somebody to tell me that all this is

mourning. I want a new god just to curse her for not telling me that you need a midwife for death too. None of this wisdom you come to on your own, so this is it, then, this is how the gods punish me for not having any friends, nobody who I can say, We was women together.

My boy. My boy with the final look on his face that say, No, this is too new, none of this feel like something I know and I don't like it. I don't like it, Mama, make it go away, I don't like it and I can't stop it, it creeping up my feet and my knees and it is in my belly and rising, make it stop, make it stop, make it stop please Mama. I see all that in his dead face, and even that dead face stubborn, saying to me, Look what you done do. Look what you didn't save. I look at him, changed into the boy he never become, the most beautiful boy I ever done see, with his skin like coffee a grandmother would make, and lips thin like his father, and a nose so wide it almost flat, and black hair drizzling with gold. I look at him until I realize that he looking at me. And when I try to shut his eyes, the eyelids fight me, refusing to close. No, I will look at you trying to end me and I won't close, he is saying with his quiet lips. And I push and push and push so hard that it feel like violence to a boy who already suffer too much violence, and the pushing make me scream, Please close, because I can't bear to see that you see me.

Nobody was murdered. Nobody is dead. No trail of army feet track themselves to my house and no trail of blood leave. Which women had ever suffered this, I ask this man, to tell their children that instead of crying for your brother, act like he never did born? Which mother ever live to tell their children such a thing? Which child can obey it? Which mother? But Keme beg me for a cooler head, knowing it would enrage me to hear that I should put a drape over my grief.

"Itutu, my love. Please. Itutu."

I want to yell at him what he mean, telling me to be cool when everything already fucking cold like my son's body, but I let my eyes do it and he turn away. Don't make me angry, for I would swap it for whatever it is I have now, I say. A cooler head, I beg you, he say. Think of what is before us, Sogolon. We have buried not one, but ten and two. Ten and one and . . . He can't say his name. He don't ask if they did come to kill me. Soon widows of the Red Army will cry for their missing husbands. Soon some inquisitor will learn that they were last seen heading for Ibiku district. Soon somebody will wonder who was it they come looking for. I need to explode my sadness. He don't ask if they did come to kill me. For two days it even work, scooping out woe from whatever hole it settle itself in and filling it with rage. At him, at the children, at the dry ground that won't break up for graves, at my son with the hole in his chest for charging when all the other children stay still. Then I remember that Ndambi rush them too but I can't recall if he move first and she follow or the other way.

I wish I knew, for it would give me something to do with my tongue. I could say, Stupid girl, you is the one that lead him to it, so why he now dead and not you? Then my head tell me that I could never say such to my child, who was only trying to protect us after the ground swallow their father whole. Protect me. He don't ask if they did come to kill me.

But I want him to ask, because I want to give him reason to fight me. Slap my cheek or punch my face or beat me with a stick so that I can beat him back and show him who in this house really have the claws. A voice that sound like me say, **Surely this cannot be mourning, for all you want to do is break anything that can be broken.** I am filling to the brim with something and Keme know that he will not abide by whatever flow over, so he retreat down the side of the hill to roar, and wail, and punch the tree trunks until his knuckles get raw and bloody, and a river flow down his cheeks when he shift. I know he is doing it and I hate him for doing it, for making show, for letting the whole ugliness of mourning out when I have to keep it in. Because there is us and there is them, and they can never know.

"This not right," I say to him a half moon after. "I don't know the rules for the dead. I don't know no ceremony. But the gods must have their way."

"You know we can't."

"We doing something wrong, I tell you. We condemning him to something worse than death."

"You don't know that."

"I know we not giving him no peace. A mother know that."

"Sogolon."

"No. This wrong and we wrong to do it so. We wrong."

"What you want us do, Sogolon? Run out in the street and say hark, we have ten and one dead men and one boy, but we blameless? Consider you other children, Sogolon. We don't want more dead child."

This should be some sort of relief, he must be thinking. This should make me feel better. But none of this make me feel better. It make me feel vile. So vile that sometimes feeling that I am vile take the place of feeling like I am empty. Or full of shit I don't want.

It is too much. There must be women who could tell me that this is too much. So much that sometimes it make me laugh until I stupid. Nobody is here to tell me, so I don't know if a mother have a right to bawl and scream, and hiss, and spit, and hurt the wrong people, and not clean her house, or wipe away her shit, or cook, or clean, or cook too little, or clean too much, or all of these things, or none of these. Two moons after we bury him I walk up to Keme and slap him. He shift a little, sprouting his whiskers and gnashing his teeth, but he don't hit me back.

"We bury our son with no name. No glory, no notice to the ancestors, no nothing, like he is some beggar you find dead in the street. No, we worse. At least everybody in the village know where the beggar is buried. We bury him with his murderer. No ancestor going find his grave. You hear me, the otherworld will never welcome him."

"Quiet, woman."

"Is not me making noise, is him. His bones going rattle and then they going rattle this house. What wicked parents we must be, we deserve to have all our children dead."

"You really trying to tempt my hand, woman."

"Tempt to what? To do to me what you do to the trees?"

"I never lay no hand on you."

"You forget."

"Quiet, Sogolon."

But I can't keep quiet. Much is private, and much I wish I alone did know. But burying somebody is not one of them things, and the only person who keep a death secret is a murderer. The fifth time I say this to the man, he say to me, "Take what you need."

"Fuck the gods, what you talking about now?"

"You know you have children still alive."

"I say what you talking about?"

"My chest broad enough?"

"I done with you."

"You want to beat it now or tomorrow?"

"I say I done with you."

"But you not. You not done. And tomorrow you start all over again. You going to scream at who, Serwa this time? Or Matisha? Or slap Keme, or tell Ndambi that if she want food so bad to slice and carve it herself or starve? All this rage you filling up your body with. It won't—"

"You think this is me? You dumb, stupid cat. You think I just go to some stream of rage and drink till I fill myself? Is anger who keep finding me. Is anger who won't let me go."

"Why should it? Grief come to you and you banish it."

"Listen to this man telling a woman how to bear grief."

"Bear? You don't have no grief to bear. You never show it. All you do is hurt your children and yourself, because you don't want it."

"I don't want it. What you want from me, tears? You want a show, since showing is all you do? Fine, let me find a tree and scream at it."

"You want someone to eat your blame."

"I don't want nothing you can give me."

"You right. I can't give you back your son. But maybe you gone blind these two moons, Sogolon, but you have six children still living. And you treat them like it's them why he's dead."

"Don't tell me how to treat my children."

"You have six still living."

"No, I have three."

And that do it. He give me a look I don't see since he bury the bones of his children, where his eyes brim

with tears so full that he look away to blink it out.
He breathe deep. He pause. He rub one paw with the
other, for all of this make him half shift.

"You lose one. I lose five and one."

"Fuck the gods, this is no contest."

When he turn back to me those eyes look colder
than I ever see them.

"The Aesi had no cause to come after me, and certainly no cause to come after your children."

I gasp. It don't feel like gasp, but like my own wind
(not wind) knock me down.

"I never ask you why. Why even with children you
go to death fights at night. Every night I have to tell
myself this may be the night you don't come back.
And I still never forbid it. I never ask where you come
from, or why you was up that mountain, or whatever
secret come down that mountain with you. Or who
you really trying to kill every night you leave here
with your stick. Because whatever you go out to discover, you never once bring back home. Now you in
here looking for somebody to eat your blame. I don't
know no truth, Sogolon. I don't know no facts. I have
nothing to tell a judge if he ask me. But I do know
that were it not for you, my boy would be coming
through that door right now. Were it not for you,
my boy would be healthy and hungry. You think you
angry? You think you know anything about anger?
Nearly every night for the past two moons I swear to
every god I going to kill you, because I know this is
your doing. But then I think of the children you don't

think of anymore. I think even as she is they need their mother. Even if three of them she don't consider hers. So you know what you can do, Sogolon? You can take your fucking blame and eat it yourself."

He didn't need wind.

I hear tiny footsteps—some of the children watching, or maybe all. I try to talk but it come out as a wail.

"I want to die," I say. "I rather die than live so. I want to die, Keme. I want to die. I want to die. I want to die. I want to die. I want to die. I want to die. I want—"

He stoop down and grab me, crushing my words into his chest. I still want to punch that chest and rip the hair out. But my hand is weak and it can't do nothing. That night, he come to my bed, the first time in a half moon. My back is to him, but everything he need from me he can get without me facing him. I pull up my robe but he stay my hand and stop me. Instead he walk his fingers in my hair and smooth down the back of my neck.

"I've been keeping things from you. Things you might not want to know," Keme say.

"If you think—"

"I don't think. I don't presume to know you. I never presumed to know you."

Sometimes I think he don't know that his words can have the edge of a knife. But I can't see his face, so I don't know if he was cutting for real. For too long now I keep the windows closed, because dark is never just black. Black will shift on you and turn into legs and arms and sword jumping in to kill you. But this night I open every window, and the night air cool the room. I was under furs when he climb into the bed with me.

"The court went mad," he say.

Near two moons ago. Keme hear this from somebody, who hear it from somebody who attend the King. This was the custom, he say, that as soon as the King wake, especially if he rise in a bed that he was not supposed to fall asleep in, the Aesi is there to bid him good morning, tell him in which day we live—for wine would still be clouding his head—have some servant wash his face, sweeten his breath, brush his hair with warm oil, help him choose his private robe, hold his chamber pot for the royal expulsion, and wipe clean the royal backside. Always in such order. But on that morning the Aesi don't come. Kwash Moki wake up in a room he don't recognize that lead out to a hallway he don't know, to the window of a castle he can't remember. Word is wind, but word is true that terror grip the King, for first he is thinking that somebody done kidnap him. Back in the room sleep the women and men who never expect to wake up in the presence of the King either. At least one of them, a man, know that at some time in the deep night, the Aesi was supposed to appear as if he was always there and drive everybody from the room so the King could wake up thinking he rise from pure sleep. So when this King wake up naked under arms and thighs not his own, faces he don't know, bodies on top of bodies, between bodies and inside bodies, terror seize his heart. He pull himself free from the tangle of so much skin touching him, stagger to the first door he ever had to open by himself, and flee down a corridor that take him to a window with the sun waiting outside. The yelling is what wake up the castle, the King screaming that they release him right now. A serving girl see him first. A guard, second. They both have to avert their eyes since nobody dare see the King naked. Your Majesty, you are in the Red Castle, right across from your own, the guard say, but Kwash Moki not used to anybody speaking to him direct, so he don't hear. They watch him talking long enough to realize that he was speaking to the Aesi about his unforgivable mistake. The guard take to his heels, to Kwash Moki's castle, one assume, because in the quick, all five of the Aesi's attending White Guards rush to the King, surrounding him in the flurry of their white robes, scrambling and fumbling with trying to act as the Aesi would. They try to drive all the entangled men and women from the room until the King scream that he wants his own damn bedchamber. Then guards try to find his robes, as the King promise a brutal round of lashes to every single person in his presence, a lash for whatever number he count to until they find them. Somehow they get him to the castle, but put the basin below his buttocks, and the chamber pot near his face. The King bellow again, wanting to know how come nobody knows which servant to call so that he does not go through the day an untidy, shit-filled fool with foul breath. By evening three of the White Guards are whipped for mistreating the King, with two more getting the lash for failing to know the Aesi's whereabouts.

This go on for a half moon. The King waking terrified, the White Guards not knowing how to do anything in any way other than wrong, the people of court not knowing where and when to gather, the noblemen petitioning the King, not knowing how to appeal and who to, the gatehouse swelling with all the people waiting on audience with the Aesi before audience with the King. Fifth in command, stuck in all his customs and waiting on direction from fourth in command, who was waiting on third, who was waiting on second, who was waiting on the Aesi. Which mean nobody know whether to cook lamb or goat, or whether to raise the minimum or maximum price for slaves coming from the river. Nobody know whether to speak to the ambassador from Wakadishu first or Omororo. Nobody know how to rein in the unruly Sangomin, for there is nobody who don't fear them.

First thing the soldiers do, they search the home of every virgin. Green Army and Red, for nobody was there to separate men by rank or skill. That is how Keme say it, which mean that is how he hear it pronounced as royal decree. No explanation come with the order, for why would a king need to explain? But all of Fasisi know, and if everyone didn't they do now, that the Aesi has a thirst for young girls. Maybe some virgin decide she not going to give what he trying to take and take something from him instead. Keme go on three raids himself, three that he tell me, so perhaps more that he don't. The first was to a girl not even ten in years, but she know to lock her windows at night. The second practice saying **I not a virgin** but then confess that she break her own hymen with her fingers and her mother cut her finger to drip blood on the sheets many moons ago so that man would believe it. The third don't speak but the father do, shouting that he wouldn't dare take another daughter after he ruin the first one so much that not even the nuns of Mantha would take her. I don't tell Keme that I walk around Taha province hoping the wind (not wind) will blow what people saying to my ears, and this is what they say. That the Aesi visit girls' houses at night and you can tell because before, the girl is all sweetness, and take care of her younger brothers, and is ready to marry. But after, she grow distant with eyes always open but looking at nothing and mouth always open but speaking air. Or she go mad, and red beside black make her scream. When the soldiers learn this, they change tactics, leaving the unspoiled girls for those talking nonsense and harming themselves. Still no Aesi.

"Mayhap he just done take leave of you, Your Majesty," say one of the White Guards.

"As one does a prostitute one is tired of?" shout the King.

"No, my lord."

"Do I tire you?"

"No, my liege."

"Oh do tell me . . . whatever your name is, if your King puts you to sleep."

A time glass don't even flip before Kwash Moki order the guards to cut out the man's tongue. That was when somebody spread word that maybe it was best to not tell the King that ten and one of the Green Army gone missing too. Everybody know this word come from the generals, in counsel with the elders, but nobody was taking credit. And keep the secret everybody do, until one of the White Guards with a little more ambition than the others, one thinking the Aesi was a position, not a man, say to the King, "Mighty Kwash Moki, there is word that ten and one of our soldiers have gone missing. Green Army, Your Magnificence."

"My chancellor and my soldiers. You telling me a whole delegation is missing? What do their wives say?"

"Whose wives, Excellency?"

"The soldiers."

"I . . . I didn't ask, Majesty."

"And what do my generals say?"

"Oh . . . I didn't ask, Majesty."

"So instead of facts, you come to me like some little eunuch spreading gossip. Hark, you must be a eunuch."

"No, my lord."

"Congratulations must be in order. For before this quartermoon is out, you shall become one."

Then he call for his generals, who admit that just as many soldiers have not reported to the Green Army barracks for near on a moon. None of their wives could tell where they went, nor any of their mistresses. This was being handled as a case of desertion, nothing more. After all, a man of such esteem and rank as the Aesi would have no business with the Green Army.

Then the King call for all fetish priests in the region and send word to Juba and Kongor and beyond. The Queen-Mother-now-Queen ask him if it was wise to have it get out that the Aesi is missing, for many will look upon it now as him being vulnerable.

"Vulnerable? Vulnerable? Is he the King here, or me?" he say, and though he don't order her tongue cut out, he make her know that he was thinking about it with a hard slap. And so it go, the King desperate to find the Aesi, but also desperate to not seem desperate.

"You think I don't hear it?" he say to nobody and to everybody gathered in the throne room. Man, woman, beast, shifter, none of them knowing how to behave without the chancellor giving instructions. Nobody answer the King's question, not even the King, but they all know what he is shouting about. Of course he hear it by now, for who is there to shield him from it, with the shield missing? The Spider King, he lose four of his legs, is what they say. They whisper it in Ugliko but shout it all over the streets of Taha, and make song and dance out of it in the floating city. The song come back to court, and somebody hear two hair crafters sing it in what they think is a locked bath chamber. The same evening Kwash Moki call them to the throne room. I hear you have a new song, so please delight us in verse, he say. The girls don't know what to do, and even people at the back of the room could see them shake. They start to weep, but Kwash Moki say, What terrible song is this? You sound like kicked dogs. Sing the song. So they sing a song, the taller one first, a child's song about a magic berry where if you bite into it everything eaten after taste sweeter than honey, even something sour, even something salty. The girls try to sing away their tears but only tremble and stammer. All everybody can do is watch as Kwash Moki rise from his seat, take a machete from one of the guards, trot over to the girls, and chop the taller one in the neck. The look in his face say it, that he was hoping to chop her head clean off. He yank away the machete and chop and chop until everything is off. Then he point the blood blade at the standing girl, blind with her own tears. She start to sing.

O' Spider King, yea Spider King, where did your four limbs go?

Burn aloe wood oh, call Assaye Yaa, maybe he know.

Maybe he—

Kwash Moki point the machete at her and she is not the only woman who jump.

"Such a golden voice on you," he say, then yell at the guard to take her away. Later that night in the jail cell, the Green Guards pour melted gold down her throat.

Is not as if people didn't know Kwash Moki was cruel. But out of the Aesi's presence, he gone so unhinged that people start saying **out of his control**. Control, at least, over the King's moods. Meanwhile the fetish priests find nothing. Many come with Ifa bowl, many come with sacks full of divining tools from years and years of craft. Two come from far west, the Purple City in the middle of Lake Abbar. All but one say the Aesi is dead, and the first six to say so get whipped to near death. "I have no love for the stinking lot of them, but give them credit for not telling the King what he want to hear," Keme say. A priest from Kongor say that he is now roaming a street in Taha district as a small beast. A rat perhaps, or a near-wild cat.

"Why would the second most significant man in the empire leave his spirit in such an insignificant animal?" another priest ask before the King ask it with the spear that he now take upon himself to throw, though he never once hit his target. All but one agree the Aesi is dead. None could agree if the death was final, even though he is just a man with perhaps some magic.

"We should ask a man who speaks to the ancestors, Most Magnificent."

"I thought that man was you. I thought my room was fat with such men," say Kwash Moki.

All but two say the Aesi is dead. All but two end up in the dungeons. Two things people know. The first that there are many cells, holes, jails, and keeps, but nobody has ever seen a man return from the dungeons. Second that despite their nuisance, without the fetish priests, many a holy place fall into disarray, run over by beggars and monkeys, for there is nobody to divine the wisdom of the gods and guide the lost. So it come that cities, towns, districts, and houses all start to shake asunder. But the two who claim the Aesi is alive didn't say he was living, but that they feel his strong presence. And that presence was in Ibiku.

Seeing as they couldn't find a dead Aesi, Kwash Moki had no confidence that his guard could find him living. So he send the Sangomin.

I remember the day.

Ibiku is not like Taha, or the floating city. Many people live together but the houses are apart and almost scattered, which is why I can never hear anybody nearby and they can never hear us. Or so I would think. But if one home don't know the other home's business, it mean that news travel slow if at all. But that day I can see clear even though it was a moon ago. See me there in the house, walking from room to room though it feeling like I am fleeing from room to room and the walls won't stop screaming at me. I stumble over little Keme, who was on the floor looking up at the ceiling, and nearly kick Aba, who was by the door saying she playing a game with Ehede but he won't come out and play. My hands push her out of the way and my feet take me out of the house to a sky that somehow look new. A sky telling me to follow it. So I follow, down the one street too wide to snake you with a twist or a turn. People are out in the street. A man I never see before say to nobody that they kick down his door and grab his wife asking where he be. He run out of the house and thought his children were running behind him. Then the ground jerk and a house down the street rumble. A crash and a scream come the same time, from the same house. The man run off and some of the neighbors follow him. Others stand still and look, but one fool move in closer. Me.

Ibiku streets not made of bricks. I stumble over stones but don't stop walking, and the voice that sound like me say, **All this mourning take away good sense.** But my mind catch fire from the moment I hear Sangomin. The house in front still shiver and shake. A woman run out clutching her baby but don't reach street before a smooth pink rope shoot out after her, wrap around her calf, and pull her down, the swaddled baby flying out of her arms. The woman scream and I am running to the baby on the ground, snug in the bundle and smiling. The pink rope start to pull her back into the yard until the source of it come through the door. Not a rope, but a tongue reeling back into a yellow face that change to green as purple eyes bulge out. At his foot, he let go of her. I never seen him before, nor the boy beside him, black as coal and his whole head one big mouth with jagged teeth hanging out. Beside him, a girl as clear and loose as water, and coming up behind her, the Sangomin witchfinder.

"Fool, where you running to? Scamper like some crab when I telling you we believe you," he say.

The chameleon boy hiss into laugh. The boy who was all mouth turn into a smile.

"Regard yourself. A lanky titty goat like you, how you going ever serve my master?"

They leave the woman house, passing me still holding her baby. My heart pounding in my chest hard enough to burst through, though I know they not supposed to know me. When the Aesi take away the King Sister from people's memory, he also wipe away everybody else who was on that mountain. They not supposed to know me. And yet when the witchfinder pass me, I catch the shudder and quake from the house.

The house still rumbling like it was trying to toss something off. Then something burst through the front, too big for the doorframe, and I almost drop the baby to stop the gasp from becoming a scream. Two jagged legs first, brown and black and furry, and two at the back that scramble like a crab. The legs passing by all taller than me and getting even longer as he stretch himself out. He, the darkchild, now a full spider, spread wider than four buffalo and higher than a giraffe. Last time I see him, he have two arms and two legs, but now he have four each, including two small baby arms bulging from his side. A young man's head, neck, and chest, enough of the boy to fool you until you look below his belly to see him sprouting a fat bulb like an insect.

He can't remember me, I whisper over and over. **He can't remember me, he won't remember me, he can't remember me.**

The darkchild scurry past me and the baby, but something catch up in his nose, for he lower himself down to the ground, his bulb twitching, and most of his legs still sticking up like stilts. He stop and sniff. He turn around to face me and sniff again. I unsettling him, I know it. I clutch the baby harder, trying to not look in his red eyes but trying to not make it look as if I trying. The smell tricking him. Maybe if I stay it will start maddening him because he can't remember. But Olu's not remembering don't stop him from being haunted by what he don't remember. And the Aesi might think his forgetting magic work on everyone, but not everybody he wipe clean. And people like me he don't wipe at all. The witchfinder yell something, perhaps his name, and the darkchild leap off. They invade another house three doors down and make it shake.

No form of the Aesi they find in Ibiku, not even after torturing many women and men and killing three. Since everybody who fail the King end up dead, maimed, or banished to prison, everybody is waiting to see what happen to the Sangomin. But nothing happen. The search for the Aesi whet their taste for terror, and with this King they do what they fancy to whoever they please. People in Ugliko used to take it for a joke until they start preying on Ugliko. People of the court take it as a joke until the random moon when they turn into prey. Grumbling turn to outcry turn to crying out to the King. But Kwash Moki do nothing.

Telling each other stories bring more light to the room than anything else in moons. I never at ease when I look at him and see a man's face. I know it was the first I ever see, but it was a false face. No, not false, just a veil. He ease into his shape as he sink into the linens, the gold hair sprouting slow, the mighty nose growing from between his eyes, the white whiskers above his lips, the yellow beard below his chin, the forest rippling across his chest, the two flesh-ripping teeth making points in his smile.

Kwash Moki lose interest in keeping lions close. Keme won't call it demotion or transfer, only that he now have freedom to be with all the children—we stop counting the number.

Kwash Moki taking counsel from the Aesi's White Guard, who even the silly waiting ladies of court know have limited sense when they not driving themselves stupid with taking up the Aesi's lust for young girls. Is a season of rape that descend on Fasisi, and all because the King have no interest in it. We forbid

Matisha from walking alone on the street at night, but soon forbid her from day too. Matisha huff and puff and the puff blow a stool across the room. I stop worrying about her after that.

The years count me off as twenty and two when the Aesi try to take me but take my son. But I been living as a woman longer than that. No name woman, one name woman, a woman with children living with a lion. We go on four more years until I say to Keme one morning, after every pot, pan, urn, and jug lift itself up and fall, that this still not settled. Our son still not sleeping peacefully so that he can wake up with the ancestors. And he not going to sleep until we bury him true. He not the only one who don't sleep in four years, for Ndambi walk the corridors and the outside like she haunted. So one night Keme come home with a woman I never see before. Old or young, I couldn't tell, for in the moonlight, scar and wrinkle look the same on a woman's face. And black, the woman wearing black so she could sink into the night, and tell us to do the same. That was it, I say to myself, that we need only one witness not from family to make a rite public. **Bezila nathi,** they mourn with us. Finally. We don't dig my lion up but we rake up the dirt and pour fresh libations. She speak a chant in a language I didn't know and write runes in the air that burn for a few blinks before they blow away. I cry loud and long like it was the night he dead, but this cry was different, this was like the cry after the baby push itself out, the cry because the burden going and you joyful that it finally leaving, but mournful as well, for there is nothing left to carry. I look at Ndambi whimpering the whole time, and know that she would sleep that night. I look at my children and name them one by one under my breath, for I know the breath was blowing goodness into their lives and whatever this is—call it family—it was going to endure. Even if this whole North empire fall down.

3

MOON
WITCH

Ban zop an
tyok kanu
rao kut

SEVENTEEN

Tail of scorpion. Blood of woman in her third moon. We might as well begin in the Sunk City. In the South lands, north of Marabanga and the Black Lake but west of Masi and south of Go. No griot sing its story, nobody know the city's true name, or who used to live there, and no verse about it survive that anybody know.

The story is this, that for ages the Sunk City stand tall and reach high until sink it did indeed do, below the dirt and beyond memory. Time run and pass, pass and run, age sit on top of age, and the land take back what the city take away, so much that it is a rain forest now, under rule of deceiving bush, aloof trees, night cats, and the backbreaker tribe of gorillas. Hear this, nobody supposed to be walking through the forest, for parts of it darker than the Darklands, but look how this is where I walking, over ferns and under trees, cutting through mist, and creeping under branches that look like the ragged legs of a giant scorpion. Deeper in the green I leap off the back of the pygmy hippopotamus, whack away the thieving hands of monkeys, and dodge the slap of a leaf that would leave an army of ants on my face.

Been living in this here bush for longer than the elephant can count, but I don't call it home. I still can't say if this place find me or I find it. All I know was that I had to get out of Omororo even if by foot was the only way. I don't want to talk about Omororo. Just so it go that one day there was me, waking up below the hundred-man-high monument that everybody call the thrusting cock, right at the neck of the city, and not knowing how it come to be. Memory cut a whole chunk out of me and turn me into a fool. How somebody can rest their head in a city far north to wake up a half a year's journey south was mystery that would drive anyone mad. I still think madness did have its way with me. And when I did get out of Omororo, and after six moons return to the place I call home, home done gone. Nothing left to do but go back to fucking Omororo. I couldn't go back. But telling myself that there is nothing in me left for that city to take didn't stop me from going. From feeling that all I had to do was get back to the place where I lose everything and I will find out why.

But the past go as it wish, refusing to tell me why it leave me this way. Life right before I wake up in that city all those years ago was so clear to me. People too. But I didn't know why I set out for a city in enemy territory, and not knowing why was pushing me from being a woman who reason to a woman who rip off her clothes, scratch her skin, and bawl. The why. I didn't have a why. I didn't know why I was there, I didn't know why I walk away from everything, and why everything walk away from me.

Enough. This is not what I want to talk about.

I know some women, none who I call friend, but they are women whose man gain everything from them, dowry, goats, house, land. Man whip, man beat, man threaten, man swallow all the space but still she won't flee, for he done leave her with nothing but the need for him. Omororo take everything and leave nothing but my need to return to it. The North close ranks and banish me back down South, and for that I would kill the world. Go, they shout, every single one of them, and who couldn't shout roar. Leave. Nobody make no space for you. Stop begging, nobody understand your tears. Stop lying, nobody hearing your voice. And this bed is not yours, nor these rugs neither. Witch. Thief. Impostor. Now you nearly kill him, monster. Leave.

Yet as soon as my sandals get within a breath of Omororo, I shift west to mountains so green they look blue. That is where I find the house that find me. Here is truth: All I was looking for was a place to lie down and never get up. When the walk to the middle of the forest finally tire me out, I sink down onto the dead leaves, close my eyes, and ponder a gorilla breaking my back, a leopard crushing my throat with his jaws, a snake coiling around me and squeezing out my life. Dying was not enough, this body was hungry for suffering too. That evening I let myself sink under rotting leaves, waiting for it to happen.

Nothing happen. Morning wake up and move on so quick that I curse out loud, for it leaving me behind. That feeling was coming, something brewing, boiling, ready to overflow, something at the back of my throat waiting to tell the gods what I think of them and their judgment. But not this day. This was the day I roll over in the dirt, pull leaves away from my eyes, and see a house looking right back at me.

Perhaps a house. Even in the morning the rain forest look like evening, and nothing is what it seem. Awake not much different from asleep, so it was a face with four or five mouths the first time I look. The second time, with sunlight cutting though with little blades, it look to be a palace, with one floor standing on another. The third time I open my eyes the full place come to me. Side of the hill to be sure, but somebody carve a grand house out of it, which make it look like the hill was swallowing it up. Trees and shrubs sprout where they will, so it was impossible to see the whole house with just one look. Right below the ridge was the ceiling, the wall, and four giant columns holding the house up. Between the columns, three dark windows at the top, with a small one on the right and left, and a middle window tall as a door. Below them an archway that was dark also. The house, looking like a face both sad and frightened. Along with the moss, and dirt, and mud, and shit, the house was the color of bone. Some of that mortar long fall away to show bricks, the muscle under the skin. No door for sure, but who need door with inside so dark? Whoever build this place didn't spend much on the entry but on the path to it, for bricks line the ground like a Fasisi road, which make me wonder if living here was a fancy witch. But nobody was living there. Inside blacker than night and as with the blind, I had to feel to know. Posts with grooves from the last animal to scratch them. Thatch screens that you could push your hand through. Smell as well, for everywhere scent was fleeing. A rug smelling of dirt and shit, a jug with a trace of wine long ago, a stool stinking of the last beast to sit on it. I couldn't tell if the floor was all dust or just dusty. Nothing to start a fire.

Making a home was easy. It didn't take long for those of the forest to learn that somebody new take lodging, and she is no beast, bird, or tree. Living through a day was harder, for no matter how much I stomp one down another was always coming. Watching the little poison frog take on a day is how I learn to live through it. First rip the day in half, time to sleep, time to walk. Then tear it down more, then more, and more after that. Tear a day into pieces you can swallow and soon the whole thing will pass. Hear this about sleep. Deep in the bush when I was starting to know plant from plant, I find one to make a tea that put me to sleep, and because that sleep didn't come from me, there was no dreaming. I do the opposite of what get done with a day. From a sleep of barely a blink, to a half day, to two days, to a quartermoon, until so long that once I wake up with mushrooms in my hair, bush sleeping between my fingers, and a colobus monkey and her child sitting on my belly. Slumber hold me for half a year—I know because summer come and gone—and in that time a tribe of them take to living in my house. I didn't care. If I wasn't going to forget, then fuck the gods, I would make sure that I never get to remember. The monkeys watch me with sad eyes as I brew more tea then go back to sleep.

The next time I wake up, a whole year pass. I know because summer arrive again. A plant that I last see as a shrub turn into a tree whose roots long crack the pot. The thought stagger me, though I tell myself that it was weakness from not moving for a whole spin around the sun. Two more days pass before I could stand it, the weight of what I do. Stand it until it come to me that there was no weight at all. The weight so light it threaten to fly away. Being long gone matter only if somebody counting your days. But even the monkeys raise no alarm in seeing me wake; they watching to see what I going to do. Hunger didn't bother me, nor thirst. But I was hoping for peace in the mind and instead terror was lingering in me like somebody who won't leave. To wake up from one year's sleep with no dreaming feel like you rising not from slumber, but death.

The house still didn't have no light, but dark is more than dark. In the room I count three monkeys, all male. As soon as they see me rise one approach me in some sort of dance while a fight break out between the other two. **Over you,** say the voice that sound like me, **Over you.** I barely think it before a strong wind roll into the hut and sweep them out. Wind (not wind). They didn't stop coming over the next few days, but they did bring food, some of which I could even eat. But this is madness, I tell myself. Sleep was no cousin of death, and no death was coming from it, but I was still looking for it. I was one of them women you call haunted, but all that haunt was behind me. **Think of the poison frog,** the voice say to me. Nobody walk backward and forward at the same time. And the three monkeys begging, pleading, and fighting their way into a fuck make me laugh.

Save for the monkeys trying to make me their woman, most of the animals leave me alone. Birds chirp and warble but none come close, not even owl or hawk. At the river the hippopotamus don't charge, nor the rhinoceros. The forest hog chase me once but the wind (not wind) slam him against a tree and he don't come for me since. The elephant didn't care, even when I walk between her and her young. The colobus monkeys didn't want me for wife or sister, but they did want me to stop eating their fruits. Especially the females. They piss and shit all around the house and even inside until one noon when my arrow kill out of the sky a hawk about to snatch one. Same story with the gorilla. I stay away from wherever they keep, didn't eat where they eat, didn't shit where they shit, didn't go north in the forest where they be, yet still I run into a pack who was quick to see me as enemy. I take to the trees, swinging from branch to vine, but they beat me to the entryway. I draw my bow. The silverback leader shuffle left, then right, then strut on his two legs and beat his chest. Two days later he rush me, but I stay still and remain so when he do it two times more. That same night, the three monkeys give me two chameleons, then huff and puff and beat their chests until I hear what they trying to tell me. You should see how he scream, the gorilla, that is, three days later when he burst through the bush only to see me dangle a chameleon. The silverback back away so quick that I was the one now chasing him. Yet even after a year of chasing and pocket full of chameleons he wouldn't stop until one wet afternoon when another, not the king, take to chasing me as well. Some young boy want to prove he is man too, and me being the fool I run up a tree. But where this silverback chief would only charge, this one look set on doing more. He leap to grab me, but his jerking crack the branch and we both fall into the river. Only one thing gorilla fear more than chameleon, this part of the deep river. Watching him splashing, scream-ing through choking, then sinking, I leave him to drown thinking this would teach the others. But the voice that sound like me decide then to bother me and wouldn't stop. I swim back out, wait until he tire himself out, then grab his arm and drag him close enough to the bank for him to pull himself out. One did tell the other after that because since then they leave me alone. More, they guard the path that lead to the clearing that lead to my house. I teach them to leave women alone. I didn't care what they do to men.

In those first years I didn't leave the bush much. Truth, it was only on a trip south to Marabanga that news reach my ears that five years done pass. Five summers since I see somebody who was neither monkey nor gorilla. Five summers since I last see the North **and five years since I think about it,** I whisper to myself though that was a lie. **That man. Those children.** Marabanga. So I was in Marabanga, the seat of the southern King. Your city in the middle of the Black Lake that one can only get to by boat. Marabanga speak a language I don't know, something like Dolingo, when they was nothing more than cow herders. But Marabanga is not like anywhere south or north. Masi rise tall, as do Nigiki, with Go rising so high it break from the ground and float. Marabanga sink low. Where other lands build on grass plains, this place was a rock in the middle of the Black Lake. Young men will say it was science and slavery, while old men will say it was the hand of the gods that build it. But these hands somehow hew through solid rock to carve and shape an entire city. Four-side towers, egg-shape obelisks, temples, houses, palaces, and roads. Weme Witu rise higher and higher, but Marabanga sink lower and lower, carving living stone until they reach water. It trick the eye from far, for the island look unspoiled, but two hundred paces from the shore the paths and steps take you down into a place like nowhere else. Every time I about to think, this place rise high, the voice say **no, this place sink low.** And far off at the edge of Marabanga is the shrine, almost as wide as the city itself, and the only structure to rise above the rock. Built by the gods, which is what priests say when they mean by the death of tens of hundreds of thousands of slaves. As for this shrine, it look like a giant man with a giant head leaning against a wall, trying to brace himself as he grasp his massive cock. Two merchants see me looking and shout that I either too early or too late.

"For what?"

"Barren women only come out at deep night."

"Oh?"

"You must come from far to be the only woman who don't know. Women sneak round in the dark to rub their koo against the rising cock," one of the merchant say. "Word is the chief prefect almost kill his wife until she rub herself one night. Now she do nothing but drop children."

Marabanga and the rising cock tell me more about the South than any record keeper could. All the cities of the South look so alike you could mistake one for the other, though the people surely don't think so. But despite all them mad kings, the territories of the South are brothers, joining together out of their own will. Most of the North join together by force and resist any move by any North king to make one land just like the other. But I don't know why I was in Marabanga, for I have no business there. The forest long smudge out any interest I would have in people, that is what I say to myself even though I been following a group of laughing children across ten and six streets. **What you looking for, you won't find here,** say the voice that sound like me. **I not looking for nothing,** I shout back, which the children hear. First they slow until they reach the mouth of a lane, and then they take off. I peep behind a wall to see two men watching the children, then looking up straight at me.

At this shrine of the rising cock, I vow to never come to this place again. Two times now I run to a city and two times that city drive me away. Fuck the gods and their people, I tell myself. I going back to the bush to hunt river fish and gather fruits and nuts, and nobody would bother me but monkeys looking for a lover. Time was no friend so I decide to be an enemy of time. Not even enemy. I choose to forget it altogether. Banish it. So when I notice that the monkeys coming to my house was not them but their sons, then their grandsons, I remark about it the way one would sunfall. Snake replace snake and hog replaced by what eat the hog. The great silverback who become friend and guardian die. I was the one who take his body to the river and send him down the falls.

After him was another leader who didn't like me and make it known by running me from their nest. After him come another, who murdered all of that leader's children, but treat me like his mother. Beasts arrive and depart, birds stop flying, and even the elephants who was with me the longest pass on to child and grandchild of elephant. On a good day I was a friend, otherwise I was just part of the bush.

More days pass, more moons, more summers. I don't look in the river much, but the sight of myself one morning jolt me. I just pass by the final resting place of an elephant to see only tusk and bone. Not even bathing, I was just trying to get to the other side, for over there was a fruit salty and sweet with no name. Looking at me from the water was somebody I did think long gone. No gray, no wrinkle, no wart, no bump, not even a mask over the brown of my eyes. A grown woman but not even a day older. Surely this river was lying to me, I was sure of it. Curse time I did surely do, but is not until the river that I grasp that I also frighten it. That was not full true. I still mark the time when I bend over to pick something up and my whole body grunt. I mark when something that was clear in my view get murky. I mark when the same climb snatch my own breath away. I mark how things that annoy many summers ago don't bother me any-more. And the monkeys I let groom my hair even as

I slap them when they touch my breast. But time was running and passing, and it didn't come near me.

More moons pass, taking more years. The Sunk City is a mystery but nobody remember why. Sometimes you see part of it poking through the ground, blocking a trail that seem clear a quartermoon ago. What look like a hill you find to be a roof, green and fuzzy from moss, and what seem to be a sinkhole reveal itself a dungeon. A pond shaped too perfect hiding what was a grand bath, with seven behind it. The line of dead tree stumps shed dirt in the rain to reveal warrior statues in ruin. On colder nights three or four fellow travelers appear on the widest trail, quarreling about which way to go. It is only when they walk right through you that you see that here be ghosts, still bound to the city that fall dead without warning, so quick on that day that even death didn't come to collect. Whispers in and out of the forest say that I am a ghost too, one that death forget to collect, for no beast but the elephant could still be alive from that first day anybody see or hear of me. The say it in Masi and Marabanga, even in Omororo, that she must did sacrifice ten and six babies or fuck a house of devils to still be roaming this place. She.

Me. I didn't seek no name. I didn't seek no person, no company, and nobody to call friend. For if is truth we speaking, then I was angry at the gorillas for not killing the botheration before they start to bother me. Waking me up was the first annoyance. Only the night before, the colobus monkey women stop looking at me as the enemy and invite me to sleep in the tree with them. No, none of them was looking for a friend, they was looking for me to use my bow and arrow to kill the eagle picking them off when they climb too high. So I was sleeping between two branches when the little girl's whimpering wake me up. Only grunts was coming from the men, and cussing in the Marabangan tongue that I still didn't know. The girl look no older than ten and her whimpering make me as furious as seeing the man grabbing her. **Scream, stupid fool** almost slip out of my mouth. The birds watch. The monkeys watch but none of them say a thing. Where the gorillas be, I wonder. Two men was wearing the pink and green of a nobleman while another sport the leather of a blacksmith. Another me would worry over what bring these men together, even though the reason was right there, getting dragged into hidden bush. Maybe they all meet in a tavern and after too much palm wine decide that noble and common was the same man after all, wanting the same thing. And maybe between all six of them, snatching that same girl didn't take no time. Another me, for this me didn't care. I didn't worry which careless woman lose her child either. Two of the men say something to her like they trying to soothe her, two of the men lift up their robes to piss, and two more pull down their breeches but not to piss. Their backs was to me, those two, but I know what was slapping between their palms. I draw my bow and try to not think of he who teach me archery. The first arrow go straight through a man's neck so quick and quiet that none of them notice. One of the men was pulling off the little girl's dress, so when the man with the arrow in his neck fall to his knees, the others still didn't notice. The first man to jump when this one fall drop to the ground right after as the arrow that I send straight through his eye burst through the back of his head. Then they panic. Man run into man, robe into robe, pushing, punching, yelling, running for cover behind a tree. I hop from branch to branch with three arrows between my fingers. **Zup-zup,** two to the chest of the nobleman, and he fall. **Zup-zip-zup,** one through the blacksmith neck, one through another man's calf, and another burst his belly. The last two run back where they come, right into the arms of silverback and his son. The son slap first man in the face and his head fly off. The silverback take the other man head in his hands like he about to embrace him then squash the head soft like a pumpkin.

Standing still the girl was dazed and confused like she reeling from a blow to the head. I don't have no Marabangan words for **leave, be gone,** or **run,** so I drag her to the edge of the forest and shove her in the direction of the city. In the middle of the following quartermoon, the girl come back, along with the mother dragging her. I was at the top of a tree from the moment the birds rustle from disturbance in the bush. **Don't bother trying to remember,** the voice say. No use looking for memory or origin, for you not going to remember when you start to watch mothers. Even the gorilla and monkey mothers. This one have a look I see before, one that say my daughter come to me with a story that I don't believe. A look that say my daughter come back violated yet untouched, and this bush have something to do with it. At least she believe her daughter about the forest or she wouldn't be dragging her back here. I didn't need to speak Marabangan to know. Anger quicken her all the way to the clearing, but now fear was creeping up on her a little. I hear her shaking it out of her voice.

"Uyathakatha? Ungu umtyholi? Ulidyakalashe? Thetha! Thetha!"

The girl whimper something, which make me wonder if this was her only way of speaking. But I didn't share her tongue and didn't know if she share mine, and didn't care either. The girl was looking up and pointing, but thick leaves hide me from them. The little girl turn to leave but the mother yank her back.

"Thetha!" she shout again. I slip over to a tree the monkeys don't climb and cut a vine holding one of the men's heads. Several paces from them the head fall, but it bounce and the rotting tongue slip out of the mouth. Both of them scream, but the girl point.

"Le ndoda ngomnye wabo," she say. They both look up, right at me but not seeing me. I look straight at them, until the mother grab her girl and leave.

These are the things that happen. I was not counting quartermoons, so I can't tell when it was that I go back south, but not to Marabanga. Even with so much memory gone, there was still some I was trying to forget, and the tavern at the fishing village skirting the banks of the lake was the place to do it. So there I was, my only concern being the beer in front of me. Though the thought brush me before I drop coin that a fuck would be just as useful as a drink, nobody in that room was of any interest to me. Then somebody behind me sniff as if about to sneeze, then sniff again, rapid like a dog.

"Some fool drag a wet bitch in here," he say.

"Or somebody who lie with dogs," say another and they both laugh.

"But now speak serious. Innkeeper, the room already stink as it is. What it be, you running pigpen around the back?"

"No, friend, the stink front and center. Watch this now. The closer you get to the bar, woi, what a funk."

"Can't be a . . . no . . . no woman could . . . no."

And then the voice was right behind me.

"Wouldn't be so bad if she smelled like fish," he say. I don't turn around.

"You, is you me talking to," this man say.

I still don't turn around, so he come up beside me.

"Friend, you not going believe is a woman. Listen,

is not so much that you smell like shit, is more that you smell like . . . like what, friend?"

"Like somebody wipe her down with swamp mud?" his friend say.

"No, is not that."

"Whatever you smell of, we suggest you go right back to it," the other say to me.

"I just finishing this beer," I say.

"Beer? These women nowadays, friend. Don't want to drink what lady to drink, don't want to smell how lady to smell."

"I do one thing like a lady," I say.

"Hark this now. What that be?"

"I put up with dumb shit from man whose cock so small he piss on his balls."

The South is full of rich cities. Even this fringe fishing village make and spend more silver than a big man in Weme Witu. I know, because this bartender bring me beer in a glass bottle, and glass is still a rare thing in the North and too precious to be wasted. So is sorrow I feel, for the bottle, the bartender, and the precious glass, when this man swing his hand to slap me and I swing around quicker to smash the bottle in his face. The man fall screeching, pieces of bottle sticking out of his face like scales. I push him over a stool and down he go. The other man was beside a woman who look like his wife. She start to cackle and he slap it out of her mouth.

"Another beer," I say.

"You done with drink tonight, bush bitch," say this man.

I hear him rise from his stool and make for me. The wind (not wind) sweep him right up to the bar just as I spin around with the broken bottle in my hand, aiming right for his forehead. I leave it stuck in his face and tell him to thank the gods that I go for around the eye, not in it. This infect three other men in the tavern, for now they all approach me. Here is truth. I could say that I was not looking for a fight. But I was not sad that fight find me. The stool was no stick but it work fine when I grab it and smash it in the first man's chest. The second dodge me and laugh, but the wind (not wind) trip him and I smash his balls instead. The third man kick me from behind and drop me to the floor. I try to rise on my elbow but he stoop down and punch me in the cheek.

"That make you smile, bitch? What you is, one of them northern girl?"

The wind (not wind) swoop him off me. I know the people watching, see him floating, know I am the reason. I let the wind carry him over to the edge of the bar and then drop him so his head land on it. The bartender had a knife near some fruit beside me. I grab it in the quick and throw it straight at the man who didn't think I see him coming. I hurl straight for his eye, and the knife stop just a blink away from it and hold itself in the air. A rock he become, still as a rock. I let him stand there as I order another beer, finish it, pay my silver, and leave. Only when I shut the door behind me did the knife fall. Two days later women start coming to the forest looking for the woman who can make knives fly. We don't care if you is a witch, I hear them say.

I look down from the trees and watch them. Sometimes I follow them to the clearing but stay in the bush. One or two time I let the gorillas scare them off. All this change one evening when an old woman come to the forest with another woman, but this woman speak Sosoli, the language of Wakadishu and Kalindar.

"Great woman of the forest, we know this is where you stay," she say. The words shake me, even though she didn't say nothing yet. Must be near if not over ten years that I hear a tongue that I know. They didn't hear me coming behind them until I could hear the shorter one breathe. She turn and jump.

"Igqwirha! Igqwirha!" she shout.

"Fool, akukho gqwirha," the old woman say. "I tell her that you is no witch."

"Even the South don't have many words for women," I say.

"But if you not a witch, what them call you?"

"A princess," I say.

"Funny."

"No. It is not. What you want?"

"Word spreading about you, spreading among the womenfolk, for the men don't know. You the one that little girl talk about, the one who mother think man try to spoil her. They say you chop off the men's heads and pickle their keke."

"If is so the women flighty, maybe I should be helping the men," I say, just to see her shake, but the old woman done see too much for that. Two moons ago they take her, she say. The woman's sister, a man kidnap her. A man from the Cheetah Society, for-hire warlords of the Fire Bush, the southernmost part of the South lands. Save my sister, or kill her if she spoiled, she say.

I did not tell her that I don't kill woman, and I was not going to confirm if the woman spoil or not, for woman can't spoil. The old woman look at me like she read my thoughts.

"Just bring back the girl," she say.

The old woman tell me that the Cheetah Society take the girl north of Marabanga, but wait until I take half of the pay before saying that it was in Masi, the city of thieves. No house more than one floor high, because no man ever live there who want to build anything, whether home, trade, or family. No man build nor woman either, for who could tell if that man would be still living the next day, or the woman gone from whore to thief or the reverse. Everybody passing through, but people always coming, so a crowded city it was, though Masi was not even a city. If the Cheetah Society take the girl there instead of back south, they don't plan to keep her.

"Her mother is a poor woman. She sell four hundred of her days to earn the silver."

"Talk simple, woman."

"She sell her freedom. Here you can sell yourself into slavery and buy the freedom back. People honor the agreement."

"If you buying slavery, you don't have no honor. Tell her to give the slaver back the money."

"He looking to make interest."

"Tell him that the Witch of the Full Silver Moon soon come to pay him interest."

I track them to a tunnel leading out to the Green Lake. Is not like anybody was trying to hide. The smell tell you why nobody swim or fish here. None of these men was a shapeshifter, and cheetah hide is not the only animal skin they wear, even though the killing of a shapeshifting cat was murder in the South. Too many of them, I was counting at least ten and three, and the wind (not wind) was still picking odd times to tell me I am not her master. Mortar and mud, this tunnel, and the entrance deep in the city was so blocked with garbage that only one man could slip through at a time. Dirt soft and wet to trap your foot if you stomp heavy, and with the dirt, shit from every beast. The narrow entrance spread to a wide middle, wider than two tall men lying flat. Wind come up from the lake and drop a chill that shake the bone. Sometimes is not the situation but how you choose to read it. Me in a tunnel with all these men. Them in a tunnel with me. Only two directions for me to go. Only two ways for them to run. They have clubs and flint stones sharp as a dagger. I have a dagger, and one of their clubs is on the ground. They have seven torches to light their way. I don't need light to see in the dark. The wind (not wind) hear me. A little gust blow every torch out.

I bring back the girl. When I was done with the Cheetah Society, those who still live fumble through the dark on broken bones, searching for limbs that no science will sew back. Those who die lie stuck in the mud, but their blood wash out into the lake, making the mouth of the tunnel look like it bleed. Hairy feet I kick out of the way, hairy heads the wind (not wind) sweep in and crack open. A dagger fall out of the hand when I kick an arm and break the elbow. I stomp right to the end of the tunnel, stabbing, slicing, kicking, chopping, and slamming any limb that come across my way. The wind (not wind) do everything else. When I come upon the girl, she couldn't see who was grabbing her. The bird they feed her was still on her breath, and her arm was not a young girl's.

"They take you much longer than two moons, ago," I say.

"You learn their tongue."

"A tongue sound better with a click."

"Who say they take me?" she reply and I hear the air just in time to dodge her blade. Fury she have, strength too, or no cheetah would go from taking her to keeping her. Skill she don't, for no man want to teach her how to beat them. She been with them too long. Spoilt yes, but not in the way her sister was thinking.

"Your sister want you back," I say.

"I don't have no back," she say and lunge for me. The night was deepening and there was beer, or wine, or spirit in some bar waiting on me. Or at least a fight that would be a little harder to win. The thought take me away and she cut my arm. And proud of herself she was, too proud, spending too long standing and laughing. One swing of the club to her belly and she bowl over, and another to the back of her head knock her out.

From then on the old woman bring plenty women, most of them she don't know. I warn them that I was a ruthless woman, and if you send me into any place, save for any woman or child, I am the only one leaving there alive. That send away certain women but urge others.

"I can know your name?" she ask me one night.

"No."

"You don't want to know mine?"

"No."

"The women, they add name where name missing. Witch of the Full Silver Moon is what they call you."

"I got no quarrel with the name."

She laugh. "Is too fussy-fussy. Witch of the Full Silver Moon who have time to say all that? In Sosoli they would just call you Moon Witch." One day that old woman stop coming. Dead, I assume but didn't ask. It didn't stop the women, who either come with somebody who speak a North tongue, or leave a note on parchment if they have money, leaf if they don't. Sometimes not even words, but glyphs, maps, or runes. One leave a drawing of a man with his head exploding into a cloud, which make me laugh. Famous indeed.

There is no woman called Sogolon. Nobody in this region need that name, so nobody use it. The Moon Witch cheat death more than once, more than twice, more than ten times, so she cannot die. The Moon Witch is death herself. She been roaming the South lands from before Kwash Moki die, after being King for twenty and five years. And she keep roaming after his son take the name Liongo, become King for seventy and one years, until he too, die. So yes a witch, though she never once take up witchcraft. So yes a ghost, though she don't haunt the living. For what reason any woman have for living that long? they say. They, the women who find themselves calling on help for peculiar problems, or the men quaking in their bones when they find out that they are the problem.

This is what the women say, that she only help women (despite the men who beg, plead, command, or bribe). Each one reach one, who tell another, who claim to know her, or at least where in the Sunk City you can leave a message that she will get. Those who cannot leave a note whisper their desire and leave a down payment in silver. She don't take gold or cowrie. You will feel like a fool, they say, whispering your business out in the wild, like you confessing a crime.

But the gray parrots hear and they take the words to her as exactly as you say it. For if you come to the Moon Witch it is because you don't have nowhere left to go and nobody left to help. It is because every other ending better than the one you living in, and you so desperate for deliverance that even a change to nothing is something. So yes, women come to her with a mountain of problems, and nine times out of ten, that problem is a man.

This is what the men say. Whether I drinking wahaba beer in a tavern in Masi or watching them lose themselves while I sip wine in an opium den in west Omororo, the men speak the same. The first moon, nothing. Six moons later one or two man talking about a string of murders in Masi and Marabanga and how this secret police don't know murderer keeping secret from them. One year later two drunkards wondering if the gods have set vengeance on some men, but no women? Man losing their sleep and now afraid to walk alone down certain streets, but the women don't feel unsafe at all. Now they be the ones walking alone or among their kind at night. Two years after that, they learn that their women keeping secrets, as if that was something new. Five years or six, seven men in Weme Witu form a search gang, to find out who is this killer of the new moon, that no sheriff think live. He among us, they say. He. Eight years in and it turn into song and joke, how some evil spirit or monstrous beast roaming the streets, and the country roads and the hillsides, and it is a tokoloshe grown too big, or an Eloko who learn to be crafty. It tempt me to take piece of their bodies just so they can ponder what creature this is to take that as a trophy. It take ten and one years for any man to notice that the women know. When a man say that to me, I ask him if that mean it take ten years for him to finally listen to his woman.

"Oh she never say nothing to me," he say.

Certain man start to see that women know something. Or they know too little. Not that, care too little, for the prime desire of a woman must be for the safety of her man. Some of the women start to use it as a threat, saying, Hit me, cut me, even cheat me and I going pray for this Moon Witch to come. So I stop being a woman, stop being an instrument of revenge, and start to be folklore. Days come and gone, kings live and die, but the women, they keep it as a woman's affair. Not a secret, just not for man's knowledge. All but two, whose husband and father beat it out of them. The husband take himself to the Sunk City, but the gorillas deal with him before I even see. The father come to the forest dressed like a woman, and even whisper a request to the parrots. But he keep demanding to see me, which is something no woman ever demand. That one I let live, when the sight of mighty gorillas, one with the rotting head of the husband, make him piss and shit himself.

This is what the women say. That this here Moon Witch been haunting the Sunk City for over a century, so maybe she was a real woman once, but she is something else now. Sogolon would laugh at such talk, for nothing about this world worth living so long in it, but I don't go by Sogolon. Everybody else in this forest get by with no name. A no name woman is what I was before all that happen, and that is what I return to, though the voice that sound like me say, **Look how the people name you anyway, Moon Witch. Listen to what they say about you, that she run across the top of trees, sleep at the bottom of the lake, and while she put an entire river tribe to sleep, suck out the blood of their cows. They say other things too, that she eat Yumboes raw, have two holes where her breasts used to be, and kill all of her children. That she use mud and magic to coax a cock out of the ground so that it can fuck her, for her swampy koo will kill any man. And that breeze in the bush people hear is she warning them to think twice before coming in too close.**

But come they continue to do. Soon word get sent from all over the South, from Nigiki, from Lish, from even the North. We find weselves in a situation where we need you. We have a need most peculiar. A man who beat his wife to death and now rape his daughters. A man who sell his sister to a slaver who paint her skin red and sell her to an ivory and salt merchant. A woman whose brother blind her, then leave her in the alley. Ten and seven rich men, whose wives wake to them dead in bed with their mouths stuffed with their own cocks. And man who did throw his wife from his window somehow get thrown from a roof. That man who hang his daughter because she rude is who people find in the market square hanging from a noose around his balls. Another who killed his sister's family to get their land found upside down, his head buried in the dirt. And then the exploded heads, so many men with exploded heads and bellies, and three that witnesses say just blow up and popped into nothing but red mist. She always come in darkness and leave with no trace, just as night leave day. **We hear to leave you silver and never leave you gold, that you would prefer a full wineskin before that. We hear that you is not just yourself but an army, otherwise how can you be in Weme Witu and the Storm Keys the same night?** You, meaning me.

So, tail of scorpion and blood of woman in her third moon, which only certain kind of market will sell. Also, venom from the bush viper, sap of palmyra, and seeds of onaye. And stem and root of winter sweet. Shed all clothes, put on the loincloth from the skin of an animal killed with two knives, pound the ingredients into a paste, mix with water, and boil from sunrise to sunfall until nothing leave in the pot but that what is black and sticky. Then I dip in it the arrows and three small daggers, and scoop the rest into a small bottle. Somebody leave silver in the clearing and a note about a man in Go, which was a moon and few days by foot. This man take a piece of every woman he touch, first whores, then a tradesman's daughter, and then a nun. And then another nun. **Be clear that whatever the nuns was trying to**

gain, they didn't need to both lose a finger and an ear, the note say. I see behind the double-talk in the words, **not about killing him but restoring grace,** and know that is the nuns who commission this kill. And that this man take more than a finger. Also this, they didn't want blood, which is why I bring the poison. The arrows was for if he decide not to die nice—or if I say fuck the gods and fuck the nuns, you call on the Moon Witch because there is blood to let. I take the trail around the Wagono Mountains and in a moon I am outside the entrance to Go.

The sun take leave before I reach the gate, and Go is rumbling. This is the first I hear it, the sound of the land about to break away. Whoever have business within was already in, and who have business without by now long gone. The city already break from the ground to rise as high as a tall man. I can already see under it, the dirt and stones that rise and those that fall off, with the underneath looking like a tree that somebody just dig out to plant elsewhere. Already too high to jump, and Go is only rising higher. I run, trying to find something hanging off, hoping the wind (not wind) would give me a push, but of course nothing come. A man hear me cuss.

"Lingqekembe ezimbini zegolide. Unyuka ileli," he say.

"I don't speak your tongue."

"Which tongue you want? North? We don't speak North here."

"And yet is North we speaking."

"Two gold pieces. You climb the ladder."

"I only have silver."

"Five pieces of silver," he say.

"Curse you and your five pieces of silver. You don't want to know what happen between me and the last thief."

"Suit yourself, for I not the one needing you," he say.

The city bound up again. I throw him three coins and he let down a rope. When he turn to me and demand the rest, I pull my sword and dagger and say, "Come and take it."

He back off, and run to some other place he hear somebody shouting for a ladder.

Here is truth. You never really believe that a city will fly until you stand and feel it rise. Sometimes the whole place shudder and throw off your balance. I look around and see nobody losing step, nobody tripping, nobody acting as if the ground they standing and walking on will rise above the clouds. I don't know what quarter I am in, but the men and women here wear the clothes of those who never think about protection, robes that look like they spend too much time pondering deep things. Go was like Marabanga, with towers reaching too high. **Why reach for the sky when you already floating all the way up to it,** I am thinking until I see the shrine and remember why a house built by a man always reaching up. This

shrine look like an obelisk toppling down but refusing to hit the ground. I hear they call it the leaning
cock. Unlike Marabanga, Go pack itself tight, with
roads small as lanes, and lanes small as paths, and
paths not big enough for a cat to pass. Running out of
space this city, with all the enchanted earth supporting some shit that man make. Last time I was here, it
was over a man stealing a deed to a widow's property,
not some cruelty he deal to a woman.

Look for a white house with a red roof, the note
say, but didn't say that most houses in this quarter
look white, and in the dark the black patterns on
every wall glow like a red fire. I've seen this before.
By now Go floating higher than the thickest cloud
and I am cursing, for the air is wet as rain and there
be nowhere to go until the city sink back down. Not
even a tavern, for the citizens of Go look and sound
like the pious sort. I cut loose the thought that the
other kind of Go people must be the ones who ages
ago take themselves north to Fasisi. I soon grasp it
that while every place on this street is white, with
black marks that turn red in the dark and a red roof
as well, none but one is a house. Only one is burning
a light within, and from this house smoke is leaving
from the top. Wind (not wind) feel like helping me
tonight. She lift me right up to the window, which
was open and ready. Too ready. Too easy. For all I
have is a note, which could have come from anybody,
including a man with a grudge who beat my secret out

of some woman and lure me into a trap. I pull three
arrows between my fingers and load one. Somebody
is brewing tea in the next room, from where the light
is coming. In this room, two stools, a large carving
of either a leopard or a woman lion, and cushions all
around for people to kneel. A house of worship then,
this place, blazing up my suspicion that Go is one big
cult. A woman start talking and I follow the voice.

"This woman look ready to kill, oh," she say before
I see her.

"Unless you is one of those fancy men, point to
who supposed to get dead," I say, still in the dark.
The woman laugh.

"No man among us. Well, alas, there is one, but
I doubt any person ever call him a man, not true?
Present yourself, Moon Witch."

"You present yourself first," I say.

"Very well," the voice say, but I jump, for the voice
now come from behind me.

Movement in the dark. The black turn restless
with a quiet rumble. I spin and fire an arrow that
enter the dark like a stick entering honey. From the
restless black come two hands and a head, that climb
out of the thickness as one would from a lake. A
black shape, twisting, bending, and shaping itself into
woman form, a long neck, one breast, then another,
hip swaying, a knee rising and a leg stepping out, or
so it look when black separating itself from dark and
bounce off the dim yellow of the lamp.

"You a god?" I ask, as if gods making themselves known was common to me.

"Gods don't call me god, but some people call me Popele."

"I don't need to call you nothing."

"Anybody ever call you polite?"

"I must be in the wrong house."

"You come killing, and pick the wrong house? Pity the man who get kill by mistake. But your feet take you to the right place, Moon Witch."

"This a house of games," I say and turn to leave.

"Sogolon," Popele say. "Yes, I know your name. I also know that it must be a hundred thirty and six or seven years since anybody call you so."

"If this is a trap, you taking a long time trapping me."

"Not a trap, just a lure," say a voice in the next room. Another woman. Popele head there, nodding at me to follow. Truth, the woman was all shadow, or all tar, and at the top of her head, a fin going all the way down her back. Also this, when she walk through the space, through air, it sound like when I walk through water.

"So, what get credit for your long life? Magic?"

"I stop counting years."

"Just like so? Tell me which magic, which enchantment."

"You taking this Moon Witch thing too far."

"Not an enchantment, then surely a curse."

"Why, because long life is a curse to you?"

She don't answer. I watch the question pierce her and she try to hide it.

"Like I say, years stop mattering when I stop counting. One day is just like the one gone and the one coming. Man's nature don't change in one hundred years and not going change in five," I say.

"You stop counting, but you still waiting," Popele say.

"For who?"

"I didn't call a who. Maybe you forget."

"You see yourself as somebody who know me."

"I know enough."

"Good. Then you know why I walking out the door," I say as I head to it. The air around grow thick, then wet like mist, then like rain, then like sea with me drowning in it.

"I told you either she come willing or we leave her alone, sprite," say the other voice in the room. The water turn to vapor, then vanish. Popele retreat to the back like some child who get scold. The woman is in the room, an old man scuttling behind her. Tall she is, and thin with her hair plait in wild directions like a mad tree. Her gown close on her body with a split in the middle almost up to her koo, and black. The old man follow, carrying an oil lamp, which light up the copper dust covering his face below the nose. A sack on his back with eight or nine scrolls sticking out. River tribe, Luala Luala, or Gangatom, I would guess.

"The dust know you or you know the dust?" I ask. The old man smile.

"You know our ways," he say, not as a question.

"I come here to kill a man and collect the rest of my pay. I doing one even if I don't do the other."

The woman with mad tree hair laugh.

"Tell me. Is it the southern living that take away your humor? You behind enemy lines."

"They not my enemy," I say, and she laugh again, loud enough to make me ask where was the joke.

"It's the joke of recognition," she say, then turn to Popele. "She said that I wouldn't believe it even if I see you."

"Right now I not believing I am still in this room."

The woman grin again. Annoying me.

"Sorry, when we set out looking for you, I didn't count on finding myself," she say.

"You looking for me too, Luala Luala man?"

"He was the one who was looking for you first," the woman say. "My name is Nsaka Ne Vampi. And you? You must be my great-great-grandmother."

"What?"

"Matisha, she of the wind powers, she was your daughter. My great-grandmother."

"I don't have no kin."

"I know what happen to you."

"You. A girl. You don't know nothing."

"Matisha left me with words. A lot of words."

"I don't know no Matisha."

"She knew you. 'I was the only one who remember,' she used to say."

"Get out."

"You in our house."

"Then watch me leave."

"Sogolon."

"Which man from the North set this up? You making joke before you kill me?"

"Popele know about you from before you leave for Omororo."

"I didn't leave with nobody."

"No. From the first time you leave. The voyage you don't remember," say the old man for the first time. "You think the gods just pick you up and put you down in that city?"

"Fucking gods, who you be?"

"Is Ikede they call me. I am a—"

"Griot. Coppermouth griot. Devils all of you must be. Devils."

"I too know of that first voyage to Omororo. It is all there in the text. The griot who sail with you was my grandfather."

I laugh out loud. And even when the laugh done I keep cackling to drive the bitterness off my tongue.

"Every one of my arrows dip with enough poison to kill a devil."

"You wake one morning in Omororo and from that day, your memory ever fail to tell why. Not true?" Popele say.

"And what if it is?"

"And then when you finally walk, ride, fly, and sail back to Ibiku, nobody remember you."

"But Matisha remember you," say Nsaka Ne Vampi.

"Quiet your mouth."

"Great-Grandmother was the only one who re-member that she supposed to know you, that you were close, maybe even blood."

"I was blood! I was the fucking blood! All of them come out of me, all the blood of my own damn blood!" I shout. "Not a single one. Not a single . . ."

I curse the tears as soon as I feel them and wipe them before they leave my cheek. I curse them too be-cause they quiet themselves to make space for what-ever flood of feeling they expect to come. Nobody was going to see me take leave of myself, certainly not three devils who claim to know me.

"You want to know why," Nsaka say.

"I want to leave."

"But you don't. Not yet," the griot say.

"I stomp on that grief one hundred thirty and six years ago. Not that you say, one hundred thirty and six? I try ten times. Then I say goodbye to that house, and good riddance. And now come the three of you, sprite, griot, and whoever you think you are."

"You think this is the first time we meet?" Popele say. "Here is truth. This is the tenth time I am talking to you, and the fourth city too. As for his grandfather, Bolom was with you until the day you wake up with no memory."

"Indeed. He wake up right beside you but think you was a beggar. He didn't remember you either. Nobody remembered nobody, you understand? But trust the gods. Trust the gods, for my name is Ikede and I am a southern griot."

He say that four more times before I catch what he mean. Southern griots, the only clan that write the history down.

"Paper don't forget, nor ink neither," he say. "Paper is where I find you. And where you going to find yourself."

EIGHTEEN

So this ship set sail for the wild sea with twelve man, one woman, and me. See us now, five days passed since we pull up anchor under a morning with a waking sun, but a morning cool also, this a trick of the gods. For gods of sea have fickle understanding and uncertain temper, and whoever sail around the south horn do so at their whim, and not from whatever wisdom a sailor could give you. But many a boatsman going tell you this. Don't get caught in open sea if the gods change their mind suddensome and blow a wind west. Spirits of air will work mischief with spirits of water and lure you into a moonless current that throw a wave as high as fifty man-lengths, a wave that break the back of the biggest ship. Hear this, a quartermaster say to me at this inn one night. Not even six moons pass since three slave ships bound for Weme Witu take foolish wisdom from a star watcher and sail out in wild sky. Three ship, seventy crew, and four hundred slave all disappear without a whisper. Disappear in that same current we sailing to.

We push off from Kwakubioko Port in a ship that people in the South call a baghlah, and people in the North call a ganjah, but most just call it a dhow. Kwakubioko Port sit on the southwest nose of the princedom of Lish. So behold Lish, rising out of the sea, but bigger than two large kingdoms put together. Long time ago man from far lands meet with, trade with, live with, then breed with the many woman of Lish and produce their own people, who look nothing like people from either North or South. People with lips thick but pink, and skin like tamarind shell, and hair woolly but soft, and eyelash thin. People who build their life so much around the sea that some of them breathe like fish. I see it. Five day now out to sea and the smell of them still follow we.

This is how I get to Lish. From the Blood Swamp I come, and before that a no name forest the river split from Wakadishu, and before that a place you don't need to know. But for the most part I take the lower Ubangta

River as it run into the Kegere. By the time I reach the forest I was wearing the look of the people I was moving with, the Bintuin, the nomad tribe of horse and camel lords that settle on the land until they devour it, then move to the next and do the same. If the sand sea was a sort of plague, then they was the spreader. But I hide in the cover of their great number, and their purple-and-blue robes that cover everything but eyes. With the Bintuin I was neither man nor woman, for that is only two, and among the Bintuin there is many. Which is to say that I pass as one of them without help of magic.

Wicked forces lead me to move with this tribe, and I couldn't hide in their numbers forever. When they make camp at the mouth of the Blood Swamp, I break from them and head south. That place proud of the trick in it name, for the Blood Swamp is the one place in the North Kingdom with no evil, ill will, or malcontent. Even the river mothers, fat and round, with bald head and no speech, approach you only to kiss in welcome, not to drag you to the bottom of sea. But I couldn't stay in the Blood Swamp. I couldn't stay nowhere. Through thick bush and deep river I dash, jump, climb, and run until I reach the edge of the swamp, also the edge of the North lands. There a man sit in a canoe like he was waiting for me all night. The man name a price so deep that I work up a quick wind and blow him out of his own boat. I row it myself, following along the coastline of the South lands until it appear out in the sea.

Lish.

But I get there too late, for only one ship was at the dock, with none on the horizon. As for this ship, a slave ship with the massive lower deck to prove it. In the torchlight, it look like it soon sink. Whoever was at my heel would catch up to me while I wait here. For somebody was at my heel again, somebody with more craft than the others.

At the inn I find not the captain but the cook, sprawling himself out in a dim corner of the room. For the right money, he don't care who or what sail with him, this captain, he say.

"I seek passage to the South. My reason is nobody business but mine. I hear that this ship sail south in two days."

"We already south," he say.

"South around the horn, then west. To Omororo."

"Illicit journey like that? You want we to sail into enemy territory? My ship don't carry no Southern mark."

"I have a passport mask in the mark that say Omororo," I say and take out the mask, small

as my palm, with white lines circling the eyes
and nose and a cross carved into the mouth.
The mask that give the owner free passage to
the land it come from—if there are four gold
dots on the inside.

"Besides, you sail with Lish colors. Neutral
ships don't need no mark."

"We don't sail for another three days," he
say to me, adding one more day.

This he say to me also, that the captain
sleep in the room right above this tavern and
whatever ails your voice to make you sound
like an owl with a rat stuck in the throat,
fix it. This fool thinking I was a man with
a throat malady, but better he think I was a
sick man than a woman, for a woman with
no man company would never get passage
to Omororo.

Deep in the night the air in my room go
cool and heavy, with a new smell above the
tobacco and old sheets, the smell of rain set
to fall. She was in my room. Not the reason
why I sharpen my dagger, but the reason why
I didn't sleep. Thickness like whale oil bubble
up on the windowsill and trickle down to the
floor. Popele.

Watch out for those things that can be
surprising and fated at the same time. Popele
is a river nymph much like a river fish, and
river fish can't swim in seawater. So how she

get to the island, I ask her. River running underground bigger and wider and longer than any above, she say.

"You following me."

"Many a man on a mission get distracted by the smallest thing."

"Good thing you don't trust a man with this mission, then. You the one who seek me, remember. I not no warrior nor spy."

"Just the woman who did something that neither man could do."

"Now you sound like you trying to convince yourself, not me."

Popele, the water sprite. She is the reason I have a mission in my dreams and a dagger under my pillow. Not only she, but Popele is the one who keep appearing, like a thought you keep thinking you forget. Ten and one moons ago she was the one who made me mark my name in blood and bind me to the promise to find him. But now she shaky as if I was the one who cut blood with her and she the one trying to break the vow.

"Leave me to sleep," I say.

"Maybe there is another way."

"You the one who choose this way, water sprite. Now you losing stomach?"

"Don't tell me what I have the stomach for. I am—"

"Divine born." More like a god, but less

than a child, I didn't say. I know that would
anger her. She would do it, make the air
around me heavy with vapor until it turn
into a ball of water covering my head, prying
into my nose and trying to drown me. I see
it in her face, she was thinking it. Three times
past she come to me in Ibiku, the first time
frightening the children. Yet she was the one
in terror and nerves, jumping from being in
a house of lions. But whatever scare her do it
long before she bring dust to my doorway. I
drive her from my house twice, until she tell
me words I never expect to hear. Words that
would pull me from my man and my children
without even a word why.

"Mission is afoot, Popele. Nothing you can
do to stop it now."

"I not trying to."

"Then what you doing? First you on fire,
now you slipping through my window, all
unsure like some virgin about to marry. You
want me to tell you what you tell me? How this
is a right so right it will undo one hundred
wrongs, one thousand? How this is the kind
of thing that no man have strength for, and
only womankind can do? I losing sleep, oh."

"I come to tell you something."

"Stop your coming and tell."

"He will be on the ship."

"He? And how you know what ship? What we just say about mankind, Popele?"

"He is not help. He is a griot."

"I look like somebody who need his balls stroked? What I need griot for?"

"He is a southern griot. He put words down on paper."

Southern griot, like all other griot, is the son of a griot, whose son will also be a griot. They hide from the eyes and spies of the North King. They don't leave story to the tongue, but put it to parchment and paper. And though any fool with money can buy a story, no amount of money can buy a southern griot, which is why they now hide from the eyes and spies of the North King.

"Of course. Now that I know you, this making perfect sense. All the way to Lish I was saying to myself, Sogolon, you know what you missing? A sniveling, singing jackass playing kora right behind you when you slash, kill, and burn. But I see you, sprite. No songs for you, you want a record that won't fade along with man memory. Because you want acknowledgment of all your ways. Praise. Glory. You more like a god than you think."

Even with her black skin in the black night I could see her face twitch.

"You didn't tell me I was guiding myself,

when I am no traveler. I don't think I see you in two moons. But you know who I see? Three times if you believe it."

"Can't say."

"Sangomin. Yes. After you tell me to head south, with no guide, or no way, I just walk against the third star. The first one pick up my smell as soon as I cross Two Sisters River. Second one try to cook me in my own skin. That be him at bottom of the White Lake. Third one jump me just as I was leaving Kalindar. His headless body might still be running mad for all I know. Three of the Sangomin ambush me in two moons."

"Where is this talk going?"

"This secret mission not so secret."

Trick of the eye, perhaps, for she is black in black. But it look like she was backing away into the shadow.

"Didn't know you was one for so much killing," she say. Popele slip away from the matter as fast as it come and I let her, for now.

"Say the one who send me off to kill."

"You not killing."

"Still hiding behind words, oh. I only ending a life."

"You not ending—"

"What you want, Popele?"

"I . . . I come to see what you need."

"Sleep, sprite. I need sleep."

Before I get to that Sangomin in Kalindar, she set a pigeon loose. What message this bird flee with I didn't know, and not even the slow move of my knife across her throat would make her talk. I knew the body would horrify Popele just as I knew she would follow me and see it. She, who asking for a death but have no bravery for killing. But hear her reasoning on the edge of a knife, speaking from a belief I know she don't hold. That if you kill him in the middle of the right season then it is not murder at all, for he is not a him to kill. She even think such thinking make sense. Folly with some wisdom in it. I tell her to do whatever she need to wash the blood off her hands, since the sight of it bother her even if the blood shedder get what he deserve. But yes, a pigeon that lead me to the Sangoma. After I fail to follow the smell of evil magic, the direction of arrows, and the false divination of fetish priest, I start to watch the birds. Near every pigeon in the sky was in service to somebody, and many in service to the Sangomin.

I let the wind (not wind) push me to great leaps, other times I ride a stolen horse. More than that I let wind show me the trail of those birds, which lead me to Kalindar. Sangomin don't have a hierarchy of knowledge. That mean even the least of them know as much as the most. But they have hierarchy of wisdom. Is one thing to give the young learning, another thing to teach them how to guard it. By the time she tell me where exactly to find him—we already know he was living down South—neither hand was of any more use. Then I throw a flame to her dress and burn down her house.

Popele leave my room thinking this woman too far gone. Poor she, divine born and still didn't know how much further I would soon go.

The night before this ship set sail, I sleep with both eye open, which mean I didn't sleep. To board this ship I was to forget woman ways. I take the cloth I buy from the bazaar and wrap around me tight. I fill out waist and squeeze in hips and bind up breasts to deny they nature. I steal sandals from the man who sell me this brown leather cloak, and make a pledge to come back after this is all done to deal with him for giving his wife the scar right below her left eye. On my person, a belt from which hang a pouch of silver, cowrie, and ingot. Strapped around my thigh, a knife. In my two earlobes, two new plates as big as my palm, and hanging from my head down to my shoulder, a headdress of a loop of rope, few coil of iron, and two tusks that stick out from the hood to give me the look of a standing boar. When I make that Sangoma burn, she didn't scream. She laugh. Once they sense me dead they going know you coming, she say.

Lish is a city of many faithful and many scared. I pass many a lodging with dimming fire, and many a window shut as tight as the door, then turn down the bazaar street, where everything shut up from stall to cart to shop, and nothing moving but mouse. I continue. Something just then disturb the air and I pull my new dagger. Walking past a perfume merchant, jasmine and myrrh follow me for ten steps. A knocking jump me, a wood bucket tumble, a cat chase and catch a mouse. He gnaw the prize and watch me as he pass by. I give it space, moving closer to the door of a fabric seller. The door, warm to the touch of my hand, strike me as strange, but then the door smile at me.

Two yellow eyes pop open and I jump back just as shiny blade slice through the space and miss my right hand. I stagger and fall back in the alley as a boy the color of the door jump at me. Truly he was the color of the wood, right down to grain, crack, and line. I roll out as he pounce and chop the road, striking off sparks. Couldn't be more than ten and four years. He say nothing but swing to chop my left foot just as I dodge, then quick as light stab for my right. With his blade hand down I kick him hard in the head and he stumble, roll, hit into the yellow wall of a shop and vanish into it.

I jump up. Grab dagger and sack. Run. So I run back where I come from, and hear footsteps on the roof right above me, though I see nothing but trick of light. A shift in the air, a wall that pop out a boy in the color of mortar. Another wall that pop out a boy in the color of northern blue. This alley longer than I remember. I keep running, hearing the running above me, then dash quick down a lane on the right, this one with more people. I hear him landing on a pile of garbage. I break left when a blow slam into my chest and knock me down. He kick the breath out of me. I roll and roll and roll on the stone road, sticking out my arms to stop. I scramble to my feet, but my chest is heaving, the coughing take away my breath. Part of the road rise up in the shape of the boy and run after me. I will not outrun him. He run straight into the wall beside him as if he just run into cream. Alongside me he is now, the wall looking like a silk sheet with a body running right underneath it. This boy is too fast. Faster. He catching up. We running away from the ship. No choice now but to run till I reach the water, then turn left and run along the seaside till I get to the port. But I mistake the city and run into a dead end. Nothing but walls surround me, no door, no window. The footsteps follow me before I see a foot. He step in mud and stop. I watch him take the color of mud, watch the boy again shape into a boy before me. A tall boy, all muscle, skin, and bone with a black bead belt around the waist. Face, arm, leg, belly, all shiny like he just rub down in clay and fat. He pull the blade again and just then I identify the like. An ida sword coat in pepper poison that if you get the slightest graze, you stop moving. The boy smile impish, like this is some favorite game. Dash at me him do, and him skin turn dry like dust, then as he jump into the air, it turn into nothing, like sky. But I know sky. He land just as I whip wind (not wind) to blast him back and far, and he hit a wall. The boy just shake him head and smile again. The wind (not wind) throw me up on a rooftop and I run and jump from roof to roof. He at my heels. Green boy when he run on green roof, gray when he run on gray, rust when he run on rust. The poison sword glint with each color. Young devil. Sangomin child assassin.

I strike my foot against a loose tile and trip. In the quick, the boy upon me. He thrust the sword, I slip out of the way but smell the pepper race past my nose. He jump back and then stomp with the right foot—somebody school him. But I get schooling too. Here is how he hope it go. He stomp hard so that I look at his foot so he can chop me or stab me as I look down. But I stay up and block his jab with my dagger. I swing away his sword hand with my left hand and stab him straight in the side. The boy hiss, pull back, and clutch him side. He look like old wood now. Smile again the boy do, then charge again like a stick fighter, sweeping that blade wide. The wind (not wind) rise up again, but the blade cut through it. He spinning faster and faster like dervish, and all I can do is stay low like a spider. One little graze was all he need. He coming closer and closer, sweeping the sword wider and wider, the air smelling of pepper poison. He step on a loose tile. I stir my hands and the air stir the tile, and up quick it clobber the back of his head. The boy stagger and drop the sword. My wind swoop the sword and hurl it to the boy neck. The boy clap him hand just in time and catch the blade between him two palm. If he weaken his grip, he die. But if I stay here I will miss the ship. And there it flash for little more than a blink, the wide eye and hanging lips of a boy afraid. The same eyes you see on a dying child who just realize he soon dead. The thought distract me only a little, but that be all he need. He dip out of the way, the sword fall, he catch it and is about to throw it, but the wind (not wind) sweep hard under, throw him up in the sky, then fling him far off before he fall, like a wet sack, ten roofs away.

The ship already push off. One of the sailors say to me later that either his eye was crossed or God was foolish because he never see a man jump that far. Reaching late will cost me a space belowdecks, so I going have to sleep between the two mast.

"Your old shoga already down below," the sailor say.

You think this story is about revenge. This is about the divine order of goodness and plenty, and how we lose our way because of one wicked imp who think such things shouldn't be in the world, but only in him. This is about malcontent growing in land and sea, like a lump that grow to a coral that burst out of a woman breast. This is about lands awash in war blood because many more going to suffer. This is not about me. This is not about me, oh. There is a boy in Omororo who is ten and one year in age, soon to be ten and two.

And I going to kill him.

Kill who?" I say.

The three of them look at me as if I supposed to know. Worse, as if I supposed to tell them.

"Answer me. This griot telling me the tail as if I know the head, and what kind of song man this is who don't even sing, nor speak in verse?"

The old man and the water sprite huddle. Nsaka Ne Vampi look straight at me, locking her eyes with mine for a while before she approach.

"They all gone now, you know. Everyone from that house in Ibiku. Your daughter, she live the longest, some would say out of pure cantankerousness and spite. Mama used to say that even death scared to come near her. Mama also said that she used to fly, but I never see it. You fly? Matisha, she live the longest, oh. Great-Grandmother was always looking off into some place nobody else could see. If we passed a road heading south, somebody would have to grab her or she going down it. Every time the sun set in the west, she look south. Mama used to say that she reach the age where her mind already gone to be with the ancestors, even if her head was still here. But I didn't think so. I think she was looking south because she knew somebody was coming. Maybe coming back."

"When did Keme . . . ?"

"Before I was born. You know, Mama, she hold us tight even when we get too big for her hands. Ten and one years old I was before I realize that she used to have pigeons following me. Regard that shit. They would land and snatch something, a grain, a piece of cloth, one time an earring, to report back to my mother. Even the neighbors hear us cussing when I find out. Loosen your grip, woman, or better yet cut us loose, I say. But she couldn't do that, my mother. She didn't want to turn into Matisha. Poor Great-Grandmother never stop waiting on the mother who leave her."

"Is so they tell the story up north?"

"Your story different?"

"I don't owe you any story."

"You don't owe me a thing. Matisha is who you leave bitter, not me. I admire that a woman can do people like a man. You just get up one day and gone. No drums, no pigeons, no note, no word, no nothing."

"And you never ask yourself why Matisha was the only one who miss me."

"Couldn't ask your other children, they all dead. They . . ."

I don't know what I show her or what she see on my face, but she let her words fade to air. Maybe she see me searching for it, the part of me that hear that my children are dead, long dead, and as soon as I find it, I hide it again. Good. For no part of me ready for the wrongness of it, the same wrongness when you see a man about to take a nine-year-old wife, or a boy watching his father kill his mother slow. The wrongness of burying my own children, that I didn't even get to bury. For the first time I find myself thinking about my long life and wondering if it was a curse, not a blessing. It don't matter how old one get, mother or child, no child supposed to be buried by their mother. And I didn't get to bury nobody. Grief lurking at the back of my head, but it is a sound, maybe even a mark on parchment, not a thing living inside me threatening to come out and take over my face. I not going to allow it. I never going to allow it.

"How come you still alive?"

"I don't know."

"Matisha too, at one time she look as young as Mama herself. People use to think they were sisters. And neither of them looked as young as you look now. You barely look like a mother, much less a great-great-grandmother. If I didn't know I would say you just turn sixty. Witchcraft?"

"Again with the witchcraft."

"And yet they call you Moon Witch."

"What you do with yourself, great-great-granddaughter?"

"Call it the family business," she say.

"You two done settle on what to say to me next?" I say to the two of them still huddled together.

"I . . . I didn't know he took so much, or I would have come before. This Aesi, he rape everything that is normal and good. He disrupt the line of kings. He turn necromancy into science and science into necromancy. And none of it ever come back?" Popele ask.

"What?"

"Your memory."

"My memory fine. Is my own blood that did forget. Even Matisha, she didn't remember me, she just know that she forget me and not supposed to."

"Is more than that," say Nsaka Ne Vampi.

"You was there?" I say, which shut her up.

"Neither him nor me thought there would be so much to tell you. Thank the gods that most make it to paper. The rest I didn't forget. None of us who live in the trees or in the waters forget."

"You the one who send me to Omororo."

"Yes."

"You don't look like somebody whose orders I would follow."

"You choose to go when I tell who you'd be hunting."

"Hunting. Your words telling me more about you than your face or your smell."

"Do you know of the Aesi?"

"Who?"

"The right hand of the King of the North. He is why you was in Omororo. We sent you to kill him."

"What? Who you to send me killing? Did you pay my weight in gold?"

"You did it for free."

"And I kill him?"

"The griot have your story."

"It's a yes or no. And . . . but wait, you said this Aesi sit at the right hand of the King. The same Aesi? So I kill him or what?"

The old man and the water sprite glance at each other, trying to not move their heads, hoping I didn't notice.

"Speak your story," I say.

"How far back you want to go?" Nsaka ask.

"Further than what they tell you," I say.

"Forgive the griot, he only know you since the slave ship. He only write what you tell him to, and in the way you tell it," say Popele.

"But why you send him?"

"Because if you succeed, you would have changed the world. But if you fail, that would change the world too. Either way one smarter than me say let there be records for we don't know if we will need them. And look, now we do."

"You all better tell me this story before I really kill somebody tonight."

Here is what that water sprite say to me.

This was time of Kwash Liongo, who become King after the sudden death of Kwash Moki in his twenty and fifth year as King. Liongo the Good they call him for three years, for both his father and his twin brother was nothing but wickedness, and both meet their deserved end, but that is someone else's story to tell. But I tell you this one true, that this is not the first time we meet, nor the second,

nor the tenth time either. The first time, there you was down by the river that run behind the Ibiku quarter in Fasisi. You washing clothes for a home where few wear any, when up from the river jump me. Here is truth, I was watching you for days, long enough that the bisimbi nymphs warn me that these were not my waters, and they have the craving of the crocodile when they get hungry. But I was regarding you for days, your shape and your manner, and for days I was asking myself if this really is the one who killed the Aesi. Hard as it was to believe that you kill him, it was harder to believe that he only manage to kill one of you. Four days I watch you and your house and your family. Your lions, and your girl Matisha, who touched with the same thing you touched with. I watch how your oldest children come and go, some of them done gone for good, for all was past twenty in age and the ones from your lion's marriage were older. And your youngest children, all of them ten, they already start pulling from you as well, for your grip on them was too tight, even you did know.

Day twenty of the Sadasaa moon. I watching you while the bisimbi watch me and I wonder if you know anything about your line, how you not the first of your blood who can do things with air and sky and ground and fire. Like

I say, you were washing when I rise behind you. I am there thinking you didn't hear me, for I rise quiet like a thought, but then you swing around quick with a knife and try to slash me. You strike first then ask questions later? is what I ask you but you didn't answer. You slash right through me and I let you, for you might as well cut through butter. Then I make myself like the river, thin and loose as water, and fling myself on you, race up your legs, cover past your waist, rush into your mouth before you shout and cover your head. I was about to be gone with you for I didn't have time to waste when a spear burst right through my shoulder. I turn around and there was you.

"My wind will blow you apart if you don't give me back my daughter," you say.

You will blow your daughter apart as well, I say, but it shame me that I couldn't tell daughter from mother. I use my own finger to cut open my belly and the daughter, Matisha, tumble out. A wall of water rise up quick and tall and violent and I know it is their doing.

And what you have is not wind, I say.

Oh, you think you know me. What is it then?

Force.

What is force?

What you have. You not blowing a man against a wall, you pushing him.

Woman or man makes no difference, for you all are still strange to me, even after watching you for age upon age. I turn both my hands into blades sharper than any knife and you don't even budge, but my saying that I see that you will kill yourself before you let another one die makes you fall to your knees as if going to bawl. But you don't. Ten years gone and the day as fresh as yesterday, you say. The worst is that it feel like something long gone, and something soon coming. Like it is something going happen tomorrow, but I can't stop it. You ever feel that? you ask and I want to say no, but you continue, that every morning it is as though he is not dead but about to die and you cannot stop it. Here is truth, you perplex me, for I could see that you waiting years to ask somebody that question and yet I was not the one to answer. When I say that I come to you on other business, you look relieved and that is no lie.

You ask what I want and I say there is no time to waste. There is a man who used to shadow the King so much that they call the two of them one spider. Don't lose valuable time telling me you don't know what I am talking about, because ten and one men and the Aesi entered your house and no man leave. That was years ago, and they was just robbers, you say. Listen, we don't have time for this game, I say louder and step out of the river. You make from pitch or tar? you ask but I don't answer you. Where can we go, for I have news that going sit heavy with you, I say and we go to your grain keep. People above sky and under land all see when you kill the Aesi, and some of them were not happy, I say to you and you say that you would kill him again if he came for another of your children. When I say that was good, you both perplexed and insulted.

I don't mean for harm to come to your children, but you just voice why I come here. We need to make haste, for the time glass already flip and it running out.

Stop talking in riddles, whatever you be, and tell me what you come for, you say and I almost laugh at your toughness. You already said what I come for. The Aesi you kill? Death you certainly bring to him, but this is the world, these are the times, and gods will be gods.

And he who you kill get born again.

"Wait. I kill this Aesi before?"
"Yes."
"You remember how your son Ehede die?"

"Bandits, robbers, somebody thinking he was a wild lion."

"You really don't know?"

"Me getting tired of you talking to me like I some ignorant fool."

"The Aesi and his men ambush you in your own house. They kill Ehede and you kill him. The second ever that the Aesi didn't die from his own hand."

"Poachers kill my son. I know because their corpses all buried in the backyard."

"Those were soldiers, not poachers."

"And this Aesi? His body in my backyard too?"

"No. You set off your gift inside him and he explode into mist."

"Continue your story."

Popele continue.

I knew to stop because the news was like a tree falling, quiet at first, with only the crackle of leaves tearing, and twigs breaking, and then the whole thing tumble down, smash onto the ground and rock like thunder. You look at me stunned, like you unaware somebody is slapping you. But we don't have time to waste, so I say, He you must again kill. How you mean he born again, you ask and I don't want to answer because that is a long answer, which can be told on the way. So I say right now he is not at court, he's not even a man. And still

you say, weak like a hurt child, How you mean
he is still alive? He really come back from the
dead? You ask if I was sure. And even when
I say yes, you ask again. I thought you was
going to cry. Your face thought it was going
to cry until your will stop it. It chose anger
instead. What kind of nasty trick is this, and
if not from you then what god playing with
such fuckery? This is why nobody worship the
gods anymore other than fetish priest. How is
it that he living again? He going come for me?
How he living again? You ask and ask until I
say to you that I misspeak. It is not that you
going to kill him. He lives, that is sure, but
you not going to kill him, you going to make
sure he never born.

Hear this now. It don't matter how he
die, but the Aesi is the kind that return to
the otherworld along with all whose spirit
is restless, and then eight summers later he
is born again. Most of those spirits are born
to the same woman and die young, and born
again to again die, leaving that woman know
nothing but heartbreak. But the Aesi is born
to a different woman every time and the
gods choose no favorites between North and
South, though in all the times I know he only
serve the North. That is why we reaching to
you now, for one born always to a different
mother is one difficult to find. But this story

running too fast and your head spinning. I say it unto you again, that eight years after you kill him when Moki was still King, he was born again. When you twenty and nine. The Aesi is not even his name, for nobody know his real name except for what his mother call him. So eight years after he die, the Aesi born again in Omororo, to a woman in the Asakin tribe out in the wild bush between the city and the sea. Kwash Moki die the same year he turn eight. It take up to ten years to find him, and five moons to find you, and now we near out of time.

How you know all this? you ask.

One day we finally get wise and start to follow they who follow him, I answer.

Sangomin?

Sangomin. A Sangoma and her wretched children killers, they been watching over the boy from afar, and it didn't look like he know. He don't know anything, for to himself he is just a boy wanting boy things and having boy wants. You ask me how I know which woman, and I tell you that I don't. Only that if he was born, then surely he born to a woman, and this also, the gray-and-yellow pigeon, the eyes of the Sangomin been flying low over that tribe for years now. No way to come in close without them catching that spying is afoot. Which woman is the mother and which boy is the son? We don't know, for the Asakin tribe have their peculiar ways, which mean that one boy is never born alone, but when seven, eight, or even ten are born within the same moon that count as one birth. One boy not more special than the other, for they call all woman Mother and all man Father. They born as a group, raised as a group, learn as a group. When one show bravery all get reward, and when one commit sin, all get punished.

And so they move through the years until it is time to turn man. The Asakin don't believe that a boy just age, but that a boy and his group grow until they reach the boundaries of youth and cannot grow no more. At ten and two, like the caterpillar, the boy must close down so that the man can come out. And like the caterpillar to the butterfly, the boy have no connection to the man other than the husk from which a grown man come. Even his birthday start again from one. But though he go through the initiation with all the boys, he is not like the other boys.

I not killing no boy, you say. I not killing no boy.

Like I say, he is no boy. You will see it in his bearing, you will see it in his eyes.

You ever see a dead child?

What if this boy grow into he who would kill the world? What if you live long enough to see it? What then? He is not a young boy but a small something else, even if he look like the other boys, I say to you.

Hear me now, for this is from the one time a griot mark it in letters, which is the only reason why we know. I see the scroll myself. The griot write it down seven hundred years ago, and even then he couldn't finish it. Truly the unfinished line turn into a riddle until somebody finish it. All the other boys, on the night they reach ten and two, pass through the ritual and become men in the eyes of the people. But when the Aesi reach ten and two, he reset the world. The griot write this, that the time soon coming, the time done coming, the time is here. Lightning cut across the sky though no rain threatening to come. He is turning, somewhere in the world, and the world is already on fire. Maybe if I keep writing and not stop then I will write my way on to the other side, for now I know his ways. I know he will re . . . s . . . Then ink spill and quill, hands, and finger smudge the scroll in black ink. Only at the bottom of the scroll the writing resume, and though it is the same hand, the griot dismiss the writing as that of a madman. We had to hunt down every script by this chapter of griots to find any more writing over the age. Some about the wretched boy who keep getting born again.

One griot write that an elder told him to watch the sky for the flight of gray pigeons. Another from five hundred years ago say to watch for those years when there is only the King and keep writing, for when the Aesi return somebody will notice the change in the script if not the world. Then there is just the scrolls that trying to do nothing but record, scrolls that mention the same Aesi over and over and over, from even before the house of Akum. Seven hundred years and only now we learn that when the Aesi reach ten and two, not only does he change, but everybody who ever see or hear or touch or breathe air with him change too. They forget him, you hear me, as if he was never born, and as for him, he change into a man, not like those boys who become man only in name, but a tall, thin man of a man. Skin so black it blue and hair red, and always he is beside the King, but nobody can tell when first he get to the King side, or who he come from, or how he get to the right of the throne. The Aesi don't have no beginning or end, he just is.

But learn this, just because you forget him don't mean he will forget you. A King Sister along with a fetish priest and ten witches hatched a plot that killed him, two hundred years before the house of Akum. He put his own vendetta on princesses and has been coming for them ever since. Mark that he will remember the woman who killed him and come for you. And yours. And gods help you but you won't even know why, which is why I say to you that to kill him you cannot kill him. Get him as a boy or a man and this is a kill. Get him when he stop being the boy but before he become the man, and it is not a killing, for he is not born. A man not born cannot die and cannot be born again. But we have to reach him on the eve of his ten and two. It is the only way.

You take one look at your youngest children and decide right then to do it. Your lion didn't like that at all. You trying to kill him as prevention or revenge? he ask you but you didn't answer. I doing this for them, you say but he say you doing it for you. Then he say that when the Aesi came killing it was you who lure him here.

"He say more but you look like you don't want to hear the rest."

"Tell me," I say.

"You call the oldest to take care of the youngest, and leave the house with ill feelings and poison words hanging between you and the lion."

"Tell me."

"Very well. He say what kind of mother can forsake her children, one who is dead because of you.

Is because I don't want any more dead, why I have to go, you say. He say is because you just can't lose the taste for blood, for even now you sneak out some nights to go fight in the donga, which shock you because you didn't think anybody knew. You tell him that you didn't bring any fight to the Aesi's door, you didn't even bring yourself to this fuckery city, he is the one who take you back here. Then you say if he was a real man instead of half of one, then he would have protected his children instead of blaming the woman. Then he say you right, the real cursed day was the day he bring you back from that mountain, and drive out a real mother instead of one who just breed and drop, truly who is the real beast here. Then you say—"

"Enough."

"He try to strike you."

"Enough, I say."

"Like I said. You leave the house with ill feelings and poison words hanging between you and the lion."

Popele continue.

It would take too long to get to the south by land, even on horseback, but going the whole way by sea was too treacherous, with the bad-temper weather being the least of it. Quickest and safest mean journey by river, riding southwest to Juba, and paying passage south on lower Ubangta River to Dolingo, then leaving water to travel through no name forest, then through the Blood Swamp to the coastline where you would take a boat to Lish, and from Lish a ship sailing south to Weme Witu and Omororo. In all, four moons' journey. Before the Aesi turn ten and two.

"In what moon was his birthday?"

"We use the best intelligence we have."

"So you didn't know. And where was you when I was traveling south?"

"I was with you always, below water. My form still too strange even for people who have seen strange."

"With me all the time. The old man say Sangomin attack me twice. You heard him. Sound like you didn't do nothing. You know what I still don't know? If you divine born and can't get your hands dirty with people business, or if you just love to watch."

"I . . . I . . . I not one to be on land too long. Water on ground, the ground suck me up and then . . . No I cannot. Just cannot. . . ."

"Popele, go back to the story," Ne Vampi say.

I couldn't say no more. Instead I tell you that though you packed light, your burden was heavy. Twice you leave the river, one time to Mitu, to a village too small to be on any King's map. You wouldn't stop until you reach three small huts, out of which pour many children, with four of them not noticing that they walk on air. A man call out to them and you shudder when you see him, as if you know him. You wouldn't leave until you saw their field, and a mound of red dirt that mean nothing to any of them. You wouldn't leave until you grab three of the girls to stare at them and they fuss and pull away from you. And my name is Popele, I feel the flow of all rivers, even the red streams running underneath skin, so I knew you and them was kin.

The first boat leave you behind, so you take another to Dolingo. From there you was to go by horseback straight to the Blood Swamp, but you stop again. Yes I followed you, anybody would wonder what business you would have in that backward sheepherder territory. I don't think you choose it, maybe it was just the last stop before bush. But you walked all over until you find a man in four huts making a house, who hoard book and parchments that he wrap in goatskin and leather. I see it. You not one for modesty. You lift up your dress, and unwrap a long scroll of linen or parchment, full of marks from your waist. Spin and spin, and spool and spool you do until it was all on the floor. Keep it secret, and keep it safe, you say, because you was wearing it as a reminder of your resolve, but come to see how that was another woman's fight and you have your own revenge. The book binder didn't know what you mean, but promise to keep it safe, among his leaning towers of books and scrolls, after you leave him much in silver.

"Tell me what happen after I get to Omororo."

"Ikede?" Popele say, turning to the griot, who unroll one scroll, then another, then five more.

"My life take up all of that?" I ask and for a blink impressed with myself.

And so he continue.

Day three. We sail in good wind, but this sky was promising nothing. There we was, out to sea in a rotten ship bound for the largest territory of the South Kingdom. A domain under the rule of a King not yet mad, but doom to be as sure as a bird dead in flight must soon fall from sky. Two nights done and seven more to come. This also. People on the ship somehow take me for a man, so a man I am. That was what the quartermaster tell the crew when I reach late, that we missing one man who already pay for his passage, a man with a matter in Omororo.

I rise every morning damp from either dew or sea spray, and head to breakfast before the biggest of the crew get up with meanness from afore and muscle everybody out of the way. Only last supper, one push me down to get to the galley and when I tell him that next time he won't have a hand left to push, he giggle like a hyena. The cook give us meals at sunrise and sunset, but in truth, there was no difference between the two. Both taste like he scoop slop from the stinking hull itself.

The captain, when I visit his quarters to pay my passage, look me over before he inspect the coin and grumble to himself. The wind blow to me the secret whisper from his lip, that I look too meager to be good slave flesh, so he might as well keep me on deck, for what money is there to be made in trading the likes of him? Plus, from the looks of me I could be a conjurer or wonderman that could curse the ship. From the looks of him, he could be a captain from a wild sea story about a captain. I watch him still eyeing me, forcing me to eye him back. Any other man would look away by now, in the agreement two people make when they talk. You look at me and speak, but look away before you finish, so I look at you with no awkwardness. None of that with this man, for he fix his eye on you like a hawk and didn't stop looking. Truth, his eye was a red fire in a thick, dark face. Beard red from dye, like a northern monk. Hair curly and wild like he from above the sand sea and tunic like one as well. Yellow and red stripe, covering the chest like a vest and reaching past the knee. Knees bare where there should be pants, but he didn't see no need to dress just to see me.

"'Tis a ten-day sail, nine if the gods are kind," he say though I didn't ask. "Three hundred sixty and five miles around the horn. Then six hundred before we get to Omororo. Do you understand?"

"You think I born in bush?"

"So you smell. As for me I see no fault. You smell nothing worse than anything else belowdeck. No shame in wherever you're born or whatever you drop out of. I sail to the East plenty so I count their way."

"Long time now since I see the East."

"Long? Surely thirty years have not passed from what I see of your face. You a monk?"

"A Bintuin."

He shake his head once, like he settle on something. I wonder right then what he, or the quartermaster, or even the boy cook say about me when they talk. Four days I stay out of everybody way, me thinking that the more I out of sight, the more I out of notice. I think wrong. My being quiet make them want to hear more, me out of their way make them stand in mine.

"Bintuin. People who live on sand, but never see the sea? You a peculiar sort. What in Omororo for a man like you?"

"Trade."

"Now who think who born in bush? Nothing a Bintuin have that anybody in Omororo could want. All you have on you is a sack."

"I can tell you a lie, or tell you nothing," I say.

The captain laugh. "Some of my crew, they think you—"

"Think me what?"

"I could tell you a lie or I could tell you nothing," he say, and wave me away like dismissing a boy. I nod and step out backways, not taking my eyes off him even though he long take him eye off me.

Day five. I am a man like all the other men on board, except the one with a wife, and that wife I only see once, hiding her little head in a massive gele that she had to grab to stop wind from blowing it to sea. Not long after that, the husband, a chief too fat for somebody so young, lock her up in the cabin, like she was just another thing to keep safe. But I sail like the sailors do, sleeping under the shed of the stern, kicking away rats, kicking away the drunk quartermaster prowling the deck for the boy cook to rape, and securing the boom when the captain shout secure the boom, tossing the shit bucket when the captain shout toss the shit bucket, mopping the deck when the captain shout mop the deck, and earning my keep when the captain shout earn your keep, even though I did pay my way with a fat pouch of silver.

To be a man you do as man do. Master one thing and you can fail at everything else, for to be a man is to fail at everything else. Here is the one thing. What man do in all things, more than anything, is take up space, whether he be priest, king, beggar, or hunter. Whether he living or dead. More space than he need, and more space than he will use.

"We can skip that," Ikede say.
"No, that I want to hear," I say.

A man sit on a small stool, but spread wider than a buffalo. Mark how he sprawl in the dirt, wash in the river, and lean by a tree. Mark how he stand to piss and squat to shit. How he swing him arms wide when he walk. He will call you with a voice that reach up a hill even though who he speak to is a breath away. Mark how he will pick nose, grab balls, and scratch ass, then dip that finger into the soup without thinking, for thinking is like fear, and fear is for womanfolk. So I was a man spreading my two leg when I sit or squat, as if left leg had hatred for right, and walking like each step was a stomp. And gripping the bulwark like I about to ride it, grabbing the boom like I was about to swing on it like a monkey, and not even frown when one of the crew fart, or toss the shit bucket the wrong way, or joke that the wife belowdeck look like one of them from the near east that have her koo cut out before she reach ten and two. Too hard and too easy, being a man. Too easy to spit, and snore, and fart, but too hard to remember. And too foolish sitting in a pose begging for kick.

And this ship. Bigger than most dhow because it was a merchant vessel, but also because of the cargo it usually carry.

And this crew. After the captain, the quartermaster, who dress more eastern than the captain and look more so as well. Younger and taller and lighter, with higher cheekbones and a straighter nose, and wearing a turban he didn't take off, a blue boubou tunic one day, a black one the next, and always black yata breeches. And a saber hanging from the shoulder, which he tap every time my eye land on him looking at me. The big cook who hide his big belly under his big agbada, while the boy cook hide his boy frame under a sheath that tie at the waist with a small rope. The young boy with picky hair, full now of teeth and an always frighten look, like he was set to flee anytime, which was every night the quartermaster not too drunk to rape him. A medicine man who look like the cook, except for the two feather sticking out of his hair, the four cheetah hide he wrap himself in, and a sword that no healer supposed to need. He come up for air two time, then decide the air below was better, for he never come back up again. As for the rest of the crew, ten men though sometimes I count nine, for they all look alike, some barefoot and in white breeches they roll up for walking, the rest barefoot and in white skirts they sometimes don't wear, all of them without shirt. In the hot day, no pants neither.

And then there was the navigator, the last man I see when I sleep and the first when I wake, standing at the bow in the night, and the stern in the day. A man from Malakal, I judge from the tongue, though the checia on his head was from lands above the sand sea. Not old, for his face was smooth like a boy, and with almost no hair, even on the brow. But not young, for in his eye was a grave look from seeing too much. Next to the captain he was the only man from whom I would choose to have words, so I follow him belowdecks. He open the door just as I raise my hand to knock.

"Magic, or fate?" he ask, smiling.

Candlewax light, but also two lanterns burning fish oil. The room, spreading the whole width of the hull, must be the biggest

on the ship. That he be the one in it and
not the captain confirm everything I suspect
about the rare wisdom of this navigator. But
the room is full with so much paper, chart,
map, and scroll, and books on top of books
in towers that soon topple, that it looked
like the smallest on the ship. I didn't see
them until they fly around me, surveying my
face and my eyes, one of them even landing
on my shoulder before flying off. The one
staring at me with blue skin and blue wings
with markings like runes. The one flying
off from shoulder with pearl skin but green
wings. Both of them as big as my elbow to
my fingertip.

"How you feed a Yumboe at sea?"

"Look here. With no grub, no cricket, no
locust, maggots will have to do. And a ship's
galley bring no shortage of maggots."

The Yumboes, both of them female, look at
him like they about to vomit. They flap their
wings so fast it look like balls of light dancing
to the window.

"Truth? They just steal my fish. Fish bigger
than the two of them. Nobody warned me
about their enchanted appetite."

"Your slaves?"

The navigator laugh out loud. The Yumboes
let out a little hiss.

"My wives."

He know that I would have a hundred questions. He look at me like he readying himself to answer them.

"What use quarter of an astrolabe have?" I ask and watch him looking at me like he is now the one with the questions.

"Correct enough," he say picking it up. "Correct enough. They even call it a quadrant. More useful. In these seas there's no North Star to follow at night, so we must use the sun in the day. Surprised that you would know the like of either."

"Because I am Bintuin?"

His laugh say to me, don't take me for a fool.

"You lucky that this quartermaster only fancy holes with a boy attached to it."

He step past me and grab a map. The Yumboes grab the two ends and hold it up by the only empty space on the wall. He hammer it down, then start to travel from land to land by finger.

"Hear this. I get paid more coin than every man on this ship, except the captain. You know why? Any navigator can reach east or west. All you need is a piece of wood and some string. But north from south? Few, only a few. Most seamen, even if they good, just follow the sun, or flee from it, then guess. Bad for a ship, bad for a crew. A voyage of nine days turn into mutiny at nine weeks."

"You tell me this because—"

"Don't take me for a fool. How the others don't see, I want to know."

"Don't take much to be a man."

"Men know this?"

He look at me like this is a game that he not playing, but want to see who win. For the first time on this ship I unwrap the kaffiyeh from my face. He raise eyebrow and smile, his face saying you look better than I was guessing. Long time since I care how a man take my looks.

"How soon you need to get to Omororo?"

"The captain say this voyage was nine days."

"Captain change his name to navigator?"

"Then how long?"

"Depends on when this same captain will go back to listening to me. At present he not. But you. I tell you before, I read things. I see what the sky don't want to show. Right now the only thing on you is weapons. You know that kohl dust have a smell, you just hope nobody here know it. I starting to feel sorry for whoever you looking for."

He sit down. He content with all he just say.

Navigator do many a thing, but more than anything else, he watch. Whatever happen next at sea, whether from sky or sea or the action of men, that was all he was going to do.

Day nine. This is the day we supposed to land in Omororo. Popele don't seem to notice that we off course. But she is not one for seawater, now that I remember, so she don't know. The captain and the navigator still shouting at each other, and the crew still have murder in their looks toward me. At this point Sangomin knowing my whereabouts was not my worry. One night I go without sleeping and the one following I set myself that I would roll on some shells and wake myself up before any man pounce me. But this is insufferable and that is no lie. There won't be any more me by the morning I get to Omororo. If I get to Omororo.

Day ten. I wake up rolling and spread my arms to stop myself. My head spinning mad until I see that it is the ship. My face cold and wet and getting wetter. But I see nothing but dark until the lightning blaze everything white. Then black again and I hear boom crash boom. Black sea, black sky, then white lightning cutting through clouds, and I see the sea, wild and unruly, waves crashing into waves to make a big surge fifty times higher than the ship. And this ship, instead of rising high, sink so low that it feel as we falling through air. We hit the bottom of the wave and ride over, but the wind beat into the side and near pitch us over. Wind lash rain at me. Spirits of sea and spirits of sky doing nasty work. Lightning slash and thunder boom then roll like it will drop out of sky on top of us. Another wave rise like a mountain and rush into us but we climb over, then drop down like we rolling downhill and can't stop. The sky bellow as it tear itself open. Another wave slam into starboard and twist us around. We roll and scramble. The bow drop under water that rush across the deck all the way to me. I grab the mast. I try to stand, but a wave slam into the port side now and throw me into the air and I flip and flip and grab a rope and hang on until the wind stop flapping like a ribbon. Wind. I hear the rough whisper of it trying to blow anybody off the ship. The bow sink under again, and deck wash soaking me. I hang on to the mast, and only then see men around me, trying to lower the sails, securing the boom, staggering to go belowdecks, running back above deck, shouting into a wind that suck in whatever they say. The wind whispering, howling, screaming, laughing. And this, though it dark, though I keep slipping and falling, though the crew scramble all around

me, and though rain keep blurring my sight.
The boy cook running up on deck, naked
and blank, then walking almost peaceful as
the ship thrashing around like caught fish.
Nobody see him but I, walking right up to the
bowsprit, and when the bow plunge undersea
and come up again, he gone. The bow ride
over a wave then down again, and again, each
time lower and lower, each time us looking
that we won't come back up. The ship lean
left, almost flat on the side, and sink down
into the water again. The water unruly, in the
dark it is mountains rising and falling inside
and on top of each other, and white spray that
hit us again. One of the crew stagger past me,
trying to tie down the second boom, which
had come loose and swinging so hard that it
soon break off. He look at me, nod, make a
run, and white spray sweep him up and fling
him off the ship. Black clouds break apart,
and thunder drop on us again. Lightning
whiten the air and somebody else is at the
bow but is not the boy. The ship dip again,
slam down into the black as if somebody drop
it on ground. I thought the ship would come
apart but another wave sweep it up again.
That was the first time I wondered if I had
any quarrel with the gods of air or sea that I
forget. Then a wave rise from beneath we and
throw the ship in the air. Another crewman

trip and tumble overboard. We land with a crash on a wall of water that pull out quick under us, leaving the ship on nothing. We fall into the dark.

The dark was a wave as big as a mountain. But when wave move in close, to starboard, somebody shout that it is not a wave. Is a fish. A fish as big as this boat when it pull up beside and frighten sailor who up to now act like they see every beast and monster. I thought the fish was as big as the ship until I realize that was only the head. I lean over too low and wind from behind almost kick me off the deck. Almost, if not for the griot, who grab my hand. The quartermaster scream for weapons, but this was a slave ship, not a warship, with no weapon bigger than a spear. He is more worried about this fish ramming into the hull than the storm wrecking us. I try to run to the stern of the ship but trip and slide to it, and see the fish's fins as far back as the edge of a rice field. It going swallow us alive, say one of the crew, while another scream like a baby. One shout for the cook to bring fire while another ask how you going throw fire on water. In a fucking storm. The fish swerve, knock the ship, and throw everybody off their feet. That bring up the captain screaming about the incompetent crew who fling his ship against rocks. The quartermaster point to the fish as it slam into the ship again. Slack the mainsheets, he say to slow the boat to a stop. A command that he should have give before the storm. The quartermaster yell that now they just sitting and waiting for the fish to ram into them like sea monsters always do, but captain yell back that if he don't shut up he will put him in chains and have the cook do to him with a pot handle what the quartermaster do to the boy cook. The ship come to as much a stop as it can on raucous sea. One sailor shout that the fish was no longer starboard. Another shout that he see a fin aft, until a gust blow him off the deck into the black. The captain look at me like there be nothing to do but wait on the whim of this storm or the pleasure of this big fish. Behind the ship, the fish rise again, enough of him that to new eyes a great mountain did rise from sea. The fish almost still but for the tail whipping.

"Chipfalambula," the griot say. "Giant of the rivers, what she doing out in the sea?"

Giant indeed. Wide as the ship. The top half of her is clear as sand, so clear you can almost see through the scales, while the lower half, from her mouth down, as blue as the sea. Eyes so big they pop out of her head like balls.

How you know Chipfalambula is a woman?
I ask the griot. The men only grow half as
big, big enough to go down in two bites, he
say, and was about to say more when his voice
get lost in gasp. The Chipfalambula open her
mouth, a little at first, then so wide that sailor
scream that it is about to swallow the ship.
The griot walk over to aft and I follow. Inside
the mouth darker than night, but from deep
come a light, like a lamp, but surely there
could be no fire in this storm. The wave rush
the floor again and nearly sweep both of us
off. The light shine on the hand holding it.
A hand! I yell at the griot, who put his hand
to his chin. The fish swim in close to the
point where it did look like she was about to
swallow the ship. Then I see whose hand was
holding the light. Popele.

"She beckoning us," the griot say.

"She mad?"

"Maybe, but she beckoning us."

Popele was standing on Chipfalambula's
tongue. The griot look at me and say, "I
can't jump first, I have to witness and write
about it."

I don't think. I just climb up the railing
and as soon as I remember my bag, sack, and
weapons, I jump. Bolom jump down right
after me and almost roll into the water. The
storm wind slam into the ship and whip it

sideways again. The ship's mast dip below the water. Chipfalambula close her mouth.

The griot continue.

The fish take us to the coast of Omororo, and the whole time Popele say nothing more than to look for a green witch who will give us room and board for the night, but we must set out at dawn. The fish almost beach herself, swimming right up to the rockier part of the shore at the south end of Weme Witu bay. From where we land, getting to the central city by foot would take us into nightfall. And even from where we was in the outskirt where most of the citizens lived, and even in near dusk, you could see the temple of the Sky God, which people rumor to be the tallest building in the world. And yet even higher was the monument to the God of Fertility and War, the stone arch half as wide the central city, with a massive pillar in the center looking like it was propping the whole thing up and ramming into the ground. The thrusting cock, that's what everybody call it, the griot say and laugh.

Omororo look like seven people plan seven cities at once. At the shore was a village with people in loincloths when they wasn't naked, people who don't seem to know that one of the

four brothers of the South empire was behind
them. The kind of people who done fishing for
the day so wasn't present for when a gigantic
fish swim herself to shore. Beyond the sea
huts, from what I could see, was a settlement,
one of four outside of the central city where
most of the people live. Settlement as big as a
city itself. Most of it was homes, taverns, inns,
and temples, most of them one floor, several
of them two, nearly all of them having some
little smoke escaping into the morning. All
of this I am watching from Chipfalambula's
mouth. Behind me, her throat and her belly,
where I sleep for one night, which look like the
inside of a hollow baobab tree, empty for now
because according to Popele, it is another two
moons before she feed. Follow the Cadanga
Road, though it winding through the people's
district, until it take you between the father
and son temples, and continue, though you
will see the central city in all its magnificence,
until the stone buildings get fewer and fewer,
mud houses get more and more, until you
come to a thick bush, with antelope and huts
like bosoms. The Asakin tribe. You will know
them by the splendid cows with horns as tall
as you. Where pigeons circle, that is where he
lives. When pigeons land, that is who he is,
she say. Sending us out, she is meaning she

will not follow. Popele already tire me with all her whimpering about dry earth sucking up too much of her, which make me think that for somebody divine born she don't seem to have much to her if she is nothing but thinking water.

Bolom set out but he can't go too far without me. I turn to go but swing around back quick and grab Popele's neck.

"You want to tell me why Sangomin keep following me?" I ask.

"I don't know the ways of the Sangoma."

"You don't seem to care either."

"This mission can't lose."

"Mission. As if we doing holy work. This is the killing of Asakin boy. And you know what? I wrong. They not following me, for that would mean behind me, and they always ahead. Who else know about this?"

"Nobody who would be in league with Sangomin."

"You know or you think? If is one thing I know about divine born is that none of you steadfast in anything. Maybe this is how one of you get his pleasure."

"By laying out a plan only to sabotage it? Maybe more people know that the Aesi died by your hands than you think."

"Then it would be a risk, using me. Which

mean you would never approach me in the first place. No, somebody getting intelligence after I agree to go."

"Sangomas share knowledge, mind to mind. You know that. Once you kill one . . ."

"But who tell that first one?"

I don't wait for her to answer. For to tell true, I didn't care for whatever she was going to say. Given how people always shouting to gods, nobody expect anything divine born to keep anything quiet, not even for their own good. But as I walk away, it swoop down on me that while I know my reason for doing this, I didn't know hers. Yes, she talk all she can about divine this and that, but she didn't come to me just to feed my revenge. Something about this Aesi is a threat to all like her, and for now my cause and hers align. I remember she mention divine right of kings which make me snort, but the more I hear from her, the more I know those words didn't first come from her mouth. Speaking of mouth, the less she heard from mine, the less likely others hear it too. That mean skipping any road she sending us. Instead I tap the griot's shoulder and dash down the first lane on the left, as if I catch on to somebody following me. Indeed, I stop once to look up for pigeons. As for this green witch, she could take a slimy fish and give herself a thousand fucks before I go to her door.

I take the first road heading north and walk right though the house of a woman too shocked to shout. Her house lead me to the back of another, which I walk around, then back onto a new lane leading me to a clearing with man, horse, donkey, and mule resting. I skip past them and take to my heels down a wide road with trade houses on either side. You going to have to turn south soon, say the voice that sound like me, the first I hear her on this trip. I turn south, but turn and dip west again, following a line of trees, and still looking above me. Only then I join this main road, which take me to this vast space of dirt and dust, more than I did expect for a city as famous as Omororo. I could see it in the distance, the great central closure, the walls higher than the highest trees, with ramparts every few paces and guards patrolling. The temple and palace beyond it rising higher, the gate between two towers being the only way out or in. But I didn't have no business there. I turn south back to the sea.

Popele wrong. I find the Asakin, and their village was right there skirting the sea, but no boy of the Aesi's age live among them. A good thing it was then that this griot speak their tongue since this was too different from Marabangan, which I barely understand even after all these years. He tell a man chewing a stalk that me and him were grandparents who want to leave something for their grandson. They know it is forbidden to come in contact with them as they become men, but even the gods know better than to deny a grandmother. The man shake his head and laugh, as if he and this griot have the same woman trouble. Yes, the boys leave for initiation near a moon ago, but no they not in the village. They not even on the land. All boy must die, and all man must be born on the Wakeda, the island right off the sea. Why this bitch and her fish didn't just take us there? I say quiet, hoping the griot didn't hear.

We steal a canoe with a hole in it. Yes, we. I didn't push off that canoe by myself, and is not my heel that plug the hole. All Popele tell me about the initiation was to look for boys in white. But as soon as we land, and as soon as I scale up a tree for a wider view, one thing become clear. Every single boy was white. Below me a branch snap, the griot, clumsy with climbing. I tell him to find a good branch and stay there. As for the white boys, they cover the whole bodies in ash and their hair with a paste, maybe a mix of same ash and cream, or clay. It make them look like statues until they move. See the alabaster boys move, four in a circle and sitting in the dirt, drinking from one small gourd. See two more crouch down by embers still smoking, one of them all white save for his face, the other with two clumps of ash in his hands that he bury his face in. See more boys, four, five, six with beaded belt around the waist, and staffs like stick fighters as they march off into the bush. More boys sit and drink from a larger gourd. For boys not yet men but they look like men even now, chest done broad, hips done thin, buttocks done big and strong, balls and cock done heavy with seed to create more warriors. This was it about boys, how sometimes they just look ready—for a fight or a fuck make no difference. They look like men even now. Popele's word was no use. Every single one was a boy in white and I couldn't tell one from the other, much less what a young Aesi would look like. Three bites from flies and I see why the ash make sense. I wait for them all to leave before jumping into it and covering myself. Only then do the insects stop biting and the air grow cool. In the gourds, I smell the last of the durra porridge.

I don't need her voice to tell me that any moment the Aesi can become what he is to become. But I hear Popele anyway, the annoying childlike bleat in it. I starting to realize that I don't like this water sprite at all. Here I was back in a tree, waiting to end the life of he who is not to be born yet is still alive and walking below me. She figure that my revenge was all I would need to feed on, and she figure right. As for how letting this man live would change the world, I don't know the world, and what little I know I long stop caring for. I care that my children move through it alive and unharmed, in any way they see fit, and I would kill all who stand in the way of that. It is something that feel like the damnation of the gods, the moment when you realize that not only would you die for your children, but you would kill as well. When the boys come back it was too dark, and soon there was nothing but shapes and shadows by the fire. Two of them, one in full ash and the other with two stripes running from face down to knee, stood by the clay sleeping hut, playing the lyre and singing.

Morning. I have to grab the sleeping griot before he fall to the ground, and drag him to a different tree when he just whip it out to piss. Nobody below expecting a golden shower, I whisper to him as I slap his face. Bow and arrow both lost with the ship. The only weapons that come with me was what I keep on me, the dagger, the machete, and the stick. When it come to killing this boy

I will have to do it up close. Not kill, I have
to remember, though that language was for
the water sprite, not me. I don't need to hide
behind any cleverness. But he is just a boy, say
the voice that sound like me. Is just a boy. A
boy is not a boy, a boy is never a boy. A boy
is potential. So I look up to the sky for where
the birds circle, and a shudder run through
me, for their eyes are the Sangomin's eyes.
Watching for something, yes, but watching
over something too. Watching with all their
focus, tightening their attention until they
are so close together that they form a black
cloud. The boys were climbing out of the hut
entrance. They reach for ash to cover what
night sweat clean away, and soon the whole
yard is thick with white dust. But they all the
same. They look the same, sound the same,
laugh the same, squat the same, even piss
the same.

Pigeons are already on the ground. They
peck and prod for food, but most start to
gather around one boy before another shoo
them away. That boy. That is the boy. The
one rubbing his forehead and revealing his
skin. The shorter one standing still, while a
taller one rub ash on his forehead and nose.
The one with a ring in his right ear and left
nose hole. He ask somebody a question, I can
tell from the tone. He don't like the answer, I

can tell from the frown. This is the boy who might not even know who he is.

Noon is threatening to push me out of this tree. I can't tell if the griot is asleep or sun drunk. Or maybe he is just lodged between two branches making up his mind about what to write. The drum been sounding since morning and while I know some Marabangan drum language, this is not Marabanga. First all the boys are jumping up again and again, then they shuffle around the dead fire. The older boy is beating the drum and shouting what sound like orders. The boys drink from a gourd, grab spears, then form a line and head into the bush. I shake the griot out of his stupor and leave him by the shore while I follow them into the forest, hiding behind wild leaves and thorns and watching for their footprints. Not many trees in this forest. Come to think of it, this is not much forest, but at the biggest tree somebody build a canopy with four blackish-red posts, with black moss all down the legs, and the roof lost in branches and leaves. They are lying down, still, as the drum beat slower and slower. The pigeons still peck and poke the ground around one boy. That boy. I approach. All of them so still, even the drummer is a statue except for the right hand beating the drum. I am closer, close enough that it is the pigeons that start. Now is the time. I think. I don't know, for the useless water sprite didn't tell me what to look for when a boy is dying and a man is being born, and right now only the gods must think this is something to look at. The posts are drawing me more, craft that I didn't expect in this province, thin at the base, thin as a tree, that is, then bulbing wider at the middle like a fruit, then narrow again, ending with a top that is arrowpoint sharp. Right now the boys are lying down still as death, and maybe from this they rise. This must be the moment, I can't wait for anything else. But he is just a boy. Is just a boy. A boy is not a boy, a boy is never a boy. A boy is potential. Ehede was just a boy, and now he will be nothing else. I don't know what to think, but the pigeons know that I am thinking. They knowing too much. First one looking at me, then another, then all of them. I pull my knife, counting how many throats I will have to cut.

Bird shrieks and fly off, so I look up. But then the ground shudder and that didn't come from sky. Boom the ground go again and more birds take off from branches above. The posts are jerking up and down, stomping into the ground and causing the rumble. The boys don't move. Above, the branches and leaves twist and turn and sway and break, even though there is no storm wind. The posts are still jerking and stomping, leaning left then right, and then just so, canopy sink down then rise back up, and something black, like hands, start to rip away the leaves. A shrieking rush through the air and hit my ears. The posts, already tall as trees, now reveal more, a lower leg as long as the leg, another just as long going up into the ceiling that threaten to drop again. I stand there looking at this confounding house when I see the house looking at me. Those joints are joints but those posts are not posts. The black fuzz is not fuzz. The shriek is not wind slipping through tight space. The black arms ripping away leaves are arms, swinging from the sides of black body with a black head with one giant horn at the back. He rip away the last branches to show all of himself, and below his belly sprout a huge, fat bulb like the end of a wasp. Spider. This can't be, I know I say out loud. But here he is, the darkchild, the black spider boy, now both man and spider and ten times taller than the last time I see him. Not a face but a snout, with only the red eyes left over from a boy's face. Three houses stacked on top of each other still wouldn't be as tall as him.

He can't remember me, I whisper over and over. He can't remember me, he won't remember me, he can't remember me. He see me and shriek. I run but there is nowhere to run and nowhere to hide. He break free from the last branches and chase. I want to look back, I want to see the small trees and branches he is breaking apart. I head for the one patch of trees, hoping it would slow him down, but the crackling, breaking, shrieking, and stomping is coming up right behind me. Dagger, machete, and a stick, what in all the fucks I going to do with a dagger, machete, and a stick? He catching up to me, his shadow is upon me already. A post fall out of sky and jab the ground right in front of me. I run into it hard, and fall back on the ground. I scramble backward, under him. His body, the shell moving and locking, the legs scrambling like they each have their own mind. I try to run, hoping that a body this large take too long to turn, but he just turn his head and scramble backward after me. I come to a patch of trees hoping to hide under them, but he climb over and catch me on the other side. He kick out one of his legs, which hit me in the back, sweep me up in the air, and toss me off into some wild bush. Then just so, dust whip up—no, he is whipping up the dust and is not until it settle that I see that he spin around. A hand come out the dust and punch me down. Wind blowing the dust away.

My wind not coming though I am begging and screaming for it. He lower himself and bend over until his head right over me. No face, just the eyes. Two long fangs where the mouth would be, and between them his feelers start to rattle. Then he lunge, his fangs snapping, and I swing the machete. He jump back quick. I run and don't get far before something wet hit my back leg, wet and milky that run hard in a blink. He hit me with his web, and was reeling me back in. I know I am screaming, I know it. He pull me right back under him and as I get near he bend over again and I close my eyes and swing the machete. It chop something, which fall to the ground. He scream this time. I open my eyes to see hand on the ground. He waving his arms wild, but from the wound something sprouting already. I run while I watch him regrow. I can't beat this spider, I have nothing. His pillar leg knock me down hard then pin one of my hands, crushing it into the dirt. I swing the machete but this time he slap it out of my hand. My legs go wet again, his web sticking me to the dirt. His face is right in front of mine now, his feelers rattling and his claws snapping. But his eyes look at me curious. I not his enemy, I am his food. One of his arms is pinning my free hand, two are on my face. One is growing back. His hand is stroking my face, poking against my eye, nose, and then shoving in my mouth, which kill the screaming. Each hand, three fingers covered in fuzz, he grab my mouth and pull it open wide, so wide that my lips stretch to tearing. His feelers separate and from a small hole a juice start to drip out. I try to flail, try to shift, try to bawl out, kick, shake, scream, twist, but nothing there is I can do. The first drop miss my mouth but hit my shoulder and it is like a flame burst on my skin. I know I am screaming no. I know he is trying to get this burning liquid down my mouth so he can turn my insides into juice and suck me out. All I see is the back of his hands now as he hold my mouth open.

Then he bawl out something, not a shriek but a scream. I smell it first, the harsh stink, hear it first, the crackle and whip, then see it only when the spider see it for himself, his back leg burning. He jump off me and try to rub it in the dust, and he is so huge that it look like a tent collapsing over me. The spider covered in fuzz and the fuzz catching like brushfire. He run, trip over his own legs as they burst into flame, roll, and tumble, trying to get to the stream but collapsing first.

I dash dirt on my shoulder to stop the burning. It stop the juice eating my flesh but not the pain.

"How long you see him there killing me?"

"I . . . I . . . I not supposed to mess in your mess. I not supposed to. I supposed to chronicle, no matter what come to pass. I . . ."

This really shake him. Not just what he see, but that he go against what man like him doing for hundred of years. Thanking him for what he did would just hammer down that he do it. I remember the boy, the one with the ring in his nose. The drummer is away from the tree and still drumming, in a trance like all the boys, with his eyes open but not seeing. None of them did even budge. I press the tip of the dagger to the boy's throat and this boy, but not just he, but the other boys all around him and the drummer all crumble to ash.

"Decoy!" I shout and run to the canoe. The griot was standing by ready to push off. "They set a decoy," I shout again. I know, he say. The sun was shimmering on the sea and blinding me. Soon come noon. I was waiting around throughout the night for signs and wonders when evil was coming at noon. And this griot. I shouting at the fool that now is not the time to write, but he still scratching on animal skin with a stick and, fuck the gods, blood. I ask whose blood but he don't answer.

"Watch the birds!" I shout and point up, but then I look up and learn something. That black cloud was not pigeons, but crows. The sight leave my eyes and sit inside my mind. When the Aesi attack my house he come with a legion of crows. Popele was a fool and so was I, for pigeon might be the sign of the Sangomin, but crows are the sign of the Aesi. And that black cloud of crows already gone from the island to the shore. Paddle! I shout to the griot but he still scratching away on the skin and gone deaf to me. A rumble come up from the water and the waves start to go wild. But I was going to find that boy and those birds were going to lead me to him. Waves were breaking against the boat, twisting us left and right like the slave ship, but as each wave pass I could see the shore. First nothing, then a wave rise like a hill that I had to row over. On the shore, still nobody. Then another wave, higher than the first, that almost flip the boat as it go over. And on the shore . . .

. . . A woman. It look like a woman. Tall, I could tell from far, naked, shiny, and black from head to toe, black like pitch, like tar. Shock take my voice and fright silence the griot. Fright, fury, pumping my chest, robbing me of the voice to even whisper her name. The woman carrying a boy in her arms like she about to place him on a table, the boy white from head to foot and loose, not like he is dead but asleep. His head leaning against her chest. And so they be, she standing at the shore looking at me, the boy like a baby asleep. Row, I shout to the griot, who is scratching words on the skin like he is about to cut through it. Sea water blind my eyes, then burn them, and when I see them again, the black tar woman is still holding the boy. The boy nudge his head against her chest and wake up. He look at her and my boat finally pick up speed and my shoulder burn from pain. The boy look at her again, then turn to look at us and then burst into a glow. Brighter, whiter, bri—

Quiet is growing thick in the room and taking away the air. All I can do is clutch my right shoulder at the burn scars that I thought were a large, nasty birthmark. Popele start talking.

"I say it before that for three years they call the North King Liongo the Good. Nobody call him that after his third year, nobody even remember other than the pages of the southern griots. Because right at the beginning of the fourth year there was Aesi, grown as a man can grow and right behind Liongo. Oh he good in his way, Liongo, he try to be. He even fight the Aesi influence better than anybody. But he bring the Sangomin back to court after Moki the Wicked banish them. And he more brutal in conquest and war than any King before. And when Paki succeed him but die after one year and his brother Aduware become King, there was the Aesi right beside him, the mentor yet again chancellor. And when Aduware die after twenty and five years and Netu turn King, who is there with him? The Aesi, looking like he don't age a day, much less a generation. Then the Aesi die. We don't know how, for by then no southern griot allowed in the Fasisi court. But somebody was writing, somebody was always writing. Then the same thing happen that happen with you. Eight years after he die he is born again, and twelve years after that, there is the Aesi, the second four limbs of the Spider King, right by Kwash Netu's side as if he never leave. Again he ageless. Again nobody make note, this time not even the southern griots, for by now Kwash Netu and Dara hunting down all the griots and killing them. And the Sangomin, after centuries of doing the Aesi's bidding, he banish them too. Many a witch laugh at that, I can tell you. Many a worshipper of the water spirits as well. Now people from city to village know that if a mingi child is born best you kill him or a Sangoma will find him. And now we in the age where Netu dead and Kwash Dara is King and still the Aesi—"

I pull three arrow at once and fire them, one two three, into Popele. She stagger back hard but didn't fall. I go to pull two more, but Nsaka Ne Vampi grab two throwing daggers from the gods know where. Popele raise her hand and she stay. She pull the arrows out of her chest and side, and I hear the holes close up.

"You was the one on the shore," I say.

"No."

"He write it down right there. Something about you was stinking up my head from the moment I meet you."

"Why plot to stop him, only to save him?"

"Black bitch, your name down on the fucking goatskin."

"Many move with the name Popele."

"That is your answer?"

"Believe it or don't. But calling me Popele is like calling a man master, or a woman queen. I am called Bunshi, Popele is what man call all in my clan. Many moving about with that name. Not all of them working for good in this world."

"So none of you can be trusted."

"Believe or not—"

"Not. I choose not. Telling people that danger is a boy when the real threat is that you can't even control your fucking kin. Who look exactly like you, something you didn't feel to tell anybody."

"We don't look alike."

"Alike enough, you stupid tar bitch. You know what? I don't even care."

"Your great-great-granddaughter was about to kill you for trying to kill me."

"She was about to try," I say.

"Blood mean to you same that it mean to me," Nsaka Ne Vampi say. "Popele, we—"

"Stop calling her that, like you worship her. Anyway, what happen next?" I ask.

"Next? Next we need to restore the—"

"I look like I talking to you?" I say to Bunshi, then turn to Ikede. "What happen next?"

This griot is trying to not look at Bunshi, trying to get some direction from her face.

"She your fucking master? I say, what happen next?"

"We don't have it, a master library. Somebody . . . somebody wise decide long time ago that if all the writing was in one place, all it take is one flame and hundreds of years burn to nothing just like so. The writing, it is scattered, from place to place, paper to paper, sometimes not on papers, sometimes on walls in the caves, or on goatskin or swineskin, one of us take to tattooing it on his body and another scar out an entire verse on his chest."

"Talk plain, old man."

"It take near a hundred years just for five griots to see that there is written four parts to this same story. **'One morning I wake up under the great monument in Omororo and have no recollection how I get there. I say to myself it is I, Bolom. What is the meaning of me waking up with beggars? I know I am a southern griot, and I know that goatskin on my chest has writing, but I don't remember writing it. Count it now, three days since. I leave it now, in the Omororo hall of records with another griot, who don't care about any business of the North.'** That was the last thing the goatskin say."

"One man born and everybody forget the world?"

"No. If he touch you—"

"You watch what you mean by 'touch.'"

"I mean if your life and his ever tangle, you forget that he was in it. The mind is a tricky thing. Memory even trickier. If your memory find a loose strand it will find a way to tie it. Which is why you think poachers kill your son when is the Aesi who kill him."

"I making tracks," I say.

"I opened the window," Nsaka Ne Vampi say.

"Cunt, you think you cute?"

"You look like you need air. We all need—"

"I don't care what you all need."

"Sogolon, I know—"

"Stop telling me what you fucking know! You understand me? I don't care what you fucking know. So what this is, this secret meeting like you all plotting big things. A nothing sprite, a nothing griot, and she who is nothing to me."

"You fool, we can still change the world," Bunshi say.

"You know what you not changing? My mind."

"I told you two this was a waste of time. She living in bush and talking to monkey for over a hundred years," say Nsaka Ne Vampi.

"Yeah? And why they don't listen to you?"

"Because according to she, you been there. You been in the Court of Kings. You know what is at stake because you see it yourself."

"Court of Kings? I been in the Court of Kings?"

"You used to be right there with the King of Fasisi.

They have more to tell you, but you don't . . . Bunshi, make we leave. Leave her."

"Bunshi?" I say.

"We need her."

"No we don't."

"You know what I tired of?" she shout. Bunshi shout so loud that the floor shake. And she grow too, taller and don't stop growing till her head near bump the ceiling and her shadow creep across it. Fins pop out of her elbows and her hands turn sharp as knives. Truth, she look like a shark.

"I tired of explaining," she say.

"I can still kill you," I say.

"Before or after I turn into a mist and reform in your lungs? Or your heart? You think only you can make man explode? You was there, woman, when you was just a girl. You was there when Kwash Moki disrupt the line of kings and drive this whole North into decadence and wickedness. Not even Liongo the Good was good enough to stop it. Every King destroy his oldest sister or send her to Mantha as a nun. They been doing it so long they don't even know why. Kwash Moki's father was the last true King to sit on the throne in Fasisi, and nothing in the North going be good until a true King rule again."

"Which North? The North that beat the South in every single war? The North that expand east and west? Which North this is that failing?"

"Oh the years of plenty soon done, mark my word."

"I don't mark nothing you—"

"Mark my word. When years of nothing come, it going to sweep north and south, and not even the gods going to stop it."

"So this is it. You hatching secret plan so that fat swine in the North won't starve."

"Fuck the gods, stop being such a provincial bush bitch," Nsaka Ne Vampi say. The wind (not wind)—the push rise up in the room and blow every lamp out. Nsaka Ne Vampi wave her hand and every lamp burst back into flame. I try to not look like that shake me. You not the only one blessed with gifts, her glare say to me.

"She is not even a North woman. Not anymore."

"You don't tell me where I belong."

"You the one saying you don't belong nowhere. When the great witch purge happen in Fasisi over a century ago, you do anything about it? Mourning song pass down from woman to woman for years. Some of the women wasn't even women yet. Some get burned because it was cheaper to let the crown kill your wife than divorce her. You never cared about anybody but yourself then, so why would you care about anybody else now? All this long life for no purpose other than living it? Well, I hope I die sooner than you. The text say it correct. You the one who abandon your own—"

"Don't think I won't shut that mouth if you won't shut it."

"You about to try?"

"Enough! Both of you!" Bunshi say.

"Should have offered her money, or nuts, or whatever it is monkeys use. Don't know what in all the fucks you were trying to appeal to with her."

"Point me to this Aesi so I can kill him," I say to Bunshi.

"You fail the second time, be—"

"I succeed the first time, though. Point where he is, I say."

"So you can strike your blow? Watch how he came back. You listen to what any of us say? He comes back. He will come back. He will never stop coming back. We have a different plan," Nsaka Ne Vampi say.

"We kill him, wait eight years, find him, and kill him again."

"You talk to her, Bunshi, because I done."

"Kill him now, me say."

"You can't kill him."

"Who going stop me? What kind of devil this be that can't stay dead?"

"He is not a devil," Bunshi say.

I look around for something to smash. I glare at her, asking the question without my tongue.

"He is not a devil," she say again. "He is a god."

NINETEEN

Fasisi have no spite for me. Fasisi have nothing. I don't know if I was yearning or dreading. If I was a counting woman I would say that one hundred thirty and six years pass since my foot touch this ground, my nose smell the river at the bottom of Ibiku district. We not staying, Nsaka Ne Vampi say. This is just a stop on the way to Mantha, but that fortress would have to wait, something we both know even before we set out. Besides, I don't take orders from my great-great-granddaughter, or the shifty blob of tar who shape herself a woman whenever she feel like it, but more often than not content just to be a puddle on the floor, pooling into people's rooms and learning their business. They should count themselves lucky after what they done tell me, I think but don't say when we leave Omororo two moons ago. If you don't come with expectations then you don't leave with disappointment, I been telling myself since we set out from the South, by sea. Why we didn't take the quicker way? Ne Vampi ask the sprite, but she didn't answer.

I want to remember the last things they said, even though it was ugly, but I long forget, which leave me feeling a way. Not angry, but not . . . the word I am looking for is not **sad,** but I don't know what the word is. They, my family. I remember what they do and I remember what I do too. I remember my lions start to maul me, and the wind (not wind) blowing one off so hard that when she hit the wall I hear Ndambi's ribs crack. A roar, a slash, a scream, somebody begging that she stop tormenting us, these come to my mind and run with it, but I can't see no face and the time lost to me. Things different, was all Nsaka Ne Vampi say, for it was all she could say.

The house standing as it do the last time I see it. **But where would it be running to?** say the voice in my head that sound like me. Somebody is smoothing clay onto the outside walls, for rain season just done pass, some woman is shelling peas, some girl is grinding grain, and another is smashing to juice the spider that sneak into the house and frighten the children. I look for it in the width of an eye, or the sharpness of a jaw, or legs too thin, something that I know is of me. And Nsaka is all these things and yet I don't see none of me in her. Where the men be I don't know, and she never said if this is still a warrior family, but from the new moat around the royal enclosure to the soldiers marching down the odd street, I can tell Fasisi is still war territory.

Fasisi is different. Bigger, wider, more crowded, and louder, but that is not it. For all its loud noise something about it quiet in a way that take me a while to hear. No music. Some drumming, and from temple nearby some chanting, but no kora, no kalimba, and no ngoni. No harp, no bow, no balafon either. And nobody who play them or sing. I was there when they come from the griots, I know it. I who lose music walking among people who never have, and I don't know who the gods would call worse off.

Fasisi is different. King after king serving themselves take their toll on even the tiniest street. A land reshaping itself for war mean a land where nobody build a house to stand higher than two floors and most times not even that. A land shaped for war build a wall right around it that take at least fifty years and tens of thousands of men. A land shaped for war now have forts with lookouts at the high point of every district, even the floating district. But the house is still standing, and I am in the outer yard and don't move until Nsaka say, Follow me.

"There used to be nkisi nkondi right there. Bigger than a small child it was," I say. Nsaka nod but don't say nothing. "What they do with it?"

"You going have to ask . . ." She say, but stop. I want her to continue, especially if it lead to a fight. I don't know why, maybe because the last time I leave this house I could kill the people in it. At least that is how I did sometimes feel. Instead she turn to me and say, "I know it seem like just a few summers to you."

"I know how much time pass."

"I didn't say know, I said seem."

"First time I ever come through this door, somebody say I look underfed."

"Still look like you never take heed," she say, and lead me into my own welcome room.

We pass a room where I expect to hear a lion roar, but instead children squeal. Two boys and two girls, no, three, for one in the dark who I didn't see until her eyes trap the lamplight. A picky-hair woman with thick arms also come out of the dark.

"You again, sister? Every time you say you making tracks, the tracks lead you right back here," she say, all the while looking at me.

"Must be your fufu that keep luring me back."

"Uh-huh. She come all the way back for mash-down cassava with no flavor. Who you, a fellow adventuress?" the picky-hair woman say.

Nsaka giggle. "No, she your great-great-grandmother," she say.

The sister put down the bundle in her hand and approach me. She look at my hands first, then my face.

"Is that right? Mother and Grandmother and Great-Grandmother all dead, and all three look older than this one when they dead. You the one she get it from? Nsaka and some of the other relations. Her gifts, I mean."

I turn to Nsaka. "You call it curse last moon."

"Some things are two things at once." Nsaka say.

"Great-Grandma never say nothing about you. She

live extra long, longer than Mama, but even she never get as old as you must be. And yet you look like you could be we mother. Where you been living all this time?" the sister say.

"In the South."

"I hear all the women there chest flat and the men fuck each other. Children, come in here and meet you great-great-great-grandmother."

The boys and girls tumble in one after the other. One ask if I was older than a tree. Another ask what great-great-great-grandmother mean. The youngest girl and boy, twins, both touch my face and grab my hair. The boy grab my breast and I almost slap him. They look over me like they seeing a strange beast before it become their own. I look over them, searching for something in their eyes maybe, or voice, or how they feel when they touch me to see if I real. I don't know what I looking for, but I don't find it.

"You can cook?"

"Oseye, stop looking for a housemaid," Nsaka say.

"She look like she need the work. At least a meal. Nobody ever take you to a fatting house?"

"So she can waddle like you?"

"There are other things you learn at the fatting house. Like how to comb your hair and stand like a woman."

"She is your great-great-grandmother," Nsaka say. I turn to her.

"Who else of family still live in—"

"Ibiku?"

"The North," I say.

"Too damn many if you ask me," say Oseye. "And none of them good for no housework. Is you they get that from? Our no-use brothers either selling contraband in Baganda or serving in the King's corps like their fathers before them. You have a cousin who is a fetish priest in Juba, another that teach at the Palace of Wisdom, I hear. And if you never heard of your relation Dunsimi, count yourself lucky, for he rape a noblewoman and kill her husband who was a lord near ten years ago. The women holding together the family that the men keep trying to tear apart. Great-grandfather have a stone in his name in the royal graveyard. Seems he became a distinguished guard to the King. Men even recall him when they recall great men. What we get from your side of the family."

"Woman who don't settle," Nsaka say.

"And where that get you?" ask the sister.

"Far away from here."

"And look who just walk through the door."

"Didn't do it for me or for you, but for her."

I want to see the room where me and Keme used to sleep. I feel like this is my house, but I also know that it is not. In this house, with these women, I can't remember my children. They refuse to come to mind. Instead all I remember is Keme coming to me in the backyard and how us talking turn into us fucking all the time, with me twitching from him inside me, but also not being able to stop, considering the space we was in and who else was in it. And how big my grip was on his cock, and how loud we would fuck in this room and that room when the children all gone sporting, and how he smell when he was half lion, which was different from when he was full. The thought should shame me, but it don't. It's the living, the sweating, marking this place in my piss and moonblood and his sperm that I remember.

"I could swear that great-great-grandmother died years ago."

"Oseye."

"What? I only going by what I know and what Grandma remember. And I could swear—"

"Oseye!"

"What! Oh . . ."

"She was nice? Keme's second wife?" I ask.

"She was here. At least that is what Great-Grandma say. Matisha was not one for talking about the past. You two here for supper or just passing through?"

Neither of us answer.

"You keep looking down there. If you want to go look I not stopping you," Oseye say, after I glance down the hallway leading to the bedchamber for the third or fourth time. I don't remember anything in this room, and don't know why I was expecting to. Yes they are blood, but they are different people living in a different way, which make this a different house. Children's clothes, and little girl trinkets. And sacks that smell like grain. And gold jewelry hanging from a stick, and stools and chairs all over because the house run out of space. The strangeness make me weak and I sit on a stool too low. **You was looking for a welcome,** say the voice that sound like me. **You was looking for somebody to call you Mama, though all of them long dead. But get the truth of what you feel. That you miss the children, yes, but not as much as your man. Your lion.** I bowl over as if about to cry, but tears don't come.

Oseye stare me down, then stare down Ne Vampi. "I finally make sense to you?" Nsaka say, taking the thought right out of my head.

"You will never make sense," she say and run after a boy who say he was going to fly out the back door down to the river. Nsaka fidget with the black obsidian pendant riding her neck, the first time I noticing it.

"To think Mama named her Oseye. The happy one."

"Where are the lions?"

"Lions? No cat live in this house or any house from before I was born."

"They just vanish from the bloodline?"

"No they vanish from this house. It just come to pass one day that lion wanted to be lion, and anybody born full lion or shapeshifter go to live with them. Two of the uncles—your grandsons—even take lioness for wife. Their sons, our cousins, are the ones running the pride now, in the grasslands west of—"

"Take me there."

We get there the following noon. Ne Vampi voice concern about Bunshi and her time, but I say that we too far inland for her to risk coming to bother me. Plus for the tenth time, I don't take orders from Bunshi. The grasslands west of Fasisi don't have a name, for no beast living there ever had a need to call it. I don't come here much, she say. I don't say of course, for I never see nothing of the lion in her. Open savanna, with the grass going tall and gold and wispy, like lion hair, it occur to me. A different river from the one that run behind Ibiku, and still flooding the banks, for this is just the beginning of dry season and water not scarce. Trees spot the land as if the gods stingy, but so much gazelle and impala that I would stay too if I did still eat meat much. Having only monkey and gorilla as family for hundred-plus years will change a woman. I still can't bring myself to count it. Hundred-plus years. The number seem so big until you remember waking up one morning and just like that you is fifty and cannot account for it. So what is one hundred then, or one hundred thirty and six? I thought it was because I just wake up one morning and tell the world that I refuse it, and all of it. I refuse space coming in on me, and I refuse time coming after me. I never said I refuse death, for that can come whenever, from spear or claws or venom. And now this water sprite is saying that is the blood that run through me, through the women—some, not all—from before man start count time. Me, Matisha, who know who else now that this family scattered? But also the lions, for before my children lions would die after just ten and two years, maybe ten and four.

But my lions lived longer than any cat supposed to, which bring me joy, but also more years of remembering that they were the same ones who drive me from my house and call me stranger. Three scars over my right breast, three claws. It come over me in a flash that this is a mistake. I not supposed to be here.

"Perhaps we go back. Before they see us."

"They see us from before we tie off the horses all the way back in the valley. Take it as a good sign that they might still be there when we get back."

A roar, far off but still loud enough to quake the ground. Then they come running, five, no six, no eight of them, three men, one of them white like a roaming cloud and the others gold. Five women, their little ears twitching. No running now. In the quick they surround us, growling, snarling, purring, and sniffing.

"Get down," Nsaka say. "Don't matter if you call them family."

One of the women approach Nsaka and growl at her.

"Didn't miss you either, bitch," she say. The lioness knock her over but Nsaka scratch behind her ears. One lick the obsidian pendant and Nsaka shove it in her dress, between her breasts. Two of them approach me, man and woman.

"Don't disrespect. This your—"

"No," I say, which throw off the male one, who make a sound that I can't tell if friendly. And he come right up to me and sniff. I know lions, I know he can clamp onto my neck and bite my head off. And my neck is what he go for. He search it with his nose and then rub his massive neck against mine. I slip my head under his so that he rub the back of my neck, then lift up my head slow to rub my cheek against his. Then this, he roll his head under mine so that I can rub my neck against his head. And the women come over and do the same. Ooooh, oooh, I say, trying to match their voice, when another knock me down, but only because I wasn't ready. A younger one, deciding she can play with me. "They know who you are," Nsaka say. I try to say I know but the words don't come. Three more approach and we rub neck against neck, head against head, hair against hair, and they purr and ooh to my purr and ooh and the tears just come. And come. And come. And I try not to cry, but instead I bawl. It's the leaning that do it, not just when they rub their head against yours, but when they lean into you and rest a weight you can barely hold, but the trust make you forget the burden.

"Great-Great-Grandmother," one finally say. He, a shapeshifter with the face of a lion and the body of a lean man. Claws at the tip of fingers, but fingers nonetheless. The man is so striking and beautiful that it must be only gods that have words to describe him. I try not to think how he look like Keme.

"Meet the fruits of your tree," he say.

———

I tell Ne Vampi that I can find my way back alone and will leave when I wish. She frown as she leave. That night I sleep in the open, my pillow and my warmth being the living skin of lions. Come morning I rub my neck against every lion I meet, rub their heads, scratch their hair, and touch forehead with all who shapeshift. On my way back to the city, I stop by a river.

"I know you was following me," I say. She take her time, but soon up from the river jump she, Bunshi.

"Tell me everything I forget. I not going to Mantha until you do. Tell me everything."

On the way to Mantha, what I see fighting against what I remember.

"From how Bunshi tell it, you is the one who do this," Nsaka say when we pass the crater, but I remember it through the sound of Bunshi's voice, not as memory. My mind have a different memory of those days, of being in the service of Mistress Komwono until she present me as a gift to the prince of Fasisi, who become Kwash Moki. Emini is a name in a scroll, not a face I put a name to. But now, on the way to Mantha, some parts of memory come for me whether I want them to or no. So Nsaka point out the crater and my mind hear boom.

Mantha. Seven nights west of Fasisi and climbing the whole time. The thing about Mantha is that for most there is no such place, even for travelers who journey past it nine times, if not ten. For they journey past a mountain, strange-looking but a mountain nonetheless, all around it flat and bare, less like a hill with a peak and more like a giant rock shooting straight up out of the ground, as wide as high. No tree or green until the very top and at the top many trees, and between rock and trees, no sign that any soul live there. For some of the way we travel by horse, yet by the time morning turn to afternoon, we have to go by foot. It is evening before we get to the stairs on the far side of the mount, cut from the rock, eight hundred and eight of them. At the top of the stairs, the rock go from being steep to straight, and we have to grab on to shrubs, roots, and spaces between stone to pull ourselves up. This place quit being a fortress seven hundred years ago. It go from somewhere to look out for foes to somewhere to hide them, especially if that foe was in your own royal house. Now it is where nuns in service to Ishpali, the goddess of childbirth and fertility, call home. That news was from Nsaka, not the nuns, some of whom act like they never even heard of any goddess. It is there that we would meet her, and there that we would set the plan afoot.

A new plan, for the Aesi is not a demon, but a god. More than a demigod but less than the gods of sky and earth, and each time he is reborn, the less like them he become. He come back quicker after death but he come back weaker, Bunshi say, but when I say that must mean that more than ever we kill him, she rebuke the remark like I was some girl. I could slap her then, I really could, but firing three arrows into her maybe was enough. Things I learn about this new Aesi, that he can control countless bodies to do what they don't wish to do, but not so much their minds, which might be bad for him but worse for the man who now witness his own hand and feet work against him. He mess with minds and make women disappear, but now people remember they are gone even if the vanishing come with a new and fishy reason, and nobody know where to find the body. Crows are still under his command, as some pigeons are for the Sangomin. As for the mind games, he come to you in dreams and play in them, even control them, and he can still cast power over you, when you are slightly awake. Before, all he did need was his own power, but now he also need cunning. Bunshi say this also to Nsaka, when they thinking I was asleep, that the Aesi find a way to take strength from the gods, and that might be why more and more people losing faith, and since the gods in turn draw from faith they grow even weaker. All the more reason to kill him, then, I resolve in my mind. All the more reason to kill him. And this time I know that to kill him good is to kill him twice. And I will do it too. Explode him now, then wait. There. Decided.

"You have to join the divine sisterhood to get in," Nsaka say.

"I don't join nothing," I say.

"How great-great-grandfather ever tame you?" she say.

"That lion never tame me. Not once."

"Something did."

"No thought is wise just because you have it, girl."

She about to reply but then we come upon a narrow path with nothing but the drop to the right of us, so narrow at one point that we had to pass by with a shuffle, our backs scraping against the rock. Nsaka shuffle on stone. It break loose. She slip and fall and before I could use my wind (not wind)—she wave a hand and everything reverse itself, she leap backways to the rock wall, the loose stone jump back and lodge itself, and she lift her foot off it. This time she view the stone and shuffle over it, and I do the same.

"What is that gift, girl?"

"Gift? Is gift you call it? When boys jump you in the street just out of fun for that is what little boys do, but you send them back—that's what I call it, a send-back—so yes when you reverse them and they walk back right into squadron of galloping riders that trample them to nothing. And an old woman see the whole thing and come to my mother's house to warn her that her little girl is a necromancer who is already causing death, just like some of the other women in your family, and this King don't decide yet his ruling on witches, so don't be surprised if we come one day and burn your house down with all of you in it. So don't think I am too much of a bitch when I say fuck you and your gifts."

"None of that was an answer, girl."

"You for real?" she say and laugh out loud. "Anything that happen, most anything that happen to me, if I see and catch it in the quick, I can reverse it. Most things. That first time it was nothing but a wish that my friends get off me. That first time I didn't even believe it was me who do it, not matter what that old woman say."

"I did think—"

"That another woman would be just like you? Great-Grandmother, yes, but I don't hear of anyone else. Would make things easier if we knew what to expect, to tell truth. It is fine, I come to terms. It don't make me happy, if that is what you asking. But I not unhappy about it."

"Never once think about that, I think."

"Think what?"

"If it ever make me sad or happy. It just is."

"You must be one of them women who was always old," she say, and point to a stack of rocks that look like giant steps, with shrubs poking through. "Watch your step, old woman."

This is how you know you are at the mouth of Mantha. You don't. A wall of rock is a wall of rock is a wall of rock, but then you stop by a side with the marking of three red circles and wait. Then in the middle of this wait, two leather straps drop down and before you can ask, What in all the fucks is this shittery? Nsaka start climbing, and you remember that she call you old woman, which is not false but still deserving of a slap, and you grab the second strap and pull yourself up, and try to ignore that twice you realize that this is just straps tied together, which mean it must did burst with someone once. And when you climb to the top and pull yourself through a chamber that look like a tomb, you come to wide-open lands with sky and mountains surrounding you. And an archway cut from stone, and the fortress I was first supposed to see over one hundred years ago.

"It look like a Kwash palace," I say.

"Because it was," say a woman I never see before, dressed all in white, a nun. "It was both palace and fort in its first life. And a prison." This nun take we inside past several rooms with devoted men painted on the ceilings, and several women in white, walking together, talking together, pouring libations in the open yard, tending to a rich garden, and sitting by their lonesome, eyes closed or staring at sky. One of them approach us and Nsaka nod her head, then kneel halfway. I just look at the woman, who don't seem like anything until three women not far away scramble toward us and stoop behind her.

"How I supposed to be one with all sisterhood, if the sisterhood keep treating me like one apart?" she ask. "You hear the latest on me, Ne Vampi? That I take to the corridors at night and whisper to the gods that I curse them. Can you imagine? Was any woman ever so brave, or foolish?"

"Not you, Your Highness."

"Only thing high about me now is where I live. And who is this?"

"My great-great-grandmother, Highness."

"Great-great-grandmother. She barely looks like a mother. And you. What is your use?"

"To bring you into your royal purpose, Princess," Nsaka say.

"Is she mute, Ne Vampi? No? Then let her speak."

The princess lean in to me as if she was expecting to hear more. Nsaka glare at me and I look at her blank, even though I know full well why. But if she is just like any other nun in Mantha, I was not going to regard her any other way. I done with acknowledging royal anybody.

"Nothing about my purpose is royal and I am no princess, not anymore," she say. "So why is great-great-grandmother here? For certain she doesn't believe in the cause."

"The river goddess—"

"Sprite. She is a sprite."

"Bunshi thought she would be of use."

"Of use. What kind of—"

"I kill people," I say and observe the long silence that follow. "People call me the Moon Witch."

"Witch. The world is fickle about witches."

"The world is fickle about women."

"Where in all this do you fit?"

"I not trying to fit," I say.

———

There is a spring on the sunset side of Mantha, and from that spring, water rush down into a waterfall that gather in a pool in which the divine sisters, all one hundred twenty and nine, bathe. It is from this pool that up jump Bunshi, who frighten the younger sisters.

"We will send a man. It has all been arranged," Bunshi say to Lissisolo in her chamber.

"I miss sweets. Did you bring any?" she reply.

"Highness?"

"No question was ever simpler. Yes or no?"

Bunshi, all black, still somehow looking confused. She turn to Nsaka.

"No sex, no sweets, no song, no joy, no men, no books, no verse, no wonder it is dark up here, even at noon," Lissisolo say.

"I . . . I . . . It has been arranged, Your Highness."

"Arranged. All this arranging going on and not a hand I had in it."

"It was what was best, Princess."

"Says who? Is my mind, my body, I dare to say that it is even my damn koo since I'm the one pissing out of it."

"We can't risk a—"

"Don't interrupt me, Ne Vampi. Look at my life. All of it around a hole owned, ordered, and arranged by men. Now I must take that from womankind too? You know nothing of sisterhood. You're just a pale echo of men."

"What she was about to say, Highness, was that we

couldn't risk any trace coming back to you. The Aesi has spies still. Even in the sky."

"So you find a man who will arouse no suspicion? You expect my son to be some plain man's bastard?"

"No, Your Most Excellent. We have found a prince in—"

"Kalindar. Another one? They seem to be everywhere, like lice, these kingdomless princes of Kalindar."

"From Mitu. He will make your child legitimate. And when the true line of kings return he can claim the North before all lords."

"Fuck all lords. All these kings also come from the womb of woman. What is to stop this man-child from doing just as all other man has done? Kill all men."

I laugh, but I am the only one doing it.

"Then rule them, Princess. Rule them through him."

"Him. Rule through him. Why only him? What if it's a girl? How come neither of you, none of you even bother to think that maybe what we need is a Queen? Surrounded by women, even a divine-born one and all you can plan for is yet another man to come and rule you. You have nothing to say to that?"

Even the breeze was making more sound than they. Nsaka look off into space, when I wanted her to look at my face and see the same question on it.

"You, you have anything to say?"

"It will be as the gods will it, Highness," say Bunshi. "Make your destiny and leave this place."

"What if I like this place? In Fasisi even the winds conspire against you."

"If it is your wish to stay, then stay, Mistress. But as long as your brother is King, plagues above the earth and below will visit even this place."

"No plague has visited so far. Six kings—well, five and a quarter. And in that time, the empire expand to Wakadishu, the Purple City, all the way west to the Mweru and all the way south to the Blood Swamp. Not to mention even the river tribes send tribute and pay taxes. So when is this pestilence taking place? Why not now?"

"Maybe the gods give you time to prevent it, Your Excellency," Nsaka say.

"Your tongue is too smooth. I do not fully trust it. Is your great-great-grandmother like you?"

"She is nothing like me, Highness."

"Oh. I like her already," Lissisolo say.

Though Kwash Dara banish the King Sister to where she would be all but dead to him, still he want her dead for real. All of this was clear as the smell of shit from that of a flower. And yet she struggle to believe it, for banishment was already like death, so why kill the dead? This is why you are here, Bunshi say to me, for there was a part of Lissisolo that still think the heart will in its time heal, that her love for her brother would overcome her hatred of him, and one day, not soon but still coming, he will himself come begging forgiveness and restore her to her rightful

place. Instead he send an assassin every other moon
to kill her. He, meaning the Spider King, meaning
he, being the Aesi. First he send a flock of crows that
swarm above us one evening as we walk. She didn't
even notice the light drizzle of blood landing on her
white shoulders as I let the push explode each bird one
by one. The second assassin Bunshi enter through the
nostril and boil him from the inside. Four more I
kill myself. In the forest between Mantha and Fasisi,
one jump me from a tree and almost cut my throat.
Another, because he knock me down, make the mistake of thinking he going to rape me first. I fuck
him with a dagger and cut a koo all the way up to
him neck. Sometimes the murder come in the food
and wine to kill the hungry, greedy sister who steal a
mouthful. Fruits that kill the cow we feed it to. Rice
that burn a goat's tongue off.

"Who knew the company of women could be so
boring?" Lissisolo say to me on a hot night with most
of the moon eaten away. She of late take to having
me with her as some sort of guard. First I thought it
was against any threat that might come to Mantha,
until I see that it was to scare away the other nuns.
But listener is really what she take me for. They have
heard of your power, that you blew up the Aesi like a
puffer fish until he exploded, she say.

"Show me. I am so very bored."

I don't waste time. The desire appear in my head,
and out in the space it happen. The wind, the force,

the push thicken the air enough that I walk up into the sky as if on steps. I climb high enough to spook birds. The princess clap as I step back down.

"You're the closest thing to a not-boring woman that we have here."

We're out in the ramparts of Mantha's highest tower. At two corners rise tall posts with roots and branches and leaves curling around up to the top, where stand two massive statues of dragons folding their wings, and two women with spears standing guard at the base. Two moons since I come here and I never seen this part, never seen the sky or the straight drop below.

"They tell me he will come disguised as a eunuch. If he please me then we will find an elder who cares for our cause."

"An elder? So we are doomed to be betrayed then," I say.

"I think you are here to make sure that doesn't happen," say the princess.

Then this happen in the quick. The nuns raise their spears at the sunset and the dragon statues blow fire and light them. My gasp turn into a quick scream that turn into a gasp. I didn't run, for nobody else was running, but my feet set themselves to run like they have never set themselves ever. One hundred thirty and six years where I done see everything, and the two of them, with a flap of their wings and a snort of smoke, say that is not true.

"And they are just babies, I hear. A few more years and there is no controlling them," Lissisolo say.

"Ninki nankas? Fuck the gods, how?"

I blink and stare at the post again. No thick roots, just a long, scaly, shiny tail wrapped all around the base. Head like a horse, ears like fans, with two small horns above the forehead and two large ones behind them. Neck as long as a giraffe before it reach the shoulder and the long limbs and claws like blades. Hair running all the way down the spine as if it just catch fire, but back skin like a crocodile. And wings. The little I know of ninki nankas never say nothing about wings. I can't take my eyes off the dragons and the woman warriors at their feet, as if one is protecting the other. Then just so, the ninki nankas push themselves off the base and fly off, high first, then deep into the valley below. Both of them as long as six men head to foot, and they are just babies. I forget what she was saying to me and what I was going to say to her.

"You can stay and watch dragons. But bring yourself to my chambers as soon as night fall," Lissisolo say.

The river sprite say preparations already afoot," Lissisolo say in her room, which look like the room I stay in, like everybody else's room, with linens on the floor, a headrest for sleeping, a jug for drinking, and a pot for pissing and shitting. Different rooms have different charms for different gods, and judging from all the blue gems and beads, and stone, and statues, this room was in devotion to the gods of lakes and sea. Rivers would be green, I guess.

"Maybe I am exactly where I supposed to be, anybody thinking about that? No. Not a one. All this thinking of history makes my head hurt. Both your great-great-granddaughter and your river sprite care about this more than me. I already had a son. Your kin and the goddess, are they together in an intimate way?"

"What? No! I never hear of it."

"Hear of it? You two far from close, so why would you hear of it?"

"She talk of a man. Call him hers."

"Like that mean anything in this world. My husband's father's father claimed me before I was born. Bunshi is here because a divine sprite need a purpose, something to bring her glory, otherwise the world forget her and she blow away like chalk dust. She will become immortal in the minds of men, not just with river spirits whispering. Even if not one word that come out her mouth is her own. Speak true, what this silly river sprite know about the natural order of the nine worlds? She still getting lost in this one. The gods feed her words, for whatever this Aesi is doing, it is harming the gods."

"What he do?"

"Gods never tell, not even the fetish priests, for then we will know what make them weak."

"Nobody cares."

"Which is a symptom of their weakness. This time two years ago I was planning my son's birthday ceremony. Take one whole year to plan his . . ."

Lissisolo stop. I think she is being silent until I see her trying to weep in secret. It make the room stop, waiting on her to let it out and regain herself. But she keep weeping, refusing to wipe her face, until the lamplight reflect itself in the wetness.

"Now I find myself thinking about the strange things. Why nobody ever tell me these things about death and living. That you remember the strange things, like the fact that we loved each other, my husband and I. A princess don't need love, not really, certainly not the love of a man, but I did love him and something about the love made me stronger. Too bold, perhaps. Is boldness why I end up in this place."

"Tell me about it," I say.

"So I can flush it all out of my system and leave my head several weights lighter? So that I will walk like on air for the first time in years, and coo like a bird? So that I will get some peace magic, miss woman?"

"Because I want to know."

She study my face hard, asking with her eyes if I really want to know. I reply with my eyes.

"My father, Kwash Netu. Really no different from his grandfather. He didn't make it a royal decree that the firstborn sister must join the divine sisterhood, but he was going to uphold it. And he would say the same thing to me, that it's not me, it's the decree.

After I reach ten and three, but before I reach ten
and eight, I am to give myself over to the divine sisterhood, which sound like it is something I choose.
Well, let ugly woman no man want become divine
sister. Why would I push away great meats and soups
and breads to eat millet and drink water with bitter, wrinkled dogs, and wear white for the rest of my
days? Just so I ask all these wise men, including my
father. Even that coward the Aesi, who hitch himself behind my father so tight that once I asked him
if he's a living chamber pot, just opening his mouth
wide to receive my father's shit. You should have seen
the court laugh, indeed what a day! But he didn't answer me and no other man either. Instead the men do
like they say woman do and start rumors about me.
This princess forget that she be princess and start to
walk like a prince. A crown prince. Look how she ride
horse, and strike and parry with sword, and string
the bow, and play the lute, and amuse her father and
scare her mother. My own mother say, What happen
to the girl who used to live for new dresses, and food
from the sand and sea. As if that have anything to do
with what I want. So I say to my father, Send me to
join the women warriors in Wakadishu, or send me
to be hostage in a court in the South, and I will be
your spy.

"'What I should do is send you to a prince who will
beat your thick head down soft,' he say.

"I tickle his fingers with my fingers and say, 'I am

Kwash Netu's daughter. Are you ready for the war that will break out after I murder this prince?'

"He laugh, then he remembered that I am the only one of his children who work his mind, and make him laugh. Plus he didn't want to send me to no southern land, because he know I would end up strengthening it against him. You too quick of wit, he would say to me, also this, that the gods jump the line of children when they were offering wisdom, which words I know, I for certain know, get back to my brother. Hunting down women and sporting with hogs, hunting down hogs and sporting with women, who know what he was doing when he walk into my bedchamber one morning and say how much more like a son I am to our father than he. I remember how he sound like he mourning when he say it, but in a blink he grin it off.

"Brother, brother, brother. I tell you true that for all his jealousy I was the only one who saw that he was no fool. Wicked, flippant, vengeful, and so petty that he nearly killed servant for serving him warm instead of hot coffee, but no, he was no fool. And by the gods, no warrior. The way he tell it to court now, it was he who tell my father to consider making Kalindar neutral territory with free trade with the South, after the elders all tell him to keep the spoils from the Nine-Day War with the South and spare none to the enemy, for they will think him weak. Especially when he had no more claim on Wakadishu. But Kalindar is a shit stain on the empire. No good fruit, pure silver, or strong slave comes from there, and the Massykin King is so mad he will think all this free trade means he won. And of course as soon as my brother becomes Kwash Dara, he goes around saying it, but what he don't say is that the reason he knows all this is because my father said to me what I say to you, and this also. How much like a son I was to him, more than this one, and he was behind the curtain and heard it.

"Thirtieth year of his reign. Carra day of the Abrasa moon. I still remember the morning. My ladies-in-waiting rushing into my chamber, pulling back the curtains, and me saying I don't know who is assaulting me more, these women or this sunlight, when one of them say, You have to rise and wash, my lady, we have to make haste, for the King called a session and all must present themselves at court before the flip of the time glass. Late my father called me. Late. How you going to be late, daughter, when this concerns you? Of course I love my father, but I'm frightened of him too. All he say is make it so and the Aesi himself had to read the proclamation. My father. My beloved Netu couldn't bear to see me leave his side so he said, You, my darling Lissisolo, shall never have to join the divine sisterhood. But you must find a husband. A lord, or a prince, but not a chief.

"Oh I found a prince. The rare prince among princes, I would say, for the gods know how the North is infested with them. He had nothing to offer me other than pleasant company and the promise that when the North liberate Wakadishu from the South he shall have his lands again. If nothing else he did give me four children in seven years, I even enjoyed what we do to conceive them. My mother was terrible example, and my grandmother as well, so nobody was more surprised that I find myself loving my husband than me. Nobody could ask for better days, you understand me? Nobody could ask for better days. That is until my brother find my father dead, right there in his tent at the battle camp. Choke on a chicken bone he say. I guess I should appreciate that he at least try to look sad, because he was far from it at the camp. Father's body not even cold before he turn to the generals, saying that he is King now and they should worship him. It take a general to tell him that he become a god when he die, not when he become King. I leave it to you to imagine how my brother react to such news.

"My brother become King and name himself Kwash Dara. As for that general, they found his armor in a crocodile's stomach all the way west in the Blood Swamp. This godforsaken, sniveling man-bitch. So he is celebrating his anniversary as King even though only six moons pass. Wine, goat, chicken, cheap magic, the whole court is celebrating when he turn to me and ask who is smarter, him or me. He thought I wouldn't answer the question, that it would silence me, but I just tell him that it is a question he should ask our mother, or our teachers. You should see him try to not look angry. He finally stop with the playing and tell me that the divine King has ears everywhere, Sister. Which King you talking about, since the newly divine King is our father who is now with the ancestors, I say, then laugh. I look at this boy who look like he still in the royal bed, still saying what is mine is mine and what is yours is mine, and I just laugh. Laugh long enough that it slip between the lulls in the guitar strumming, and jump over everybody else's voice. As soon as everybody turn around to see me, he slap me in the face. No, he didn't slap me. He strike me down so hard that I fall off the throne platform, and nobody help me up. Oh he was about to let it out now, this man who think he is King. He let it out.

"Your plot has been found out, he say. You, dearest Lissisolo, on this my first anniversary, your plot has been found out. Did you think that you could slip it past a King and a god? All I could do was stare at him like a stunned goat because I didn't know what he was talking about. All I could say was But you are not a god, and then I laugh again, for what else could this be but a joke? Then he goes into some long rant about how I was always Father's favorite, and how he would have used surgery to put his own cock on me in order to make me a son. And all I could think was this was my brother's way with words, to put my father's cock in me to suggest some sick business. Then he say that I was working witchcraft all those years ago when Father decide not to send me to the divine sisterhood, that I violate the gods, that my husband and children one could call abominations, but not him because he is a kind King. Good King Dara. It's not him that is treating me this way, it is the gods. And if Kwash Dara has to bow to the will of the gods, why not me?

"I serve who deserve serving, I say. Did you hear, excellent people of the court, did you hear? he say. Seems all kings and gods must make themselves worthy of Princess Lissisolo's service.

"That's when new wisdom clubbed me. I know my brother. He is not an idiot but he is limited in his ways, narrow by choice because why be wide? He is King. People learn to climb to the top but if you born at the top why learn? No, never was smart, my brother, but somebody was giving him smart counsel. I tell the whole court that only the gods know my heart.

"So we agree. For I certainly know yours, Sister, he say, then tell us all to eat and even then my brother can't resist making ceremony. At one point he is demanding milk with a little cow's blood in it so he can be like river folk. Honey and milk, mutton cooked, mutton raw, chicken, vulture, and stuffed doves, even now I can smell the garlic, and pepper, and powdered crawfish, and locust bean. And wine, so much wine. And beer too. All of this at the great table, all of them the servant present, one after the other as if it was some pageant. I remember one manservant not seeing that my brother's wineskin was empty so the guards took him outside to flog him. And the court, these men and women, these carrion. They love to mock river folk and to tell truth I used to do so as well.

But you should see them attack the table like hyena stealing a lion's meal. All of them eating, drinking, gorging, fattening, noble women with blood running down their dresses because the raw goat must have been divine blessed, I tell you, divine blessed! All this time I am just standing and watching because I know better than to sit without his permission. Finally he wave at me to sit and I am about to take my place, three chairs down on his left, where I always sit, and he says, Sister. Sit at the foot of the table, for we are one flesh. And who else would I want to see when I look up from my meat? All these people still eating, then eating more and drinking too. Grabbing meat, grabbing fruits, grabbing raised bread, grabbing flatbread, calling for honey wine and daro beer, while musicians with little of the skill of the past play kora and drum and sing of how the great Kwash Dara is even greater one year in the reign. Maybe the reason why I remember all this is because all I could do was watch. I turn to look at my brother to see him looking at me. Then he clap and two palace guards bring to the table this large basket.

"Listen to me now, he say. I brought in a special delicacy, both of them from the noble houses in the South. For you, Sister. So there is no malice between us and we are again equal.

"He wave his goblet at me, then at the men. They turn over the basket, and this happen: Two severed heads fall on the table. Yes I jump, why wouldn't anybody do anything but jump if they see two heads dumped on a platter as if it was food. And he wait, my brother did. He wait until I recognize the faces. He wait until he could catch me shudder, or cry, or gasp, or scream, because that is what everybody else in the room was doing. But I just look at him. Julani of the house of Ishl was one of them, who knew my father. Nwangaya was the other, an elder. Both of them from the South Kingdom.

"My brother wave and everybody shut down. Then he grabs Nwangaya's head and lift up this face like he will have words with it. Nwangaya's eyes were still open. These are men who do nothing more than bring light to my days because I wanted to know more about the South. All my life I heard how different they were from us. I just want to know. Nwangaya was the one who told me about the southern song men who were exiled from the North, and that they had stories that would interest everyone, but especially me. This is what my brother say to the whole court:

"'Now this one, this boy lover. Is he a boy lover? He must be a boy lover to think that my sister, a princess, can become a king. What kind of witchcraft they must work on him to scheme and plot, and re-member, eh, Sister? Take some wise words from your wise King. As you drag a man into a plot, so you should also drag the wife, or she will think it a plot against her. Next time you get this plotting sickness, try not to infect anybody else with it, Sister. Play a game of Bawo.'

"Then he drop the head in my bowl, and say,

Remove her from me. Guards lock me in what lords called the midnight hole and had more guards at the top waiting to report whether I cry or scream or go mad. Most times he order them to feed me only scraps from the royal table. Either he was giving the guards direction or they learn cruelty on their own, because it was quite the problem, wasn't it? How do you hurt the princess without touching her? One day they bring me a bowl of water and say it was soup with a special seasoning most excellent, and as they place it down I see a rat floating in it. There they stand by the bars, grinning, looking at me like they aiming to ask, What now, woman? So I grab the rat, drink some of the water, then I bite into the rat and spit right into the guard's face. He try to rush me, the imbecile. I dare them to come touch divine flesh.

"Ten and four days pass. I know because the head guard always piss right as dawn break. Right in front of my cell, did I tell you this? Nonetheless, my brother come to my little room and first he do, he ask me if I didn't have a chamber pot. I say to him, Brother I thought we long pass those days when you fuss over my koo. He try to grin it away, but I know this fool. The same pissing guard had to go down on all fours in his own piss when his Kwash Dara say he need something to sit on. Then he say to me that he misses me. I say this to him:

"'I miss me too.'

"Whatever he was looking for me to say, that was not it. Then he start to go on about this and that, but conversation is not one of my brother's skills. He care too little to be interested in whatever people have to say. Painful it was, to hear him trying to make talk, and I don't remember most of what he said. Except that even though I betrayed the North, blood is blood. And this, that my sorrow is his sorrow.

"I didn't betray the North, I don't have no reason to. And if I listened to ambassadors from the South because somebody need to bring reason and wisdom to the latest dispute, then so be it. I would do it again. I didn't even know about the line of succession until I come here. I didn't betray anybody, but what I said to him was, You have no proof that I betrayed you. Then he strayed off his own path and went down some strange roads indeed, about truth being with the King, who is the godhead, and in all of this I am realizing that this is not him, for my brother don't have the kind of head from which would come those words. Not at all. Even in the dark I could see he who was behind the words lurking in the shadows. Foolish to hide in the shadows when your hair is redder than a whore's mouth, I say to the Aesi. That make him leave the dark.

"We come bearing news, Sister. It is not good, my brother say. That the prince consort and the children all fell from air sickness, for it is the season and they went where malevolent airs were prominent. They will be buried tomorrow, in ceremonies fit for princes, of course. But not near the royal enclosure, for they may still carry disease. He say more but I interrupt him. I mean this speck of shit on donkey's backside that the tail can't flick off, calling himself King— who I didn't betray.

"What did you come down here for? A scream? A plea for my children? You sitting on a man's back waiting for a woman to come undone? Is that what you waiting for? He tell me that he would leave me to grieve. I ask him if his wife hear him calling my name when he fuck her yet. I knew that would get to him. He jump up and kick out the guard, then leave the Aesi. Me and him alone, I almost say finally. He tell me the very next day I am to join the divine sisterhood, since that was my original destiny. He even wished me abiding peace. Give your peace to the grieving, I say. Grief sound like this is a tragedy, but this is a disgrace. I curse him so bad that he finally lose all Itutu and say he will kill me too. This imbecile compel me ask him if he really just come to my cell to confess murder. I curse him and his children and he run."

That was enough talking for the night. I didn't have anything to say to her, not even goodbye. She was doing all the talking, but I was the one who wake up tired. And yet as soon as she see me, she have more to say. And ask.

"I know why Bunshi is involved, but I don't know what motivate Nsaka Ne Vampi," she say.

"Money," I say.

"No, that is you. There's more to it for her. No. I am wrong. There is more for you as well. What is it?"

"Because a man take what is not his to take and it's the same man who take everything from me. Then he take everything again. I am helping you because fuck him and fuck your brother. Fuck your kings and fuck all gods."

"Your plan don't sound like their plan. Yours sound like revenge."

"Revenge? How am I going to take revenge on a god?"

"They say you killed him once."

"I would kill him for good the next time but Bunshi have other plans."

"Yes, I know about her plans. But I would want this Aesi dead too."

"She say that is the wrong road to travel. That in his own way the Aesi is as bound to order as anybody else and if what we do line up in the order of things then even he have to submit to it."

"You ever submit to order?" Lissisolo ask.

"No."

"From what I know, whenever he is reborn he is weaker, is he not?"

"Yes. Sound like more reason to kill him, but Bunshi, like I say, have other plans."

"Does that mean you think this is a good plan?"

I didn't answer. She take that as the answer.

I meet the Prince of Mitu in the Longclaw woods, the cold mountain forest between the Mantha trail and the Fasisi border. I come on horseback, he come with five more men than we plan. I take the one with the gold helmet to be him and say that there is only passage for one. The others protest before he say that it will be only because they are dead why they would not be accompanying their liege, and I fight the urge to say that I can arrange that. No man should ever enter the sacred fortress of Mantha, so just one is already too much. That is when this prince say that this could be an ambush for all he know, and if his men can't come then he don't go. Nobody is paying me to reason with him, I am thinking, but losing him is a loss for me too, not just the princess. And this prince: tall and dark, thick in hair, brown in eyes, full and dark in lips, pattern scars above the brows and down both arms, and many years younger in age.

"I am sure they tell you the arrangement, Prince."

"Well, yes, but . . . but now there is nothing but doubt."

"I know one thing that is without doubt."

"Without doubt, what?" he say, nodding at me, like that title he's so hungry to hear will ever leave my mouth.

"Without doubt, if she can't have Your Grace, she will find another. Think of where this will place you when all it come to pass. You will be exalted above all other princes. You won't even be called Prince."

That is all I had to say, so if he isn't taking to it, I am setting to leave them all here.

"Wait," he say.

Morning come before we reach halfway and evening arrive before we are near the Mantha rock.

"Why do we stop? Shouldn't we make haste? Enough with this foolishness, we need to make haste now, or I swear I will turn back."

He say something else, but I stop listening and dismount.

"Anyway, they give me instructions for you, which I don't feel like repeating. No man put down foot in Mantha for one hundred years, but many eunuchs. None of the women would ask the eunuch to lift he robes, for the scars show horrendous knife craft. But at the great entrance stand the big guard, daughter from a line of the tallest women in Fasisi, who grab the crotch and squeeze. So listen to me now, forget you great discomfort and do not betray your unease or they will kill you at the gate and not care you are a prince."

"What? This is outrageous, I—"

"I not giving these instructions twice. You can do this in front of me or behind me, I don't care. Take off your armor and tunic."

"I will do no such—"

"Take them off!"

He jump. I wish he remove his clothes as quick.

"You want me remove my undergarment too?"

"Your choice, Prince. But this is what you going need to do. Take your balls and feel for each, then push them out of the sac up into your bush. Take your penis and pull it hard between your legs until

it touch near your bottom hole. The guard will feel
your ball skin hanging on both sides of the penis, and
think you are a woman. She won't even look you in
the face."

His mouth gape open in silence, but his eyes say,
You cannot be serious.

"I can grab it and pull it back for you," I say and his
face take it like a punch.

"Absolutely not," he say and suck his teeth as he go
behind the horse.

"He will do," Lissisolo say, when we get him to
her chamber.

Six moons later and the divine sisters still don't know
what kind of white science or black math leave
Lissisolo pregnant. Ne Vampi, gone for half of those
moons, come back heavy with tidings. We smile at
each other until we both notice that we smiling, then
we nod, then we make one step to reach each other,
but reach and do what? The question stop both of us.
So we nod at each other again and wait for the princess to ask where she was and what bring her back.

"We find the source of the Ewe drum from the
west. And Bunshi guess right that here we find a man
devoted to the cause."

Ne Vampi tell her of Basu Fumanguru. This man
from Fasisi, who had the ear of this King even before
he become King, but withdraw once the King appoint

him as elder. The dead elder he replace breathe his last on top of the latest sacrificial virgin, and didn't come back to the council as spirit, as was the custom. The King was looking for eyes and ears within this secret bunch of bastards, but Fumanguru had his own ambitions. He was the one who push the King to appoint him, saying, You have my eyes and ears as surely as you have my love, so put me in this position where all three can serve you. So Kwash Dara appoint him because Basu was like him in all ways. Or so the King lead himself to think. Fumanguru may have been like him when they were young and sporting, and drinking and whoring with women who were not whores, but when he become elder, he truly become like an elder. See, the man became devout and pious and annoy both temple and royal house. No law was there written that the King like that Basu didn't challenge. And many customs too. Letters he write plenty, writs he post until the walls were exhausted from bearing so much parchment. Fumanguru take his old ease with the King as liberty to visit court whenever he please, without announcement. Sometimes even the King's bedchambers. I already know that cock as much as my own, he say to King, who just throw his hands up. If the King take an order to the nobles, Fumanguru take it to the people and whisper that the land is only a quartermoon away from rebellion to get his way. Indeed many people start to ask who is King and who is elder? Before Kwash Dara even produce a prince, Fumanguru take a pious wife and breed many boys.

Hear this now, Bunshi say, for the elder was making more trouble for the benefit of the realm. But he was also arrogant and boastful, and nobody was convinced of his intellect more than he. Even in this noble move, we had to make him think that the idea was first his. One morning the people passing by the dungeons hear a cry coming from it, and the cry was from Fumanguru. He shout that the King imprison him to stop him from speaking out against his brutal and barbaric grain tax on old men while his own friends remain rich and fat.

"Woe will hit this land, you hear me. I prophesy it," he say.

Not a quartermoon pass when there it come, flood rains even though it was not rain season, that sink towns and villages, sweep away hundreds of people, destroy crops and kill hundreds of cows. The flood waters even come for the mountain of Fasisi, turning every road in and out into a river. The King relent, but he also release himself from their friendship after that. But imprisonment didn't stop Fumanguru. It take a smart one to see the method, the heart of all his actions, and we in Mantha see it first.

So Fumanguru make enemy of the King, but he also make enemy of his fellow elders. Who know which step was the step too far—the writs or the beating. Listen here about this beating. People called the elders fat and corrupt, but they were wise and wicked too. Along come this Fumanguru to challenge their ways, which didn't please them at all. I say before that the last dead elder die on top of a little girl they was about to take turns raping. When will they stop coming for our girls, the people ask. They are taking them younger and younger, and no man will marry them. People say, Go to Basu if that elder took your crops. Go to Basu if a witch spun a curse. Go to Basu for he is the one with reason. Go to Basu.

So an elder spot someone barely older than a maiden selling necklaces and bracelets in Baganda district and decide not to make his manhood go to waste. My words, not Bunshi's, since she never seem to find any reason to speak bitter. This is what he tell the father, that unless he hand over the girl for the divine privilege of serving as maid to the water goddess, no wind or sun will prevent his sorghum fields from blight. The mother didn't even have time to make her a new dress before the elder arrive to take her away. The girl don't take the basket off her head before he set upon her. Basu was in another room tying the neck of his nkita nsumbu bag. He was setting to go hunting down the evil besetting an old Taha clan when the screaming beset his room, followed by the slaps and grunts of the elder. Right beside Basu was a gold staff of correction. March into the room he do, he waste no time, and strike the elder five time in the back of his head. Of course he killed the elder, of course after that come nothing but wahala. The year don't pass before he move his entire family to Kongor, where they live now.

Listen here about these writs, Bunshi say to me. **Being a Writ in the Presence of the King, by his most humble and loyal servant, Basu Fumanguru.** That is how they begin and they are thirty in number. Basu do with the writs as he do with anything to be taken to the King—he bring it to the people first. I remember as soon as she say so, that day before we head to Mantha, me walking through the floating district. Other than Ibiku this was the only place in Fasisi that I tell myself that I must see. The floating city still float, but now they call it Mijagham, and where it used to house all who barely belong in Fasisi, now it overrun with those ruling it, who come with their magnificent dwellings and torchlit streets and no taverns or houses of pleasurable goods and services. I thought the rich and noble lived in Ugliko, I say to nobody. Yet it was on the walls of Mijagham that I see them, red letters, on wood, on linen, and sometimes right on the wall. **A free man can never be enslaved again,** say one. **The property of a dead man should go to his first wife,** say another. Another call the royal house corrupted, though that was a mark on paper. Still another on a floating rock call for a return to the real line of kings, wrong for seven generations. Not until a half a day's ride from Fasisi that I remember that I live through the rule of six Kings, seven if you count

Paki who last only a few moons, one that you didn't need the Aesi's magic to forget.

"So the man write a few grievances down on paper. That's all we need to trust him?" Lissisolo ask.

"He is a voice against the King."

"Many have voice. What mark him special?"

"He's still alive. But more than that, Highness, he was looking for you."

That is true. Fumanguru finish the writs, then send a message under the Ewe drum that only devout women could hear, for he play it like a devotional, saying he have words for the princess and tidings that may be good, may be bad, but will certainly be wise.

Bunshi rise out of the window frame and form herself.

"The Aesi is not what he was, I say that before. He came back weaker. No more can he wave a hand and wipe a woman's entire history from our people's memory. Even he will have to bow to the divine right of kings. But that just mean that now he move like any other man. Plot and scheme and kill. But keeping the prince secret and safe is all for nothing if he is born a bastard."

I ride back to the Longclaw woods for the elder Fumanguru, who then wed Lissisolo and the prince before most of the divine sisters see what is happening. My thinking was that the sister regent either didn't know or didn't care about the princess, at least no more than any other sister. But the night of the wedding there she was in the garden with us, and two moons later there she is, ready to deliver Lissisolo's baby. A boy.

"The only place safe for him is the Mweru," she say. How much she know was a mystery to me.

Nsaka look not at her but me and say, "You been in the South, you don't know the Mweru."

"It is an evil place. Nothing good grow in the Mweru," Bunshi say.

"But you never been there," Nsaka cut back. "I agree with the sister regent."

"But we know nothing of it. The place is mystery even to the divine."

"Because there is no divinity in it. You scared because it is a place gods can neither account for nor control."

"Even from far it smell like it's always burning. The smell it carry on the air, it—"

"Sangomin will not follow him there," I say.

This is what the sister regent say of the Mweru. The farthest place west in the North Kingdom yet not even Kwash Dara would dare try to conquer it. People, if you call them people, are taller than a castle pillar, have fangs instead of teeth and skin whiter than the white scientists. Rumor is that while anybody can enter, no man can leave. Now when a man or boy go missing people whisper that they kidnap him to the Mweru.

"But if you take the boy there, he might never leave," Bunshi say. "The Mweru has giant trees, none of them green, clouds in the sky but none of them is air, and giant towers and tunnels of iron and wood but nobody knows who built them. And no man ever leave the Mweru."

"That is the shit old men say."

But it is shit that the princess believe. A quarter-moon don't pass before we send two pigeons, one as decoy straight to Fumanguru's house, knowing that some crow or wicked hawk would cut it off, and another taking the longer way on a stranger wind, to Fumanguru's study. We in Lissisolo's room, trying to feed a boy who don't want her breast anymore. I about to say that he is full.

"He not even done with milk yet. How we going send off a boy who don't wean yet?"

"A wet nurse. Fumanguru will arrange it," I say.

"No."

"How you mean no? If you was a princess in a palace the boy would not even know your breast."

"I'm not a princess, and this is no palace."

"You know what I—"

"Don't presume to know how I raised my own children. Or that every mother is like you who leave her own. Oh I know about you. Must be so easy to tell me, Give up your child."

I open my mouth to say something but don't.

"Sogolon, wait!" Nsaka shout after me but I am already out of this princess's room, out the hall, down the corridor, when I hear her shout for me again. I open the great door and step outside, but then this.

I step backways, landing exactly in each footprint I make before, and as I step back to the door it opens, the knob swinging right into my hands, and I push the door back shut.

"Use your trick on me again and I kill you," I say.

"You wouldn't be the first woman she have to apologize to for her loose tongue," Nsaka say.

"Oh you think she going to ask forgiveness. Woman like that don't even know how that word feel in her mouth."

"I not saying forgive the princess. I saying have a care for a woman who lose her whole family."

"I lose mine too!"

"Is not a cont—"

"Finish that line and you never see me again."

"I hear you."

"And you. What the fuck is you all about? First you act like you don't even want to see me, and now you telling me not to leave, and showing kindness like I either ask for it or need it. What you want?"

"What I want?"

"Yes, what you want for yourself?"

"If I was a man, you would never ask me that. A man tell you he putting his own life down for a cause, even stupid one, and nobody ask any more questions. Sure, they ask question about the cause, but they never ask any more about him. Maybe the world they want to make is the world I want to live in and that is that."

"You and the water sprite rubbing koo together?"

Nsaka sigh.

"One hundred seventy and three years old but only twenty years deep. I have a man. Before you ask where, he is in hyena country because somebody called in a debt. Also my work is my work and I don't need him in it. Either way, if I was taking a buffalo's cock while kissing his granduncle, is none of your fucking business. They will triple the money if that is all that matters to you."

"Don't talk down to me and I won't talk down to you," I say. It is a relief that she think I am only here for the money.

The sister regent dash in the hallway. "A sister missing. Go by the name Lethabo," she say.

"Shit," I say. "How long?"

"Don't know, but she going by foot."

Another divine sister rush into the room. "Is Lethabo," she say. "She here longer than the princess, but still new. A help in the cookroom, but she didn't report to cook dinner. Her room empty. All sort of white splats in one corner of the room."

"I leave now."

"We can intercept her before she reach Fasisi," Nsaka say.

"She not trying to reach Fasisi."

I don't waste time telling her that this woman was trying to get out of the view of the sentries. Bird shit. She was keeping a pigeon. Or maybe a crow.

"Saddle two horses," Nsaka say.

"Need something quicker than horses," I say.

We in the sky quicker than a loose thought. Me and a sentry on the back of a ninki nanka. Wind (not wind) take me up in the sky all the time, and more than one time I leap over an entire forest, but wind rush by so fast on this dragon's back that it take me out of why we was in the air. And the air colder than the white dirt and solid water up in the mountains, and wind whipping past quick and forceful as a storm. Open my eyes too wide and the wind blast the tears out of them. I grab on to the sentry tighter than I would like, but she don't notice. Underneath us muscles more powerful than an elephant or rhinoceros and scales trapping the last orange of the sunset. The ninki nanka shriek. The sentry grip the reins tighter, which the beast take as command to flap her wings and rise higher into colder sky. Over her shoulder I see the dragon's impossible neck and the thick ridge of scales leading all the way to her head full of horns. She snort and black smoke leave her nose. Behind me, her tail stretching far back, whipping in the air. I want to stay in the air on this fantastic beast's back, and the voice in my head is telling me that I would if not for the reason why we flying in the first place. I want to ask the sentry if she ever get used to this, flying so light on the mighty back of one so heavy, and I would if not for the reason why we flying in the first place. I was about to say that we need to be lower when dip the ninki nanka do and I try not to scream as we go lower and lower and lower until we less than two men high above ground and rustling up dust. It's only one trail, and some parts barely wide enough for a small wagon. And every fabric, skin, and wool in Mantha is white so she will never be one with the dim or the dark.

"I don't see her," I say.

"Leave it to Ningiri," say the sentry. "She see heat, especially in prey."

What I was going to say next I leave stuck in my throat. We almost touching the ground now, but dashing so fast that ground, rock, and mist blur. Ninki nanka shriek again. I grab the sentry tighter, right before the dragon rise, spin twice, spread twice, then dash down a small valley. There we see the one named Lethabo, running wild, then trying to hide by a tall rock. The sentry pull reins the way one would with a horse and the dragon flap her wings to stop. Lethabo try to run again, but ninki nanka blast a stream of flame in her way.

"Where is the bird?" I yell down to her on the ground.

"Take off and gone," she yell back. "You hear me? Take off and gone."

"To who?"

"If I was so the fool he wouldn't send me."

"Bigger fool than you know not to say he. So who is he?"

She purse her lips and look away like that is all that will be said on the matter. I nod at the sentry and

the ninki nanka approach her. She scramble backways and stumble on the ground. The dragon lower
her head right in front of Lethabo and shriek so loud
that it blow her clothes like wind. Lethabo scream.
The ninki nanka puff a small flame in her face. She
scream again.

"Two elder send me. They behind everything, even
the name."

"You not Lethabo."

"Which mother ever name a daughter so? They
guess that the regent would think whoever name me
never want me. She drawn to them kind of woman."

"First a he, then a two, now a they. Talk, woman,
or she going start with burning off your hands first."

The ninki nanka purr. She understand me. And now
she expecting supper. She approach Lethabo again.

"Move it from me!"

"She look like anybody moving her?"

"The bird long gone. Nothing you can do about
it now."

"But still there is something you can do. I not
asking again."

"One of them was some fat man name Belekun.
The other don't say nothing. He don't look like an
elder now that I think about it. More like a warrior.
Black robes, no blue, no blue and black. He make
the fat one nervous. Is the black one who give me
the crow. And say if I see any strangeness from the
woman you call princess to release the bird."

"With no message?"

"If they did want message they would done send a woman who can read and write."

"Strangeness, eh?"

"You know anything stranger than a nun with big belly in front of her?"

"You lying."

"Me going lie with . . . with that thing looking me down?"

"Strangeness could mean anything. They would expect more. You use word or glyph?"

"I say—"

"A crow will get to Fasisi before the end of the night. Go on like this you won't live to see it."

"I draw a stick! A stick with a belly and a dot in it."

The Aesi. Perhaps. **But if not him then who else?** ask the voice that sound like me. How we get this far not assuming that behind him must be a legion? Eyes and ears, and nose everywhere, even beyond the so-called sacred hymen of Mantha.

"The whole of you good. I almost did think that she just stop move with the rest of we because she remember that her blood richer. Is not until she start to birth-bawl that I know."

Nothing left to learn from this one, but she is just beginning to talk. And so she go on, about what a simple life she used to have as a thief before this fat monk smelling of rape come to her with a black robed man smelling of murder. And she, just a thief. All she want now is to stay out of whatever is going on with all involved and whatever wahala going burst loose.

"I don't even know this woman name. I don't—"

She didn't see me nod at the ninki nanka. He spit a blast of flames that roast her faster than she could scream. Then she eat her own cooking.

So here is the plan. The boy we send with Nsaka to Basu Fumanguru, who two days after we release the pigeon respond by secret women's drum to **come, come now.** But if our pigeon can reach Kongor in two days, theirs will reach Fasisi in one. The princess we escorting to Dolingo, the independent land of blue-skin people, that is not under the Fasisi King's dominion, though he love to say so. She is a supporter of the cause, the Queen of Dolingo, Nsaka say. We will be women together, she say in a message sent two moons ago with the Bultungi, shapeshifting hyenas of the Forest Lands. Only two other realms have a Queen, and neither of them is like Dolingo, which even I in a southern bush hear legends and rumors of the new domain built there. A giant land with a citadel sitting on top of giant trees and all sort of caravans, wagons, carts, doors, ladders, hatches, baths, and windows that operate by their own.

"I hear that is more than a moon to get to Dolingo. She in enough danger already."

"By land it is, but you going by river," Nsaka say.

"That is still too long to stay hid. Crows fly every sky and pigeon too."

"We not going the whole way by river, Sogolon," Bunshi say. "Chipfalambula will take us down lower Ubangta, until we reach Mitu."

"You didn't hear me? By land too long and too dangerous."

"We not going by land," she say.

Lissisolo demand one more night with her baby and scream when we say she have to leave tonight. Scream louder when we say now. She not parting with child unless you pry her fingers away one by one and tolerate her spitting in your eye, or biting your hand with each try. You don't understand, she say while looking at me. You don't understand what it mean when you realize you would die for thing, but kill also. This woman talking to me like I didn't have children from before her grandmother was even born. Then keep him and lose another child, fool, I say, knowing that deep within there is some other King Sister I am really talking to. She say something about how I dare to, but I don't listen to the rest. The sister regent say give her till dawn, or there will be no peace. Even at their swiftest, nobody reaching this place before a quartermoon, and that is assuming we let the straps down to welcome them.

Chipfalambula take us all the way down Ubangta River, bending around the Juba pass, then turning south to the lower Ubangta. Once clear of Juba and Kongor the great fish open his mouth.

"This one different?" I ask but Bunshi don't answer. Indeed he different, for half of him always above water. And to his side right above his right eye is a rung.

"Of a ladder?" I ask. Soon we on the back of this fish, and being stunned at what I didn't see in the night. Dirt under my feet rich as any farm, also grass, a small puddle with small fish, and trees. Tall trees with mighty branches and lush leaves all growing on this fish's back as if we not on a fish at all but a small island. An island drifting down the river. How many times people sail pass him in one of the great rivers and wonder how long an island been there? And where it vanish to the day after? Nine nights later we on the banks of Mitu. We remove the hoods from the horses, for surely they would have been frightened by being in the workings of the great fish belly. Two more nights and I know he would have eaten them, or swallowed all of us.

Grasslands and farmers, just as I remember this land. We ride on a dusty trail that lead us to a wider road going south. On that road we continue passing sleeping cows and dark huts until we get to another road crossing it. At the edge of the sky dawn is about to break.

"Sangomas think this secret only they know," Bunshi say.

"That two roads sometimes cross is nobody's idea of secret," Lissisolo say. Bunshi give a little girl chuckle that annoy me. Right at the cross she cup her hands and whisper. See it now, four or five hand lengths above her head, a spark catching fire that split and race down two sides of a circle until both ends strike and puff out.

"A magic trick. Is the world different?" Lissisolo ask.

"Not the world. Just that spot right in the middle of it," I say and point to a small space, about the size of a door, a space unlike ours where it was still night. Bunshi walk through the space first. Too curious, I walk around the shape thinking I would still see her, but instead see the clear road I walking on, all the way to the sky. Lissisolo already gone through when I step back around. As I step through, the space squeeze in on itself until with a **pfft** it is gone. All around me the air is new. And the road is five times wider than in Mitu and all cut stone. Greener, and with trees, but not the green of the trees set by gods. People tended to this space and it go as far as one can see.

"It's like somebody made a garden five days wide," say Lissisolo.

"We still a day or two from the citadel," Bunshi say. Dolingo.

Something about a horse throw a shudder in Bunshi. Her body will not take to it and even with her black eyes, mouth, and teeth we can see the fear. Instead she fall like a stream into a leather wineskin strapped to Lissisolo's side. That was all the water, she say as she ride off. I am riding close behind, picking up her horse's pace and wondering how Bunshi giving her directions. We riding along this stone road, going up what one can only call a cultivated mountain, when a cackle burst into a wild laugh. I look behind me but nobody was on my heels. Wind, then, and tiredness. I almost catch up to Lissisolo when the cackle break out again, louder. I slow the horse and turn around. Nothing. Then somebody slap me in the face but I see nothing and the nothing slap me again. I block my face but a kick come to my chest and a hand grab mine and yank me off the horse. I fall and hit the ground hard. A clump of dirt block the yell in my mouth. Then I start to roll and roll and can't stop rolling until a leg I don't see block me with a kick in the chest that make me cough. The nothing grab my hair and drag me across the road. It can grab me, but I grasp and grasp and can't grab it. I shout Who! and the word get stuck in my throat—who, who—I couldn't stop. Lissisolo finally see something wrong and ride back toward me. I swing at the air and miss, but the air swing and hit, knocking the breath out my chest, then stomping me into the stone. Screaming finally leaving my mouth.

How you managing the life, Moon Bitch? snarl the voice in my head.

But it don't sound like me.

TWENTY

Sometimes a door is more than a door. Sometimes a door is black secret mathematics. Sometimes when you make a way through, you think you opened it, but is the door who opened you. And there are many such doors, or maybe a few, the truth is few people know, and of them few will say. Some doors take you up to the gods of sky, some down in the otherworld. Some doors pass you through only once. Some turn the journey of a half year into less than a day and quicker still. Work your mind to it, the sight of one leg in Dolingo while the other steps into Mitu. One far south that opens to the North, or as far as lands of the eastern light, or beyond the sand sea.

"We don't know how many they be. Some say it is the causeway of the gods. How they can move from one land to another or one world to another in the quick. How when you call a god he can appear, or just as quick leave. Go behind the hills of the

Purple City and there is one that open at the edge of the Mweru. Somebody claim to open one in the Hills of Enchantment, and walk through to a flood drain in Lish. One from the edge of the East to the Uwomowomowo Valley. Three hundred years past, so it might not be true, but word is the Kwash at the time march a whole army though a door near Ku and just like so—the army quash a rebellion in Kalindar. Belief come in short supply, for none of these doors open for long. Sometimes a door is standing there, sometimes a door already open, sometimes the door is very much a door, like the one rumored to be in the Darklands. One at the edge of the sand sea that lead out to sea. And one on the road to Mitu that instead lead you to Dolingo. Ten and nine that we know or hear about, but yes, there might be more. But few know how to sniff them out, and that few is either Sangomin or divine born. How you open it?"

This woman that I never see before crane her neck to hear me even though I not speaking low and she not deaf.

"This the Dolingon tongue. I know it and can speak it," I say.

"That remarkable where you come from?"

"If me not from Dolingo, yes."

"You don't remember when you learn it?"

"No."

"But you know enough to open the fire doors."

"I didn't open no door. The water sprite do it."

"Don't matter who was the key or who open the door, you should never have gone through it."

Unless I look up, all I see is feet. They have me lying on flat cushions on the floor, in a room weaved of wicker or bush, with no window, and a light coming through with no heat. They, the others in the room. A young woman, a woman older dressed the same, and a man wearing a light gown like big minds do, his skin gone past black to blue. And another man, who have wrinkles but don't look old, scars maybe. Also this, he is white. Not without color, like an albino, but white like milk. Is the older woman who is talking to me—not to them, she just don't care if they hear.

"Where is Popel— Bunshi? Where is the princess?" I say.

"Enjoying the hospitality of Her Glorious Eminence."

"And those who sick don't get none of her gloriousness?"

"I think she is protesting your accommodation," the old woman say to the white man. Truth I speaking here: The sight of him is making me feel sicker and my head was not yet my own. Even in the bush I hear of white scientists. Men (all of them is man) working forbidden magic, making nasty sacrifice, mixing their knowledge with abominations, and brewing hard potions with sulfur for so long that they burn all the brown off their skin. Now the skin whitening is the initiation to join their number. And even after that is another thirty years before one can call himself a scientist. Theirs is the way of pain because to them pain is growth and one must only grow. He remove his hood and his white locks slither down his shoulders. Other than his cloak, the only part not white on this man is his eye, and all of it, not just the pupil, is black. Left is an eye, right is a patch. I want to ask how after all these years of deep learning he never learn what any young witch could do, which is to return a gone eye.

"More light and air," he say and just like so the ceiling pull black slow to show sky and parts of the wall crack open and rise like window shades pulling up themselves.

"What kind of place this?" I say.

"Dolingo. Where even the small wonders make the world's wonders wonder," the white scientist say.

"Any sense ever come out of your mouth?" I say and the old woman laugh. A voice in my head say that the old woman is younger than me, but I don't want to hear it. Of her like I never see either. But I hear of people like her too, a Nnimnim woman. The sunburst of feathers is what you see first, red and white and a long one sticking out the back of her head, long enough to bend like a tail. The crown she can remove, but the bow feather grow from her head. Then there is the monkey bones sticking from the sides of the headdress. The dress covered in cowries and little calabashes all carrying little potions and poisons, but wide, with waves and waves of fabric also. The face she paint in white, but not like Ku or Gangatom, this hand is sure and precise, each line even and sharp. I never hear of Nnimnim women this far west, but I also never hear of anybody telling them where the fuck they can go. Word is they get summoned by the god of sky, which is why they come back down growing that feather in the back of their head. Nnimnim older than the ancient masters of war and nobody call them unless they trying to vanquish a great evil.

"Who summon you?" I ask.

"Her Glorious Majesty herself. Great friends you must have."

"I don't have friends."

"Great something, then."

"What they call this place, a sickroom? I sick?"

"You not sick."

"Then what I doing in this room?"

"Time now to talk clear with no fuss. You not well, woman. And you never will be again."

"You just say I not sick. Whatever riddle you talking in, it neither good nor funny."

"I said I talking clear, but let me make it clearer. Those who die wrong might be dead but they not gone. However they get gone, their death was neither wanted nor desired by the god of the otherworld, so he not taking them. But they have no body other than the flesh that rot away, so they can't walk among the living either. So they walk, and scream, and pick up anything to lash against the cause of their death.

Or the who. Sometimes the might of their rage strong enough to blow off your hat, or make goblet drop, or even blow under your dress, but they neither resting nor living, so they walk in a place where they can't reach the land of either. Good tidings for if you are the wrong that lead to their deaths."

"Wrong for who? The wife who can't walk anymore, or the lover who can't see? Or maybe the maiden who drop a baby because a man punch her in the belly, because babies is a task for his wife, not his mistress."

"I make no judgment, just letting facts rest where they rest. Many a man roam bodiless because of you, and the years of roaming leave them with only rage. None of that did matter because not a single man could touch you. Then you walk through one of the doors."

"I don't remember no door."

"You heard the man. The door is not always a door. But the door take space and time and flatten it like a flounder. But just because it flat don't mean it's not wide. Understand what I saying to you. Door is just another word for portal and each of them is a portal where every kind of world might meet. This is what it mean for you. When you cross through that door, you step through every portal to get to the other side. You just didn't know it, or feel it. Every portal, every world, even the one where the wronged dead stay. Here is truth, you was like fresh flesh for hungry wild dogs, worse when they smell the flesh and see that they know it. You let slip the dogs, woman."

I know I am trembling and I want to curse myself for it. I not angry and I not afraid, so why am I trembling?

"That is your body shaking as the whole world shakes," she say. "Your first time through the door can leave you feeling like you still in there."

"The men. The men I kill, where they live now?"

"Wherever they want. Most people they can't touch because they don't know or won't remember. Some won't even remember you, not fully, perhaps not your name. But they know their eternal misery and they know you are the cause. They will come for you whenever you go through one of these doors again, or if you around anywhere with a trace of Sangoma magic. Or in a land enchanted, or with people enchanted. Any craft that shake the world as we see it will also shake them loose. Understand? The doors are magic and magic is a door, so either will loosen them on you. You a witch?"

"No."

"They call you Moon Witch."

"Is just a name! Is just a name."

"If I was you, I would become an enemy of all kind of craft. Except the one you born with. But force, what you call the push, is of the world and they not of it."

"They going torment me the rest of my days? What kind of revenge is this?"

"You the one who go through the door."

"No. Bunshi lead me. I . . ."

The rest of it don't come. I know I am on the floor all this time, but it feel like I just collapse to it. Bad tidings is afoot and it is crushing my neck. A voice, me this time, say, He kicks out the guard so he and the Aesi are alone. But I can't keep doing that, just the thought of it is already exhausting. I about to cry, but then I hear cry as just a voice and don't know if that voice is me.

"How many men you kill?"

"You think I keep accounts in my head?"

"Would do you good to know."

"I don't know. Why, they all coming back?"

"Only the gods know."

"The gods always taking step with me. And every time I think I win they just change the game. What kind of fuckery is this?"

All she do is nod, which enrage me.

"Why throw all this shit down on me if I can't lift it off?"

"You would rather think you was going mad?"

"Yes. I would rather think I was going mad. What in all the fucks do you think?"

"There is still something you can do," she say.

H er first lesson was the next day, right there in the sickroom. She take a rock of chalk and make marks on the wall, a curve going up, under it a curve going down, the two of them meeting at the ends. It look like a cave drawing of a fish. When I say they look like runes she snort. Man is who write runes, and five out of every ten mean nothing, and ten out of ten do nothing. This is not runes, this is nsibidi. Some people call them the cruel letters because **sibidi** used to mean "out for blood." Rumor was that this was the mark of executioners, but the truth is that the first of these marks come from the jenga in the river. Two lands, four eyes, the fish, and the King, these are the words of mystic vision. This is the power to note significant things, power that last as long as the mark. Mark it on the door, the table, the chair. Meditate on it deep until you lift off the floor and mark it on air.

"This is what I saying to you, girl. To keep spirits at bay and to send them back, you have to lock them in the words, imprison them in the marks. Is not enough to speak the invocation, though you will for sure learn it. It is not enough to write the invocation, for some marks you will need on you always. Tomorrow we will begin the scarring, marking some on your arm. Take this, for this is the ukara ngbe cloth and the pattern is nsibidi script. You will have to be on your guard for the rest of your days, woman. For there are men out there with grievance against you. And they coming."

All this is too much for one woman to believe, so I don't believe it. Enchantments put on you don't leave this room, the Nnimnim woman say to me. Every day and every room, she say. Now I have to mark wherever I enter, for every door is a portal. No trouble come to my mind for two quartermoons now, which

is enough to make me wonder if this nsibidi was foolishness and what happen to me was just troubles of
the mind. Old age been threatening to catch up with
me for a long while now. And if a man didn't frighten
me when he was living, he sure don't frighten me
when he is dead. I write each nsibidi over and over,
until the room start to remind me of another's room,
a person I can't remember but I am sure is a man.
I write them because she continue to show me, but
I not learning them. I not recalling anything. You
don't leave until you learn all you need to learn, she
say, but I been in this room for a moon. Long enough
to see that she is keeping me in here not on a promise
but by fear. **I am done with her and her magic,** say
the voice, which shake me before I see that it is mine.
I will see Dolingo. I approach the door and it open
without reaching for the knob. I don't know why I
do it but I step back just a few paces and door pull
itself closed. But then I nudge to the door and it open
again, step back, and again it close. I couldn't tell the
last time a laugh or anything close to the sort come
to my face, so I do it longer than I would—nudging
forward and back, as the door open and close. Back
and forth, back and forth, back and forth, then back
and . . . back! I jump back suddensome, but the door
open anyway. Ha! I shout. White science have skill,
but white science not perfect, I am thinking when I
leave the room.

Dolingo. This must be some place to see when
you looking up from the ground, but I am up here

with the birds, in what must be the highest tower. Melelek, the hall of white science. And yet when I was expecting to see clouds, what I see is leaves. Plenty people live in trees, and some build houses up in there, but I never see a whole city resting in trees, nor this—trees tall and wide as city quarter. Trees tall enough to touch the moon, tall as the world itself. It make no sense looking down, for the distance from tower to ground is too high. One can only look across, at the sky caravan coming to a dock right out the window from me, a wagon—sky caravan being my words, not theirs, big as a dhow and moving on a pulley system of ropes. Caravans taking themselves from one tree to the next—tree being my word not theirs, and each tree far off as well, so these caravans travel a great distance. A city in the tree, and another farther off, and ropes connecting the two, ropes carrying cargo, carts, and beasts in cages. My head feeling the rare air, it is spinning from seeing waterfalls far off, and aqueducts they call the floating rivers, and great pools. How? Water running in and out this citadel, with no sign of how it could reach this high. All of this is too much to just look at, so I slip out of the white science hall, make for the sky docks and take the first caravan about to pull away.

Dolingon people, with skin past black into blue. Most of them standing and holding on to a post in this caravan. Men mostly, in robes and caps, carrying books and scrolls. None of them a white scientist. Some talking to each other, not arguing, for they

seem to agree on everything, but most just standing
and thinking deep things. A wind push the caravan to
sway, but I am the only one who jump. I grab for the
post but grip the arm of a man who look at me like he
will wash it as soon as we reach where I don't know.
And this caravan, fat like inside the Chipfalambula,
but windows running down both sides, like a gallery
for plants that only the rich in Marabanga have. I
couldn't see them but I feel them, wheels on top moving along these great ropes, big caterpillars crawling
through sky. And even from this view Dolingo look
like it is still growing, house on top of house on top
of house again, all the way past clouds into sky. Cogs
and gears pull us into the hub, an open area round like
the sun, with a thatch roof and pillars made of gold.

"This is Mungunga, the heart," say a voice with
no speaker, a voice that hover in space, and I am the
only one who think it strange. At the center of the
heart, big wheels connecting to small wheels, connecting to big wheels again. All of it in the mysteri-
ous Dolingon magic of making thing push and pull
themselves. From Mungunga, caravans come and go,
but my knees buckle at the thought of another trip,
which perplex me, since I am no stranger to sky. **Is
not the fear of flying but of falling that grip you,**
say the voice that sound like me. **You should fall and
land in a field of spears that stab you and fuck
your life out,** say another voice that I don't know.
The voice make me stagger, but I still go. Outside of
the hub was a long walkway of cut stone road, with

wide chairs for anyone to sit, and fountains that I only see in Fasisi but bigger, statues of creatures looking like Bunshi spurting water out of their mouths and nipples. I stop at another platform, which turn out to be another dock with a loud voice coming from no one saying, Court common. A slow old cart pass by, followed by a swift new chariot with two riders. Mungunga must be in the center, because from there I can see everywhere. These are indeed the trees of gods and giants, though I never hear any story of giants living in the North. The court common is a series of grand halls, stacked like an arrangement of goods at a market, and from here I could see pillars and columns and wide-open spaces full of people. And other halls that look like storehouses, or yards for the clearing of foreign goods. It is behind Mungunga that make me gasp. Far enough that I can see most of the tree, though the bottom yet hide in mist. But near the top the grand trunk split in three, and sitting on the two horns are two full districts, or towns, maybe even small cities.

On the right, they replace the trunk with fort walls, or maybe they build around it. But the fort wall rise high, and behind the wall rise higher. Castles, one could call them, with floors numbering past five to six, seven, even eight. On the fifth floor a platform hanging off that jolt me when it start to lower itself down with thick ropes. Behind those castles and rising higher are roads, and bridges, and more waterways, and townhomes that ride high instead of spread wide, higher than the people-dwelling obelisks in Omororo. So many people about, walking, talking, sitting among others, off by his or her own, that I wonder who in this city do any labor, not just slave labor, but any labor. So many long gowns, no armor, no tunics, no gele, no agbada, no skirts, no breeches, no bare breasts, no bare feet.

On the left branch, the Queen's enclosure, I was sure of it. I know enough to know when a place with one hundred roofs is the residence of just one ruler. A courtyard, yes, and filled with many palaces, but a place for the rulers and who the rulers wish to see. Purple, red, and gold. One caravan going back and forth, which I don't need to see to know that it is packed with guards. I circle back around the hub and take a caravan heading north. The air have the scorch that lightning leave behind, but I don't remember a storm. This is Mkora, the great twin legs, the voice say. My legs are moving faster than my thoughts, they skip over to another caravan about to leave. This is Mwaliganza, the hub of the ever flowing right hand river, say the voice. And a river is what we land in the middle of, this hub right in the center, both banks made of brick, so more of a canal than a river. Every roof was near the same height, so this is where the common folk live. Though so far I still don't know what is common for Dolingo. But this is where I finally see them, people doing the things city people do. Donkey carts with nobody driving the donkeys, the same for the mule carts. Tall men riding tall

horses, stout women pushing carts, fruit sellers off
in a section with their legs spread wide around baskets. Men like the men in other districts, in robes
and caps, with scrolls and books. Silk mongers, fruit
mongers, trinket sellers, men and women buying silk,
fruits, and trinkets. And everywhere: ropes creaking
from pulling hard, cogs squeaking, a giant water-
wheel crackling. The caravan to the next tree say it is
going to Mupongoro. I look around and see nothing
new to discover. I am right by the bank of the canal
with a guard noticing me, when I see why. Everything
look the same, not the buildings or the colors, but the
thinking behind them.

Choose which breast I chop off first, say a voice
that don't sound like me. I shake it off. **No, stab
into the sweetest part of her neck, the part that
will make blood burst like a fountain,** say another.
**Seize her mind, control her feet, and let them take
us to the house of her kin so we can choose which
girl to rape,** another voice say. **Is that what excite
you, girl? How you take to a man wearing nothing
but himself?**

Remember they don't always come with words, I
say to myself. I say it again and again until the guard
hear me and turn around. I am seeing nothing, but
the nothing grab my neck and try to push me to the
ground. **You passing so many days as my wife's little
pet that you forget that whoring is what you do.**
I push and slap and kick and try to free my right hand
because a hand is pinning my left, even though there

is no hand. Nsibidi. Cruel letters. Write them on air if you cannot mark them on the ground, that is what the woman say. I try to draw just one letter. Just one.

So the Moon Witch just plunge into the river like she drowning herself?"

I am in different room, with the Nnimnim woman standing over me.

"Where this is?"

"Mupongoro. Far west. Unless you want to go back to sleeping with white scientist watching you."

"No. And I didn't plunge into no river. He push me in."

"He who?"

"You know who."

"This one announce himself?"

"I look like I waiting for no introduction? And your ukara ngbe cloth don't work a damn."

"By itself, no. Is that what you waiting for, girl, the one trick to blow all of this away? If such magic coming, it don't come yet."

"Then what is the damn use?"

"They have to work together. And not everything work the same way with everybody. It depends on the woman. It also depend on that woman's will or desire."

"You think I don't have enough will? You think I desire anything else?"

"I don't know what you think. I only know what I know."

"What a fucking bush bitch answer."

"Then get other counsel, if the bush too lowly for you. Go on then, Sogolon the Wise."

"What if I go back through the same door?"

"What? That nasty white man didn't tell you? No, Moon Witch. You can't go backwards. You go through that gate as much as you want, though most only do it once. But you can't go backwards until you been through all the doors. And nobody know for sure how many, so nobody really know when you done."

"What happen when you go back?"

"So far nobody who do live to tell it, so nobody know for sure. Some believe that to go backwards is to flip the way inside out, and so the same go for your body."

"I will find this door."

"You need Sangomin magic for that."

"Or a useless water sprite who turn out to have one use."

But Bunshi don't come to my room. The guard stationed at my door tell me that she enter a room then disappear—after he spend near all of the morning telling me about the glorious feats of his astonishing Queen, in whose presence every head will bow and every knee will kneel. And so beautiful she is too, have I gazed upon her? Bunshi gone indeed. Coward is not what I would call her, but fear seem to be her natural state. Or she know that I blame her for this, and Lissisolo too, for I didn't have any reason to go through any enchanted door. Sorry for what come to you, this princess say, not sorry for causing it. Not sorry for now making me hesitate before all kind of door.

"Sit," Lissisolo say. I look around but see no other stool nor cushion.

"I not sitting on no damn floor just so you can have somebody lower than you."

"Fuck the gods, Sogolon. I didn't say sit on the floor. I said sit."

Maybe she just want me to fall. Maybe she want me to look and feel a way. Maybe I should just squat like I going to piss. I sit and just like so, a door cut itself open from the wall and a chair push itself out to catch me.

"Remarkable, is it not?"

"Not the word coming to my mouth."

"Science, or magic?"

"I don't know."

"It must be neither. Who told us they were at war? No such war going on in Dolingo. I almost wish I was a princess of this kingdom. Queendom. Has ever a place been so perfect in all its ways? Perfect."

"Again, not the word coming to my mouth."

"Then run outside and swing in a tree if it suit you. The Queen just told me how it must be the gods bless her with a sister, for we shall rule together."

"You want to be Queen now."

"Of course not. I must be regent for the true King, who else will protect him?"

"Can't answer that question for you."

"You will cease with that tone. I am still royal blood in a kingdom that recognizes my title. You would do well to do the same."

"Yes . . . Highness," I say. But then her face change as she smile at me again, like we are sisters about to share wicked secrets.

"But our Queen, do you know what she just told me? That I waste precious time and cause too much danger trying to beget an heir in such a backward, barbarian way. I could have just come to Dolingo and a son would have been born to me in three moons."

I want to tell this bitch that hers is not the time that done waste but instead I say, "What that mean?"

"Breed with a minor demigod, perhaps. She wants to meet you."

"What if I don't want to meet her?"

"Your great-great-granddaughter never mentioned your humor," she say.

"I wasn't making joke."

"Nor was I. You seem to think the Queen is making a request. You also seem to think we are women together. On both counts you are wrong. Know your place before somebody here has to remind you," she say. I hold my tongue, for I see her for who she always was, somebody who couldn't wait to close ranks and leave me on the outside. I done serve my use.

Even when it is full, I feel alone in the sky caravan,

perhaps because it is the only place I don't feel watched. No voice unlike mine bother me in the sky. I take the caravan to the Branch of Court Nobles, then take another to Mluma, the brightest district because its wings catch the sunlight all day and then light up the sky at night. I follow the small group to a platform that lower itself one floor. Nobody move to get off, so I do. I pass through hall made out of clay, rough and uneven like hand work. In the corner is the statue of a man and woman sitting by a fire, everything form from clay as well. The swamp grass is what tell me that this is a tribute to old Dolingo. The hall spread out from the entrance in a circle, and on the left wall are drums, spears, lion skins, cheetah skins, parts of a dhow, and two skeletons wearing crowns and carrying scepters. On the right is a scroll, unrolled all along the wall. Testimony to some glorious age that was not so glorious, I am thinking, until I move in closer. This is not papyrus or leaf, but linen, and on the linen is Dolingo. The linen have nothing about it to say what it is, who make it, or how. Maybe this is the work of the land's grand designer, and all of this spring from his head. The first drawing is a tree tall past the moon, and a city or citadel on top. Beside it a road snaking around branches and a river going up instead of falling down. A palace in a tree, and another farther off, and ropes connecting the two, ropes carrying cargo, carts, and beasts in cages. Rope in knots, rope on wood, rope connecting big wheels to small wheels and big wheels again. House on top of house on top of house on top of house.

"So high they would frighten the gods." The whisper barely leave my mouth.

I don't hear from my great-great-granddaughter since she take that baby to Basu Fumanguru. Word that his writs to the King was all the talk of Fasisi, Malakal, and Juba, and spreading to Kongor, though few have read all of them.

"No writ pass my eye, except for the writing on the wall," I say to the Queen of Dolingo. She will know of the writs and she will know now. Does it speak out against all monarchy or just the Fasisi King? And this Queen haughty, harsh, and sharp with everybody. No patience for fools but it seem that to her everyone is a fool. Especially her chancellor, who translate for her even though her tongue was not much different from most of the North once one get used to it. This tall, thin Queen wearing a gold peacock crown that her ladies-in-waiting had to catch from slipping off her head. Gold also on her eyelashes, dotting her lips, and cupping her nipples. A magnificent throne behind her, but she remain standing. And this throne room, this great hall, with gold columns racing up to a ceiling so high it might as well be sky. The throne, a pyramid rising out of a low platform where everybody else stay standing. At the base of the pyramid, a platform littered with women and with soldiers on the left and right flanks. **Soldier** being a word I use loose. Those gold throwing daggers and ceremony swords not ready for even a rumor of war.

"Next time bring me this Basu Fumanguru. 'Tis been a long time since I heard any such wisdom coming from a man. I find this funny," she say with a smile that shift into a scowl when no reaction come from the court.

"I said I find this funny."

The whole room burst into laughing, clapping, whistling, and shouts to the gods. One wave and they quit in a blink.

"You interest me," she say looking at me. "Chancellor, is she not interesting?"

"Yes, Most Magnificent."

"Very interesting, in just one flip of the time glass you have done four things that would have gotten you beheaded, if not five. And yet it is not disrespect I am getting from you, but that you simply do not know. How old are you?"

"I don't have no official count," I say.

"Misstep number six. Tell her, Chancellor."

"It is, 'I don't have an official count, Your Majesty.' Address the liege in front of you."

"Who else I would be addressing? For certain I not speaking to you."

She laugh. "I hear you are one hundred and seventy years old. Of course. You have seen too much to still be standing on ceremony. Where is your princess?"

"I not her lady-in-waiting, Queen."

"Of course. She never told me what it is you do exactly."

"I kill whoever come near her that she don't know."

"Man? Beast? Bird?"

"Yes."

"How frightening. And how delicious. This King Sister wants my allegiance and my help, and why not? Dolingo is the light of the world and who else but us will show the way out of these beast kings and barbarians? Brother and sister fighting over a throne neither has ever truly earned, the whole thing make for mild amusement. But we shall be Queens together—even if she is just a regent. But she has nothing to offer this kingdom. But you. You, lowly as you are, you, on the other hand, just might."

The whole court shudder so hard the floor shake when I tell the Queen that I will think about her offer. She herself drop back like I hit her with a punch when she was expecting a slap. I live in the bush too long to care about offending queens or kings. Or lords, or chiefs, or the wives of them for that matter. If they come for me, they come. I exploding at least four heads before they come for mine, one of which might be the Queen, and even the dumbest of them know that I have nothing to lose. I am in my quarters gathering my things, for it is long past time I cut this place loose. The King Sister is safe as she can be, escaping a pack of wolves by hiding in a nest of snakes. Word was that the Aesi was coming as part of a diplomatic mission, maybe to ask things this Queen will neither confirm nor deny. For all my talking, he was still the one thing I could never be indifferent about. Too much time pass before I realize I am holding the same wineskin in my hand as I was since evening, because I done trapped myself into thinking of the Aesi. There was no presence of rage, but I know that I didn't have to give myself too much time to work it up. Standing here, with this wineskin in my hand, I am wondering why I come here in the first place. Money, yes, but I was not lacking money and even a little was more than I need. Seeing my family, most certain, but that thought would never come to me had my great-great-granddaughter not arrived to disturb my peace. To know her, my great-great-granddaughter? We know the other enough to know that there can never be love between us, not even liking. To love her, to love them, would take great work, mostly on myself, too much work. Just because you are blood don't mean you are family. And this Aesi. I still remember how Bunshi warn me against taking up anything with him, for according to her he is a god. Demigod. Some kind of diminished divine thing. Still a man I kill once, and nearly kill a second time. I feel a voice coming, one with a filthy taste in my mouth, and I draw an nsibidi mark in the air just as he announce his name and that he was coming to free my head from my neck. Jakwu, he call himself. I remember him from sixty and seven years ago. A warrior that even the South King has honored with gold. A rapist and killer of girls, from

Weme Witu. I sneak into his house thinking I could disguise myself as his victim, a move that fail as soon as I see that not a single living or dead girl hanging in his dungeon had hair anywhere else but on her head. Him I remember because he make me enjoy cruelty. It give me pleasure to kill him slow, and watch him suffer till the end only to see me push the end back even longer. Long enough that some of the living girls start to wonder how many monsters was in the room. And even then I leave his body in way that his here-after would be of suffering. But now he is back. I grab a chalk and draw a line of nsibidi on the door. He still manage to slam my head into it. I know I feel them—one hand grabbing my right hand, the other grabbing my neck. The push, the wind, the whatever her name is still an erratic bitch, coming to help only when she feel like it. Then just as I start to feel fin-gernails digging into my skin, nsibidi appear on the wall, writing themselves with fire. They blaze, burn, and leave a smoking mark in just a blink. Behind me, the Nnimnim woman.

"You not ready," she say.

"Nevertheless, it is time to leave."

"You couldn't even fight two. What you going to do with twenty attacking you at once?"

"Take them to the river and drown them."

"Them already dead."

"Then I will just—"

"Abandon humor, girl, that is not for you."

"You just call me girl? Who now making jokes? I

taking what I know and leaving in the morning. If you want to show me more between now and then it is welcome. If not, then get out."

In the morning a voice wake me up. It didn't sound like me, but it didn't sound like them. Urgent and weak at the same time, like somebody at the door calling me with a whisper. But nobody is at the door and nobody in the room. And the voice not saying any word of harm, not saying any word at all. I shrug it off, saying it must be wind slipping through a small crack somewhere. I head to where I remember the window to be and it open itself, which still put me off. Outside the window, Mluma, the district with the iron wings, attracting sunglow. The district that look like it will any moment take flight. Hanging down the side wall right now are men, fifty, seventy, maybe one hundred tied to ropes and painting the Queen's face in black. This Queen promised me a horse and chariot to go and come, because she is still thinking I was coming back. Defiance, something so foreign to her that it bump against her ear and bounce right back off.

The Nnimnim woman pack me a sack of charms, spell binders, vulture bones, chalk, and stones from the bottom of a bottomless pool. I put it with my bundle and turn to set off. Another me would have bid the King Sister goodbye, but this me knows her place. I say to the air that I hope the gods give her much favor and turn to leave when the voice tease me behind my ear. My hand is in the chalk and writing

beside the window before a devil could blink. But
it is hard to bind a voice that is saying nothing, no
word at all. A sound hard to follow, though follow
it I try, right up to the door, which open, then back
a few steps, then to the left as the door close, then
right against the wall. People in the next room perhaps, except this is neither hostel nor inn. Soon the
truth come to me that the sound is not beyond
the wall, but inside it. The push obey me before I
give the order, slipping behind the wood panels and
punching them out.

Is a man I am seeing.

Eye wide open but no dark in the middle. Arms
thick, thighs big, belly small. No mouth, for something is in his mouth, like a tail as thick as a fist.
Leaning back against dry grass is this man I am seeing. First I see a web and him trapped in it. Three
or four blinks pass and all I see is rope. The band
around his neck, a rope. The band around his arm, a
rope. Everywhere—legs, feet, toes, arms, hands, neck,
even each finger—also they tie to a rope, and every
move he make pull something in the house. Nobody
pulling my jaw shut, it hanging loose about to touch
the floor. I back away, not thinking much, but as I
approach the window, the man pull his middle finger as if beckoning me, and look, the window pull
open. The Queen's voice come back to me right there
she saying, It's neither spell nor craft why Dolingo is
Dolingo—it is iron and rope. Is a man I am seeing,
but it is a woman I am hearing, a woman I either hear

once but don't know or know but don't remember. Not this Queen, but somebody else asking, If rope pulling everything, what pulls the rope? Outside, wind slip through the window and rush his skin, which make him panic. The room abandon its cool and go wild, windows open and closing, the door swinging open and slamming, the table rushing from the side, then rushing back. Is a man I am seeing and up to now he never feel wind. I don't know when it happen, but my last meal is a puddle on the floor and my mouth is bitter and my throat is burning. My chest heave again, but my belly is empty. From the ceiling it come, a bucket that lower itself and overturn water right above the floor. I jump out of the way. Planks in that part of the floor split, flip to drain the water off, then right themselves as if nothing just happen.

I grab my sacks, mount my horse, and leave to never come back.

4

THE WOLF AND THE LIGHTNING BIRD

Igegenechi o ma za okawunaro

TWENTY-ONE

They lose the boy.

The black bitch and them, they lose the boy. This must be sad tidings for some, maybe many, but all I could do is laugh. Live as long as me and there is not much that don't turn funny, even grief, even cruelty, even loss. Because here is truth. Between gods and princesses and kings and noble people, all of this is a game, so how can one not laugh when they can't play? And this water sprite, with her usual judgment of character, give away the child, then declare him lost. No, taken, for even she cannot abide by the term **lost,** as it can also mean dead. Bad circumstances fall on the boy, they say, as if somebody didn't drop those circumstances on him.

Like I say, I laugh.

So, Malakal. Now I am in the city she summon me to, despite all I know of her foolishness. What that make me, I don't know. Two quartermoons ago I board a dhow at Lish sporting merchant flags to escape war boats and berserker stripes to scare off pirates. I do likewise and put on the air of a necromancer to scare off whoever on the ship would test me. The dhow leave me on the coast far west, a coast with no name, not giving me the choice but telling me to either get off or become cargo. I know why they choose this place, because I know who choose it. Only a little farther north and the coastline would be closer to Malakal, which was still seven days out or more. But not far from this shore stand one of the ten and nine doors, which would land me just outside the city. In that, at least, this water sprite was still true to nature, sending people down a road, but never the one to pay the toll. She know what walking through that door would cost me, but already she consider it done. And yet look at me, following her instructions to the crossroads where waiting was a boy once a Sangoma, who switch sides for the true cause when he start to bulge into a man. What cause that be and why he think it true I don't ask. I just wrap the Nnimnim woman's cloth—nothing but tatters now around my neck—scrawl ten nsibidi on my clothes, and scratch another on my shoulder with a fingernail. Yet as soon as I walk through, a spirit push me down in the Malakal dirt and try to stomp my head in it before I could free my own hand and draw marks on the ground to banish him. Not Jakwu, I think, for he love to announce himself, but some other man who put himself in the way of my killing knife.

I take one more night before I show myself, because there was no way I would let anyone see me weakened from this door. But also, fuck her. A hundred curses to that water sprite for thinking that all she have to do is beckon and I will come running. And yet here I am, so what that make me, I don't answer. That night I pass in the lodgings of a man who teach laws to those who can't read. He couldn't stop telling me what come to pass between North and South. Tensions rising again, he say. At one time when Netu was King, the reigning mad southern King move from war talk to full war, and despite or because of his madness take not just Wakadishu, but conquer all the way to Kalindar and redraw the map of North and South. He lead the attack himself, and shame Kwash Netu, who spend the war on his throne and his shitpot.

Nine years pass before the people of Kalindar themselves drive the South back below the Kegere River and liberate Wakadishu as well. Wakadishu just as quick declare that they are independent and won't take dominance from either North or South, even though there was never a time that this place could defend itself from either. Things calm from Netu's last days into Dara's reign, but calm never mean cool. Not much news come to the forest, but enough to know that North and South all but coming to war. Again. Living in the South didn't give me sympathy for the South, but it did give me indifference to the North. **Indifference to kings and princesses,** say the voice that sound like me. This man look at me like he expecting gratitude for telling me news, some of which I already know. As for me, I did wonder if sucking his tongue instead of his cock would make him talk less. I leave before he wake up to tell me that I look different in the dark.

After we deliver the King Sister to Dolingo and the boy to Fumanguru, I deliver myself back to the bush. By the time I get back South to the woods by the Sunk City, woman stop sending word for the Moon Witch. It make me burn that a few women, all suffering, one or two probably dead now, braved the woods for the Moon Witch's help, only to find her gone. To help royals she care nothing about. So like a hermit woman I be then, until they send word.

Word that bring me to Malakal, the other mountain, but nothing like Fasisi. Fasisi start at the foot of the mount, but the desire of people to lord over people, with the King of the North lording the most, lead them to building higher. Malakal start high and build lower. Old Malakal start at the foot of the mountain and drive itself into ruin. New Malakal, founded three hundred years later, change their tactic from breaking ground at the bottom and building up, to the reverse.

Come to it straight and you can see why some people call it the great lighthouse, or used to back when I still mess with the North. When Malakal start to burst, they build another wall lower to swallow the first, a wall that also surround the mountain. But that wall couldn't hold a growing province either, hence another wall, lower and wider, and yet another. House below house, window below window, and towers like needles, the towers Malakal is famous for, some so skinny that they forget to have steps. Some so lean that lean is what they do, collapsing on each other like spent lovers. Also this, they build the third wall after the fourth, not because that wall was swelling to burst but because over the years rise many who think themselves too good for the bottom, but who run into other people who don't think them good enough for the top. I never could settle my thought on this city. Roads snaking and pointing, rising then plunging, as if they can't decide where they want to go. Four forts for a city still acting like it was the last stand of the North, which it was before even Netu was King, when the South invade everywhere but here. Malakal is barely a day away from the Hills of Enchantment, Sangomin territory and another reason why I don't give no fucks for this place. But they do produce gold and they do reach to the sea.

Somebody book me a lodging at an inn behind Malakal's second wall, a room with a mirror hanging by the door. And this mirror, the like of which I don't see in at least an age, hanging but looking like it is floating, which make it appear like an enchanted window, one that curse you to see only what is behind, never what is ahead of you. A past that flip on itself, warped, impossible to read. I look in the mirror and see an old woman at last. Head near total white, hair shaved all around, leaving just the tree on top. But I can't trust it, for the mirror flip my face, put my right-arm scars on the left, and draw a crooked line under my jaw. Some women regard just one strand of white hair with more fear than they would a demon, but I been waiting for white and gray for over a hundred years. As for years, it take them three before they finally send word to me, three years that might be two years and ten moons too late. It come from the whisper of a Yumbo, who get it from a Yumbo, who get it from a Yumbo, who get it from Bunshi, who would never tell me herself that the boy gone missing.

So when Nsaka come to tell me, I say nothing at first. They lose the boy before the mother name him, which mean he is three years old now, if not dead. Bunshi didn't check for his whereabouts in the Malangika, the tunnel city and the secret underground witches' market, and I know why. For Bunshi know that if she so much as slither down there, a necromancer mightier than she would trap and sell her whole or butcher her for parts, upping the price for each piece cut while she was still alive. But I don't need the voice to tell me that if a little boy long done gone, that is the first place to look. So before I sail from Lish, that was where I head, above the Blood Swamp but below Wakadishu to find out what become of this no name boy.

Somebody come looking before you, say a man who work a spell to flip his street cart in one movement and turn potions into toys and jewelry. Not the mother but a man on her behalf, he say. Well not a man but a snake, who say he looking for a no name boy and whoever it be that was selling him. Truly I never see this sort of man but I hear of them, built with two arms and two legs—but this is how you know, for the eyes lighter than most people, the skin colder than mountain water, and his tongue, mark how it is forked. Not a shapeshifter, a man. But praise the gods that he don't bother with clothes and should really call that thing his third leg, mansnake, who shed his skin every two moons and who have forked tongue and cold blood. He speaking of Nyka, who Ne Vampi is still pretending not to fuck. I used to fuck a lion, I want to tell her. No shame in fucking a snake.

The child is gone, Basu Fumanguru's corpse is in a crouch, and in an urn and long past rot, but that is neither the beginning nor the end of the story. I didn't like the man when I meet him, so news of his death didn't move me one way or another. This is what I know, that Fumanguru produce writs against the house of Akum, in particular this King, but other than passages on walls in Fasisi and Juba, nobody see the actual writs. Writs is serious business in the North Kingdom, for once the people read or hear them they can never be unread or unheard. But writing on the wall with no purpose or author is writing people forget as soon as they walk past the next wall. Nsaka speak of outcome before cause, saying that only Basu know where he keep the writs, but if one was to kill him, and one did, then the secret of their location die with him. But that was assuming evil come for Basu because of something he was about to do, and if the answer was so simple, then I wouldn't be here. Writs contain a serious rebuke to the King, but that man is Kwash Dara, and to be scared of a scroll's power he would first have to read it. Evil come for Basu because of what he already done do.

I come back from the Malangika and Nsaka is waiting for me in the room like me never leave. "How her version go?" I ask. "The water sprite," I add.

"I know who you're talking about," Ne Vampi say, then tell the sprite's account. "Night of the Skulls they call it in Kongor, though the night earn the name long before this come to pass. Fumanguru's wife and six sons, plus the baby boy he raising as his own, all fast asleep as night was reaching the middle. Also asleep, most of the servants and the grounds and garden slaves. Here is who was not asleep: Wangechi, his oldest wife; Militu, his youngest; two of the cooks; and Basu himself. We don't know who arrange it, but it smelled of the elders, first for a witch to work the spell, then for a sullen slave to gather the youngest wife's moonblood to set off the roof walkers. If you know nothing of the Omoluzu, know that their hunger is as monstrous as it is unending, and all they need is the smell of one person's blood for them to hunt without tiring until they drinking the source of it. This slave dig up her blood cloths, then wait until dark to throw them up to the ceiling. Those awake and those rustling from sleep must have thought they were hearing a rainstorm. But it was darkness consuming the ceiling, darkness thick and unruly like waves. That is what she say, waves. Like waves on rocks, so both the rush and rumble, but also the cracking. And these devils, shaped like men and black like coal, start to pull themselves out of the ceiling the way you would rise from a lake. They run and hop and jump along the ceiling as you would the floor and have blades that look like bone and giant claws that look like blades.

"The blackness sweep the rooms, slicing and chopping the crying slaves first. One get away and she is yelling that it is coming for them, the night. Bunshi crawl through the window just in time—"

"Don't come here with some tall story and not mention that they look exactly like her, Or perhaps she didn't tell you," I say.

"She said Omoluzu or roof walkers, demons of the shadows. Bunshi is not a shadow, she is—"

"Water, I hear."

"Bunshi don't sink from the ceiling," say Ne Vampi.

"Bunshi can sink from anything they choose."

"This is not her kind."

"Her kind was who guard the Aesi for him to be born again, so I don't know what in the fucks you talking about. With my own eyes I see her."

"You want the rest of the story or no?" she ask.

"Talk your talk," I say.

"So. Basu is screaming for his family to get away, and grab the only one he find, the King Sister's son. The slave run to the wife and from above the Omoluzu chop them down to chunks. The children they kill quick, not out of mercy but because it is quicker to kill a child. Then the slaves in the grain keep. Everybody but Basu and the child, who run to Bunshi for her to save them, but the Omoluzu is right at their backs, black racing across the ceiling. Give me your child if you want him to live, she say. I can't save both of you, she say. You should never have brought him to me, he say and toss the boy. That is not true. He place the boy in her hands like is his own for real. I am his father, he say. The boy was one year old then, just over. Bunshi turn her finger into a claw and cut her own belly open to stuff the baby in there like a womb. Basu Fumanguru was brave till the end, but he didn't have a blade. She had the kind of knife that cuts them—"

"Because she and them are one."

"Quiet. She couldn't kill them all, so she escape through the window."

"Most heroic thing I ever hear her do. Most times she just slither into a corner and look overcome."

This is where the story should end, but she never say finish.

"And all of this was three years ago?" I say.

"That is not all," Ne Vampi say.

"Bunshi is neither warrior, hunter, protector, nor assassin. This sound like the part where she should have called you. But you never hear a word from her, not so? This fool only seem to come to you when it too late."

Now she turn quiet.

"She is here? Come out from the shadows, you coward," I say.

"Why you hate her so?"

"Hate. I too old to hate anybody. At best what passed between me and she is indifference."

"Whatever you say. You still blame her for stopping you from killing the Aesi, even though it wasn't her."

"She never seem keen on me trying again," I say.

"So he can be born again? Maybe you have been living too long. You certainly never get tired of tiresome talk. The Aesi can't change minds like he used to, she told you that. You want change, restore the King, and even he won't stop that truth when it unfold."

"You ground that on what?"

"Even he in his own way respect the order of things."

"You ground that on what?"

"Disrupting the line of kings didn't come from him. Read the griots. He only about serving authority, and believe it or not, he don't care which authority. He don't care who he serve, but once he in their service . . ."

"I don't believe it."

"I don't care. Calling on you was, as always, the water sprite's idea."

"I know why she do it, you know. Why she keep calling on me."

"Must be your one hundred years of good deeds."

"She only come to me when the time too late. Or when others fail before."

"You mean me? I never get any call. All I did was deliver the boy. But what a thing to be proud of, to get a call only after people exhaust everything else. Good for you, Great-Great-Grandmother," Ne Vampi say.

I want to say that I see it, this grievance that you have against me, so just give it air and be done with it. I want to say it, but I don't.

"You never finish the story," I say, and wait.

"Bunshi take the baby to a blind woman still in Kongor. The boy was still a milkbaby and she could give suckle. And she was one of the few women in that land who was not a witch."

"Good."

"No, not good. Her husband beat her to near death for taking a child in without permission, then sell the baby to a trader as soon as he could get a price."

"Peerless, she is, this water sprite. Peerless in how she judge character."

"Her was fine. Is the wife's judgment that fuck all things up."

"No sale happen in the Malangika, at least."

"No. You leave before I could tell you there was no point in checking the Malangika. He take the boy to a slave market in the Purple City, near Lake Abbar. That was when Bunshi send word for me. I track the boy to a perfume and silver merchant whose plan was to sell him in the far east markets where little dark boys go for gold. While I was looking for him, I learn that mercenaries already find the caravan on the Mitu border of the Darklands. Somebody ransack it and kill everyone."

"The Mituti usually a peace-loving sort of thief," I say.

"This not the Mituti. Nor robbers, for they didn't take a thing, not the silver, civet, or even the myrrh. Only the boy. And something else."

The dead look like the oldest of the old, was what she first say to me, until she look at me and remember that I am what old look like, at least in this room. What she wanted to say was they look like somebody wither them down to a husk, so "Like a husk?" is what I ask her. She shake her head. Like somebody pierce a hole at the chest and suck everything out. Every tear, blood, bile, juice, marrow, suck out every single thing that power whatever one call life, leaving skin and bone. And even that skin go from coffee to ash. And all of them with eyes gone gray and hazy, like the war-stunned. Maybe that was why though everybody was dead, some didn't carry a death stink. The mercenaries say the whole place smell like heavy rain about to fall.

"You wasting time not telling me the entire truth."

"What you think I not telling you?"

"Ipundulu never move alone. They just don't move with other Ipundulu."

"I never said it was Ipundulu."

"I never ask. Ipundulu, if he travel with others, is leading them, all except his witch. She beckon when he have use, but up to his own mischief when she don't. Not all bodies accounted for, including the boy. The only reason that boy alive is that make for good bait."

I can tell she don't believe me.

"You ever cross one?" I say.

"N—"

"No. For if you and him ever meet, you would not be here right now."

"But not you, Sogolon the baddest woman alive."

"Never meet one to take the claim from me."

"We not getting anywhere. So what so wicked about this Ipundulu and why you think some bodies unaccounted for?"

"The lightning bird, he go by also. A vampire to shame vampires. Handsome white man, hair stringy like a horse, you have to be close to see that it's not hair but feathers. White like a cloud, whiter than an albino who still have blood coursing close to skin. They not from one region because they love to move and hide tracks. And so they do, from one place to the next, always looking for the next heart to cut out of chest, and next body to drink blood. From when he see you, he work your mind against you, so much that night is day and only you don't know that the white gown he wearing is wings. Woman mostly but children and men too. Some he kill, some he change, all he rape. Worst is when he get filled with rage and turn to full bird, for one flap of those wings loosen enough thunder to knock down a wall and lightning to kill everybody behind it."

"You ever kill one?"

"No, I never kill one. But I kill his witch."

"And that end him. Easy then."

"No. It free him. He terrorize a little village between Masi and Nigiki every night for a moon until he try to pull a little boy by the foot from his mother's hut, and she grab the first thing she could throw at him, a lamp. He burst into flame and run away. The next morning they find dead man right at the edge of the river. Body burned black with two wings, but no feathers. All these years I hear of twenty, but there must be more. And not all of them under command of a witch."

"Not every victim have their heart cut out."

"I say he don't move alone. Just not with other Ipundulu. Obayifo, who leave his own body to attack, was but bad blood come between the two. Also, not everybody the Ipundulu kill. Some of them, he change."

"You cross one before?"

"And live to tell you about it."

"Nobody bad like Miss Sogolon."

"He did already drink his full, so he didn't have no need to attack me. But a little girl walk travel with him. She is the one that get woman to open her door. A girl her mother pay me to find."

Let us make this quick. That Ipundulu poison that girl's mind in barely a quartermoon, and this boy in their clutches for three years. I don't tell Nsaka that whatever we find at the end of this search will not be a child, won't be a son and will certainly never be King. I saw a little daughter who in five nights done know desire, done know lust, barely a girl yet coming to the vampire like a lover. No return to the true line of kings is going to happen for Lissisolo, and the last time I face an Ipundulu, all I do was make him laugh. Yet I ask Nsaka where and when we meeting next, which she take as a yes. Which it is, not for this child, but for he who I know is searching for him too. The Aesi. Only one use that child have left, which is to smoke out this scheming son of a jackal bitch, who don't seem to know much about the vampire or he would know the work he seeking to do was already done. None of this I tell Nsaka Ne Vampi.

"You should know, the Aesi and his royal guard searching for him too," Nsaka say. I don't feign indifference, and she wouldn't believe it anyway.

"Then he already ahead," I say. The thought of Bunshi and Ne Vampi grabbing the boy in a race for throne, the Aesi at their heels make me laugh.

Some people believe that time bring Itutu to all things, that as days arrive and depart you can quench all malcontent with mystic coolness. But my malcontent don't cool, it fester. Everything annoy me, everything aggravate me, and all things work together to make me bitter. All that time away helping the King Sister breed another man King who would be just as bad as all the others before cause me to lose the name of the Moon Witch. The woman who lose her child to Ipundulu was the last one to come to the clearing and call out that name. A voice that sound like me say, **You gone back to being a no name woman again,** and I couldn't disagree. In all time away helping this princess to breed, the monkeys abandon the house, the hawks return to the treetops, and the gorillas forget me. I know because three charge me, one right into the house and didn't stop until I blast him out the door. They didn't quit until one come for me in my sleep and my wind (not wind) slam against him in the quick and break his neck. That was when I burn off the welcome I enjoy for near one hundred years, and slip away like some thief before the whole tribe come for revenge. Coming back was a mistake that somebody else pay for. And like I say, all that my malcontent do was fester.

I have this feeling that people who lose everything have a different kind of grief from people who have everything taken away, for all I could do for days, moons, and then years was let my rage simmer, let it all boil down to just one focus. And if the focus start to blur, I put myself back in my welcome room as I watch my son die, and the front yard where my own family look me in the face and declare they don't know me. And that they all long dead didn't take away the anger or give me relief. The only relief was the lions in the wild who didn't want nothing but for my head rub theirs. The North see me several times, something I would never admit to Nsaka. But I couldn't quit the Aesi. Every connection reminded me of loneliness, every new lion child that I meet remind me of the child that I lose, every handsome shapeshifting lion make me desperate to run up to him and say, Give me tidings of love and joy, for the last thing I say to my lion was nothing but bitchery. Here is truth—I was doing worse than when I lose Ehede, even worse than when I lose my whole family. No, not worse. I didn't feel worse. I feel somebody sharpen me down like the edge of a knife. I feel nothing.

But the nothing is something. It have weight and shape. Like I say, it is like the sharpened edge of a knife. When I had people to live for, one of them died. Then it come to pass that to the others I was dead. I could claim the lions as my own but nobody own them, and as for Nsaka, me and she never did become . . . even the word **family** sound like saying too much. The voice that sound like me say what I won't, that this is the one real bond you been having for years now. **You grow it, you nurture it, and worst of all, you choose not to fulfill it, for once you do, then you have nothing.** So call it what it is, years in the wilderness growing my malcontent until I can bear to then live with nothing, if live is what I do. Because all of me is about all of him and when I end him, I will end me too, and why not? One hundred seventy and seven is a longer life than devils. A gift I never asked for and never did need. There. Decided. We can find the child, but I already know that he is lost.

So, Malakal. Not much of what Ne Vampi tell me was of use, but it did prick up my ears when she say that the sprite summon more than me and her. None of them Bultungi, even though the shapeshifting hyena women are the best hunters in the North, when they not trying to eat what they find. No warrior women, none of the Seven Wings mercenaries, and no former guard or soldier. Who that leave would be a mystery until I get there.

Is a long trek up to the first wall, too hard for a horse. Most of the dwellings in this enclosure long past old, but none as old as those to the south, including one that people call the Collapsed Tower, which is actually two towers, with one crumpled and leaning against the other. A joke that run on for too long if you ask me, since all these towers look near collapse. Ne Vampi say they would meet on the top floor, but she leave out that most of the stairs long broken away, and what she call a climb was a jump that could turn to a death fall, and that don't count for the steps ready to break off with you. The whole time I am wondering why hire so many in number. The Moon Witch work alone, I say to her, but she act like I just pass wind. She don't say it was because they just done try with one, but Nyka didn't find the boy.

All I see is columns until one move. An Ogo, tall

enough to brush against the ceiling and looking like he supporting it. The light throw shape to the scar pattern on his forehead, the two tusks poking a little out his mouth, as well as the mountain of necklaces covering a bare chest. Around his waist look like a cloth but it could also be animal skin, and nothing on his feet but feet. A North mountain giant that the South army use as berserker, so I was surprised that anybody would employ one for something else. I nod, he grunt, and that was all. I was second but he make me feel like I reach first, with nothing to do but consider the room with its blue walls, dim torchlight, and cushions nobody sit on in least an age. At the far end of this room hang another, with more light and a table laid out with food. Just so, the others come at once. Amadu the slave trader who join the cause and who was making the down payments. Another man behind him with the shuffling walk of a manservant. And Nsaka.

"No big cat?" she ask.

"The Leopard should be coming shortly. He bringing another. I heard of him, they say he has a nose," say the slave trader.

"What he going to do, sniff the boy out half a year away?"

"That is exactly what he do," he say.

Nsaka turn to approach me but jump when the Ogo scratch his face.

"Fuck the gods, I thought you were a statue."

"Thank the gods that this Ogo considers every move before he make it," say the slaver.

"This Ogo have a name?"

"Sadogo," is all the giant say.

"An Ogo named Sadogo. Poor giant, is it because—"

"Nsaka."

"What, old woman?"

"Nobody need a probe from a woman he don't know."

She take that as a hint to come talk to me. Somebody spend some serious time twisting her hair into branches so that her head look like a baobab tree. Didn't hate it, but don't like her enough to tell her I like it. But the gown cut low down the front making me wonder if she either coming from somewhere better, or heading there after.

"A lightning lady. We capture one. She will lead us back to him."

I about to ask which him she was talking about when two people coming up the half stairs make the slaver jump up from the cushions. Two men enter, one dark and shiny with a skirt around his waist, beads around his neck, and two axes on his back, the other tall, bearded, and hairy, wearing only himself.

"Three eyes, shining in the dark. The Leopard and . . . what they call you, half wolf?" ask the slaver.

"Wolf Eye, but I prefer Tracker," he say.

More people I don't know and from the look on her face neither do Nsaka. The Ogo's face don't change. But the slaver is delighted to see this one he call Leopard. "In the inner room," Amadu say, and Leopard is what he become, stooping to the floor the way Keme used to, shrinking and stretching at the same time, brown skin to black fur, shorter legs, bigger head, thicker legs, hairy head, two paws, two more, and claws. The cat trot off to the inner room and snag something fleshy and wet.

"An Ogo? Mind this collapsing tower finally collapse," the Tracker say and laugh out loud, though nobody else find it funny. "I hear Prince Moki was the fool that build this four hundred years ago. Collapsed as soon as they blessed it with chicken blood."

"Four hundred years? River folk count lion years, or dog?" Nsaka say.

"Juba I hail from, not some river," he say.

"You dress like a Ku," she say.

"In the finest Malakal cloth?"

"Not when it reek of Ku. Now I feel like I'm passing through the swamp."

"You sound like somebody the swamp passed through," he say with a grin.

Nsaka follow the Leopard to the inner room and return with a bowl of plums. The manservant offer the slaver a tray of berries, the Ogo still standing as if holding up the roof, and the Leopard chomping and swallowing the last of the okapi flesh. I write three nsibidi on air just to make sure.

"We losing time," I say.

"It's yours to lose?" say the Tracker.

"Oh. Thought you were done."

"Done what?"

"Looking around for anybody worthy."

"True, good sense telling me to leave, but why disappoint my furry friend after he go through so much trouble to find me. And where you hail from, old woman? Writing runes on air. Something nasty must be following you."

I was about to tell this man which part of a dead sow he should fuck first when the slaver say, "I tell you true and I tell you wise. Three years now they take the child, a boy. Long time he walking and nana was most of what come out of his mouth. Taken from his home right there in the night. They take nothing else, they don't once call for ransom. Maybe they sell him in the Malangika—yes I know of the place— but by now surely he too old for the uses of a witch. This child was living with his aunt, in the city of Kongor. Then one night the child was stolen and the aunt's husband's throat cut. Her family of eleven children, all murdered," he say and go quiet. For effect, I think. When I turn to Nsaka, the only thing on my mind is what in the name of gods is he lying for. She nod and shrug, then look over to see if Wolf Eye was watching her.

"Kongor is but the beginning, but it could be the end too," say the slave trader. "You can leave for the house at first light. There will be horses for those who ride, but the best way is by the White Lake, then around the Darklands, and cross lower Ubangta. And when you come to Kongor—"

"You enslave lost boys, not save them. What is he to you?" say the Leopard, taking the words out of my mouth. I wish he did ask about Kongor being the end too. Nsaka know that I am glaring at her, which mean she don't look my way. The Tracker is looking at me, though.

"The boy? Son of the friend who is dead. That is all. I will see rescue for him," the slaver say.

"The boy is most likely dead," say the Tracker.

"Then I will see justice," say the slaver.

"And I would seek better answers, slave trader. Why was the child by an aunt and not the mother?"

"I was going to tell you. His mother and father died, from river sickness. The elders said the father fished in the wrong river, took fish meant for the water lords, and the bisimbi nymphs who swam underwater and stood guard struck him with illness. He spread it to the boy's mother. The father was my old friend and a partner in this business. His fortune is the boy's."

The Leopard go right up to the slaver and sniff. Nsaka and the manservant clutch their swords.

"Do you know how to tell a good lie, Master Amadu? I know how to tell a bad one. When people talk false, words plop muddy where they should land clear, but clear on shit nobody expect clarity on. Something that sounds like it might be true. But it's always the wrong thing. Everything you just said, you tell me different three nights ago," the Leopard say.

"Which he then tell me," say the Tracker.

"Truth don't lie," the slave trader say.

"But it sure can change. I believe there is a boy. And I believe a boy is missing, and if he's missing many years, dead. I even believe that you want us to find him. But four days ago, the boy child was living with a housekeeper. Today you say aunt. By the time we get to Kongor it will be a eunuch monkey. What do you believe, Tracker?" ask the Leopard.

"I don't believe. How about you, old witch?"

"I believe I want less interruption," I say.

"Good, good, wonderful, fine," say the slaver.

"Why you need so many of us? Between the Ogo's sharp mind and the old woman's mighty strength, people wouldn't hide shit from you," the Tracker say.

"Sadogo, he is calling you stupid," Nsaka say.

That pull the Ogo out of his giant corner, not stomping, but walking most surely to the Tracker.

"I said you was sharp! Everybody hear me say sharp!" he say, backing away quick. The Tracker pull the axes from his back. The Leopard stoop to the floor slow. Nsaka stand by the manservant, both clutching the handle of their blades. The Ogo is still.

"If this is an ambush I will rip your throat out before he splits your heads in two," the Leopard say.

"Who is looking for you?" I ask.

People taking sides. The Ogo standing alone. I done see enough.

"How one small room hold so many fools, I don't know," I say.

"Something a witch don't know? You must be a rare one. I mean, you have the airs of a witch. Your calf-hide clothes, underarm funk, your lemongrass, fish, and blood—no, moonblood from, well, clearly not you."

"And you have the air of the Sangomin. They get you young, or you come to this kind of mind all by yourself?"

He laugh. This sparring was sport.

"What do you know of the men who took the boy?" the Leopard ask.

Something catch the Tracker's nose and he sniff all the way to the window. The scent pull him so hard that he sit in the sill and stay, looking out.

"Tracker?"

"Nothing, cat."

Tracker. Cat. I am in a room stinking of boys. Boys. Even this Ogo.

"I tell you true, we know nothing," the slaver say. "Night is not when they came, but in the noon of day. Few, maybe four, maybe five, maybe five and one, but they were men of strange and terrible looks. I can read the—"

"I can also read," the Tracker say. I can't tell if I find the whole room tiresome or just him. But I don't know what game this slaver is playing and can't tell if Nsaka know either. Of course they smell lie, because a lie what this man is telling them. I set myself to just leave, then I look out the window and picture the dark being nothing but crows.

"Nobody saw them enter. Nobody saw them leave," the slave trader say.

"Why we back here? How this help us find the boy when who take him last is not who try to take him first? Stop wasting everybody's time, you stupid water sprite," I say.

"Sogolon."

"You shut up too, Ne Vampi. Bunshi, come out of the fucking window frame."

"Who this old woman talking to?" the Tracker ask the Leopard.

"Bunshi!"

"Tracker, time to leave," the Leopard say. "Tracker?"

The Tracker is by the window looking out again. "Yes, yes, cut this place loose," he say.

They about to leave when the doorway melt. Bunshi. Long time pass since I see people jump at the sight of her. Bunshi flow down slow like honey and pool on the floor. The pool start to rise and bend and shape and Leopard and Tracker draw arms again. Work of devils, the cat say but the Tracker say he seen this kind of devil before and I know he is thinking what I often say. The Tracker chuck a dagger into the black mass, which suck it in then all suddensome chuck the dagger right for his eye. The Leopard catch it, quick as a blink. I want to scream, Quit with all this show, you black bitch, but hold my tongue. Bunshi continue with herself, rolling up and around like injera dough, twisting, squeezing, spreading wider. The Leopard snarling, the slaver fidgeting because it is his wishy-washy words that draw her out. Well, you is the fool for telling him to lie first, I want to say to her. Finally she curve herself out of her own mass and stand there, like she waiting for a clap. Nsaka know not to look at me, for she know the look I going give her back.

"I am—"

"Omoluzu. Everybody can see that," the Tracker say, and I couldn't stop the snort.

"Bunshi. Some people call me Popele."

"What are you, some water imp?"

"This Leopard spoke much about your nose. He never said anything about your mouth," Bunshi say.

"How he keep putting his foot in it?" Nsaka Ne Vampi say.

The slaver laugh first, then Nsaka, even the Ogo look away to hide his smile. Even in the dim light I can see the grin burn away from the Tracker's face. He reach for an ax.

"You forget what I do with your knife?"

"Leopard, I tire of this room," the Tracker say.

"Hear the full story, then decide if you want to stay," Bunshi say.

"Another? Promise me somebody fucks in this one."

Bunshi continue, telling him about Kwash Dara, Basu Fumanguru, and how this man that the King love the most soon run afoul of him. Basu have visions of what a King, a country should be, which make him win the people but lose all who prefer the North just as it is, among them the royal house and the elders. Then one night he catch an elder raping a girl and kill him. Good for the girl, good for all who seek justice, but bad for Fumanguru. He flee to Kongor with his family and fool himself after a few years that he safe. Then come Omoluzu and the Night of the Skulls, and her saving his youngest son. I knew Nsaka wouldn't be looking at me when I turn to her, but I stare her down anyway. Glare her down. Dare her to see the scowl on my face. This water sprite is telling them that the heir to the throne was Basu Fumanguru's child. I want to tell them that I done with this, but I look in the dark and swear I see crows.

Then the Tracker say that maybe this child is better off wherever he is, with whoever he is with. Certainly better than this water sprite who couldn't keep him safe in the first place. Seriously, you look like a walking target begging for an arrow, he say. More words like this and I might almost start to like him, especially when the holes in Bunshi stories get so big they start to whistle.

"She's not paying you to ask or to think. Just to smell," say Nsaka. "You the one with the all-smelling nose. If this job too much for you, then leave."

"Is I who decide who stay and who leave," say Bunshi.

The Tracker not listening to either. He back by the window, sniffing again. A door swing open and the only person I can think coming upstairs is the one person missing.

"In two days we ride for Kongor. Come or don't come, it makes no difference to me. She's the one that wants you two," Nsaka say. The footsteps draw her ears too, she hop a little then settle into a walk, trying to not look eager. She is for certain fucking this snake.

"You are late. Everyone is—"

The hatchet slice off her sentence, zip past her face, and lodge in the door.

"You full crazed? You barely missed me, old friend," Nyka say and step in with a smile. Truth, I want to step past my great-great-granddaughter and touch the skin of a man who feel he don't need to wear nothing else. **Snakeskin, furskin, you just want to touch,** say the voice that sound like me, but I don't know what she mean.

"I wasn't trying to miss!" shout the Tracker and fling his second ax straight for Nyka's face. He dodge but it almost hit Nsaka. Nyka yank the ax and throw it right back at the Tracker, but the ax either lose flight or dodge, hard to know in the dark. Nyka say something about enchantments when in the quick the Tracker jump him and they tumble out the door and roll down the stairs. Nsaka run behind, screaming at the two of them, as if she don't know that the last place you want to be is between two men fighting.

That make me follow, not for them, but for her. I reach the doorway, see them still tumbling down into the dark and sparks going off, their weapons stabbing and scraping the mortar more than their skin. Nyka! Ne Vampi shout. The light dim but we can see them hit the landing where Nyka jump the Tracker, but the Tracker kick him off, and there again, the glint of a blade. Nyka quick, he bash it out of the Tracker's hand and punch him in the belly, which make him bowl over, his face right into Nyka's knee. Tracker yell and stagger but he not done. He block the snake's right hand, upper-punch him in the chin and straight into the face. The air change for me, change to something I know too well and like too much. All that missing is the stick, I don't think and I certainly don't say. Ne Vampi shouting at me to stop them and all I can think of is how much I miss how a fight smell. The Leopard run past me but what he was going to stop as a cat? Nyka is the more skilled fighter, but the Tracker don't care if he lose. Nsaka stop screaming at me and rush down the stairs. The Tracker throw himself at Nyka's back and grab around his neck. Then just so it happen, Tracker's hand yank away from the snake's neck, Nyka slip from Tracker's grip and dip to the ground, Tracker pull his hand back to his side and he reverse-jump right back onto the step.

"The fuck!" he yell. Nsaka and her gift. He jump backways right into the knife that she press against his throat.

"Don't think I won't cut a dog," she say.

"I can slip out of this and punch your koo," the Tracker say.

"And the next time I reverse you, my knife will be at your balls. Cool your foot."

"Next time he fuck you, wash yourself after," he say.

"What a man lover like you doing smelling a woman's koo?" she say, which drop shock on his face, then rage.

So it is shot, an arrow straight missing her forehead. Some boy, several steps below, already drawing his bow. I done see enough. The wind (not wind) drop like a blast on the landing, and blow them all away. All of them I pin against the wall as I step past them, the Leopard snarling, the Tracker cursing, the arrowman barreling down more steps, Nyka laughing out loud, and Ne Vampi yelling at me to quit. A weight touch my shoulder and make me stagger. I am thinking a pillar fall on me but it is the Ogo. My wind (not wind) let everybody drop. The Tracker howl in rage.

"So you know each other?" say Bunshi, and I remember how many times I want to slap her.

"This is who you think going find this boy?" I say.

"You two know each other," Bunshi say, not even hearing me.

"Black mistress, have you not heard? We are old friends. Better than lovers since I shared his bed for six moons. And yet nothing came to pass, eh, Tracker? Did I ever tell you I was disappointed?" Nyka say.

"Who is this man?" Leopard asked.

"No word on me? But he told me so much about you, Leopard."

"This son of a leprous jackal bitch is nothing, but some call him Nyka," the Tracker say, then go on about how the son of a bitch sell him off to the Bultungi just for sport. "They took my eye!" he shout.

"And now you have a better one," Nyka say. Even I was getting tired of his smirk.

"You leave them to kill me."

"And yet look how they still leave you alive. Better than how you left their sisters. What my brother chose to skip is that he killed five of their number once, two of them children. All for sport."

"You is scum too."

"Not scum enough to kill infants."

"I swore to every fucking god I could name that when I see you next I would kill you," he say.

"That day is not today," say Nsaka.

"This reunion not going well, it looking," I say.

"You didn't even do it for gold. Not even silver," the Tracker shout.

"Still such a fool. You think I do it for money?" Nyka say.

"Leave now, or I swear I won't care who I kill to get to you."

"You leave instead, but stay, Leopard," I say, but from what I see of him, the cat would not.

"Where he goes, I go," he say.

"Then both of you leave," Bunshi try to shout but it come out as a yelp. Truly, I want to slap this woman. The Tracker, the Leopard, and the archer all leave.

I wake up and all of Malakal turn gold and black. So much gold that at first I am thinking the sun was rising lower or shining twice as bright. But when I look out the window there it is, shirting every roof, every arch, every doorway, pole, and flagstaff, strands of gold and black stripes, the colors that tell of the richness of the North empire and the ruler, Kwash Dara. Windows with patterns in gold leaf, plants hanging from gold rings, and also this—nobody stealing them. Malakal was never a realm to wake up early, but everybody done start the day without me. Perplex me is what they do with all this preparation for there is no sign of it last night or the night previous. Banners on walls, crowns on heads, sashes on women, robes on men, even a path for the royal procession flanked with gold spears, all of which somebody do last night.

Memory was forcing me to think of the Nnimnim woman who restore chunks of my past but not all of it, saying no science, math, or enchantment that powerful. But there is one memory so fresh, real, and raw that I can almost smell it. Kwash Dara coming to Malakal. Kwash Dara, the spider king, with his extra four limbs ahead of him. Some sores heal and some sores fester. The sharpened edge of the knife getting sharper and is two more days before we leave this place. I leave my room, but it feel like the room push me out. See me walking down Malakal's tricky roads, a steep climb to a steep drop, to snake around a corner and jump over a dead end. One gold-and-black flag lead me to the next, one gold ribbon lead me to the next, one woman with gold-and-black breasts lead me to another, on and on until I reach the palace of the Malakal grand chief.

"Is here he going stay?" I ask a woman whose face split in half, black and gold.

"You would put the king someplace else?" she say and dance away.

"They arrive in two days," say the next woman I ask.

If I know Bunshi, she spend all night convincing the Wolf Eye to join the search. Woman who don't feel secure unless a man at the helm is an argument I stop having back when somebody once ask who is the Moon Sorcerer guiding the Witch. Always blinkered, that sprite. Seeing what she want to, and blind to what she don't, even if it in front of her.

Two nights now I sit in my room and stew. Curse this red hair man for making my wounds fresh. Nsaka Ne Vampi come calling the second night but cease knocking when I don't answer. Meanwhile I sharpening my rage in daydreams, the side of my hand, a blade to slice the Aesi's neck, my breath a fire to burn down to nothing. I don't just want him dead; I want him to suffer. The third morning I streak my face in black and gold and vanish in the crowd. It still annoying me that nobody in Malakal know their own history, thanking this King who should be thanking them. I want to think that this too is the Aesi, but nobody need enchantment to write history any way they wish. The King is here and because so many road are steep, they will travel by foot. They, his soldiers, for the King will travel by palanquin. Another woman tell me that even the poor get their share of gold to wear but will be executed if they try to sell any of it. I don't ask. As for me, I am remembering that the Aesi can't read my head but can tell where there is a spot in the crowd that he can't read. Drummers heat up the drumming and my heart is pounding with them. The voice want to say that is gold dust fly up in my head to make me feverish, but I know my hand is shaking, and my neck running sweat, because my head is hot with the thought of killing a man. God. Demigod. I let the push of the crowd take me far down the street. How to get close to him? Maybe use this same crowd's push to ram into him, my knife ready for his side, to kill him before he notice. Or to stab him at that place in the neck where his feet won't even know he is dead. **Or touch him and make him explode again, his head alone this time,** say the voice, surprising me with her helping. Inside my head as I am, I don't hear the drumming shift and the crowd shifting with it, going **baka baka boom.** The whole street sweep up like a wave even though there is no sign yet of the procession. But they must be near.

Soldiers march past. This King want to show his might, even though it was mercenaries who saved Malakal. One would think the mighty Fasisi army, with their mighty spears, knives, clubs, and bow will cool me but they don't. Maybe I am still the woman who think I have nothing left to live for and nothing left to lose but that leave my thought funny, like the right fruit having the wrong taste. Soldiers pass, drummers drum, women and children cheer. I jump to the side of the street to walk against the procession, to walk towards him. Too many shoulders are hitting mine, knocking me back around, almost knocking me down. Too thick this crowd, and all I have is one dagger. They squeeze in too tight, light me off my feet, and take me with them into an alley. I shout, and grab, and kick, and punch my way back out to the street, but the King done pass. Truth, I could grab anyone right now and kill them in my anger. You all in league with him, I am thinking. You all in league.

The rooftops are the only way I can follow and I running along rooftops before thinking about it. The wind (not wind) making me jump over roofs, and skip across alleys, and for once I shouting at her to stop. As if anybody looking above to see me ride sky. You really going do it this time, you going to find him in this crowd, for you know he is there, and kill a demigod. It don't matter that he will re-born himself in eight years, because then you will find him and kill too. **If you find him,** say the voice. But I not killing the man to stop him from being born. I not looking for peace, and I not looking to close no void. I killing him to kill him. There, in a gold palanquin carried by four tall men is Kwash Dara. He almost lost in the gold drapes that keep blowing in his face, looking like a child somebody scoop up. Spearmen march along his left, archers along his right. White guard pick up the rear, but no Aesi. Of course, he not one for the middle of a parade, he not one for black and gold. Man like him work in shadow, and everything casting shadow. Maybe he gone long ahead or he far behind, maybe he walking in the crowd, maybe he already seen me. Maybe he is watching me all this time or watching out for wherever could come an attack on the king, including above. Red hair. Weaving the people on the other side of the road. Is him, have to be him. No, red feathers on woman's head. Red again. No. Red hair again. No. Maybe he see me. Maybe I am not hunter but prey. He is hunting me. Bunshi's voice at the back of my head, a whisper telling me not to go after him. I know he is here. He must be. Shadows moving along the roof, clouds blocking the sun. But then I look up and is not clouds, but crows.

I run, but they diving after me. I don't get to the edge of the roof before some snag my hair, some flapping wings in my hair, and some clawing at my chest and back. My wind (not wind) not helping, and I scream a curse that get lost in their shrieking. Then just so my feet get cold, then my calves, then my knees. I pull crows away from my face long enough to see black fluid pooling around my feet, riding up my legs, covering me until it reach all the way to my eyes and all I see is black.

The next thing I see is my room, with Bunshi by the window about to leave.

"He didn't march in the parade," she say.

"I never—"

"If he was in Kongor, I would have sensed him."

"Why I should believe you?"

"Because if he was here, I wouldn't have come to save you."

"I don't need no saving."

"Of course. Your wind was going to sweep down in a blink and blow everything away."

"You pick up wisdom now? Then why the crows if he not here?"

"You think he wouldn't send an enchantment to protect the king? Everybody marching north, but you walking south. Everybody on the street, you on the roof. I also stopped the two archers in the tower across the street aiming for your heart," she say, and leave before I could say anything.

Six days later, at the foot of Malakal mountain and right at the mouth of the Uwomowomowo Valley, who I should see coming to join our riding party but the Leopard, the archer, and the Tracker, who ask for the Ogo. Seems they change their minds and will not be driven away.

"You going to need his nose," the slaver say to me when I confront him in his cabin.

"We need a hound, not a wolf," I say.

"This wolf have an uncanny nose. Besides, how you going find a child who leave no trace? Nobody have a thing, not a swaddling cloth, not a rag, not a hair, nothing. He will find in Kongor what many have not."

"And if he don't?"

"He will."

"Those words yours or Bunshi's?"

"The water goddess, she—"

I cut him off. "Sprite. Sprite is what she is," I say.

"She say he ride with you."

"You expect me to trust him?"

"I don't have expectations for none of you. Ask Bunshi," he say.

The slaver give us silver for expected and unexpected costs, then bid goodbye to the manservant, who mount a horse and say he is coming with us. The Ogo, back from the river, nod with that look on his face that say what must happen will happen. Nyka and Nsaka not having that at all. They don't have to, Nsaka say and pull the tapestry off a cage to reveal a lightning madwoman, silver light flashing from inside her head all the way down to her toes. I grab Nsaka.

"Which Ipundulu she follow? How you know is the right one?"

She look at me like the look alone is an answer.

Nyka open the cage and the woman spring out, sniff the air, then dash off like a mad dog, heading east.

"Your hound head the wrong way, oh," the Tracker shout, but neither pay him any mind. They mount a chariot and ride off.

listen for lions moving through the night, hoping that they be ones that I know. **Oh they will find you, they will catch the smell of your koo gone sour,** say Jakwu. His voice been gone for so long that I almost miss it. Two slaps and a punch to my chest he get in before I scribble a nsibidi that robs spirits of flight and tongue, for here is truth—I can take his punch or his kick but is his voice that vex me the most. And vexing is all he is doing as we rest on the lone road around the Darklands. In the Uwomowomowo Valley we met as eight, head out as six, and now as we take rest from riding around the Darklands, we down to two. This is what the slaver say, that there are two ways to get to Kongor. Head west till you reach the White Lake. From there you can go around it, which will add two days to your journey, or cross, which will take a day, for the lake is narrow. When you get to the mystic forest you can go around, or through. But think good on it before you ride through the Darklands.

Let us make this quick. Two of us now left riding around the mystic forest, and one of us not among who set out from Uwomowowomowo. Two nights ago, darkness catch us on the valley trail on the way to the White Lake. I say we should continue, but the Tracker say we should rest, and his words infect the group. So rest is what we do, what we try to do, but then this Wolf Eye man ask the giant some question, which give him a warrant to chat most of the night. Two time he wake the manservant, who shout about how much he prize the precious gift of sleep. The Leopard climb up the same tree we tie the horses, change form, and start snoring quick. The Tracker set himself down beside the Ogo, who wouldn't stop talking until he doze off and even in that he still mumble to himself until he drift off into a dream where still he mumble.

The Tracker take off for a thicket of trees we pass on the way. Not long after that the Leopard's archer, whose name I don't know, follow, so I of course follow him, for if I not going to get sleep, I at least going to get knowledge. The trees dot the land in clumps all over, like groups of gossiping men who have no business with the other group. But I get close enough to hear the archer spitting two times into his hand, and doing something with the Tracker's ass as he bend over in front. The archer's breeches drop, as he slap slap

slap his cock awake then push himself straight into this Wolf Eye, who yelp into his own hand. There they go, two shadows slam and bounce, the slap slap slap of skin on skin, both trying to fuck wild yet quiet.

Because you scare them off with you secret loving, I say to myself when the archer wonder out loud where all the beasts gone. But he was not wrong, for the tall tree plains leading up to the Darklands is much loved by giraffe, zebra, and dik-dik, much packed with wildebeest, much noisy with monkeys and I was yet to see any. Nor a hog, or okapi, or any prey, or any cat after prey, or even a bird.

Consider another route, I say to the group, but the Tracker push ahead, then his new mate the Ogo follow, and so do everybody else. He is the one with the nose, but I am the one who smell it first, firewood, ash, popping fat and burning hair, which drop on us a ruthless stink. The trees are wilder here, the bush taller, and hiding the source of the smell until we stumble right upon it. Open flame flaring with each drip of fat. A whole leg cooking on a spit, a leg from a boy hanging from a tree, his right arm, his last limb remaining, tied up. Hanging beside him, a girl untouched and unspoiled. The Tracker chop the rope and free her, which should cause her to give thanks, but instead she scream. Three of them, not far from the fire, jump up.

"Zogbanu!" the manservant say.

Swamp trolls. Nobody have time to ask what they doing on the plains by a clean river, so far from the nearest swamp. Sadogo swat the first into a tree. The Leopard jump the second while the manservant thrust a sword into his neck. I grab one of their spears and hurl at the second troll's back, and he run until he fall. We don't have time to look, but look we do, at the white skin, the tusks popping all over his head, lining his brow, poking out of his mouth. Little skulls around his waist. We hear a shout like a war cry and grab horses to take off, but they chase after us, twenty, thirty in number, running near as fast as the horses can gallop. The girl is screaming that she is the glorious offering to the Zogbanu and fighting me off, so the Ogo throw her over his shoulder and run. From all around us come a rumble in the bush and it closing in. My horse is ahead and so is the manservant, until a Zogbanu jump from a tree and knock him off. The Tracker yell Bibi! but keep riding.

To the river we come and in the water is an island I know, a mound of sand, dirt, and trees. The Leopard with the archer at his back ride past me. I shout for him to make for the landing and take the island. We making distance between us and the trolls when first come a **zip zip zip** and then a shower of daggers, arrows, spears, and rocks. Something burst my left shoulder and the burn follow me all the way to the river. Nothing to do but slash, chop, and ride. Slash, chop, and ride. The Tracker ride past me and I see it again, daggers, small spears, anything iron or iron-tipped skip, dodge, or stop short of him. Some bounce off a barrier not there. The Ogo hop onto the island

and it sink a little before rising to meet the Leopard's horse. The island—Chipfalambula—push away with us right before the whole tribe of Zogbanu throng the shore. On the island waiting for us, Bunshi.

Is not until the next evening that we reach the shore that leads to Darklands. Bunshi come ashore, a surprise to me. There is no time lose, the only thing on which we agree. I can feel the voices coming for me, more than just Jakwu, and know it is because they smell the enchantment in the forest. The only way is around, I say.

"The only way is around," mock the Tracker in an old witch voice. "The only person you speaking for is you," he add. Then he ask the girl what she think and laugh when she say that she is the glorious offering to the Zogbanu. He is taking the route right through because he had no time for delay, nor cowardice. I almost call on the wind (not wind) to grab and fling him up a tree. So he turn to go and the archer turn to follow. Only the Leopard call this out as possible madness.

"This is a place of bad enchantments. You won't be able to trust anyone, not even yourself," the Leopard say.

"Who feed you that foolishness, mama or papa cat? Around the lands is three days. A man with sense would make the choice. A flighty woman? Who's to say," say the Tracker.

No woman ever take a cock the way you take it two nights ago, I don't say.

"Pick your choice, but we go round," I say.

"Make sense to me. Come, Fumeli," say the Leopard.

"Come where? What me wasting precious days for?" the archer say.

The Leopard confused. He don't see the smile on the Tracker's face, but I see it, and he see me seeing it.

"Won't be waiting for you in Kongor," the Tracker say and ride off. The archer run after him. Then the Ogo.

"Sadogo, why?" the Leopard ask, but he only grunt and follow.

The girl is holding on to me now that she is on a horse and frightened. Evening was going to outrun us, but the Leopard is still watching where the Darklands swallow them up.

"You ever travel through the Darklands?" I ask.

"A small patch to get to lower Ubangta."

"And?"

"And even then I barely make it out."

"What about the Tracker?"

"His nose travel to more places than his self."

"Not just his nose."

"What?"

"They won't reach the other side. You already know that."

"Each is a grown man."

"That a word for me, or you?"

I ride off. He don't follow. Bunshi gone too.

———

The slaver say it was two days around the Darklands, but three nights now pass and we still not even around the horn. The girl ask so many questions that I thought **Venin** was another one until I realize it was her name. But then she recall the names of all the glorious sacrifices of the Zogbanu through the ages and all of them named Venin. All were raised to be blessed offerings to the Zogbanu, so the trolls wouldn't terrorize their village, which mean her own people raise her to be food. The first night she jump off the horse, land hard on her left foot, and try to limp away, crying that she will not be cheated out of her glory. The second night, Venin was crafty. She wait until I was asleep and make a run for it, but I done tie her ankle to a rope that done tie to the horse. The third day and night I let the horse rest. By the fourth night, we run out of food and all she do is whine and bawl, and I start to picture smashing her head in and cooking it. Late in the night wild dogs start to circle, but they run when my wind (not wind) fling one up in the sky so high that he don't come back.

Near daybreak I feel a hand around my neck. Here is truth, that while the spirit can throw and punch and land a blow, and while they can put on force, they can't hold it for long. The grip squeeze tight, then vanish like dust blowing away.

Give me the girl, he say.

Other voices come to me, including one that say I deceive his mistress, then him, and where is my heart, girl, where is my heart? But Jakwu is the one that torment me the most, so much that I learn his name. Sometimes I find myself trying to understand him, but all I grasp is that what was a crucial moment for him, his death, a murder by a woman's hands, was just another notch on an arm full of scars for me. Jakwu, the prized warrior tactician of the South King, who once honor his noble warrior with a statue of his likeness in gold. Jakwu, who everybody long know was raping and killing girls but it did not affect his warring skill, and those girls hail from Weme Witu. Maybe he remember me because I did go out of my way to make his killing memorable.

Give me the girl, he say.

"I wouldn't give you my morning piss," I say to the wind. The girl is still asleep after I rustle up enough insects to roast and feed her.

I know what you want. What you really want. I alone know.

"Yes? And how you know that?"

Stupid bitch, I live in your head.

Lie, lie, he lie, I tell myself. He is the father of deceit, after all not a single woman I find in his house come there by their own will. I've been living with his yapping for years and am not about to take his words to mind, much less to heart, now. But he's been worse of late, even with me writing nsibidi to shut him up. He is crowding me and know it. He might even know why. **You know it too,** say the voice that sound like me. That voice and Jakwu trading harsh words with each other day and night, and about to

drive me mad. I pull myself out of drowsiness and
stand, telling myself to not let them clutter. Don't let
them clutter your mind. I was expecting a legion, but
the only one bothering me is Jakwu.

He live in your head too, Jakwu say.

The "he" that I should be thinking about is this
boy, and the vampires he travel with. That though he
will serve no use as King, he will be excellent as bait.
Bait? the voice ask. **What it say about you that all
he be is a little piece of fish set to catch a shark?**
I snarl back, saying that given that all kings, queens,
and nobles ever did to me was eat me whole, then
shit me out, I have no problem with treating this
child as just a thing with little use. Besides, I live long
enough to see Moki the Wicked, Liongo the Good,
Paki the Unlucky, Aduware the Defeated, Netu the
Vengeful, and Dara the whatever, and in all regimes
those fat was still getting fatter and those starving
still starve.

I come to realize that Bunshi abhor violence against
man. Oh she abhor violence that man commit too,
why would she not? But for a divine-born being she
still accept that this is province of men, something
to skip, avoid, or endure. That wickedness is part of
maleness whether King or Aesi and is not that he have
the right to it so much as we don't have the right to
fight it. Or avenge it. Or maybe the silly black bitch
don't even think that deep. But even when she agree
to me going after the Aesi as a boy, it was never to
set right the wrong he do, but to stop his influence

on court. His influence on other man. Well fuck the gods, for if a man leave me with suffering I can leave him with violence. And maybe there is something to restoring the line of kings, other than just one king taking power from another because power is there to take. I am a woman of the world and in the world, so why wouldn't I want justice, or the order that men keep confusing with justice? But justice don't consume you. Helping one power take another power is not what keep my days moving slow but my years moving quick. **And all you do is keep him in your head glutting on him until you wet.**

Jakwu.

Some of we live here because you trap us, but him you invite. Also Jakwu.

"If I was going to trap a man, I would pick one that delight me," I say.

You going tell me that none of this is delight? Look at you, fooling you. All consumed with raging fire, and yet all you do is go to sleep in a mountain house and let monkey fuck you.

"No monkey fuck me."

That what they tell you? You deep in sleep for moons.

He stun me, so hard it might as well he used a brick to slam in my face. Jakwu know what he do, know how much doubt can shake a woman, when she cannot account for own body. I see what he doing, he is trying to strip away all I know, leaving only what I believe, an easier thing for him to snatch.

**Even Mistress Vengeance can't account for when
she sleep.**

I take too long before I say, "Nor you." He laugh
loud and long.

"Whatever truth there, your tongue don't know it,"
I say.

Give me the girl.

"Shut up."

Give me the girl.

"Shut up!"

And so we go until morning come and my shouting finally wake the girl.

We get to Kongor by night, after six days going
around the forest and one more day to get to the
riverside. Take the bend around the Darklands and
you arrive at the narrowest point in the river and the
shortest ferry from coastline to island, which is what
the people call Kongor even though the city get cut
off for only four moons in the rain season. This river
is something to see, for I remember when water was
the enemy of Kongor. Never a place for much rain,
certainly no flood, and not much of a river. First the
ferryman charge us more because of the horse. Then
he add another charge for the time of night, saying
he risking never seeing his children again for landing
this late at the rough and illegal Gallunkobe/Matyube
port. We not going there, I say, but he ignore me. I
already resolve that we will either take this raft all

the way up to that quarter and then take the border roads to where we were going, or force him to let us off at the Nimbe canal. But before I can cuss, we land ashore and he push off. Maybe he see the scowl on my face in the dark, for the short trip across must mean that he leave us at bank of the Tarobe quarter. Illegal is right, I can't imagine the good people of Tarobe being comfortable with some no name raft depositing any sort of person in their midst, even under night cover. I try not to think of it, how many years pass since I last see Kongor. Tens of tens.

Bunshi and the slaver give instructions to head east along the border road, take the second road right, then left and left again to get to this master's house, a man in the Nyembe merchant quarter. This man she long know to be southern griot, but now he deny it with such ire that she doubt herself. Along the way to his house, I keep looking across to Tarobe quarter and not recognizing what I see. Why would any place hold on to its looks over so many years, is a question I didn't need to ask. But too many things striking me as uncanny. Torchlights few and far between in a quarter that used to be so bright you would confuse night with day. At one point I leave the border road to go south and almost ride into the river. But it is not the river, not really, it is still Tarobe, an entire street with houses third-way, halfway, and full-way under- water. We so tired when we get to the man's house that I barely bid him good night or check where to lay my head before I fall asleep.

No sign of the Ogo, the Leopard, the archer, or the Tracker. It supposed to take only one day through the Darklands, two at the most, if nothing rumored about this place was true. But with the seven nights before I land in Kongor and the three nights since, ten days done gone and none of the four Bunshi hire yet to appear. No Bunshi either, not because she don't know the way, but that she know I will declare them and this mission dead. From the lies she tell the men, to this first stop in Kongor to pick up clues that any informant could find, Bunshi already blighting a mission she think is pure and righteous. Her desperation to hide that they looking for the future King lead her to wasting people's time and killing off four men. And yet I still find myself lingering in Kongor, an itch telling me that this place will yet have use.

Kongor. Once in this place I was a runaway, then a whore, then a gift. One I remember more than the others. The shape of the land now smaller, and I never once see so much water. There are places I supposed to know, names to remember if not faces, but nothing will come back to me, because of this Aesi. As for this house. I wake up in a room hiding from morning light, the girl snuggling up to me like a pet, even though she have her own bed. So many tall statues in the rooms that I imagine Venin waking up screaming that a chamber full of men set to take her. I leave the bed and step on a dirt floor somebody pound down to a shine. A love for tapestries this man have, a love that come from going beyond the sand sea and liking all he see. They seem to be in talks with one another, these red and brown tapestries running from ceiling to floor, with patterns of lions, cobras, beasts unknown, and lovers. Arch windows big as doors. Archways instead of doors. From the window I see the street creeping up then snaking around, also that my window was on a floor six floors up, with open shutters. Other windows sport platforms with hanging plants. I am at the window wondering who would wake up first, the girl in my bed or the street. As for the man, there he is in some sort of cookroom, even though I don't see no cook. She soon come to start the coffee, he say, though I didn't ask for it. I really want to ask what his use is to Bunshi, but figure one should at first be polite.

"People call me Sogolon."

"What you call yourself?" he say.

"Clever."

"One of the nicer things somebody me call this quartermoon. Nine days ago it was old, blaspheming, cocksucking man whore, so the sun is definitely shining on me today."

My laughter surprise me.

"Bunshi tell me much about you," he say.

"Uncanny, for she tell me nothing about you."

"Nothing to tell. I am a simple man given to the cause. Also an old man with nothing much to do and not much living left to do it. I figure we be the same age?"

"You figure wrong."

"Oh. What bring you to the cause?"

"Money."

Here he remember that there is another room to build to the rear of the house so he need to get on with building it, meaning get the strapping young men, so proud of their muscles, to build it.

"Before you go. Rain season still many moons away. So what happen to Tarobe quarter?"

"Tarobe? What you mean?" he ask.

"I nearly drown my horse last night just heading south. Some houses the river claim full."

With the look on his face, I might as well be talking about the sand sea.

"Why go south to Tarobe, when it is north?"

"North?"

"That I say. If you was riding south, that was the slave and servant quarter."

"Gallunkobe? How? When?"

"Tarobe being north and Gallunkobe being south? Is so I born and come see it."

"This place about to drive me mad."

"I don't—"

"Is not a question."

"I . . . I mean I don't trouble my head with what come to pass, but there was great and terrible rains many years ago, either before or right as I born, that flood out Tarobe so bad that one-third of the quarter drown. The rest move north."

"To the one people they could drive out easy."

I laugh. He nod and leave me.

My memory of Kongor is barely anything, but it is enough to know that in nearly every way I walk through a different city. Yes, some building and dwelling look as they always do, but everything else is now set to disturb me. I remember stick fights and boys wearing nothing but the attitude of a warrior and showman. And I remember some women wearing skirts that stop below the breast, never above it. So when I walk through the Nyembe quarter and see women covering up not just breast, but arms, legs, fingers, hair, sometimes even face, I keep thinking I trip and land in another place. I walk down roads where I know the smell, but not the look, paths where the color come back but not the sounds. Maybe because this place never think me somebody to claim. I ask an old man going nowhere what happen to Kongor. First he look at me confused, after all Kongor was always like this.

"I mean the flood," I say.

"Which one?"

"The one that move Tarobe."

"Ah. Ah. Barely a boy when that shit come to pass. Before the flood was the drought, understand. After nine moons, people demand that the elders beg and sacrifice to the gods—well, they do more than demand. They drag three visiting elders out in the street and beat them until they start to work cloud magic. One of them warn the people that all they can do is start the rain. Only the gods decide what to do next. But hear this now, the begging work, but just as they warn it work too good, for rain wouldn't stop for a moon. The biggest flood, and quick too, so big that it swallow most of Tarobe and kill plenty from the quarter. Here is truth—nobody grieve over that loss. Anyway, when the flood recede half of Tarobe remain underwater. They move north and didn't care who they root up to do it."

"But what happen to Kongor?"

"How you mean? I just tell you. . . . Oh. Oh, that. Me old enough to remember before that too. Well after the great flood Kongor start to fear the gods, you understand? Fear of punishment for not being strict against sin, so the whole place turn pious, even the whores wear veil now. And the littlest thing can bring some quick, severe justice, oh. Severe justice."

I don't ask him why Seven Wings mercenaries is everywhere amassing, for it can't just be because they answering roll call at the Tower of the Black Sparrowhawk.

Bunshi show herself two times more. The first was before me and Venin come. Spook the shit out of me, the master of his house say, but he quiet when I ask why he would get spook by who he worship. The word make him frown, **worship,** and it make me remember that praise is not the same as fear. Me performing my ablutions in the bath when the window frame melt like oil and the oil mold into her, he say. He didn't stop screaming until she wrap her fingers around his mouth. What is the news? Where are they?

she demand from him and then scream when he say he don't know.

"I mean, since she is the divine one, isn't she the one who supposed to know? The day after you two come she appear again," he say.

"She look any better when you tell her I was here?"

"No. I tell her that you and the girl sleep upstairs, but she leave as soon as she come."

"Uncanny."

"You talk like there is a canny."

"How you so sharp, old man? I thought you was down for the cause."

"The cause have my head, it might even have my eyes. But my heart?" he say.

"Say more."

"This grand peace is walking on a crocodile's back, Sogolon. All you see is men of the Black Sparrowhawk, but they not the only ones who assemble. Man from Juba getting word—unofficial of course—to find the sword they long put away and the shield they long retire. Seven Wings assemble in Malakal, even Mitu, and soldiers long on leave getting called back to barracks. I can't speak for this King, but when his father used to gather mercenary it was only for one thing."

"Something that nobody want."

"We not the correct nobody. Ambassadors from Weme Witu coming in two quartermoons. To settle disputes, they say."

"What they disputing?"

"Better question is will it get settle. You can guess my answer."

"Kwash Netu should have never given spoils of war he didn't lose."

"Spoils? What? Kalindar and Wakadishu? Wakadishu is an independent nation and Kalindar was never spoils."

"Look like that news never reach the South. I hear the Marabangan tongue there more than once."

"He didn't give the South Kalindar. No treaty ever say so. He give them free passage and a trade agreement, gold for salt. The South take it to mean they have land title and start to move in like a soft invasion."

"And how the people of Kalindar take to that?"

"Before or after they start burning down things South man build?"

He leave me to the food somebody cook. I stop asking for the mistress or the woman he claim come to cook and clean. It become a joke the next three nights between me and he, whether that water sprite will show and will she come as a trickle through the window, a pool under the door, or a lump in the shit bucket. So when she do show on the fourth night, as Bunshi always do, trickling down the window to pool at the sill, I don't bother to explain why I cackle. In the quick Venin is annoyed with her, as Bunshi is with she.

"How go your fellowship now?" I ask.

"Is not yet two quartermoons," she say.

"Who marking your time, Bunshi? Time running

fast. Days going faster than that. You and Mistress King Sister need another tack."

"They may still show."

"When? It looking like anytime is just in time for you. If I did know I was going to be so free, I would have tell the ferryman to take me to Juba."

"We need the Tracker."

"What you need is another plan, water sprite. This mission, if we going call it such, on the edge of a knife."

"We need them."

"Him or them? And which him, the Leopard?"

"The wolf."

"The Wolf Eye? What he call himself, Tracker? Which mother name their son Tracker? What his brother name, Guard? The man sound like he sit down on a cactus and it still there."

"He have a nose."

"Everybody have a nose, sprite."

"Nobody have his nose. When he pick up a smell of a man or beast he can follow the source."

"So he really is the wolf."

"You don't understand. He can follow it across the land no matter how far, across the sea, even the sand sea. And he can follow it from a quartermoon to a year. He get ahold of the boy's smell, all left for him to do is point. The only reason I approach the Leopard is to approach him."

"Crafty. The water sprite is crafty. Well, the rest of us who don't have a nose will have to use our head."

"That is just one of his gifts," she say.

"What a man this is. He demigod or sorcerer? Or just another man deceiving you?"

"You won't get to where you need to go without him."

"His gift must be wings. He is a bird?"

"You think this is a joke."

"I don't say nothing."

"I never say you say it."

"All this fuss over replacing one head with another head, when the present one wicked enough? No, water sprite, nothing about it funny. I must be laughing at something else."

"Purging of women all by just calling them witch funny to you?"

"I never say anything about—"

"Nine hundred ninety and six under Kwash Moki. Six hundred and two under Liongo the so-called Good."

"Listen here—"

"Five hundred under Aduware. Three hundred seventy and six under Kwash Netu. All of them women who somebody call witch. Sometimes just once. So maybe it is funny. Maybe everything that happen under the rule of the Spider King is funny. Everything. Maybe the Aesi set loose to do this King's bidding is funny. Hark, I just had a funny thought. The killing of a lion cub. Somebody's son, spear right through the heart. Funny, no?"

"You piece of dog shit."

"A spear is a funny weapon. Just a long, long stick—"

"Don't."

"But watch it pierce right through to a little boy's heart."

"I swear."

"No no no! Let us take things and make joke. Surely when your own son died in front of you because of that fucking chancellor in service to that fucking King, you laugh instead of weep?"

"Bunshi."

"And since every king is the same, it doesn't matter then. Different king, same dead boy."

Maybe the wind (not wind) scream, or maybe me. Maybe it is just force as the Nnimnim woman say, but it come down in the room like a tremor, shake the walls, fling the bed, the stools, the jugs, the basin, the water all up in the air to smash into each other, then suck itself into Bunshi, blow her up like a sheep stomach, and explode her. All around the room, splats and splotches of black, dripping from the ceiling, rolling along the floor, speckling the tapestry, turning me and the bawling Venin into leopards with all these spots. I grab the girl to leave, only to see a stream of black run around the seam of the door and seal it tight, no matter how hard I pull. Venin bawl again. I turn around to see droplets, drips, and puddles run into each other, rising into one pole. The pole bend and twist, then shoot shards at me that

zip past my neck and pin me to the door. I make the
mistake of a gasp but couldn't shut my mouth before
Bunshi shoot herself into my throat, skip where food
go to invade where I breathe. I begin to choke, lose
my breathing, she is drowning me, she will kill me
right here. Venin scream three times before she stop.
I still choking, still growing weak, still falling on my
knees before Bunshi pull herself out of me. Every spot
of black rush from all the corners of the room to form
her. Then she jump out the window.

Another quartermoon later and I could kill her for
what she say, I really could. I sit in the room and
boil. Without thinking I raise a fruit and a jug in the
air and blast them apart. But then I stop the blast to
a still, and watch the parts suspended, walking in the
middle of the scatter. This is what I have done—will
do to his head. What I have done—will do to her
body. What I will do to the whole world. Then I sleep
off my temper and wake up empty and sore. **Good
riddance to she,** say the voice that sound like me.
I going take a knife and enlarge your cunt, say
the voice that don't. I mock it, saying, You have all
sorts of designs for inside me, yet I am one hundred
and seventy years older than what usually bewitch
you. When a girl ten and three too old for your spear,
maybe all you have is a thimble. Is that why, Jakwu?
Why everything that come out of your mouth just
scream little penis? Jakwu have no words for my voice

being as savage as his, so he back away, at least for a few days.

A few days when there is nothing to do but sit stunned by the quiet. Or pass sharp words with the master of this house, who seem content that the only name I have for him is "You." A word come to me one morning, to just leave as you be, with your sack and your revenge hunger, and take the river to as close to far north as you can get, the Forest Lands or Ku. And from there to as close to Fasisi as you can get. Then the city, then the royal enclosure, then him. Then wait eight years to either torture one of the Sangomin or watch for where pigeons fly. But these thoughts I think before. I not bringing anything new to them and can already smell them going stale. The truth is that the sprite leave words that stain me. I will not call it shame. That I pass life so close to crowns and kings and still leave thinking they have no bearing on how a woman in her house live or how a man die, when I, Sogolon, should be the one woman who know different. Maybe if there was the true line of kings I wouldn't have the death of my son turning fresh every day. I don't want to think about loss.

Instead I am in the great hall of records. Four quartermoons come to pass and those men not coming. I don't see Bunshi for days now, but I can imagine her in whatever window frame she hiding in, telling herself that they will come soon, because they have to. Meanwhile news arrive from carrier pigeon that they **closing in on the Ipundulu.** Nsaka, I assume, though no name on the note. They convinced that this Ipundulu is the one we looking for even though it sound like he move alone, and we looking for one with company. "They" meaning him, for he is the one convinced. She is just the one convinced in the snake.

The grand egg in the center of Nimbe quarter, this great hall of records didn't just keep account of Kongor, but all of the North. Rumor is that it also hold a secret vault of verse from the southern griots, but either it is in a corner that no person living ever see or it is as true as Yumboes the size of a man. This is a place where people seldom go, run by a man who look to me like he prefer it that way.

"You practice that scowl in a looking glass?" I ask.

"What?"

"Nothing."

"You want something other than to bother an old man?"

I am about to answer but then the hall distract me. Great indeed, this place, five tall floors, each floor taller than a three-story house, and stacked with so many scrolls, books, satchels, and loose paper that the recordkeeper must did dispense with order a long time ago. Impossible as it might look, something is telling me that he do all this stacking himself, or maybe he start stacking when he was but a boy and never stopped. Sometimes a scroll slip away, fall, flap like wings, and land somewhere else, while on some shelves the books let slip out whispers on what they contain.

"Shut it, little whores," the old man say and they go quiet in the quick.

First I think he has a hunchback, but he pull himself out of the book on his table long enough to look at me again. White scarf around a head that is mostly cheekbones and chin, white brows and beard. Eyes looking river blind but here he is over a book.

"Woman, what you want?"

"What you know of blood drinkers?"

"You asking me if I know any myself?"

"I asking what is written."

"You want me to tell you so that you don't read it yourself?"

"Fuck the gods, is every old man a crabby bitch in Kongor?"

He look at me like he is truly looking for an answer to the question but it confound him. Is not his fault that he long forget how to talk with people.

"Your reading travels ever come across writing on the lightning bird?" I ask.

His face wake up when I call his reading travels. I am somebody he would engage after all. He stroke his chin and take a quick sweep of the space.

"He known by any other name?"

"Chi . . . Chi . . . I can't remember—"

"Chimungu. Also, the Inyoni Yezulu. You asking about creatures who roam a realm most people don't know even though it right beside them, breathing the same air. Some of we call them creatures of the high noon. Why? Because is only when the sun highest in the sky that some people know to lock their door, or if they don't have door, hunch into a corner and pray. By people I mean the river tribes who don't read or write so they have no record. But some Chimungu not sated by river folk. And just as many prefer to make their moves at night. Come with me."

We turn down an aisle where the books start to whisper again until he shush them.

"Some of these parchments are older than the children of the gods. Word is divine wish, they say. Word is invisible to all but the gods. So when woman or man write words, they dare to look at the divine. Oh, what power. But this is so new that it is not yet book, just loose pages and a half-done scroll. Hark, on some of the leaves you can still smell the ink. Learn this, some of the ink is not ink but the creature own blood— don't ask me how that come to pass. Not every leaf come from the same scribe either."

"How come you by all of this?"

"How? The way I always do. Some I seek, some seek me. A man on a tired horse leave it twelve moons ago, saying to keep it secret and safe."

A leaf float on top. Then another, then one more.

"They fighting," he say. "Fighting over which account get read first." He go off, return holding a candleholder with four alight.

"You are my first visitor in seven moons," he say.

The pages won't stop spreading and unrolling themselves.

"New knowledge. They scared of turning into an archive nobody but an old man read. I mean, look around you. Look at the wisdom banished to a dark corner," he say pointing to the walls. But I don't recognize the writing. The old man don't have to ask.

"This is a journal from somebody who claim people call her the Nun."

"For real?"

"That is what I reading in the pages. You going to ask more questions or listen? She leave her children, and her husband . . . no the husband died . . . killed. Yes killed. 'He' enchant her, but didn't turn her or kill her, he want her to remember who kill her husband. He catch her unawares when she was grinding yam in the backyard. This she remember: him taking her out of the trance long enough to see what he doing to her, then bewitching her again so she can't do nothing about it."

"How long ago was this?"

"Likely from you was a girl. He enchant me because he was enchanting, it read. Why everybody feel they have to be clever?"

"Old man."

"Sorry. But husband and children? Then how she can be a nun?"

"Old man."

"Sorry. He enchant her, then he rape her, then kill her husband while she watch. Then he make thunderstorm in her bedroom and fly away. Baby and other children with grandmother. She tell them that they can't come back. Go off near the sand sea until her womb too heavy. Uncanny, I never hear of an Ipundulu carrying living seed."

"Ipundulu he name, not zombi," I say.

"Yes. She in Malakal next—"

"What happen to the baby?"

"Stillborn or she kill it. Oh. Oh my. Trust the gods," he say in a hush.

"Why?"

"What?"

"Continue."

"Oh. Yes. I—"

"This narrative seem to be surprising you, old man. You never read it?"

"Never seemed interesting, an account from a wo—"

"Nun?"

"Oh. Yes. Anyway, she go to Malakal. She gather weapons, things that can kill it. Spear and stakes made from assegai wood. Poison milk, for it love woman milk as much as blood. That's why he didn't kill her, for she was still nursing a child. She track him down to one of the salt routes going out of Malakal. Here she say that is not the same Ipundulu who kill her husband. There might be five or six—there used to be more, but who know how many?"

"More. I looking mention of one."

"Not this one. She wound him with an assegai spear then burn him alive."

He skip two pages.

"This one, she follow back to his witch in the hills behind the Purple City. It just say he dead. But another one, he keep escaping, just like that, just as soon as she get information he vanish. Vanish leaving sucked-out bodies, usually the entire family with one he leave as the lightning slave. Different, she keep saying this one different. A lightning slave lead her to the place he was hunting. But he not alone. Eloko is with him, three of them, grass demons, each with two bones sharpened like a dagger. And more, like the spirit vampire, Obayifo, but he and the Ipundulu turn enemy and part ways. Ipundulu use little children. Obayifo eat them. The entry is three years after her husband murdered."

"She readying herself."

"Maybe. Nothing in here other than she tracking them. Gathering intelligence, maybe she get news from others. Here it say she talk to those who people stop listening to, and people who others think mad. You say you hunting Ipundulu?"

"I never say I hunting nobody."

"No, you was just looking for a nighttime story to tell the children and that dagger under your leather is for peeling grapes," he say and scoff. "Here somebody just listing attacks and victims. She couldn't be in all these place at once. Hark, that look like the last thing she write. The rest here is from somebody else, maybe several people. This one say he hear that they used to call her the Nun because she only dress in green. She track them down to the border of the sand sea. If another is writing this, then it must mean that she . . . that she . . ."

"Find her a spot on the ancestors' tree."

"Brave woman."

"She wasn't supposed to be. No woman supposed to be brave if they don't want to."

He look at me and nod. The next few pages pass by in silence.

"Wait, these leaves new for I can still smell the ink. The Blood Swamp—three women, sisters. Luala Luala—family near banks with Nyangatom. Seven days later, Enchantment Hills, then Nigiki—a girl and a boy. . . . In a quartermoon, Dolingo—man, wife, and seven children. . . . Next page, five days later, the Mitu-Kongor Road—hunting party looking for them. Next page is a moon later. . . . Hmmm."

"Hmmm what?"

"At the top is the Darklands, not a killing, but a witness sailing the White Lake say he see a big black beast with bat wings flying over to some people already on shore. They didn't anchor. Then a report from Kongor, then this part, Mitu-Kongor Road—family running a roadside inn—"

"Skip the bodies."

"Mitu-Kongor Road again, then eight days later, Dolingo. A quartermoon later, Nigiki, Luala Luala, Blood Swamp."

"The same places in reverse, give or take a place.

They following a pattern. Since when vampire have such discipline?"

"You asking me? That not even the strangest thing. Mitu-Kongor Road, then eight days later, Dolingo? New page, another entry over half year later, Dolingo again, then five days later, the same road? From Dolingo to Mitu is almost three moons, and that is by horse. Maybe a moon and a half by river. How they getting to these places so quick?"

"She ever mention Malakal?"

"Up here, yes."

"I going guess that either before or after it is the east coast."

"Yes, yes, right here."

"That black bitch."

"Who?"

"Somebody from the river who should stay there."

That water sprite must did know. Have to, and just waiting on me to discover it myself. Ipundulu and his band of blood drinkers are using the doors.

"How many names listed before a repeat?" I ask him.

"Ten and nine," he say.

"I need a list in a tongue I can read."

"Hold, there is more, on this new leaf. Somewhere between Mitu and Dolingo. They don't say for sure. They pick up a boy."

"What? What else it say? What else?"

"Nothing, just that it is a boy. They traveling with

a boy. Here is what they say. The boy come to a door with all sort of crying, and they let him in."

"That entry, where from?"

"The Enchantment Hi— Hills of Enchantment."

"You say before this was a new book."

"Yeah, not even here a year, but I can confirm with the records."

"I need news newer than this, old man."

"Is bookkeeper me name. If it not written then I don't know."

"Or you don't care?"

"It not real until it on the page."

"It too late by the time it get to the page."

"You judging me? You think this is some archive?"

"This is a tomb. By the time we read what is in your walls, it no longer have no use."

"You telling me that my hall don't serve no use? If it wasn't for these dead words some people would never know who they be. You out here thinking you doing what? Fixing a wrong? You think your wrong is the first? If all of your kind did read, then maybe the last wrong would stay last and you wouldn't be here insulting books that do nothing but hold truth you can't keep. Get out!"

"That is not what I say."

"You just call my hall a tomb!"

"All I want—"

"And yet you still want something on top of your insult. Which of the nine world shit you out?"

I don't want to fight this man. So I tell him that all I want is news so new that he will have to write it himself. All these years, all these books, all of it the words of others. What about your voice, I ask him. Your book? He see through my words but they work anyway.

"Only one way to hear tidings before they tide," he say and disappear down a dark corridor. Many things shift, slip, fall, and crash in the dark before he return with a talking drum.

"The strings too loose. When I squeeze the body under my arm the note might not be high enough. I can't swear for the pitch. You understand me? Tapping the high note four times mean 'tell me what you know.' Ease the string and let one beat hum low, then tighten in the middle of the same beat, and it say, 'the strange people' and 'people of the blood.' But if the string come lose in the middle of the hum that all I telling them is that the 'moon is full and beautiful.' Alas the drum is many tones just as your tongue is many tones. Maybe who hear it will know what I asking and reply," he say, then take the stairs far back and go to the roof.

Night lose herself to day when he come knocking on my door. I did tell that I would come back, but the freshness of the tidings give him plenty vigor. He still pounding into air when I open the door.

"The Hills of Enchantment! Tidings come that they last seen in the hills."

"When?"

"Little over a moon. So if one moon ago they set upon the hills, where next they going to be?"

"Nigiki," I say. "No door waiting nearby so they might still be in the south. Maybe they stop in Wakadishu."

"Something still too uncanny," he say.

"These accounts, they mention Ipundulu and others, and this boy. But who they don't mention is his witch. Ipundulu still answer to his witch. She command him as much as she can, he do her bidding, as much as he wants, and she the one who direct him to fresh blood. But none of this mention a witch. Which mean you not looking for Ipundulu at all, woman. You looking for a masterless bird. An Ishologu."

"That sound bad."

"Praise the gods, it worse than worse. At least an Ipundulu under some control. Ishologu under nobody, so he just acting out of pure bloodlust. No teacher, no master, no method, no nothing but chaos."

TWENTY-THREE

Only Kongor put the dead in urns big enough for a living woman to hide in with her child. Maybe they offering the dead to the gods as nourishment in a vessel meant for storing water or oil, but nobody is around to ask. There is only the dead. Basu Fumanguru, his wife and children murdered, embalmed and left alone in his house. This I know, that after the Kongori place the dead in these large jars, they bury them. They do it with some care. But nobody come for this family, nobody want to touch them, nobody bury them. Judging from the overgrowth of thornbush all around the house, nobody come to the house since.

I don't need to be here. The Tracker might smell something if he was here, but all I finding is the dead. The welcome room beside the grain keep is where they sit, for these bodies for certain don't lie. The sun gone some time ago, but last light is yet to leave. This room hold nothing but the urns, three of them as tall as my chest, one below my waist. I think it then make it, the wind (not wind) shifting the lids off and placing them down gently. Big man Fumanguru get the biggest urn. No face and the skull smashed in. They dress him in his elder robes and leave the staff leaning behind him, try to give him back dignity in the sitting pose. But only one leg is a leg, the other is wood and cloth. The second urn have smells both rotten and sweet, something for the Tracker to figure out. But the perfume and the blue linen tell me that this is the wife. She look like those bodies in the north that they preserve by drying out the water. But the top of her body is facing north while below the waist turn to south. In the third urn, what remain of two children, and the fourth urn holding one. Three children here mean three they didn't find. Nothing left for me to see, so I leave.

They who kill the family is not they who have the boy, but Bunshi have us all come to Kongor so that the Tracker can find him with his magic nose. Except I all but sure where this boy is, and where he will be. But Bunshi not around to hear and the Tracker not around to smell and I in no mood to tell. She keep herself scarce ever since she try to drown me, which suit me well, for if I knew a way to kill her that night I would. For all this talk about the Wolf Eye, for all the needing of these men, none of them spend over one hundred years killing man just like them. None of them can stand up to the Aesi she keep stopping me from killing. Her voice keep barging in my head, telling me that if I kill him, he will only come back. But I know what she don't, or won't admit, which is that this empire have no future in the King Sister. **You could leave,** say the voice that sound like me. Go right now and head them off. Maybe not in time for Wakadishu, but perhaps for the Blood Swamp, or Dolingo. There. Decided. Find them some way, somehow with some other hound. Find the boy, kill the vampire, put the boy to the only use he have left. There. Decided.

I know what you planning, Jakwu say, as usual picking the perfect time to invade my head.

"This little fool keep thinking he know me," I say.

This whore keep forgetting I live in her head, he say.

"Invade but you still can't conquer."

Give me the girl.

"I wouldn't give you the shit I leave on the ground."

Who you fooling, woman? You think you is master and she is apprentice. She more dull than a rock and have less of a mind. Even she know that she is nothing but blank flesh for use.

"And you already have a plan for how to use her."

I know the mission you going on. I even know that you waiting on some man or some beast that will never come. If where you heading call for a fight, that girl is no use to you. Better for she and you that you leave her in Kongor. Or sell to the slaver. Or give her to me.

"As bad as the other choices be, both still better than putting any part of you inside that girl."

You need a spear. You need sword. You need a skilled warrior that can wield both.

"So I should give her body to a man who used to take women's bodies, for what now? So you can stab me in the back as soon as you can? I only look like I plop out of cow koo."

Warm wishes to you then, he say and leave. It stun me that he quit just so, and I steel myself, waiting for a punch or slap. But nothing come. He think it is enough to leave me with thoughts I don't want to think. That whether I choose to go after the Ipundulu or the Aesi, this girl will not be a help, but a hindrance, a danger even. Yet I can't bring myself to set her loose, right into the arms of another man waiting to devour her.

I leave Tarobe quarter and take the border road east. The housemaster is fussing over more pots than usual, all but beckoning me to ask who he preparing feast for.

"No feast, just more mouths to feed. They find your Tracker. And your giant. And two more."

"You tell the Leopard not to follow me?" say the Tracker, alive and unspoiled.

"I tell him you won't reach the other side, but look at you—alive and unspoiled. Trust the gods."

The Tracker right now looking like he don't trust the room. I don't blame him, for it is dim and musty, and can't be much peace for his nose. The fowl-shit green not much peace for his eyes either. In Kongor it seem the crabby old men with no women keep together. At least they share something. That is how the master of this house get word that some truly strange men appear in a dim room in the hall of records. A room all but sealed off by a wall of books not touched in one hundred years. This master must did tell somebody that he was expecting exactly such strange men.

Here is truth: It is only now, lying in bed and not able to move far, that I finally see him. Certain woman would even call the Tracker handsome, that certain woman being a younger me. Not like the Leopard—that cat is a walking reason to always stay naked and ready. The thought make me chuckle, which make the Tracker frown, which bring me back to him and his hair cut down close to scalp to show the shape of his head and his skin, darker than pure coffee. He look more Jubite than Ku, no scars except for healed wounds, traces of kaolin on his neck that he never learn to use as a child. Thick dark lips revealing that he still have all his teeth to gnash. I try to smile, which make him scowl. He hate that the world did move on without him. The Tracker hate it so much that even this sunset—another day leaving—is making him angry. Making him say things like, "Those gods told you to forget us after only one night?"

"You leave your whole mind back in the forest," I say.

"How one night take my whole mind?" he ask.

"Be glad it didn't take something else."

"Meaning what, woman? Soon as I pick up a scent at Fumanguru's house we can leave before this quartermoon is out."

"Ay, we doing this again."

"Don't tell me what I doing, woman."

"You lost in that forest twenty and eight days, Tracker."

"What?"

"A whole moon come and go since you go into that bush."

He do it again, slump back down on the rugs and linen like somebody shove him. You can see it on his face, him staggering to grasp what he hear more than once, his lips quivering, his eye twitching, him turning away from me, for he must know that all this anguish is playing out on his face.

"Yes, a whole moon," I say.

"Is not my first time in the Darklands. Time never stopped then."

"Who say it stop?"

"You tire me," he say.

Outside, Seven Wings gather in the street to march, three and four to a group, to the Tower of the Black Sparrowhawk. This is the first time I am seeing some on horseback, white horses and black with red reins, men in black veils and black robes under chain mail and armor. I don't hear the Tracker until he is right beside me.

"Coming from all corners of the North and some

from the South border. The border men wear a red
scarf on the left arm. Do you see them?" I ask.

"This is whose army?" he ask.

"Mercenaries."

"Who? I spend so little time in Kongor."

"Seven Wings. Black garments on the outer, white on
the inner, like their symbol, the Black Sparrowhawk."

"What Kongor need mercenaries for? Young girls
dancing too wild in Gallunkobe?"

I laugh. "Tell me something," I say. "The forest
don't lead into this city. It don't even lead to Mitu. So
how you get here?"

"There are doors, and there are doors, woman."

"Yes. I too know these doors."

"Old people always seem to know everything. What
kind of door turn one night's ride into just one step?"

"Ten and nine doors. I don't know if they have a
name. Ten and nine door counted so far. A door that
cut a trip to the Blood Swamp down to one step."

"Madness. Just fucking madness."

"Yet look at you, right now looking at me. How
long you apprentice under a Sangoma?"

"I not no apprentice."

"You have training. And if not training then some
form of enchantment to open a door."

"I didn't open any door in the Darklands."

"A door can't open itself. Like I say, if not training then some sort of Sangoma enchantment. When
Bunshi said you have gifts, this must be what she

mean. Must be why she never seem worried about losing time, no matter how long you gone. Why, when you can eat time in just one step? Only people I see with that gift are divine born and Sangomin."

"I used to live with one. Me and the Leopard. Well, visit."

"Don't need to stay long to learn necromancy."

"You seem to be confusing her with a witch. You the one who slice up babies. We used to save mingi children."

"No, you used to recruit for a Sangomin child army. And I not a witch."

"Is you they call the Moon Witch, not me. So if I— if we really been gone for a whole moon, what did you and the water goddess find about the child? About Fumanguru? Nothing? Nothing in the whole moon."

I just look at him.

"You go by his house?" he ask.

"The house was waiting on your skills, not mine."

"Hmph. Maybe your skills don't call for much mind work."

"I must be a blunt instrument," I say.

"Well, no wonder I still think only a day pass if after twenty and eight we not any closer to Fumanguru's boy. Or maybe nobody is earnest about finding him except Bunshi."

"See to your cat and giant," I say. "And your—and the archer."

The Ogo is more blank than when last I see him, and the Leopard is more snarly than the Wolf Eye.

Neither strong enough to stand for long, much less walk. Both talk about a man monkey in the bush, working up to a mania before they fall asleep again. I pass the giant's room later in the day. The Tracker is in there with him, sitting on the floor, while the giant is punching his palms in his iron gloves and setting off sparks.

"I itch to kill," he say.

"That might happen soon."

"When do we go back to the Darklands?"

"When? Never."

At least the Ogo could punch and shake the floor. The Leopard shaking only himself when he stand. He almost fall before I run into the room and catch his shoulder, which still bring us down to our knees. The Leopard apologize. He don't know why his legs still won't work, and when they do, why not for long. Most of the day he is just lying on these sheets like a dying cat. I almost ask where he is, the archer, but then picture him already making it to the Tracker's floor. I almost became prey, he mumble to himself, the third time I hear him say it, as if it mystify him even more so than scare. I look at him and wonder about my lion, even though lions hate leopards.

"You're the Moon Witch," he say.

"Yes," I say, girding myself for another argument.

"A lot of the wrongs in this world you have righted. That I know for a fact."

"I . . . what?"

"I have many sisters, in spirit if not in blood. Walk

with heads high they do, and brave as warriors because looking out for them is the Moon Witch. They will not believe I have met you."

"I don't know what to say," I reply. But quick as a blink his mind gone somewhere else.

"There are holes in the ground, baked clay and hollow like bamboos," he say.

"Piss and shit in them and the hole take it away. Kongor is unlike other cities in what she does with piss and shit. Apologies. My head is going again. Who put us in this place?" he say, pulling himself up to his elbows.

"Some old pervert who like to cook," the Tracker say. He is in the doorway looking as bad as the cat, but at least he is standing. "Oh it was nothing, saving you."

"So it's thanks you want? You the reason we end up in the damn forest."

"I will leave you two," I say.

"Stay," say the Leopard. "Not much I want to hear from him anyway."

"We have to stay and find the boy since this witch wasted a full moon," the Tracker say.

"If you stay, then I leave," say the Leopard.

"As you wish. Is that Fumeli's wish?"

"Fuck the gods, what a question."

"Tell me, can you stand? Change form? Even a lazy, half-blind bowman with lousy aim wouldn't miss you. I will tell the slaver that you no longer wish to find her slaver," the Tracker say.

"Don't speak for me."

"Fumeli can speak for you. He already doing the thinking."

"Speak like that again and—"

"And what? Change into a cat or some sniveling little bitch?"

The Tracker laugh. The Leopard is furious. He rise from the rugs but stumble.

"Get out," I say.

"Don't give two fucks for your orders," the Tracker say. "You who couldn't manage a little search in a whole moon. I—"

The wind (not wind) sweep him off his feet, throw him out the door, and slam it before he could bang at it. All the shouting soon tire him out, and he go away.

"You two look like friends the first time I see you."

"Well, appearances," the Leopard say.

"Not you the one who bring him along?"

"Not me, Bunshi. I just made the offer. And yes he was a friend until the Darklands, when he chose to only save himself."

"In the Darklands many a man is not himself."

"Except that is exactly what he is. It's the Ogo who turn back to save us, and only because he saw the door was still open. He didn't even try to get us. Didn't even look back. I'm sure he told the others that it's the Ogudu, the little curse. And none of us remembering right. But I remember. If he staying with this mission, I leaving."

"And the archer?"

"He can speak for himself."

The boy enter right then as if the words summon him. He carrying bow and quiver and standing up too straight, puffing his chest out too far. Trying to look like a man but the Darklands put a spell on him too. I look at him and wonder what truly is his use.

"Tracker's chamber is on the second floor, if you wish to stay out of his way," I say.

"No it not, it's on the third," the boy say, as quick as I knew he would. He shut himself up and look away, glancing at me twice to see me looking at him.

"We hunt a boy, do we not?" the Leopard ask.

"You don't remember?"

"Yes and no."

"Catch up with your sleep, Leopard," I say.

That night, when the Tracker set out, I follow him. Bunshi not above giving people working together different instruction, but for a man who only this morning couldn't move, he moving strong. I would think he sniff something out but he is yet to go to Fumanguru's house. Truth, the Tracker is moving at his own pace, near slow. The voice want to tell me that I have better things to do, but when I ask her like what, she shut up. Bunshi tell this Tracker to do something as soon as he reach Kongor and he setting about doing it. The Ukuru cloth that was on his bed is now around his waist and over his head like a hood. Surely with my smell, he can tell I am on his tail, but from what I know, if he don't choose to lock on my smell, then mine is just like any other. So I follow him as he trace steps I already step, visit places I already go to, come to knowledge I already know. In the Nimbe quarter, he try to talk to a boy, who shout Bingingun without stopping. Then his feet take him to a place I would never expect. A place that a market woman done with her day say is Mistress Wadada's House of Pleasurable Goods and Services.

A whorehouse.

The next day, Leopard shouting how many times he must smell the Tracker on the archer's cock. The fight brewing, I thinking to stop it, then I think better. The Tracker don't deny it, he just don't know why the Leopard putting this **appendage** over their friendship. The boy don't know what appendage mean, but he know it not good. He say something, but loose is all I hear. Fuck the gods and fuck this little shit, the Tracker yell and jump at the archer, who is useless without his weapon. Leopard change full cat and knock him over. Tracker is slapping and punching but in the quick Leopard clamp his jaw on the Tracker's neck.

"Leopard!" I shout.

The Leopard drop him. The Tracker, coughing, turn to leave.

"Don't be here tomorrow," he say. "Neither of you."

"I don't take orders from you," the Leopard say.

"Don't be here tomorrow," the Tracker say, then stagger out.

And then Bingingun come. Somebody who know Kongor only by name would be surprised and aghast by the festival, because yes what just flash past him is bare breasts and what just slap that woman's thigh is a real penis. A man here for just a day would scream hypocrisy, not knowing that it is the pious nature of Kongor that beget a thing like Bingingun. Only in a place like Kongor, where everybody lock themselves down so tight, would they burst so loose. Only in a place like Kongor, and at a festival like Bingingun, would I spend most of it in the alleyways and gullies, because that is where men drag off girls under the cover of bright colors and noise. I watch them as they pass, the barrel drummers and bata drummers, small bata drummers, grounding the chant and calling to dance. Behind them jump the actual Bingingun. Watch the trickster and his tricking robes keep sucking in, then blowing out in a new color, the Ancestor King in royal purple, hiding his face behind a curtain of cowries, and more jumping as high as a man is tall, in red, gold, pink, and blue, and silver, in bush, coins, braids, tassels, and amulets. Face nets to hide what man see, hand nets to hide what man do. The drummers shift the beat and the whole procession change. Bingingun cut loose. In a half moon they will whip a woman for doing these very things, yet give the man only a warning to not let himself fall prey to temptation. I catch up to the

Tracker, this time with the Ogo, and lose him in a wave of masqueraders. But I know where he go and is about time. Fumanguru's house. In the morning he will tell me that he and he alone know where the boy had been going, and where he will appear next. He will also tell me how the Fumanguru house die, as if he discover it first.

By morning, the Leopard and the archer both gone. The Tracker and the Ogo return in the evening. The Ogo, happier than I ever see him, go straight to the massive meal I never see this old man cook. Her fellowship dwindling by the day, but even this don't bring out Bunshi. My guess is that as long as the one person she deem irreplaceable is still willing, then everybody else can go. So going is what I spend most of the day thinking about. I was set to go only five days ago. Bunshi have her reasons for not telling these men who they are looking for.

And this girl, Venin. She taking to things most girl like, running down to markets to wrap her fingers around precious fabrics and fragrant oils, not knowing that she can't take something without paying first. I want to follow the Tracker but instead I have to follow her, sometimes to pay the merchant before he scream thief. Or whip up a wind (not wind) when the seller start to chase her. In all of this she is unmindful, thinking I am only following her to check her freedom. Not follow! is all she shout, for now she resisting all things Sogolon, especially teaching. I can't control her so I think to consult a witch to put on a spell that make her fall asleep if she walk too far, but that would leave a sleeping girl at the mercy of whoever find her.

Give me the girl. Jakwu.

"Murderer, I don't know them kind of sorcery."

You don't need no craft. You need to get out of the fucking way.

I should be waiting until the Tracker wake to hear what he will do, or see where he will go. But instead I go as soon as first light, looking for the hut behind the house of a witch who will put a spell on the girl. I don't do it with pride. But I do it. The witch don't take kind to me finding her out, and is not until I threaten to not only reveal that she is a witch but also a man, that she open the door.

"Kongor is for the pious. No witchcraft going on here," she say.

"So let us not call it a spell, then," I say and enter without her invite. In my wineskin, a piece of the string the Zogbanu use to tie Venin up. After the ritual, the witch braid it into an anklet and dip it in incense.

"Tell her it is a gift," she say.

Jakwu know something is afoot.

Give me the girl now, he say.

"Now? How come you the only one that want the girl?" I ask. "Also, for years upon years there was a whole army of malcontented men in my head waiting to strike me down. Now there's only you. What you do?"

Jakwu, never one for answering questions I actually ask him, quiet again.

Back to the master's house. As soon as I step into my room I can tell, even though I am not the one with the nose, that this Tracker been in here. She leave her smell here as well, Bunshi. I gathering my thing to go when Venin start to fuss. "First here is a gift from a precious musk merchant," I say, which delight her. Then I tell her that where we going there are wonders, like water that run upward, wagons that travel through the sky, and dresses that dress you. We setting to leave when the smell of that damn sprite, only trace up to now, suddenly come on pungent, present. She shaking so bad that she shifting in and out of her self.

"Hall of records . . . something happening . . . Tracker!"

Bunshi don't have time for more words, and is shaking too hard to utter them. I say we take the Ogo and she scream that we need a blade not a battering ram, which he don't take offense to. She say she will lead Sadogo and the girl to a road heading to Mitu. And a crossroads.

"You and your damn doors. This go to Dolingo?"

"You know that's where it go."

"If they using the doors, maybe we wait until they get to Kongor."

"No. We can't stay in Kongor. Not anymore. Go!"

"Maybe the Tracker should save himself. You the one who need him."

"And if they decide to stay in the Blood Swamp how would you know? If they come to Dolingo, how you going to find them in a place that take three days to cover? Guess? Write a rune? Maybe ask market women until somebody say yes, I did see a white gentleman over there buying magic berry."

"Now you think you cute."

"Go help him, or just go!"

Is the faces we see first, me and the housemaster, faces orange and flickering, the crowd watching the hall of records on fire. Kongori make note of everything, even of things not Kongori, so I can feel it with them, the sight of everything that make them who they are going up in flames. The great hall of records now like some great bonfire of a wicked god, blazing so tall that it light up the whole quarter. I wonder if the whispering books are screaming. Just as my mind run on him, somebody in the crowd shout, No man, no! The bookkeeper. As if to say, No your help won't do, the roof collapse and embers explode. Tears, sweat, or both, faces are wet. While everything in that place could catch fire, fire don't catch itself. The Tracker, I am sure, will have a lot of explaining to do. Or maybe he in the blaze.

And the people.

People crying.

People screaming.

People quiet.

Just so, not quieting down, no hush, whispering, just all of a sudden quiet. Fire will entrance, that I know, but the face nearest to me is looking past the blaze, past everything, even past himself. He and everyone near him not only quiet but still. Stiff. Sweat run into his eye and he don't blink. Every man, woman, and child in the street stiff like wood until their heads all turn left. No other limb, not even a finger. Then a woman yell from two streets over, and all of them take to their heels, running like they fleeing an actual fire, all of them, even the very old and the very young, turning into a stampede that knock down and trample whoever can't run as fast. Nobody saying nothing and nothing to do but go with them. They all dash for this lane, where I see the Tracker just as he elbow a woman rushing at him in the face while a man, dressed like a magistrate, slapping people away with the flat side of his sword. A mother drop her own child and attack the Tracker while another boy leap onto his back. The magistrate pull him off. Then the crowd swarm them, people they trying not to kill, who have no such thought of the two of them. Who don't have any thought. It take me too long to realize who is doing the thinking, and before I realize that it is him at the other end of the lane, he vanish. The hair like flame topping his head. His hair short and red. His earplugs, his black cape with the red underneath. The cape flying even though it is a hot, dry night.

The Aesi. In Kongor.

Which mean he following us, maybe by himself or with an army. Which mean he follow us from Malakal. Which mean he know us, for he have no other reason to attack the Tracker. Which mean somebody spying for him. I spend so long trying to cut this mission loose so I can trail him that it never even come to me that he would be trailing us. Many things he can't do. He can't fly, he can't disappear, he can't blow himself away like a wish. If I hunt him down I will find him, and I am one of the few, maybe the only one, who ever kill him. I can kill him. He will kill them. I don't know them, or care. But still he will kill them, and also these people will wake up tomorrow missing a sister, a brother, a child, maybe just a limb, but even hand is one limb too much. Anger rising and I can't control it—for the only one losing here is me. The people on top of them now, the Tracker and the magistrate, and soon they will have no choice but to kill their way out. And despite knowing all that I still make a step in his direction before I stop myself.

"You not one of them woman with secret craft?" the housemaster ask, and jolt me back.

"Is not a secret," I say.

I jump off the horse just as my skin ripple. Wind (not wind) push up the dust first, then knock off all the torches, rip off loose windows, and before anybody notice, start throwing people against the wall and up in the air. As I walk it run ahead of me, barreling down or flinging up every woman, man, child, and beast. My force plow down right up to them two.

"He own every mind in this alley," I say as we ride up to the magistrate and Tracker.

"I know," the Tracker say.

"But yours."

"Who are these people?" the magistrate say to me. His light skin startle both me and the housemaster. I don't see such skin since I was too far north.

"We should leave now," I say.

Some of the people start to rise and stare.

"I don't need saving from them."

"But they will soon need saving from you," I say. More man, woman, and child rise.

While I take too long to get to my horse, the people start to gather. And run. The wind (not wind) don't wait. It sweep everyone and everything down alley, all the way down to the end.

"This man coming?" I ask the Tracker.

"I'm not the commander of his movements."

"Oh will you shut up," the magistrate say and mount the housemaster's horse.

"Where's Sadogo?"

"Waiting with the girl."

We leave the housemaster back at his house, and find the most shallow part of the river, where one could still cross to the shore by horse. The Tracker can't stop whining that I am trying to drown him, while the magistrate ask if he is always like this? On the other side is the long road to Mitu. We coming to a crossroad when Sadogo come out with the girl. The Tracker shout his name. The Ogo do the closest thing to a smile I was ever going see. But the sight of the magistrate distract him.

"So who you?" I ask.

"He is one of the Kongori chieftain army—"

"His mouth, it's like a loose bowel. Mossi is my name."

I am trying to see this man in the night, but only his big hoop earrings, his silver necklace, and his long hair are clear to me.

"This is not your business," I say.

"A thought you all should have had before you broke into Basu Fumanguru's house. Did this Tracker tell you where he spent the night?"

With whores, I don't say.

"Late of this night, wherever I go you seem to follow. High time you quit that," say the Tracker.

"High time you all stop telling me what to do," say the magistrate.

"Look, he was as interested in Fumanguru's fate as you are, and that nearly got him killed. Now he has nowhere to go back to," the Tracker say to me.

"Sound like his problem," I say.

"Oh, you think the Aesi hunting him won't become your problem? Yes, woman, we know of the Aesi too. Among other things."

"I told you not to speak for me," say the magistrate, Mossi.

"Oh shut up, Mossi," the Tracker say.

The Ogo help down Venin from a tree with a care I didn't think the giant was capable of. She hold on to his arm, even when she firm on the ground. We walk a little farther, right to the center of where the roads meet.

"You commanded the wind back there? Fascinating," the magistrate say.

"Is not wind."

"Oh? What is it?"

"F—"

"You witches and your crossroads," the Tracker say.

"Is for you, not me," I say, amazed at how quickly he can irritate me. "You and Bunshi done have words already."

"I can't tell if your mood is sour or if that is how you always look. I know who he is, you know. The boy."

"Aje o ma pa ita yi onyin auhe."

"The hen doesn't even know when she will be cooked so perhaps she should listen to the egg," he say and wink at me.

"Who you think he is, this boy?" I ask.

"Somebody this Aesi is trying with all his might to find before you do. And it all points to the King in one way or another. And don't tell me it's Fumanguru's son, because I don't like time wasting any more than you do."

"The King want to erase the Night of the Skulls, that child—"

"That child is who he was after all along. I have read Fumanguru's writs, woman."

"You find them."

"People really should read more. That's what libraries are for. But you pass through only a few days ago."

"My smell."

"Still there. And you didn't find it? The great Moon Witch. Or it's not what you went looking for. That is it."

"You still think I care about the writs."

"You should," the Tracker say. "He was giving instructions on what to do with the child when we find him. Word on top of words was a big thing with your elder."

"Talk plain."

"What I said. He wrote notes on top of the words in milk. He said to take the child to the Mweru. You stare at me. So quiet you are. Walk through Mweru and let it eat your trail, that is what he said."

"Of course. Of course. No man ever map the Mweru, and no god either. The child would be safe."

"Might as well say he will be safe in hell."

"Bunshi lead us here because there is a door, Tracker," I say.

"Tell me who the child is before I find out. You know I will," say he.

"Open it."

"Who is the boy?"

"You all keep talking about this boy. This is about the doll, isn't it?" ask the magistrate.

"A doll?" This come out of nowhere.

"Some family this is, where nobody speaks. No—you're exactly like family," say the magistrate. "So yes, a doll found in the house, a child's toy. Except no mother of Kongor would have given her child a doll. Terrible sin, you see, to train a child to have idols. A child **in** Kongor, on the other hand, doesn't have to be Kongori. So whoever killed the Fumangurus failed to kill one . . . which I will guess is this child you all speak of. No? Clearly a child of great import to have such . . . people hunting him. I thought this Tracker was holding back, but he clearly doesn't know."

I liking this magistrate. But this don't explain why he is here, or why I should let him come with us instead of killing him.

"Whoever following us is still following," the Ogo say to the Tracker, and he finally nod, step away from us, clasp his hands, and whisper some chant. Sangoma antimagic. A spark set off, then split in two, spreading into a fiery circle big as a house, then dying out.

"There it is, witch, the flame died and there is no door. Because we are in the crossroads, where there would be no door in the first place. I know you are from lower folk, but even up to a few days ago you must have seen what we call a door," the Tracker say.

"Will he shut up soon?" Mossi say to the girl and even she laugh. I smile too, knowing how much it enraged the Wolf Eye. We don't go too far before we on a different road, not more mud, but stone, no warm air but cold, not flat path but a slight uphill.

"This . . . this is neither Mitu nor Kongor," Mossi say.

"Even a Sangoma, when she's not whining like an unfed bitch, can do mighty feats. Or just this," I say and ride off, leaving the magistrate exclaiming to the girl and annoying the Ogo. I am too old now, clearly. Too old to see when a man, even this giant, have warm feelings for a woman. I slow down for the Tracker to mount my horse.

"The Aesi might be following you through dreams," I say.

"I only had one dream with him."

"Don't sleep tonight. Neither you nor the magistrate."

"But sleep already claims me, Moon Witch."

"Then find something to do."

"I know who your boy is," the Tracker whisper.

"You mean Bunshi's boy," I say.

We won't be getting anywhere this night but lost, so we take rest off the road. Mossi and the Tracker build a fire and watching them I can't help but wonder how the fire in the Hall of Records start. Then the Tracker try to annoy everybody to keep himself awake, so much that the magistrate finally pull him away and they go off to the river, running along part of the trail. I hear him explaining to the magistrate how his nose work, how once he have a smell he can follow it anywhere over land and sea, and how the first time he discover his gift he nearly cut his nose off from madness. And how he can follow that scent until the person die, and how the living, woman, man, beast, all smell different, but the dead all smell the same. He picked up the boy's smell at Fumanguru's house and now the smell is pulling him south, maybe Dolingo, maybe farther. But before, his smell would fade only to come back strong, like the boy couldn't make up his mind where to go. Now it get stronger the more they travel, and when they came through that door it was as if the boy ran right into his face.

Then one of them scream and before I jump, a splash in the river. Then another splash, then no talking. I can't tell in the time of silence if the fire eat itself out, or if I am just thinking it. I roll over to sleep, knowing—no, hoping that my mind is still unknowable to the Aesi. But it is too quiet.

It is their clothes at the edge of it that stop me from falling off the cliff. Below, the river. On the banks with moonlight riding their skin, the Tracker on his back with his legs spread like they running away from each other, the magistrate above him, in him, fucking him.

TWENTY-FOUR

So they knock me clean off my horse. Knock me so hard that I think is my own wind (not wind) that hit me. Kick me clean off my horse, fling me high up in the air, to fall flat on my back and coughing. In the quick Venin dismount and run to me, but they slap her down so hard that she twist and fall, crying. They, not just him, not just Jakwu. Maybe five or ten, maybe every single man I kill. I try to get up but they knock me down again, then hands—I can feel them grab my legs and drag me across the road. Mossi jump off his horse, pull his two sword, but they circle around him, pitch him forward and twist his own sword toward him, trying to get him to fall on it. The Tracker run and pull back. The hands at my ankles are pulling me into bush, too fast for me to write any nsibidi. And I have no words. The Nnimnim woman tell me more than once to learn the words, to practice invoking them, but I never did. Somebody's word riding the air, and is not Jakwu. Somebody chanting something. Mossi charge after me but they knock him down again. Only the Ogo stand. When he go to stand before me, they prod and push and slap but none move him. Venin, I don't know what she doing, but she grab a stick and mark in the dirt. Maybe she been looking at me writing nsibidi long enough to know the shapes if not the meaning.

It work. They sound like wind squealing. All of them going back to wherever they come from. One grab my hair and pull a chunk out.

Mossi run over to help me, but Venin jump between me and him.

"She not to be touch by no man," she say.

The Tracker's face as surprised as mine. The Ogo lift me up on her horse she is fine with, though. We continue on the road until the path narrow into one smooth stretch. My head is coming back but still don't feel like my own, and if I dismount I will likely fall. A causeway built by some long-gone empire, must be, Mossi say. In daylight it come to me that while just about everything about this Tracker strike me as flawed, stupid, ridiculous, or wrong, I have no gripe over his pick of men. And this one. Even with skin the color of what you use to mark skin, he is striking form of man. And a real warrior, unlike everybody else here. The one man not picked by the water sprite might be the one man of use. Nothing like the men I always see save for the thick lips. Hair wild and loose like my horse. Beard riding up a sharp face, nose hanging over like hawk's beak, and when he pass close, eye like a pool of water. Also this, he is taller than the Tracker. But so is every other man, not just the Ogo.

"Am I alone in hearing that?" Mossi say.

"I hear it too," say the Ogo.

Just as the Tracker nod, from both flanks it come, a rumble, a crack, then a wave of cracks, then a thunder from below, coming from deep, and coming up.

"Fuck the gods, what else going trouble us this morning?" I say.

Venin grab her staff and pull it apart into two lances. Must be from the housemaster, I say to myself. Sadogo sniff the air. Heat break from the earth and with it a stink that burn the nose. This also break from the ground, wicked wild laughter from women. Wilder as they get closer and closer and closer until they erupt from the ground.

"Gentlewomen and -men. Go!" Mossi shout.

Four at once, two to a side. Blasting chunks of earth with them that rain down on us like boulders. See how they rise, taller than the Black Sparrowhawk tower, hear how they cackle and scream. Women, the breasts, chest, waists of women, but the hands of giants and below the belly, a body of serpents as thick as tree trunks. Rising high out of the ground and reaching higher, then suddensome they mark us and dive. The frightened horses throw us off. Skinny, scrawny, scaly, and black, hair red, eyes red also, fangs snapping for flesh. The ground crack open and two more surge up. One swoop down and knock over the

Tracker, then flick out her claws, but right then come Mossi with his two swords, spinning like a whirlwind, slicing and chopping off the devil's hands. She scream and duck back into the ground.

"Mawana witches!" Sadogo shout.

They smell food. They smell us. I too weak to summon wind (not wind).

Sadogo charge one just as she grab a horse. She will take it down with her but the giant jump on her snake end, thumping and punching until she let slip the horse. Sadogo climb her like a tree. One dip in for me but Venin run in front of me, swinging and jabbing with her two lances just as how Mossi was swinging and jabbing with two swords. Where she get this skill from, she will have to answer me. The witch tremble and swing and dive trying to toss the Ogo, but he hold on and his weight alone push her down. At her face, her breath smoking, he punch her forehead over and over until her head crack and she fall. That frighten the others still trying to grab Mossi, claw the Ogo, and swoop up the horses. A witch catch one, take him up too high before she let go. I watch Sadogo watch the horse smash and die. He furious now, and is a long time since I see an Ogo let loose. He jump another one, lock his arms around her neck. Neither her breath nor her claws save her from him strangling her to death. One of them try to swoop the Tracker, but pull back when he turn around to face her. And Venin. This girl run all the way up Sadogo's back, leap off his shoulder, and scream all the way over to a witch she land on by pinning both lances in her back. As some start to fall the witches start to falter. The Tracker take advantage, chasing after the younger one with his two axes out. She try to dip back into the dirt before he reach, but not before he swing both axes at her neck. Another, seeing that I am the only one too weak to fight, make for me, diving in fast. Venin run before me, right underneath the witch, who can't stop herself from smashing her chest against Venin's blades. She fall over, yelping until black blood fill her throat. The other witches stop shrieking and dive back into the ground. We huddle together, all weapons ready, and stay there, hearing nothing but our heavy breathing, until the rumble underfoot go quiet.

"Well, look at witch attack witch," the Tracker say.

"Well, look how none attack you," I say.

"You see it by now. Iron have no power over me. Nor gold, nor silver or bronze," he say.

"All of them are flesh. Don't tell me that you never see the last one backing away from you."

"Running scared."

"You not the one among us to be scared of."

"Where you going with this, woman?"

"You sleep last night?"

"What you think, witch?"

"I say did you sleep?"

"Just about the only thing I didn't do last night. You witness it yourself, didn't you? Back up on the cliff."

Whatever word is in me, he take it.

"Best we go. Now!" I shout.

Now we down to one horse. Mossi walk, while Tracker for a time ride Sadogo's shoulders until it come to him that he look like a child doing it. I on the horse, with Venin behind.

"Where you learn such skill with a lance?" I ask.

"Skill? I been playing with spears since I stop sucking my mother's teat."

"What?"

"I will have a sword. Maybe two, like the pale one. Tell me, which of those two is the fucker and who is getting fucked? They both walk like somebody gave their assholes some brutal business."

"Venin?"

"You know better, moon bitch."

"Jakwu."

"I love it when you say my name. Say it again."

This road is not the only one to Dolingo. We come upon a fork where the way left would be quicker, under cover of trees, some of them with fruit. But I stay on the right and don't answer the Tracker when he question why. Nobody take the route on the right because the rumor is that you can't travel one league without running into devils. No devil live on this road, but the man who start the rumor do. He and his kind scattered north and south out of fear. He, the southern griot.

Ikede.

Yet it surprise me when I first see his house. We approach it slow. **Who know what else await us?** The voice that sound like me say. Jakwu try to grab my waist again and I elbow him.

"I can't wait to try out being a woman. Tell me true, how you don't just stay under the sheets and play with your breasts all day?" he ask.

"Do anything to Venin and I swear—"

"It done, moon bitch. It already done."

"Venin, if you hearing me, fight this."

"Stinking cunt bitch, you not hearing me? She gone and she not coming back. Don't worry, you soon hear her whispering, although she don't know much words."

"How you make this come to pass? Talk."

"Me? You do most of it, going through a door you shouldn't go through. Some of the other men do the rest. Fight you down enough, where you too weak to rein in every spirit. And we do it too, but then they get too strong. You think it was Venin marking nsibidi in the dirt to lock them off? It was me. What me to say? Of all my mother's children I love me best. And this girl so blank that anybody could slip in her head and find enough space. But here is truth. Not going lie. I always wondered what it feel like to take a cock like mine. And this Venin look like a virgin. Can't wait, and I wasn't even a man lover. Them peaks and valleys that no man get to have. Can't wait. Should I try the Ogo? Him taking more than a fancy, but I don't want to kill the girl."

"I kill you before that happen."

"Look who have words. Venin not going need words. Her mouth will be full with something else."

"If you—"

"You keep using if like we not done past if. All of this is when, woman. Learn that."

"You think I won't kill her to save her?"

"You can try."

And so we go to Ikede's house, almost as tall as the master's house in Kongor, but nowhere as wide. It so thin you might as well call it a tower, which is what I say to Ikede when we arrive to see him sitting outside his door, chewing khat, expecting us.

"You have them ready?" he ask. "Bunshi—"

"Yes, I hear from the water sprite. They ready."

The Tracker look at me like he about to ask a question I not about to answer. Jakwu size up the southern griot and follow the rest of them into the house.

"I leaving soon. And I taking the horse," Jakwu say. "But this game you playing. I like it. They know they hunting the next King yet? How much that secret worth to you?"

"Is not my secret, fool."

He laugh. I will never call him she. The pigeons are in a cage, ready to go to Dolingo, with a note written by the griot that I check twice because the time for trusting long pass. On the second pigeon I tie another note. I am in a house with one man who witches don't touch, one man that is all might and no head, one man who cheat a woman out of her own body, and one man who up to a few days ago I didn't even know, an arm of the chief who is the arm of the King. In the house of a man who once hold my whole past over me. I might not fall asleep this night. The Tracker is at my door as I set the second pigeon loose, arguing with Jakwu and trying to slip past him, and not knowing that in the girl is a man who has killed tens upon tens of men like him. But Jakwu let him through because he know that will annoy me.

"A message for the Queen of Dolingo to expect us," I say.

"Wasn't asking."

"They don't show kind to people who come with no announcement."

"If you say so. But we shall have words, woman," the Tracker say.

"Oh we going have words now?"

"Words, yes. On this boy, for one. Your Aesi is after him. And since he only acts in interest of the King, then Kwash Dara is after him."

"You find out much in that library."

"Admit it. You're surprised I read."

"You don't have to read to know the Aesi act for the King, or even think for him. Even children call Kwash Dara the Spider King."

"Everything about the boy was in the writs."

"Look at you, the reader. You and the pretty magistrate."

"If you say he is."

"How you two escape such a blaze? Either you too hard to kill or he not trying hard to kill you."

I go over to the door to show him out.

"We two not done," he say.

"Lovely, because I'm just starting," Mossi say, and walk in the room.

"How many women either of you know that would just walk into a man room like that?" I say.

The magistrate look taken aback. Unlike the Tracker, he have good breeding. He motion to go but then stand his ground.

"Magistrate," I say.

"My friends call me Mossi."

"Magistrate, this not for you. Best thing to do is go back."

"Too late for that. You have all left me with nothing to go back to. The chieftain army will think I killed my own men on that roof."

"You two was out killing magistrates when the hall burn?"

"They tried to kill us first. Besides, a few were already dead. Some the Aesi controlled," the Tracker say.

"And some he bought," Mossi say, and sit down on the floor and pull a batch of paper out of his satchel.

"Fuck the gods, you took the writs?" the Tracker ask.

"They had an air of importance. Or maybe just sour milk," he say and laugh.

The papers are drawing me closer. I can't help it. All I know of the writs is what Fumanguru write on the wall. But this is it, a sign that people of the empire was thinking for themselves and not believing that every thought must be in lockstep with the King.

"Glyphs," say the Tracker. "Northern-style in the first two lines, coastal below. He wrote them down in sheep milk."

"Your nose."

The papers draw in even Jakwu.

"Fumanguru's great new idea for empire was a return to old. There, I sum it up for all of you," I say.

"You read the whole writ?" the Tracker ask.

"Was around when he write them. Boring once he stop talking about the King. Then he just turn into one more man telling woman what to do. But for what he say about the King, he might have been of great use."

"But did you read it?"

"What you think?"

"I think you think you have smart tongue."

"You read the part about the history of kings? That who succeed the King changed with Moki? Every King before him was the oldest son of the King's oldest sister."

"Yes, you fucking hound I was there. I live it, and I survive it when that same Kwash Moki and that same Aesi decide that all woman of her own means must be witch, and drive a stake from her bottom hole right through her mouth. At least Fumanguru didn't tell you that part because for all his nobleness even he can't see any woman beyond her koo's use. Not even a royal one. But Bunshi didn't tell that part? I was there, and I suffer all of that before most of you was even born."

"Most?" ask Mossi.

"Shut you face whoever you is!" I say, not taking my eye off Jakwu.

"I only ask how he became King?" Mossi say with sorrow.

"Banish his sister for adultery and plotting to install a false king. I was serving the princess when it happen. Banish her all the way to Mantha to join the divine sisters, then he send this Tracker's Sangomin brethren to murder us before we get halfway."

"Of course. My murderous brethren," the Tracker say with a laugh.

"You act like you never ever see what they do."

"After seeing the nastiness that you witches do, I would say they justified. Like you alone know atrocity. I survive your wickedness too."

"Tracker," Mossi say.

"No. This woman will have words so I will give her words. I see Sangomin protecting people who nobody else protect. I see little babies' bones because woman like you judge them as abomination, so you let them starve and die slow, because to you that is mercy. And yet all they do is protect the same people that try to destroy them from they born. Last time I see it, nobody call the Malangika the Sangomin market."

"Tracker."

"What, Mossi? Listen to her slander children?"

"If they are anything like the Sangomin in Kongor, then she is not wrong for feeling her way in my eyes."

The Tracker frown and gripe, but he shut up.

"After Moki even good King Liongo follow his father lead. Then the Aesi make the whole empire forget. That used to be one of his gifts. Now he less powerful," I say.

"Old age come for everyone but you, I hear. Three hundred seventy and three years old?" Mossi ask.

"That what this Tracker tell you?" I laugh. "In any case, Bunshi think the land cursed ever since this Aesi take hold."

"All this expansion and bounty? What curse?"

"The South nearly win the Areri Dulla war at one point, if that mean anything. And I been behind those palace walls. One of Kwash Moki's twins drown. Liongo lose his firstborn so they have to crown his second. And the children of their concubines turn as mad as a southern king. Rot run through the whole family. Yes, the great kings of the North make war and win plenty, but they lose where it count, and they always want more. Free lands, lands in fuss. Realms that don't take a side. They cannot help themself, man raised by man, not woman. Woman not like man, they don't know gluttony. And as each kingdom spread wider, each King get worse. The South kings get madder and madder because they keep making incest with one another. The North kings get a different kind of mad. Evil curse them, because they whole line come out of the worst kind of evil, for what kind of evil kill his own blood?"

"Only care about questions where the answer is the boy," the Tracker say. I come this close to blasting him out the window.

"If you can't answer those questions by now, your mother probably still worry about you," I say.

He try to enter my face, but Mossi stop him.

"Mossi, read it," he say, and the magistrate reach for the papers.

Gods of sky—no, lords of sky. They no longer speak to spirits of the ground. The voice of kings is becoming the new voice of the gods. Break the silence of the gods. Mark the god butcher, for he marks the killer of kings. The god butcher in black wings.

"Pompous, silly, stupid man, even on paper he must puff his chest bigger."

"You want the rest or no? Continue, Mossi."

Take him to Mitu, to the guided hand of the one-eyed one, walk through Mweru and let it eat your trail. Take no rest till Go.

"Go. Take the child south to the floating city? Fumanguru is guessing. Guessing because he don't know much about the Mweru. And why would a man know?" I say.

"The god butcher, for he marks the killer of kings. The god butcher in black wings. The Aesi?" the Tracker ask and I nod.

"That is why he is trying to get this boy either before us or from us, not so? The boy will grow up to kill the King," say Mossi. The magistrate in him on alert. He will not quit that soon, his nature to protect the King. I laugh.

"Is not prophecy," I say.

"What, you're deaf? It's a prophecy resting hope on a child. Which prophet so foolish? Witch bitches from the Ku? On a little thing that not going live ten years? And you, Mossi, are you not from countries where people never stop with the talk of magic children? Children of fate, people put all hope in them. All hope in a thing that sticks a finger in his nose and eats what he pulls out," the Tracker say.

"Is not prophecy, even though he pompous. He pointing to a way," I say.

"Listen to you. You still think I don't know. That night Bunshi told me all that shit about Fumanguru and the elders, I went to see an elder. Killed him too, which happens when you try to kill me. He also wanted to know about the writs. He even knew about Omoluzu. Your fish told me the boy was Fumanguru's son, but he had six sons, not seven. Even the people sent to kill him didn't know, which is why they thought, mission accomplished. Also this. The day before we met you, the Leopard and I tail the slave trader to a tower in Malakal, for no other reason than somebody was calling a fish a dog. So you see, we saw that woman with lightning sickness that Nsaka let loose the next day. So either you all were dropping nuts like a trail for the bird to follow, or you don't know a thing."

"I know of ten and nine doors," I say.

"And not one lead you to him. At this rate, the Aesi will either find him first, or will be right there to snatch him when you do."

"The man knows his importance," say Mossi.

"The man knows his worth. I can find this boy; your door only make it quicker," the Tracker say.

"And this magistrate with you."

"Mossi is his own man. We have come a long way, Sogolon. Longer than I would have ever gone on half-truths and lies, but something about this story . . . no, that's not it. Something about you and the fish shaping this story, controlling so hard how each of us read it, that turned into the only reason I came. Now it will be the only reason I leave," the Tracker say.

He turn to leave. Mossi follow for a step then stop.

"It's right there. Not so? Everything is in there. Now you waiting on us to put it all together like we're children," he say.

"I will be a mother then. Pretty magistrate, read the line. Again."

"Mark the god butcher, for he marks the killer of kings."

"Stop."

I look at them. They not going to catch it. And this no longer feel like a game.

"Still sounds like your little boy is a prophesied as-sassin to kill the King, which is treason," Mossi say.

"No. Killer of kings mean killer of the depraved line, rejected by the gods, under the influence of demigod getting his power from other gods. No, I don't have time to make all that clear. This is what you need to know. The boy not here to kill the King."

I pause. **You really want to take them there,** ask the voice that sound like me. **Go down that road and nobody coming back.**

"He, that little boy, is the King," I say.

Both of them back away, almost staggering, drunk on sudden truth. Then I tell them to sit down, for this day just starting. I tell them about Kwash Dara, Princess Lissisolo, the murders, the banishment, the plot to get her married and produce another heir, hid-ing the boy, losing the boy, and Basu Fumanguru. Is near evening when I finish.

"Why not tell us this from the beginning?"

"You all working for money. Greater money might be in killing him than saving him."

"The only true killer among us is you, Moon Witch," the Tracker say. I don't say anything.

"How come this Aesi doesn't use these doors?" Mossi ask.

"The one sharing secrets with him should ask."

"From idiots to traitors in just one day. My own speed is making me dizzy. Yet you trusted a prince to a woman who sold him as soon as she had the chance. You don't even need traitors," the Tracker say.

"Her husband do the deed. And Bunshi was the one doing all the trusting."

"But who has the boy?" Mossi ask.

"So there is one of you who don't care about royal intrigue," Ikede say and enter the room. "Even you, Sogolon, forgetting that to save the boy from the Aesi, first you have to save him from those who drink blood. And he might not want to be saved."

"I know they're using the ten and nine doors, another thing this witch didn't tell us."

"Bunshi," I say.

"Whatever."

"My head is already spinning from king, princes, and plots. Which they is this now?" Mossi ask.

"I know of two by name. Two are Eloko, grass demons. But he too wild to be the leader. And too stupid. An Ipundulu among their number," I say.

"Lightning bird," whispered the old man. "You find his witch?"

"A masterless one."

"Dear lords of sky, what you bring on us? Dear lords of sky, an Ishologu."

He curse under his breath and head to the window. A weight drop on him and the whole room. "Lightning bird, lightning bird, woman beware of the lightning bird," he say.

"You about to give us song, brother?" I say but he frown.

"I talking 'bout the lightning bird. Talk is just talk," Ikede say.

"And song is how you talk," I say.

"Way of song long gone, Sogolon. Singer man don't sing songs no more."

"Just because you not writing down deeds don't mean you stop singing. How you keep to memory what the world tell you to forget?"

"Maybe I want to forget! You ever think that?"

"Southern griots speak the truth of the King since before Kagar. If it wasn't for you we wouldn't know that the King supposed to descend from sister, not brother. If not for you preserving memory none of us would be in this room. If not for you, well . . ."

Ikede nod, knowing what I couldn't finish.

"Southern griots gone the way of witches, Sogolon. You know what I mean," he say.

The old man pull away a stack of rugs and uncover a buried kora.

"Kwash Aduware, this King's grandfather, six of we his soldiers discover. That King, he kill them all. You want to know if he kill them quick? No is your answer. No. Sogolon, remember Babuta? Maybe you never know him. Babuta, son of Babuta. One night he come where six of us gather with proclamations heavy on his chest. Enough with hiding in caves for no reason, we sing the true story of kings! Then he recite one long poem about the purpose of truth that I don't remember. Babuta say he know a man in the court of the Kwash Aduware who serve the King but loyal to the truth. The man say the King come into knowledge of us since he have belly walkers on the ground and pigeons in the sky. So gather your griots and set eyes for Kongor, for they can live safe among the books in the House of Records. For the age of the voice is over and we in the age of the written mark. The word on stone, the word on parchment, the word on cloth, the word that is even greater than the glyph, for the word provoke a sound in the mouth. And once in Kongor, let men of writing save words from lips and in that way the griot may die, but never the word. He sell it to us as such a wonderful thing. Sanctuary for the southern griots at least, whose only crime was that to power we speak true. We will no longer live like dogs, this is what Babuta say. Hear this, for he say this also. That when the pigeon land at the mouth of this cave, in the evening two days from now, take the note from its right foot and follow whatever it say. Do you know who the pigeon in service to? Sogolon know. Babuta, mark whatever occur with great care, but none of that ever stop him from being a total fool. I tell him, Read the songs of your fathers. People in the King's court only a fool would trust. And he say, Go lick a wild dog's koo for calling me a fool, and leave if you don't want to stay. So I leave. Nobody ever see them men again. Same thing come to pass in nearly every other cave. So there be no southern griot. There be me."

"You not the last."

"I the last you going see."

"The day passing and running, old man. Tell them about the lightning bird. And who travel with him."

"You see how they work."

"So have you."

"Fuck the living gods, will one of you tell us the story?" Mossi say. He was on the floor, head raised like a dog, almost smiling, for he will have this tale. The griot take the stool and begin.

"A wicked word come from the West, two quarter-moons previous. A village right by the Red Lake."

"The last word I hear was that they leave the Hills of Enchantment for Nigiki. They cross the river already?" I ask.

"This is what come by talking drum. People come across a hut in a village above the Blood Swamp, but below the Red Lake. All around the hut death is stinking, but the foulness coming from dead cows and goats not the people and yes, they dead. The fisherman, his first wife and second wife, and three sons, but none of them stinking, oh. You couldn't even call it rot. How to describe a sight strange even to the gods? Skin like tree bark. Like the blood, the flesh, the humors, the rivers of life, something suck it all out. The first and second wife, both of them with their chest cut open and they heart done rip out. But not before he bite them all over the neck and leaving his dead seed to grow decay in them. And now you saying he don't answer to no witch."

"Yes," I say.

"Ishologu, he the handsomest of men, skin white like clay, whiter than this one, but pretty like him too," Ikede say, looking at Mossi.

"Ayet bu ajijiyat kanon," Mossi say. My eye spread wide open before I could pretend no surprise.

"A white bird. He surely is, yes, but he not good. He more evil than people can even think. And Ishologu ever worse. Because he handsome and he in a gown white like he skin, woman think they come to him free, but Ishologu infecting they mind as soon as he enter the room. And he open he gown which is not no gown but his wings and he not wearing no robes, and he make woman do what they don't choose to do, and some men too, when he feel the desire. Most he kill, some he make live, but they not living, they living dead with lightning running through they body where blood used to run. I hear rumors that he change man too. And watch if you step to the lightning bird and he know, for he change into something big and furious and when he flap his wings he let loose thunder which shake the ground and deafen the ear and knock down a whole house, and lightning that shock your blood and burn you to a husk.

"This is how it happen before that, in Nigiki. A hot night. See a man and a woman in a room, and a cloud of flies above a bed mat. He a handsome man, neck long, hair black, eyes bright, lips thick. Too tall for the room. He grin at the cloud of flies. He nod at the woman and she, naked, bleeding from the shoulder, walk over. Her eyes, they gone up in her skull and her lips, just quivering. She covered in wetness. She walking to him, her hands stiff at the side, stepping over her own clothes and scattered sorghum from a bowl that shatter. She come closer, her blood still in his mouth.

"He grab her neck with one hand and feel her belly for sign of the child with the other. Dog teeth grow out of his mouth and past his chin. His fingers roughing between her legs, but she still. Ipundulu point a finger at the woman's breast and a claw pop through the middle finger. He press deep into her chest and blood pump up, as he cut her chest open for the heart. The grass troll, Eloko, he don't care for the heart. He only hunt alone or with his kind, but since the King burn down his forest to plant tobacco and millet, he join anyone. Maybe they don't know if is two of them or one get mention twice. And then picture this. A cloud of flies swarming and buzzing, and fattening up with blood. Flies pull away for a blink and is a boy on the mat, covered in pox holes like chigger. From the pox holes worm burrow out, ten, dozens, hundreds, pop out of the boy's skin, unfold wings and flying off. The boy's eyes wide open, his blood dripping onto the bed mat also covered in flies. Bite, burrow, suck. Him mouth crack open and a groan come out. The boy is a wasp nest."

"Adze? You telling me an Adze moving with them? They used to only like cold country," I say.

"Times change. Somebody had to take Obayifo's place. This is what happen when Ipundulu suck out all the blood but stop before he suck out the life. He breed lightning into her which drive her mad. A magistrate pull all of this out of her mouth, but he is not a griot to make verse. There be those three and two more, and another one. This is what I telling you. They working together. But is an Ishologu leading them. And then this boy."

"What of the boy?" I ask.

"Don't play fool to catch wise. You know they use the boy to get into the woman house."

"They forcing boy," I say.

"Now you sound like the water sprite. Also this, Sogolon. Another one. He following them one or two days later, for by then the rotting bodies that Ishologu didn't kill is a pleasing scent to him. He used to have a brother till somebody kill him in the Hills of Enchantment."

The Tracker just then look away then turn back just as quick, thinking nobody see.

"By force, by choice, neither matter. They putting the boy to use, certainly as lure," Ikede say.

"You get no dispute from me," I say.

"And the boy has been gone three years?" Mossi ask.

"Yes."

Everybody in the room know the words that would follow, so nobody say them.

"How they know of the ten and nine doors, and how they use them?" Mossi ask.

"You have to ask. One of those bloodsuckers was a Sangomin, or under their magic," I say.

"Woman, you really are tiresome," the Tracker say.

"Fools, we losing time," the old man say to all of us.

Over by the chest he take out a thick parchment.

"Too much for one afternoon, old man, show us tonight," I say. And everybody make to leave before the griot object. Only then I notice that Jakwu don't leave because he gone long ago.

This old man. This damn griot. He not only know of the ten and nine doors, but he mark them on a map. Tracker never see a map before, but Mossi, who come here by sea, gaze at it like one entranced. I thought these were uncharted lands, he say, then ask if they were drawn by masters from the East. Ikede ask if he think that only man the color of sand can draw, which quiet him a little.

"You mark them in red? Based on what wisdom?" I ask.

"Mathematics and measuring arts. Nobody travel four moons in one flip of a sand glass, unless they move like the gods, or they using the ten and nine doors."

"And this is them," I said. "All of them?"

"All that we know. But there may be more, down south perhaps."

"What else we know about them?"

"You already know plenty."

"Not that, old man."

"Oh." He chuckle. "More things we know. Once you set through a door, you can go through it again as much as you wish, but you can't go retrace your steps, not until you complete all the doors. If them vampires stopping anywhere from five days to eight, then they make a full cycle three times a year. Perhaps."

"So what happens if I go back to the hall of records?" the Tracker ask.

"It's no more," Mossi say.

"But the door still stands. What happens if I go backwards to the Darklands?"

"We don't know. Nobody ever survive it to tell us," Ikede say. "They must be using them for two years now, Sogolon. House of Records have papers that say for longer."

"Used to have," I say.

"They near impossible to keep track, even if we know they pattern. Some places rich in victims, some places poor. And some places fight back. But they stay the course until the journey complete, then they go backways. That's why I draw each line with an arrow at the two ends. That way they kill at night, kill only one house, maybe two, maybe four, all the killing they can do in seven or eight days, then vanish before they leave any real mark."

Tracker point at the map and say, "If I was going from the Darklands to Kongor, then here, not far from Mitu to Dolingo, then I would have to ride through Wakadishu if I feel like to feed more, or just go straight south, to Nigiki. If they travel in reverse, and the last we heard of them was north of Nigiki, even north of the Kegere River, then they headed to—"

"Dolingo," Mossi say as he press his finger on the map. "Dolingo."

TWENTY-FIVE

She mount your horse and just take off, it seem," Ikede say.

"Don't fuss. She not going far," I say.

He is still staring at his kora when I leave him, me envying that no matter how much Ikede cut himself off from his past, he can still look at it as one solid thing, unlike me. I know that is unfair, that he looking at just a symbol that mean more, and the weight of it still heavy, but at least when he look at his past he remember it. When I look at my past I remember somebody telling me about it, and I don't know how much of what bloom in my head is memory or fancy. The Ogo, who take to sleeping on the roof, watch me leave. I follow the hoof trails, down the road for a bit before veering off into the rocky bush. Night, yes, but full darkness never come to these parts. The horse I see first. Jakwu, he barely twenty paces ahead, still in the dirt, but sitting up and dabbing a bruise on his knee. I know he hear me coming but he don't bother to budge.

"Ingenious, bitch. Fucking ingenious."

"Don't pretend to know what that word mean," I say.

"I would say I could kill you, but now we know that won't be true."

So about this spell I have that witch put on the girl. We speak my desire in an old north tongue, which I know Jakwu can't speak, just in case he is alert and hearing. Is a binding spell, on the girl and on the rope that I fashion into an anklet because I know the girl love fashion. Jakwu don't care about fashion, so he leave it on her ankle. I forget how far she can run, or ride, or swim, but if she go too far in the quick she will slam into an unseen wall only there for her. I burst out laughing at the thought, Jakwu on my horse, galloping away, only to smash into a barrier of air while the horse under him keep running. I still laughing when he jump up and make mad rush for me.

"Fucking jungle bitch!"

He still yelling and cursing when my wind (not wind) throw him up in the sky and leave him there, spinning head over heel. It come to my mind to raise him higher, so higher he go, confusing birds now below him. I tempt myself to throw him so high that frost form on his nose, but then I remember that is not his nose. Nearer to the ground, he is a mad cat trying to scratch.

"You can't harm me," I say.

"You see how that Ogo look at me? He will kill this body with just a finger fuck."

"And where you go after that, Jakwu? A wandering spirit with no body, plenty creatures out there feed on the likes of you."

"You don't know that."

"Try it then. Also, the Ogo can't touch her. She free from violation because I bind her from pain and pleasure. So try it, oh. Try to get fucked. Eh, try to fuck yourself and see what happen to your finger."

I let go and he tumble. But he jump up on his legs, quick, also like a cat. He look ready to attack, but change his mind and stand, smoothing himself out.

"I know what ingenious mean."

"It look like you do, after all."

"So what you want?"

We come back in the early afternoon, for me to see the Tracker looking bothered, then hiding it as soon as he see me.

"Your girl called Sadogo simple," he say.

"Then he should stop being simple," I say. I got no feelings good or ill for the giant, but will not have this man with his two little hatchets start no fuss with me. "I have nothing against the giant, but maybe he leave Venin alone."

"Don't call him giant."

I know we have nothing more to say, so I leave

without nodding. Then he say, "Your old man, he was singing."

"You lie."

"Got no cause to lie, old woman. No fear neither."

"The same man, who only this morning refuse to sing."

"I know what I heard," the Tracker say.

"He don't sing in thirty years, maybe more, but he sing in front of you?"

"Truth, his back was to me."

"A silent griot don't just open his mouth."

"Maybe you are the one he didn't want to hear."

"Maybe he was singing about you." My words sting him, and he not swift enough to throw it off.

"Me. A nothing."

"A griot never going explain a song, only repeat it, maybe with something new, otherwise he cheat you out of drawing your own meaning. Nothing about the King?"

"No."

"Or the boy?"

"What you think?"

"Then he singing about love," I say.

"Nobody loves no one," Tracker say, and right there it come over me, immense sadness for this boy who don't realize he still just a boy.

Ikede used to have a love. When Kwash Dara's father realize he not going to catch every southern griot, that he not going to stop the song about kings, he hatch a new plan. Must be the Aesi who teach him that you don't have to kill a man to destroy him. That's when the wives and children start to float up in rivers with their head cut off.

The next morning he and I wake up to the Ogo weeping and Ikede dead on the ground. He throw himself off the roof. Me and Tracker hide the body, take his horse, and we all set off.

Dolingo. We get there at nightfall, a day and a half's journey. Nobody notice the trees when right under them, not until I instruct them to look up. I pretend that the sight not new, but there is no way to come upon Dolingo and not lose your breath in wonder. Coming from south, we reach the three-prong Mkololo tree first. The tree of the great citadel center, halls of governments, and the palace of the Queen. A platform above us lower itself, and following the Tracker, everybody draw their weapons.

"Return your weapons. Dolingon can win a fight without a sword," I say.

"What is this place?" Mossi say.

"Dolingo, it seem," say the Tracker.

"I have never seen such magnificence. Do gods live here? Is this home of gods?" Mossi say.

"Is the home of white science and black math," I say, but he furrow his brow more. The Ogo seem to have been here before, stepping onto the platform from before it reach the ground. Both Mossi and Tracker dismount as we rise but Jakwu stay on the horse. I look at Mossi's face and see that never in his life he ever rise this high. He come from those lands where they believe in one god and that god live in the sky. The grinding of gears and wheels I remember, but the sight of rope I push out of my mind, trying to forget. They see it as I see it, the painting of the profile of the Queen with her royal gele on her head, covering six floors and still not done, which surprise me given this Queen. When the platform level, the Tracker have to nudge Mossi to move.

"This is Mkololo, the first tree and seat of the Queen," Sadogo say just as that ghost voice drop on us saying the same thing.

"Sadogo, when you come upon this place?" I ask.

"Two years ago. Dolingons will pay big coin for fights."

Fights. I couldn't tell the last time I think about fights, much less see one. Much less fight.

"We should talk on this more sometime," I say and he nod.

The last time I was close to this river, I fall into it. A lot of this, the wide stone bridge, the straight road that disappear at the end, even the parts where the river flow upward, I forget because in Dolingo there is too much to remember. Mostly I just watch the shock of those with me. Around heights so high, we look like bugs. Two sentries in green armor rising all the way to their nose let us through the door. All of them, including Jakwu, reach for their weapons again.

"Don't insult the Queen's hospitality," I say.

I do remember that the Dolingo court out-magnificent magnificence. Woman, man, and beast as courtiers. Too many bald men in expensive wool, too many women with fabric towers on their heads, shapeshifting lions, leopards, hyenas. Mighty guards with ceremonial swords and spears not mighty, for nobody in neutral Dolingo ever need to use them. The Tracker look taken with the gold pillars. Mossi and Venin with everything else. So much to look at with amazement that one can almost miss the Queen. But there is no missing the Queen of Dolingo. She will make sure of it. The golden bird perched on her head—her crown, of course—the gold dots on her eyelids and lips, the frowning face of somebody who done hear all there is to hear, the towering height, the gold running along the seams of her dress that make it seem as if the metal is pouring out of her. This Queen she stand more than she sit, hands on her hips, and looking down as she hold her chin high.

"Sogolon, this is a surprise. When the sentries describe who approach, I say it can only be the Moon Witch. Put no obstacle between our meeting. Friends, how tired you must be from your journey. First you rest, and then we will have words," she say.

"But there is—" I say.

She cut me off. "Matters of state that I must attend to. Be off with you and expect the greatest care," she say as two fat men with robes scraping the ground approach us.

"Needing a bath, no, yes? And some scrumptious food, no, yes? Yes!" they say at the same time.

"Most Excellent Queen, remember we on urgent business," I say.

"Urgent is what I say is urgent."

Later that night she call me back to court. Only about a third of the people stand and sit with her now—her chancellors, handmaidens, the four sentries of the throne room.

"The warrior with the horsehair, I have never seen such skin. Is it a disease?"

"It is how most men who live beyond the sea look, Majesty."

"What? How frightening. And how delicious. Sit," she say, but as usual she prefer to stand. Two men rush a stool under me and push me down to sit.

"And the King Sister? Where is Lissisolo?" she ask.

"Your guess good as mine, Majesty. I only hear from Bunshi and that was days ago."

"So after all the trouble to produce an heir, and in gods know what barbaric fashion, they lose the boy? I will hear this story."

I am thinking she know the story, but I tell her what I know.

"And she trusted this decision to the water sprite."

"She pick a woman devoted to the cause, Majesty. But a husband not so."

"No. She didn't choose a woman devoted to the cause, she chose one devoted to her. These sprites thinking they are gods, when nobody want to be gods. I don't wait for devotion, Sogolon. I enforce obedience. Simpler. But given how short me and Lissisolo's sisterhood lasted I am surprised you are here. How is she managing in the Mweru?"

"She the one to answer that question, Majesty."

I surprised she is surprised but don't know yet if this is one of her games, only that it is already afoot and I have no choice but to play.

"I tell you most of this in the note, Queen."

"Note? Don't remember any note."

Of course you don't, I think but don't say. Why bother your imperial head with a matter fit for the chancellors?

"They find a portal, somewhere in Dolingo. We believe they been using it for years."

"Who?"

"Majesty?"

"Who?"

"Ipund— Ishologu and his others. Vampires, if you want to call them that. They move with the boy. We think they use him as a lure."

"What horrible luck, is it not, to escape one set of monsters to somehow land in with another?"

"It is a dangerous road," I say, but I really don't know. Yet something else is missing here, but I don't know if I would ever find out. But I think as she do, that something here is at once too neat and too awry.

"And now you believe that this little band, the baby and the bloodsuckers, are on their way here?

To Dolingo. And that they have been here before? Madness. The dead don't just disappear in Dolingo. There are records, attendances. Requirements. Obligations. Even a dead scribe would be missed."

"They smart enough to not leave much trace, Majesty. So they might not be killing in Dolingo, only using here for passage. Or they killing slaves."

"We don't have slaves."

I know she see me blink the frown off my face. "One have the power of persuasion and one can make himself invisible, Majesty," I say. They totally killing slaves. Dolingon just don't know how to treat a slave killing as a death.

She turn to her chancellors, but they look as blank as her. That something might be happening, something so insidious without her knowing, is making her angry and them afraid. Somebody will pay for this ignorance, I can already see this on her face. I don't want to tell her of the ten and nine doors, even though it is nothing to me if she use them. **But if it is nothing to me, why don't I tell her?** say the voice, annoying me.

"I will know more of this portal," she say.

"It in Dolingo, but not in the citadel. Three days away by horse."

I tell her what I know of the ten and nine doors. First she promise to whip all her chancellors and science men this coming dawn, for they are supposed to be the great repositories of knowledge and they didn't know a thing. I want to say that they are rumored to be the pathways of gods, but Dolingo has no use for gods, so why would they know, but I quiet myself. This Queen is acting even stranger than the last time I see her.

"With permission, Majesty, is everything in place?"

"Is what in place? This bush lady has so many requests of this Queen. Did we switch positions?"

The court whisper and hush out a No, could not be, Majesty.

"The prince will need the protection of your troops, first to deliver him from Ishologu, then safe passage to the Mweru. And from there up to his mother, the King Sister."

"I thought no man who enter the Mweru ever leave," the Queen say.

"I didn't make the plan, Majesty."

"But you have no problem enforcing it. You always struck me as your own woman. Also that you are long tired of royal affairs. How did they convince you?"

"Good coin, Majesty."

"But you are the Moon Witch. You already make good coin. Is this golden boy the fish or the bait?"

Right there I tell myself that this is not about the Aesi, this is something else.

"Majesty?"

"How long have you known of this portal?"

"Not long. I only know of three, but there might be more. To tell truth, if there was no portal in Dolingo, we would not be here."

I know that face. Plotting already—if not plotting,

then conceiving, taking stock of the marvel of the door, now even less interested in the boy.

"If Bunshi had more wisdom about people you would not be here. I offered to hide the boy. Instead they took him to some man because he wrote some writs. Another man with a mission—all of them make me sick. I told Lissisolo that I was pleased with her plan. Too many inbred kings and their inbred cocks when what we need are Queens to rule. And even though I was disappointed that all she wanted to do is put yet another man on the throne, I was happy that she would be regent. The real power. We would be women together. But her steady belief in nothing but her son began to displease me. How long this boy been with vampires? Don't lie to me."

"Three years."

"Three. So vampire is all he know?"

"Bunshi swear he is unspoiled, Majesty."

"But does Bunshi know? Yes? No? I must say this is all too surprising. When my sentries said you approach and with who, I was thinking old business."

Now I am the one confused. I don't have no business with this woman. I certainly don't have no business with queens.

"And how you plan to find the child? Shall you knock on doors and ask politely are there vampires within?"

"One who ride with us, the Tracker, he have a nose. He is the one who track his moving. He is the one who know the boy coming and where he going be."

"Fascinating."

"I send two notes, Majesty. One of where we were and when we coming. One with what we need."

"Chancellor, what notes does she speak of?"

"There is no word of any note, Majesty. None in the provinces, none in the great hall. Nothing on the drums or in the clouds."

"Two pigeons. It was two pigeons."

"Chancellor," she say to another, "it's your business to watch sky. What news from pigeons?"

"No news, Majesty."

"But . . . but . . ."

"Somebody intercepted your birds, Sogolon," she say.

It come over and crush me, a feeling so weak that I need a seat, even though a seat is under me. To not fall on the floor is all I can think.

"This dance we're having, this peculiar dance. You thought I knew. No, I didn't get your pigeons. But we did get a crow."

"A crow?"

"I know you're not deaf."

"The Aesi."

"Already sending a delegation. Won't be here for a moon and a half at least, and that is if they take the river, but they are coming. How is it that Fasisi's chancellor is right behind and far ahead of you?"

"I don't know."

"Yes, you do. You have a spy. We will be women to-gether, your King Sister said to me. Yet at every turn she depends on the work of men. And here you come with three, and none of them like you. Either one of them is a spy, or you're the spy. A better question is how is he contacting them. Crows?"

"I don't see no crows."

"You have a mystery, then," she say.

No, I already solve it.

"Bunshi is the one who insist on the Tracker. Delay us a whole moon just to wait for him. If not for those twenty plus days we would be in Nigiki, or even Juba, not here," I say.

"And the Ogo? The horsehair one?"

"Bunshi choose the Ogo. The magistrate is with the Tracker."

"And the girl?"

"With me."

"Some fellowship this is."

"My Queen, you have an agreement with the King Sister."

"Don't you tell me what I have and don't have. 'Twas different when all of this was a secret. You think I would anger the King of the North lands, for some princess itching for the throne but no desire to rule it herself? If she wanted to be Queen, that would be one thing, but she's just fighting for a boy. Why, because she bred him? What a stupid reason. Meanwhile your Aesi is coming."

"I am sure the King Sister will make you some offer."

"I am sure the King of the North will offer more.

Truth, your King Sister has nothing to give me. You, however, are a different story. So tell me, who do you think is your spy?"

She want me to see. The Queen continue. "You want truth? That is what I am looking for, Sogolon. I am looking for truth. Our truth is that intimacy is the threat, carnality the assault, and since we have long separated barbarism from reproduction, who needs the diseased or the deformed? Mingi children, simplistic pleasure—who needs the sweat of a man or the violence of him? Who needs children—beings when they are the most demanding yet the least useful—when through science and math we can hatch livelings fully grown and ready to work?"

There she is as her women wash and dress her, wanting to win my mind. Instead I give her silence. Her chambers are as big as her throne room, with a bed at the center as wide as a Fasisi pool. Everything is blue, the walls, the bed linen, and the veils skirting the bedposts, making everything within it a blue haze. The bath push itself out of the wall, as do the table with oils and perfumes, and the stools for her handmaidens to sit and wash her. They put me to stand by the far south window, beside a white scientist trying to make it look like he is not pulling baby mice from a bag and popping them in his mouth. A little tail is dangling out his mouth before he suck it in and smile. My head leave this room for another, where I see rope around a neck, around an arm, on both legs, and around the tip of each finger. And eyes seeing whatever people see beyond terror. And a door that open and shut, open and shut, open and shut.

The Queen say something to her head maiden, who clap twice. Her doors open and in march two guards in front, two at the back, Mossi between them, fascinated, confused, wearing that grin that might be a mask. They dress him in the long robes I see the old men wear. I can't imagine him speaking Dolingon and when the maiden start talking he look at her dumbstruck. I try to push myself into the dark of the window, but this white scientist is still trying to slip mice into his mouth. I would go over and say he not one for woman flesh, but then they might ask how I know. The Queen shout at him three times to remove it, and when he don't the guards grab him. He try to fight and punch two before they hold him down. A handmaiden slap them away and touch his face. He don't resist when she lift the caftan off him.

And there he stand by the bed, still bewildered, but liking the women's hands rubbing oil over him. At least this is gentler than the bath, he say, and they rub his chest, arms, back, and lower. He is something to behold, his limbs dark as sand and his chest and thighs almost as white as a white scientist. His lips like an open wound, she say. This Queen really don't know anything about intimacy and refuse to hear counsel. Then again, who here would be able to give it to her? An old man, not a scientist, whisper something to a woman, who whisper to another, who whisper to the head maiden, who whisper to the Queen. She slap the head maiden and shout, You think I don't know that? and raise her hand so that they can pull off her gown. Him, naked and white, she naked and blue, and room of people who don't know what to do next.

A guard push Mossi to the bed, but they all stare at his cock, waiting for the moment when it will wake up. A twitch and they all gasp, but that is all. They fumble, they ponder, the women shake their head and the men stroke their chins. And the Queen, she is standing on the bed asking, Why is this not happening? What else is there to the barbarian way? She was told by her elders that there would be a change in penis. This would go on all night if nothing change. Her handmaiden suggest she rub her breasts together and smile at him. Another takes off her own clothes and stroke it, but the most she get is a shy smile. Harder, but not hard enough, and gone before they could push him into the bed.

"He need a boy," I say in their tongue. Mossi look up to see me through the veil. I turn away before his eyes ask questions. In come two Dolingon boys about Venin's age, whatever that was, and they remove caftans before being asked. Something tell me that all these Dolingons thinking the same thing, **What great science! What great science!** The boys are eager. One from behind start to work his tongue on Mossi's neck. The other use his mouth to wake his cock up finally, and behold the wakeness. The Queen applaud as both boys pull him to bed. Is looking beyond them when I first see it, a golden cage and in it two pigeons. All white, not like mine. Is around the time when Mossi stop hiding how much he enjoying himself that the head handmaiden tell us to leave. Us, the white scientist and me.

"Barbaric, yes, but if she conceive it she won't have to carry it," he say, as if I ask him a question. "You want to see how we reproduce? How generation beget generation?" he ask me.

The next day. Afternoon already. Is only when you get what you think you want that you realize you don't want it. The Queen is getting what she want. Lissisolo, even. Maybe. I want to save the child more out of still lingering malice to Bunshi than anything else. To say, Here is your child, so go fuck yourself a thousand times for saying that my child's death is my fault. The voice that sound like me say that is not what she said. That it is folly to think lives are not tied to the fate of kings, for your family's fate and yours have been because of kings. The wrong kings. Not that the right kings would be better, but that the evil that visited my house would never have visited. It still sound like she blaming what happen to my family on me letting a King rule, as if I am the Aesi.

The Tracker. I tell him not to sleep, neither him nor the magistrate. Yet the Aesi is following us, and also moving leagues ahead of us, which means he must be following him, them, one of them, in dreams. Venin is gone, Jakwu he has never seen, and the Ogo is the

Ogo. That leave them two, and the Tracker is the one who call him by his name. Bunshi is the one who believe in him. Nyka is the one who send him to his death, only the Bultungi didn't kill him. I don't know him much, and the little I know I don't like. I ask myself over and over why this Tracker would betray, and answer myself with that he care so little for this mission, this rescue, that to save him comes down to the coin. What to expect of a mercenary but the mercenary?

Dolingon constables tell them that it's because of the falling boy, but they know that story will change. But two things I know: He fall from the Tracker's balcony, and he is a rope slave. I don't have another word for him. The great pull that move everything in Dolingo is slavery. The power behind the gears was a riddle somebody did have, somebody I don't remember. This realm solve it with the hands and feet of slaves. At the caravan platform and it is all everyone is talking about how nothing is working. My chair refusing to seat me this morning, say one. My bathwater run cold when I said hot, say another. My door refused to open—can you imagine opening one's own door? and No, there was no fan when I said fan, so I just stood there and watch it still—are our houses getting testy with us? Talk of the boy is gone in a blink. I come to realize these people don't know what make their houses work. They don't know a single thing, because they never have to. They don't know that a chair that hesitate is actually hesitating, and a fan unwilling is actually unwilling. I would do as they do, sit and ponder long on these things, except there is a chancellor at my door who take me to where they keep the Tracker.

"I will speak to neither you nor your Queen. Only the witch. Those were his exact words. Filth just to say them," this chancellor say to me.

"Ah, the Sogolon smell," the Tracker say.

"It pleasing to you?"

"No. They going arrest us for murdering that slave boy?"

"Perhaps."

"That poor boy jump to what he thought was freedom. You knew the workings of this place."

For a place so forward in its ways, their cell look more backward than black holes of Juba. Dirt floor, and stone walls, a thick wood door with a slot big enough for his head but nothing else. Nowhere to shit, for shit is all that one smell.

"Some loose tongue spread word that metals fear me," he say.

"How long you working with the Aesi?"

"I at least finish the job with someone before I start working for their enemy."

"You do something to get his attention. Kill a spy? A witch? He would notice the killing of a witch."

"Don't think there's much my dead can tell him."

"He follow you in dreams."

"Best you ask my dreams."

"I tell you not to sleep that night."

"And while I don't take orders from you, the one thing I didn't do was sleep. You would know since you watch the magistrate fuck me all the way into morning," the Tracker say.

"Didn't stay till you finish."

"Was one for the gods, that finish."

"And yet even a god do only one thing after . . . if he's a man."

"I say no sleep come for me."

"The Aesi already sending a troop to Dolingo," I say.

"So somebody did betray you? Bunshi? She's been missing for a long time, but I just assumed you two had words."

"He not the one coming. Just the troops."

"No? But still. Sound like you need to find this child quick. How you plan to do so?"

"I never understand why she need any of you. Any five or six warriors and a hound would do. You, perhaps since you closer to dog even before the Wolf Eye. And yet the first thing you do is set off for the Darklands for no other reason than it burn you to take wisdom from a woman."

"Wisdom? You ride all the way around the forest because you were a coward, not because you wise. Same reason you stay away from all things enchanted. Same reason you hate those doors," he say.

"You sure whatever fall on you in that forest not still in you?"

"What you want, Sogolon?"

"What I want?"

"Yes, you. Or the King Sister, or Bunshi or whoever."

"Tell us where the boy is."

"Who is us? Because I know it's not what this Queen wants. Mossi already gave her some of what she is looking for. So if this is where you tell me how I can free myself from the prison, then this is where I tell you to take a shit stick and fuck yourself with it."

"Who say I promising you freedom?"

"Then what you promising, everlasting inner peace? Where they get you from? You still don't tell me what you want."

"The child you going still help me find," I say.

"You been around royals too long. Say one thing and mean something else, for a woman who don't have a thing you certainly have their ways. In the royal enclosure but having none of their power. And you can quit this shit about the child. You mentioned him less than five times since we set out. The Aesi, on the other hand, him you mention plenty. Including just now. Didn't you just hear yourself? Before you even ask me where is the child, what did you say? Repeat it for me," the Tracker say.

"The one thing about devils. They don't need acknowledgment in their ways."

"Your head is just all over the fucking place to-night, woman."

"He can't win again, you hear me? Not a third time, and you not going to help him. I kill you first."

"Finally. I been waiting for the real Sogolon for over a moon now. So this is a game between you and the Aesi."

"Not a game. I don't play."

"Play is exactly what you're doing. So what is the play here? Sadogo in on the game? Mossi?"

"I don't play."

"You mean you don't enjoy it," the Tracker say. "But it is a game. You're not a true believer like the girl Nyka is fucking. Not a zealot like the water goddess—"

"Sprite."

"Whatever. In fact you're more indifferent than a lizard in a cockfight. Except for the Aesi. What did he take from you?"

"You the one with answers, not me."

"They still talk to you, the spirits he took from you?"

"No."

"That is a shame. You look like you could use a kind word from dead kin. Unless . . . Of course."

"What now?"

"Word from dead kin is the last thing you want. You're responsible. Fuck the gods, Sogolon."

"Done talk?"

"Now you want silence?"

"Tell me where the boy is."

"Now it's me. Just a blink ago you said us. In exchange for what, freedom?"

"Look through that slot behind and you will see the prison and torture chamber."

"Between you me and the gods? A fist up my asshole is not torture."

"No, fool, out there is the prison. You not in the prison."

I been waiting for that smirk to leave his face this whole time.

"I know you wonder it, how come you never see a single child in Dolingo? Some cities rear cattle, other cities grow wheat. Dolingo grow men, and not in no natural way. You don't need explanation and your head can't swell to take it. So know this. For moon after moon, year after year, a cluster of years after cluster of years, the seed and the wombs of the Dolingon become useless."

"The white scientists?" Tracker ask.

"That is misadventure, not breeding. What is not barren breeds monsters unspeakable in look. Bad seed going into bad wombs, the same families over and over, and the Dolingon go from the most wise of children to the most foolish. It take them fifty years to say to one another, Look at us, we need new seed and new wombs."

"Tell me there will be monsters soon," he say.

"It greater than magic. If she conceive—she, the

Queen, that is a man like no other. He will live like no other except that he fathering hundreds upon hundreds. He is the tap and they drain him. Other men they drain for the rest of the people. Even your Ogo, whose seed useless, their scientist and witchman can make it sow and breed."

"What happen when they done draining?"

"You live life as full as any other life."

"Of course. All they want for me is a full life. I'm taken with this draining. A tube? I would far prefer a mouth. This don't answer why there are no children," the Tracker say.

"The hall outside your window. They call it the great womb. They suspend them in womb juice. Feed them and grow them, until they as big as you. Only then they hatch. But they healthy and they live long."

From him a smart line will come. Is coming. But not yet.

"This is the great Dolingo."

"Three days done pass, counting today. Where is the boy?"

"No children, no slaves, no travelers either."

"Nobody get safe passage in Dolingo," I say. "They use anyone who they find at the foot of the trunks for breeding and kill whoever they can't put to use. You at least have use. Even in this, is the man who have use."

"Go fuck a lame god with that logic. You sold us off."

"The Queen will treat you, the prefect, and the Ogo better than concubines."

"Will she give us each a palace that she never visits?" the Tracker ask.

"All my life men telling me this would be the life above all lives. Well, here come the Queen of Dolingo saying, That is all you have to be for however long you live. From how man talk, this should be the greatest gift."

"I'd rather a choice then a gift."

"So now you is like a woman in all things. Tell me how it feel one day."

"Thought I was just a nose."

"A nose with some use. The rest of you just in the way. And when we get the boy, know that you help restore the natural rule to the North."

"Like you care about the natural rule of the North. Now you sound like Bunshi. You will use the child to draw him out. The Aesi. Does Bunshi know?

"Tell them what they need to know. These scientists, I hear they like finding new ways to make you talk," I say and turn to leave.

"One thing, Moon Witch. You don't know me well but you know enough. By the time I kill half the guards in this room, they will have to kill me. So my question is this. How many runes will you have to write each night to stop me coming for you?"

I turn from him to the shadow. He is in the cell but I am the one who feel the wall just close in on me.

But just in the corner of my eye, so in the quick that I almost miss it, he jerk his head. Like somebody call him name.

"The boy. He is here," I say.

He shout curses at me, but I leave him for the room outside. Two guards stand at a door, three more across from me, in a green room, dim and with torch lights. Just then the torch lights blow out. Come on again. Blow out. So we go again with this shit, one of the guards say. Then the door open, slam shut, then open again. A guard rush in, saying that the cell gates keep unlocking again, and this wild shit been happening all quartermoon. The door slam again, right on a guard's finger. One of them say they done with it now, leave and come back with a ladder, which he use to climb into a hatch in the ceiling. A thump first, a punch, a slap, then a squeal, more grunts, and cursing. And while all this going on, torch fire come, then go, then come back, doors swing in and out, and the one window swing open, then close. Everything shudder, then everything still.

Two enter, three leave. Both of them, hoods hiding their heads, robes hiding the rest. The guards so fast to get out of their way that one walk into the wall. One remove the hood to reveal his spidery white locks. The other loosen his robe enough to expose the shifty, meaty hump on his right shoulder. They close the door behind them. The Tracker is the Tracker, laughing, mocking, insulting, saying something smart that I don't hear. But I hear something muffling his throat. And then nothing. For a long time, maybe too long. Long enough for me to see from the guards' nodding and whispering what this mean. And then it come, a mumble first, and shout into the gag—words he trying to say. And then a bawl. Then he scream, then he scream louder, and louder than that, and louder still. And he scream into a cough, which turn into a bawl like somebody cutting his leg off without opium. Then he scream again, long and loud, a scream that run all the way down the corridor and vanish into the dark. And still he screaming. One of the guards vomit.

"Mwaliganza, the fifth tree. We see him there, and others. Find him in the old apothecary and her house," the first scientist say as he leave.

The second emerge, his body bare down to his waist. White and thin his skin, I can see the blood routes and how they work. He is following the first when a slab of flesh slither out the door. The guard jump. The slab look like the hind quarter of a pig. It wail and squeal and pop an eye open. Not a head, a lump with lumps and a mouth always open and drooling spit along the floor. He pull himself along with his long bony hands, still shrieking, until he catch the scientist, yank himself up to his waist, crawl slow up his back, then wrap one hand around his waist, where it disappear in fold of skin. The other hand pop claws and dig into his chest. I couldn't see and don't want to. The hump settle back on his right shoulder as the scientist cover himself and walk away.

"Mwaliganza! Now!" I shout. The soldiers outside, twenty and nine more all run. Venin not running.

"Not in this world or another I fighting your fucking fight," he say.

"You still not going get far," I say.

"Unless you die," Venin say.

No sky caravan take us direct to Mwaliganza. We have to take it to Mungunga, rush to another one heading to Mkora, and from there take the only caravan leaving. The craft almost clear of Mkora when we see it several floors below in the big public square. An explosion of brown, like something drop on an ant's nest to make them scatter. "What is that?" one of the guards shout. We at least ten floors above it. Them. The mass is brown because they all naked, except for the pieces of rope probably still on them. Another explosion of brown, like a wave upon a wave spilling more into the plaza. The slaves? one ask. The slaves! another shout. What slaves? shout another. But they overrun the square, trampling everyone underfoot. The slaves done rebel. They sweeping Mkora like a flood, shocking and confusing the soldiers. Nobody read anything into the chairs sticking, the doors slamming, the boy jumping from the Tracker's ledge. That the fan refuse to swing was a slave refusing to swing it, and the bath refuse to fill itself with water was a slave refusing to fill it. Truth, I never think nothing of any of it. The soldiers all shouting for this caravan to move faster, still not thinking that is slaves pulling it. Until, several paces from the dock, they stop. We kick out the front doors and jump into the river. A soldier thank the gods that it was not deep. From the dock we looking over at Mkora, as slaves keep bursting through doors like flood. An explosion shake us. An explosion now at Mwaliganza.

"You know your orders!" I shout at them.

But I can't tear myself from the sight either. The slaves rebelling. I try to cut off what they brimming up in me. No, flooding me. Royal Courts. Kings, King Sisters, and Queens. A trail of impaled bodies all because of the word of one King. Me taking all of it as just the way. Even when I hate it, I accept it, even when I hate fate, I accept it. Shock come but it don't push out the shame. Rebellion. We suffer, we survive, we endure. None of us ever think, we rebel. I snap myself back.

"Go!" I say.

We at the door of the old apothecary's house and shop. The door is open, most likely because no slave is keeping it shut. I don't know soldier tactics and they don't know to take orders from any woman save their Queen. And these gold ceremonial weapons for people who never had to fight in any war. These damn gold weapons. Two step in ahead of me and before the third one pass, my wind (not wind) push him back. Behind us the tumble of slaves bursting borders, the good nobles screaming, bawling, and getting ripped to bits. I imagine the rebels sun-shocked, staggering, powering themselves with hate if might won't do. The soldiers jump with every explosion, with every shout, with every roar, and with every shake. Some run off.

"You can't beat a fight with a dance," I say to those near me. "Your Queen give you orders."

Upstairs is a room, just a room, like a lesson hall. But up another floor, a child's cry. Quiet but forlorn and insisting that you hear it. The two in front of me march up one more flight. Nobody have any tactics, nobody speaking any code, nobody given any signs. Keme had signs, Keme and his Red Army. I don't know why that thought choose now to come, but I dismiss it. This floor is emptier than the one before, making me wonder what exactly this apothecary sell. Gray walls wearing away back to the orange behind it. But it is not empty, just misty. Banking us on both sides, stools with oils, potions, powders, a line of birthing chairs, odd since nobody in Dolingo birthing the barbarian way. I about to curse myself for thinking like them when the boy's cry draw me further in. We shuffle over to him and see the shape of two boys. One floating in the air, still, with bugs buzzing around him, perhaps dead. The other, his back to us, still crying.

"Little boy, little boy, come now. End with the crying," say a soldier.

"Shut up," I whisper.

We shuffle closer. The boy's cry turn into a full bawl, but as he turn around only his mouth crying.

His body still as a statue, his eyes as blank and calm as somebody waking up. His face perfectly peaceful even as loud bawling come from his mouth. And the other boy, the shape of a boy, blood is dripping from his feet. His eyes wide open but nothing he see. All over his skin pop open with holes like a wasp nest, while in, out, and all over come bugs. Several squeeze through his eyes and fly up to the ceiling, where up to now nobody look. Eloko the green-hair grass demon I see first, then I blink and see two. Then a short one, all black hair, fingers and toes, then him, Ishologu, still in his handsome man form, his wings spread as wide as the room. Their back against the ceiling as if they lying down on floor and we hanging upside down. The boy cry again. Above! a guard shout, but then Ishologu flap his wings, thunder shake the room, and lightning cram the whole room with bright.

Burning hair bring me back, but the blinding bright take me out. My eyes open but they feel like somebody opening them. They open to everything hazy, then they shut, then the fear hit me that my skin is burning, burning up, my skin roasting and roasting quick, blinding white, blinding burn. I wake up screaming, but everything is still a haze. One Eloko, then two, then two more, one with something dangling from his mouth, a leg, then a foot, then a toe, he swallowing it. Bodies of soldiers burst apart and scattered, while some soldiers run around crackling lightning without and within. Smoke—no, mist. A cloud of flies swarm two soldiers and lift them off the ground and they scream until bugs fill their mouths and pop into their skin until they are just a host for flies. Two flies fat with blood pass my eyes. The swarm leave the bodies and I can see right through the holes as the corpses fall. The swarm clump together to form a ghoul with yellow eyes and claws. My eyes go dark again and open to gold. Swords fly while monsters laugh. The room blur and all the screaming make my ears hurt. Then right in front of me, green hair above a face like an arrowpoint, red with white stripes— no, white with red stripes, eyes spinning, his bone dagger about to go into my chest. He pull back to stab but somebody yank him away so hard that his leg kick my face and my eyes shut again. And air is under my feet, my body is rising and is not my wind (not wind) doing it. His hand wrap around my neck firm, but not a squeeze. I open my eyes to his square jaw and moonlight-white skin. White hair streaking black hair and leading into feathers at the back of his head. I blink and his face is all eyes and beak, blink again and he is a man and my voice slur about how he handsome. See his hair come down to a point between brows and his lips curl unto a wicked smile. He open his mouth but I still hearing thunder echo. I can't look down. Ipundulu. No, Ishologu. My head start to burn . . . not from the lightning . . . he trying to enter my head . . . just like the Aesi. He curse something. I hear him. Then he flick a claw and touch between my breasts.

And my chest is on fire, then my chest is wet and

I open my eyes again to see him cutting in me. But then he jump—a knife is in his shoulder and his blood is black. He let me go and I fly, no I fall, I hit the ground—my feet, my knees my belly, my head—black again. Eyes open and Jakwu cackling as the two Eloko jump him, one from the floor and one from the ceiling. Ceiling Eloko swing right into Jakwu, clobbering him in the chest. Floor Eloko slash his thigh but he laugh again, dodge a blow and smash his face. Third one I don't see what he do, but I hear him scream and grab his belly. Jakwu don't wait, he smash the grass demon into the floor. The cloud of bugs swarm Sadogo, who swat and swat and crush but can't stop them piercing his skin until a bottle of oil smash on his chest. Rub it on your arm! somebody shout. Tracker. My eyes dip. They return as Adze's bugs drip out of the Ogo. Lightning men fight Mossi and his two swords. Two swords are blurs and spilled lightning is everywhere. I try to get up but under my skin start to roast again. Ishologu's lightning leaping from his chest onto me. He whip his wings open and drop a thunder that make everything shake and fall. And break off. The room don't move, for everyone get knock down. Ishologu turn back to me and just then a torch hit him in the back. He look at me as confused as a baby before he burst into flames.

They hang over him, I can count them all. Nobody come for me. I cough and my chest spit blood. I smell who they hang over. At my side I see a cooked bird. All his wings roast off, skin black and red, charred like a goat. Smelling like a botched sacrifice. They talking hard about him, but then they look at me and the harshness don't change.

"What is his name?" Mossi ask.

"Nobody ever name him," Tracker say.

"Then what do we call him, Boy?"

They gather around Ishologu. Jakwu coming up from behind me, kick me in the back.

"Moon Bitch don't rise soon, all her spirits will know she is weak," he say.

"What should we do with this one?" Mossi say, pointing to Ishologu.

"Kill him," Jakwu say. "Kill him. Then kill he—"

The wall and window break away and in come a ninki nanka. No, not a dragon, something with wings, bigger wings than Ipundulu. A big chunk of wall knock Sadogo down. Not a dragon, he have legs like a man. Not a man, his legs have claws. The feet kick Mossi through a wall. He knocking over stuff with his wings, black skin with no feathers, like a bat, not an Ipundulu. Sasabonsam, somebody shout. He turn to go for the Tracker, and I squeeze my hand and the wind (not wind) knock him off his feet and pin him down. I hold him down, but each time he push my chest hurt. I can't hold him no more. Sadogo rise to his feet. Sasabonsam grab Ishologu's leg with his iron claw hand, take up the boy with the other hand—the boy run to him—and fly away.

The noise of rebellion swell and burst over my ears, then fade as another mob move away. Now I am outside on a wet floor. Above, one caravan is burning and another just fall. The Queen's palace don't have any ropes. They surround me and I go out again. I wake up in night almost falling off a horse riding through the dark, fall asleep again, wake up feeling rope tying me to somebody's back, fall asleep again, then wake in the morning.

"There is no way we'll catch them," Mossi say, eyeing the door still open.

Outer Dolingo.

"She didn't send those pigeons to Dolingo. She send them to the Aesi," Tracker say. It inflame my mouth, but not the rest of me.

"You lie, you . . . you is lying child of a bitch . . ." I say.

"He already dispatched an army to Dolingo. See her plan? To imprison us, snatch the child for herself. Present both to the Aesi like a fucking gift. Aesi kills the child and this corrupt monarchy is saved," the Tracker say.

"How fares that enterprise?" ask Mossi.

"You don't care about no damn monarchy! None of you," I say.

"You were the one Bunshi warned me about," say the Tracker. "You the only one. Don't trust a witch, she say."

"I not a . . . I not a witch. I not a witch."

"And you, Jakwu, is it? How come you to be in this girl's body?" Mossi ask.

"Ask the Moon Witch."

"Everything is me, oh? Everything is me. Sunrise and sunfall must be me . . ."

"Sane is definitely not you," the Tracker say.

"Still, Mossi fucking the Queen for the rest of your days is no punishment?"

"You didn't feel inside her koo," Mossi say as they laugh and go off to discuss me. The Tracker, now paces away, whisper into the air and the flame spark, blaze, and cut the door open.

"What do I see through this hole?" Jakwu ask.

"The way to Mitu," Sadogo say.

"I shall take it."

"All might not be fine with you. Jakwu has never seen the ten and nine doors, but Venin has," the Tracker say.

"What that mean?" Jakwu ask.

"He means, though your soul is new, your body might burn," Mossi say.

"I might still be tethered to this one, but I shall take it," Jakwu say.

I finally pull myself to stand, but stumble and almost fall. None of them come to catch me, not even the Ogo. They all decide to pursue the boy. Jakwu take a look at me trying to stand, and laugh. But he still shuffle timid as he step through the door. The door shrink some more as the three men turn to leave. I stumble again, landing on my knee, and the Tracker run over to help me up.

"Just this, Sogolon. The Aesi never once find me in my dreams."

He lean in so close that his lips touch my ear.

"I am the one who went searching for him in his. And you, you are the fucking fool that let a Sangomin run loose."

Before I could say anything, before my wind (not wind) could do anything, he grab my back and shove me through the door.

And all I remember is fire.

5

NO ORIKI

Ko oroji
adekwu ebila
afingwi

TWENTY-SIX

Y ou want to know about my list. All this time, and all these words, all that ink and all that paper, when you could have asked this from the beginning. Look at you, hotting up yourself with glut, saying you come here for facts, but fact is not why you come here every morning before the rooster even crow. You come here for story not so the Tracker tell you? I hear him. I hear some of his tale. Some of it even have one or two women he neither call witch nor bitch. But all of this—some of which I don't remember, some I recall as a tale being told to me—not something I see, hear, or smell myself. You know how you remember what you sweat through? I have no memory of sweat. Some of this is the testimony of Ikede, who preserve my life on page when it go up in smoke, before he throw himself from his own roof. Tell me what it mean that my memory is of a man telling me what my life was and me choosing to believe it, when even the gentlest of men can tell only so much story about a woman. But look at you. All you really want to know is who on my list.

No paper. You taking this witch thing too far. Yes, too far, for I know witches of the North and South and none of them move in the way you think. What next, that I flay a child and write my list on his skin? This I will tell you, that one time I write every name down on piece of red linen, tie it around a nkisi nkondi that I steal, and then bury it in the same ground where before lie a necromancer who practice shameful science with plants and beast until people bury him alive. And if you believe that, then who know what else you take for truth these days? Funny thinking for a man living a lie.

I see Inquisitor, but I hear southern griot. Look at you, shifting on your stool, the only devil in this room is the past right behind your ear. Work hard you do, so hard on that voice, yet you still sound like any moment you will break into verse. Your left ass is tired, Inquisitor, shift to the right. You wondering if I have contempt for you. You don't know what I talking about. Bet that before we finish you will check the door again to make sure no guard hearing us, even though you say "leave us" twice. They won't know who a southern griot is, but they might ask. I thought your kind was safe in the South, unless what you preparing is a report for the North. I hear southern griot, oh. I even smell it. But let no woman say you never make good for yourself. Nor man either, for this here man have ambition. To climb your way all up into the grand chamber of inquisitors and makers of law sure did take some sort of cunning. Intelligence too, of course, not to mention that rare discerning eye. Either that or standards run so low in Nigiki that a commonplace recordkeeper can climb to the highest rank of the lowest rank of power—yes I insult you. Don't call a crow a hawk when everybody can see the feathers. So let us make this quick.

Any griot would say, But what can a man do but flee? People's eyes allow more and condemn less in the kingdom of the four brothers. I don't abhor you because you are a liar. I don't even despise you because you are a coward. I dislike you because you still sit there smug in thinking that you must be smarter than who you talking to, for your task is to take from them what they not willing to give. Look at you, taking down as many of my words as you can, thinking you will sift through the lies later. You, the same inquisitor who just listen to a man sell you truth about an ingenious buffalo. Oh, I heard that part too. Such a shrewd beast. Canny, shifty, with such an impish whip of tail, such a fine friend indeed. Them kind of animal more steadfast than man, constant and true, and as for his mirth? Bottomless. Yet you didn't even question it when this beast among beasts just done vanish from the last part of his story? And for no other reason than he get bored telling it. A smart buffalo? Eh, a smart buffalo would never be so foolish as to mix with people. Nor a smart leopard neither. Ingenious beast—ingenious lie is more like it.

Long time I pondering what I was going to say when I finally meet one like you, one who betray his own brothers. No? You not a betrayer? You just a man who leave right before the purge. Chance of the gods, coincidence, them white scientists call it. No warning come to your window by whisper or pigeon, then. One day you gone, next day ax come for the griot head. I know one man who survive, but the guilt of not dying make him take his own life. But here you come, alive, for now.

You think this is about setting aright what is askew, disorder back into order. That is the shit men think, to make any wicked action right in their eyes. No, fool, this is about revenge. I just done say that I don't call a hawk a crow. And even revenge is not about revenge, not really. The planning too long and the execution too quick. What really fire up revenge is desire. You want to know why it take five years to do what would take another person five moons, when the answer right in front of you. Is the desire. Desire is what rush under your skin, through your bones, flowing where blood used to flow. Wanting to kill a man, living to kill a man, sharpening my whole life to the fine point of being nothing more than a tool to kill, that give me more reason to wake up every dawn than killing him for real. You grow it, you nurture it, you prune like a plant, bend and twist it as well. Plus, it is something to do and a woman need work. You want to know who is on my list so you can tie their death to me.

The Mweru. She is the one I hunt first. She and him, two targets that I would chop to death in the height of my rage or invade their hearts and let them explode. The King Sister post sentries from her rebel army on the skirt of the Mweru. To stop enemy approach, go the thinking. Who stand guard once inside the Mweru is a mystery. No man know for sure that if a man enter, he never leave, but few been foolish enough to test it. I wait until night and slip through on foot, hopping over potholes deeper than chasms and creeping around pools and springs more foul than a burning dog, with shooting steam that would burn my flesh off. It mystify me how she live here, since nothing here is ever green, nothing here ever grow. No trees, so no cover, but I wear black and this night have no moon. So much strangeness in these lands that nobody going notice a moving shadow. The ten nameless tunnels of the Mweru. People say they look like overturned urns of the gods. People also say that each go in a different direction, one of them to a lake of fire, another to the otherworld. All I know is that compared to their height I was an ant. The one I choose wider than a causeway but something was glowing at the end of it. The skin of the palace, for skin is what you call the walls of something that look like a whale in death stretch. Sails too, as if this was a ship in another age, or mockery for any who think they going leave this place. I see myself in a puddle and stomp in it.

The guards see me. My wind (not wind) kick two

far off into the sky and slam two against the corridor walls. One I throw up in the high ceiling and he don't come down, one try to grab me but below his neck reach me before above. I slice, stab, slam, and throw my way into the great hall, but nowhere to be seen is this Queen. In the throne room, two women stand guard by the empty seat. The women raise their spears. I tell them that I try within my power not to kill women but push me beyond the edge of my temper and I will dispatch a bitch.

"I know you."

"Is Sogolon," I say.

"No you're not. I know her."

I don't tell her that she both right and wrong. Instead I let her think that I'm just some woman who infiltrate her throne room. Savior or executioner, she don't care. I come to see.

"Some days I think he take him. Some days I think he leave."

The voice is so weak that first I thought it's one of my own, coming back. He didn't raise no alarm, didn't scream, or shout, or even weep, she say. She, Lissisolo, stumbling onto the black throne, sleep controlling her and liquor the cause. I smell the herb and know it from the Sunk City. Two tusks rise from the foot of throne right into the ceiling. Her headdress on the floor, her gown open at the top with her breasts falling out. His hunger for the milk never quit, even though no milk was going to come, she say. First she think he a strange boy who miss being close to his mother. Soon she think he a strange boy always wanting to lick his mother's nipple. Later she think he strange after he stop licking her breast and bite it, deep enough to draw the blood that he lick. No, suck.

"He didn't even cry, you understand? He didn't even cry."

This is how it go. One of the vampire who run with Ishologu, the one they didn't kill, come for the boy. This boy who displeased with everything, who fall asleep in the position of one murdered, who stab one servant, kick another, and nearly gouge the eyes out of one more, he didn't say nothing when the monster come for him. Instead he crawl up to the monster chest and let it cradle him. This boy, long pass when you could call him infant. Of course she whip the women who swear he go willingly. Her son was stolen. But from the beginning I never have hopes for this boy, I say to her.

"Shut up."

"Your little boy drinking from monster teat from the day he move with Ishologu."

"I say shut up, you."

"Thinking he was your boy. He was never your boy. Now he not Ipundulu or Ishologu, but worse."

"No."

"Among the living, but he drinking blood anyway. Drinking vampire blood the way some man take opium. Kidnapping? He couldn't wait to flee from you. And why would he need you? He already have a mother."

"Kill her!"

The women guard both throw spears, one I dodge, one I let the wind (not wind) halt midair, flip and hurl right back at them, bursting through the neck of one and pinning her to the wall. The other pull her sword. I put away my knives and leave her perplexed.

"Is true. I had to call the healers the last time he set on my breasts."

"He no longer your boy."

"Stop talking about my son."

"What you name him?"

"Liongo, after his ancestor."

"What he answer to?"

"I . . ."

"What he answer to?"

"He have a name!"

"What he answer to?"

"He is the future of the North," Lissisolo say.

"He don't have no future," I say.

"Wh-who are you, eh? Who she think she is that she can speak evil to me? I have my own army."

She willed her son to be unharmed and unspoiled for so many years that the will is what she have in place of him. I can imagine when she finally see him for who he was, and choosing the son of her longing instead. Trying every day to will that son into being from the mass of flesh and bone before her. And this army. Her rebel army. I see them, not even two thousand strong, they join forces with the South so that

if they defeat the North, then she would be crowned
Queen. Regent, of course, she just holding the place
for true King of the true North. Then the South King
suddenly dead, his forces banished farther south than
in any war before, and all she have to show for it is a
scattered force.

"Where the water sprite keep herself?"

"Who are you to want news of the water sprite?"

I just look at her.

"Is not secret, after all. The dead can't hold on to
any secrets, they dead. I was there, and even I didn't
believe it. The Aesi slash her throat."

I shift as if dodging her words. The news so shocking and so inevitable at the same time that I both
shake my head and gasp. Divine born, killed at the
hand of a demigod make for a wicked kind of joke.
But the last time we meet I try to kill her myself. I
have no grief to fill the space that her death leave, but
an empty space there is.

"What they call you?"

"Sogolon," I said.

"I say I know a Sogolon and she is not you. She's
dead, not so? Or she another one who won't stay
gone? Are you here to save my boy? He is just a little
boy, my little boy. Yet so many wicked people want
to hurt him."

Then she do something neither me nor her guard
expect. Break from the throne like she trying to escape and run toward me, grabbing my hand. Either

she weak or she begging, for her knees on the floor. She still don't see that is me. First name on my list and I don't kill her because I don't have to.

"My son, my son, you going to find him for me? You going to bring back my precious boy?"

I look at her, not even seeing me, though to tell the truth if I was looking with her eyes, I wouldn't see me either. Instead I find part of myself in her. When the desire is all you have left. No boy, just the longing for the boy. What she will never say is that she did still have longing for the boy even when he was right there. And that is what buckle her knees and bring her down to the floor.

"No," I say, then leave.

I lose memory of who find me. But I remember that everything, even a gentle touch, burn. Just a breath on me would make me scream. I hear then through what did leave of my ears that this is either the gods' wickedness or mercy. The two times I look at my hand I see charred meat so I stop looking. I just lie there on the dirt trail, hearing Jakwu's laugh getting fainter and fainter, and knowing that if the laugh vanish, it mean the spell on him was broken too. But that thought come and vanish like smoke. The Tracker push me through the door, violating the door. It do nothing for Jakwu's body, while mine explode in fire. All I see is fire. All I remember is flame. I have no recall of running, or dropping to the ground and rolling, or screaming over the crackling of my own flesh. The burning don't stop even when the fire gone. The burning don't stop during sleep, and even when I drag myself to a pond, the water taste red. Like I say, I don't know who find me. My head was not keeping anything, not the horse, the wagon, feet, bed, sheets, cot, healing herbs, nothing. I do remember a plant rubbing all over me that burn first, then cool, colder than the white dirt in the mountains.

She find me. Who know how many days pass, or moons? You wouldn't stop calling it, a man's voice in a dark room say to me, after he squeeze water on my forehead and peel fruits to stick in my mouth. You wouldn't stop calling it so we ask around for who go by that name. Nobody round here answer to that, but from Kongor come one who do. I couldn't talk much so I don't know how to ask anything. Another voice I feel nearby and ask if she call for the Nnimnim today. The next day a woman come, make herself known in the dark. Why the black? she ask, and the man say that she think even daylight burning her. The woman tell them she will take me now and leave by boat at night. I don't know where we going, only that wind was blowing against that direction, and over the Ubangta, wind blow south.

"Nnimnim . . . Dolingo . . ." I whisper.

"There is no Dolingo," she say.

One moon later it was the fall of Dolingo that shock me the most. Yes, the slaves kill nearly every noble, counsel, delegate, every master of verse and song, and every white scientist they could throw from their own tower, the Nnimnim woman say. Then they burned the halls of white science. Everybody wild, nobody thinking, everybody wanting blood. Most of the slaves couldn't even speak since they didn't know they had tongues. The Queen they give to a man not slave but not free either, who was to find one of the thousands of secret chambers in all of Dolingo, bind every limb up in rope, shove the feeder down her throat, and lock her away for as long as she live. Then they kill the man so that the location die with him. It don't take long for Kwash Dara to send troops to restore the peace. That and a chief from Malakal to ease the people of Dolingo into a new era of further peace and cooperation. But Dolingo have the ropes and they have the gears. They don't have the pull. We going to need the pull, he say, right as Kwash Dara send more troops.

Wild dakka to keep me in sleep, for when there is sleeping, there is healing. A bath in black plum leaves for open wounds. South people call this iputumame, but we call it kiluma, she say, as she bring a spiky plant in the room. It bring life, heal life, lengthen life, the only thing it don't do is take it. She and the women slice the thick leaves, scoop out the gel, and rub it deep into my skin, then they wrap the leaves all around me, and give me tea from a sister plant to drink away infection. I wake up and see my skin green and scream until she say, Hush girl, these are the things that must happen to you. Another night the other women, seeing that I still can't do anything with my hands and fingers, grind a paste out of the blister beetle and rub it in. Is days later when I can hold the bowl of tea myself.

"This tea, it different," I say.

"You first words other than Nnimnim or Dolingo."

"The tea."

"Mkonde-konde in the North, umkakase in the East. It stop your mind running away from you. Skin no the only thing that need the healing," she say.

The Nnimnim woman look at me, not pleased but satisfied.

"Your body take you far, Sogolon. Time now you give it rest."

"You telling me to die?"

"No. You know what me telling you."

I don't catch what she saying, until I catch it.

"No," I say.

"Many a woman out there with no use. You know there is a way because you seen it."

"No."

"This here body can only do so much for you."

"I not taking no girl body, you hear me? I rather dead. Make death come first."

"Death not coming for you, woman."

"Then poison me."

"If you was going die, you would have been dead long time now."

On a day I didn't count, I climb out of the bed. I walk but not far. I bend over and feel kiluma leaves pop and think it is the skin on my back. The next day I make a great error turning at my waist and more than the leaves pop. When I clutch my sides I see that I gone from four fingers to two. All the healing couldn't stop my fingers from fusing together. I fling away my hand with fury, as if I could fling the thing off. The rest of my body I don't dare look at. Not once. We bathe you in every healing herb, every tonic, every ground magic, everything to make your skin stretch and move, but you still burned girl, she say. You hair not coming back. Your skin going always be like charcoal. The burning smell branded in your mind, it never going leave your nose. But there is still something we can do.

The Nnimnim woman offer me a spell and I take it. Two of her kind come to my room that night. No, this is not possession, this is something else, they say. Who do I want to look like? It can be anybody.

"An old Mitu woman," I say.

They describe the woman to me. Jaw more square than mine, cheekbones higher and wider, forehead big and flat with tracks, nose straight and pushing out, like a sand sea woman. Wide shoulders, lanky and strong like a running messenger, hair braided with dry fruit, hard flowers, bones, tusks, and long feathers of the hawk. Then they mark white clay down my breasts, down to my belly, and with wet fingers, divide the clay into stripes. Another woman wrap ripped leather around my hips. Every soul that look at you will see the woman you describe. That is how all we see you. But the enchantment won't deceive any kind of mirror, not glass, not iron or copper, nor the puddle nor the river. Nothing that woman use to look at their face. This is how everybody will see you, but you will never see yourself.

More women come into the room as it get lighter. And still more women, or perhaps I was seeing them all for the first time. You don't remember me, one of them say. She wear a band around the eyes that her husband take away from her. After you right the wrong done to me, the women teach me how to see, with my fingers, my ears, and my nose, she say as she paint clay on my skin with grace. After my father kill my mother he take to raping me, say another. The night you come, he was heading to my sister's bed. You don't know me, for then I was no woman, say yet another. I call each of those women my sisters since then, you remember us? The girls kidnapped in that caravan headed to Marabanga. They was taking us out to sea to sell us off as wife and concubines. We was seven and eight. Each night they take away one of us to test the goods and that girl would never return. That night you swoop down on we roof was the night I know the gods didn't forget us.

"Every woman in this room touched by the Moon Witch, step forward," the Nnimnim woman say, and every woman in the room look at me and approach the bed and surround it. They take their time and let the quiet shuffle do the talking. Some look like faces I supposed to remember, some look like faces I used to know. Many of them old, some of them older than the child they was when they see the Moon Witch. Woman with the gele of the East on her head, woman with the ighiya of the South on her. Woman in white like nuns, woman in rainbow like Queens. Mother and daughter and sister and woman with no one. Woman with one eye, one ear, one leg, no legs, woman other women holding up. Woman from the top of Mantha and from the bottom of Marabanga. Ghosts of women who come back from the other-world to see the Moon Witch, and a crabby one who say, Boy she did love that silver. Some with mouths pack to the brim with words waiting to explode, some nodding quietly, their eyes saying, We see you, sister. Woman who steal a touch of my shoulder, fore-head, woman who grab my hand until another pull my hand into theirs. They pack the room right up to the doorway, and still more was outside, waiting to squeeze themselves in. A girl worm through them to touch me and say, They couldn't move my mother, so she send me.

"Moon Witch still flying through the trees," say another. "Now plenty women righting the wrongs. Plenty in North and South saying, Moon Witch, she is me."

Healing, restoring, remembering, feeling myself take one year. Then I leave. The Nnimnim woman see me trying to write on parchment with my fused fingers. I give up, grab the stick like an ape, and scrape the words. She ask me what I planning to do but my look was the answer.

"No peace in revenge," she say.

"The vengeful not looking for peace," I say.

Mitu. You want to know how I find him. How I find them. Is not like any of them was trying to hide. Is not like the slaver didn't pay him what was owed enough for him to believe that the road ahead was the comfortable life, and the comfortable life was for him. Is not like they didn't all assume I long dead. Is not like I couldn't find where they living after I threaten to cut this man's throat, then chop off a finger and promise him that I will come back for more if word ever set loose that I was looking for this man. He fearful but still he laugh, too long for the laughter to be about me. Talk, fat man, I say, and talk he do. His tongue was a stream, oh. About how the Tracker and them sniff the boy all the way to Kongor, where they was hiding out in the flooded section of Old Tarobe. And of course, the Ishologu just a husk with nobody to work a healing spell, since he long ago kill his witch. All but one of his group dead, yet he still head to Kongor, which mean he is the one with knowledge of the ten and nine doors. Cornered animal. Wounded animal. Dangerous animal, but a beast going nowhere. That is when the Tracker send pigeon to the slaver with a note for three times the money, or he, the magistrate, the Leopard, and the bowman was going take off and leave the boy, or worse, save the boy but hand him over to the Aesi. The Tracker seem to be many things, but liar was not one of them, say the slaver. So when he say he already in communication with the Aesi, we believe him. So they save the boy, but lose the Ogo. He take the Ogo's share.

A riverboat on lower Ubangta take me there. I ask around for the two men living like brothers, then wink and say, But really like husband and wife, and that was all I need to say. Nothing about the Tracker's thin body or the magistrate's sand skin. He long ago charm the women in the market, who say, He used to have hair like a horse and hark his fearsome children, but then he say we bountiful in wit and bosom, so we love him now, oh. He, Mossi. The two men and the six mingi children who live in the baobab tree beyond the city. Beyond the great central outpost, beyond the villages but above the river. From down by the river I watch them. The Tracker's nose don't worry me, for I no longer smell like Sogolon.

They live inside and outside the tree, which give much to them despite heavy use. Cooking they do on open fire away from the branches, but everything else is within the trunk, and hanging steady or loose from the branches. A tree house then, with many rooms not together but scattered all over the top.

The tree not far from the river, so I watch them from the river. There is an old hut on the other side of the banks. The old woman in it long dead, but no-body ever come to check on her it seem, because now her dress holding only bones that rattle when breezes blow. Maybe the Tracker keep to his own and have no care for an old woman who die alone. The older children draw water as they need it. The younger children play nearby, though Mossi don't like when they go too far. The smoky girl one appear before me one noon, but I grab my cloak and make like a washerwoman. She make like one too, shaping her cloud into a hand scrubbing up and down until she get bored and poof into the air, only to form again several paces away. Meanwhile I watch and work up my rage at men who can be villainous to all but virtuous to some. Watching them be kind to children should make me think of them as better men, but it make them worse, for no other wickedness more wicked than choosing with who you dole out kindness. Seeing them wrap their children in loving don't make me want to spare them. It make me want to watch them suffer. The old man who live with them write pretty oriki, but the Tracker slap him every time he hear it. One quartermoon, all of them go to the river lands, but I couldn't follow in such open country without somebody seeing me, so I don't know what they go do. But they come back even more loving, joking about the strange, smelly priest who was so excited to cut Papa's keke skin off, and I think of the family I have and lose, and I hate them even more.

This evening they leave the children in the care

of the old man and sneak away. I see them coming
to the river, moonlight making the water shimmer
silver. They throw off clothes before they even get to
the river, and I not going watch them fuck. But the
trees too sparse and the rocks too little and I won't
get to the shed without them seeing me. The wind
(not wind) blow a ball around me, which become a
bubble and I sink underwater. I see them only once,
two white legs fluttering past me, two dark hands
grabbing his ass.

One day, the old man leave with as much ceremony
as I assume he did come. The quartermoon don't even
blink before the Leopard arrive without the bowman.
I have no quarrel with the Leopard, but I surprised
to see him back as friend. The Leopard entice him to
leave. Entice him so good that not even a loud argument with Mossi couldn't stop him. I don't know the
Tracker, yet I know the Tracker, so I know he didn't
need much convincing. I would have his head, but like
I done say, I don't have no quarrel with the Leopard.
A fight against one would be a fight against two, and
that cat not on my list. First I think to follow them,
then I think to stay—after all, how long can one man
be away from his family? And like I done say, I don't
have no quarrel with the Leopard. So I stay in the
shack, long enough that the smoke girl get too close.
Tracker and the cat gone a quartermoon, then half,
then full moon. I wait and I nurse my hate, for I am
an old woman, wait is all that is left to do.

But waiting lead to thinking, and my own mind

ask me if I want to kill the Tracker or destroy him, for those was two different things. If I want to find the Tracker, I only need to find who commission the Leopard. If I want to destroy the Tracker, all I need to do is head to his house. The thought seize me, and I glut full on the conceit of it, but hold my place in the shed. I not going after people I don't have no malice toward, not even the consort who believe him, and his whole brood of little Sangomin.

Is the loud crash that wake me up. A door kicked down, a roof cave in, I don't know what rush me to the window. The tree jerk and shake and from inside come yelling, growling, and screaming. Things smash, things crack, a boy's yell smash in half. The tall albino Sangomin, the handsome one, yes he and Mossi grab swords and jump from the shack up highest branch and kick down the back door at the trunk. Squeal, screech, yelp, bark, cry, and the tree shaking. And bursting through the window, the wing of giant bat. Mossi, grabbing two of the children, run outside, put them on a horse, yell, and slap the horse for them to gallop. Is then I see the boy, who I don't see since he born but know is him, even though that don't make no sense. He coming to the river, coming to me. From in the house Mossi bellow, curse, and chop and whoever in there squeal like a pig. Then there he fly, Mossi, flung from the house, landing, rolling, stopping in the dirt. He only have one sword now, one sword to hold as the whoever come out.

He taller than three men standing on shoulders,

hand for feet, foot for hands, both with iron claws like daggers. Black fur, horse ears, tusks sticking out of his mouth, and the wings all gray skin, no feathers. Blood dripping from the ass he keep touching. Even in a crouch he taller than a tree. The boy is by the river, giggling like he hearing a silly uncle. The beast shriek, but Mossi not scared. He stand his ground and raise his sword. I never know the magistrate so fast. He dash between the beast's legs and slash his back, slip back around and cut his thigh, then stab him in the crotch. He laugh, I know the beast laugh, and swat Mossi away. Mossi still leave a sword in the beast's hand, which he pull out. Mossi on the ground and he can't even get up, but he try anyway. The beast, he grab Mossi and take his claw and slash his throat. Then he eat him.

I trip back to the floor, stunned. To the second window I scramble as quiet as I can keep it, to see if my noise catch the boy. The boy must be near ten in age now, and yet he staring at his reflection as if this is the first he seeing it, and is not a reflection at all, but another him that keep doing what he do. Of course he splash the water, he, the future King. My mockery must did make a sound, for he look up again. A big, bushy hand grasp his waist and the beast with bat wings take off into the sky.

The voice that sound like me say, Come, make we leave, but I stay. I sit there in that hut and watch day lose to night, which lose back to day again. I stay and watch even as vultures land from sky to start cleaning up the ground. The tree stand still as if nothing even trouble it. I watch Tracker coming back, his hand full of gifts. Watch him as he sniff, but he too far for me to see if his face perplex. Living people have thousands of smell, but all dead people smell the same. I watch him run right up to the tree, see what left of Mossi scattered outside, and faint. I watch him wake up and fall to his knees again, bawling and scream. Then it slip like a loose thought. No! No! No! he shouting, wishing fate away as he dash inside. Things get tossed, things smash, things break. He scream again. Then he bawl so loud that it shudder the river and beyond. He bawl through the day, bawl through the night and the day after. He find enough of Mossi to cradle him, and take to talking to him as if he being stubborn and won't put his body back together. Come now, magistrate, your children need you. Your children need you. I said you fucking children need you come now! Then he will see what in his lap, the light skin turning gray, the vultures behind him, quiet but insistent, and he bawl all over again. I watch him bury each one with whatever left to bury. A day later that smoke one appear. He chase after her, try to grab her, beg her to stop, then curse her. She keep coming together then breaking apart and not even him opening his arms wide to embrace would stop her mad movements. She break apart and don't come back together.

Learn this, I set myself on killing the Tracker, but after this, death would come a mercy. And I all out of mercy. It make us one, brother and sister in some way, with all this loss too heavy to ever speak it. I whisper from far, for he never did see me near, that from now on you will ache as I ache. The Sasabonsam come a killing, with a boy on his back. The same boy the Tracker save, I whisper from far, for he never did see me near. And I never hear of a such story where you save someone's life and in reward they destroy yours. Mighty grief that would make a giant buckle.

But for what happen to the Tracker's house, the Tracker blame the Leopard. Blame the Leopard for luring him away from the arms of home, as if the cat ever force him to go. I understand his ache, but understanding don't make me wish it would lighten. I glad he suffer. I glad that seven dead mean seven times and seven ways his grief cut open every day. I look at him, staggering drunk from the one tavern in Mitu, trying to say he will kill the world, but it come out as a torrent of vomit and tears. Pity is a dhow that sail away long time. Fuck the gods and fuck your grief. My only worry is that he would get to the others on my list before me.

But I don't kill him.

In five years and a moon, war go from rumor to real. Nobody can ignore it for too long because even when you not near battle, war is upon you. Who know what start it, whether it was when ambassadors from Weme Witu go missing in Kongor, or when the South King send four thousand troops to Wakadishu

and Kalindar, even though Wakadishu keep screaming they independent and Kalindar is the free movement of people and trade between North and South,
not no occupation. Maybe mad people hearing the
same things a different way. But battles break out
and both claiming victories, which mean neither side
winning. The North push back against the South in
Kalindar. The South reach above Wakadishu, trod
through the Blood Swamp, and set sight on the now
weak Dolingo. North have a wiser and more vicious
King. South have greater warriors. Battle after bloody
battle, none changing the outcome of this war. And
then Lissisolo and her rebel army declare war on
her brother.

Omororo. Five streets away from the hundred-man-
high shrine that people call the thrusting cock. The
city where I remember forgetting everything. What
the Nnimnim woman don't tell me until the day I
leave is that I can shape the look of my face. With just
the palm of my hand I can smooth her out younger,
or squeeze the breasts bigger, push the nose to flat-
ter, purse the lips to thicker. I don't care, a shape is a
shape, and while all of them is mine, none of them
is me. I look down and see five fingers and that is
enough. This place is not even a tavern, or an opium
den, but a tearoom. This man not looking for another
wife, or mistress, or concubine and even if he do, the
tearoom is not where he go looking for her. He don't

walk like a warrior, but he dressed for war, with his shield, heeding his King call that every man should get ready. I tell him that I done come from one of the grassland tribes, I don't know the North tongue well. My husband gone west to find a lion to kill to prove he can join the society of men even though lion kill get declared murder in Omororo. In the closet—for this was barely a room—he grab and throw me to the bed, for he think in this way he would have me. He promise to lick my clay off. I pull my skirt and he say praise the gods for I thought I was going smell bush koo. I say thank the lords indeed, because I was expecting fish cock. Talk like sex, I tell him and he go on to tell me all he going to do to me, is doing to me, will do to me. He saying things that would make an old me laugh. But is calling my younger self older me that make me giggle. He wasting my time talking so I climb on top of the bed and guide him in me. He still talking like sex when I reach behind myself and tug his balls hard, jolting him. Fuck like you never going set eyes on me again, I say, but I don't wait, I fuck him. I ram him. I crush him. I am the one who have his legs in the air. I make him start say oh . . . wait . . . I . . . like he the one who whip out more than he can spend. I almost call him a weak bitch but his cock was doing the work. I squeeze him to a cum, which he do, jerking like lightning strike him. Good man he keep saying he is because he stay hard until I cum too. I miss it, but it also shake my nerves, because no matter how much people claim that is you feeling yourself, a cum is still something you giving to somebody, and you give it too naked, too defenseless, too spent. He still below me when I look up and see a black husk in the back of the iron shield he leave in the corner. Looking like Bunshi made out of burned wood about to lick this man's cock. He shout, What happen? What me do? even after me long fly out of that bed and take off by horse.

This is how you reduce a woman.

Call it a quartermoon ago, when a memory come and ambush me the night. In the memory is a woman. See the woman. No name woman, for one used to have several but lose them all, for nobody leave in the world to call her. Nobody who can say I know her and this is who she be. She outlive her kin, her children, and her children's children. Hear what they say about her, that she will never die even if she get very old. She is old. Three hundred and seventeen, go the rumor in the North, one hundred and seventy-seven go the rumor in the South. She used to be the witch of the southern bush, and she used to be the ghost of the Blood Swamp, but there was a time she was a woman and a mother and a warrior and a whore and a thief. For these are things people call her, but nobody ask her what she call herself.

Even Sogolon is somebody else's name. Some would claim it is the name of her mother, but all she ever know was a rumor. A loose whisper from when brothers talk, and not meant for her ears, so the name could have been Sugulun, Sogola, Songulun, or nothing at all. The whisper could have been talk about another woman, a dog, or a place that no longer appear on a map. Long time now she should be dead, even she know, but look how she still living, still suffering, still chasing him down, for nothing left now but the thing.

The thing that she stop giving name.

The Malangika. The secret witch market. The place that prove it to be true, everything people say they hunt and kill witches for. Don't look for the city on no map, for you won't find it. Take the deepest salt mine, dig three times that, and the Tunnel City is still lower. People get lost between the Blood Swamp and Wakadishu, but it is of neither place. Word is that gold, not salt, is the reason the old people dig so deep, sticking tree trunks all around so that the tunnels never collapse. The old people stay down here digging so much that start to build house, and stable, and town, punching holes in the ceiling to let sunlight through, but depending more and more on lamplight. Then they vanish, like so many old people and old cities vanish. The whisper was that they fall in love with the gold so hard that they couldn't bear to part with it, so they lock themselves off underground and die with it. Dead city like this, it was only time before it attract necromancers, and those who make business with them.

But first the Mweru. I didn't leave the old shack

but stay and watch the Tracker go through the many seasons of his grief. When rage move him to saddle his horse, I put myself in his head as to where he would go. The boy, of course, but they didn't fly west, which is where the Tracker was heading. So he wasn't following a smell, then. Or maybe the boy don't have a smell no more. As for the monster, everything that would have his scent he eat. The Tracker ride several horses hard until he break into the Mweru. I only have one horse so it take me days longer. He would have words with this Queen about her boy. Maybe even kill the Queen, and this boy. But Lissisolo don't know where her boy be, and she have most of her rebel army looking, even the regiment of women, who marching to Nigiki to join a South army that they don't know already retreating. I know because I stay on pigeon routes and knock them out of the sky. The Mweru hide me the same way it do the last time, in the long tail of shadows. I stay out there and wait for days.

What happen next the voice in my head swear could never happen. **That is because you are a fool and always was a fool. Who else would be coming? Who else could pull a man out of the Mweru?** The Tracker and his horse galloping out of a tunnel, with Lissisolo's small infantry hot behind him. Where he think he riding to? I ask myself, my eyes following him right to the answer. There he was, sitting cross-legged, floating and writing in the air. He put both feet down as coming off a stool, rub something in his hand, rock, mud, and then throw it.

Is not that something happen next. Nothing happen next. Meaning nothing stop the Tracker from leaving the Mweru.

With the Aesi.

A horseman reach just a length from them before he and horse slam into a wall that nobody could see. It happen to many more.

The Aesi. He still wake up the red in me. I want to say that it make me feel something, as if the something was unknowable, but I know it. He wake up my desire. With this list I was rope and gear without the pull. He give me the power.

So, the Malangika. The Tracker go in alone, but he come out with an Ipundulu. Ishologu, for I don't think this one have a witch either. I can't move in too close, for either the Tracker will notice my scent or the Aesi will pick up a dead area that his mind can't scan. But they have an Ishologu, and the young prince don't suck any vampire blood in years. I laugh. They won't even need to search. He and the bat wing will come to them.

Let us make this quick. I watch them go to that village. I watch them from the woods and nearly get caught by the monster they was waiting to catch. They didn't catch him even with the lure of the Ishologu. The monster, the Sasabonsam, attack from behind the village, grab a woman, and fly off. They chase after him, both of them moving away from me, who didn't forget how to stand on the top of trees. They chase after the bat wing and run into Lissisolo's rebel

army. I see this section before and know them to be
all women. The Aesi work his magic and get them
to attack each other, killing most of their number and
all but a few of their horses. Neither the Tracker nor
the Ishologu do anything. Not long after they leave,
one of the riders, one of the few the Aesi couldn't control, find a horse and take after them. I ride in pursuit
but take a different trail up to a mound that I know
they will all pass. Here is truth, I didn't expect to
get there before they pass, but that rider must did
delay them somehow. He wasn't with them.

On that hill I stand and watch them as they approach. None of them see me. I don't know if some
part of me did already choose this place, or if the
place choose me. Or the times is the times and it say
right here, right now, this is it. So strange that something you wait your whole life for would just come
on in a rush. This was the time. And he would know
too. I whisper his name and let me wind (not wind)
throw it through the air at him. Is my head playing
with me but I would swear that I see my voice flying
down this mound, through the air, and dodging dust
to get to him. The Aesi. In the quick he leave the
other two and head toward me. I long down the little
hill when I hear his horse, then his feet behind me.

"Your head, it is closed to me," he say. I don't say anything. "I must have mistaken you for something . . .
considerable."

Yet you come for me anyway, I don't say.

I throw two daggers at him. In the quick he catch

one, but the other dodge his hand, up, down, under, then behind, where I cut the back of his neck. He smile and say something about how he should know me, but I don't look like anyone he has crossed paths with. Not that any of them ever lived to give good or bad report, he say. I don't remember him talking so much. The ground underneath me begin to shake, split, tear in two. I jump on the side of a chasm ever widening, when a chunk break off and hurl itself at me. I try to dodge but it hit my right thigh and knock me over into the dirt. Bigger pieces break off. He would crush me with them, but the wind (not wind) dome over my head and the boulders crack into dust, the same dust that I whip into a storm to blind him. Run right up to him I do as he fumble around, but he catch my hand, grip it, swing me, and slam me into the ground, killing the dust cloud. He have a sword now, swinging to chop and chop and chop, but I roll and roll and roll. My wind (not wind) knock him off his feet and he land on his back. I leap at him but a tree knock me away. He say enough with the tricks and grab his sword, then kick me my daggers. He say something about how is long years now that he don't have any sport. I don't say that this must be his first time since his last birth that he find a mind he can't read or control. He catch me going too deep in the thought and swing for my head. I block but he knock me over and I roll again out of a jab to the ground. He swing low and I block low, push him back, and jab high, but he block high. I kick him in the belly and he stagger back just enough to steady himself and charge back, spinning like a whirlwind. Swing and chop left and I block left, swing and chop right and I block right, he have me only defending blows and he know it, so he swing hard and faster, and I let the wind (not wind) bounce me over his head and slice across his face. He yell, then spit, then laugh. So we're cheating, then, he say, and a block of dirt burst in my face. I can't wipe my eyes before his hand is on my neck, and I remember the last time his hand grab my neck.

"I know you," he say. "But I don't remember your face. Not even the real one behind your false face."

This enrage me. After all he done to me, it's that he don't even remember that make me scream and my wind (not wind) blast him off me. I go inside and explode people before. I can do it to man a great distance from me. But maybe I need to touch him because all I am getting is a headache. Maybe the body learn from the old even if it new. He land at the side of the mound, saying something about my wind.

"Is not wind," I say. And then a hole open up and suck me down. I not even thinking of the wind (not wind) when the earth pull me down deeper, deeper, and deeper still, past new roots, past old root, past layer of rock, layer of mud, and deeper, deeper, deeper. The wind (not wind) have to choose between attack and protect, and it choose protect, with a barrier around my head. And still the underground suck me under the dirt, crackling, shifting, and trickling as I go down, down, and down. I try to get the wind (not wind) to blast, but it won't leave my protection. It won't attack. So far down in the earth he leave me, yet I can still hear the fucking Aesi.

About how war was coming, not the one that is here. That it was vital that the North win. That this latest mad King of the line of mad kings of the South was the craziest because he wanted to rule all kingdoms. So maybe he was not that mad. Maybe foolish. But a threat is coming, from neither South, North, nor East. But the West. Fire and disease and death and slavery will come across from the sea, and nobody, none of the great elders, fetish priests, and yerewolos have seen it. But he has seen it with the third eye. And only one unified kingdom, only one strong King, not a mad one, and not a blood-hungry abomination can alter what he has seen. He leave me with the echo of his voice, buried deep in the earth.

The Red Lake. When I finally claw my way back to the top it was morning. But it was also morning when this ground suck me under, so this was a new day. The Aesi leave my horse, likely thinking I would never free myself from the ground. I didn't know where to go or where to look except ahead is the Red Lake. I get there to see Lissisolo's soldiers, only ten or twelve in number, all on the inlet almost surrounded by river that people call the skull. One of them holding her son. Separated by that thin turn of the lake was the Tracker and the Ishologu. I don't know what I was watching. Some sort of drama with no sound. The Ishologu spreading his wings and the boy fighting the stronger hands restraining him. He want to run to the Ishologu and is screeching, that I hear. I don't know what they saying. The soldier holding the boy remove his helmet and I am shocked to see the Leopard. He was the one I wondered most about, for if the Tracker didn't blame him for what happened, then surely he blame himself. Then the boy break free, and the Leopard chase after him, two spears fly, both hitting him in the chest. The Aesi coming up from behind, as he always seem to do. The Tracker shouting Leopard's name, dashing into the water after him, swimming to catch him before he float away. The Aesi, I know it is him, appear to do nothing, but every soldier fall to the ground, just like so. The Tracker is bawling over his cat, who seem to still be alive.

And then this, the boy run to the Ishologu. Everybody is so taken with this, Ishologu holding the boy, hugging him, that nobody see me approach. The Aesi is going around making sure the soldiers are either deep in sleep or dead. The Tracker is still cradling the Leopard and kissing him on the forehead, telling him that he was the great love, the only one he could call love. The Leopard say that if he love any one person as much as he loved his own cock then that would have been enough love to fill the whole world. Nobody else would need any, he say, and die mid-laugh. Ishologu turn around and for the first time I see that it is Nyka, the snake. It rush to my mouth to ask him where is Nsaka Ne Vampi, where is my great-great-granddaughter, but he is an Ishologu now and in his eyes I know. And this boy. He lean into Nyka's chest, resting, nuzzling like a baby lamb, but was just aiming for the nipple to bite into. This boy, who look like he only a few years from a Zareba. Nyka wince, but he also smile. He wrap his arms tighter around him, and flap his wings until he was flying. The boy stop sucking when he see they in the air and smile with black and red lips. In the quick, Nyka flap his wings again and a lightning bolt, tall as the sky, strike them two. The dirt shiver and knock me off me feet. The lightning stay, not jumping around, not hopping, not vanishing, just dropping a shower of shock on the two. Nyka hold on tight to the boy kicking and screaming, until they both burst into flame that explode, leaving nothing but smoke. And the Tracker, still whimpering.

A hand grab my neck from behind.

"This is the third time you grab my neck," I say to the Aesi.

"Oh is so? What happen the first time?"

"Second time more interesting."

"Tell us," he say.

"Second time is when I remember that you are the only one I need touch first."

"Touch for wha—"

I don't look back, not once. I been doing this for over one hundred years. First a big pop in his left eye, then his right. He too shocked to do anything before his right ear pop. Before he can shout or scream, his tongue swell and burst. He drop the hand now, trying to get away from me. I still don't turn around when the back of his head explode and he fall. I don't know why I don't turn. **Yes you do,** say the voice in my head. Turn around and you will see that this is not the peak you come here expecting, that his dead body won't give you anything more than the last time you kill him. That this close nothing and end nothing, for his death is just the beginning of killing him.

Then he grab my hair and pull me to him. The Aesi. I turn around and see the bloody, pulpy head trying to tell me something. I cut his throat.

The Tracker still have the dead cat in his arms, still crying and kissing him.

"He the only man who ever love me," he say.

"Nobody love no one," I say.

You want to know about my kill list. Some list this be, where only one man on it I actually kill. You looking for something profound to come from my mouth.

J uba. He cross a bridge east that nobody ever name, the one they call the Bridge That Has a Name Not Even the Old Know, and enter the city before sentries return for the night and close the gate. The sun dip in the west and the east already dark. Three days since he leave the Purple City, and nobody there shedding no tears that he gone. Five years in the North and still not much knowledge of it, so he do what men do when they reach a road they don't know. Turn left. He hoping this will open up Juba, even though it is small road, too small for big sport, but perhaps the kind of street for the kind of pleasure that like to hide in a dark corner. Man like him don't want what the city show; he want what it hide. So, the horse he leave at a stable that promise fresh grass and good housing from the rain coming. But he threaten to behead the stable keeper if tomorrow he don't find his horse unweary and unspoiled. And the stable keeper look at him and take his word for joke until he brandish a dagger longer than a sword and shove it by his balls before the man could jump. I know why this kind of threat give him glee, just as I know that this kind of threat he would carry out, just so. Anybody can still see the east gate from where he standing, and the aqueduct running over it, so he walk in the other direction, ignoring what this thunder is promising, leaving this little road for one bigger. He will have drinking and carousing and masquerading and big adventure. And fucking, and hurting, and sporting, and whoever come at him with the wrong intent will get a knife in their gut. Or their back.

He wearing clothes off the back of a man he kill in the Purple City. The voice that sound like me ask, **What it make you that you just want to watch a man die?** I tell the whimpering bitch that not a single person's world is all the poorer from that loss, as that man was scum too. Steal from a thief, gods laugh. Kill a murderer and gods whoop and holler. If you believe in gods. I once hear the Tracker say that is not that he don't believe in gods, but that he don't believe in belief.

First he hide for two years, for every single day he think I was coming. I let him think I was dead, which is what time always let us think, and it make him bold. His sort always go where his urges lead, which mean a place that don't ask questions, and don't leave tracks, where nobody ever come looking, and where nobody place value on whoever live there. Masi then, or Juba, the nasty shitholes of the South and North. Two years I take to get this close to him, and is not because he was always moving. Is not like he was covering tracks. Is because I was making myself ready and he not the first name on my list.

Here is truth. The first time I follow him was to see how he making out in the world. He knew war was coming, that in the mind of many war was already here, and there he is, the master war tactician from the South, but from war over one hundred years ago. Skill is skill, and skill can't kill, he say to the army officer recruiting men in Malakal. I follow him right up to the window but can't hear what they say. I see him, though, losing his temper, slamming his hand down on their table, probably screaming about his quality. About how in his day he was the master tactician of a great army even though he look like he don't reach twenty years. The marshal sigh, the look on his face saying so young, yet mad already. The deputy looking like he say that at least our Kwash Dara inspiring everybody to take up arms, even the women. Jakwu, still in Venin's body no matter how much hard work he push it through to shape himself a man. I watch that too, how he let his hair go wild and knotty. How he rub certain bush to grow a beard but leave only a mark, smoke all sort of wicked grass to pound and grate his voice, but now sound like a eunuch, how in his room he wrap a tight linen around his breasts to keep them down before he go sporting, or whoring. How plenty time he will fuck a whore with his finger and his tongue, which make one laugh—yes, I watch while he beat her. Then one day when that Kampara actor troupe was passing through the city, he sneak into the caravan and steal one of their wood cocks. Now he fuck whoever with it, causing them great damage, but woe to the woman who laugh.

So, see him walking down this street closing up day business for night work. Hunter swagger. Walking like he don't know that hunter become game. Here is truth, he should have been dead from half a year ago, and every single weapon I own have come close to his neck, face, back, even heart, but I let him go. Is only since the last quartermoon that I admit why. That the hunt is what I did want, not the kill, at least not yet. Because I already know that once I take him away, only one thing left. Also because one can't hunt the dead. Jakwu going down this street because he looking for something so secret that he keep it from his own self. Down this street, he lose all swagger and walk the way hips and legs shape him to walk, looking for a man who think he will have to pay, and he will, just not money. I remember the first days he was in Venin's body saying to me, No lie, I did ever wonder it. And envy it, that peak after peak when woman cum that men don't get to have. I tell him what a mystery it is to me that you know, for I sure not a single woman ever suffer that with you. It would obsess and disgust him, that I know. Also that he would seek it out but hate whoever bring him to it.

He go into a smoke hut that don't serve opium. It don't take much to gain the attention of a man, for all a woman need to be is next. I stay outside the door and listen to Jakwu telling the man to mete out whatever punishment he think he can deliver. He make all sort of moaning, bawling, and hollering, as if he expect that people out his door listening. Not long after the man shudder and cum, he is shouting at him to shut up and get out. This is part Jakwu like the best, the part where he can burn off his shame with anger, the part where the man never fail to put this one in her place for being a impudent bitch. Jakwu never strike first because he never have to. Somebody will clean up the mess—he pay for that too.

He want to tell somebody how it make him feel, but who in this world hearing him wouldn't judge? Unless they think him a virgin or a fool. You the one who steal her body, I want to say. What you want to tell somebody is that she in turn steal your wanting to be a man. Is not just that you coming into the shape of the woman you steal, but you starting to like it.

All of which must be an abomination somewhere, but I done with feeling outrage. Or shock, or horror, or even disgust. I tell you what I did feel and I didn't feel it, I heard it. The voices of all those women in the room who called me the Moon Witch. Who now call themselves the Moon Witch. And with that, I knew that the void I was hoping revenge would fill did fill to overflow. It just take me this long to see it.

That don't mean I didn't kill that fucking bitch Jakwu. In the same smoke hut I walk up right beside him, say Venin talk to me when I see the ancestors, which was not true, but it make his head turn, which make my wind (not wind) wrench his head until it snap.

Some days later news make it all the way up to the North, even a sorry place like Juba, that somebody kill King Sister Lissisolo's son, which mean Lissisolo had a son, even though she was a nun. And because the King Sister form an alliance with the South King (who was now dead) to make this boy Kwash **something,** this Tracker who was being detained might stand trial for regicide. Kwash Dara, taking leave from the search for the Aesi, declare that the North had no hand in any killings, and if anything the South should answer for the disappearance of his chancellor. I take passage down the river, and in my own time sail all the way to Nigiki, using a pirate vessel to dodge the river blockades between North and South.

It tickle my nose and wake me up. I slap it away, but there it come again, tickling my nose, making me sneeze, making me annoyed. I roll away from it, but then it stick itself into my ear, which feel worse. Fuck the gods, I shout and slap it away. But again, he tickle.

"I going bite you if you don't stop," I say.

"Promise?" he say. This lion already straddling me, his mighty legs like two towers, his tail between them, misbehaving with my breasts, the rest of him far too ready for whatever he looking to do this morning. People warn me about you cats and your constant hunger, but I didn't listen, I say, to which he grin.

"That don't sound like disagreement," he say, and just so, his massive head, with his massive gold mane, and his big round ears, and his rough whiskers is rubbing against my left cheek then my right. First day in the Buffalo Legion, he say. I leaving soon.

"Leaving? No," I say.

To a dim, empty room.

When I turn myself in to this prison, the guards didn't know what to do. I tell them that if they are looking for people of interest in the matter of a dead prince, then they should be talking to me. Though I didn't kill him, I was there when somebody did. And then you search me and find the list, which have the boy's name on it. Then you lock me in here, and why not? I have nowhere else to go, for eight years at least, and twenty if we counting when that demigod will again come of age. I done outlive everybody there is to know, and if I leave it to just him, then the only story of this business will be the Tracker's, and that silly, slutty fool don't even know that this tale is not just bigger than him, but one hundred seventy and seven years older. Because for all his love and all his loss, that man with a nose is just a boy. And truth speaking? This is woman work.

So let us make this quick.

ACKNOWLEDGMENTS

Maybe it will be called a plague year. But 2021 was the year that saw me fleeing a devastating disease, from city to country, as if this were 1665. Which means I began this novel far way from home, at the dining table of Abbie Boggs and Milo Theissen, who opened a home that they had only just bought to houseguests who ended up staying over six months. The gratitude I have for them is beyond words, but here are words just the same said from the bottom of my heart: Thank you.

As always, for support, guidance, generosity, free meals, and blind faith: Ellen Levine, Jake Morrissey, Jeff Bennett, Claire McGinnis, Jynne Dilling Martin, Geoffrey Kloske, Simon Prosser, Jackie Shost, everyone at Riverhead Books, the Macalester College English Department, Ingrid Riley, Ano Okera, Lisa Lucas, Steven Barclay, Pablo Camacho for another stunning cover, Neil Gaiman, the James Merrill House for a wonderful residency, and, for deep trust, deep understanding, and even deeper love, Nicholas Boggs.

My mother is allowed to read all of this book.

ABOUT THE AUTHOR

MARLON JAMES is the author of the **New York Times** bestselling National Book Award finalist **Black Leopard, Red Wolf,** the Booker Prize–winning **A Brief History of Seven Killings,** and **The Book of Night Women** and **John Crow's Devil.** In addition to the Booker Prize, his novels have won the American Book Award, the Los Angeles Times Ray Bradbury Prize for Science Fiction, the Anisfield-Wolf Book Award, and the Dayton Literary Peace Prize. Born in Jamaica, James lives in New York City.